Texas Destiny
Texas Glory
Texas Splendor

Lorraine Heath

Texas Destiny
Texas Glory
Texas Splendor

Rhapsody
Garden City, New York

Texas Destiny
Copyright © 1997 by Jan Nowasky

Texas Glory
Copyright © 1998 by Jan Nowasky

Texas Splendor
Copyright © 1999 by Jan Nowasky

This edition was especially created in 2004 for Rhapsody by arrangement with Signet.

Published by Rhapsody, 401 Franklin Avenue, Garden City, New York 11530

ISBN: 1-58288-113-8

Book design by Christos Peterson

Printed in the United States of America

Contents

❧

Texas Destiny

For Curtis

When it was most needed,
you gave us all a strong shoulder to lean on.

How proud I am that you are my brother.

$\mathcal{A}$cknowledgments

$\mathcal{I}$ HAVE OFTEN heard that a writer's life is a solitary one. To those who proved the myth untrue, I offer my sincerest appreciation. Without your help and guidance, this story would not have been written.

Jennifer Sawyer Fisher, who saw the potential and encouraged me to reach for it.

Robin Rue, who views detours as opportunity.

Chris and Jim Armstrong, for providing medical information as well as answering my questions about weapons and the Civil War.

Alan Beaubien, for going above and beyond when sharing his knowledge on the Civil War.

Susan Broadwater-Chen, for extensively researching mail-order brides and sharing all that she learned.

Stef Ann Holm, for taking the time from her own writing schedule to offer assistance with my research.

The reference librarians at the Plano Public Library, for their exhaustive research on mail-order brides.

The many readers who have taken the time to let me know that my stories and characters have touched their hearts, just as their letters touch mine.

And Jack Thomaston, who not only shares his knowledge of horses, any time, day or night, but who also graciously forgives me when I steal away his wife, Carmel, so she can critique my work.

Thank you, all.

Chapter 1

᪡

*H*E HATED THE railroad with a passion.

Fort Worth had been fading into obscurity, turning into a ghost town, before the citizens extended the town's boundaries so the railroad could reach its outermost edge. It had taken nothing more than a whispered promise to change the fading cow town into a thriving boomtown that the elected officials boasted would one day be known as the Queen of the Prairie.

The Queen of the Prairie.

Houston groaned. His brother had taken to calling his mail-order bride that very name, and Dallas had never even set eyes on the woman.

Hell, she could be the court jester for all Dallas knew, but he'd spent a good portion of his money—and his brothers' money—building this woman a palace at the far side of nowhere.

"We just need to get one woman out here and the rest will follow," Dallas had assured his brothers, a wide confident grin easing onto his darkly handsome face.

Only Houston didn't want women sashaying across the windswept prairie. Their soft smiles and gentle laughter had a way of making a man yearn for the simple dreams of his youth, dreams he'd abandoned to the harshness of reality.

Houston had known men who had been disfigured less. Men who had taken a rifle and ended their misery shortly after gazing into a mirror for the first time after they were wounded. Had he been a man of courage, he might have done the same. But if he had been a man of courage, he wouldn't have been left with a face that his older brother couldn't stomach.

He saw the faint wisp of smoke curling in the distance. Its anticipated presence lured people toward the depot the way water enticed a man crossing the desert. Turning slightly, Houston pressed his left shoulder against the new wood.

Damn Dallas, anyway, for making Houston leave his horses and come to this godforsaken place of women, children, and men too young to have fought in the War Between the States. If Houston hadn't been stunned speechless when Dallas had ordered him to come to Fort Worth to fetch his bride, he would have broken Dallas's other leg.

He still might when he got back to the ranch.

He heard the rumbling train's coarse whistle and shoved his sweating hands into his duster pockets. His rough fingers touched the soft material inside. Against his will, they searched for the delicate threads.

The woman had sent Dallas a long, narrow piece of white muslin decorated with finely stitched flowers that he was supposed to have wrapped around the crown of his hat so she could easily identify him.

Flowers, for God's sake.

A man didn't wear flowers on his hat. If he wore anything at all, he wore the dried-out scales of a rattlesnake that he'd killed and skinned himself, or a strip of leather that he'd tanned, or . . . or anything but daintily embroidered pink petals.

Houston was beginning to wonder if Dallas had broken his leg on purpose just to get out of wearing this silly scrap of cloth. It wouldn't do to anger the woman before she became his wife.

Well, Houston wasn't going to marry her so he could anger her all he wanted, and he wasn't going to wrap flowers around the crown of his brown broad-brimmed hat.

No, ma'am. No, sir.

He hadn't stood firm on many things in his life, but by God, he was going to stand firm on this matter.

No goddamn flowers on his hat.

He squeezed his eye shut and thought about breaking Dallas's other leg. The idea's appeal grew as he heard more people arrive, their high-pitched voices grating on his nerves like a metal fork across a tin plate. A harsh whisper penetrated the cacophony of sound surrounding him.

"Dare you!"

"Double-dare you!"

The two voices fell into silence, and he could feel the boys' gazes boring into him. God, he wished he'd never shut his eye. It was harder to scare people off once they'd taken to staring at him.

"Looks like he's asleep."

"But he's standin'."

"My pa can sleep while he's sittin' in the saddle. Seen him do it once."

"So touch him and see."

A suffocating expectation filled the air with tension. Then the touch came. A quick jab just above his knee.

Damn! He'd hoped the boys were older, bigger, so he could grab one by the scruff of his shirt, hoist him to eye level, and scare the holy hell out of him. Only he knew a bigger boy wouldn't have jabbed him so low.

Reluctantly, Houston slowly opened his eye and glanced down. Two ragamuffins not much older than six stared up at him.

"Git," he growled.

"Heh, mister, you a train robber?" one asked. "Is that how come you're standin' over here so no one can see ya?"

"I said to git."

"How'd you lose your eye?" the other asked.

His eye? Houston had lost a good deal more than his eye. Trust boys to overlook the obvious. His younger brother had. Austin had never seemed to notice that his brother had left the better part of his face on some godforsaken battlefield.

"Git outta here," Houston ordered, deepening his voice.

Blinking, the boys studied him as though he were a ragged scarecrow standing in a cornfield.

With a quickness they obviously weren't expecting, he stomped his foot in their direction, leaned low, and pulled his lips back into a snarl. The boys' eyes grew as large as their hollering mouths just before they took off at a run. Watching their bare feet stir up the dry dirt in the street leading away from the depot, Houston wished he could run with them, but family obligations forced him to remain.

In resignation, he repositioned himself against the wall, slipped his hand inside the opening of his duster, and stroked the smooth handle of the Colt revolver. The thought of breaking Dallas's leg no longer held enough satisfaction.

Houston decided he'd shoot his brother when he got back to the ranch.

Amelia Carson had never been so terrified in all her nineteen years.

Afraid the train might hurtle her onto the platform before she was ready to disembark, she clung to her seat as the huffing beast lurched to a stop. The wheels squealed over the wobbly tracks, the whistle blew, and the bell clanged as the engine settled with an ominous hiss. The pungent smell of wood smoke worked its way into the compartment as the passengers flung open the doors, forgetting their manners as they shoved each other aside in their hurry to scramble off the train. Amelia had never seen such an odd collection of people crammed together in one space.

Women with throaty voices and low-necked bodices had graced the compartment. A few well-groomed men had worn tailored suits as though they'd been invited to dine with a queen. Only the guns bulging beneath their jackets indicated otherwise. Some men, smelling of sweat and tobacco, had squinted at her as though contemplating the idea of slitting her throat if she closed her eyes. So she'd rarely slept.

Instead, she had spent her time reading the letters that Dallas Leigh had written to her. She was certain the bold, strong handwriting was a reflection of the man who had responded to her advertisement indicating she had a desire to travel west and become a wife. He was a hero— inasmuch as the South could claim a hero in a war that it had lost. He had been a lieutenant at seventeen, a captain at nineteen. He owned his land, his cattle, and his destiny.

He had wrapped his proposal for marriage around dreams, dreams of building a ranching empire and having a son with whom to share them.

Amelia knew a great deal about dreams and how frightening it was to reach for them alone. Together she and Dallas Leigh could do more than reach for the dreams. They would hold them in the palm of their hands.

Countless times during her journey, she had envisioned Dallas Leigh waiting for her in Fort Worth, impatiently pacing the platform. Once the train arrived, he would crane his neck to see into the cars, anxious to find her. She had imagined him losing his patience and barging onto the train, yelling her name and knocking people out of the way, desperate to hold her within his arms.

With her dreams rekindled and her heart fluttering, she gazed out the window, hoping to catch sight of her future husband.

She saw many impatient men, but they were all rushing away from the train, yelling and shoving through the crowd, anxious to make their mark on the westernmost railhead. None wore her handiwork wrapped around the crown of his hat. None glanced at the train as though he cared who might still be on board.

She fought off her disappointment and turned away from the window. Perhaps he was simply being considerate, giving her time to compose herself after the arduous journey.

She pulled her carpetbag onto the bench beside her and opened it. With a shaky breath, she stared at the conglomeration of ribbons, flowers, and a stuffed brown bird that her betrothed had labeled a hat. Since she had no portrait to send him, he had sent her something to wear that he could identify.

She was grateful. . . .

She stared at the hat.

She was grateful . . . grateful . . .

She furrowed her brow, searching for something about the hat for which she could be grateful. It wasn't an easy quest, but then nothing in her life had been easy since the war. Suddenly she smiled.

She was grateful Mr. Leigh had not met her in Georgia. She was grateful that she didn't have to place the hat on her head until this moment, that none of her fellow passengers had ever seen it.

She plucked it out of her bag, settled it on her head, and took a deep breath. Her future husband was waiting for her.

She just hoped none of the cowboys still mingling at the depot took a notion into their heads to shoot the bird off her hat before Mr. Leigh found her.

Standing, she stepped into the aisle, lifted her bag, and marched to the open doorway with all the determination she could muster. She smiled at the porter as he helped her descend the steps, and then she found herself standing on the wooden platform amid chaos.

Tightening her grip on the bag, she eased farther away from the train. She felt as though she were a shrub surrounded by mighty oak trees. She had little doubt that even the hat was not visible among all these men asking directions, exchanging money and paper with a purpose, and shouldering each other aside.

She considered calling out for Mr. Dallas Leigh, but she didn't think she could lift her voice above the horrendous yelling that surrounded her. She had expected Texas to be quiet and unsettled, not reminiscent of all the carpetbaggers who had come to stake a claim in the rebuilding of Georgia.

She shuddered as the blurred memories, images of Georgia during and after the war, rushed through her mind. With tremendous effort, she shoved them back into their dark corner where they couldn't touch her.

The men and women began to drift away. Amelia considered following them, but Mr. Leigh had written that he would meet her at the train station in Fort Worth. The sign on the wooden framed building proudly boasted "Fort Worth." She was certain she had arrived at the correct depot.

Slowly she turned, searching among the few remaining people for a man wearing a hat that bore her flowers. What if he had been here? What if he had seen her and found her lacking? Perhaps he had expected her to be prettier or made of sturdier stock. She had always been small of stature, but she was competent. If he'd give her the chance, she could prove that she was not afraid of hard, honest work.

She dropped her carpetbag and the platform rattled. Tears stung her eyes. She wanted so little. Just a place away from the memories, a place where the nightmares didn't dwell. She squeezed her eyes shut, trying to sort through her disappointment.

No man would send a woman tickets for a journey and then not come to meet her. Somehow, she had already disappointed him . . . or a tragedy had befallen him, preventing his arrival.

People referred to portions of Texas as a frontier, a dangerous wilderness, a haven for outlaws. Newspaper accounts drifted through her mind. She latched onto one, and her imagination surged forward. Outlaws had ambushed him. On his way to Fort Worth, on his way to meet her, he had been brutally attacked, and now, his body riddled with bullets, her name on his lips, he was crawling across the sun-baked prairie—

"Miss Carson?"

Amelia's eyes flew open as the deep voice enveloped her like a warm blanket on an autumn evening. Through her tears, she saw the profile of a tall man wearing a long black coat. His very presence was strong enough to block out the afternoon sun.

She could tell little about his appearance except that he'd obviously bought a new hat in order to impress her. He wore it low so it cast a dark shadow over his face, a shadow that shimmered through her tears. Although he wasn't wearing her flowers on his hat, she was certain she was meeting her future husband.

Brushing the tears away from her eyes, she gave him a tremulous smile. "Mr. Leigh?"

"Yes, ma'am." Slowly, he pulled his hat from his head. The shadows retreated to reveal a strong, bold profile. His black hair curled over his collar. A strip of leather creased his forehead and circled his head.

Amelia had seen enough soldiers return from the war to recognize that he wore a patch over the eye she couldn't see. He had failed to mention in his letters that he had sacrificed a portion of his sight for the South.

His obvious discomfort caused an ache to settle within her heart. Anxious to reassure him that his loss mattered not at all, she stepped in front of him. With a tiny gasp, she caught her breath. She had expected the black eye patch. She was unprepared for the uneven scars that bordered it and trailed down his cheek like an unsightly frame of wax melting in the sun. With fresh tears welling in her eyes, she reached out to touch his marred flesh. His powerful hand grabbed her trembling fingers, halting their journey of comfort.

"I'm sorry," she whispered as she searched for words of reassurance. "I didn't know. You didn't mention . . . but it doesn't matter. Truly it doesn't. I'm so grateful—"

"I'm not Dallas," he said quietly as he released her hand. "I'm Houston. Dallas busted his leg and couldn't make the journey. He sent me to fetch you." He reached into his pocket and withdrew her embroidered cloth. "He sent this along so you'd know you'd be safe with me."

If his knuckles hadn't turned white as he held the linen, Amelia would have taken it from him. He had shifted his stance slightly so only his profile filled her vision.

A perfect profile.

"He mentioned you in his letters," she stammered. "He didn't say a great deal—"

"There's not much to tell." He settled his hat on his head. "If you'll show me where your other bags are, we can get goin'."

"I only have the one bag."

He leveled his brown-eyed gaze on her. "One bag?"

"Yes. You can't imagine how grateful I was every time we had to get off the train that I only had the one bag to worry over."

No, Houston couldn't imagine her being grateful for one bag. He allowed his gaze to wander slowly over her white bodice and black skirt, taking note of the worn fabric. Wouldn't a woman wear her best clothing when she met the man she was to marry?

Hell, he'd worn his best clothing, and he'd only come to fetch her.

He wrapped his fingers around the bag and lifted it off the ground. Judging by its weight, he figured she was hauling nothing but air, and they had plenty of that in West Texas.

She needed to be carrying all the things that they didn't have at the far side of nowhere. Hadn't Dallas told the woman anything about the ranch when he wrote her? Hadn't he told her they were miles from a town, from neighbors, from any conveniences?

Two bullets. He was going to fire two bullets into his brother.

"I'm ready to go," she said brightly, interrupting his thoughts.

No, she wasn't ready to go. Only he didn't know how to tell her without offending her. Without thinking, he removed his hat to wipe his brow. Her green eyes brightened, as though she were pleased with his gesture, as though she thought he'd done it for her benefit as a gentleman would. He fought the urge to jam his hat back on his head and explain the situation to her from beneath the shadows. "Did Dallas mention how long the journey would take?"

"He wrote that it was a far piece. I thought of a piece of cloth that I might use for quilting." She spread her hands apart slightly and her smooth-skinned cheeks flamed red. "But that's wrong, isn't it?"

Three bullets. He was going to shoot three bullets into his brother.

"It's at least three weeks by wagon."

She lowered her gaze, her eyelashes resting gently on her cheeks. They were golden and so delicate—not thick like his. He wondered if they'd be able to keep the West Texas dust out of her eyes.

"You must think I'm an idiot," she said quietly.

"I don't think that at all, but I need you to understand that this is the last town of any size you'll see. If there's anything you need, you need to purchase it before we leave."

"I have everything I need," she said.

"If there's anything you want—"

"I have everything," she assured him. "We can leave for the ranch whenever you're ready."

He'd been ready three hours ago, consciously packing and arranging all his supplies so he left half the wagon available for her belongings— only she didn't have any belongings. No boxes, no trunks, no bags. He cleared his throat. "I . . . I still need to pick up some supplies." He crammed his hat on his head, spun on his heel, and started walking. He heard the rapid patter of her feet and slowed the urgency of his stride.

"Excuse me, Mr. Leigh, but how did my fiancé break his leg?" she called from behind him in a voice sweeter than the memory he held of his mother's voice.

He turned to face her, and she came to a staggering stop, the bird on her hat bobbing like an apple in a bucket of water. Balling his free hand into a fist to prevent it from snatching off the bird, he wished now that he'd given Dallas his honest opinion on the damn thing when he'd asked him what he thought of it. "He fell off a horse."

Her delicate brows drew together. "As a rancher, surely he knows how to ride a horse."

"He can ride just fine. He took it into his head that he could break this rangy mustang, and it broke him instead." He spun back around, increasing the length of his stride. If Dallas had just listened to him, heeded Houston's warning, Houston would be back at his own place smelling the sweat of horses instead of the flowery scent of a woman, hearing the harsh snort of horses instead of a woman's gentle voice. He wouldn't have to watch a stupid bird nod. He wouldn't be carrying a bag, wondering what the hell she didn't have.

Four bullets. And even then he wasn't certain that thought could sustain him through the hell that tomorrow was sure to bring.

Chapter 2

꒐

AMELIA FOLLOWED THE towering man as his long, even strides stirred up the dust and took them past several storefronts. His spurs jangled, his coat flapped around his calves, and he pulled his hat farther down on the left side.

He stepped on the boardwalk, sending the harsh sound reverberating around her. He seemed as impatient as she was to begin the journey, and she wondered why he hadn't thought to purchase his supplies before she'd arrived. She could only be grateful that he wasn't the man she'd come to Texas to marry.

He hesitated before shoving open the door to a hotel. He moved back slightly, waiting for her to go inside. She felt as though she were still on the train, traveling headlong toward a destination she wasn't even certain was right for her.

"Why are we going in here?" she asked.

His jaw tightened as three people barged past him. "I figure by the time we're done gettin' the supplies, it'll be too late to travel today, and considering how many people got off that train, I figure we ought to get the rooms before we get the supplies."

"A very wise decision," she acknowledged as she slipped past him and entered the hotel. People crowded the lobby, closing in around her. Fighting the urge to run, she struggled to draw in air. As long as she could breathe, she could live.

Houston dropped her bag to the floor. "Wait here while I see about some rooms."

She watched him walk to the front desk, tugging on his hat. She was greatly disappointed that Dallas Leigh had not met her. She had hoped to become better acquainted with him before they exchanged their vows. But she had little hope of that happening now. Once she arrived at his ranch, she was certain they would be married. She'd have no opportunity to change her mind, return to Fort Worth, or travel home.

Home. How easily the word slipped into her mind. How difficult to remember that she no longer had a home or a family. Everything of importance, everything that meant anything to her at all was carefully packed away in the bag resting near her feet, along with the marriage contract Dallas Leigh had asked her to sign. His wording had been practical and straightforward, a guarantee that he would take her as his wife if she journeyed to Fort Worth, a guarantee that she would take him as her husband if he provided her with the funds with which to travel.

She did not begrudge him his caution. He knew as little about her as she knew of him. Trust, like love, would come with time.

As the scowling man returned to her side, she could only hope that Dallas's moods were not as dark.

"This way," he grumbled as he snatched up her bag.

She followed him through the lobby and up a distant set of stairs. At the top landing, he took a right and charged down the hallway. He inserted a key into the lock, turned it, and flung open the door. He stepped back and waited for her to enter the room.

Amelia walked into the small room. The bed beside the window immediately drew her attention. Dallas had sent her tickets that allowed her to sleep in a berth. She had taken one look at the small compartment and traded in the tickets, using the refunded money to purchase him a wedding gift—a gold pocket watch, second hand.

During her journey, she had snatched sleep here and there, sitting up, whenever she'd dared to sleep. She'd almost forgotten what it felt like to sleep in a bed.

She faced the man standing in the doorway. He was holding his hat, presenting her with his right side.

"I need to take the wagon and animals to the livery and let the hostler know I'll be keeping them there overnight. I thought you might want to"—he waved his hat helplessly by his thigh—"do whatever it is ladies do when they get off a train. I'll meet you in the lobby in an hour, and we'll go get those supplies."

"Where is your room?" she asked.

"This was the last room. I'll stay at the livery."

"That hardly seems fair. You're paying for the room—"

"You're gonna sleep with the horses?"

"I've slept with worse." Amelia dropped her gaze as the heat rushed to her face. She should explain that statement, but she couldn't. She didn't want to give freedom to the blurred memory lurking in a shadowed corner of her mind. "I simply meant . . . I am most grateful for the room, but if you wished to share it—"

"That wouldn't be proper."

She forced herself to meet his gaze. "Won't we be sleeping together while we travel?"

The cheek that was visible to her reddened as he turned his hat in his hands. "No, ma'am. You'll sleep in a tent, and I'll sleep by the fire." He settled his hat onto his head. "Tonight I'll sleep at the livery. I'll be back in an hour. I'd appreciate not havin' to wait on you."

Before she could remind him that she'd had to wait on him at the depot, he slammed the door closed. She didn't know whether to laugh or cry. Three weeks. She would be in that man's company for three weeks, and if the past fifteen minutes were any indication of what she could expect on the journey, she anticipated an extremely lengthy three weeks.

She closed her eyes. Grateful, grateful, grateful. He had to possess some redeeming quality. She opened her eyes and smiled. She could be grateful that he appeared to be a man of few words, and she was incredibly grateful that he'd left.

He no doubt thought she had the brain of a gnat, and perhaps she did: traveling from Georgia to Texas in order to marry a man she knew only through correspondence. What if she had misjudged the tone of Dallas Leigh's letters? What if she had created in her mind a man who did not exist beyond her imagination?

Since the war, she had received offers to better her life, but none had carried the respectability of marriage. To the victor go the spoils. Her father's plantation, his wife, and his daughters had been the spoils.

Shuddering, she squeezed her eyes shut and wrapped her arms around herself. She was too tired to hold the memories and fears at bay. Too tired.

With longing, she gazed at the bed. She would sleep for just a few moments. Then she would wash away the dust of her journey and meet Houston Leigh in the lobby. She imagined it would be quite interesting to watch him bargain for supplies. With his temperament, she had little doubt he would end up paying double for anything he wanted.

She eased onto the bed, sighing with contentment. The mattress, as soft as a cloud, sank beneath her weight.

Heaven.

Just a few moments of heaven.

Hell's fury had surrounded Houston for so long that he couldn't remember if he'd ever known heaven's touch. He was afraid that if he wasn't careful, he'd drag the woman into hell with him.

He'd already hurt her feelings. He knew he had. Otherwise, she would have met him in the lobby.

He was angry at Dallas, and he had taken his anger out on the woman. He hadn't meant to, but in looking back he could see that he had.

He stood outside her door, practicing his apology. He couldn't recall ever giving an apology, and the best words to use wouldn't come to his mind. An apology to a woman should be like the piece of cloth she'd sewn for Dallas: flowery, dainty, and pretty.

Hell, he didn't know any words like that. She'd just have to be happy with the words he knew, sorely lacking though they were.

Thank God, he wasn't the one she was going to marry. He'd spent the whole morning thinking about what he would say when he met her. When he'd seen the tears glistening within her green eyes, shame had risen up and sent every word he'd practiced scattering like dust across the prairie. Shame that it had taken him so long to gather his courage and cross that platform to greet her. Shame that he hadn't considered how she might feel standing alone in a strange town waiting for a man who wasn't going to come.

At the livery, he'd thought about how he might explain the supplies. Their purchase was sure to be a delicate matter. After all his thinking and word gathering, she hadn't met him.

Now he was having to think of an apology.

He just wanted to be back at the ranch, where he could walk alone and think alone. He didn't want to answer questions, or consider another's feelings, or remove his hat.

With a heavy sigh, he removed his hat, knocked lightly on her door, and waited, the apology waiting with him, ready to be spoken as soon as she opened the door.

Only she didn't open the door.

She was either angrier than he figured or she'd left. If she'd left, he'd be the one with four bullets in his hide because Dallas always hit what he aimed at.

Earlier, without thinking, he'd placed the key to her room in his pocket, leaving her without a way to lock her door. What if someone had stolen her? Women were rare . . . so rare . . .

He knocked a little harder. "Miss Carson?"

He pressed his good ear to the door. The blast that had torn through the left side of his face had taken his hearing from that side as well. He heard nothing but silence on the other side of the door.

Gingerly, he opened the door and peered inside. The late-afternoon sun streamed through the window, bathing the woman in its honeyed glow. Curled on the bed, asleep, she looked so young, so innocent, so unworthy of his temper.

He slipped inside and quietly closed the door. He crossed the room, set his saddlebags on the floor, and sat in the plush velvet chair beside the bed. He dug his elbows into his thighs and leaned forward.

Dear God, but she was lovely, like a spring sunrise tempting the flowers to unfurl their petals. Her pale lashes rested on her pink-tinged cheeks. Her lips, even in sleep, curved into the barest hint of a smile.

He had spotted her right off, as soon as she'd arrived at the door of the railway car. Beneath that godawful ugly hat, the sun had glinted off hair that looked as though it had been woven from moonbeams. The smile she had given the porter as he'd helped her down the steps—even at a distance—had knocked the breath out of Houston.

He still wasn't breathing right. Every time he looked at her, his gut clenched as though he'd received a quick kick from a wild mustang.

She wasn't at all what he'd expected of a heart-and-hand woman. He'd expected her to look like an old shirt, washed so many times that it had lost its color and the strength of its threads. He knew women like that. Women who had traveled rough roads, become hard and coarse themselves, with harsh laughter and smiles that were too bright to be sincere. Women who knew better than to trust.

But Amelia Carson did trust. She was a heart-in-her-eyes woman. Everything she thought, everything she felt reflected clearly in her eyes. In her green, green eyes.

The warm depths reminded him of fields of clover he'd run through as a boy. Barefoot. The clover had resembled velvet caressing his rough soles. For a brief moment, he actually relished the thought of holding her gaze.

His brown eye could serve as the soil in which her green clover took root.

What an idiotic notion! The next thing he knew he'd be spouting poetry. He shuddered at the thought. Wearing flowers and spouting poetry. His pa would have tanned his hide good for either one of those unmanly actions.

He watched her sleep until the final rays of the sun gave way to the pale moonlight. He shivered as the chill of the night settled over him. Standing, he reached across the woman and folded the blankets over her. A warmth suffused him, and he imagined drawing the blankets over her every night for the rest of his life.

Only that privilege belonged to his brother. Houston had witnessed the document Dallas had drawn up, something as close to a marriage contract as he could arrange without the "I do's." For all practical purposes, Amelia Carson belonged to Dallas.

Which was as it should be. Dallas had spent a month thumbing through the tattered magazine he'd found when they'd driven the cattle to Wichita, Kansas, in the spring of seventy-five. Houston knew desperation for a son had driven Dallas to write his first letter to Amelia.

He could only wonder what had compelled her to reply, to accept his brother's offer of marriage. He settled back in the chair. It wasn't his place to wonder about her. He didn't have to like her. He didn't have to talk to her. He didn't have to be nice to her. He just had to get her to the ranch . . . and by God, that was all he planned to do.

Through a waking haze in which dreams still lingered in the corners of her mind, Amelia snuggled beneath the blankets, relishing the comfort of the soft bed. She had no recollection of drawing the blankets over herself, but she welcomed their protection against the chill permeating the room.

Complacent and rested, like a kitten that had spent the better part of the day lazing in the sun, she stretched languorously, inhaled deeply, and froze.

The aromas of bacon, coffee, and freshly baked bread teased her nostrils. Slowly she opened her eyes, expecting the harsh glare of the afternoon sun to streak across her vision. Instead, the soft glow of early-morning light cast its halo over the furnishings, directing most of its attention on a small cloth-covered table set in the middle of the room. The sunlight shimmered over an assortment of covered dishes.

Amelia's mouth watered at the same time that alarm rushed through her. She hadn't heard anyone come into the room.

Unexpectedly, she detected another scent, much fainter than the food causing her stomach to rumble, fainter, and yet in an odd way more powerful. Leather and horses.

She spotted saddlebags leaning against a chair near the bed. Cautiously, moving only her eyes, she allowed her gaze to sweep over the room.

Her heart stilled when she noticed the long shadow stretching across her bed. The shadow of a man. She bolted upright and jerked her gaze over her shoulder.

His left shoulder pressed against the wall, Houston Leigh stood beside the window watching her. The sunlight took a moment to outline a portion of his tall, lean frame before completing its journey into the room.

Amelia threw off the blankets and scrambled out of bed, her knees almost hitting the floor before she jumped upright. She pressed a trembling hand to her chest, the rapid thudding of her heart vibrating beneath her fingers. "Mr. Leigh, it's morning."

"Yes, ma'am," he acknowledged with a slow drawl that did nothing to calm her erratic heart.

"You must think me terribly rude. I only meant to sleep for a moment—"

"Didn't think you were rude at all. Just figured you were tired. Figure now you're probably hungry." He inclined his head slightly in the direction of the table.

"You did this?" she asked as she cautiously neared the table.

He lifted one shoulder in a careless shrug. "Needed to make up for yesterday. Dallas would have my hide if he knew how I treated you yesterday."

"Does he anger easily?"

"He's not a man you want to rile." He settled his hat into place. "Enjoy your meal."

He had picked up the saddlebags, slung them over his shoulder, and walked halfway across the room, his hat pulled low on the left side before Amelia realized he was leaving. "Aren't you going to join me?"

"I've already eaten."

"Then just keep me company." He hesitated, and she knew she should let him leave, but she was incredibly tired of being alone. "Please."

His answer came in the form of a movement toward the table as he removed his hat and draped the saddlebags over the back of a nearby chair.

Amelia rushed to take her seat. He took the chair opposite her, turned it slightly so she had a clear view of his profile, and stared at the hat he held on his lap.

Houston searched the farthest recesses of his mind, but he couldn't locate anything worth commenting on. He thought about telling her that her hair was falling down on the left side, but he was afraid she'd hop up and straighten it, pulling it back into that coil she was wearing the day before. He liked the way it looked now, drooping as it was. He secretly hoped it might work its way free and tumble down her back.

Dallas would, of course, prefer to see every strand pulled back and held in its proper place. The man was a stickler for orderliness, but Houston had always thought a woman's hair should flow around her as freely as the wind blew across the prairie.

He thought about describing Dallas's ranch, but she'd see it soon enough, and he didn't have the skill with words to do the place justice. A discussion of his own place probably wouldn't interest her. It was a pretty piece of land, but it would never bring a man wealth or glory.

"Are you sure you don't want anything?" she asked.

"I'm sure," he replied, cursing his gut for jumping into his throat at the sound of her voice. All he had to do was sit still while she ate and give her no reason to bring up her breakfast. The sight of his face had made him bring up his meals a few times in the beginning, but that was years ago when the wounds were still raw . . . and the guilt still festering.

Amelia tore off a piece of warm bread and lathered it with butter, quietly studying the man sitting across from her. His gaze remained fixed on his hat, his brow furrowed as though he were desperately searching for something just beyond reach.

"How did you and your brothers come by your names?" she asked before she bit into the bread with enthusiasm.

"Our parents lacked imagination. They just named us after wherever it was they were living at the time we were born."

"I suppose you're grateful that they weren't living in Galveston when you were born."

He seemed to contemplate her answer for a moment, as though she'd made her comment in all earnestness. His jaw tensed. "I reckon I would be if I'd ever thought about it."

She had hoped for a smile, a chuckle, a laugh, but Houston Leigh appeared to be a man who did not give into lighthearted banter or teasing. That knowledge saddened her. Everyone needed smiles and laughter to replace the absence of sunshine in a stormy life. She hoped the brothers didn't share this stern outlook on life. "Do you think Dallas will want to carry on the family tradition and name our children after towns in Texas?"

"I'm not sure what names he favors." He shifted in his chair and brought one foot up, resting it on his knee.

Amelia chewed slowly on the bacon and eggs, savoring the flavors, wondering how she could gather all the information about her future husband that she didn't have. Letters could only reveal a man's thoughts. She did not know his smile, the sound of his laughter, or the way emotions might play across his features. She was incredibly curious about every aspect of him and his life. "Dallas mentioned Austin quite often in his letters."

Houston gave a brusque nod. "He's right fond of Austin. You'll like him, too. He's the sort people take to right away."

As he spoke of his younger brother, a trace of warmth flowed through his voice, reminding her of snuggling before a fire on a cold winter's night. She wanted to keep the flames flickering. "I don't remember how old Austin is."

"Sixteen."

"Then he's spared any memories of the war."

"I doubt that."

Amelia set her fork down. "But he would have been so young. Surely he doesn't remember—"

Houston slid his foot off his knee, and it hit the floor with a resounding thud. He shifted in the chair. "I'd rather not talk about the war, if you don't mind."

"No, I don't mind," she said softly, aware that she'd lost the warmth in his voice, in his manner. He clenched his jaw as though he were fighting desperately to remain where he was. She could feel the tension radiating around him, palpable in its intensity. Although more than ten long years had passed, the war still continued to rip through people's lives. "Do you think Dallas will try to break that mustang again when his leg heals?"

He scooted up in the chair, then slid back. "I let it go," he said in a voice so low she wasn't quite certain she heard him correctly.

"I beg your pardon?"

He grimaced slightly. "I set the horse free."

"Why?"

He slowly waved his large hand through the air as though it were a curtain billowing in a spring breeze. "The horse had a heavy, wavy mane and tail. That marks it as tricky and dangerous. Figured Dallas would eventually kill the horse or it would kill him." He sighed. "So I set it free."

"You said he wasn't a man you wanted to rile. Didn't that rile him?"

"He was still laid up in bed. I was long gone by the time he discovered what I'd done."

"So you'll have to deal with his anger once you return to the ranch."

"I'm hoping your presence will distract him, and he'll forget about the horse."

Amelia cleared her throat. Houston shifted his gaze to her, and she lifted an eyebrow. "So, shortly after I meet your brother in person, I'll learn whether or not he values me more than he does a horse?"

Horror swept over his face. "I didn't mean—"

"I know you didn't," Amelia said, smiling as she carefully folded her napkin and placed it on the table. "I've finished eating."

Houston bolted from the chair. "Good. I'll have someone send up some hot water for a bath. It'll be some time before you'll have that luxury."

He crammed his hat on his head, adjusting it to the lopsided angle to which she'd grown accustomed. He slung his saddlebags over his shoulder and walked to the door in long strides that complemented his height.

"Is Dallas as tall as you?" she asked.

He halted, one hand on the doorknob. "Taller."

He opened the door and hesitated. "I'll be back in about an hour. Then we'll go get the last of the supplies." He slipped into the hallway, closing the door behind him.

Amelia shoved away from the table, walked to the washstand, and glanced in the mirror. She groaned. Her hair had come loose and was sticking out like the raised fur on an angry cat.

Little wonder Houston Leigh had avoided looking at her.

She heaved a deep sigh of longing. A warm bath. The purchase of a few supplies. Then she would begin what she was certain would be the most important journey of her life.

Chapter 3

❧

CLUTCHING DALLAS'S LETTERS to her breast, Amelia sat in front of the window and watched as the sun chased the early-morning shadows away from the dusty street. Gathering her courage had never seemed quite so difficult.

Soon Houston would come for her, and she had to be ready to travel toward a dream.

She had read each of Dallas's letters after her bath. He was not a man given to flowery prose, yet she always found beauty within his simple words. During the time they had corresponded, she had come to know the man behind the letters well enough that she had not hesitated to accept his offer of marriage.

She pressed his letters to her lips. Already, she fostered a hint of affection for Dallas Leigh. Surely, love could not be far behind.

The rapping on her door came as softly as the pale sunlight easing through her window.

Taking a shaky breath, she placed the precious letters in her carpetbag, picked up her hat, and walked to the mirror. Ignoring the bobbing bird, she worked a hatpin through the narrow brim. Although it would probably be at least another three weeks before she met her betrothed, she hoped he would recover quickly enough to meet them before the end of the journey.

She anxiously crossed the room, wrapped her trembling fingers around the doorknob, and pulled open the door. Her apprehension receded as she looked at the profile of the man standing in the hallway.

The damp ends of his black hair dragged along the collar of his duster. He smelled of soap, and she realized he'd indulged in a bath as well. She supposed the journey would hold no luxuries for him, either.

"Ready?" he asked in a low voice.

"As ready as I'll ever be, I guess." She stepped into the hallway as he walked into the room and retrieved her bag.

She could think of nothing to say as the click of the closing door echoed along the hallway, effectively drawing to a close one phase of her life. She averted her gaze from the tall man standing beside her. She didn't want him to see the doubts darting in and out like a naughty child searching for mischief: One moment they were gone and the next they were playing havoc with her emotions. She placed her palm over the watch she'd safely stored within a hidden pocket in her skirt. She imagined she could hear its steady ticking as it patiently marked the passing moments until she placed her gift into Dallas Leigh's hand, a hand she was certain was as large and as bronzed as his brother's.

"We'd best get goin'," Houston said.

Breathing deeply, she once again forced her qualms to retreat. "Yes, I suppose we should. Do you have many supplies to purchase?"

"Not many."

In silence, she followed him out of the hotel and onto the board-walk. His strides weren't as long or as hurried as they'd been the day before. Enjoying the leisurely pace as she walked by his side, Amelia studied the clapboard buildings, the men hunched over as they drove wagons down the street, and the horses carrying riders toward destinations unknown to her. Anticipation thrummed through the warming breeze. Savoring the excitement, she hoarded the images, knowing a time would come when she'd share them with her children, her first impressions of a town that had brought her closer to her destiny.

She was so absorbed in her musings that she nearly bumped into Houston when he came to a dead halt in front of a dress shop.

He glared at the simple plank of wood as though it were a despised enemy. Considering his previous hurry to be on his way to the ranch, she thought his time would be better spent picking up the supplies he needed. She was on the verge of suggesting he move on when he took a deep breath and shoved open the door. Bells tinkled above his head, and he cringed.

"Get inside," he said in a low voice.

Baffled by his choice of stores, Amelia strolled into the small shop ahead of him. When she thought of supplies, she thought of canned goods, cooking utensils, and an assortment of odds and ends that a person would usually purchase at the mercantile or general store. She wondered if he had a wife for whom he wished to purchase some clothing. She knew very little about Houston, but it warmed her to think she might be traveling with a man who would be somewhere he obviously didn't want to be in order to obtain a gift. She imagined his wife would be as dark as he was, small, and quiet. Very quiet.

A buxom woman with bright red hair threw aside the curtains behind the counter and waltzed into the room. "I thought I heard my little bells," she exclaimed in a voice hinting at a French ancestry. Her hands fluttered over the counter. "I am Mimi St. Claire. Proprietor and expert dressmaker."

Amelia watched as Houston clenched and unclenched his hand before reaching up to remove his hat.

"Oh, my," Mimi St. Claire squeaked, pressing her hand above her bosom. She laughed nervously. "You took me unawares, sir. Shadows one moment, none zee next. What can I do for you?"

"She needs to be outfitted," Houston said in a taut voice.

"Outfitted?" Mimi questioned.

Houston gave a brusque nod.

Stunned, Amelia stared at the man. "You don't mean to purchase clothes for *me,* do you?"

"Dallas told me to get you everything you needed before we headed back."

"These are the supplies?"

"Yep."

She wrapped her fingers around his arm and pulled him away from the counter, seeking a small measure of privacy.

"You can't purchase me clothes," she whispered. He stared at her hand as though he couldn't quite figure out how it had come to be on his arm. She snapped her fingers in front of his eye, gaining his attention, and tightened her hold on his arm for emphasis. "You can't purchase me clothes," she repeated.

He shifted his gaze back to her hand. "Dallas is purchasing the clothing."

With a sigh, she released his arm. "He already purchased the tickets for my journey. I don't feel comfortable having him spend more of his hard-earned money on me. What if he changes his mind about marrying me?"

Houston's Adam's apple slid slowly up and down. "He won't change his mind."

She tilted her head slightly. "You don't think so?"

"I'm not a man who lies."

But he was a man easily offended, if the tone in his voice was any indication. One brother who was easily angered, another who was easily offended. She would have to learn to deal with both.

Fingering the collar of her worn bodice, she glanced with longing around the dress shop. "I suppose one—"

"Five."

"I couldn't possibly accept five."

Ignoring her, he directed his attention to Mimi St. Claire, who was leaning over the counter, straining to hear every word. She didn't bother to appear embarrassed at her actions, but simply straightened her back and wrapped a loose strand of red hair around her finger.

"She needs five outfits," Houston said. "Make a couple of them fancy for entertaining. We need them today."

Mimi's eyes widened. "Five? Today?" She patted her chest and smiled brightly. "Sit in zee chair, and I'll show you what I have already sewn."

With a whirl, Mimi disappeared behind the curtains as Houston walked to the corner. Instead of sitting in the chair with the delicate spindly legs that looked as though they could easily snap beneath his weight, he pressed his left shoulder against the wall.

Clasping her hands tightly together, Amelia walked across the small shop. "I can't possibly accept five—"

"Five."

She sighed deeply. "Don't I have a say in this matter?"

He took a long slow nod. "As long as you say five."

She narrowed her eyes, scrutinizing the man standing before her, trying to determine if he was teasing her. His lips curled up not at all, his eye didn't glint with mischief. If anything, he seemed more serious than before.

"Mademoiselle!" Mimi St. Claire stuck her head between the drawn curtains. "Quickly, come in here. We must show zee gentleman zee clothes."

As Amelia passed through the waving curtains, Houston set her bag on the floor and slipped his hand inside his duster pocket. He heard Mimi St. Claire's deep-throated chuckle. Amelia's gentle laughter quickly followed, reminding him of spring rain, soothing and sweet, the kind of rain that a man simply removed his hat to enjoy as it washed over him.

Her touch had been as soft as her laughter, but he'd felt the determination in her fingers. He'd been surprised when the warmth from her small hand had penetrated the material of his duster and shirt to fan out over his skin.

He strained to hear their voices, but could decipher none of the hushed words. He wondered if Dallas had explained in his letters that Amelia would have no woman with whom she could whisper secrets. Tightening his hold on his hat, he wondered if Amelia knew she was traveling toward godawful loneliness.

She stepped between the curtains, wearing a yellow dress that had ruffles and bows sewn over it. She glanced his way with uncertainty.

Mimi St. Claire came out and waved her hand in a circle. "Turn, turn so he may see all of it."

Amelia pivoted on the balls of her feet. The dress had more ruffles in the back than in the front. Houston imagined if a strong wind blew through, it would carry Amelia Carson and that frilly dress across the plains like the petals of a dandelion.

Dallas would like that dress. He'd like it a lot. Too damn bad he'd broken his leg.

Shaking his head, Houston thought he saw relief fill Amelia's eyes. "You got something that looks like the earth?" he asked.

Mimi St. Claire's face puckered as though she'd just bitten into a lemon. "Zee earth?"

She grabbed Amelia's arm, and they disappeared behind the curtain. When next Amelia emerged, she wore a dark brown dress that perfectly matched the hat with the bird. Houston hated it.

"I didn't say dirt," he grumbled. "Something that looks like the earth. Something like clover."

"Clover?" Mimi asked. "You want green?"

Houston nodded slightly, not really certain what he wanted, just certain he'd know when he saw it.

Mimi rolled her eyes. "Trust men to speak in riddles. Why could he not just say green?"

She pulled a smiling Amelia back behind the curtain. Houston wondered how often Amelia would smile in West Texas, when the sun beat down on her, the dust rose up to choke her, and the nearest neighbor was a day's ride away on a fast horse.

He wished he could ignore her laughter coming from the back room, but he embraced the melodious sound as easily as his fingers stroked the delicate embroidery threads buried deep within his pocket. He no longer had a reason to keep the cloth on his person. He'd identified himself. He could give the embroidered linen back to her or stuff it into his saddlebags. Instead he found himself constantly rubbing the only soft thing in his life.

And staring at the curtain, waiting impatiently to see Amelia again, the sparkle in her eyes, the way her lips curled up as though she found this whole situation amusing.

The curtain billowed out and she slipped through, wearing a dress the shade of clover. It had no frills, no bows, no lace, no ruffles. Simply made, it hugged her curves as a lover might.

Warily studying him, she turned slowly, keeping her gaze on him until she was forced to snap her head around. "You don't like it either?" she asked.

"I like it just fine," he said as he settled his hat on his head and picked up her bag. "Get it and anything else you want. Take your time. I'm gonna fetch the wagon."

He ignored her crestfallen expression and walked out of the shop, the door rattling behind him. He'd hurt her feelings again, but this time he'd had no choice. If he'd stayed in that room, he would have crossed that wooden floor and trailed his finger along the delicate column of her ivory throat.

Just one finger, just one touch, just one sweet moment . . . but buried deep within his own personal hell, he knew he had no right to claim any sweet moments, especially from the woman pledged to his brother.

Breathing heavily, he came to a staggering stop and dropped his chin to his chest. After years of wanting and waiting, he finally had the opportunity to prove himself. He had only to deliver Amelia Carson safely and *untouched* into Dallas's arms.

He'd never realized how heavy a burden trust was.

Amelia stared at the door, willing the man who'd just stormed through it to return. One moment he seemed interested in her wardrobe, and the next, he was walking out as though he couldn't escape fast enough.

"He does not like zis one either?" Mimi asked, irritation laced through her voice.

"No, he did like this one. It's me he doesn't like."

Mimi threw up a hand in a dramatic gesture. "Nonsense! He adores you."

Amelia walked into the back room. "Actually, I'm a burden to him."

Mimi began unbuttoning the back of the dress. "Oh, little one, I think you must not be wise in zee ways of love. A man sees a woman as a burden only if he thinks he cannot please her."

"All he has to do is escort me to his brother's ranch. How hard can that be?"

"That, little one, depends on zee journey. For you, it will be easy. Your heart belongs to another, yes?"

With the hope that she would indeed give her heart to Dallas shortly after meeting him, Amelia nodded.

"When a heart belongs to no one, zee journey is never easy." With a flourish, Mimi spun around. "Now, let's see what else I have that looks like zee ground!"

An hour later, Amelia breathed a deep sigh of relief and walked out of Mimi's shop wearing her own clothes. She would save the new clothing until they neared the ranch.

"Did you get five outfits?" a deep voice asked.

Amelia spun around. Within the late-morning shadows, Houston leaned against the wall.

"Yes, she just needs you to pay for them, and she'll wrap them up.

Although I can't imagine what I could possibly want with so many clothes."

He shoved away from the wall. "Dallas figures other women will come farther west once you get there. He thinks he'll be the king of West Texas." He held her gaze. "You'll be his queen."

"Is he that successful?"

"He's got a good start, he's smart, and he's not a man to let anything stand in his way."

"Are you successful?"

He shook his head. "Nah, I leave the glory of success to Dallas and men like him. I'd just like to watch the sunset in peace."

He tugged on his hat, and Amelia had the feeling something deeper dwelled within his words, something he had no desire to discuss. Although she could not see it, she was certain that he'd just thrown up a wall.

"Take a look around and see if you can think of anything else you need while I purchase the clothes. If not, we'll be leavin'."

He went into Mimi's shop and returned a few minutes later with two large parcels. "Did you think of anything?" he asked.

"No, I feel guilty about all that you've purchased already."

"Don't feel guilty. Dallas won't begrudge the purchase. He's generous to a fault when it comes to those he cares about."

"And you think he'll come to care about me?"

"He already does, Miss Carson. Give you my word on that," he said as he stepped off the boardwalk.

Amelia's apprehensions began melting away. Perhaps the man behind the letters was as she had imagined him. She thought of Houston's comment that she needed clothing for entertaining. One day she would delight the ladies of West Texas with parties and social calls—just as her mother had charmed the women from the neighboring plantations. Perhaps as the wife of a rancher, she would find a semblance of the life she'd known before the war, a life she'd thought would one day be hers.

A life shattered by men in blue and men in tattered gray.

Shuddering, she squeezed her eyes shut and forced the past back into the recesses of her mind. Her future lay before her, clear and untarnished, with a man who had shown her nothing but compassion and respect in his letters.

Amelia came to a halt as Houston placed the packages in the back of a wagon laden with supplies. A brown horse, tethered at the rear, nudged Houston's shoulder. He reached into his duster pocket and brought out an apple. The mare grabbed it and began chomping greedily.

As Houston pulled a tarpaulin over the supplies, securing it in place with ropes, Amelia traced her fingers over an emblem burned into the side of the wagon. An "A" leaned over until its right side touched the left side of a "D."

"What's this?" she asked.

"Dallas's brand. An 'A' and a 'D.' Joined."

Joined. As in a partnership. As in a marriage. "Has he always had this brand?"

"Nope. In the beginning, he just had the 'D.' He added the 'A' when you accepted his offer of marriage."

Deeply touched, she wished Dallas could have shared this moment when she discovered his gift. "He never mentioned it in his letters."

"Reckon he wanted it to be a surprise."

"A brand is important, isn't it?"

"The choosing of it isn't something a man takes lightly. Neither is the changing of it."

"Is this why you think he cares about me?"

"It's one of the reasons."

"And the other reasons?"

"I reckon they'll be real obvious when we get to the ranch." He tied a final knot in the rope. "Ready?"

More than ready, she nodded. He placed his large hands on her waist. She grabbed his shoulders as he swung her onto the wagon. She sat and arranged her skirt, trying not to think about how the warmth of his hands had soaked through her worn clothing. Dallas's hands would be that warm, his shoulders that steady.

Houston climbed in and settled onto the bench seat beside her. He released the brake and slapped the reins over the backs of the four mules harnessed before them. "Well, Miss Carson, take a last look around because where we're headed there's nothing but open land, cows, and cowboys."

Chapter 4

❧

$\mathcal{I}$T WAS WELL past noon before they reached a small stream. As Houston watered and fed the mules and his horse, Amelia sat on a log, using a fork to dig beans out of a can that he had opened for her.

She couldn't hear his words, only his voice, as he talked to the mare. Neither of them had spoken as the wagon had traveled away from Fort Worth. From time to time, she had glanced over her shoulder. He had never once looked back.

He crossed the clearing and hunkered down before her, his right shoulder close to her drawn-up knees. His black duster parted, revealing the gun strapped to his thigh. It served as a gentle reminder that she was headed toward an untamed land.

"My apologies for the simple meal, but I didn't want to take the time for a fire," he said quietly. "We'll have a better meal come evening."

"I'm truly grateful that you thought to bring some canned goods."

Removing his hat, he studied her. "You've eaten worse."

She smiled softly. "As a matter of fact, I have."

"Yep, me, too."

Standing, he settled his hat on his head. "You can wash up by the stream. We'll be leaving soon."

Amelia rose and began to walk toward the water.

"Miss Carson?"

She glanced over her shoulder. His profile was to her again, and he seemed to be studying something in the distance. "Yes, Mr. Leigh?"

"Once, when I stopped by a stream to wash the dust off, I laid my hat beside me. A raccoon carted it away." He ground his jaw back and forth. "If you were to take off your hat while you were washing up, some critter might haul it away."

"I'm so grateful you shared that with me. I'll make certain I guard the hat well."

She thought he grimaced before he turned away. She strolled to the water's edge and knelt beside the stream. The hat, with all its accessories, weighed heavy on her head. She had considered removing the bird or some of the ribbons. She had even considered pretending that she had never received the hat, but she had no talent for telling lies. Dallas would see through her deceit, and she didn't want to risk hurting his feelings after he'd gone to so much trouble.

She dipped her hands into the cool water. She couldn't recall Houston's ever initiating a conversation between them. He politely answered her questions, but for the most part he kept quiet. Yet he had openly shared the story of the raccoon and his hat, although he had appeared uncomfortable reciting his tale as though he had feared offending her. She imagined he had been quite put out not to have his hat, since he seldom removed it.

She caught sight of her reflection wavering in the water, the bird bobbing with her movements. The hat was so incredibly unattractive. She wore it because Dallas had sent it to her, because it was a gift and she had received so few in her life.

She glanced over her shoulder and wondered if Houston wasn't offering her a gift as well: an honorable way to lose the hat without hurting anyone's feelings.

She rose and walked to the wagon where he was tightening the ropes that held the tarpaulin in place over the supplies. "You don't like my hat," she stated in as flat a tone as she could manage.

He visibly stiffened, his hands stilling. "No, ma'am." He removed his hat and met her gaze. "I think it's the most godawful ugly thing I've ever seen."

Amelia released a tiny squeal and covered her mouth.

Regret reshaped his features. "My apologies, Miss Carson. I had no right—"

"No!" She held up a hand to stay his apology and moved her other hand away from her face to reveal her smile. "I think it's awful, too."

"Then why in God's name are you wearing it?" he asked, clearly stunned.

"Because it was a gift from your brother."

He slapped his hat against his duster. "Well, it's not very practical. Your nose is already turning red."

Amelia pressed her fingers to the tip of her nose. She could feel the slight prickling of her skin. She had worn a bonnet to protect her face when she'd worked in the cotton fields following the war. She'd hoped never to have to wear a bonnet again. "I'm not overly fond of bonnets," she said as she gnawed on her lower lip.

"If a raccoon were to carry your hat away, you could borrow the hat I bought for Austin," he offered.

"Do you think he would mind?"

He shrugged. "If he minds, he can keep his old hat. I just bought it because I didn't know what else to get him, and we don't get into town much. He might not even want it."

"I don't want to hurt Dallas's feelings. The hat was a gift—"

"The hat was a way for me to recognize you. You've been recognized."

A twinge of guilt still pricked at her conscience. "Do you think he'll wear the band I embroidered around his hat?"

"No, ma'am. I can guarantee you he won't be wearing it."

"I could just pack the hat away, I suppose."

"Got no room in the wagon for anything else."

She knew that for the lie it was. A little less than half the wagon remained empty. "You really dislike the hat."

"If you pack it away, there's gonna come a day when company's gonna come to call, and he's gonna want you to wear it . . . in front of people who need to respect him. The way I see it, in the long run, you'll be doing him a favor if it goes no farther west than this."

"Are there raccoons around here?"

"Yes, ma'am."

"I think I need to give my face a good scrubbing."

He nodded. "I'll find Austin's hat."

Amelia walked to the stream and knelt. Reaching up, she removed the hat and studied it. Dallas had bought it for her so he could identify her. It had served its purpose. She set it beside her and viciously scrubbed her face, praying he would never discover her deceit. She lifted her skirt and wiped the cool water from her face before casting a sideways glance at the hat. It remained untouched.

She rose to her feet and walked to the wagon. Houston handed her a black broad-brimmed hat.

"Are you sure Austin won't mind?" she asked as she adjusted the positioning of the hat on her head.

"I'm sure." He placed his hands on her waist and lifted her onto the wagon, then settled in beside her.

"I feel guilty," she said as he reached for the reins.

"Don't."

He flicked the reins and the mules began to pull the wagon across the stream. Amelia waited until the wagon had cleared the shallow stream before glancing back. The hat remained where she'd left it.

"Do you really think a raccoon will take it away?" she asked.

"Yes, ma'am. Maybe not today or tomorrow. But someday."

The fire crackled softly, shooting sparks into the night. Despite the vastness of the black sky, an intimacy dwelled within the small camp, an intimacy that hadn't existed in Fort Worth. Amelia wondered if perhaps it existed here because there were only the two of them, alone, surrounded by nothing but the dark shadows of the unknown.

She stole a sideways glance at her traveling companion as he sat on a nearby log and forked beans into his mouth. They had traveled through the afternoon in silence, her thoughts directed toward her hat and the raccoon, his thoughts . . . she had no idea where his thoughts had traveled.

He had set up a tent, tended the animals, and cooked a meal, speaking only when necessary to convey his needs. As he prepared the camp, he had moved with an effortless grace that always kept the right side of his body facing her. She wasn't certain if he sought to protect his scarred face or to protect her from the sight of it. Perhaps it was a little of both.

"Are you married?" she asked quietly.

He jumped as though she'd fired a rifle into the night. His fork clattered onto the tin plate and flipped to the ground. He picked it up, wiped it on the leg of his trousers, and started moving the few remaining beans around on his plate. "Nope."

He jammed the bean-laden fork into his mouth.

She knew his parents had lived in Texas when their children were born. She wondered if they'd lived elsewhere. "Did you grow up in Texas?" she asked, hoping to entice him into discussing his childhood, a childhood that had included Dallas.

"Nope. Lived in Texas when I was boy. Grew up outside of Texas."

She furrowed her brow. "When did you leave Texas?"

"When the war started. When Pa enlisted, he signed me and Dallas up to go with him."

Threads of Dallas's letters wove through her mind. His military life had astounded her, given her cause for pride, but she had thought Dallas was nearly thirty and based on that knowledge, she'd assumed he had enlisted near the end of the war. She wondered if she had misread his letters, misjudged his age. "How old were you?"

"Twelve. Dallas was fourteen."

"You were children," she whispered, remembering so many young faces parading along the dirt road in front of their plantation.

"Pa thought we were old enough. Dallas was commanding his own unit by the time he was sixteen."

The food she'd eaten rolled over in her stomach. "Yes, he gave me a detailed accounting of his accomplishments. I just didn't stop to think how young he would have been when he enlisted. Sometimes, I wonder if it wasn't actually a children's war."

He moved to the fire. "More coffee?"

"No, thank you."

She watched as he poured the black brew into his tin cup before moving back. She had a feeling his movement to the fire was his way of signaling that he wanted to end that particular vein of conversation. Since he had an aversion to talking about the war, she decided to oblige him.

"Could I ask a favor of you?" she asked.

Houston had been waging a battle all evening, fighting to keep his attention focused on the writhing flames dancing in the night instead of on the woman sitting beside him. He didn't think Dallas would appreciate how much pleasure it gave him to watch Amelia, but the lilt of her voice, a soft southern drawl that hinted at no hurry to be anywhere, the hope echoed in her words, was his undoing. Admitting defeat, he shifted slightly, met her gaze, and nodded.

"When your brother and I wrote each other, we didn't describe ourselves, which is why we had to send something for identification. I was wondering if I could tell you what I think he looks like and you tell me if I'm wrong."

"I could just tell you what he looks like."

She shook her head vigorously. "No, I want to see how close I am to imagining him as he truly is."

She sat on a small log, looking like a little girl waiting to be handed a piece of candy. He was willing to give her the whole jar, but in deference to his older brother, Houston merely shrugged. "Go ahead."

She bit her lower lip. "All right. I know he's tall, since you told me that. And I always thought of him as having black hair, like yours. Only it wouldn't be as long. I think his hair might just cover his ears. It wouldn't reach down to his shoulders."

Houston nodded slowly, and her eyes brightened. He imagined the fun Dallas would have keeping those eyes shining. She seemed incredibly easy to please.

She closed her eyes a moment, then popped them open wide. "Blue eyes."

Damn! He hated to disappoint her. He shook his head slowly. "Austin got our ma's blue eyes."

"Are Dallas's brown, like yours?"

"Same color, but he's got two."

She leaned forward, pity filling her eyes, and he wished he'd just kept his mouth shut and not tried to tease her. What the hell did he know about teasing? For some reason, he wanted to hear her laugh again as she had with Mimi St. Claire. And he wanted absolutely none of her pity.

"How old were you when you were wounded?" she asked quietly.

"Fifteen. Thought you wanted to know about Dallas."

Straightening, she gave him a quivering smile, and he knew he'd hurt her feelings again. Damn, he hated when he did that.

"You're right," she admitted. "My interests lie with Dallas." She furrowed her delicate brow. "His nose is straight, not too big, not too small, and it sits right in the middle of his face."

He was on the verge of asking her where else she thought she might find a nose when he noticed the glint in her eyes. She'd already forgiven him for his rudeness, was teasing him. She did it with such ease. He envied her that ability and could do no more than nod.

"He has a strong jaw," she said.

He shook his head slightly, and the sparkle dimmed in her eyes.

"He doesn't have a strong jaw?" she asked.

"Ain't never seen it wrestle a steer to the ground."

The sparkle that lit up her eyes was enough to blind a man. And her smile. Her laughter. Dear God, but a man could start to believe in heaven and angels and an eternity of peace.

She wiped a tear of joy from the corner of her eye. "I meant that his jaw was well-defined, like yours." She reached out and trailed her fingers along his jaw.

He jerked back as though she'd seared his flesh with a red-hot branding iron. He could see the hurt and confusion swimming in her eyes, but he couldn't explain to her about the needs that surged through his body with her simple touch, a touch that belonged exclusively to his brother.

"I'm sorry," she stammered.

He crouched before the fire. "Nothing to apologize for. Tomorrow's gonna be a long day. You'd best get some rest. You can take the lantern into the tent with you. I'll want to leave at dawn."

"Shall I wash the plate in that bucket of hot water?"

"Nope. I heated that up for you. Just leave your plate by the log, and I'll take care of it."

Picking up the lantern and bucket of water, Amelia began walking toward the tent.

"Miss Carson?"

Stopping, Amelia turned around. He stood beside the fire, the shadows playing over his profile.

"Yes, Mr. Leigh."

"Dallas has a mustache."

"A mustache?"

"Yeah, one of those big bushy ones. The sides fall down around his mouth. Heard a woman say once that he was handsome as sin."

"Thank you for sharing that with me. I never imagined him with a mustache. Good night, Mr. Leigh."

" 'Night, ma'am."

She walked into the canvas tent, the tarpaulin he'd used to cover the supplies serving as her floor. She set the lantern on the small table and opened her bag. Gingerly, she brought out a stack of letters. She untied the ribbon and removed the letter from the first envelope. Sitting on the edge of the narrow cot, she tried to conjure up an image of Dallas Leigh as she now knew him to be. Brown eyes. Thick mustache.

April 21, 1875

Dear Miss Carson:

I read in your advertisement that you are seeking a husband. If you are still available, I am seeking a wife.

I am in good health, have all my teeth, and consider myself fairly easy on the eyes. I have land, cattle, and a dream to build a cattle empire the likes of which this great state has never seen.

Please write back if you are not yet married, and I will be pleased to bore you with the details.

Yours,
Dallas Leigh

An honorable man would have looked away.

But Houston Leigh had never been an honorable man.

He lay on his pallet beside the fire, the covers drawn over him, his gaze riveted on the tent.

He hadn't realized until he'd banked the fire and thrown the camp into near darkness that the light from the lantern created shadows inside the tent, shadows visible from the outside.

He could see the woman sitting on the cot reading a letter. Reading with those green eyes of clover that darkened each time she spoke.

She had been reading for some time now. He liked to watch her put one letter away and remove another from the envelope. Her movements were elegant, refined, practiced, as though she often read the letters. He wondered if she was reading the letters Dallas had written her. He wondered exactly what Dallas had told her about his brothers, then he damned himself for caring.

She set the letters on a small table beside the cot, the table that held the lantern. She raised her arms over her head and reached toward the top of the tent.

When she lowered her arms, she began to remove the pins from her hair. He watched as the shadow of her hair tumbled over her shoulders and along her back.

His hands clenched, and he was powerless to look away. She reached into her bag and withdrew her brush. Slowly, she pulled the brush through her hair.

He counted the strokes.

And envied the brush.

And envied his brother, who would have the privilege of watching the woman with no canvas cloth separating them.

A hundred strokes. A hundred long, torturous strokes.

She braided her hair. He thought it a crime to confine something so beautiful. To confine her glorious hair into a braid, to confine a lovely woman to an isolated ranch in West Texas.

Slowly, she peeled away her clothing, every stitch, until nothing remained but the shadow of her flesh. His body reacted to the sight and his hand fisted around the blanket. Sweat beaded his brow, his chest, his throat.

He prayed for a cool breeze to whisper along his flesh and remove some of the heat, but the heat only intensified when she dropped a rag into the bucket and bent over to retrieve it. She tilted her head back, lifted her arms, squeezed the cloth, and let the drops rain over her face, her shoulders . . . her breasts.

Leisurely, she wiped the cloth along her throat, following the trail of droplets coursing down her body.

Houston imagined he could feel the pulse of her heart, the warmth of her flesh. He imagined it was his hand gliding over her body instead of the cloth, his hand touching her curves, his lips leaving a damp trail over her skin.

Rolling to his side, he brought his knees toward his chest and huddled like a child trying to protect himself from the aching loneliness. A solitary tear slid along his cheek.

He had his horses. He had his solitude. And on nights when the moon was full, he could look across the vast prairie and hear nothing but the lowing of distant cattle, the whisper of the wind, and the promise of tomorrow.

And if there were moments like this one, when he wished for more, he had but to catch a glimpse of his reflection in the still waters of a pond to remember that he deserved less.

So much less.

Chapter 5

~

AMELIA AWOKE TO the scent of strong coffee permeating the air. She had a feeling it would be as thick as molasses on a winter's day. Grimacing slightly, she rolled off the cot. Every muscle, every bone she possessed protested her movements.

Standing, she pressed her fists into the small of her back and stretched backward. She wondered if she would be better off walking part of the day. Sitting in a jostling wagon was hard on the body.

Using the remaining water from last night, she quickly washed her face, then separated the strands of her braid, brushed her hair, and swept it into a coil. She glanced at her clothing, wishing now that she'd taken the time to wash it while they were near a creek. She had no idea if they would have water every night.

She carefully placed all her belongings into her carpetbag, folded the blankets that had covered the cot, and put out the flame in the lantern. It was a childish thing, really, to sleep with a flame burning beside her.

Cautiously, not certain what she would find beyond the tent this morning, she slipped her fingers between the tent opening and peered through the small slit. She could see Houston crouched before a boulder, a razor in his hand. He had set a jagged mirror no larger than the palm of her hand on the rock so it rested against the tree. He tilted his head slightly and slid the razor up his throat, scraping away the shaving lather and his morning beard.

Amelia withdrew from the opening, and with excitement thrumming through her veins, she snapped open her bag and reached inside. She withdrew her mirror, a large hand mirror that had belonged to her mother.

She rushed out of the tent, grateful that at last she had a way to thank him for all he'd done for her: the tent, the fire, the meals, the warm water. "Mr. Leigh!"

He turned, a furrow creasing his brow.

"You can use my mirror," she said ecstatically as she thrust it toward him.

Waving his hand through the air, he jumped back as though she had offered him a snake. "God Almighty, get that away from me!"

Amelia hugged the mirror against her chest. "But it's so much larger than yours. I thought it would make shaving easier."

"I don't even know why I bother to shave," he mumbled as he picked up the small mirror and dropped it into a box along with the rest of his shaving gear. "Do whatever it is you need to do to be ready. Coffee and biscuits are by the fire. We'll be leavin' right after breakfast."

Tears filled her eyes as she watched him rush out of the camp as though his life depended on it. She pressed the mirror closer to her chest. She wondered if he used the smaller mirror so he wouldn't have to see all of his face at the same time, if in small pieces, perhaps he could pretend he wasn't disfigured.

He'd only been fifteen when he had been wounded. She tried to imagine how devastating it would have been for a fifteen-year-old boy to awaken from battle to discover that a portion of his face had been ravaged by enemy fire. An older man who had learned not to place much value in appearances might have adjusted, but a young man who had yet to court and marry might have withdrawn from the world.

Every conversation they had shared—with the exception of one— had begun when she had asked a question. She had assumed that he considered her a burden. Now, she wondered if perhaps he simply had no experience at socializing. He always looked as though he was searching for something. Could he possibly be searching for something to say?

She held out her mirror and studied her reflection. She wasn't prone to vanity, but she couldn't imagine avoiding the sight of her face. She thought of him tugging his hat brim down, leaning against walls, and standing in shadows. She had a feeling Houston Leigh carried other scars that were visible only to the heart.

Houston knelt beside the creek, habit forcing him to stir up the water before he leaned over to fill the canteens. Still waters could throw a man's reflection back at him.

He dropped to his backside, closed the canteens, and rubbed his hands over his face. He owed her another apology. His reaction to her kindness had frightened her. He'd seen it in those eyes of clover that reflected her heart as openly as a book. They had been filled with joy when he'd turned around, and he'd walked away leaving them filled with despair.

He felt as though he'd just squashed a beautiful butterfly for doing little more than innocently landing on his shoulder.

He closed his eye against the memory of last night. He owed her an apology for that as well, even though she had no way of knowing what had transpired by the campfire after she had walked into the tent. How did a man apologize for taking advantage of a situation without causing more harm?

One way or another he needed to make amends. His lustful thoughts had no place on this journey.

He picked up a stick and drew an "A" in the mud. He traced the right side until the groove was deep and water began to seep into it. Then he carved the "D" and stared at his brother's brand, emblazoning the sight in his mind and on his heart.

He knew that the marriage ceremony that would take place when they arrived at the ranch was only a formality. As far as Dallas was concerned, Amelia had become his wife the day he had joined her initial to his. Houston would do well to remember that.

He tossed the muddy stick aside, forced himself to his feet, and wandered back to camp, his apology tagging along like an unwanted puppy.

He stopped dead in his tracks, his practiced words forgotten as he stared at Amelia walking through the camp, her hand covering her left eye. She tripped over a rock, stumbled, caught her balance, glanced down, her eye still covered, and spoke to the rock as though it were some child who had wandered across her path. "Oh, I didn't see you."

She lifted her gaze and continued to roam the small area, her skirt coming dangerously close to the fire.

"What do you think you're doing?" he bellowed.

She spun around. Her cheeks flamed red as she lowered her hand. "I was trying to see the world as you see it."

He hunkered down before the fire and poured the remaining coffee over the low flames. "Believe me, you don't want to see the world as I see it."

With small hesitant steps, she eased closer to the fire, wringing her hands. He knew he should apologize now, but damn if he could remember the words he wanted to use.

"I've noticed that you try to keep . . . your . . . your right side facing me. I thought it was because you were trying to spare me the sight of your scars . . ."

Her words sliced through him like a knife. If he could, he'd spare her his presence altogether. Damn Dallas. All six bullets wouldn't be enough satisfaction.

"I realize now that your vision is hampered," she continued.

"I'm like a horse that wears blinders on one side, so just stay to the right of me," he said gruffly.

"I didn't mean to embarrass you."

"You didn't embarrass me. You just came dang close to setting your skirt on fire."

"Oh." She gnawed on her lower lip. "At least you don't have to squint when you aim a rifle."

His gaze hardened on hers. Sympathy filled those green eyes, along with the tears.

"I was trying to think of a reason why you might be grateful that you lost an eye. I know it's a silly reason, but sometimes when I'm bothered by something if I can find a reason to be grateful—"

Drawing himself up to his full height, he glared down on her. "Do you know what would have made me grateful, Miss Carson?"

She shook her head slightly.

"If I'd lost both eyes."

As dusk settled in, Amelia scrubbed her blouse viciously in the warm bucket of water Houston had brought her—in silence. He hadn't spoken a full sentence since that morning. He'd grunted, yepped, noped, and for the most part left her alone.

They'd set up camp a little earlier than they did yesterday because he wanted to keep them near water as long as possible. He'd shot a hare for the evening meal. Amelia had wanted to crawl into the dirt and hide when he strode into camp with the hare and his rifle. How could she have said what she did this morning? How could she have thought he'd be grateful for the loss of an eye or the scarring of a face that she was certain would have made women swoon with its rugged beauty?

She knew she could apologize a hundred times, but that wasn't what Houston Leigh wanted . . . or needed. He needed to be accepted as he was, to learn that he didn't have to hug walls or view life through shadows of his own making.

Rising, she slapped her blouse over the side of the wagon, smoothing out the wrinkles so the material could dry through the night. She trailed her fingers over Dallas's brand. She had expected so much more from this trip: laughter, stolen kisses, promises of happiness.

She should leave Houston to mope around in the world he had no desire to share. She should focus her thoughts on Dallas and how she could best make him happy. She wasn't learning much about him from his brother, but perhaps if she read his letters again, she would discover something she'd missed.

She dumped the water out of the bucket, straightened her back with a sigh, and began walking toward the tent and solitude.

A horse's whinny caught her attention. Glancing toward the area where Houston had tethered the mules, she stumbled to a stop.

Houston sat on a log, his left side to her so she was not visible to him. He'd laid a checkerboard on a tree stump. Beside his feet lay his folded duster, his hat on top of it.

He was leaner than she'd expected, and yet his shoulders fanned out as he planted his elbow on his thigh and cupped his chin in his palm. He had rolled up his sleeves, and she could see the strength in his forearm. Before him, his horse snorted.

"You sure?" Houston asked.

The horse bobbed her head.

"All right," Houston replied and moved a black checker piece across the board. He promptly picked up his own red disk and jumped the black one he'd just moved.

The horse whinnied, dipped her head, and nudged the checkerboard off the tree stump.

"God damn! You're a sorry loser," Houston whispered harshly.

Laughing, Amelia approached the duo. In one seamless movement, Houston grabbed his hat, settled it on his head, sprang to his feet, and spun around.

"Thought you were washin' your clothes," he said from beneath the shadows of his brim.

She took no offense at his actions, but the sadness swept through her. He trusted his horse, but not her. She fought to keep her feelings from showing on her face as she rubbed the horse's shoulder. "I was, but it doesn't take long to wash a blouse." She eyed him speculatively. "I suppose I should have offered to wash your shirt."

"That's not necessary. On a cattle drive, a man gets used to having dirty clothes for a while."

"But we're not on a cattle drive. I'll wash your shirt tomorrow."

He opened his mouth as though to protest, and then snapped it shut.

Amelia pressed her face against the horse's neck. "I never mentioned that I think your horse is beautiful. I thought she was brown, but sometimes when the sun hits her coat just right, she looks red."

"She's a sorrel. Got speed and endurance bred into her, and she's smart as a whip."

She studied the man who was watching the horse with obvious affection. She remembered his description of the horse that had broken Dallas's leg. "You know a lot about horses."

"I'm a mustanger. It's my job to know a horse's temperament. With mustangs, it's usually easy. Their coloring gives them away. A dun with a black mane and tail is hardy, an albino is worthless, a black is a good horse unless he has a wavy tail and mane."

"That's amazing," she said quietly, more impressed with how much he'd spoken rather than what he'd said. "Do you raise them?"

"Startin' to. They used to run wild over Texas, but they're gettin' harder to find so I've taken to breedin' 'em."

She rubbed the horse's muzzle. "What's her name?"

"Sorrel." He lifted a shoulder in a careless shrug. "Reckon I got as much imagination as my parents."

She laughed lightly, delighted with the conversation. Although he still wore his hat, he had relaxed his stance. He appeared to be more at ease with horses than with people. She wondered what would make him comfortable around her, what would have to happen in order for him to leave his hat on the ground. "I play checkers. Probably better than your horse."

He narrowed his eye. "My horse is pretty good."

She tilted her chin. "I'm better."

"You willin' to put that claim to a test?"

She'd thought he would never ask, but decided against showing too much enthusiasm. She didn't want to frighten away the easy companionship that was settling in beneath the shade. She simply waltzed to the log where he'd been sitting and tilted up her face, offering the challenge, "Why not?"

He shot across the short space like a bullet fired from a gun, gathered his playing board and pieces, and set them carefully on the tree stump. He playfully shoved Sorrel aside when the horse nudged his shoulder. "This ain't your game. Get outta here." Then he dropped down, sitting back on his haunches, and the game began.

Amelia had never seen anyone concentrate so hard on a game. Houston balanced himself on the balls of his feet, his elbow resting on his thigh, his chin in his palm, studying each move she made as though each move were equally important.

She remembered playing checkers with her father before the war. Their games went quickly, and usually ended with both of them laughing, neither of them winning. She was beginning to understand why Houston's horse had tipped over the board.

"My father taught me to play checkers," she said. "If I thought I was going to lose, I'd move the pieces when he wasn't looking. He always pretended not to notice."

"You say that like you loved him."

"Of course I loved him. Very much. He was my father. Didn't you love your father?"

"Not particularly."

She sensed from the tightening of his jaw that he might have regretted voicing his feelings.

"Your move," he grumbled.

She promptly removed another one of his pieces from the board and settled in for the long wait as he contemplated his strategy. With his thumb, he tipped his hat off his brow. His attention clearly focused on the game, she was certain he didn't realize that he'd allowed the shadows to slip away from his face. She welcomed the opportunity to view more than his profile. The black patch was larger than many she'd seen. She supposed that he wanted to leave as few scars visible as he could. Her fingers flexed, and just as she had when she had first met him, she felt an overwhelming desire to touch the unsightly scars with compassion. She imagined holding him to her breast, easing the pain that still lingered within his remaining eye.

An unexpected warmth suffused her as though she'd wandered too close to a roaring blaze. She balled her hands into tight fists to stop her fingers from trembling, from reaching toward a face that fascinated her with the history it revealed. Houston's marred features left no doubt that he'd fought in the war. She wondered if Dallas's countenance revealed as much.

"Was Dallas wounded during the war?" she asked.

Houston tugged on the brim of his hat, bringing the shadows home. "Nope."

She chastised herself, wondering if she'd ever remember how quickly talk of the war distanced Houston. Although he sat across from her, she sensed that he was retreating. She wanted desperately to keep him near.

"Does Dallas play?" she asked, grateful to see the stiffness roll out of Houston's shoulders as he leaned forward.

"With all he has goin', I don't imagine he has time."

"Don't the two of you ever play?"

He reached toward a piece, then pulled back his hand without touching or moving the disk. "No."

He scrutinized the board with such intensity that Amelia wished she had planned to lose. With a sigh, he moved a piece forward, placing it so she had no choice but to jump over and claim it. She was certain he intended to forfeit his piece in order to gain two of hers, but she didn't think it would be enough of a sacrifice for him to win. She somehow knew that her winning would also be her loss.

She slipped her fingers beneath the board and quickly tossed it off the stump.

"What the—" He glared at her with obvious displeasure.

Amelia smiled sheepishly. "I thought I might lose."

"You knew darn good and well that you weren't gonna lose."

He reached for the board, and Amelia wrapped her fingers around his arm. He stilled, the muscles beneath her fingers tensing. "It was only a game. You're supposed to have fun when you're playing a game."

"I was havin' fun," he said gruffly.

"You were?"

He nodded, but the muscles beneath her hand didn't relax.

"Then let's play again." She settled into place while he set up the game. She allowed him to have five moves before she dumped the board over.

"Dang it!" he roared.

"You weren't having fun," she said.

"I sure as heck was. I was gonna win that time."

She smiled sweetly. "No, you weren't."

"You're aggravating, you know that?" he said as he collected his board and pieces.

"Does Dallas smile more often than you do?" she asked.

"Everyone smiles more than I do." He laid the board on the stump and put the pieces into place. "Go ahead and move."

Amelia leaned forward and placed her elbow on the stump of the tree, cradling her chin in her palm. "Why don't you smile?"

He averted his gaze, and Amelia studied his perfect profile, imagining how he might have looked if a portion of his face hadn't been torn to shreds when he was a young man. Women would have fallen over themselves to gain his attention. They might have said he was handsome as sin.

He certainly had the temperament of the devil.

"You feel up to riding?" he asked.

His words startled her. The shadows were lengthening. "You want to travel at night?"

He drew his gaze back to hers. "No, I just want to show you somethin' if you feel up to riding. Of course, you'll have to ride on the horse with me."

She glanced at Sorrel and the saddle on the ground. She hadn't ridden in years, not since her father had died. A horse wasn't nearly as wide as the seat of a wagon. She wouldn't be able to avoid the accidental brushing of thighs or elbows. She wouldn't be able to ignore the closeness of Houston's body. Her mouth went dry with the thought, her heart pounding. He wanted to share something with her. No matter how small, friendship was built on sharing. "What are you going to show me?"

"If I could describe it, I wouldn't have to show you."

She rose from the log. "Then I'd like to see it."

A few minutes later, he led Sorrel over to her and lifted her onto the saddle. She clung to the pommel as he slipped a booted foot into the stirrup and threw a leg over the back of the horse.

Reaching around her, he took hold of the reins. "Relax," he ordered. "You'll make the horse nervous."

"I am relaxed," she squeaked, nestled between his thighs, her shoulder bumping against his chest.

"Yeah, and I was having fun playing checkers," he said in a low voice as he prodded the horse forward.

The gently rolling plains stretched out before them. She glanced over her shoulder, but Fort Worth was beyond her vision, a piece of her past now. Her future lay ahead.

Sorrel plodded up a steep rise. When they reached the crest of the hill, Houston brought the horse to a halt, dismounted, and gazed toward the horizon.

"See where the sun touches the land?" he asked in a reverent voice.

"Yes."

"That's where you'll be living."

Amelia admired the tranquil splendor of the distant site. Lavender and blue hues swept across the sky, reached down, and melted into the green horizon.

"See all the people?" he asked.

"No."

Too late she realized his question required no answer. She glanced down. The dark depths of his eye held a profound sadness, and the purpose of his question struck her hard with its intensity. She looked back at the majestic land, the scattered trees, the vast emptiness.

"Who will you talk to, Miss Carson?" he asked.

"I'll talk with my husband."

"And when he's not there?"

"Our children."

"I don't know what Dallas told you in his letters, but you're heading into a loneliness so deep that it hurts the heart."

"Only if you let it, Mr. Leigh."

Houston didn't know if he'd ever heard words spoken with so much determination or if he'd ever seen anyone look as serene as Amelia did. The breeze blew wisps of her hair over her face, and her lips curved into a smile.

"I think it's beautiful," she said quietly.

"You have no idea what you're heading toward."

"No, I don't. But I know what I've come from. And I have no desire to return to it." Turning her head slightly, she glanced down at him and gave him a rueful smile. "You were right this morning when you said I didn't want to view the world as you do. You see only the emptiness. I see a place that's waiting to be filled with dreams."

Chapter 6

୬

"DALLAS? DALLAS, I'M *scared.*"

"*Don't be.*"

But Houston was afraid. The clouds passing across the midnight sky reminded him of ghosts, and he imagined that he could hear their tortured cries in the rushing waters of nearby Chickamauga Creek. He drew the blanket up to his chin, but it didn't stop his shivering.

"Dallas, I'm scared about tomorrow." His harsh whisper echoed around him, more frightening because his pa had told him that Chickamauga meant "river of death" in Cherokee.

Lying on the pallet beside him, Dallas rolled over and mumbled, "I ain't gonna hold you, but you can scoot a little closer to me if you want. Just don't let anybody see you doin' it."

Houston inched over until he could feel the warmth of Dallas's body, but not the solidness of his touch. He didn't want his father to find him sleeping right beside his brother.

"What if I die?" Houston whispered.

"You won't. Just stay by my side. I won't let nothin' happen to you."

"Swear?"

"Give you my word."

Amelia awoke to an anguished wail that ripped through her dream into her heart. With trembling fingers, she turned up the flame in the lantern.

Her blood pounded at her temples; her breath came in short gasps.

She took a deep breath to steady herself. In her dream, she and a man she wanted to believe was Dallas—but who had looked remarkably like Houston—had been walking through a field of clover. His arm had been around her, and she had felt safer than she had felt in years. She didn't think the cry had come from her.

She slipped off the cot and eased into her night wrapper, drawing it tightly around her as though it had the power to ward off her fears.

She tiptoed across the tent, guided her fingers through the tent flap, and peered through the small opening her narrow fingers created. She could see Houston hunkered down before the fire, wearing his duster, his hat drawn low over his brow as though he had plans to ride out.

She widened the opening in the tent. "I thought I heard a cry," she said, her voice quivering.

He visibly stiffened. "It was just an animal. Go back to sleep."

His rough voice didn't ease her doubts. He reached for the pot of coffee. As he poured the coffee, he trembled with such intensity that the brew sloshed over the sides of his tin cup.

Amelia pulled her wrapper closer, gathering her courage within its folds. Leaving the tent, she padded across the campsite and knelt beside Houston.

"I said to go back to bed," he said gruffly.

"Do you think we're in danger?"

"No."

He gripped the handle of the pot so tightly that his bones were visible against his skin. Reaching out, Amelia covered his hand, her palm cradling his knuckles. He jerked at her touch, but he didn't attempt to pull away.

She rubbed her hand over his, surprised to find his so cold. Slowly he relaxed, his fingers loosening their grip on the handle. She eased the pot away from him and set it near the fire.

He wrapped his hand around the tin cup. She was amazed that the cup didn't dent with the strength of his grip.

"When I was a child," she said quietly, "I used to have nightmares, and I would pray that I would grow up fast so that the nightmares would go away." She gently placed her hand on his arm, hoping to gain his attention. Ignoring her, he focused his gaze on the fire and clenched his jaw tightly. "When I grew up, I learned that nightmares don't go away. They just become more terrifying because we understand so much more."

She worked the tin cup from his grip, held his hands, and willed him to look at her. He continued to stare into the fire. "Do you want to talk about your dream?"

"Nope."

"You don't have to be embarrassed because you were frightened by a dream."

He broke free of her hold and surged to his feet. "Frightened by a dream? Woman, I'm afraid of life!"

"Do you think you're alone—"

"Yes! Goddamn it! I'm alone!"

Houston regretted his outburst as soon as he saw the stricken expression fall across Amelia's lovely face. She looked as though he'd taken his fist to her. He'd had moments in his life when he'd felt small, but he'd never felt this small or this ashamed. Lord knew, he'd done plenty that he could be ashamed of.

He took a step toward her, his hands moving like a windmill in a slow breeze. He didn't know what to do with them. He didn't want to frighten her, but he was afraid she might grab his hands if he held them still, and he'd end up wrapping his arms around her just so he'd have a tether to hang onto so he'd feel safe. Only a woman shouldn't make a man feel safe. A man was supposed to protect a woman. "Amelia—"

She tilted her head slightly, the wounded expression retreating until she smiled so sweetly that he thought his heart might shatter. Every word he'd ever known rushed out of his head.

"I remember the first time I slept alone," she said softly, her voice drifting on the calm breeze as she shifted her gaze to the fire. "The bed was so large. The night so dark. I thought surely both would devour me. And the sounds. I heard a door creak and a board moan. I felt so incredibly alone." She wrapped her arms around herself and began to rock back and forth. "My father died during the war. And my sisters. Allison and Amanda."

The serenity of her gaze fascinated him. His hands had settled into a stillness as her voice floated toward him. She had a hell of a way of distracting a man. Her remembrances had lulled his memories back into oblivion, his shakes and sweats going along with them. She glanced up at him.

"My mother liked names that began with A. My father's name was Andrew, and I often wondered if that was why she married him."

"That's not a very practical reason for marrying someone," he said.

"Is my reason for marrying your brother practical?"

He stepped closer to the fire, wishing he could attain her composure. She always seemed at peace, relishing each moment as it came. Resting on the balls of his feet, he cautiously bent his knees until his gaze was only slightly higher than hers. "I don't know your reason."

"Because I hate being alone." She closed her eyes. "And because I want to share someone's dream."

"Don't you have your own dream?"

She opened her eyes and smiled mischievously. "A question?"

Lord, he loved the glimmer in her eyes as though she'd trapped him, and he wasn't altogether certain that she hadn't. He lowered his gaze to the fire and watched the orange and red flames writhing in a contorted waltz. "I had no right to ask." But damn, he wanted to know everything about her, about her dreams, her reasons for traveling such a great distance to marry his brother.

"I dream of not being hungry. I dream of being warm."

He shifted his gaze to her. The smile had left her face.

"I dream of regaining something of what I lost during the war: a family, a promise that tomorrow will come, and that it will be worth living, savoring, and remembering."

"And you think Dallas will give you all of that?"

Her lips tilted up. "Another question. I'm impressed."

He wanted to look away, but her eyes held him captive. At that moment, with those green eyes boring into him, Houston almost had an overwhelming desire to search for his own dreams. "You don't have to answer it."

She scooted closer to him. "I think I do. No, I don't think he will *give* me my dreams, but I think we'll work together to gain them. I've always believed that dreams were meant to be shared. Where's the joy in reaching for something if you have no one to see you capture it?"

He had no idea. He'd stopped reaching long ago.

She laid her hand on his arm. "I don't expect you to answer that."

"That's good because I wouldn't know how."

She laughed, tilted her head back, and looked at the canopy of stars. "Oh, the sky is beautiful tonight. I almost envy you sleeping outside."

"It has its moments." Just as she did. Sweet moments, gentle moments. Moments that filled him with awe.

She smiled softly. "I should stop pestering you and let you go back to sleep."

He unfolded his body as she rose gracefully to her feet and turned away from the fire.

"Oh, look. I can see the shadow of a moth that's flying inside the tent. Isn't it pretty?" The smile eased off her face. "I can see the moth's shadow," she said in a hushed voice, "and everything inside the tent."

Houston stiffened as her gaze streaked to his pallet. With his saddle at one end, it didn't take much imagination to figure out which way he'd been lying or what had been in his line of sight.

Her gaze flew back to the tent, then to the pallet before she snapped accusing eyes his way. "I can see everything. Everything. Have you been watching me each evening?"

Sweet Lord, he wanted to speak but anything he could have uttered would have condemned him. As it turned out, his silence condemned him.

As she drew back her hand, he forced himself to give her an easy target. The blow came, jerking his head to the side.

She stormed into the tent, the flap momentarily billowing and slapping after her. Her shadow reflected as much hurt and anger as he imagined she felt. Then the shadow disappeared into the darkness as she extinguished the flame in the lantern.

Houston felt as though all the light had suddenly gone out of his life. He broke out in a cold sweat as his gaze swept over the camp. He'd told her he was alone, but until this moment he didn't know the true meaning of the word.

She'd shut him out of her life with a single breath. She'd ask no more questions of him, of that he was certain. He should have been relieved. Instead, he thought he might keel over and die. With trepidation, he neared the tent. "Miss Carson?"

A thick heavy silence was her reply. For some reason, he thought he'd feel a sight better if he could hear her sobbing or throwing things around.

"Miss Carson, you need to step outside and slap me again. The side you hit is mostly dead. You need to hit the other side of my face so I can feel it like I should."

He could hear nothing but the heavy pounding of his heart. He could see nothing but a vast emptiness filling the coming days. Dear God, what words could atone for what he'd done?

"Miss Carson, I know what I did was wrong. It was shameful, and I regretted it even as I did it, but dear Lord, woman, I swear to God, I've never seen a sweeter shadow than yours . . . and that's all I saw. Just your shadow."

"Without clothes! Washing up! Enjoying a few moments of freedom!"

Sweet Lord, yes, and he'd enjoyed her moments of freedom most of all, but he didn't think she'd appreciate hearing that at this moment.

"Miss Carson, if I could undo what I'd done, I would. But I can't. If you just knew how beautiful—"

"I don't want to hear it, Mr. Leigh. Just leave me alone."

"You have every right to be upset—" He heard a sob. He'd been wrong. Hearing a noise was worse than hearing the silence.

"Miss Carson, I'd do anything on God's green earth to make this up to you. I'd pluck out my eye—"

A light flared inside the tent, and the flap flew open. She stood before him, her eyes rimmed in red, and he could see the faintest trail of tears along her cheeks. In all his life, he'd never loathed himself more.

She sniffed. "Do you mean it? Would you do anything?"

He glanced at her hands, expecting to see the knife she no doubt planned to use to remove his remaining eye. But her hands held nothing but the cool night air.

He swallowed hard. "Yes, ma'am. Anything."

She folded her arms beneath her breasts and swept out of the tent like a queen granting her least favorite subject an audience. She held her chin high with a dignity unlike any he'd ever seen. Dallas had been right to refer to her as the Queen of the Prairie.

She spun about and looked down her nose at him—as much as she was able, considering the top of her head didn't reach the height of his shoulder.

"You may sleep in the tent tonight."

Although her words had come softly, she'd spoken them with the force of a hissing snake. His gut clenched. He wasn't exactly sure where she was headed with this train of thought, and he wasn't certain that he wanted to know, but she appeared to be waiting on him to respond.

"Excuse me?"

"You may sleep in the tent," she repeated slowly as though he hadn't a lick of sense, and he was beginning to think that he might not have any sense at all. "Undress. Wash up. Do whatever it is men do before they go to sleep." She dropped to the log, placed her elbows on her thighs, cupped her chin, and smiled sweetly. "And I'll watch."

"Are you out of your mind?" he roared.

"You said you'd do anything. Well, Mr. Leigh, you have just heard my idea of anything."

He glared at the tent. The goddamn moth was still flying around. If he stepped into that tent, his first order of business would be to murder that pesky critter. He glanced at the woman sitting on the log. "No, ma'am, I can't do it."

"Why not? What's good for the goose is good for the gander."

"It ain't the same at all. I'll know you're watching."

She came off the log like vengeance sweeping through hell. "And you think my *not* knowing made what you did acceptable?"

No, it didn't make it acceptable at all.

"What if I gave you a real pretty apology with some fancy words—"

"No."

"If I don't do this, you're gonna stay mad, aren't you?"

"Yes."

Good Lord, based on the delivery of that one simple word, she'd stay angry until they reached the ranch . . . and maybe beyond that. He'd be traveling through hell when he was just getting used to being near heaven.

His stomach was knotted so tightly that he didn't know if he could even walk into the tent. But it was the tear shimmering in the corner of her eye that decided him. The firelight caught it, and he could see himself as she must see him: a man who had shattered her trust.

Without another word, he flung back the tent flap and stormed inside, allowing the flap to fall behind him, encasing him in the golden haze that filled the tent.

He could smell her sweetness surrounding him. He couldn't identify the scent. It wasn't horses, or leather, or sweat. It was soft, reminding him of something so far back in his memory that he didn't know if he could pull it forward. His mother, perhaps, leaning over him, brushing the hair off his brow, telling him not to be afraid.

"You can't just stand there, Mr. Leigh. You have to wash up!"

Her voice penetrated his memories, reminding him more of his father than his mother. "Don't just stand there, boy! When the battle starts, you march into the thick of it."

And he'd marched, while everything inside him had screamed for him to run.

He took a step toward the small bucket and glanced at the water. With no steam rising up, it looked cold, but he'd taken cold baths before.

"Mr. Leigh!"

"All right!" Damn impatient woman. He tore his hat off his head and tossed it onto the rumpled covers of the bed where she'd been sleeping before he'd cried out like a baby. He was tempted to place his palm on the bed and see if it still carried her warmth, but she was watching him now, watching him as he'd watched her. Damn his eye for remaining open when it should have been closed.

Rolling his shoulders, he worked his way out of his duster and laid it beside his hat. He sat on the edge of the cot and discreetly placed his hand near her pillow. His fingers lightly brushed the area, searching for her warmth and finding only the cold.

She wouldn't be giving off any warmth until he'd done what she asked. *Anything*, he'd said. In the future, he wouldn't use *that* word around her.

He jerked off his boots. Unbuttoning his shirt, he stood, pulled it over his head, and dropped it on his duster.

He turned, presenting the silhouette of his backside to the front of the tent. Praying that she wasn't circling the tent, he began to unbutton his trousers.

Amelia watched, mesmerized. The shadows were distorted, not

nearly as clear as she'd imagined, but that didn't change the fact that he'd wronged her. Considering the slowness with which he was removing his clothing, she assumed he was beginning to understand that.

With a quickness she wasn't expecting, he dropped his trousers. She buried her face in her hands. Dallas would no doubt send her back to Georgia if he found out what she'd required of his brother. It didn't matter that she couldn't actually see his flesh or the rigid contours that probably ran along his body.

He was standing inside her tent, buck naked. Whatever had she been thinking to require such a thing of him? She had wanted him to experience the humiliation that she'd felt when she'd discovered that he'd been watching her.

Only now mortification swamped her. The warmth flamed her cheeks as her mind brought up images of Houston washing himself. She couldn't bring herself to look, but in her mind's eye, she could see the glistening drops of water trailing down his throat, over his chest, along his stomach, traveling down . . .

She doubled over and pressed her face against her knees, but she couldn't block out the images. She had always been a dreamer, but no decent woman would conjure up the fantasy swirling inside her head.

Had he been content to stare at her silhouette or had he imagined the drops of water—

"I learned my lesson."

Amelia screeched and shot off the log, but not before she caught sight of a knee resting above a hairy calf. She hadn't heard him kneel beside her, but she was listening now, listening hard for his approach as she stood near the edge of the shadows, within the ring of light that the fire created. "I said you were to sleep in the tent," she reminded the man behind her, grateful she couldn't see him.

"I don't think you're really interested in watching me sleep. I gave you your show. Now, get inside the tent and get some sleep. We'll be leaving at dawn."

"That wasn't the bargain."

She heard his knee pop and assumed he'd risen to his feet. She was tempted to step beyond the light, to disappear into the night, but she feared the darkness while she was only wary of the man.

"I'm used to sleeping outside. I'm not sure you'll know what to do if you wake up with a snake coiled on your chest."

"A snake?" Without thinking, she spun around and found the breath knocked out of her. He stood stiffly beside the fire, his clothes bunched before him offering him some protection from her wandering gaze.

The firelight played over his flesh like a lover's caress. He had additional scars on his left shoulder, healed flesh that trailed down his chest toward his stomach and finally blended into oblivion. Old wounds the water may have kissed on its journey.

He shifted his stance, and his muscles rippled with the slight movement. He appeared much stronger than she'd imagined. She lowered her gaze as his hands tightened their hold on his clothing. She could see the veins and muscles in his arms straining with the force of his grip.

"Git inside the tent," he growled in a low, warning voice, "or you're gonna see a lot more than my shadow."

With a quick nod, Amelia scurried into the tent.

Houston fought to hold back his laughter. The woman was precious. Bold as brass one minute, ordering him into her tent; timid as a mouse the next, with wide eyes and a blush that just begged a man to touch her cheek.

Dropping to his pallet, he worked his way back into his clothes. Inside his cabin, he did sleep without a stitch of clothing, but not out here where a man *could* wake up with a snake curled over him.

He hefted his saddle to the other end of his pallet and stretched out, his gaze focused on the mules instead of the tent. He should have done it this way the first night.

He chuckled low, remembering the relief he'd experienced when he'd peered out the tent and seen Amelia crouching on the log, her face hidden. He wondered at what point she'd covered her eyes. Maybe he could have spared himself the cold wash-up. He'd done it so quickly that his body had barely noticed the touch of the cloth. He supposed out of fairness, he should have let the cloth caress his body the way she did when she washed. He should have slowly removed every speck of dust and every remnant of dried sweat until he could have come out of that tent smelling like she did: clean, pure and tempting.

How could a woman be both pure and tempting? A decent woman

shouldn't wash herself the way Amelia did. A decent woman shouldn't travel halfway across the country to marry a man she only knew through letters. Maybe Amelia Carson wasn't a decent woman. Maybe—

"Mr. Leigh?"

Her soft, gentle voice brushed over him like the finest of linen rubbing against his coarse body, sending his thoughts, to perdition where they belonged.

Rolling over, he came up on his elbow and met her troubled gaze as she knelt beside his pallet, her hands folded primly in her lap. "Amelia, don't you think after what we learned about each other tonight that we can call each other by our first names?"

Even in the night shadows, he could see the flush in her cheeks as she lowered her gaze to her clenched hands.

"That's what I wanted to explain. I didn't watch for very long so I just . . . I just didn't want you to think I was wanton."

He didn't know what possessed him to slip his finger beneath her chin and lift her gaze back to his. He could feel the slight quiver beneath her soft skin and hated himself because his weakness—and not hers— had brought them to this moment.

"I don't think that."

Her green eyes held a depth of sadness. "Dallas might feel differently if he were to find out about tonight."

"He won't hear it from me."

His fingers ached to spread out across her face, his palm to cup her cheek, his thumb to graze her softness, his hand to draw her heart-shaped mouth to his. In all his life, he'd kissed only one woman—a whore whose breath had carried the stench of all the men who had come before him.

He had a feeling that the first time Dallas kissed Amelia, he'd taste nothing but her sweetness . . . as he should. Dallas had earned the right to nibble on those tempting lips because he'd dared to offer her a portion of his dream.

Houston drew his hand away before his fingers stopped listening to his head and started listening to his erratic heart.

"You'd best go back to bed now," he said in a rough voice he hardly recognized as his own.

"I don't like to be inside the darkness, but if I keep the lantern burning, I'll create shadows."

"I won't be lookin'."

"Promise?"

He deserved that hesitancy, that lack of trust. Dallas had told him once that if a man went back on his word one time, his reputation as a man of honor became little more than dust. He'd never known Dallas to break a promise. The strength of his word had laid the foundation for his empire. "I give you my word."

She pushed to her feet. "Sleep well."

Nodding, he settled back against his saddle, resisting the urge to watch her walk into the tent, knowing if he did, he might never find the strength to look away.

Chapter 7

❧

MORNING BROUGHT WITH it the glaring sun and harsh reality. Amelia had avoided Houston's gaze as she had eaten her breakfast. When he had begun packing their belongings into the wagon, she'd come to the stream seeking solace.

It had been one thing to meet Houston's gaze by the campfire, with more shadows than light, but when no shadows separated them . . . she couldn't meet his gaze, knowing what he had seen, what she had seen.

She had issued her challenge last night much as she had often dared her sisters—much as they had dared her—to step beyond the rigid guidelines their parents had set for them. But as imaginative as the dares had been, they had been children's dares, designed to make hearts race and giggles erupt, designed to strengthen a bond.

Last night her heart had raced, but she'd felt no desire to giggle, to laugh, or to smile. No bond existed between her and Houston that could be strengthened.

She stared at the small stream and listened to the gurgling water. She felt soiled, inside more than out. She wished Dallas had come for her. She wished they would reach the ranch today. She wished she'd never seen the firelight skim over Houston's bronzed skin.

She dropped to her backside, removed her shoes and stockings, and wiggled her toes in the cold water. It wasn't enough to wash away the memories of last night, to make her forget how for one insane moment she had envied the firelight.

Lifting her skirt higher, she waded into the stream until the brown water lapped at her calves. Brown like Houston's gaze, Dallas's eyes. Brown like fertile soil.

"Amelia?"

Refusing to acknowledge Houston's presence by turning around, she glared at the trees lining the opposite bank. Anger swelled anew, anger at herself because she liked the way her name sounded coming from his lips, with his deep timbre wrapped around the sounds. She hoped Dallas's voice would carry the same resonance.

"You got any plans to look at me or talk to me today?" he asked.

"Perhaps at nightfall. It's easier with the shadows around us."

"Then I reckon we'll wait here till nightfall."

She clenched her hands. "I thought if I did to you what you had done to me, I would find what you took from me. But trust isn't gained back that easily." She pivoted in the water and tilted her face up slightly.

He wasn't wearing his hat. No shadows kept his gaze from hers. Within the dark depths, she read sorrow, shame, and a profound apology that almost made her weep. "I'm sorry," she whispered hoarsely.

"No need to apologize. It was all my doing. I have a habit of taking the easy road. It was easier to watch than it was to turn away." He settled his hat on his head. "The wagon's loaded. We can leave whenever you're ready."

"Just a few—Oh!" The sharp pain came suddenly, without warning. She stumbled back, falling into the cold water.

Houston thrashed through the water, lifted her into his arms, and carried her out of the stream. "What happened?"

"My leg. Something bit me. A fish or something."

Gingerly he set her on the grassy bank and knelt beside her.

"Close your eyes," he demanded tersely as he tore the hat from his head. "God damn it! Close your eyes!"

He had only sworn at her once—last night—and normally she would have obeyed anyone who yelled at her with such urgency. But she couldn't bring herself to move, to act, to do anything but stare at the two puncture marks in her calf and the blood trailing toward her ankle.

"What happened?" she asked.

"Snake," he replied as he wrapped a strip of leather around her calf before unsheathing the knife he carried at his side. The early-morning sunlight glinted off the steel.

"It's gonna hurt. I'm sorry," he said quietly as he sliced the blade across her calf. She clenched her teeth and balled her hands into fists, wishing she could reassure him, but afraid if she opened her mouth to speak, she'd scream.

He dropped the knife. Wrapping his warm hands around her calf, he lowered his mouth to the wound. His jaws worked feverishly as he sucked and spit. Sucked and spit. Over and over.

She touched her finger to the black patch dangling from her calf and shifted her gaze. No strip of leather indented his brow as he worked. His thick black hair fell over his face, and she had a strong urge to brush it back.

"Am I going to die?" she asked quietly.

He jerked his head up, apparently forgetting or unaware that he wasn't shielding his face from her gaze. Nothing remained of his left eye or cheek. His tangled flesh was stretched taut in places, ridged and heavily scarred in others, as though his ravaged face hadn't quite known how to repair itself. She wanted to weep for the pain he must have endured, for the wounded child he had once been.

"No," he said with conviction. "No, you're not gonna die."

He scooped her into his arms as though she were little more than a bouquet of flowers, freshly picked. She pressed her face against his chest as he carried her in long strides back to the camp. She could hear the pounding of his heart, so hard, so fast that she was certain he was in pain. He set her down near the cold ashes of their campfire.

"I'm still bleeding."

"That's all right. Let your leg bleed for a while. I'm going to set the tent back up."

"Why?" she asked, the panic knotting her stomach.

Gently, he cradled her cheek. She felt the slight trembling in his fingers and placed her hand over his. His Adam's apple slowly slid up and down.

"You're gonna get sick," he said, his voice ragged. "Real sick."

"I didn't see a snake," she said, hopefully.

"He left his mark. Probably a water moccasin, maybe a rattler that close to shore."

He withdrew his fingers, and a coldness seeped through her. A shudder racked her body.

He tore off his duster and gently slipped it over her shoulders, tucking it in around her. He pulled his shirt over his head and wadded it up. "Here, lie down."

She curled up on the ground. "I'm tired," she said, her tongue feeling thick. "Didn't sleep well last night."

"You'll sleep today. I'll be back for you."

Before she could reply, he raced to the wagon and began searching through its contents, an urgency to his movements. Her eyelids grew heavy, but she forced them to remain open as she watched him set up the tent beneath the shade of a tree.

His back was lean, tanned, and she wondered if he often worked without a shirt. His muscles reminded her of a stallion's, sleek but powerful, bunching with an easy grace as he worked.

She closed her eyes and the dizziness assaulted her as the blackness swirled around her. Jerking her eyes open, she fought to ignore the throbbing pain in her calf and concentrated instead on the plainness of the patch that usually covered the harshest of Houston's scars. Perhaps she would decorate it with tiny flowers before she gave it back to him.

As she reached for it, to examine it more closely, so did long brown fingers. She watched as Houston removed the strip of leather from her leg and tied it around his head, the patch falling into place to cover his loss.

He wrapped a strip of cloth around her wound. Then he lifted her into his arms and carried her into the tent, gingerly setting her on the cot.

"Do you think you can get out of your wet clothes or do you need me to help?" he asked.

She glanced at her nightgown waiting on her pillow. She nodded lethargically, her tongue struggling to form the words. "I . . . can."

"Good. I'll be back in a few minutes."

He disappeared before she could say more. Sluggishly, she worked her way out of her clothes, leaving them heaped on the floor. She slipped on her nightgown before curling up on her side and drifting off to sleep, trusting her life to Houston's keeping.

Houston scooped the mud out of the bowl and patted it over the swollen flesh on Amelia's calf, hoping the coolness would reduce the swelling.

Damn, he didn't want to have to cut out part of her muscle. He knew the venom could kill the flesh, the muscle, and in rare instances, the victim.

The thought of her dying caused a hard, painful knot to settle deep in his chest. He was certain she had more questions she wanted to ask, discoveries she wanted to make.

He wanted her to see a sunset from the porch of his cabin, with the far off horizon a distant haze. He wanted to learn to answer her questions with patience.

He wanted to watch her daughter grow up.

For some ungodly reason, he thought she'd give Dallas a little girl instead of the son he craved. He imagined a little girl with Amelia's golden hair, her green eyes, and her tiny tipped-up nose, running over Dallas's ranch, wrapping cowhands around her tiny finger. He hoped sometime she'd visit with her Uncle Houston. He'd give her a gentle mare to ride and share his secret place with her where the wildflowers bloomed, the water misted, and the sky was always blue.

And he'd love her. If she was half as sweet as her mother, he'd love her.

He shifted his gaze to Amelia's face. Dear God, but she was pale. He brushed his mud-caked fingers over his trousers until they felt clean, then he gently wiped away the dewy sweat beading above her upper lip.

He wished he'd been able to spare her the sight of his face uncovered. He'd told her to close her eyes, but she hadn't obeyed him, and he hadn't had time to press the issue.

If Dallas had told her to close her eyes, she'd have closed them. His voice carried the mark of authority. If the man said, "Jump!", every other man within earshot would ask, "How high?"

Hell, Houston hadn't been able to make those two ragamuffins at the train depot follow his order to leave him alone. Maybe that was the reason he enjoyed working with horses so much. They listened to him.

Amelia's eyes fluttered open, her green gaze vacant. Damn, he wished the snake had chosen him.

Her lips lifted slightly, and a small spark glinted in her eyes. "No shadow show tonight."

He swallowed hard, wondering how she could tease him when she was feeling so poorly. "You get to feeling better, and I'll give you one," he promised, knowing he'd give her anything, do anything if she just wouldn't die on him.

Her smile withered away like flowers pulled from the earth and left too long without water. Reaching out, she pressed her palm against his left shoulder, her warmth seeping through his flannel shirt. "Did you get this wound at the same time?"

"Yes. I'm sorry you had to see my face—"

She moved her hand up to palm his left jaw. The scars were fewer there, and he could feel the gentleness of her touch.

"The scars suit you," she said quietly.

Yeah, the scars suited him. A man should be as ugly on the outside as he was on the inside.

Self-consciously he wrapped his fingers around her hand and placed it on the cot. She tucked it beneath her chin and drew her legs up as she lay on her side, vulnerable as the day she was born. He brought a blanket up to her shoulders, but it could only protect her from the chill of the evening, not the harshness of life. Offering comfort was as foreign to him as giving an apology. He desperately searched the recesses of his mind for some memory to help him.

An image came to him, so powerful that his hands shook. A time when he'd had nothing but pain, fear, and the overwhelming desire to die. Another memory teased the back of his mind. Small hands, a nurse's hands, rubbing his back, making the pain tolerable with her sweetness. Like most of the young wounded soldiers, he'd entertained the idea of marrying her . . . until he'd caught sight of his reflection in a mirror.

He placed his hand against the small of Amelia's back and felt her stiffen beneath his fingertips. "I won't hurt you," he reassured her. "Just gonna help you forget."

Awkwardly, he rubbed his splayed fingers over her back. She had such a small back. He wondered if she'd have the strength to bear Dallas the son he wanted . . . or the daughter Houston thought she would have.

He stroked her shoulders, stopping just short of the nape of her neck. Touching her flesh, absorbing her warmth appealed to him, appealed to him as it shouldn't. He had no right to feel her skin beneath his fingers, even if he was only offering comfort.

"My mother used to rub my back when I was sick," she said quietly, and his fingers faltered.

His thoughts were anything but motherly. "I just thought it might help."

"It does."

His hand continued its slow sojourn over her slender back. Touching her in a less than intimate manner warranted a bit of reverence that could best be appreciated with silence: like watching the rising of a full yellow moon or hearing a wolf calling out to his mate.

"Would you mind reading one of Dallas's letters to me? I always find comfort in his words. They're in my bag." Her mouth curved up. "But I suppose you know that."

He preferred stroking her back to reading, but his desires didn't seem nearly as important as hers. Opening her bag, he removed the bundle of letters. His fingers felt clumsy as they untied the delicate ribbon that held the letters together.

"Take one from the middle," she said. "Any one."

He took the one that looked the most worn, figuring it would be her favorite. He removed the letter from the envelope. "You sure you want me to read it?"

She nodded. He turned up the flame in the lantern and angled the letter so the faint light could home in on his brother's words. He cleared his throat.

April 6, 1876

My dear Miss Carson,

The wind blew through this afternoon, turning the wheel on my windmill for the first time. The wheel groaned and complained as some men are wont to do, but eventually, it worked hard enough to bring up the water. I enjoyed listening to its steady clack. Hopefully, many a night it will serenade my family to sleep.

Loneliness does not exist for me when I am surrounded by the vast expanse of land and the endless possibilities. I think you would find much here to ease your loneliness—the land, the howling wind, the braying of cattle, the sun, the moon, the stars. When I ride out at night alone, I find companionship in all that surrounds me. I tell you this because I do not want you to think that loneliness is responsible for the following words.

*I believe a wife and sons would enrich my life beyond mea-
sure. And I would do all in my power to enrich theirs.*

*After a year of corresponding, I am convinced you and I are
well suited, and I would be honored to have you as my wife. I
shall anxiously await your reply.*

Yours,
Dallas Leigh

"I said yes," Amelia stated softly.

Houston set the letters aside, picked up the cloth, and wiped her
brow. "Yep. Dallas was grinning like a fool for a week after he got your
letter."

Her laughter washed over him as gentle as a spring rain. He
couldn't recall ever making someone laugh . . . or causing them happiness. A measure of disquiet swept through him. He didn't want her depending on him for laughter, happiness, or comfort because eventually
she'd learn the truth about him: He wasn't a man that a person could
depend on.

He knew Dallas had experienced qualms about sending him to
fetch his future wife, but he'd had no choice. He wanted to believe Dallas had sent him because he trusted him and had gained a measure of
respect for him, but he knew the truth: Dallas had no one else to send.

Her laughter drifted into silence, and she placed her hand on his
arm. "You really can be quite charming." Her cheeks flushed, and he
wasn't altogether certain it was from the fever. "Dallas will be a good
husband, won't he?"

"The best." He dropped the cloth in the bowl of water. "I'll get you
some water to drink."

He started to rise. She reached out, wrapping her fingers around his
hand. "Thank you for saving my life."

He didn't have the heart to tell her the worst was still to come.

Amelia prayed for death when she thought she was going to live, prayed
to live when she thought she was going to die. She prayed while she
heaved up her breakfast. She prayed when she had nothing left to heave
but her body insisted on trying anyway. She prayed when she was shaking from cold and prayed while she was burning with fever.

She prayed Houston wouldn't leave her. It was the only prayer answered to her satisfaction. He stayed with her throughout her ordeal, lying constantly.

He'd tell her the worst was over when it wasn't so she wouldn't give up. He'd tell her the chills were a good sign, then he'd say the fever was good. Using a cool cloth, he'd wipe the sweat from her brow, cheeks, and throat, all the while saying she would be all right in his deep voice.

She decided that she loved that voice, even when it was lying. It had a soothing, calming quality about it. She imagined the horses responded well to it. She wanted to live long enough to watch him train a horse, her horse, the horse he'd promised her when she'd felt certain she would die.

She watched him now as he gently washed the mud from her calf. His brow didn't furrow as deeply at the sight of the discolored and slightly swollen flesh as it had when he had examined it before. She wondered if anyone had cared for him this tenderly when he had been injured. She couldn't imagine with all the war casualties that anyone would have found time for a fifteen-year-old boy so badly wounded. She was surprised he'd come through his ordeal.

But he had survived, and she was determined not to let a little snake claim her life.

"Did your father take care of you when you were hurt?" she asked.

He visibly stiffened. He so hated talking about the war, and yet it was such a part of his past and Dallas's. How could she understand the men she would live with if she didn't understand their history?

"Our pa was dead by then. Dallas saw after me."

"Dallas seems to have a habit of taking care of people."

"He has a knack for it. He'd have taken better care of you than I have."

"I can't imagine how he could have," she said as she placed her hand over his. His eye was red rimmed, his face haggard. "You need to sleep," she said.

"I will as soon as your fever breaks."

"When will that be?"

"Soon."

Soon could be any moment, any day. Soon could be when death came.

"Tell me something nice," she said. "Something nice about the place where we're going."

He touched the damp cloth to her throat. "Flowers. You'll see beautiful flowers come spring: blue, red, yellow. Not as pretty as what you sew, but pretty just the same."

"What else?"

"There's nothing to block your view of the sunset. You can just watch it sweep across the land, making you feel so small."

"I am small."

He lifted a corner of his mouth. "Yeah, you are small."

Smiling softly, she touched the corner of his mouth. "A smile. I thought I'd die without ever seeing you smile."

"You're not gonna die."

She lifted a brow. "Dallas will have your hide if I do."

Leaning low, he brushed a strand of hair from her cheek. "Damn right, he will."

"Can't let that happen," she said as she drifted off to sleep.

He had the longest eyelashes she'd ever seen. She'd never noticed before, but as he slept with his face pressed to the cot near her hip, she could clearly see the length and thickness of his lashes. His hair—black as a midnight sky with no stars—curled over his ear, rested against his chin. He needed to shave.

Staring at his profile, she no longer tried to imagine how he might have looked if he'd never been wounded, but she found herself mourning what he might have had. A life that included a wife and children. A smile that would have warmed many a woman's heart. A laugh that would have rung out strong and true.

She'd never heard him laugh, had only seen a ghost of a smile. He wasn't hers to care about, but she did care. She wanted to hear him laugh. She wanted him to smile without feeling self-conscious. He had fought to give her back her life. Giving him a smile was a small payment.

She combed her fingers through the thick strands of his hair. It was coarser than hers, as though the wind and sun had battled against it.

He awakened with a jolt. "Your fever broke."

She smiled softly. "I know. You were sleeping."

He sat up and stretched his shoulders back. "How do you feel?"

"Tired."

"You'll be weak for a couple of days."

"Have you ever been bitten by a snake?"

"Nope, but it happens now and then to men on the trail."

"Do you take care of the men then?"

"Nope. The cook usually does the doctoring. Think you could eat a little something?"

"I'll try. Are we going to travel today?"

"Nah, we'll let you rest for a couple of days."

"Won't Dallas worry if we're not there on time?"

"I don't think he'll start to worry unless we're not there within a month."

Houston carried her outside during the day to enjoy the sun and carried her back into the tent at night to sleep. He'd taken to sleeping on his pallet, his saddle placed so he was watching the tent. Under the circumstances, he didn't think she'd mind. She wasn't giving any shadow shows.

On the morning of the third day after her fever broke, he awoke, his gaze fixed on the tent. With the early light of dawn filtering through the leaves and dancing over the canvas, he couldn't see any shadows or movements within the tent, but he could envision Amelia clearly, lying on the cot, sleeping soundly. In the past two days, she'd slept more than she'd been awake.

He thought they'd be able to travel today. He supposed he should get up and wake her, but he liked the thought of letting her sleep, letting her wake up on her own, stretching, washing her face, brushing her hair. He would be able to see none of the movements, but knowing they would take place almost made him smile.

She was sweet, so incredibly sweet.

He threw off the blanket, scrambled to his knees, rested his hands on his thighs, and continued to look at the tent. He'd make her some coffee before he woke her. Thicken it with sugar just the way she liked it. He'd warm up some water for her.

He turned and froze. She was sitting on a log, her hands pressed between her knees.

"Good morning," she said softly.

"You're awake," he croaked, grimacing for telling her something she obviously knew.

She smiled, and he lost the ability to draw air into his lungs.

"I wanted to see a Texas sunrise. It was beautiful."

He sank to his backside, fighting off the urge to tell her that she was more beautiful than any sunrise he'd ever seen. Her braided hair was draped over one shoulder, her face pink from an early-morning scrubbing, her green eyes bright with appreciation. He thought he'd never again be able to look at the sun easing over the horizon without thinking of her, just so, enjoying the start of a new day. To him, a day was just something to be gotten through.

"I guess when you think you're going to die, you start to appreciate things a little more. What was the first thing you wanted to see after you were wounded?" she asked.

"My ma." He grabbed his hat and settled it into place. He'd never told anyone that. He'd wanted his ma so badly that he'd felt like a baby.

"But she was too far away to come to you."

Her eyes held so much understanding that he couldn't stop himself from dredging up the memories. "Yeah, she was too far away, and she had Austin to care for, so even if she'd known I'd been hurt, she wouldn't have been able to come."

"You didn't tell her you were hurt?"

He shook his head. "Dallas said knowing would just make her worry. After the war ended, we headed home. When we got there, it was so quiet. You could feel in your bones that something wasn't right . . ."

His voice trailed off into the dawn.

"What wasn't right?" she asked, gently prodding him to continue.

Houston shifted his backside over the hard ground. Physical comfort eluded him as easily as peace of mind. He'd never discussed that day with anyone, not even Dallas. Sometimes, he felt a strong need to discuss it with Austin, to see if he remembered, but if Austin held no memories of that time, he didn't want to give him any. "We found our ma in her bed. She'd been dead for some time. I was glad then that Dallas hadn't written her about me, that we hadn't give her more cause to worry."

"Do you know how your mother died?" she asked.

"Figured she'd taken the fever. Our pa wasn't one to make friends so no one checked at the farm while we were gone. We don't know how Austin managed to survive. He was like a wild animal when we found him."

"Those are the memories you think Austin has of the war?"

"I've got no idea what memories he has. If he doesn't have any, I don't want to give him mine."

"So you never talk about it."

"Nope." He stood and rubbed his hands along his thighs. "If you're feeling strong enough, we'll head out this morning."

She smiled then, a smile that made his heart ache, a smile that made him wish that, in his youth, he'd traveled a different path.

Chapter 8

❧

$\mathcal{A}$S THE WAGON rumbled over the uneven ground, Amelia clung tenaciously to the seat. She was regaining her strength with each passing day, and with each passing mile, she grew closer to Houston.

She knew she *shouldn't* have these feelings. She knew she *couldn't* have these feelings. She had signed a contract stating she would travel west to marry Dallas. She didn't think he was a man prone to breaking contracts or dismissing them. She had been wallowing in the depths of despair, her world closing in on her, her options dwindling when she'd received his letter of hope. She owed him for lifting her out of the mire into which the war had dropped her, for altering her destiny.

She read his letters each night before she went to sleep, trying to hold an image of the man within her heart, but it was Houston she heard whimper in the hours past midnight, it was Houston she would sneak out of the tent to watch sleeping.

He never seemed truly at rest. As he slept, beads of sweat would coat his face and neck. He would begin to breathe hard as though he were running a great distance.

She told him she awoke early to appreciate the sunrise, but the truth was she enjoyed those moments before dawn when the sun's feathery fingers would touch his face and his breathing would calm as though in sleep he recognized that he'd survived another night.

Amelia spotted the small log cabin near dusk. Her heart tripped over itself when she saw the few cattle grazing in the fields beyond. "Are we already at Dallas's ranch?" she asked.

"Nope. Just stopping to look in on some of Dallas's neighbors."

"So we're close."

"Nope. Out here, anyone you pass along the way is considered a neighbor." He pulled the wagon to a halt between the house and a weathered barn.

A tall gangly man holding a rifle stepped out of the house. He cupped a hand over his brow and squinted against the setting sun. "Houston, that you?"

"Yep, Dallas told me to stop by." Houston climbed off the wagon and held his arms up to Amelia.

She scooted over the bench as the man ambled over.

"You got you a woman there?" the man asked.

Houston wrapped his hands around her waist and lifted her to the ground. "Yep. Miss Carson is betrothed to Dallas. He busted his leg. Sent me to fetch her."

A wide grin split the man's face. "Well, I'll be. She a heart-and-hand woman?"

"Yep."

"Dallas sure got himself a pretty one, didn't he?"

"Reckon he did," Houston said quietly. "Miss Carson, this here's John Denton."

Smiling, Amelia brushed her hand over her dusty skirt and toyed with the brim of Austin's hat. At the moment she imagined she looked anything but pretty.

"Beth, we got company!" John hollered.

A young, dark-haired woman rushed onto the porch, wiping her hands on her apron. A little girl, with a rag doll draped over her arm, clutched the woman's skirt and peered around her. "Land sake's, company. John, don't just stand there. Invite them in for supper."

Amelia glanced at Houston. He gave her a brusque nod. "I'll see to the animals' needs, then I'll join you."

John trailed after Houston as he led the mules to a trough. Amelia strolled to the house.

The woman's smile grew brighter. "I'm Beth." She rested her hand on the child's dark head. "This is Sarah. She's four years old and into everything."

Amelia knelt before the child. She had her father's blue eyes, her mother's dark hair. "Hello, Sarah. I'm Amelia."

Sarah held out her doll. "This is Mary Margaret."

Amelia touched the doll's cloth arm. "She's very pretty, just like you."

Sarah pressed her face against her mother's skirt and giggled.

"You'll have to forgive her shyness. We don't get much company out here."

Amelia rose to her feet. "I guess that's something I'm going to have to get used to."

"I never expected Houston to take a wife."

"Actually, I'm going to marry Dallas."

Beth's eyes widened. "Dallas? Have you met him?"

Amelia shook her head. Beth slapped her hand over her breast. "Handsome as sin." She eyed Amelia speculatively. "Are you a heart-and-hand woman?"

"I just heard Houston say I was, so I guess I am, although I'm not sure what that is."

Beth slipped her arm through Amelia's and led her into the house. "A mail-order bride. Cowboys call us heart-and-hand women because most place their orders from *The Heart and Hand*. That's where John found me. Our little house might not look like much, but what I have here is a hundred times better than what I had before."

The furniture looked as though it had all been carefully crafted. The fire crackled in the hearth. The room smelled of freshly baked bread and cinnamon.

Beth reached into a cabinet and brought out wooden bowls, setting them at the square oak table. She picked up Sarah and plopped her into a chair that was taller than the others. "John made all the furniture."

"It's lovely."

"He works hard, trying to keep me happy. I imagine Dallas will do the same for you."

"I only know Dallas through correspondence. I was hoping to learn more about him as we traveled, but Houston isn't very talkative."

Beth looked at her, complete understanding reflected in her eyes.

"Oh, Amelia, none of the men out here are. They won't ask you for the time of day. They figure if you want to share that information, you'll take out your pocket watch and tell them."

"Why do you think they are like that?"

Beth brought a pot from the hearth and began to ladle stew into the bowls. "I think it's because a lot of the men came here after the war to start over. Or they had a past they weren't particularly proud of. A lot of them change their names, or just go by their first names. No one questions them. That's why they come out here. If they want to be alone, they're left alone."

"And if they don't want to be alone?"

Beth smiled. "Then they order themselves a bride." She placed the pot on the table and returned to the hearth, bringing back a black pan that held something that reminded Amelia of a yellow cake.

"Corn dodgers and stew," Beth explained. "It's not fancy, but it's filling and out here the men need something that fills up their bellies." She looked past Amelia and pointed a finger. "Keep that dust out there where it belongs!"

John and Houston stomped their feet on the porch for a minute before walking in and taking their seats. Amelia sat beside Sarah, across from Houston, who had angled his chair so he sat with the scarred side of his face away from the table.

When Beth took her chair, everyone bowed their heads.

"Dear Lord," John began, "thank you for bringing company to take the burden of talking off me for a day or so. Amen."

Grinning, he looked up at Beth. She wagged a finger at him. "You were listening at the door."

"No, missus, but I've been married to you long enough to know poor Miss Carson here is gonna get her ear chewed off afore the evening's over."

"Please, call me Amelia."

He blushed before digging into his stew.

Beth placed her hand over Amelia's and squeezed. "You'll have to forgive me," she said. "As much as I've come to love John, I miss a woman's voice from time to time."

Amelia cast a furtive glance Houston's way. He watched her in seeming innocence, but she wondered if Dallas had indeed told him to stop by here or if he was just trying to bring home his point regarding the absence of company in this part of Texas.

"I think you're delightful," Amelia said with all sincerity. "And I know what it is to long for a gentle voice."

Amelia received a good dose of what Houston endured each evening as Beth fired off questions, one after another. She wanted to know about life back East, the journey on the train, and how fashions had changed. She talked about everything but the weather. John commented from time to time, but Houston held his silence on all matters.

When John's bowl was empty, he leaned back in his chair and asked a question only Houston could answer. "How many head of cattle does Dallas have now?"

Houston glanced up from his stew as though he hadn't noticed that the majority of the previous conversation had not included him. He had asked no questions, prompted no replies, and caused no soft chuckles. "Around two thousand."

John released a low whistle. "Have him send word if he needs some help getting 'em to market. I could bring Beth to the ranch and she and Amelia here could visit."

"I'll let him know."

"John, why don't you drag out the bundle board? We'll let Amelia and Houston sleep in the bed tonight. You and I can sleep in the loft."

Amelia's heart slammed against her ribs. She thought the intimacy surrounding her and Houston as they sat beside a campfire would pale in comparison to the intimacy that would surround them if they slept in the same room, the same bed, beneath the same covers.

John cleared his throat. "I'm not sure that would be proper, Beth. Usually, we pull the bundle board out when the two people are engaged."

"Don't be silly. Dallas trusts Houston, or he wouldn't have sent him to get Amelia. And she must trust him, or she wouldn't be traveling with him. Nothing will happen in that bedroom that couldn't happen on the trail."

John shrugged. "I reckon you got a point there."

"I appreciate the kindness, but I'll sleep in the barn," Houston said.

"Nonsense," Beth said, slapping her hand on the table for emphasis. "When was the last time you slept in a bed?"

Houston looked as though he'd been trapped which Amelia realized he had been. He couldn't even claim to have slept in a bed while they were in Fort Worth.

"A while, but I'm used to sleeping on the ground."

"Then tonight you will sleep in a bed, and we'll prepare you each a bath. A good hot meal, a hot bath, and a soft bed. I would have sold my soul for those when I was traveling out here. It warms my heart to be able to offer them to you."

Amelia met Houston's gaze, and she knew he wanted an honorable way out of the situation, knew she should help him find one. But he had made one sacrifice after another for her on this trip. Surely Dallas would find no fault with her for making this one sacrifice for Houston.

"I truly appreciate your generosity, Beth," she said quietly. "I would love to have a hot bath."

Beth slapped her hand on the table in front of her daughter. "Sarah, stop staring. It's not polite."

Amelia glanced down at the little girl. She bowed her head, but Amelia could see that her gaze was still trained on Houston.

Houston shoved his bowl back. "It was a fine meal, ma'am. If you'll excuse me, I need to check on the mules." He scraped the chair across the floor, stood, and headed out the door.

Beth sighed. "That's such a shame he had to get wounded like that, but I imagine Dallas sleeps better at night."

"What do you mean?" Amelia asked.

"It's not unusual for a mail-order bride to meet someone along the way and never make it to the man who sent for her. Imagine Dallas figured that wouldn't happen if he made Houston come after you. You're not going to fall in love with him."

Houston crossed his forearms over the fence railing. Sorrel snorted and nudged his elbow.

"No apples." He scratched behind the horse's ear. Most cowboys wouldn't be caught dead riding a she-horse, but Houston had discovered he could approach a herd of wild mustangs with more success when he rode a mare. Although wary of a strange horse, a stallion was more likely to accept a female into his domain. He'd viciously fight another stallion. "You'd best get some sleep, old friend. I sure as hell won't get any tonight."

The horse nudged Houston's elbow again and when no apple was forthcoming, she trotted away, leaving Houston to enjoy the solitude he craved.

He knew it wasn't uncommon for people to offer their bed to visitors, even when the travelers weren't married. The lack of towns and hotels had resulted in a code of hospitality across the plains that Houston couldn't help but admire. Still, he wasn't certain that Dallas would appreciate his neighbors' generosity. He could only hope that his brother would understand that Beth couldn't have spoken truer words: Nothing was going to happen in that bed. Nothing at all. Hell, he probably wouldn't even be able to sleep.

Houston felt someone watching him, the gaze more of a tickle than a stare. He glanced down. Big blue eyes looked up at him. Incredibly innocent. He wished he could give the little girl a smile, but he knew no matter how hard he tried that the left side of his face wouldn't cooperate, and he'd end up giving her something distorted and uglier than what she was looking at now, something that might frighten her.

"I got a hurt," she said. She lifted her skirt until her white bloomers came into view along with her scraped knee. "My ma kissed it and made it better." She released her skirt and pointed her finger. "You got a hurt."

"Yeah, reckon I do." Right in the center of his heart.

She scrunched up her face. "I can kiss it and make it better."

Something inside his chest grew so tight that he thought he might not be able to breathe. She crooked her little finger and wiggled it at him. "Come here."

Holding on to the railing for support, he bent his knees, squatting until he was as close to her height as he could get. Her eyes grew large and serious. She puckered her tiny lips, bobbed her head forward, then ran off. The brush of her mouth against his cheek had been as faint as the first breath of dawn. Deep inside, he smiled.

Standing a few feet away and slightly behind his left side, Amelia knew that his hampered vision prevented him from seeing her. She also realized with awe that he was smiling. Not on the outside where it would show, but within a secret place where he harbored his fears and his doubts, where she imagined a fifteen-year-old boy mourned the loss of his youth.

She knew that she was wrong to watch him without his knowledge, but she wanted to understand him as much as she needed to understand Dallas. With Dallas, she would have an advantage. She was certain he would talk with her and ask her questions. His brother would hold his hurts, his longings, his dreams close to his heart where no one could share them.

She turned and walked back to the house, where her bath waited. She hadn't seen Houston's smile, but it hovered around him, like a whispered sigh, sweet and unexpected.

Houston sank into the steaming hot water and released a slow, appreciative breath. Beth had draped blankets over the back porch railing to give him a measure of privacy. He could feel the cool night air moving in. In the distance, he could see orange and lavender sweeping across the sky.

A man couldn't ask for much more than that.

He closed his eye. Amelia had been in the water before him. Although Beth had added more hot water to the tub after Amelia got out, if he concentrated hard enough, he imagined he could smell her sweet scent. Her scent had to be that of a flower, but it wasn't any flower he knew. He imagined her tiny feet resting against the bottom of the wooden tub where his were now. He imagined the lye soap skimming over her body, touching her before it touched him. It seemed such an intimate image, to have the same water, soap, and air caressing both their bodies.

His mouth went as dry as the West Texas breeze. He was sitting in a tub of water, dying of thirst. He opened his eye. The cake of soap slipped out of his hands, spiraled through the air, hit the porch, and skidded toward the dirt.

Amelia bent down and picked it up.

"What are you doing out here?" he croaked.

She straightened and leaned against the porch railing, her gaze holding his. "I've never seen you enjoy anything."

"I was enjoying the bath."

"I know." She smiled so sweetly that he wondered if his thoughts had been visible. He held out his hand. "I need the soap and some privacy."

She handed him the soap and held up a cup brimming with shaving lather. "The beard doesn't suit you."

He rubbed his hand over his hand over his rough jaw. "I'll shave it, then."

"I'd be happy to shave it for you."

"I can do it."

She gnawed on her lower lip. "I'm very experienced at shaving a man's face. I shaved Mr. Bryant every morning."

Amelia watched the expressions flitting over his face, and she knew that he wanted to ask, but as always, with rare exception, he held his silence.

She walked forward and knelt beside the tub, her courage faltering as he plunged his hands under the murky water, splashing her with his frantic efforts.

"Woman, I'm not wearing any clothes!"

She'd seen him without clothes, but she saw no reason to remind him of that fact. He'd argue that the circumstances had been different, and she'd have no choice but to agree. Although she had no intentions of dropping her gaze below his bare shoulders, she jerked a blanket off the porch railing and draped it over the tub. "I can't see anything but your face and shoulders now. I'd like very much to shave you. It's such a small thing, a way to thank you for caring for me while I was sick."

He glanced around the porch.

"Beth and Sarah have already gone to bed. John's closing the barn."

Watching his throat muscles work, she would have sworn he was terrified. "I won't hurt you," she assured him, smiling softly. "I just want to help you forget."

"You're using my words," he grumbled.

"They're easy to remember. You don't say very many."

"You're aggravating, you know that?"

She smiled warmly at his disgruntled expression and began to swish the brush in the cup, hoping to put them both at ease before night fell, and they found themselves together in the same bed.

"My father owned a plantation before the war." She had his undivided attention as she brushed the lather over his face and along his throat. "We had slaves, cotton fields, a big house. I had two sisters. No brothers. I was the youngest. Papa's favorite. I was quite pudgy and he used to call me his little pumpkin."

He furrowed his brow. "Can't imagine you pudgy."

"War changes people."

His brow relaxed. "Yeah, I reckon it does."

She set the lather cup down and slipped the razor out of her pocket, giving him time to ask a question, but no question came.

Placing her finger beneath his chin, she tilted his head back. "I told you that Papa died. It was just before the war ended. Mama said he took the fever, but I think he just grieved for the South he loved, the South that was disappearing. My sisters died shortly after he did. Then it was just Mama and me."

She took a moment to enjoy the sound of the razor scraping over his unmarred jaw. "Mr. Bryant came from the north and paid the taxes on the plantation. He let me and Mama stay on to serve him. We moved to the slave quarters."

His jaw dropped. She pushed it back up. "You need to keep still so I don't cut you."

"He shouldn't have done that."

She shrugged. "I'm just grateful he didn't make us sleep in the fields or turn us out completely. When he planted cotton, we picked it."

"Me and Dallas used to pick cotton when we were young."

She sat back on her heels. "You did?"

He nodded. "I didn't mind it so much, but Dallas hated it. Swore when he got old enough, he'd find himself a job that didn't involve plowing fields or picking crops. Reckon that's why he likes cattle."

She stood and walked to the other side.

"I can finish shaving," he said, reaching for the razor.

She batted his hand away. "I can do it." Carefully, she began to shave the area below the patch, to work her way around his scars. "Anyway, eventually, Mr. Bryant let Mama work in the house. When she died, I took over her chores. I tended to his needs when he got too feeble to take care of himself. He was such a proud man. In the end, I grew rather fond of him, even though he was a Yankee."

She angled her head to study Houston's face. "Shall I leave the whiskers above your lip so you can grow a mustache?"

"If you want. A man with a face like mine doesn't put much stock in how he looks."

But he did care, she realized, thinking back to the day she'd met him. He'd been clean shaven then. The morning they were to leave, he'd bathed and shaved. And he'd brought along his shaving equipment and a tiny mirror so he could keep up his appearance as they traveled. If he had wanted a mustache, he would have grown one without her suggesting it. She pursed her lips and narrowed her eyes. "No, I think a mustache would hide your mouth, and you have such a nice-looking mouth."

In the fading light, she could see the blush creep over his face. Gingerly, she shaved over his lip. A shiver shimmied up her spine when his breath fanned her knuckles.

She wiped the remnants of lather away and trailed her fingers along his smooth jaw, across his chin, and up his cheek until her palm cradled the side of his face, her fingertips resting lightly against the patch. It pleased her that he didn't grab her wrist and pull her hand away. "Does it still hurt?"

She watched as he swallowed. "Sometimes . . . when a Norther blows through, it'll ache."

Her gaze drifted back to his lips. They looked incredibly soft and out of place on a face as rugged as his. She lifted her eyes and discovered that he was studying her mouth as well. Self-consciously, she licked her lips.

His gaze slowly roamed over her features until they settled on her eyes. "It'll be dark soon. You'd best get inside. All manner of animals come out at night."

Withdrawing her hand from his cheek, she rose. "I set some towels by the fire to warm. The breeze can be quite chilling when you're wet. I'll get them for you."

As calmly as she could, her stomach quivering, she strolled away, knowing that she shouldn't have enjoyed shaving Houston as much as she had, knowing that she shouldn't wonder if his lips were as soft and warm as they appeared. She made a silent vow that on the morning following her wedding, she'd shave Dallas.

*   *   *

Amelia sat on the edge of the bed, waiting for her sleeping companion. She'd put on a clean blouse and skirt that she'd brought from Georgia. She couldn't quite bring herself to sleep in her nightgown. She heard a soft tapping and rose to her feet. "Come in."

The door opened, and Houston peered into the room. "You ready for me to come inside?"

She nodded. With one long stride, he was in the room, looking as uncomfortable as she felt.

"You want the door closed?" he asked.

She nodded again, not certain her voice had come into the room with her.

He set his saddlebags near the door and glanced around the room, looking at everything but Amelia and the bed. Finally, he released a long, slow breath and met her gaze. "I figure we got two choices here. I can either sneak out the window and sneak back in at dawn, or I can sleep on the floor."

"Or you can sleep in the bed."

His gaze darted over to the bed.

"I think it would hurt Beth's feelings if she somehow discovered that you hadn't slept in the bed."

"Yeah, well, right now I'm more concerned with your feelings."

"Are you?"

He swept his gaze over to her. "Yes."

"Well, right now, I'm tired and would love to sleep in a bed. If we keep our clothes on, with the bundle board between us, I see no problem with us sharing the bed."

A corner of his mouth crooked up. "You don't think I could crawl over that?"

She angled her chin. "I don't think you *would* crawl over it."

He met her challenge gracefully. "All right. Which side do you want?"

"I'll take this side next to the table."

He walked across the room and sat on the side of the bed nearest the window. The rope bed creaked beneath his weight. "Can I take off my boots?"

"And your hat and your coat."

Amelia took a last glance around the room. Beth's clothes hung in a wardrobe with no doors. Her wardrobe contained fewer clothes than Amelia's new wardrobe, but Beth possessed something Amelia didn't.

"Oh, isn't this beautiful?" she asked in a quiet voice of reverence as she crossed the room and touched her fingers to the finely detailed white lace covering the silk gown.

"White's not very practical," Houston said. "It'd be showing all the dirt before the morning was half over."

"A woman would only wear it once."

"Seems like a waste of money then."

"I suppose, but I guess you're paying for all the memories it would hold."

"Memories?"

"Yes," she replied, glancing over her shoulder at the man sitting on the bed, wondering briefly if men held onto memories as women did. "A woman would wear it on her wedding day."

He furrowed his brow. "What are you gonna wear when you marry Dallas?"

She shrugged and walked to the bed. "Something that we purchased in Fort Worth, I imagine."

"You should have told me you needed something special."

She sat on the bed with her back to him and removed her shoes. "I don't need something special." She quickly slipped beneath the covers and rolled to her side, her back against the bundle board.

The bed shifted as he stretched out on the other side of the board.

"Do you mind if I keep the lamp burning?" she asked.

"Don't mind at all."

"Will it keep you awake?"

"No. I always sleep with a light burning."

Amelia rolled to her back. "You do?"

"Yep. The light from a campfire or the lamp beside my bed."

The gruffness of his voice stated more clearly than his words that it had cost him dearly to admit that, to reveal a part of himself that she imagined no one else knew. She hugged herself, hoarding the information he'd shared with her. "Is Dallas's house like this one?"

"Nope."

"What does it look like?"

He took a long moment to answer. "It's big."

"Is it pretty?"

"Dallas thinks so."

"But you don't think so."

He heaved a deep sigh. "I don't think you can really appreciate it until you've seen it."

"Do you live there?"

"No, I got my own place about an hour's ride away."

"Is it big?" she asked.

"No. It's smaller than this place. Just one room, but it suits me."

Amelia drew the covers up to her chin and watched the shadows play over the wall as the flame inside the lamp quivered. She could well imagine Houston in a one-room house, tending his horses during the day and watching the stars at night.

"Good night," she said softly, rolling over to her side.

"Amelia?"

"Yes?"

"If you hear that animal cry out like you did some time back . . . just ignore it."

She had suspected all along that it was his cry she had heard, but the sound hadn't been that of an animal; rather the wail of someone who was lost.

"Sometimes, I cry out at night, too," she said softly.

He didn't reply. She didn't really expect him to. She allowed the silence to ease in around her. She closed her eyes. The light from the lantern danced across her eyelids, comforting her with its presence. The bed shifted.

"Amelia?"

Rolling over, she came up on her elbow, only to find Houston had done the same. Their gazes locked, his only slightly higher than hers. She stilled, her breath held. She watched his Adam's apple slowly slide up and down.

"I . . . uh . . . I wanted to thank you for the shave. I've never felt anything so fine in my whole life."

"It was my pleasure. I . . . I'm going to shave Dallas after we're married," she felt compelled to add.

He gave a brusque nod. "He'll like that. 'Night."

"Good night." She snuggled beneath the covers, trying to forget the feel of Houston's jaw cradled within her palm. Once she had tried to imagine what his smile might look like. Now she wondered how his mouth would look poised for a kiss.

She squeezed her eyes shut. She had done nothing wrong. She'd simply shaved her fiancé's brother as a way to repay him for his kindness . . . but her reasoning did little to ease her guilt.

Chapter 9

༄

As dawn eased over the horizon, Amelia hugged Beth tightly.

"We'll try and come in the spring, during round-up," Beth promised.

"I'll look forward to it," Amelia assured her just before she allowed Houston to hoist her onto the wagon. She tightened the ribbons on the bonnet Beth had given her. As the wagon began to roll forward, she turned and waved at the family left behind.

John slipped his arm around his wife. Amelia smiled. Soon she would have a husband to do the same with her. If only he would love her as much as John loved Beth.

Amelia faced forward. "Wasn't it nice of Beth to give me a bonnet?"

Houston kept his opinion on that to himself. All he could see was the tip of her nose and as cute as it was, it wasn't enough. He knew the bonnet would protect her from the sun and wind, would keep her face soft, her skin pale. But it didn't mean he had to like it.

"Will we be meeting any other neighbors?" Amelia asked.

"Not that I know of."

"How much longer until we're at the ranch?"

"A good fifteen days." Or a bad fifteen days, depending on how he looked at it. He'd drop her off at Dallas's door and head on to his own small place, where he ate alone, slept alone, and dreamed alone.

If he dared to dream. He'd been right in the beginning. Having a woman around made a man long for things he shouldn't. He'd stayed up all night listening to her even breathing, watching her snuggle beneath the blankets, and wishing that damn bundle board hadn't been there so she could have snuggled against him.

His stomach tightened as he thought of Dallas's holding this woman through the night, protecting her from whatever it was that made her sleep with a light burning.

A light seldom kept his own demons at bay. He sure as hell couldn't keep hers away.

They traveled four days, the land growing flatter, the trees scarcer. Amelia imagined in summer, when the sun baked the earth, that men worshipped the shade they found beneath the few trees scattered about. As Houston had promised, nothing blocked her view of the sunset.

As dusk settled in, she glanced at the scattered trees, the brush, and the withering grass blowing in the breeze, rippling across the land like the sea washing over the shore.

"What can I do to help?" she asked as she followed Houston from the wagon, his arms loaded with supplies while hers remained empty.

"You can gather up some prairie coal."

"Prairie coal?"

A corner of his mouth tipped up. "Cow dung."

"What are you going to do with it?"

"When there's no wood, we burn cow dung."

She wrinkled her nose. "Isn't that rather unpleasant?"

"You get used to it." The corner of his mouth lifted a little higher. "But I'll gather it up. Why don't you look in the wagon and decide which can I should open for tonight's meal?"

She angled her chin. "You've done everything since we left Fort Worth. I can handle prairie coal." She walked back to the wagon, picked up her reticule, and pulled out a white linen handkerchief with tatted edges.

She marched to the first brown lump she could see peering through the tall prairie grasses. Carefully, she placed her handkerchief over the object and gingerly lifted it off the ground, making certain her fingers never actually touched anything other than the linen.

Holding the coal—she much preferred to think of it as coal rather than dung—as far away from her as possible, holding her breath as well, she walked back into the camp. "Where do you want the fire?"

Working to stretch the tent into place, Houston glanced over his shoulder and a shaft of warmth pierced his heart. He'd never thought of Amelia as prim and proper, but she sure as hell looked prim and proper with some lacy thing hanging over cow dung. "Right there ought to do just fine."

She started to bend down.

"No, no," he amended. "A little closer to the tent might be better."

She straightened and walked toward him. "Here?" she asked.

"Yep."

She placed the dung on the ground and began shaking out her linen.

"On second thought, that might be too close. A strong wind comes through here and the tent would go up in flames."

"Where do you want it, then?" she asked, her lips pursed.

He wondered what the hell he thought he was doing. He'd often seen cowboys pull pranks on each other, but he hadn't been on the giving or the receiving end of a prank in years, and he had forgotten how it was done so everyone ended up laughing.

He wanted to hear her laugh, but playing with manure sure as hell wasn't the way to accomplish that goal. Irritated with his stupidity, he released his hold on the tent, and it fell into a heap. He picked up the cow dung and tossed it a foot or so away. "Right there ought to do it."

A look of horror crossed her face. "You touched it."

"It makes the chore go quicker."

She visibly shuddered. "Should I set it on fire or do you want to?"

"We're gonna need a few more. Since my hands are dirty, I'll gather them. You check the cans."

This time Amelia didn't protest. She scurried back to the wagon and studied their supplies. Nothing appealed to her.

A shiver raced down her spine, and she shuddered with the realization of how quiet everything had suddenly become. Silent and still, like a funeral. Even the mules and Sorrel seemed to sense it as they lifted their noses and turned their ears back.

She glanced at the sky. It was growing darker, but not from the approaching night. Blocking out the late afternoon sun, black clouds rolled in as though pushed by the mighty hand of a giant.

Without warning, the wind rose, sweeping up the dirt, whipping it around her, and startling her with its ferocity. A fat raindrop splattered on her nose.

She heard a harsh curse and spun around. Houston was fighting the wind to get her tent into place and having very little luck. She wondered if he would stay in the tent with her if it rained.

She heard a crack of thunder. A sheet of lightning flashed, igniting the sky so brightly she would have sworn she was standing in the center of it. Houston flung the tent to the ground and strode toward her, seemingly a man with a purpose.

A wide arrow of white lightning streaked to the ground. Sorrel whinnied and dropped her head between her knees. The sky reverberated with rolling thunder as another streak of lightning burst through the darkening sky. Houston reached her.

"Climb inside the wagon," he ordered as he began to unbuckle his gunbelt.

Amelia backed up a step. "I don't mind getting wet."

"It's not the rain I'm worried about," he said as he laid his gun on the floorboards. "It's the lightning. Now, get inside." Kneeling, he removed his spurs and tossed them into the wagon.

"Are you going to get in the wagon?"

"No, I need to get all the metal off the animals." As though tired of waiting on her, he quickly came to his feet, grabbed her waist, and hoisted her into the back as though she was nothing more than a sack of flour.

The wind wailed, thunder roared, and lightning flashed across the sky.

"Get down, damn it! I don't have much time!"

It was the desperation in his voice that convinced her. She lay on her side and wrapped her arms around her drawn-up knees as he brought the tarpaulin over her. Darkness enclosed her, encircled her, and taunted her with the memories of another time when she'd been huddled in a wooden box.

The rain began to pelt the tarpaulin, a steady staccato beat, like the distant sound of long-ago gunfire, the pounding of a thousand hooves . . . or so it had seemed at the time.

The terrifying darkness trapped her inside its windowless cocoon, blacker than night with no stars, no moon. She was a little girl again, eight years old. Too small. Too frightened. And the enemy was coming.

Amelia grew hot. Breathing became difficult . . . just as before. The memories rose up and howled louder than the wind that rushed past the wagon.

She could hear her mother's frightened voice. "Hurry, Amelia. Hurry!"

"No, Mama! No!"

Her mother's fingers dug into the delicate flesh of her arm as Amelia tried to dig her heels into the wooden floor. Her mother jerked her so hard that she thought surely her arm would come off her body. "Come on, child. Your papa will protect you. You'll be safe with him."

"No, Mama! No!"

The room loomed closer and closer. The shadowed room. The flames from the candles flickered, and the ghosts danced along the wall.

"Hurry, Amelia. Papa will save you."

"No, Mama! No, please! Papa can't save me. Papa's dead!"

Amelia couldn't breathe. She was suffocating, drowning in the memories. She yanked on the ribbons and jerked the bonnet off her head. Still she couldn't draw air into her lungs. Desperately she tore at the tarpaulin.

Houston was working to get the harness off the mules when he saw Amelia scramble out of the wagon and begin running toward . . . nothing but a distant horizon. He was familiar enough with lightning storms to know the damage they could do on the flat open plains. With a harsh curse, he bolted after her.

She stumbled, her knees hitting the ground. She scrambled back to her feet and continued to run, her arms waving around her as though she were warding off the very demons of hell.

His legs were longer, churning faster than hers. He caught her, totally unprepared for the stark terror in her eyes when he swung her around. She flailed her arms, hitting his face, his shoulders, his chest.

"Don't put me back in there! Please, don't put me back in there! I'll die! I swear to God, I'll die if you put me back in there!"

He wrapped his arms around her, drawing her against his chest. "I won't," he promised, his breathing labored, his heart pounding so hard he was certain she could feel it. "I won't."

She slumped against him. Still holding her, he brought his duster around her and eased them both to the ground. She trembled violently.

"It's all right," he cooed as though she were a horse he wanted to tame. "It's all right." He began to rock gently back and forth while the mild rain splattered his back and dripped slowly from his hat. Lightning flashed around them, so brilliant, so close that he thought it might blind him. He pulled the right side of his hat down and ducked his head, hoping to give her more shelter. A short distance away, lightning struck the ground, igniting a fire that the rain quickly drenched. Smoldering smoke trailed along the ground.

"If it hits us, we'll die, won't we?" she asked in a quiet calm voice, a voice too calm, too quiet.

"Probably."

"Do you think it'll hurt?"

"No," he replied, tightening his hold. "We'll just see a flash of bright light, and everything will go black."

She tilted her face. "You don't have to wait here with me."

"You'll get wet."

She smiled, an endearing crooked grin, and right then, he didn't care if the lightning did strike him. Dying with her in his arms couldn't be worse than living a life alone.

His backside was drenched, mud coated his trousers, rivulets of water ran into his boots, and water dripped off the brim of his hat onto his shoulders. His muscles ached from the unnatural way he held his body, trying to shield her from the storm. He brushed his knuckles over her tear-streaked face and lowered his mouth until it rested beside her ear. "Tell me," he said simply.

The crack of thunder filled the air. The smile eased off her face, and a great sadness filled her eyes. He wished he had the power to remove the sadness from her life—forever.

The rain lessened, falling softly, its patter a somber melody to accompany her words.

"I told you that my father died during the war. The day we were to bury him . . ." She swallowed and turned her gaze toward the darkening sky. "Some men came. I don't know if they were soldiers or deserters. They wore blue uniforms, but no one seemed in charge. My mother was terrified, so she hid me."

A tremor traveled the length of her slight body. He remembered that she'd told him that she didn't like being inside the darkness. Not in the dark, not afraid of the dark. But inside the darkness. Dread crept through him. "Where did she hide you?"

"With my father." She looked at him then, tears welling in her eyes. "Inside his coffin. It was so dark. I was afraid that no one would find me. That they would bury me with him. I cried until I fell asleep."

"You said at the hotel that you'd slept with worse."

She nodded, her voice growing ragged. "He was so cold. When I woke up, Mama was holding me, but she was different. I don't know what they did to her. Her face and her throat were bruised. Her dress was torn. I always thought that she should have been crying, but she wasn't. She just stared, but not at anything I could see. It was like she was staring inside herself, like her mind, her heart had gone away, and only her body remained to hold me."

The bile rose in his throat. "Your sisters?"

She pressed her face harder against his shoulder until he thought she might crack his bones. She moved her head back and forth, and the warmth of her tears soaked through the flannel of his shirt. "They were staring, too," she rasped. "Staring at the sky. They were lying side by side, holding hands . . . and there wasn't much left of their clothes. It was so ugly." She dug her fingers into his sides.

"Don't think about it," he ordered. He hated the war. It had brought out the best in men like his brother, the worst in men like him, and turned the rest into animals.

She sobbed. "I didn't want to look at my sisters, but I did. I didn't want to see the blood, but I did. So much of it. I think I know what those men did—"

"They weren't men. Animals, maybe, but not men. Men don't harm the innocent." He cupped her cheek and pressed her face against his chest. "They didn't hurt you?"

"Not my body, but my heart. I wanted to leave the plantation then, but I was only eight. And Mama was in no condition to travel. So we stayed and survived as best we could."

She tilted her head back, her eyes as dark as the storm clouds. "That's when I began searching for things, small things, for which I could be grateful. It didn't matter how trivial, how silly. I just needed something each day to make me go on to the next day."

He knew that feeling. Damn, he knew that feeling all too well.

"When Mama died, I placed my ad to travel west and become a wife. I had to leave, to get away from the land that had soaked up my sisters' blood, away from the memories. I need new memories to replace those that haunt me when darkness closes in."

The thunder echoed around them, the lightning shimmered through the air, and the rain began to fall again, harder than before. She nestled up against his shoulder.

Houston removed his hat, giving the rain the freedom to wash over them, to wipe the tears from her face, and to ease the hurt in her heart.

The deluge prevented him from hearing her voice, but the shape of her lips revealed the words "Thank you."

He could only nod and pray that when the storm ended, he would find the strength to let her go.

Chapter 10

❧

*H*OUSTON STARED AT the roiling brown river and cursed last night's storm. It lingered on the air, threatening to return, leaving gray clouds hovering low and a strong brisk wind toying with the prairie grasses. If the storm returned, it had the power to make the river impassable for days, leaving Houston's options damn limited as far as he was concerned.

They could wait until the water receded and hope the storm moved on with no others coming to take its place. But they were already behind schedule. As it was now, they wouldn't arrive when Dallas was expecting them. He didn't think Dallas could afford to send his men out on a wild-goose chase, so instead, his brother would be pacing on his bad leg, staring toward the rising sun, and working himself into a slow simmering temper.

Or Houston could haul Amelia and the wagon across the river, and hope the good fortune he'd lost somewhere along the way would catch up with him. Not one thing had delayed him in reaching Fort Worth. Nothing should have delayed him in returning to the ranch.

He prodded Sorrel forward. The horse moved cautiously through the swirling water, but she didn't hesitate. Houston trusted the animal's instincts. If the horse had balked, he wouldn't have pressed her on.

The cold water lapped at Houston's calves. Crossing rivers had never been his favorite part of trailing cattle or moving from one spot to the next.

They reached the middle of the river. The small waves slapped at

Sorrel's sides, but the river itself wasn't as deep as Houston had expected it to be. He glanced over his shoulder. Amelia sat in the wagon, worry etched along her delicate features.

Despite the cold water, her concern warmed him. She would soon become his sister by marriage, but he seemed unable to steer his feelings toward brotherly concern. They ran deeper, so much deeper. He pulled the reins to the right, guiding the horse back to the bank from which they'd come.

"What do you think?" Amelia asked as they cleared the water.

"I think it's safe, but I want to take you over on the horse. Then I'll come back for the wagon."

"Why are wooden crosses lining the bank?" she asked.

He glanced toward the crude markers, made from tree limbs. "It's not unusual to lose a man when you're crossing a river, herding cows. Horse gets spooked, cows get spooked. Man goes under, can't swim, the cows stop him from coming back up."

"I suppose, then, that I should be grateful we're not herding cows."

"Yep. Reckon you should be."

She gnawed her bottom lip. "Do you swim?"

"Yep."

Relief quickly flickered in her eyes, trust soon replacing it. Dallas's trust had been heavy enough to bear, hers seemed incredibly heavier.

He positioned his horse and held out his hand, anticipating the warmth of her fingers within his grasp. She slipped elegantly onto the back of the horse and wrapped her arms around him.

"The water's cold," he said as the horse skidded down the bank and splashed into the river.

Releasing a small gasp when the water rose up to their calves, she tightened her hold on him. "How many more rivers do we have to cross?" she asked.

"Not many, but this is the widest and deepest. It would have been better if we'd been able to cross before the storm."

Sorrel momentarily lost her footing. Houston's heart leapt into his throat, nearly suffocating him with the thought of Amelia's falling from her precarious perch behind him, but she clung tenaciously to him while he held fast to the saddle horn, calming the horse with the pressure of his thighs, his sure hand on the reins.

He knew the moment the horse regained her footing. He urged Sorrel forward, breathing an unsteady sigh of relief as the water grew shallow. Sorrel struggled up the muddy tree-lined bank.

Reaching behind him, Houston helped Amelia slide off the horse. He shrugged out of his duster and draped it over her shoulders. "Why don't you see if you can find some dry wood so we can warm up before we head out?"

With concern clearly reflected in her eyes, she rested her hand on his thigh. He would have sworn her touch latched onto his heart.

"Please be careful," she said quietly.

He gave her what he hoped was a smile. He couldn't remember the last time his face had broken into a real smile. The muscles felt tight, unaccustomed to the movement. He hoped he didn't look ridiculous. "Got no choice in the matter. Dallas would have my hide if I left you out here all alone."

She gave him a smile, a beautiful smile that made her green eyes sparkle and chased away the worried frown. The sight of it tightened something in his chest.

He prodded Sorrel back across the river. Once on the other side, he tied a rope to the saddle horn, his intent to lead Sorrel back across the river. He left the other end unsecured, simply threading it through his fingers along with the reins. He didn't want the horse tethered to the wagon if something should happen. Every now and then, a strong rush of water had pushed against them as they'd crossed back over.

His more practical side told him to wait . . . but the side that housed his heart urged him to take the wagon across and get Amelia to the ranch as soon as possible.

He looked across the river. She stood on the far bank, watching him, not gathering wood as he'd told her. For some reason he couldn't explain, it alarmed him and warmed him to see her watching, waiting for him.

He indulged himself for a moment and envisioned her standing within the doorway of his cabin, wearing that green dress they'd purchased in Fort Worth, her loose hair brushed to a golden sheen, the scent of fresh-baked bread wafting behind her . . .

He shook off the image. She'd be standing on Dallas's veranda. Houston Leigh would be nothing more to her than a brother by marriage, which was as it should be. Women like Amelia belonged to men like Dallas. And Dallas had branded her as his long before Houston even knew her name.

With a slap of the reins and a coarse yell, he sent the mules moving slowly toward the river's edge. The wagon teetered as it rolled over the uneven, muddy ground.

Houston whacked the reins over the mules' backsides and yelled louder, urging the animals forward into the rushing water. The four mules moved sluggishly, dragging the wagon slowly across the river. Floating brushwood rushed rapidly downstream, spinning and dipping.

The wagon jerked to a stop. Houston slapped the reins and hollered. The mules strained against the harness, strained against the water. Houston was on the verge of jumping into the water in order to work the wheels free when the wagon lurched forward, a loud crack filled the air, and all hell broke loose.

A mule brayed, and the other mules no longer worked as a team. It flashed through Houston's mind that something—possibly a snake—had spooked them.

Then nothing but panic roared through his mind as the wagon began to lean with the force of the current. He released the rope holding Sorrel and prayed the horse had the good sense to cross to the other side of the river. Then he prayed Amelia would have the good sense to ride the horse west.

A log traveling rapidly with the current rammed into the wagon. The mules screeched. Houston was losing control, losing control of the team, losing control of the wagon. He jumped into the river with the thought of gaining control by grabbing the lead mule, but the current was stronger, the river bottom slicker than he'd anticipated. His foot slid out from under him and he went under.

Amelia watched in horror as Houston disappeared beneath the raging current. When he surfaced, he plowed through the water until he reached the back of the wagon. He wrapped a hand around a wheel, then bent, his other hand disappearing under the water, and she wondered if he thought he could lift the wagon, free it, and push it across the surging water.

Then the wagon groaned and tilted further until it looked as though it might topple onto him. She balled her hands around his duster, silently urging him to leave the wagon, to escape the river. As though he heard her pleas, he began to fight the current. She barely had time to release her breath before she realized he wasn't heading toward shore, that his destination was the mules. Helplessly she watched as he struggled to release the mules. An eternity seemed to pass before one mule began to wander toward the shore where she stood.

Amelia's heart leapt into her throat when she spotted another log traveling quickly with the current. She screamed out a warning at the same moment that one of the remaining mules sidestepped and shoved its shoulder against Houston. Houston stumbled backward. The log rammed into the base of his skull. Once again, the current dragged him down.

Amelia threw off his duster and jumped into the river.

White light exploded in Houston's head before the brown water sucked him under. He heard Amelia's scream, and dear God, help him, he thought he saw her leap into the river.

He forced back the pain, forced back the welcome oblivion, and resurfaced to see her splashing in the water, screaming his name.

With long, swift strokes born of desperation, he swam toward her, fighting the current, fighting the fear. If she lost her footing as he had, she'd go under the murky waters . . . and find herself surrounded by the darkness that terrified her. No sunlight would filter through the churning river to guide her back to the surface. He wanted her to see another sunrise, to know again the feathery touch of dawn.

As he neared, he could see the fear darkening her eyes. Gaining his footing, he snaked out his arm, wrapping it around her waist and drawing her trembling body against his. The mud sucked at his boots as he hauled her to the bank of the river and collapsed in the mud, her body falling alongside his, her breathing labored, his own chest aching as he fought to draw in air. With the blinding stars dancing across his vision, he rose up on an elbow and glared at the quivering woman lying beside him. Her lips were incredibly blue in a face that was amazingly white. He pressed his wet body over hers, trying to warm her.

She laid her palm against his bristled cheek. "You're safe," she whispered.

"What the hell did you think you were doing?" he growled, his heart pounding wildly in his chest.

"I was going to save you."

He threaded his fingers through her tangled hair. She'd lost her bonnet. She was damn lucky she hadn't lost her life. "You little fool," he rasped in a voice rift with emotion. "You brave little fool."

His mouth swooped down to cover hers. Her cold, quivering lips parted slightly, and he thrust his tongue through the welcome opening like a man desperately searching for treasure.

And treasure he found.

He gentled the kiss because she wasn't a whore whose body he wanted to use to gratify his lust. She was a woman whose warmth he wanted to relish as it seeped through his body, touching his heart as none had before her. He wanted to feel the gentle swell of her curves as they pressed against the hard planes of his body. He wanted—for just one moment—to be young again and innocent. To have no knowledge of betrayal.

Her mouth was warm and sweet, so incredibly sweet. And small, just like the rest of her. She tasted so damn good. He savored her flavor the way a man might enjoy a glass of fine whiskey, leisurely, allowing the whiskey to fill his mouth before releasing the brew, allowing it to burn his throat.

He touched his tongue to hers and heard her small sigh. She scraped her fingers up the side of his face and wove them through his hair. He'd lost his hat as well, and for the first time since he'd been wounded, he welcomed the absence of the shadows.

She smelled of the river, but still he caught the slight scent that was hers and hers alone. He longed to give his mouth the freedom to warm all of her, to kiss every inch of her.

She stopped trembling from the cold, and he could feel the intoxicating warmth as their bodies pressed together. Another tremor passed through her body, a tremor that had nothing to do with the cold. He deepened the kiss, his hands bracketing her face, turning it so he could better the angle and touch her mouth with the intimacy of a long-time lover.

Kiss her as he'd never kissed another. Kiss her as he had no right.

Drawing away, he gazed at her. Her eyes were dark with passion, her lips no longer blue, but red, a deep red, swollen from his kiss.

"I shouldn't have done that," he said in a low voice.

Hurt plunged into the depths of her eyes. Gingerly, he removed his fingers from her tangled hair. "I'll get a fire going."

He struggled to his feet and staggered to the place where she'd left his duster. He snatched it up, returned to her side, and spread it over her as she lay there staring at him. A coldness seeped through his flesh and wrapped around his heart. He went in search of something—anything— with which he could build a fire.

Amelia sat up and slipped into the duster, drawing it tightly around her. It carried his scent of horses and leather.

She touched her fingers to her trembling lips. She had always imagined that Dallas Leigh would be the first to kiss her. But she had never imagined the kiss would be like the one she had just received, would make her feel so warm, so scared, so safe. All the feelings jumbling around inside her made no sense.

She watched as Houston built a fire nearby. She waited until he'd brought the fire to life, just as he'd brought feelings to life within her.

She rose to her feet, walked to the fire, and knelt beside him. "I suppose I shouldn't have kissed you back."

"No, you shouldn't have," he said, tersely, never taking his eyes away from the smoldering fire. "But I figure you were probably just scared and not thinking."

"Were you scared?"

Houston felt his stomach clench. By God, he was terrified, more now than he had been when he'd seen her rushing into the river. That kiss had him shaking clear down to his boots.

He'd expected her to be sweet. He hadn't expected her to be everything he'd ever dreamed of when he was younger and deserved dreams.

Damn Dallas! Damn him to hell for wanting women in addition to cattle, land, and wealth. Damn him for wanting this woman, for earning the right to have her.

Houston shoved himself to his feet. "I need to round up the mules. You stay here and dry off."

His long strides couldn't take him far enough, fast enough. Her flowery scent followed him like a shadow. The lingering taste of her lips taunted him, made him hungry for more. He could still feel the soft swells of her breasts shifting beneath his chest. His fingers ached to hold them, shape them, and caress them with a tenderness he'd never known existed.

He released a shudder as he skidded down the muddy bank. He needed a sporting woman. He'd gone too long without spending himself on a woman. That was the reason he found this journey so damn difficult, the reason he wanted to hold Amelia close. He just needed to purge his longings. Maria would help him. She always did. She would douse all the flames, and in total darkness, he'd take her without passion, without love, without hope. And in the darkness, she couldn't see the ugliness that made him the man he was.

He didn't want Amelia to see the ugliness, either, but she would. Sooner or later, she would.

When night fell, Amelia eased as close to the fire as she dared and wrapped the horse's blanket around herself. The wind came up off the river, damp and frigid. She shuddered.

"Cold?"

She lifted her gaze to the man sitting on the other side of the fire. He'd found the horse and three of the mules. She had a feeling that he'd found the fourth mule as well. She'd heard a gunshot, but he hadn't brought any food back to their small camp. Tomorrow, they would comb the banks of the river to see what they could recover.

"A little," she said, hating the way her teeth clicked together as she spoke. She hadn't been able to regain any warmth since he'd ended the kiss.

Watching him, if she didn't know better, she would have thought he was having an argument with someone. His brow furrowed deeply, his jaw clenched, and with his finger, he drew something in the dirt. Then like a man who had lost the battle, he shoved to his feet and walked around to her side of the fire.

Curiosity getting the better of her, she scrambled to her knees so she could see what he'd written. The light from the flames danced over Dallas's brand.

Houston sat beside her, and she met his gaze. "Why did you draw that?"

"As a reminder that he has a claim on you." He stretched out on the ground and opened his duster. "Come here."

She hesitated, her heart pounding. As an unmarried woman betrothed to his brother, she knew she should suffer through the cold, shouldn't welcome the warmth his body could provide. She closed her hand around the watch, her gift to Dallas that was still hidden in her pocket, and lay next to Houston.

He wrapped his duster and one arm around her, crooking his other arm. "Here, use my arm as a pillow," he said quietly.

She scooted back, nestling her backside against his stomach and laying her head on his arm.

"Better?" he asked.

"Warmer." She studied his curled hand, the long tanned fingers. She knew the strength those fingers held, had felt it this afternoon as he'd braced her face and lowered his mouth to hers. The pads and palms of his fingers were callused, and she resisted the urge to place her hand over his, to press palm to palm, fingertip to fingertip.

"What will we do tomorrow?" she asked.

"See what we can salvage. Use the mules as pack animals."

"I guess we should have waited to cross the river."

"Yeah."

She heard his sigh more than his word.

"Why didn't we?"

Silence fell heavy between them. Amelia rolled over within his arms and felt him stiffen. "Why didn't we wait?"

"Because we'd already lost too much time," he stated flatly.

"Why did you kiss me?"

"Because I'm a fool."

She touched her fingers to his lips. He grabbed her wrist and pulled her hand back.

"Don't do that," he said gruffly.

"We shouldn't have crossed the river. You shouldn't have kissed me. Yet, you did both. Why?"

"Because it's been too damn long since I've been with a woman. Don't read any feelings into what happened this afternoon. I'm a man and I've got needs. Needs any woman would fill. Right now, you're the only woman within two hundred miles."

"So it's not me specifically. It's only because I'm a woman."

"That's right," he said curtly.

"And why did I kiss you back?"

"I reckon women have needs, too."

"And any man would do? That makes me no better than a whore."

He released her wrist. "That's not what I meant."

"I know," she said softly. "You think it's the circumstances and not the people that made us turn to each other this afternoon."

"That's right. You won't be turning to me once we get to the ranch. Once you're with Dallas. Now go to sleep."

She rolled over, giving him her back. She watched the flames in the low fire flicker, just as her thoughts flickered. Was he right? Had she kissed him just because he was there? Because she'd been terrified? "Houston?"

She had been quiet for so long that Houston had been certain she'd fallen asleep. He'd never before heard his name come from her lips as anything but a scream. His heart tightened, and he fought against pulling her closer. "What?"

"What sort of man is Dallas?"

A better man than me. He swallowed, searching for the words that would do his brother justice, true words that would ease her doubts. "He's the kind of man who casts a long shadow . . . a shadow that reaches out to touch everyone and everything. Years from now, people who never knew him will remember him."

She rolled over, pressing her face against his shoulder. "And my shadow will be short. I worry that the man I imagined in the letters doesn't really exist. He seems almost perfect."

"All I can tell you is that I couldn't ask for a finer brother, and I don't imagine you could ask for a finer husband."

"What if he's disappointed when he meets me?"

Tenderness filled him at her insecurity. "He won't be disappointed. I can give you my word on that." Reaching over her, he tucked his duster around her. "Now you'd best get to sleep. Tomorrow's gonna be another long day."

"I'm so grateful you were with me today," she said quietly as she closed her eyes.

Houston couldn't remember if anyone had ever before been grateful for his presence. His mother, he supposed. Certainly not his father.

Unlike Dallas, Houston had never measured up to his father's expectations. He had never been strong enough, smart enough, or fast enough.

"Swear to God, I ought to dress you in girl's clothing!" his father had bellowed the day he had discovered Houston holding a rag doll in the mercantile.

The doll had looked so lonely sprawled over the counter, where a little girl had left her while she browsed the assortment of candies. And so soft. He'd just wanted to see if she was as soft as she looked.

She had been. Her embroidered face had carried a permanent smile, a smile that had made Houston grin crookedly at her.

He realized now that the smile more than the doll had probably set his father off. Or maybe it had been both. Either way, his actions hadn't been of a manly nature. When they'd returned home, his father had taken a switch to Houston's backside. A switch he'd made Houston find.

When the punishment ended, Houston had pulled his trousers up with as much dignity as he could muster. When he had turned, and his father had seen the silent tears coursing down his cheeks, he'd struck Houston's face. The switch had cut into his tender young flesh, leaving a scar that ran the length of his cheek.

He'd hated the scar, often wished it was gone. His mother had warned him to be wary of what he wished for.

When he was fifteen, his wish had come true. Yankee artillery fire had blown the scar off his face, leaving a place for thicker scars to form. He hadn't made a wish since.

But he found himself wishing now. Wishing that the arm holding Amelia hadn't grown as numb as the left side of his face. He could no longer feel the warmth of her body, the sureness of her weight. His one chance to hold a decent woman within his arms through the night, and his arm had fallen asleep.

He thought about adjusting his position, but he didn't want to wake her. His free hand hovered over her face, and like a moonbeam kissing the waters of a lake, he brushed her hair away from her cheek. So soft. So incredibly soft. Like the rag doll he'd held so long ago.

Only she wasn't a doll. She was a woman, flesh and blood, a woman whom Dallas had entrusted into his keeping.

A woman with eyes the green of clover, hair the shade of an autumn moon.

And courage as boundless as the West Texas plains.

Chapter 11

      ૐ

*E*VERYTHING. EVERYTHING WAS gone.

    Amelia stared at the brown flowing river and wondered why they even bothered to look. Her letters from Dallas were gone. A miniature of her mother. She had brought everything that had ever meant anything to her—and now everything was gone.

Everything except the pocket watch she'd purchased for Dallas.

She fought back the tears welling in her eyes. She'd lost everything once before, and somehow she'd managed to survive. She would survive again.

She lifted her chin in defiance, daring the fates to toy with her. Out of the corner of her eye, she saw the sunlight glint through the mud. Lifting her skirts, she walked cautiously to the water's edge.

Her mirror, the mirror her mother had given her, caught and reflected the sunlight. Reaching down, she pulled it from the mud and washed it gently in the water. A sweet memory from the distant past.

She dried the mirror on her skirt, then held it up to gaze at her reflection. She was a mess. Her hair tangled, a bruise on her sun-tinged cheek, a button missing from her bodice. She stared harder at the mirror. In the background, a green cloud billowed in the breeze. She gazed over her shoulder and looked down the stream.

She trudged along the water's edge until she reached the green dress, the bodice wrapped tightly around the spindly branches of a bush, the skirt flapping in the wind. Amelia gathered the skirt close, buried her face in the smooth fabric, and let the tears fall.

And that was how Houston found her. Sitting in the mud with the water lapping at her feet, her knees drawn up, her face hidden by the abundance of green silk.

He wished he could have spared her this journey, could have just plucked her up and put her in Dallas's house without asking her to endure heartache, storms, and raging rivers.

He imagined sitting on the porch years from now with his nieces and nephews circled around him, telling them about the journey he'd made with their mother. A woman of courage, he'd call her.

And he hoped that no one would hear in his voice or see reflected in his gaze that he'd fallen in love with her.

He skidded down the muddy bank and caught his balance, stopping himself before he plunged into the river. He trudged through the mud and knelt beside her. "Amelia?"

She lifted her tear-streaked face. "This was the first dress I'd had in over ten years that didn't belong to someone else first. I was going to save it for the day I married Dallas." She crushed the skirt to her chest. "It's all caught up on the branches."

He knew well the feeling of wearing someone else's hand-me-downs. He had worn Dallas's discarded clothing until the war. The first piece of clothing he had worn that had been his and his alone had been the gray jacket his mother had sewn him so he could ride off with pride alongside his father and older brother.

Only he hadn't felt pride . . . only fear, a cold dread that had slithered through his bowels. A terror as unsettling as the one surrounding him now. He wanted this woman safe, safe within his brother's arms, where Houston couldn't touch her, where he couldn't drag her down into the hell that was his life.

He removed his knife. "I'll cut the branches, and you can take your time working the dress free. Maybe you can repair the damage."

He moved around her and began hacking at the limbs.

"I found my mother's mirror," she said quietly. She touched his brim. "You found your hat."

"Yep. Other than that, I haven't had much luck. The water's too strong. The current's too fast."

"Are we going to go back to John and Beth's?"

"Didn't see that they had much to spare. Think we'd just end up losing time and gaining very little."

"Then what will we do?"

He cut through the last branch and sheathed his knife. "We'll survive. We've still got everything I'd packed on Sorrel. It's not much, but it's enough. I've traveled with less."

She bundled up the green silk and rose. Houston shoved himself to his feet, removed his hat, and extended it toward her. "You'll need to wear this."

Her eyes widened. "But that's your hat."

"I know, but I can't find Austin's hat or your bonnet, and the sun will turn your pretty skin into leather. It can't hurt mine much." He grimaced as a tear trailed along her cheek. "Don't start crying on me."

"But I know what your hat means to you."

He almost told her that she meant more, but reined in the words that he had no right to voice aloud. "Then take good care of it because I'll want it back when we get to the ranch."

The cold winds whipped through the intimate camp. Amelia pulled the blanket more closely around her, tugged Houston's hat down so the brim protected her neck, and scooted closer to the fire. They had traveled most of the day, she on Sorrel, Houston straddled across a mule. They had Sorrel's blankets and the nearby brush to ward off the winds.

"Do you think it will snow?" she asked.

He glanced up. "No. Imagine in a day or so, it'll be warm again."

"This isn't winter?"

He shook his head. She returned her gaze to the fire. She wished she had Dallas's letters. After all the times she'd read them, she should have had every word memorized, but she couldn't remember anything he'd written.

All she could remember was the way Houston's kiss had made her toes curl, the firmness of his body folded around hers last night, and the warmth of his breath fanning her cheek.

Would Dallas tuck her body protectively beneath his as they slept after they were married? Would he gently comb her hair back when he thought she was sleeping? Would he make her body grow as hot as the flames licking at the logs?

She rose to her feet, walked around the fire, and knelt beside Houston. "I've been thinking."

"Yeah, I figured that."

His words surprised her, although she supposed he was coming to know her as well as she was coming to know him. "How did you know?"

"You get this deep dent in the middle of your forehead."

"What else do you know about me?"

"That you're about to start asking me questions."

"Not exactly." She scooted a little closer to him. "You said you had needs—"

"I shouldn't have said that."

"Don't you have needs?"

"Yeah, I got needs, but I shouldn't tell a lady about them."

"Why not?"

"I just shouldn't, that's all."

She gnawed on her lip. "So I shouldn't tell you I have needs, either?"

"No, you shouldn't."

Bringing the blanket more closely around her, she stared into the fire. She tried to imagine Dallas as she stared into the fire. She tried to imagine Dallas as she had envisioned him all those months, without a mustache and with blue eyes. She concentrated on the image she now had of him: brown eyes, a mustache. A woman's dream. A dream she couldn't yet touch . . . "I do have needs," she said quietly. She turned her head slightly and thought he looked terrified. "I was thinking about what you said . . . that any woman would do. I'm wondering if it's the same for me. If any man would satisfy what I'm feeling right now."

"What exactly are you feeling?"

"That I want to be kissed. If you want to be kissed, and any woman would do, why not kiss me? Then both our needs would go away, and maybe we could both go to sleep instead of sitting here staring at the fire."

"I'd rather stare at the fire."

Pain shot through her as though he'd just sent a herd of his horses stampeding over her heart. His words shouldn't have hurt. He wasn't the man she was going to marry—

"Don't do that," he ordered. "Don't get those tears in your eyes."

She gave him her back, fighting the sorrow, the anger, and the hurt. "It's not fair. Until we crossed that river, I'd never been kissed." Surging to her feet, she turned on him like a wolf trapped in the wilderness. "It wasn't fair to give me these needs and then leave me to deal with them on my own. I've never felt like this . . . like I'll die if you don't kiss me."

She whipped around and marched into the darkness away from the fire, immediately regretting her foolishness, but having too much pride to return to the warmth and the light. Surely, Dallas would want to kiss her and satisfy her needs anytime she wanted.

A large hand cradled her shoulder. "I'm sorry," she whispered. "I made a fool of myself. I can't remember what Dallas wrote in his letters. I feel lost . . . just like all our belongings. And afraid. And—"

"He said he wasn't lonely." Gently, Houston turned her and nudged his hat up off her brow. The firelight crept over his shoulder and caressed the patch and scars while leaving his eye and unmarred cheek cast in darkness. Once, she would have wasted the moment trying to imagine him as he might have looked if he'd fought no battle. Now, she simply accepted the rugged features that war had carved into his face.

"He said a wife and sons would enrich his life." He glided his hand from her shoulder up to her cheek and tilted her face. "He asked you to become his wife."

"And I said yes, but surely a simple kiss . . ." Her voice trailed into silence as he rubbed his thumb over her lower lip. Since the war, she had always feared the dark, and it seemed as though it had swallowed them both as he lowered his mouth to hers.

Leaning against him, she twined her arms around his neck, wanting him closer, relishing his warmth as it seeped into her.

He groaned deeply, and she felt the rumble of his chest against her breasts. He plowed his hand into her hair as his mouth plundered hers, his tongue probing, seeking, causing her toes to curl.

He slipped an arm beneath her knees and lifted her against his chest. She kissed his neck, his throat, his jaw as he carried her to the fire. She clutched his shirt as he laid her on the ground and fanned out the sides of his duster before stretching his body over hers and settling his mouth against hers.

She could hear the howling of the wind, the far-off cry of a wolf, and the beating of her own heart keeping pace with his. Needs swelled up within her, needs she'd never known existed. The hard, even lines of his body melded against her soft curves. Over the worn fabric of her bodice, he palmed her breast, kneading her flesh tenderly. She couldn't hold back the whimper that rose in her throat or the desire that exploded like fireworks on the Fourth of July. She arched her back, wanting, needing him closer than he was.

He dipped his head and trailed kisses along the column of her throat.

"It's not working," she rasped.

"I know." Lifting his head, he gazed down on her, brushing the stray strands of hair away from her cheeks.

"You knew it wouldn't work, that what I was proposing was silly—"

"Not silly." A wealth of tenderness filled his gaze. "Definitely not silly."

"I need more."

He brought her hand to his lips and placed a kiss in the heart of her palm. "It's not mine to give you."

"Will Dallas give me what I need?"

"And more. He'll give you the very best. Sporting women don't even charge him for the pleasure of his company."

"Do they charge you?"

"Double." He nibbled on her lips. "Remember that. You'll be getting the best when you marry Dallas. No need to settle for less before then."

He shifted his body and wrapped the duster around her. Then he reached for the blanket, draped it over her, and tucked her in close beside him. "Go to sleep now."

But she couldn't sleep. Unfulfilled desires ravaged her body. She watched the firelight play across his features, golden shadows, amber hues. His body held a tenseness that rivaled hers. How did he expect her to sleep when her toes were still curled, her skin tingled from his touch, and her breast ached for the feel of his palm? "It would have been better if Dallas had come for me."

"Yep."

She turned into him. "Rub my back like you did when I was sick."

He splayed his fingers over her back and began the lonely sojourn.

"What I feel when you kiss me—"

"It's lust, just lust," he interjected.

"That's why you said any woman would do."

"Yep."

She snuggled against him and concentrated on the motion of his hand, the small circles, the occasional sweeps. She imagined she was lying within Dallas's arms, wanting his warmth, his touch, and his even breathing surrounding her.

But when she drifted off to sleep, she dreamed of Houston.

Amelia awoke to the sound of thunder and groaned. "Not another. storm."

"Not a storm, a stampede," Houston said, an urgency to his voice as he rolled away from her. "Get up."

She rose to her feet, the full moon playing hide-and-seek with the shadows. He grabbed her hand and tugged her toward a tree. "What are you doing?" she asked.

"Need to get you off the ground. Grab that branch," he ordered as he swung her off the ground.

She did as he instructed and scrambled into the tree. "Aren't you coming?" she yelled as the thunder grew louder.

She didn't know if he heard her as he raced to the mules and freed them from their hobbles. Then he released his horse and started running back toward the tree.

Terror swept through her heart as the tree began to shake and the air reverberated around her. "Hurry!"

He lunged toward the tree, grabbed a branch, and swung to safety just as the herd reached the outskirts of their small camp.

Amelia tightened her hold on the tree limb as the horses rushed under her. The moon sheathed their backs in pale light, outlining their muscles as they bunched and stretched with their movements. Their manes whipped through the breeze. Their galloping hooves pounded the earth and stamped out the campfire. Their frantic neighs filled the night.

Amelia watched, mesmerized by their beauty, their singular purpose. The last horse shone the brightest, the color of the moon. It came to a staggering stop, raised on its hindquarters, threw its head back, and neighed defiantly before continuing on, following the herd.

When the thundering hooves fell into an eerie silence, Houston slid down the tree. He held up a hand and waited, as though testing the night. Amelia could sense the tenseness in his stance. Slowly, he reached for her. "Come on."

She eased down, and he wrapped his hands around her waist. She could feel the trembling in his fingers, feel her own body shaking. She collapsed against him and listened to the pounding of his heart.

"That was incredible," she said on an escaping breath.

"Yeah, it was," he said quietly as he led her back to the remains of their campfire.

She sat on the ground and watched as he worked to bring the fire back to life. "That last horse . . . I've never seen a horse the color of the moon," she said in awe.

"Palomino. That shade of coloring is called palomino."

"She was beautiful."

"He."

She scooted toward Houston. "He? How could you tell?"

"The pride in the way he held himself. And the fact that he was last. That was his band of mares."

"I always expected the stallion to be the fastest. He couldn't even keep up with the others."

Houston chuckled low. "He's fast. He was putting himself between the mares and danger. The first horse that came through would have been his favored mare. She's the fastest, strongest, probably the smartest of his brood."

As the fire began to crackle, he gazed into the darkness where the retreating mustangs had disappeared. She sensed a wistfulness about him, as though he wished he could have galloped along beside them.

The mules and Sorrel had moved out of harm's way. As they meandered back to camp, Houston secured them for the night. He was quiet, contemplative when he rejoined her by the fire, lay down beside her, and took her into his arms.

"What are you thinking about?" she asked.

His hold on her tightened. "The beauty of those mustangs."

"Who do you think they belong to?"

"The land. Right now, they just belong to the land. They're wild and they're free."

"Are you going to capture them?"

"Nah, I need to get you to Dallas." His voice reflected mourning, loss.

"Will you come back for them?"

"Might. Wild mustangs usually stay in the same area for a while."

"And if they move on before you get back here?"

He shrugged as much as he was able with her in his arms. "There'll be others."

She lifted up on an elbow and met his gaze. "You told me once that the wild ones are becoming rare, that's why you're breeding them. If I wasn't here, would you take the time to capture them?"

"If you weren't here, I wouldn't be here. I never would have left my place, never would have seen them, never would have known they existed . . . so I never would have had them anyway."

She smiled and touched his rough jaw. "But I am here, and you do know they exist. When you left the ranch for Fort Worth, did anything slow you down?"

He furrowed his brow. "No."

"And yet going back, we've had one mishap—"

He chuckled low. "Mishap?"

"All right. We've had one catastrophe after another. Maybe these horses are your destiny, are the reason this journey has been so difficult. They'll give you fine horses to raise. How can you leave without at least trying to capture them?"

She thought he might have shoved her aside if she wasn't wrapped so snugly within his duster.

"We've lost too much time already." He pressed her face into his shoulder. "Go to sleep."

"Then I'm grateful for every incident that slowed us down. Just seeing those magnificent horses was worth it. Don't you agree?"

Silence was his answer. She wondered if he'd wanted other things in his life, but had put his desires aside in favor of someone else's. A horse's whinny broke through the silence. Beneath her cheek, Houston's heart thudded rapidly.

"Do you think that's him?" she whispered.

"Yep."

"And you're going to let him go?"

"Amelia?" She heard the frustration in his voice. "It's not like I'll ride out and rope him and be done with it. Capturing mustangs the way I do is slow goin'."

She came back up on her elbow. "How do you capture them?"

He sighed deeply. "I become one of them."

A warm smile crept over her face. "I'd love to see that."

"Well, you're not gonna. I need to get you to Dallas. Now go to sleep."

She snuggled back against him. "What color did you say he was?"

"Palomino."

"And the first horse that ran through, his favorite mare was the same color, wasn't she?"

"Yep."

"And their manes looked silver in the moonlight."

"They were silver."

"They ran so incredibly fast. Have you ever seen horses run that fast?"

He held his silence.

"I like the way he threw his head back—"

"You're aggravating, you know that? I'm trying to forget I ever saw them, and you won't stop talkin' about them."

"If you don't capture them while we're here, you might lose them forever." She rose back onto her elbow and cradled his unshaven cheek in her hand. "Sometimes, we only get one chance to realize our dreams."

He threaded his fingers through her hair, holding her face immobile. "I don't deserve dreams," he growled through gritted teeth.

"Everyone deserves a dream. Dallas wants a son. Our staying here a couple of more days won't stop him from obtaining what he desires. Your dream is to raise horses. Don't let Dallas's dream overshadow yours. Yours is just as important. Those horses could be part of it." She placed her hand over his. He turned his palm, intertwined his fingers with hers, and brought the back of her hand to his lips.

"You don't know what you're asking," he said, his voice taut.

She heard the palomino stallion whinny in the far distance. "I'm pledged to your brother, but that doesn't mean I've closed my heart to other dreams. If I'm with you when you capture the horses, then I'll become part of your dream as well. And years from now, someone will ride a magnificent palomino horse because we dared to reach for the dream . . . and we'll be remembered."

Chapter 12

*H*OUSTON HAD NEVER considered his desire to raise horses as a dream, but he supposed that it was. He always found a measure of peace when he worked with the mustangs, perhaps because he knew what it was to have one's spirit broken, to be beaten down, and to be left feeling worthless. As a result, he worked damn hard not to break the horse's spirit.

Some horses, like the black mustang Dallas had tried to break, simply couldn't be broken. They were too proud or just too ornery, much as his older brother was. He figured his father had recognized that stubborn trait in Dallas and realized that he couldn't be broken so he'd never tried to bend him to his will. He'd accepted him as he was.

Houston, though, had been another matter. He'd have gladly given his life if just once his father had looked at him with pride reflected in his eyes, but then he had to admit that he'd probably never given his father cause to feel pride toward him.

He glanced around the small boxed canyon. The mustangs could drink at the pond nestled in the corner and rest after the chase until he was ready to take them out. He wouldn't have enough rope to take them all, but he'd take the best. The stallion, his favored mare, and any others he thought would be worth his time. The remaining horses he'd let run free.

Wiping his brow, he watched the woman who wanted to be part of his dream, her fingers nimbly uncoiling a thick rope so he could wrap the individual strands around the tree limbs he had gathered. He didn't dare tell her that she was already in his dreams, those he had at night while he held her in his arms, those that would never become reality.

He would never wake up with her in his bed. He wouldn't grow old holding her hand. He would never see her eyes darken with passion. He would never tell her that he loved her.

He could only hope that Dallas's dreams would extend beyond wanting a son once he met Amelia. That he would cherish her as Houston wanted to.

He didn't think Dallas could avoid falling in love with Amelia. Her grit would appeal to his brother. Houston had dragged her through three weeks of hell, and she hadn't complained once. She'd make Dallas one hell of a wife.

Bending, he began to crisscross the sturdy limbs one over the other until they resembled a lengthy checkerboard. When Amelia finished her task, he would tie the branches tightly together at every juncture where they met to form a "T." The opening to the canyon was small enough that his makeshift gate would cover it. He'd secure one side of the gate to one side of the opening in such a way that Amelia could easily swing it across to block off the canyon once he'd brought the horses here.

He was probably insane to try and capture the horses with the few provisions he had and a woman at his side. Austin had been with him before when he'd captured wild mustangs, staying on the perimeter while Houston infiltrated the herd. He wouldn't have that luxury this time. He wouldn't leave Amelia to fend for herself, although he imagined she was capable of it, but time was running out. He'd only have her to himself for a little while longer . . . and then he wouldn't have her at all.

Dawn arrived. Amelia had slept little, the prospect of watching the horses race into the enclosure filling her with excitement.

Houston had doused the fire as soon as they'd finished eating breakfast. She watched him now as he readied the camp for his departure, her anticipation mounting. He placed a rope halter he'd fashioned on Sorrel. He dropped to the ground and removed his boots and socks before pulling his shirt over his head and tossing it on top of his duster.

He turned to face her, and she balled her hands into fists to prevent them from reaching out to touch the hardened contours of his body. "How long do you think you'll be gone?"

"Not long. Today, I just need to find them." He walked across the small expanse separating them and took her hand. "We need to talk."

Her breath caught. At that moment, she needed a kiss. Lord, she needed a kiss. She fought to keep her gaze locked onto his, her hands from trailing along the scars on his shoulder and chest. She licked her lips.

"I want you to come with me, but I need you to understand what I'm asking. I'm leaving everything here but my revolver, my trousers, and a canteen. I want the mustangs to get used to my smell; the less I have, the less they have to get used to. I'll stay with them until they trust me enough to follow me. I'll sneak away at night to get food and water. I'll bed down where they do. If they take it into their heads to stampede . . . I'll do all I can to protect you, but it might not be enough." He released her hand and started to pace. "Hell, this was a stupid idea. I can't leave you and I can't take you with me. I don't know what I was thinking. I wasn't thinking. If Dallas knew what I was thinking, he'd have my hide."

"I want to go."

He stopped pacing and stared at her. "This ain't no buggy ride."

She wrapped her arms around herself to keep the excitement from carrying her to the clouds. "We're going to ride with the herd? Become part of the herd? This is something I'll share with my grandchildren." She dropped to the ground and began to remove her shoes. He knelt beside her, placed her foot in his lap, and worked her shoe off.

"If something happens—"

"Nothing is going to happen." She hopped up and carefully placed her shoes alongside his boots; the action couldn't have felt more intimate if she'd done it in a bedroom that only the two of them shared. She whipped off his hat.

"Keep the hat on," he ordered.

She spun around. He had already mounted Sorrel. "We're not likely to find much shade."

She settled his hat back in place, grateful that he hadn't wanted her to leave it behind. She would have hated for a raccoon to cart it away.

"Climb on that rock," he said.

He eased the horse over and held out his hand. She slipped her hand into his, using his arm for support as she threw a leg over the horse's back and scrambled into place. She wrapped her arms around Houston's bare chest and pressed her face against his broad back.

The world seemed more beautiful than it had the day before; the leaves were just beginning to turn golden and a briskness to the air promised cooler weather would return. They rode in silence for several hours, Houston studying the ground and the terrain. She could have easily drifted off to sleep with him as her pillow. She wondered if Dallas's back would be this broad, this smooth, this warm.

Houston tensed beneath her cheek and drew the horse to a halt. "There they are."

Leaning to the side, she peered around him. The mustangs grazed in the open.

Houston prodded Sorrel forward. Amelia was certain the pounding of her heart would drive the horses away. They neared the herd. The stallion lifted his head, eyed them warily, released a shrieking neigh, and took off at a gallop. The mares rapidly caught up and passed him, his silver mane blowing in the wind, his tail lifted in the air.

Amelia wanted to weep. "They ran away."

Houston rounded his leg over his horse's head and slid to the ground. Reaching up, he placed his hands on her waist and brought her to the ground. "Expected them to, the first time. That's why I said I wouldn't be long today."

"Why didn't you chase after them?"

"They would have just run harder. This is their range; they'll come back. When they do, we'll be waiting."

"How long before they accept us?"

"Hard to say."

He slipped his arm around her, and in a gesture that seemed as natural as breathing, she leaned against him, waiting for the promise of his dream to return.

For several days, they found the herd, walked into its midst, and watched the horses scamper away, but each day the mustangs didn't run quite as far or quite as fast. On the fourth day, they didn't run.

Houston felt Amelia's arms tighten around him as he guided Sorrel into the middle of the herd. The palomino stallion eyed them warily, slowly approached, and sniffed Sorrel, sniffed Houston's leg. Houston thought he could feel Amelia holding her breath against his back. How he wished he could have turned around to watch her. He imagined her green eyes bright, her lips curved into a smile.

When the stallion had determined they were no threat, he shook his head, sending his long silver mane rippling over his neck, and sauntered away as though to say, "Do as you please."

Houston did just that. He wove his horse through the herd, studying each horse, judging its merit. He would capture them all, but he would keep only the best. He didn't have enough rope to tether them all on a lead.

The one thing he missed throughout the day was Amelia's questions. She held her silence, and he longed to hear her voice. He had a feeling his place was going to seem so much quieter for his having known her.

Amelia lost track of the days as they traveled with the mustangs. Their range covered a considerable distance, but she wouldn't have minded if they'd galloped forever toward the dawn. She loved the feel of the horse beneath her, the man before her when the herd sensed danger and ran. She loved the night sounds when the mustangs settled in around them. Houston would draw her close, and she'd sleep in his arms. Sometimes, they'd talk quietly about the horses, which ones they preferred. Or they would talk about the moments during the day when they hadn't spoken, but each had sensed the other's thoughts revolving around the same conclusions.

She knew before he told her that he preferred the stallion's lead mare over the others. She knew he would use her as the foundation of his own herd. She knew he would take care in breaking her.

And she knew in the hours before dawn when he quietly led Sorrel away from the herd and took her to the small box canyon that she'd fallen in love with him.

"I don't understand why I can't stay with you."

Cupping his hands, he brought the water from the small pond to his lips and gulped. "Because I'm gonna ride them hard, and I need someone to close the gate behind us once I lead them in here."

"What if they don't follow you?"

He stood and dried his hands on his trousers. "Then I'll have to chase them down and rope the ones we want. We've lost enough time as it is."

She wrapped her arms around herself. "I don't understand how you can view the past few days as losing anything. It was the most incredible experience of my life."

He ran his finger along her chin. "I didn't mean it that way, but you have someone waiting for you. I need to get you to him."

He strode to his horse and mounted. "Stay behind the brush until you hear me holler. Then start closing the gate. I'll get over to help you as soon as I can."

She sat on a boulder and waited. She watched the sun ease over the horizon and felt the loneliness sweep through her. Could a person love more than once in a lifetime, love more than one person this deeply, this strongly?

Dallas had answered her advertisement; she had given him her word that she would marry him. She had an obligation to fulfill, but she imagined years from now her children would circle her feet, and she'd tell them how she'd helped their uncle capture the beginning of his dream.

She heard the pounding hooves, felt the ground vibrate. She scampered behind the brush and waited. The herd came into view, thundering over the plains, their heads thrown back, their tails raised, their sleek muscles bunching and stretching as they rushed toward their destination.

Trailing behind, guiding them, keeping them on course rode Houston, low over his horse's back, the wind whipping his hair, the sweat glistening over his body. She thought if she lived to be a hundred, she'd never see anything more magnificent.

Breathing heavily, their coats shiny with exertion, the mustangs galloped into the small canyon, heading for the pond. She heard Houston call her name as he roared past.

She moved the brush aside and began pushing the gate of limbs and rope. Then he was beside her, shoving it into place as the horses milled within the canyon. He fastened it, grabbed her about the waist, and hauled her to the side. "Don't know if it'll hold them," he said as he released her.

The stallion was the first to notice that they were trapped. He reared up and rushed toward the gate of tree branches but stopped short of ramming against it. He trotted back and forth. Amelia could almost feel his anger.

"I have a feeling he's a horse you don't want to rile," she said.

"Yep." Houston dug through their belongings, located his shirt, and drew it over his head. "I could geld him. He wouldn't be so spirited then."

Amelia was appalled. "You won't, will you?"

"Nope. He wouldn't be much good to me then." He walked to the gate and held out his hand. The stallion snorted and trotted into the late-morning shadows.

"What now?" she asked.

"We'll give them a day to calm down, then we'll pick the ones we want and head out."

Amelia began to relish the approaching darkness, the coming of night. Houston never voiced his thoughts or feelings, but she thought he welcomed the night as much as she did.

They spoke seldom during the day, but at night, after they'd eaten, after he'd banked the fire and drawn her into his arms, they'd talk quietly about the past, the present, but never the future.

She came to know more about the man she was to marry in those quiet moments. Houston was more comfortable relating tales of his brother than tales of himself, but she loved best the moments when his story carried a portion of his life.

She learned that Dallas was the favored son, although Houston never came out and admitted it. From the warmth in his voice when he spoke of his mother, she knew that Houston had adored the woman who had fought to bring him into the world.

She hoarded the stories he told her like a miser might hoard gold, sifting through his words, searching for all the keys that unlocked the mysteries that were his.

Houston lost track of the number of days that they traveled, but every night when he gathered Amelia in his arms to sleep, he fought a battle with his conscience, trying to justify what he'd done. He could have taken her to the ranch and returned for the mustangs. He *should* have taken her to the ranch.

But dammit, he'd wanted her with him, to share the capture, to know the horses as he knew them, to be able to lay claim to a corner of his dream.

When he turned her over to Dallas, she'd begin to live her own dream, and he had no place in it.

He drew his mule to a halt. Amelia's mount stopped, along with the mustangs he had in tow. They'd settled on eight. One was a puny thing that he didn't think would ever amount to much, but the woman beside him was afraid it wouldn't survive on its own when they released the horses without the stallion and his favored mare to guide them. So he'd kept the gentle creature, knowing full well his world wasn't made for gentle things.

The shadows were lengthening but they had plenty of daylight left, too much daylight left. He veered his mount to the left, trusting everyone else to follow.

In awe, Amelia stared at the small spring. Three waterfalls, each no taller than a man, cascaded over the moss-covered rocks and through the brush, melting into the wide pond. The horses lapped at the clear water.

Beside her, Houston hunkered down, stirred up the water near the edge of the bank and dipped his palm beneath the surface. "It's colder than I expected it to be."

His voice reflected disappointment, and he glanced up at her. "Thought you might like a swim . . . but it's too cold."

She knelt beside him and flitted her fingers through the water. "When I was little, I used to run and hide when my mother told Dulce to get my bath ready. I thought it would be wonderful to never have to take a bath, to get as dirty as I wanted, and have no one care." She tugged on her bodice. "I have never felt so filthy in my whole life. I'm surprised you get as close to me as you do."

"I'm not too sweet smelling myself."

"I think the horses smell better than we do."

He nodded slowly. She lowered her hand into the water. "It's not too cold once you get used to it." Her gaze circled the pond. "Do you think there are snakes here?"

"I've never seen one, but let me scout around."

As he studied the perimeter of the pond, she removed her shoes, her fingers shaking with the thought of a snake digging his fangs into her again. She took a deep, calming breath, determined not to let her fears guide her life.

"Think you'll be safe. I'm gonna gather up some wood, then I'll get a fire goin'. You can wade in. Holler if you see anything."

He walked away. She didn't care how cold the water was. They'd been traveling for days with little more than shallow streams that wouldn't get her big toe wet. She wanted a warm bath in a big wooden tub, but she'd settle for this cold spring.

She'd placed his hat on a boulder and stripped down to her undergarments before she thought to glance over her shoulder. Houston was sitting back on his haunches before a pile of wood, staring at her. He scuttled around until he presented her with his back.

After all they'd been through, removing her clothes in front of him had seemed natural. She waded into the water and screeched.

Houston surged to his feet and raced across the clearing. Laughing, Amelia held up her hands. "No, it's just cold."

He skidded to a halt. "Don't go hollerin' like that. You made my heart stop beating."

Tensing, holding her breath, she sank beneath the water. She came up laughing and sputtering. "It's not so bad once you get used to it. Come join me."

He looked as though she'd just plowed her fist into his stomach. She glanced down. The white linen clung to her body, outlining her curves, shading the different facets of her body. She eased into the water, welcoming its chill. "Come join me," she repeated softly.

"Good Lord, woman, are you outta your mind?"

"Maybe I am, traveling across the country to marry a man I barely know. Traveling across Texas with a man I didn't know. You could have taken advantage of me and you didn't. I don't think you will now." She tilted her head to the side. "It feels nice to get the dust off."

Houston knew his body needed a cooling off . . . bad. He tossed his duster onto the ground and pulled his shirt over his head. He dropped down to remove his boots and socks. If his body didn't like the sight of her so much, he'd remove his trousers. As it was, he waded in, cringing as the cold seeped through his remaining clothing. "How long before I get used to it?" he said gruffly.

She laughed. Lord, he loved her laugh. He loved the sparkle in her eyes, the way her lips curved up.

She splashed water at him. He couldn't afford to play with her, afraid he'd wrap his arms around that slick body of hers, pull her against him, and never let go. Instead, he settled on the sandy bottom and leaned back on his elbows, allowing the cold water to lap around him, fighting a losing battle, trying not to notice how her white cotton was melting against her flesh.

She dropped her head back, her throat an arched column of ivory. He'd like to lay a dozen kisses from the tip of her chin to the base of her throat.

"Sometimes, I wish this journey would never end," she said, wistfully. She lowered her gaze and met his. "But it will, won't it?"

"Yeah, it will."

She slid through the water until she neared him. "And all I'll have are the memories of the time we shared," she said softly.

The molten heat flowed through him with her nearness. He was surprised the water surrounding him didn't steam. "We probably ought to get out now," he suggested as he started to rise.

She placed her hand on his bare shoulder, and he dropped back into the water. "Amelia—"

"I didn't mean to embarrass you," she said.

"You didn't embarrass me. It's just that every now and then we start heading down roads we shouldn't, and I just figured you were fixin' to get on one of those roads."

"Because I've enjoyed the time I've been with you?"

He nodded.

"That first day I met you, I expected this to be the longest trip of my life. I never thought I'd find myself hoarding moments with you as though they were gold." She pressed her finger to his lips before he could protest. "Do you know which moment was my favorite?"

He shook his head, held by the glow of her gaze.

"After we crossed the river on Sorrel, before you returned to the other side for the wagon . . . and you smiled."

He grimaced. "Woman, you must be part-near blind. If it looked anything close to what it felt like, it should have given you nightmares."

"I could pull out my mirror—"

"Nope." He sank deeper beneath the water. "I don't like mirrors."

"You're not scarred that badly."

"It's got nothing to do with my scars." And he'd be damned if he'd explain himself. Not this evening, not when their time together was drawing to a close.

She sighed heavily. "I'll admit that the left side didn't go up as high as the right side, but I still liked your smile." She touched her fingertip to the corner of his mouth. "Smile for me again."

He pressed his lips together.

She placed her thumbs on either side of his mouth and tugged up. He jerked back. "I can't smile if I'm thinkin' about it."

"Then don't think about it."

She scooted back, skimmed her hand over the top of the pond, and sprayed him.

"Don't do that," he ordered.

She smiled mischievously. "Why?" She splashed water on him again.

"Because I said, that's why."

"Oh, I'm scared," she teased as she spattered water at him again.

"You're gonna be, if you don't stop," he threatened.

She laughed then, laughed loud and clear, the melodious sound echoing around the falls. He'd probably never know what overcame him, but he lunged for her, grabbed her waist, and carried her under the water.

When he brought her back up, her arms and legs were wrapped around him. She tossed the hair out of her eyes and laughed. "I'm still not scared."

He couldn't help himself. He added his laughter to hers as it floated on the breeze. Deep and strong. The sound shook him, and he fell silent.

Amelia touched his cheek. "You've never laughed," she stated simply.

"Not as a man. Not that I can recall."

Tears welled in her eyes. "I find that incredibly sad."

He moved her aside and pushed himself to his feet. "Time to get out and get warm."

But he could still hear his laughter reverberating between the falls, and it was all he could do not to weep himself.

*　　　*　　　*

Wrapped in a blanket, Amelia huddled beside the crackling fire in her damp bodice and skirt. Her drenched undergarments were stretched over a rock to dry.

Night hovered around her. A million stars twinkled overhead. She could hear the waterfalls, the occasional splash of a fish, frogs croaking, and the silence of her traveling companion as he gazed into the fire, his brow furrowed. She wondered where his thoughts traveled tonight.

Based on the depths of his creases, she had a feeling he was traveling back toward a war that had catapulted him into adulthood, stolen a portion of his sight, his smiles, and his laughter.

"A penny for your thoughts," she said quietly.

He glanced at her. "They're not worth that much."

"They are to me."

A corner of his mouth crooked up, and the warmth raced through her. She'd given him that, small as it was, a halfhearted attempted at a smile that she hoped would one day brighten his life.

"Even when you aren't asking questions, you're asking questions," he said.

"You don't like questions."

"Don't mind the questions. It's answerin' 'em that I'm not fond of."

She eased closer to him. He'd long ago stopped shielding her from the sight of his face. She couldn't imagine him looking more perfect than he did at that moment. Nor could she imagine him asking her a question of his own free will. "Play a game with me."

"The checkerboard is at the bottom of the river."

"I know a game that doesn't require a board. A simple game, really. I used to play it with my sisters. The rules are easy. You decide if you want to truthfully answer a question or take a dare. I'll ask the questions or issue the dare." She smiled sweetly. "The question will be something you wouldn't want to answer; the dare something that frightens you."

Horror swept over his face. "You call that a game?"

She slapped his shoulder. "It's fun. We always ended up laughing. Do you want to answer a question or take a dare?"

"Neither. I'm goin' to sleep."

She placed her hand on his thigh, effectively halting his movements. "Humor me. I'll go first. Ask me a question."

"Why are you so partial to questions?"

"Oh, that's an easy one. It's the best way to find out information. Now do you want to answer a question or take a dare?"

He looked as though she'd just set his favorite horses free. "That wasn't hardly fair."

She fought the urge to squeal with the realization that he would indeed play. "You have to choose your questions carefully."

He narrowed his gaze. "I'll take a question."

"It'll probably be something you don't want to answer."

"I don't want to answer any of them."

"All right." She shifted her backside, planted her elbow on her thigh, her chin in her palm, and studied the scowling man, wondering what she could ask that would present a challenge but not scare him off. "When you cry out in your sleep, are you dreaming about the war?"

"A dream is something you want. No, I don't dream about the war." He looked toward the fire. "But it's there in my head when I sleep." He shifted his gaze back to her. "This sure ain't like any game I ever played."

"When was the last time you played a game . . . not counting checkers?"

"How many questions do you get?"

She smiled. "You're right. Your turn. I'll take a question."

"Anything?"

"Anything."

Houston stretched out beside her and traced a finger in the dirt. He could ask her anything, and she'd answer it. Maybe she would have all along, but asking questions was as foreign to him as giving an apology had once been. He didn't want to parrot her, but he couldn't think of anything to ask. "Sometimes, you whimper in your sleep. What are you thinking about then?"

"My sisters . . . as they were the last time I saw them."

"I should have figured that."

"I don't dream about them as much since the storm, since I told you about them. And more often when I do dream about them, I see them as they were before the war . . . when we played games like this. It still hurts to think about them, but it's a different sort of hurt. A good hurt."

"That doesn't make any sense. What exactly is a good hurt?"

She held up a finger. "One question. Tell me the truth or take a dare."

"A dare, I reckon. I've answered enough questions."

She eased alongside him. "Kiss me as though I had no contract binding me to another."

"You don't want that."

"Afraid?"

Hell, yes, he was afraid. Afraid he'd forget that she was bound to his brother. Afraid he wouldn't find the strength to keep riding west in the morning. Afraid she'd touch the part of him that longed for softness until he couldn't ignore it. "Unbraid your hair," he rasped.

She sat up and draped the long braid over one shoulder. Nimbly her fingers worked the strands free. The firelight sent its red glow over her golden tresses, each strand seeming to have a life of its own as it curled over her shoulder, circled the curve of her breast, trailed down to her waist.

It was her game, her rules. He'd always been afraid not to follow the rules or to stray from the path. She ran her tongue over her lips, the innocent woman he knew turning into a temptress. Raised on an elbow, he threaded his fingers through her hair and pulled her mouth down to his.

She released a sound, more of a mewl than a whimper, her lips parting slightly in invitation. He didn't have to be asked twice.

Rolling her over, he slipped his tongue into her mouth and relished the feel of heaven.

Amelia ignored the hard ground below her, and welcomed the firm man above her. His fevered kiss curled her toes as she rubbed her foot along his calf. Groaning, he slipped his knee between her thighs, and she arched up against him.

He tore his mouth from hers, his breathing labored as he laid his bristly cheek against hers. "Don't do that."

"Why?"

"Just don't," he rasped as he brought his mouth back to hers.

She thought his hot mouth might devour her, and she didn't care. She had embraced Dallas's dreams, but now she wanted more. She wanted love; she wanted to feel the sunrise in a kiss, the glow of a full moon in a touch, the warmth of the fire in a caress.

His questing mouth gentled, but his fingers tightened their hold.

"God, I want to touch you," he said in a husky voice as he trailed his mouth along the column of her throat.

"Then do."

He chuckled low. "Woman, you don't know what you're saying."

"But I know what I need. I need you to touch me."

Houston surged to his feet, stormed to the spring, and leaned against a rock. "You don't know anything. If I touch you the way I want, I'll destroy every dream you came here to find."

"We could build new dreams together."

He shook his head, refusing to acknowledge the hope in her voice. "You came here to start a new life. Dallas can give you that."

She sat up. "You could give me that."

"It's not my place. Dallas asked you, damn it. He built you a huge house and changed his brand. He can give you everything that I can't, everything you deserve . . . everything I'd want you to have. I can only give you rags, loneliness, and nightmares."

Amelia bundled up her damp clothes and stuffed them into a saddlebag. Dawn had been clear and should have filled her with joy, not despair. She had lain within Houston's arms, but he had somehow distanced himself from her. She wasn't even certain he'd slept.

He shook out the blanket, laid it over the fire, then quickly flicked it back. Black smoke spiraled into the air. He repeated his actions.

"What are you doing?" she asked.

"Letting Dallas know we're here."

Amelia's heart slammed against her ribs. "We're that close?"

He rose from his crouched position, crossed the small expanse of space separating them, and touched his rough palm to her cheek, holding her gaze. "We're that close."

"Last night was good-bye?"

"It was supposed to be. I couldn't think of the right words to use. You deserve prettier words than I can give you."

Reaching around her, he grabbed the canteens, walked to the spring, and began filling them.

As though she were ensconced in a dream, Amelia walked to the spring and knelt on his left side, her way of showing him that she didn't care if he was scarred, if he was imperfect. "I love you."

He continued his task as though she'd said nothing at all. Perhaps it was best. If he had acknowledged her feelings, she might have found it harder to honor the contract she'd signed.

"Houston?" She placed her hand on his arm.

He twisted around, meeting her gaze, his expression somber. She extended his hat toward him. "You'll want this back."

He took her offering, but didn't settle it onto his head. "Yeah, I reckon I will."

With a feather-light touch, she trailed her fingers around his patch. He went as still as stone. If he wouldn't accept her declaration of love, she'd give him something easier to accept, another version of the truth.

"When I began this journey, I cared for Dallas," she said quietly. "I still do. Only I've come to care for you more."

"That's because you've been with me for a while. Once you've spent some time with Dallas, your feelings will change back to what they were."

"And if they don't?"

"I'll take you back to Georgia."

She shook her head vigorously. "I don't want to go back to Georgia."

"Then give Dallas a chance."

"Do you care for me at all?"

He touched his knuckles to her cheek. "More than I have any right to."

Chapter 13

~

$\mathcal{H}$OUSTON SAW THE cloud of gray dust billowing in the distance, the riders shimmering against the afternoon sun. If he weren't on Dallas's land, he might have felt a measure of panic, but he was certain Dallas would have had his men out patrolling the area where he expected them to ride in. Besides, he recognized the black wide-brimmed hat that was his brother's trademark, ordered special from the Stetson factory in Philadelphia. He didn't know of any other man in the area with a hat brim that wide.

He drew the mule to an ungainly stop. He wished he'd had time to tame one of the mustangs, but his method of taming a horse was slower than his method of capturing them. He didn't relish meeting his brother with a mule beneath him. He nearly snorted at the odd timing of his pride. His pride. His father had first beat it out of him. Then the war had buried it in an unmarked grave.

Amelia brought Sorrel to a graceful halt. Houston couldn't stop himself from engaging in a moment of self-indulgence, of watching her from beneath the shadows of his hat. She was one hell of a horsewoman as far as he was concerned, an even finer lady. She'd do Dallas proud.

"Why are we stopping?" she asked.

Reaching over, Houston unwrapped the canteen from her saddle-horn and handed it to her. "Riders."

She cupped her hand over her furrowed brow and gazed into the distance. He thought of a hundred things he should say to her at this moment before she left his side, never to return.

But he held his silence because it was easier, so much easier. Or at least it should have been easier. For the first time in his life taking the easy way seemed damn hard.

He watched the column of her throat lengthen as she tilted her head back and drank deeply from the canteen. Several strands of her hair had worked their way free of her braid and the prairie breeze whipped them around her face. Her dress was soiled, her feet bare, her face kissed by the sun.

He thought she'd never looked more beautiful.

She handed the canteen back to him, worry etched within her eyes.

"The man riding in the front, the one wearing the black hat, is Dallas," he said.

She nervously combed her hair back. "I look a mess."

"You look beautiful."

He swung his gaze away from her, and Amelia wondered what it was she had briefly seen reflected in his face. Regret? Loneliness? He wore each one closely woven together, like a layered second skin.

The land surrounding her was vast, as vast as her future, her dreams. The man with whom she'd agreed to share both rode toward her. She wrung her hands together, her trepidation increasing. "I didn't expect to meet him with an audience."

"It's just his trail hands. Imagine he had them out lookin' for us."

The pounding of hooves intensified as the riders neared, a tide of dust rolling behind them. Then a deafening silence roared around Amelia as the men brought their horses to a staggering halt, as though they'd slammed against a brick wall. The horses snorted and whinnied, prancing before her. The men simply stared, slack jawed.

The man who had been in the lead removed his hat, and Amelia was struck hard by his handsome features. His black hair was cut shorter than Houston's, trimmed evenly, and indented where his hat had pressed against it. His thick black mustache draped around full lips that she longed to see shaped into a smile. His brown eyes scrutinized her as they slowly traveled from the top of her head to the tip of her tiniest toe. She fought the urge to squirm in her saddle, wishing she'd at least gone to the trouble to work her feet into her shoes.

Slowly, each of the six men surrounding him removed their hats as though in a trance, their mouths gaping open, their solemn gazes riveted on her. Only the young man who had ridden beside Dallas seemed comfortable with the sight that greeted them, his grin broad, his eyes the mesmerizing blue of the hottest flames writhing within a fire.

Dallas dismounted and, with a pronounced limp, walked toward Sorrel, his gaze never leaving Amelia. He grabbed the reins when the horse shied away, and Amelia sensed that his one movement left no doubt in the horse's mind who had just become his master.

"Miss Carson, it's a pleasure to have you here," he said, his voice rich with confidence, his stance bold as though he knew no one and nothing could topple him from the mountain of success he'd climbed.

He was all that she'd expected. He wore self-assurance the way Houston wore his duster. She touched her braid. "A raccoon ran off with my hat."

Dallas blinked hard and stared at her. Houston cleared his throat, and Amelia wished a dust storm would rise up and sweep her across the plains. After all these many months, she finally had the opportunity to speak with him in person, and she'd said something that might make him think she'd left her wits back in Georgia.

"I told you to put a rattlesnake on that hat instead of a bird. Raccoon wouldn't have touched a rattlesnake."

Dallas snapped his head around and glared so intensely at the young smiling man that she was surprised he didn't topple out of his saddle. "Was she talking to you?"

The young man's smile grew. "Nah, but I was listenin'."

Dallas's eyes narrowed. "Miss Carson, that youngster is my brother, Austin. I'll introduce you to my men in time."

Amelia smiled warmly at the young man. "It's a pleasure to meet you," she said.

Austin ducked his head, blushing clear up to the roots of his scraggly black hair. Amelia's cheeks grew warm. From the corner of her eye, she saw a muscle in Houston's jaw strain as he fought to hold back what she was certain would be a smile if he gave it freedom. He had told her the truth about Austin: He was the sort people took to right away. Even while sitting in a saddle, he was more relaxed than either of his brothers.

His dark brown gaze uncompromising, his jaw tight, and his stance foreboding, Dallas turned his attention to Houston. "You're over three weeks late, with no wagon, no supplies. Reckon you got some explaining to do."

Houston shifted his body and pulled the brim on his hat low. "Reckon I do," he said simply.

"We'll discuss it up at the house," Dallas said before he limped to his horse and pulled himself into the saddle. He urged his horse forward until it sidled up against Sorrel. "Miss Carson, will you do me the honor of riding at the front with me?"

She glanced over at Houston. He gave a brusque nod. She hadn't expected to say good-bye to him like this—without saying good-bye at all. She thought of a hundred things she should say, wanted to say. She held her silence, forced a smile, met her future husband's gaze, and nodded because at that very moment her throat was knotted with emotions. As Dallas guided her horse through the waiting men, she felt as though she was leaving something precious behind her.

Houston had expected his farewell to Amelia to consist of more than a quick nod, but at that moment he couldn't have spoken to her if his life had depended on it. He watched Dallas lead her away from him, lead her toward her rightful place at his side. He told himself it was for the best, but he hadn't hurt this badly since Yankee mortar fire had torn into him.

Austin urged his horse toward Houston. "You got some new ponies."

Houston cleared his throat. "Yep." His voice sounded as though he'd just swallowed a handful of dust. He cleared his throat again before prodding the mule forward to ride behind the awe-struck procession.

Austin kicked his horse into a short canter and caught up before slowing down to keep pace. "She's pretty, ain't she?" Austin asked.

"Yep."

"Think Dallas is pleased?"

Houston glanced over at Austin, his young face incredibly earnest. "If he ain't pleased, then he's a fool."

Austin's face split into a wide grin. "I ain't never known him to be a fool."

Houston heard Amelia's light laughter, followed quickly by Dallas's deeper chuckle. She needed a man who'd laugh with her. She'd find that in Dallas.

"She's got a pretty laugh," Austin said.

"Yep."

"Dallas was fit to be tied waiting on you to get here."

"Figured he would be."

"He ain't gonna like it at all that you took time to capture some horses."

Houston sighed deeply. "Didn't think he would."

"He said that he was gonna shoot you for lettin' that black stallion go."

Houston gave his brother a sideways glance. "Now, how'd he know it was me that let the stallion go?"

Austin shrugged. "Just guessed, I reckon. Is she gonna be my ma?"

"Hell, no, she's not gonna be your ma."

Austin looked like a puppy that had just been kicked. "It ain't fair to grow up without a ma. I was hoping Amelia might just sort of pretend she was my ma."

"She's Miss Carson to you, and she's gonna be too busy being a wife to Dallas to be pretending much of anything."

"Not until that circuit preacher gets back here, and Dallas is probably gonna shoot you on account of that, too."

Houston snapped his gaze over to his brother. "The preacher's not here?"

"Nope. He got here about three weeks ago, waited a whole week, then said he needed to get about searching for lost souls."

Houston tightened his hold on the mule's short cropped mane. Without a preacher, no marriage would take place. Until Amelia was safely tucked away as Dallas's wife, Houston wouldn't feel safe from his heart's longings.

He wondered why he thought a little piece of paper could snuff out the flames of desire building within him. He wondered how much longer he had to wait before he had to endure the hell of watching Amelia become another man's wife.

"Two months!" Dallas barked as he dropped into the leather chair behind his desk. He looked at Houston, grimaced slightly, turned the chair, and stared out the distant window. "It'll be at least two months before the circuit preacher gets back here."

Houston shifted in his chair on the other side of the desk, grateful Amelia was in a room upstairs taking a bath. He was accustomed to Dallas grimacing whenever he was in a fit of temper and looked Houston's way. When he wasn't in a fit of temper, he remembered that he couldn't stomach the sight of his brother. Houston knew the reason Dallas preferred not to look at him. It was a testament of Dallas's love and strength of character that he'd never thrown the reason into Houston's face.

"I got her here as fast as I could."

Dallas leaned back in his chair and raised a dark brow. "You just happened to find a bunch of horses tied together on a rope?"

"Wild horses are gettin' scarce. I thought—"

"I don't need horses. I need a son!"

"So send somebody to fetch the preacher back," Austin suggested as he hitched up a hip and sat on the edge of the desk.

Dallas glared at him. "Was I talking to you?"

Austin's face split into a wide grin. "Nah, but I was listenin'."

"Why don't you go listen somewhere else?" Dallas asked.

" 'Cuz I wanna know what happened to the wagon."

Dallas thrummed his fingers on the desk. His jaw clenched. "What did happen to the wagon?"

"Lost it when I tried to cross a swollen river."

"Why in the hell did you do that?" Dallas roared.

"Because we'd already lost some time, and I thought you'd be worrying."

"He was worryin' all right. Just like an old woman—"

Dallas slammed his hand on the desk and came out of his chair. Austin slid off the desk and took a step back, the grin easing off his face, his gaze never leaving his brother's.

"Children are to be seen and not heard," Dallas said in a low deep voice.

"I ain't a child," Austin said, his chin quivering, his voice anything but deep. He balled his fists at his side. Houston could see that he was trying to decide if this was the moment when he should stand his ground . . . or if he should save his hide and run.

"As long as you live under my roof, eat the food from my table . . ."

Houston resisted the urge to cover his ears as Dallas continued his tirade much as their father had before him. Houston could remember those very words directed his way. He'd been eight, sitting in a patch of clover, tying the little flowers together, making his mother a necklace. He'd made the mistake of slipping the chain of flowers over his head to see if it was big enough. His father had torn the flowers off, scattering them on the wind before he'd told Houston how he should behave in the ways of a man. Houston had felt smaller than the ants crawling beneath the clover.

"He didn't mean any harm," Houston said quietly.

Dallas stopped his tirade midsentence and shook his head. "What did you say?"

"I said that Austin didn't mean any harm. You're angry at me, not him. So take your anger out on me, not him."

"It's my fault," a soft voice said from the doorway.

Houston bolted out of the chair, nearly knocking it over.

Amelia walked into the room wearing a scoop-necked peasant blouse and skirt like the women wore in Mexico, her feet bare, her hair loose. She looked like an angel, only Houston knew differently. He could see the anger reflected in her eyes. Reflexes had him taking a step back. Curiosity had him wondering if Dallas had just met his match.

Dallas cleared his throat. "Miss Carson, I'm certain you did nothing wrong—"

"I didn't say I did anything wrong," she corrected him as she stopped before him and tilted her face. The afternoon sunlight streamed in through the window, bathing her in a yellow halo. "You're angry because our trip was delayed, and I don't blame you for that. I'm certain you were concerned and that's enough to make anyone irritable. But when we saw the horses . . ." She sighed sweetly. "They were magnificent. If you'd heard Houston's voice when he said he'd come back for them . . . I knew they'd be gone, that he knew he'd never possess them. So I talked him into taking the time to capture them. We lost a few travel days, but we're here now."

She made it sound as though they would have been fools if they'd passed up the horses. Dallas was staring at her as though he couldn't think of anything to say.

"And the horses were so important now that Houston is breeding them."

Inwardly, Houston groaned. Why hadn't she stopped talking while peace was settling within the room?

"What?" Dallas asked, apparently finding his voice. He looked at Houston and winced. "You're breeding horses?"

"Thinking about it. I'm just thinking about it."

"That's not—"

He stopped Amelia's words with as cold a glare as he could muster. She lowered her gaze but not before he saw the hurt he'd put in her eyes. He'd forever be hurting her. It was his way, and he hated when it touched her. He needed to leave, but he couldn't leave without trying to put a smile back into those green eyes. "I like those clothes. Where did you get them?"

Grabbing the sides, she fanned out the skirt. "The cook brought them to me. He said they'd belonged to his wife."

"Hand-me-downs," Houston said quietly, knowing it was no longer his place to worry about the clothing she wore. Dallas had taken over that responsibility earlier in the day, when he'd led Amelia away from Houston's side, but he found himself worrying anyway.

"She won't be wearing hand-me-downs for long. I've already sent one of my men to fetch yard goods." He looked at Amelia. "There's a small settlement to the south of us. I can't guarantee that what he selects would be your first choice in materials, but until I can find the time—"

Amelia held up her hand, warmed by Dallas's consideration. "You don't have to explain. I'm quite grateful for what I have."

"Still, I put him on a fast horse so he should be back within three or four days."

"I'm sorry we lost most of the clothes you purchased me in Fort Worth. They were lovely."

Dallas furrowed his brow. "What clothes?"

"The clothes you told Houston to purchase for me."

"He didn't tell Houston to purchase you any clothes," Austin said.

"He did tell me to purchase her some clothing," Houston said in a low voice.

"I don't recall him saying anything about clothes."

"You weren't there," Houston said.

"I was there the whole time you were talk—"

With one swift movement, Houston grabbed the scruff of Austin's shirt. Despite the boy's protest, Houston hauled him out of the room.

Dallas cleared his throat. "If you'll excuse me, I need to help settle this matter."

Amelia pressed her hand just above her pounding heart. "Certainly."

As soon as he walked out of the room, the harsh whispering in the hallway increased in volume. If she were a gambler, she would have bet money that Dallas hadn't told Houston to purchase her clothing. He'd bought her clothing because she'd been carrying one small bag with everything she owned tucked inside. The "outfits" had been a gift from Houston, a gift he'd never planned to claim. She wondered how many other gifts he might have given her: her life, a Texas sunset. She smiled with the memory of him inside her tent, stripping down. She wished now that she'd watched the entire show.

The men trudged back into Dallas's office, each wearing disgruntled expressions.

"My apologies, Miss Carson," Austin said. "Seems I was wrong. Dallas did tell Houston to purchase you some clothes."

She glanced first at Houston, then at Dallas. Their jaws were firmly set. The lie, she supposed, was for her sake. "No harm done. I'm sure quite a bit was said . . . or thought to be said before Houston was sent to fetch me."

Houston settled his hat on his head. "I need to be goin'."

"The cook said supper would be ready soon. Surely you'll stay for the meal," Amelia said, hating the thought of his leaving.

Houston watched as sadness and nervousness warred within Amelia's eyes. He wanted to stay. He wanted to leave. He wanted a few minutes alone with her so he could explain what couldn't be explained.

"You'll stay. Miss Carson wants you here," Dallas said, his tone effectively putting an end to Houston's choices.

Weary from the journey, Houston nodded. "I'll stay."

"I'm so glad," Amelia said before she turned to Dallas. "I have something for you." Holding out her hand, she unfurled her fingers to reveal a gold pocket watch. "A small token of my affection. But it broke."

"Your affection broke?" Dallas asked.

Houston wished he hadn't heard the catch in Dallas's voice, but the sound brought home how much Dallas was depending on Amelia to marry him, to give him the son he wanted.

Amelia smiled softly. "No, the watch broke. I was carrying it in a hidden pocket in my skirt, and it got ruined when I jumped into the river. If you shake it, you can hear the water that's still trapped inside."

Dallas took the gift from her, held it near his ear, and rattled it. "Well, I'll be. I'll treasure it always."

Amelia blushed. "But it no longer keeps time."

Dallas smiled warmly. "No, but it'll remind me to stay off wild horses."

Every room Amelia had set foot in was huge: her bedroom, Dallas's office, the front parlor, and the entryway. The dining room, however, was the largest of all. A chandelier hung from the ceiling towering above. The walls were bare. The hearth empty. One large oak table with four chairs resided in the room with nothing else. The furniture in each room seemed oddly matched, as though Dallas's taste in wood and fabric ran along the same lines as his taste in women's hats. Amelia didn't know if she could ever feel comfortable in any of the rooms. They seemed incredibly cold, and she sensed that fires burning within the hearths would not warm them.

The chairs scraped across the stone floor as everyone took their seats, Dallas at the head of the table to her left, Houston to her right, and Austin across from her. She was struck with the beauty of Austin's eyes, a sapphire blue that any woman would have envied. His thick black lashes framed his eyes, drawing attention to them. She thought if women did come to the area as Dallas hoped, Austin would soon be married.

A door at the back of the room was kicked open, and the cook ambled in carrying a black cast-iron pot. His white hair stood out in all directions as though it had battled the wind and lost. A bushy white beard hid his mouth. Stains splattered his white apron. He brought the ladle out of the pot and spooned the stew into Amelia's bowl. "Ain't fancy, but it's filling."

She glanced up at him and smiled. "Thank you. And thank you for the loan of the clothes."

"Ain't no loan. They're yours to keep. Got no use for 'em any more."

"Didn't know you was married, Cookie," Austin said.

"Years ago, boy, years ago. Little gal from Mexico." He placed stew in Dallas's bowl. "She up and died on me, but I kept some of her clothes. Used to take 'em out at night and just smell 'em because they smelled like her. But it's been too many years now. Can't smell her no more. Might as well let Miss Carson here get some use out of 'em."

"What was your wife's name?" Austin asked as Cookie filled his bowl until the stew dripped over onto the table.

"Juanita. Beautiful, she was. With black hair, black eyes, and red, red lips." He closed his eyes at a memory. "What those lips could do to a man." He ambled over to Houston. "If I keep thinkin' about her, I'm gonna have to hightail it up to Dusty Flats."

"Dusty Flats?" Amelia said.

What was visible of Cookie's cheeks turned as red as Juanita's lips might have been. He dropped the pot on the table. "I'll leave this with you. I ain't no butler." He went back through the door by which he'd entered, kicking it closed on his way out.

"Dusty Flats?" Amelia repeated. "Is that a town?"

Houston and Dallas both shifted in their chairs, their faces set. "It's not a town that a lady would go to," Dallas said.

"But it's got women," Austin said. "Or so I've heard." He stuck out his lower lip. "Can't get nobody to take me, though."

Dallas cleared his throat. "It's not proper conversation for the supper table."

"How come?" Austin asked.

"Because we have a lady eating with us."

Austin nodded as though what Dallas had said made sense to him, but Amelia could see confusion clearly reflected in the blue depths of his eyes.

"How do you like the house?" Dallas asked.

Amelia nearly choked on the stew. She took a sip of water, glancing down the table at Houston. He sat with his chair turned to the side. She had expected him to at least be comfortable with his disfigurement around his brothers.

"It's big," Amelia said, turning her attention back to Dallas. Those words were an understatement. The house was huge. Two stories of stone and—

"Adobe," Dallas said. "The house is built of adobe so it'll stay cooler in the summer. Gets hot here."

"Yes, that's what Houston told me. He said you can drop an egg on a rock and watch it cook."

"He said that, did he?" Dallas asked.

Amelia nodded, remembering so many things Houston had told her as they'd settled in each night, within each other's arms.

"Did he tell you that I designed the house? Made it look like a castle with turrets and such, like they have in England. Thought it would be good for defense."

She smiled. "No, he didn't mention that. He just said that he couldn't describe it. That I needed to see it. And now I've seen it. It's very unusual. Where did you learn about castles?"

He leaned forward with none of the hesitation Amelia had grown to expect from Houston when she asked him a question. "There was a fella in my company during the war who had come over from England. He believed in the South's cause more than some of my men did. We spent many a night discussing the differences between our countries. When the war ended, he returned to England." He cleared his throat and eased back in his chair. "Apparently, he had placed some rather large bets on the outcome of the war. The South losing was not to his advantage."

"He sounds like an interesting character. Houston never mentioned him."

Dallas's gaze shot to Houston, then back to Amelia. "Houston never met him. I didn't meet Winslow until after Chickamauga." He slapped his hands on the table. "But he was fascinating. Although I used much of what he told me to design this house, it still needs a lady's touch. Give some thought as to what you'd like to see in the way of furniture and decorations. Maybe in the spring, we'll go back to Fort Worth for a visit."

"I'd like that. The town had so much energy."

"I wanna go, too," Austin said. "I bet the town has a lot of women. Houston, was there a lot of women in Fort Worth?"

"Wasn't there long enough to notice."

"If I'd just been riding through, I sure as hell would have noticed the women," Austin said.

154

Houston slapped Austin's arm. "Don't use that language around Miss Carson."

Austin stared at him. "What language you want me to use? Spanish?"

Houston grabbed Austin's shirt and hauled him out of his chair. Austin protested loudly as Houston dragged him out of the room.

Dallas sighed deeply. "If you'd be so kind as to excuse me?"

Amelia swallowed her laughter and nearly choked. A woman's touch was needed with more than the house. "Certainly."

Harsh whispers filtered in from the hallway along with the sound of a possible slap on the arm or shoulder, which resulted in a young man's fervent objection. The brothers stayed in the hallway outside the dining room longer than they had stayed in the hallway outside of Dallas's office. When they finally returned, they had all set their jaws into uncompromising lines. They took their seats.

She wanted to hug Austin; his face was that of a boy trying desperately to become a man.

They ate in silence, Houston and Dallas concentrating on the meal. Amelia could see thoughts flickering across Austin's face as though he was trying to decide what he could say without being hauled out of the room. Suddenly, his face lit up like the candles on a Christmas tree.

"Dallas is gonna buy some of that new fencing."

Houston looked up at his older brother. "That barbed wire?"

"Yep," Dallas acknowledged.

With that, the conversation ended, and the meal continued in silence.

Chapter 14

❧

AMELIA DREW THE remnants of a blanket over her shoulders. Dallas had torn the woolen blanket in half, the easiest way he knew to give her something that resembled a shawl.

The sun was easing over the horizon, painting the sky in lavender, the land in shadows. Beside her, Dallas matched his pace to hers, leaning on a cane, his limp slight. She thought that without the limp, he would be able to cover twice as much ground as she.

He stopped walking and pointed toward the setting sun. "See where the sun is going down? That's where my land ends."

He met her gaze. She didn't know if she'd ever seen a more handsome man, and she thought her heart should be tripping over itself with his attentions as he took her hand.

"When you wake in the morning, look out your window. Where the sun comes up is where my land begins." He brought her hand to his warm lips, his mustache tickling her flesh as he steadily held her gaze. "You're all that I imagined," he said quietly.

Her heart did trip over itself then, pounding fast and furious as though she were running, as though she wanted to run. She could think of nothing clever to say. Her tongue grew thick and useless. "I imagined you with blue eyes," she said, cringing with the inane comment as soon as the words left her mouth.

He raised a dark brow. "Blue eyes?"

She nodded. "Houston told me they were brown. And that you had a mustache. And that you cast a tall shadow." She glanced at the ground where his shadow stretched out behind her. Smiling self-consciously at her babbling, she looked up. "And he was right."

"I can't imagine Houston doing as much talking as it sounds like he did bringing you here."

"Only because I asked questions. He doesn't volunteer the information, but if you ask, he'll answer. Besides, it was a long journey."

"I'm sorry I wasn't able to come after you." He released her hand and leaned on the cane. "It was stupid of me to try and break a horse the day before I was to leave."

"Especially a black horse with a wavy tail and mane."

"I beg your pardon?" he asked, his brow furrowing deeply.

"Houston explained that a horse's coloring often tells him about its temperament. A black horse with a wavy tail and mane is usually mean-spirited."

"He said that, did he?"

"Yes. I don't remember what all the other colors mean, but he knows. You should ask him." She heard a horse whinny and glanced over her shoulder to see Houston in the corral, gathering the mustangs. "Is he leaving?"

"I imagine."

"I need to say good-bye."

"Why don't you run ahead and I'll catch up?" Dallas suggested.

"Thank you." The dust rose up around her as she ran to the corral. Houston was leaving, and she might not see him before she was married. She couldn't bear the thought. She skidded to a stop near the corral as Houston tied the last of his horses together.

He climbed over the railing and walked toward her, removing his hat to hit the dust off his trousers. She wanted to comb the hair off his brow.

"Enjoy your evening stroll?" he asked as he stopped before her.

"Yes. It was nice. Dallas is nice."

"Nice?" He smiled. "I'm sure he'll be glad to hear that you think he's nice."

"The ranch is huge."

"Yep, and you ain't even seen all of it. A man could travel for days without leaving Dallas's land."

"That's what we did, isn't it?" she asked. "Traveled for days on his land?"

"Three days."

"You could have signaled him sooner."

"Could have. Should have, but then I did a lot of things while traveling with you that I shouldn't have done."

She was grateful for every one of them. The memories would hold her for a lifetime, even if the man standing before her didn't. "I don't suppose there's a chance that some creature might haul the house away if we leave it unattended?"

He laughed, deeply, richly, and the warmth returned to Amelia's heart, a warmth that had disappeared when she'd moved from his side that morning.

"No, I don't imagine any critter is gonna haul the house away."

"It's . . . it's . . ."

"I told you that you needed to see it."

"Why do you think—"

"A castle for his queen," he said, his smile easing away. He touched a finger to her cheek. "You're his queen."

"And if I don't want to be a queen? If I just want to be a wife?"

"He'll let you do that as well. One thing about Dallas, he's loyal to a fault. If you're by his side, he'll give you everything."

"Why didn't you tell him you don't think the barbed wire is a good idea?"

He narrowed his gaze. "What makes you think I don't think the barbed wire is a good idea?"

"I traveled with you for well over a month, shared your food, shared your bed—"

"Don't you dare tell Dallas that!" he hissed. "He'd tan my hide and hang it out to dry. You didn't share my bed, you just slept beside me."

"Is that all you think I did?" she asked.

"That is all you did."

"I came to care for you."

"You'll come to care for Dallas even more. You just haven't had much time with him."

"I'm going to miss listening to you snore at night."

"Amelia—"

"I'm going to miss you."

"I'm not that far away. If you need something, you can send Austin to fetch me."

"And you'll come?"

"I'll come."

She heard approaching footsteps and turned. Dallas and Austin walked toward her, Austin with a loose-jointed walk as though he hadn't a care in the world, Dallas stiffly as though he carried the burden of the world upon his shoulders.

The brothers stopped before her, and she felt a tension rise within Houston.

"I'll send word when the preacher gets back," Dallas said.

"I'll be waitin' for it," was all Houston said, and Amelia realized she wouldn't see him again until the day she married his brother. A keen sense of loss ricocheted through her.

"Austin and I will sleep in the bunkhouse until the preacher arrives," Dallas said.

"The bunkhouse!" Austin exclaimed, horror laced through his voice. "Why do we have to sleep in the bunkhouse?"

"Because it wouldn't be proper for an unmarried woman to sleep in a house alone with two men," Dallas explained, his voice strained.

"Why not? Houston slept with her—"

Houston grabbed Austin by the shirt and hauled him out of hearing range. Amelia thought she had heard material rip this time. The poor boy was going to need a sturdier shirt.

"You'll have to excuse Austin," Dallas said, drawing her attention away from the two men engaged in a heated discussion. "He hasn't had any women in his life and his education in certain matters is lacking."

"Houston said you're hoping more women will move out here once we're married."

He slipped his arm around hers and began walking toward the house. "I am hoping that this part of Texas will become more developed over time. My father told me once that some men are content to walk where others have gone." He turned and faced her. "I'm not one of those men. My aspirations and dreams are grander." He flushed, something she didn't think this man did often. "I know I sound like I'm full of myself, but we have an opportunity here to build an empire whose foundation is made up of dreams, hard work, and determination. I want you to share it with me. I want our children to inherit it."

He leaned down and kissed her on the brow as a brother might a favored sister. "I'm glad you're here. Sleep well."

He limped off the porch, leaving her to watch the fading sunset alone.

"Dallas? Dallas?" Austin whispered harshly.

Staring hard at the wooden beams running the length of the bunkhouse ceiling, his mind on weighty matters, Dallas sighed heavily. "What?"

"I don't recollect ever hearin' Houston laugh before. I didn't realize it until I heard him laugh this evening. You ever hear Houston laugh before?" Austin asked.

Dallas swallowed hard, fighting to push back the guilt. "He laughed a lot when we were boys . . . before the war."

"I'm thinkin' that you're right. Bringing women out here is gonna be a good thing. They sure make everything look prettier."

"Yeah, they do. Now, get yourself to sleep. We got business to tend to tomorrow. Can't stop working just because we've got a woman in the house."

"If you decide you don't want her, I'll take her."

"I'm not giving her up. Signed a contract saying I'd make her my wife if she traveled out here. A contract is like giving your word. I've never broken my word."

He slammed his eyes closed, knowing he'd find no sleep tonight. No matter what the cost, no matter who paid it . . . he'd never broken his word.

Sleep had been as elusive as the shadows hovering in the room, changing with the flickering flame from the lantern. Each time sleep drew near and Amelia grabbed it, she'd find herself searching for the feel of Houston's arms, the sound of his breathing, and the scent of horses and leather that was part of him. She'd awaken with a jolt, alone. She so hated being alone.

Sometime during the night, she'd slipped out of bed, draped a blanket over her shoulders, moved to the window, and welcomed the company of the stars. They had served as her canopy for so many nights, brought with them vivid memories of a man she didn't understand. She thought she could ask Houston questions through eternity, but his carefully guarded answers would forever keep her from understanding him fully.

She was certain that she meant more to him than he let on, thought it possible that he may have fallen in love with her, knew she'd come to love him. She wondered why he didn't act on his feelings. She wasn't married to his brother. Surely Dallas would understand if she had a change of heart. She didn't fear Dallas, but she sensed that Houston was wary of him, as though he thought his brother might strike out at him if he spoke the wrong words or took the wrong action. She wondered how much Dallas resembled his father. Houston had not been fond of his father. She wondered if he saw his father when he looked at Dallas.

In the predawn darkness, she sighed and listened to the steady clack of the windmill Dallas had built. Soon the sun would touch the earth, throwing its glow over Dallas's land. She hoped the sight would bring joy to her heart, would replace this mourning of a loss she couldn't identify or explain.

She heard a thump in the hallway. Her first thought was that Houston had sneaked in to see her, but she didn't think that would be his way. He'd said once that he always took the easy way. As much as it pained her, she had to acknowledge that for him, leaving her was easier than claiming her.

She heard the bump again. She rose from her chair and tiptoed across the room to the hearth, where the embers from the dying fire glowed red. She picked up the smallest log in the stack beside the hearth and crept to the door.

She opened the door slightly and peered out. She saw a shadow moving out of one of the far rooms. She couldn't remember if that room was another bedroom. The person was carrying something. She stepped into the hallway and held the log like a club, hoping she had the strength to carry out her threat if the thief tried to bolt. "Stop right there!"

The culprit turned, stumbled back, hit the door, and fell into the room from which he'd just come. Amelia rushed down the hallway, her heart thudding madly. She skidded to a stop and stood over the prone figure, trying to decide if she should hit him now or cry for help.

"Miss Carson! It's me! Austin."

She scrutinized the darkness, barely able to discern his features. She could hear his heavy breathing. She had no doubt frightened him as much as he'd frightened her. She lowered her raised arms. They quivered as they relaxed against her side. "What are you doing here?"

He scrambled to his feet. "Come to get my violin. Dallas didn't give me no time to get my belongings. You scared me to death."

She laughed with a crazy sort of relief. "You scared me, too."

"Sorry about that. Didn't mean to." He tilted his head. "Miss Carson, you want to come watch the sunrise with me?"

"Will Dallas be there?"

"No, ma'am. He done headed out with some of the men to check the south range. I'm supposed to watch out for you today."

"Let me get dressed."

She hurried into her room. She considered putting on her own clothes. She had washed them last night, but she had enjoyed the freedom she'd felt wearing the loose skirt and blouse. She slipped into the clothes, wrapped the makeshift shawl around her shoulders, and walked back into the hallway. Austin was plucking a string on his violin.

He shoved himself away from the wall. "Come on," he said, taking her hand and leading her down the stairs and through the house to the back porch.

He released her hand and dropped to the top step. She settled in beside him, leaning against the beam. "Dallas said that where the sun comes up is where his land begins."

"Yes, ma'am. He has a hell—excuse me, heck—of a lot of land." He leaned toward her. "Can I say heck?"

She smiled. He had lived in a world dominated by men. She didn't expect him to change his habits overnight, wasn't even certain if he should. "You can say whatever you want. I don't mind."

"Oh, no, ma'am. I'm used to seeing Dallas angry, but I ain't never seen Houston angry. I don't want to say nothing that's gonna make Houston angry, so I gotta practice talking to a lady like she's supposed to be talked to. And I sure as hell, excuse me, heck, ain't gonna mention that you slept together. I thought he was gonna tear me in two."

Amelia scooted toward him slightly, clasped her hands together tightly, and rested her elbows on her thighs. "Dallas and Houston don't seem to talk to each other much."

"No, ma'am. They surely don't. They never have as long as I can remember."

"But they talk to you?"

"Yes, ma'am. It's kinda funny. When it's just me and Dallas, he talks to me like I imagine a father would talk to a son, explaining things real patient-like. When it's just me and Houston, he talks to me like I figure brothers would talk to each other, but I never see him and Dallas talking that way. When it's the three of us, it's just best to keep quiet."

"Did you know that Houston was breeding the mustangs?"

"Oh, yes, ma'am. He told me. When he needs help, he lets me help him."

"Dallas never helps him?"

"Oh, no, ma'am. Dallas ain't never even been out to Houston's place. When he needs Houston he just sends me out there to fetch him."

"Why?"

"I reckon 'cuz he needs to talk to him."

Amelia smiled at the boy's innocence, an innocence that was belied by the revolver he wore strapped to his thigh. She wasn't certain if she'd ever grow accustomed to the abundance of guns and the ease with which young men carried them. "No, I mean why doesn't Dallas go out there?"

Austin shrugged. "Busy, I guess. Least that's what Houston says. Sometimes I think it bothers him that Dallas ain't never been out there. I asked him about it once. He said Dallas has empires to build. He's got no time for the little things, but visiting family don't seem like a little thing to me. But I'm just a kid, so what do I know?"

She placed her hand on his arm. "I think you're very close to being a man, and I think you know a lot. Could you take me to Houston's place?"

"Sure could. It's just two whoops and a holler away. As soon as the sun finishes coming up, we'll head out. If you won't tell Dallas, I'll show you what the sun sounds like when it's coming up."

"Why would he mind?" she asked, taking her hand off his arm.

He lifted a shoulder. "Cookie is a fiddle player, and he taught me to play some songs. Dallas don't mind those. But I hear songs . . . Dallas says they ain't manly so I just play 'em when he's not around. Since he ain't here, you want to hear the one that I think sounds like a sunrise?"

Amelia wrapped her arms around herself and settled against the beam. "I'd like to hear it very much."

Austin shifted his backside on the porch, brought one leg up and stretched the other one out. He slipped the rounded end of the violin beneath his chin and picked up the bow. He pointed the bow toward the far horizon. "Watch the sunrise."

Amelia turned her attention to the distance, but as soon as she heard the first low strain of music, her attention drifted back to the boy sitting on the porch with her. He'd closed his eyes and swayed slightly in rhythm to the music he created. The music rose softly in pitch just as the sun did. She could see the sunrise without watching it, could feel its warmth without touching it, could sense its power as it brought light to the land.

How could Dallas not encourage the boy to expand on his gift? If he played this beautifully after taking lessons from a cook, she couldn't imagine how well he would play if he had proper lessons. Dallas Leigh needed more than a wife. He needed someone who could teach him that life was composed of more than hard work.

The music drifted into a hushed whisper. Austin opened his eyes, tears shimmering within the incredible blue depths.

"That was beautiful," Amelia said softly.

Austin sniffed and blinked until the tears disappeared. "Dawn is my favorite time of day, but I got a song for the sunset, and for all the seasons. They just sorta come to me. Like yesterday, when I saw you for the first time, a song just went into my head, but I ain't had a chance to try it out yet."

"I'd like to hear it when you're ready to play it for me."

He smiled broadly. "I'll do that, as long as Dallas is off with the men." He stood and tucked the violin beneath his arm. "You ready to head out to Houston's place?"

She tried not to appear too eager as she stood, but the truth was: She couldn't wait to see Houston again.

* * *

He was standing on the front porch of a small log cabin, his left shoulder pressed against the beam, his gaze focused on the horses milling around in the corral. He wore no hat, and the wind blew through his black hair much as it blew through Amelia's blond tresses. She'd worn her hair pulled back, a strip of cloth keeping most of it in place, but much of it had worked itself free.

"Maybe we should yell so he'll know we're coming in," Amelia suggested, anxious to have him turn and see her, wondering if he would be as pleased to see her as she was to see him.

"Won't do no good. He can't hear from that side," Austin said.

Stunned, Amelia stared at Austin. "He's deaf?"

"Only on the left side. When he was wounded during the war, he lost his sight and hearing on that one side. Always figured that was why he sat with his right side to us, since his hearing ain't so good."

Austin's reasoning made sense, but Amelia didn't think it was correct. Near the end of their journey, Houston had never turned his face away from her. But she had whispered her heartfelt endearment near his left ear. She realized now that he hadn't been ignoring her. He simply hadn't heard her words, although she now understood that his hearing them would not have altered the journey's end.

As they neared, Houston turned slightly and shoved his hands into his trouser pockets. The morning was cool, but he wore no duster or hat. She was certain he'd expected no company.

"What brings you out?" he asked as he stepped off the porch.

"Dallas took the men to the south. He told me to watch Amelia. She wanted to see your place," Austin said as he dismounted.

"Oh, she did, did she?" Houston asked, his lip curved up slightly on one side as he placed his hands on her waist and helped her dismount.

The warmth of his touch shot clear down to her toes. His hands lingered, his fingers flexing as though he knew he should let her go, but couldn't bring himself to do it. She wanted to step forward, lean against him, and feel his arms close around her.

As though reading her thoughts, he shook his head slightly and stepped away from her. "Not much to see. House, corral, shed. Nothing fancy."

"A woman doesn't always need fancy," Amelia said softly.

"But she should have it just the same."

"You gonna let Amelia watch when a stallion mounts a mare?" Austin asked.

Houston turned swiftly to grab Austin. Austin ducked just as quickly, backing off, his fingers splayed before him. "What'd I do now?"

"You don't talk breeding around a lady," Houston said, his voice low.

"Makes no sense. You can't say nothin' around a lady. What's the point in sharing your life with her if you can't speak what's on your mind?"

"I'm not gonna marry her and neither are you. And you need to call her Miss Carson."

"Why? Dallas told me last night that she'll be my sister by marriage. I wouldn't call my sister Miss Leigh."

Houston reached to pull down a hat that wasn't on his head. Then he spun around and faced Amelia. "What do you want him to call you?"

"I'm hoping Austin will come to think of me as a sister so I'd truly prefer for him to call me Amelia."

"Fine." He waved his hand in the air. "Fine. Call her Amelia."

Austin released a whoop. "Hot diggity damn! That's the first time I've won an argument!"

Houston pointed his finger at his brother. "No swearing!"

Wearing a broad smile, Austin raised his palms as though warding off an attack. "I just forgot. Won't do it again."

"See that you don't," Houston mumbled.

"Can I ride Black Thunder to the bluff and back?" Austin asked.

"Black Thunder?" Amelia asked.

"Yeah, he's over here," Austin said, grabbing her hand and pulling her toward a distant corral, leading their horses behind him. "He ain't gelded, so Houston has to keep him apart from the mares."

The black stallion threw his head back and trotted around the enclosure. In a separate enclosure nearby, the palomino stallion whinnied.

"He's beautiful," Amelia whispered. The horse's black coat shimmered in the morning sun.

"I named him," Austin said.

"Why Black Thunder?" she asked.

"Because he runs so fast and so hard that he sounds like thunder rolling over the plains." He glanced over his shoulder. "Ain't that right, Houston?"

Reluctantly, Houston had followed them over, cursing himself for wanting to see Amelia's face when she caught sight of the stallion. He'd never given much thought to raising horses until he'd seen this black stallion on a rise. He'd pursued him for two years, wondered at times if he was a phantom, a horse of legend . . . until he'd captured him with Austin's help. He hadn't had a mare worthy of the black stallion until now.

Until Amelia had convinced him to pursue the palomino's herd. He'd carefully made his selections, choosing the mares that would service his black stallion.

"Yep, he's fast, but he's not saddle broke," Houston said.

"I love ridin' him bareback," Austin said, rubbing a hand up and down his thigh. "I can feel his power, his strength . . . Please? Amelia can wait here. I won't be long. Just a short fast ride."

Houston felt as though he was trapped between a stampeding herd and a huge abyss. What he wanted and what he knew was right were warring. Amelia looked at him, her green, green eyes filled with hope, and he couldn't say no, couldn't send her on her way, even though he knew it was best.

"Just don't be gone too long," Houston said, gruffly, offering himself a compromise.

"I won't," Austin assured him. He handed the reins of his horse and Amelia's horse over to Houston, grabbed the hackamore bridle off a post, and slipped through the railings.

The horse snorted and pranced. Amelia sidled up against Houston. "He's black. Isn't he dangerous?"

"All horses are dangerous if you don't handle them right, but he's not mean spirited."

She smiled as Austin slipped the bridle over the horse's snout, wrapped his fingers in the long black mane, and threw himself over the horse. The horse bucked once, and Austin hollered, his smile brighter than the noonday sun.

Houston pulled back the gate, and the horse with rider sprang forth, churning up the dirt as they headed out. Houston slapped Austin and Amelia's mounts, urging them into the empty corral. He closed the gate.

"I was thinking about working with the mare today. Need to get over to the other corral so she can start getting used to my scent again."

"Can I come with you?"

Houston nodded. He walked to the corral, Amelia at his side. Sweet Lord, it felt right to have her there with him, to smell her scent, to see her shadow touching his. He crossed his arms over the top railing, and the horses scattered to the far side of the corral.

"They don't trust us yet," she said quietly.

He thought now might be a good time to make sure the woman understood there was no "us," would never be an "us." But the morning was peaceful, the breeze slight, and she looked so pretty standing beside him watching the horses that she'd helped him capture.

He should have explained to Austin why a man would want a woman in his life. It had little to do with the physical release his body craved. It had everything to do with every memory he had of her from the moment she'd first stepped off the train in Fort Worth until he'd watched Dallas kiss her last night. It had to do with the softness of her voice, the way she believed in him when no one else ever had.

"They'll get used to us again in time," he said.

She turned her attention away from the horses, her delicate brows drawn together in a furrow. "Why didn't you tell Dallas that you were breeding mustangs?"

He averted his gaze, deciding it was easier to watch the horses than her. "I might not have any success at it. Dallas has seen enough of my failures."

"Such as?"

"You don't want to know."

"I don't want to know or you don't want to tell me?"

He forced himself to meet her gaze. "I don't want to tell you."

"You don't trust me," she said simply. "You're like the mustangs. You don't trust easily."

"Look what happened when they finally decided to trust us. We betrayed them."

"And you think I'll betray you?"

"No," he said, unable to stop the ragged edge in his voice. "I think you'll hate me."

Chapter 15

✌

*A*USTIN RETURNED LATE in the morning, while the breeze was still cool. Amelia wouldn't have minded spending the entire day with Houston, watching him work with the palomino mare, but she sensed that Austin was ready to move on.

As they rode back to the ranch, Amelia found herself intrigued by the young man riding beside her. Full of untamed energy, he had a restlessness about him. She supposed it had to do with youth. Something more exciting was always waiting just ahead, in the next mile, in the next moment.

Amelia drew her horse to a halt. "What in the world is that?"

Austin sidled up next to her. "What?"

She pointed toward the reddish-brown beast. Austin's eyes nearly bulged out of his head. "It's a cow. Ain't you never seen a cow before?"

She shook her head. It looked nothing like the cows of Georgia or the ones she'd seen grazing at John and Beth's. "Not one like that. Those horns look dangerous."

"They are dangerous. From tip to tip, the horns can grow as long as some men are tall. Longhorns enjoy a good stampede, too. Dallas keeps his cattle spread out over the range so they're less likely to stampede. You wanna see Dallas at work?"

"You know where he is?"

"Sure. He's gathering his cattle down on the south end, marking 'em so they'll be ready come spring."

She realized too late that she should have sought out Dallas first thing that morning, instead of Houston. When she had begun this journey, her mind was filled with thoughts of Dallas. Somewhere along the way, Houston had taken his place. "I'd like to see him working."

"Come on, then."

They rode at a gallop with the breeze circling around them. She thought she might never understand how men could look out over the land and know exactly where they were. More cattle became visible, dotting the countryside.

Then she saw what she thought must have been a whole herd, a sea of brown and red. It didn't take her long to spot Dallas. He rode through the herd obviously with a purpose. She watched as he maneuvered his horse, maneuvered the calf away from the center of the herd.

"He rides well," Amelia said.

"Yep. He's got men to do that but every now and then, he does it himself." Austin removed his hat and waved it in the air.

When the calf broke through to freedom, another cowboy lassoed it. Dallas rode past the bawling calf and caught up with Austin and Amelia. "What are you doing out here?"

"Took Amelia out to see Houston. Discovered she didn't even know what a longhorn was so figured she ain't never seen a roundup. Thought I'd show her."

Dallas nodded and glanced over his shoulder. "They're smaller in the fall. Come spring, you can hardly see for the dust the cattle stir up."

"Houston said you had two thousand head of cattle."

He smiled. "At last count."

"I thought a ranch would feel like a plantation, have its grace and charm."

"You don't find the smell of burning cowhide and the ruckus of bawling cattle charmin'?"

She laughed lightly. "I find it fascinating, but nothing like what I'd expected. It's so big. I think it takes a special breed of men to tame it."

"That it does."

"Houston mentioned that you were that sort of man."

A blush swept down Dallas's face, disappearing behind the red bandanna he wore wrapped around his neck. "I'm having a hard time believing how much that man talked. Reckon I got some catching up to do."

A tinny sound filled the air. Amelia looked toward its source: the chuckwagon. With a metal bar, the cook was hitting a metal triangle.

"Are you hungry?" Dallas asked.

Amelia smiled. "As a matter of fact, I am."

"Austin, go fetch us a couple of plates."

As Austin rode to the chuckwagon, Dallas dismounted and helped Amelia off her horse. He removed his vest and set it on the ground. "It's not fancy, but it'll protect your skirt somewhat."

"Thank you," she said as she lowered herself to the ground.

"Think we're having beefsteak today," he said, dropping down beside her.

"I suppose when you raise cattle, you always have meat to eat."

"Yes, ma'am, we do."

She sighed, her mind suddenly blank. Asking questions of Houston had come so easily. She couldn't think of a single thing to ask the man she was going to marry.

"Do you—"

"I've never—"

She laughed, he smiled as their voices bumped into each other.

"Go ahead," he said.

"No, you go first."

"All right." He yanked a spear of grass out of the ground and slipped it between his lips. "I was just gonna say that I've never had a girl before so you might need to prod me from time to time if you need or want things."

"You've never had a girl?"

He flung his arm in the direction of the cook. "No, ma'am. As you can see, my company is made up of men and cattle."

"But you've been to a brothel."

He sat straighter. "I beg your pardon?"

"Houston said that sporting women don't charge you, so I'd assumed you'd had a woman."

"I meant I've never had a steady girl." He leaned forward until she could see her reflection in the brown depths of his eyes. "Did Houston mention that I stopped visiting brothels when I got your first letter?"

"No, he didn't tell me that."

Dallas stretched out beside her, raised up on an elbow, and smiled. "Why don't you tell me everything he *did* mention?"

Dallas rode his horse hard, with the cold midnight wind circling him, and his temper hotter than a branding iron straight out of the fire.

Houston said . . . Houston thought . . . Houston had told her . . .

Dallas had spent the afternoon and early evening hearing about everything Houston had ever said to Amelia. Dallas had known Houston for twenty-eight years and his brother had never in his whole entire life talked that much! Never!

Not when he was a boy working the cotton fields, not when he was beating a drum for the Confederacy, not when they'd traveled back to Texas . . . Never!

Dallas hadn't planned to break his leg, but when he had, sending Houston after Amelia had seemed the right decision.

He'd known Amelia would be safe with Houston. Houston kept to himself, had since after the war. Dallas had moments when he felt regret over that . . . and a measure of guilt. Sometimes, he wondered if his actions on that fateful night had been self-serving. He'd never gone back on his word in his life, but he often wondered if the price of keeping his word had been worth it.

He shoved the unsettling thoughts back into the dark corner of his heart that he reserved for regrets, and set his spurs against his horse's sides.

A rough ride usually calmed him. But tonight, nothing was working. He kept hearing Amelia's voice, speaking Houston's name so softly, as though she liked the way it sounded or enjoyed saying his name. As though she spent time thinking of him . . .

He drew his sweating horse to an abrupt halt and listened to the beast's breath wheeze into the night. He wasn't a man who usually abused his animals, and any other time, he would have dismounted and asked no more of the horse than he asked of himself.

But this time he had a burning inside him that couldn't be contained. He urged the horse forward at a slower gait. He saw the lantern hanging on the front porch of the log cabin, a lantern to welcome strangers and friends alike. He hadn't expected Houston to be so accommodating.

He drew his horse to a halt just beyond the front porch and gazed at the simple log structure. Judging by the size, he didn't think it could be more than one room. It reminded him of . . . home.

Home before the war. Home, where his mother would flap her apron at them when she discovered them sticking their fingers into her precious sugar or honey. Home, where his pa would let him herd the few cattle they owned instead of making him work in the fields. He'd hated the fields, hated the cotton. Sitting on a horse with the scent of cattle riding the wind was preferable any day to tearing up the land and breaking his back to do it.

He dismounted, pushed the memories aside, and pulled on the tether that harnessed his anger. He took no pains to be quiet as he stepped on the porch and pounded the door so loudly he was certain he'd wake the dead.

If his brother didn't get his butt out here, that was exactly what he'd be—dead.

Sleeping on a pallet against the corral fence, Houston had awoken to the sound of hooves beating the earth unmercifully. His first thought as he saw his brother riding in like hell's vengeance was that something had happened to Amelia. His heart had matched the rhythm of the horse's gallop, and although the evening air was cool around him, he'd broken out in a clammy sweat.

He'd thrown off the blanket, scrambled to his feet, and would have gone tearing across the yard like a madman if Dallas hadn't brought his horse to a grinding halt, and then sat there as though he'd come in from a leisurely Sunday ride.

Now his brother was banging on his door loud enough to start a stampede.

"Goddamn it, Houston! Open the door!"

A memory flickered through Houston's mind of a time when they were boys: They'd been swimming in the cold creek. Dallas had left the water, claiming it was time to go home, ordering Houston out of the creek, always ordering Houston around. This day, Houston hadn't been in the mood for orders. Taking a deep breath, he'd gone under the water and swam to a place where the shadows were deep. He'd come up for air just as Dallas was stomping his boots into place. Then Dallas had looked out over the creek and started yelling for him. Houston had held his silence, hard as it had been, until Dallas had finally plowed back into the creek, slicing his hands through the water like he was Moses and could part the waters of the creek to reveal his brother. Houston had crept out of the water and moseyed over to where his clothes were. He'd sat there quietly waiting until Dallas stopped his thrashing and called out his name again.

"You might try lookin' a little to your left!" Houston had yelled. "I might be over there!"

Dallas had spun around so quickly that he had lost his balance and slid beneath the water. He'd come back up sputtering and angry.

They'd wrestled, as boys were prone to do, until the laughter took over, and they both agreed it had been a fine day. They'd come home covered in mud, smiling as they told the story. Unfortunately, their father hadn't shared their enthusiasm for the prank. Houston had received a lecture on the evils of crying wolf and had been sent to bed without his supper. But it had all been worth it to see the surprise on Dallas's face when he'd turned around, and the horror in his eyes when he'd realized he was going down.

Oh, yeah, it had been worth it.

Dallas's pounding hadn't abated as he yelled once again, "Houston, open the goddamn door!"

Houston stepped silently onto the porch, eased his arm beneath his brother's pounding fist, grabbed the latch, and shoved the door open. "That what you wanted?" he asked.

Dallas jerked back as though someone had just roped him and given him a sharp tug. His breathing was labored, and Houston was certain if it had been daylight, he would have seen fury within his brother's dark eyes.

"Where in the hell were you?" Dallas demanded.

"Sleeping by the corral."

Dallas turned toward the corral, and Houston almost imagined he could see the horror on Dallas's face. He couldn't stop himself from adding, "I saw you the minute you rode in."

"Then you should have spoken up, let me know you were about."

"But watching was so much more fun."

"I didn't give you anything to watch."

Houston could have argued against that statement, but decided to let sleeping dogs lie. "Has something happened to Amelia?"

"No, she's fine. I just . . ." Dallas cleared his throat. "I've just never been out to your place before."

"It looks better at night," Houston said, a bad feeling in his gut. It wasn't like Dallas to have difficulty finding the right words, and the man never explained his actions. Never. "What'd you do to Amelia?"

Dallas jerked his head around. "I didn't do anything to her, but I'd like to know what you did."

Houston narrowed his gaze. "What do you mean by that?"

Dallas took a step forward. "I mean every sentence she utters has your name in it. Houston said this . . . Houston thinks that . . . You'd think the two of you were one person. She's telling me things you think like she's an authority on what goes on in your head."

Houston shrugged. "You travel with a person, you get to know him."

"How well did you get to know Amelia?"

Houston's gut reaction was to plow his balled fist right into the center of his brother's perfect face. Instead, he did what he always did. He took the easy path. "Why don't you head on home, and I'll forget you ever came out here tonight?"

"Answer me, goddamn it!"

"I just did. Now get the hell off my land."

"You bedded her, didn't you?"

Like most cowboys, Houston had never before hit a man. Guns were a man's way, not fists. His brother's face felt like a wall of stone when Houston's tightened fist made contact with it. The pain shot up his arm as Dallas stumbled back and fell off the porch. Houston leapt off the porch and planted his foot squarely on his brother's chest. Dallas grunted and wrapped his hands around Houston's ankle. Houston pressed down.

"I told you to stay off that goddamn horse, but you wouldn't listen! And I paid the price for your stubbornness. For forty-three days I traveled through hell, wanting that woman like I've never wanted anything in my life. For forty-three days, I drew your goddamn brand in the dirt to remind myself that she belonged to you, that she deserved the best of men. Think what you want of me, but never for one goddamn minute think less of her because you forced her into my company." He jerked his foot back. "She went through hell to get to you: snake, storm, flood, hunger, and cold, and she never once complained. She's a woman of courage, Dallas, and by God, if you don't worship the ground she walks on, I'll find her a husband who will. Now, get the hell off my land."

Without looking back, Houston strode to the corral and crossed his arms over the railing. He was shaking badly and his legs felt like the thick mud of a bog. He thought they might buckle under him at any moment. That would certainly ruin the effectiveness of his tirade. He thought he might even be sick.

He heard Dallas's horse whinny and then he heard the pounding of hooves. He slid to the ground and leaned back against the fence post. His father had been a violent man, quick to raise his voice and fist in anger. Houston had never wanted to be like him. He'd kept his temper to himself, letting it gnaw at his insides, never letting it show for fear of what it might do.

Well, now he knew. He was just like the man he despised.

Within the depths of slumber, Amelia heard her name whispered frantically. She struggled through the haze, squinting against the light burning in the lantern. She could see a slender form hovering over her bed, a young man with worried eyes. Austin.

Her heart slammed against her ribs. Bad news always came at night. Houston. Something had happened to Houston. She jerked upright and grabbed his arm. "What's wrong?"

"Dallas got hurt."

"Dallas?" Her momentary relief gave way to panic and guilt. Her first waking thought should have been of Dallas. Scrambling out of bed, she wrapped a blanket around herself.

"It ain't bad," Austin explained, "but I think it's gonna need stitching."

She rushed to the chair by the window and knelt beside the green dress she'd been trying to repair. She grabbed her scissors and cut the thread before slipping the needle from the cloth. "Where is he?" she asked as she spun around. Caught off guard, she stared at Austin, who had pressed her pillow against his face.

Guiltily, he dropped her pillow to the bed. "Your pillow don't smell like mine."

"Do you want to take it?" she asked.

He hooked his thumbs on the waistband of his trousers and ducked his head. "Nah, I'd best not. The men might laugh at me. That sweet smell would surely get noticed in the bunkhouse. It's rank in there, just like old meat."

She made a quick mental note to sprinkle some fragrance in his room once he moved back into it after she and Dallas were married. "Where is Dallas?"

"Oh!" He jumped, his arms flailing out. "This way."

She followed him to the barn. Dallas was sitting just inside the doorway, his head pressed back against the wall, his eyes closed. Dust coated his clothes. Blood trailed slowly down his bruised and swelling cheek.

"Oh, my goodness, what happened?" Amelia exclaimed as she knelt beside him.

His eyes flew open, and he glared over her shoulder at Austin. "I told you to get the cook."

"I know, but I figured you probably just forgot that we had a woman here to tend to our needs."

"Amelia, go back to bed," Dallas ordered. "I'll get Cookie."

He started to rise, and Amelia placed her hand on his shoulder. "I'll take care of you, but we'll need to move to the kitchen."

"That wouldn't be proper."

"Why not?"

"Because we're not married, and it's the dead of night."

She sighed. "You're hurt. You're the man I'm going to marry. Surely the men who work for you know that I can trust you in my kitchen."

She could see the arguments running through his mind. She thought she might never understand the way a man thought. "It makes no sense that I can travel across the state with your brother and not damage my reputation, but helping you in a time of need will mark me as a loose woman."

He averted his gaze and struggled to his feet. "All right." He pointed a menacing finger at Austin. "This goes no further than you and me."

Austin nodded, but Amelia saw the confusion in his eyes, a confusion she understood.

"Dallas will be all right," she assured Austin as they walked to the house.

Once inside the kitchen, Dallas pulled a chair out from the table and dropped his aching body into place. Austin hitched up a hip and sat on the table.

"Make yourself useful and build a fire in the stove for Amelia. We'll be needing warm water."

Austin slid off the table and went about the task, dropping three logs in the process. Dallas had a feeling Austin had grown sweet on Amelia. He couldn't blame the boy. They were a young man's feelings, no threat to him.

He watched as Amelia warmed the water. He'd been so grateful to finally see her in person when she'd first arrived at the ranch that he hadn't given a lot of thought to what she'd endured in getting here. He should have. He should have grilled Houston for an accounting of every day—

"How did you get hurt?" she asked as she set a bowl of warm water on the table and sat beside him. She dipped the cloth into the water and gently dabbed at his cheek.

Humiliation swamped him. He would have preferred a bullet to a fist. "I fell off my horse."

Her hand stilled, and she searched his face. He kept it as still as stone, knowing she was looking for the truth, hoping she didn't find it. He'd never lied before, and he had no idea if he was covering it up.

"I couldn't sleep. I go riding when I can't sleep."

She smiled softly. "Well, then, I'm certainly marrying into the right family. You don't sleep. Houston doesn't sleep. I don't sleep." She glanced at Austin. He'd returned to his spot at the end of the table. "Do you sleep?"

"Not in the bunkhouse. Too many men snoring. Dallas is the worst. You won't get any sleep at all after you marry him."

"If I can sleep through Houston snoring, I can sleep through anyone snoring."

"I'm probably louder," Dallas said, wondering what had prompted such a childish response. He'd never felt competitive where Houston was concerned. He'd always known he was the better of the two. His father had drilled that lesson into him, every chance he got, pointing out Dallas's strengths and Houston's weaknesses.

Her smile increased. "I won't hold that against you." She withdrew the needle from her sleeve. "I think I should sew that up."

He nodded toward Austin. "Go get the whiskey."

Austin hopped off the table and headed for Dallas's office. Amelia continued to dab at his face, so gently. Before he could think, he'd cradled her cheek in his palm and carried his lips to hers. She sighed in surprise, and he slipped his tongue inside her mouth.

She returned the kiss timidly, almost as though she were afraid. Lord, he didn't want her to be afraid, not of him, not of anything. He drew back and studied her face. So innocent. He was ashamed of his earlier doubts. He'd deserved the punch Houston had given him; deserved it and a lot more.

"It's gonna be a long two months," he said.

She blushed prettily, so damned prettily, that for the first time, he saw the journey through his brother's eyes. And he didn't like what he saw. Not one damn bit.

Long before dawn, Amelia sat on the back porch, waiting, hoping that she was wrong.

She smiled as Austin appeared through the darkness, his long legs carrying him toward the back porch, his violin tucked beneath his arm.

"Mornin'," he said as he sat beside her and positioned his violin beneath his chin.

"Did Dallas ride out with the men?"

"No, ma'am. He rode out right after we left you. Said he had some business to take care of."

Panic swelled within her as she imagined exactly what that business might entail. She shouldn't have waited. She should have ridden out by herself. "Will you take me to see Houston?"

Grimacing, he tapped the bow on the violin. "Dallas told me not to take you out to Houston's place."

Her panic increased as she stood. "Then I'll go alone."

Austin jumped to his feet. "You can't do that."

"I need to see how badly Houston is hurt."

"What makes you think he's hurt?"

She tilted her head and studied him, wondering when it was that people lost the innocent way they viewed life. "I've seen Dallas ride. He didn't fall off his horse."

"Then what happened?"

Reaching up, she brushed the dark hair from his youthful brow. He ducked his head in embarrassment at her attentions. "I think he and Houston got into a fight."

"Houston? Ah, no, ma'am. Houston wouldn't have hit him. Houston never fights. Maybe Dallas ran into some cattle rustlers and just wanted to spare you the worry."

"Then why did he tell you not to take me to see Houston?"

"I don't know. He's not a man I question."

"I know that you're probably right, and I'm probably wrong, but I need to see Houston."

He sighed heavily. "What if I just went to check on him?"

"No, I need to see him."

"All right. I'll get our horses."

She heard him muttering oaths as he strode away. If she was right, she expected to be muttering a few of her own before the day was over.

"See? He's just fine," Austin said as they brought their horses to a halt at the edge of Houston's property. "He wouldn't be inside the corral working with the palomino if he wasn't."

"I want to see him more closely."

She started to urge the horse forward, but Austin snaked out his hand and grabbed her arm.

"We can't go ridin' in there while he's alone in the corral. We spook that horse, and she'll pound Houston into the ground."

"All right, I'll walk."

She dismounted, only to find Austin barring her way.

"You know, you are more stubborn than Dallas ever thought about being. Let me tie these horses up over at that bush and I'll walk with you. If we don't do this right, we'll get him killed."

"I know how to approach a wild mustang. I was with Houston when he rode into the herd."

Using his thumb, he tipped his hat off his brow, his blue eyes wide. "He took you with him? Into the herd?"

She smiled at the memory.

"God damn it! He never took me. He always made me wait by the corral he'd built for them so I could close the gate. How come he took you?"

"I guess he couldn't leave me alone."

"What'd it feel like?" he asked in awe. "What'd it feel like to be in the middle of all them horses?"

"Wonderful." She put her hand on his arm. "Let me see if Houston is all right, and then I'll tell you all about it."

"Wait here," he ordered before taking the horses back to the bush.

Amelia turned her attention back to the corral. Without a shirt or hat, Houston stood in the center of the corral, leading the palomino on a rope. The horse trotted in a circle.

The animal was beautiful, graceful, and carried herself proudly as though she knew her ancestors were of the best stock. Houston would be able to get a good price for her, enough that he could expand his small operation, breed more horses with earnestness.

She imagined the joy that would be found in working beside a man, helping to build and shape his dream. Dallas had already built his empire, realized all but one of his dreams. Amelia would give him his final dream: a son. She would find joy and happiness in their child. Through the years, she would guide him so, like his father, he would be a man whom other men respected and admired.

Yet, she couldn't help but wonder if a small part of her would always yearn for more.

Austin rejoined her, and together, they slowly approached the corral. She couldn't stop herself from admiring Houston's lean form. As sinewy as that of the mustang, as powerful, his muscles rippled over his back, over his chest, along his arms as he guided the horse.

As they drew nearer, she could hear the gentle timbre of his voice as he encouraged the horse. She thought the man could tame a snake if he set his mind to it.

"He doesn't look like he's been in a fight," Austin whispered, leaning low so she could hear him without disturbing the horse.

No, he didn't look as though he'd been in a fight. She could see no bruises on his face or body. She could only see the magnificence of his stance. He was in his element here, with his horses. She supposed some men were simply meant to be loners, simply preferred their solitude.

He caught sight of them then, and her heart misbehaved as it always did when he gazed upon her with such intensity. She wished for an insane minute that she was a horse, that he could love her as he did his mustangs.

With a gentle guiding hand, he slowed the horse to a walk, then brought it to a halt. He removed the rope halter and gave the horse a slap on the rump before walking toward Amelia.

The horse turned about and nudged Houston's backside. Smiling broadly, Houston reached into his pocket and withdrew an apple. The horse took it and trotted to the far side of the corral. Houston continued on and climbed over the railing.

"What brings you out here?" he asked as he grabbed his shirt and shrugged into it.

She resisted the urge to capture the bead of sweat that trailed down his chest until it found refuge behind the waistband of his trousers.

"Amelia didn't believe that Dallas fell off his horse last night and busted his face," Austin said.

Houston began to button his shirt, his gaze lowered as he concentrated on a task he should have been able to perform in the dark. "It's not unusual for a man to fall off his horse when he's riding at night. Especially when there's no moon. Horse drops a leg into a prairie dog hole, and he throws the rider."

She placed her hand over his, and he grew still. "How did you bruise your knuckles?" she asked.

He lifted his gaze. "Fell off the porch."

"How'd you do that?" Austin asked.

"A hell of a lot of falling going on around here," she said before she spun around, the anger seething within her.

"I didn't think women were supposed to swear," Austin said.

"Take Black Thunder for a ride," Houston said.

"But I wanna hear—"

She heard a gentle scuff that she was certain was Houston tapping Austin's head.

"Goddamn it!" Austin cried.

"Stop using that language around Amelia."

"Why? She uses it around me."

She heard Houston's exasperated sigh and fought back the tears burning her eyes.

"Please take the horse for a ride," Houston said in resignation.

"Will you take me into the herd with you the next time you go after wild mustangs?" Austin asked.

"Yes."

"All right. I won't be gone long."

"Fine."

She watched as Austin ran to the corral. She waited an eternity for him to mount the horse and gallop out of sight. She felt Houston's hand come to rest on her shoulder. She couldn't stop herself from turning and stepping into his embrace. He closed his arms around her, and she laid her head against his chest, relishing the steady beat of his heart.

"Dallas came here last night, didn't he?"

His arms tightened around her. "Dallas has his life planned out in detail. He's just a little frustrated right now because some of those details didn't go as planned. Once you're married—"

She lifted her gaze. "I don't love him. I don't know if I'll ever love him."

He released his hold on her and stepped back as though she'd suddenly sprouted poisonous fangs. "You knew you wouldn't be marrying for love when you placed your ad."

"Because at the time, I didn't know what it was to love, how precious a gift it is."

"If it's a gift, then it can be given away, and you'll find a way to give it to Dallas."

"I've already given it away. I can't take it back. But you don't want it, do you?"

She saw anguish reflected in the depths of his gaze. "It's not that I don't want it. It's that I don't deserve it."

"Why?"

"Ask Dallas. It's the reason he can't stand the sight of me."

Chapter 16

❧

SITTING ASTRIDE HIS horse, Dallas gazed at the tower, admiring its simple design as he admired all works of man that harnessed nature. He found comfort in the steady pounding of the hammer as Jackson worked to finish the wooden structure. Dallas already had three windmills bringing up water on his land. His first had been built where he'd always planned to build his house so he could gift his wife with the luxury of pumped-in water.

He, his brothers, and the men who worked for him had slept beneath the stars before Amelia had accepted his offer of marriage. Her simple words, "I would consider it an honor to become your wife," had set Dallas on a course toward establishing stability. He'd built the house that he had thought about for years: something grand, worthy of the family who would live within its walls. He had erected a bunkhouse to add to the feeling of permanence that Amelia's letters had stirred in him. The future would find a kitchen next to the bunkhouse to replace the chuckwagon because eventually the cook would become as stationary as the cattle.

The barbed wire would see to that. It would bring dramatic changes to their lives, just as the expansion of the railroads continued to do. Dallas fought a constant battle to stay ahead of the changes, to make decisions that wouldn't leave him trailing in the dust. He had to be the best. His father would accept no less.

Dallas shifted his backside over the saddle. He wanted to carry his son to the top of the windmill so together they could look out over all the land that he had tamed. He wanted to teach his son to appreciate nature, to understand its weaknesses, to respect its strengths. He wanted to love his son unconditionally, as his father had never loved him.

Everything he owned, all that surrounded him, he had gained through his own efforts, his own persistence, his willingness to take chances when other men held back. If he could obtain a son on his own, he would, but he was a man who acknowledged his own limitations.

He needed a wife in order to have a son. He needed Amelia. And whether or not she knew it, she needed him.

He hadn't been tactful when he'd confronted Houston last night. When Houston's fist had plowed into his face, Dallas had thought his brother intended to claim Amelia for his own. Instead, he had threatened to find her another husband. If Houston harbored feelings for Amelia, they didn't run deeply enough to overshadow Dallas's desire for a son.

As for Amelia's feelings . . . After receiving her gentle ministrations as she had repaired the damage inflicted to his cheek, Dallas had decided it was simply her nature to care about people. He would see to it that she never regretted taking him as her husband.

And the sooner she became his wife, the sooner these needless doubts would stop distracting him from the concerns of running his ranch. "Jackson!"

The pounding stopped, the silence reverberating through the air as the man at the top of the tower tilted back his hat. "Yeah, boss?"

"Need to talk to you."

Dallas eased his stallion forward as Jackson nimbly climbed down the sturdy structure. His legs were as long as a longhorn's, his body as wiry. Dallas admired his agility and respected him for doing his job when no one was around to watch him. It was the trait of a good cowboy; a trait all the men who worked for him possessed. He might know nothing of their pasts, but he knew how they worked.

The man hit the ground with both feet and swept his hat from his head. "Yes, sir?"

"I need you to go find the circuit preacher."

Jackson's jaw dropped. "What about the windmill?"

"I need a son more than I need water."

"You won't be thinkin' that if we get hit with a drought."

Dallas raised a dark brow, and the man settled his hat over his dark hair. "Yes, sir. I'll find him."

"When you do, bring him and yourself on up to the house. I'll want all the men there for the wedding—for Amelia's sake."

"Yes, sir."

Dallas prodded his horse into a gallop. This time next year, he'd be sharing that windmill and all the land surrounding it with his son.

An incredible freedom swept through Austin as he stood at the edge of the bluff and stared across the craggy rocks below to the far horizon. Here, his dream seemed attainable. Here, he could voice his heart's desire aloud, and it didn't sound foolish with only the wind to listen.

Someday, he'd find the courage to tell his brothers. Or maybe he'd just leave, and when he'd realized his dream, he'd return to share the glorious moment with them. He knew once he'd proven himself, they wouldn't laugh, but until that moment of success, he feared their lack of faith or interest might destroy what he hoped to have.

One violin . . . created by his hands . . . that would make the sweetest music ever heard.

Rising in crescendo, soft as a spring breeze, strong as a winter storm, the gentle strains flowed through his heart, his mind, so clearly . . . so clearly and so loudly that he didn't hear the scattering of rocks soon enough. Black Thunder snorted and pawed the ground as Austin spun around.

He was a dead man.

He balled his hand into a fist to keep it from reaching for his gun. He'd never drawn on a man . . . much less six.

"Howdy, boy." His lips raised in a sneer, the bearded man leaned forward and crossed his arms over the saddle horn. "Nice horse you got there."

"Ain't worth nothin'. He ain't saddle broke."

The man laughed. "I can break him. Could break you if I wanted."

Austin didn't doubt that for a second as his gaze dropped to the man's big beefy hands. He had a godawful feeling in the pit of his stomach that the man liked to draw out killing. "Look, mister, I don't want no trouble."

The man's grin spread like an evil plague. "That's good, boy, 'cuz I don't neither." He drew his gun from his holster and five other guns were quickly drawn.

Austin's mouth went as dry as dust, his heart pounding so hard and fast that he could hear little else.

"Mead, get the horse."

A man built like a bull climbed off his horse, lumbered over to Black Thunder, and grabbed the dangling reins. The horse jerked his head up and the man yanked hard, pulling the horse after him.

Without warning, the bearded man fired a bullet near Austin's feet. Austin jumped back. The man laughed.

"Just keep goin' back, boy."

Austin held up his hands. "Mister, I'm standing on the edge of a cliff. If I go back—"

"I know, boy. You can holler all you want on your way down."

He again fired at the ground, the bullet spitting up dirt between Austin's boots. Austin scrambled back.

"The next one's going to take your big toe with it, the one after that your knee."

Austin heard the explosion, jumped back, and found himself surrounded by nothing but air and demented laughter.

Cowboys weren't meant to walk. Aching and sore from his head to his toes, Austin dropped to his backside and jerked off his boots.

He'd gone over the edge of the cliff, grabbed a scraggly bush, and clung tenaciously to it, his toes searching for a hold on the side of the rocky gorge. He'd waited until he heard the riders galloping away before he'd started working his way up.

He'd been walking for hours, the sun beating down on him, the dry wind whipping around him, and the dust choking him. Standing, he drew his gun from his holster and fired it into the air, realizing too late that he might alert the horse thieves to the fact that he'd survived.

Angrily, he swiped at the tears streaming down his face. He should have taken a stand. He shouldn't have allowed those men to run off with Houston's best horse. He should have pulled his gun—he would have been killed for sure.

He should have been paying attention, not daydreaming. If Dallas and Houston discovered what had happened today, they would never trust him again, would see him as the boy they thought he was instead of the man he was becoming.

He'd been irresponsible and stupid. Dallas was always lecturing him on the dangers that abounded out here, where they were isolated from the law. He'd taught him how to use his gun. Austin just hadn't had the guts to test that knowledge.

He saw two riders in the distance. He aimed his gun, his intent to kill them both. He dropped his hand to his side when he recognized Houston and Amelia. They'd no doubt grown worried and ridden out to find him.

He wiped the fresh tears from his cheeks. He'd rather face the horse thieves again than Houston.

Houston and Amelia brought their horses to a halt. Houston was out of his saddle and grabbing Austin's shoulder before Austin had time to blink back any more tears. "Are you hurt?" Houston asked, his voice ragged with concern.

"No, just bruised. I wasn't paying attention." He sniffed, wishing to God he wasn't crying like a baby. "Black Thunder hit a prairie dog hole. Snapped his leg in two. I had to shoot him."

Houston jerked his head back as though Austin had just slapped him. "Where is he?"

Austin hadn't expected him to want to see the horse. He rubbed his finger beneath his nose, buying himself some time while he thought of another lie. "I heard coyotes. I don't think you want to find him."

"No, I don't reckon I do." Houston removed his hand from Austin's shoulder and walked past him.

Austin turned to watch his brother come to a stop and drop his chin to his chest. He knew Houston was hurting, and his guilt increased because he had no idea how to ease his brother's pain. He was startled when Amelia took hold of his hand.

"Are you all right?" she asked.

"Yep. I didn't mean to lose the horse."

"He knows that."

She strolled to Houston and he wrapped his arm around her, drawing her against him.

Austin didn't think they were talking, just holding each other as though that was enough. He wished Amelia had kept touching him, but he figured Houston needed her more right now. Austin couldn't remember how he'd felt when he'd lost his ma, he just knew the ache stayed with him, always there as though a part of him was missing. He imagined Houston was feeling that right now, and he was glad Dallas had brought a woman out here to ease their hurts because he and his brothers sure as hell knew nothing about giving comfort. A glare, a shout, a slap up side of the head was all they knew.

Amelia tipped her lovely face up and said something to Houston, and Austin would have sworn the man smiled. He drew Amelia closer until it looked as though they were one person before he moved away from her and walked back to Austin, Amelia strolling along behind him.

"I appreciate that you put an end to Black Thunder's suffering. Putting a horse down ain't an easy thing to do."

The tears welled back up in Austin's eyes. "What'll you do for a stallion now?"

"As Amelia so kindly reminded me, I've got the palomino. Come spring, you and me will go find another stallion. I'll take you into the herd with me then."

Austin felt as though Houston was rewarding him for an action that he should have punished him for. "You don't have to take me into the herd."

"Said I would. A man's gotta keep his word. Why don't you mount up behind me, and we'll get you home so Amelia can tend to your cuts and scrapes?"

Austin nodded in mute agony. His conscience had him feeling lower than a snake's belly.

As night fell, Amelia sat on the front porch, lanterns on either side of her providing the light by which she worked, using patience, care, and delicate stitches to mend the torn green silk, wishing she could mend the tear in her heart as easily.

Her mother had told her once that it hurt to love a man. Her mother had been crying at the time. Amelia had decided then that she would never love a man who'd hurt her.

Yet she had fallen in love with a man who was determined to hurt her as his way of protecting her. She didn't think she'd ever feel this yearning for Dallas.

She would care for him and grow fond of him. She would be a good wife, a wonderful mother to his children. She would gain his respect, his trust, but never his love.

And he would never hurt her. It was impossible to hurt someone who had given her heart to another.

She heard the mournful strains of the violin serenade the night. She would have joined Austin on the back porch, but she sensed that he needed to be alone. He hadn't wanted her patience or her attentions when they'd returned to Dallas's house. If she didn't know better, she'd think he was trying to punish himself for something that wasn't his fault.

She had admired the manner in which Houston had handled the loss of his horse: without blaming Austin. She knew Houston was hurting tonight, had lost one corner of his dream. She wished she could be with him to ease his pain, but her place was here, waiting on the porch Dallas had built for her, waiting on the future that she had once anticipated.

Dallas was the man to whom she had given a promise, a promise she would keep no matter what the cost to her heart. He didn't deserve her doubts or the betrayal of her feelings.

Austin's music drifted into silence just as Amelia saw the rider coming in . . . at long last. She'd been waiting for Dallas, needed to speak with him. He rode to the house, dismounted, and wrapped the reins around the railing.

His spurs jangling, he stepped onto the porch. He wore a vest over his light brown shirt, chaps over his dark brown trousers. He swept his hat from his head and knelt beside her, his large tanned finger touching the green silk. "What's this?"

"One of the dresses Houston purchased. It got torn when the wagon overturned, but I can fix it."

Furrowing his brow, he rubbed the silk cloth between his callused fingers. "It doesn't have any ribbons or bows."

She secured the needle in the cloth. "It's really a simple evening dress, but I think it looks quite elegant when I'm wearing it."

He looked up and the light from the lanterns shimmered over his black hair. "Don't ladies like frilly things?"

She thought of the hat he'd sent her and tried to find the right words. "We like some frilly things. It depends on the occasion."

"You must have been grateful, then, when that raccoon took off with your hat."

"I was . . . I was greatly relieved."

"Too many ribbons, huh?"

"Too many birds," she confessed.

He nodded sagely and smiled. "Think a rattlesnake would have been better?"

"If I had opened that box and seen the head of a rattlesnake, I'm not certain I would have come."

The smile eased off his face. "Why didn't you tell me you were doing without? I would have sent money."

"Your letters were comfort enough."

His fingers skimmed along her cheek. "Too proud. I could always sense that in your letters. We're well suited to each other, Amelia, and after waiting so long to finally have you here, two months seems like an eternity. I've sent one of my men to find the circuit preacher. Hopefully within the month, we'll be married."

She held his gaze. If she could not have a marriage built on a foundation of love, she at least would insist that it be built on trust and honesty. Lies from the past, hers and his, she would forgive and forget. But their future demanded a stronger foundation. "I want your word that you will never again lie to me."

He clenched his jaw. "You saw Houston today?"

She nodded. "He wouldn't tell me why he hit you, but I suspect it had something to do with me. I don't imagine he told you that during the time we were together, he was always respectful of me and loyal to you."

"No, he didn't mention that, but I'm beginning to see that's the way it was."

"He became my friend, and I'd like to think that I became his. You're his brother, and yet I don't understand why you didn't know he was raising mustangs, why you never went to his home before last night—"

Dallas surged to his feet. "He never asked! Not once. He likes his solitude, and by God, I owe him that if that's what he wants."

"But you sent him to fetch me."

"To protect your reputation. No one would question your reputation knowing you'd traveled with him."

"Because of his disfigurement?"

Dallas had the grace to blush. "That and his temperament. He keeps to himself, or at least he did until he made this journey."

She lowered her gaze. He knelt beside her and touched her cheek. "Amelia, I need a wife that people will respect."

She lifted her eyes to his. "I need a husband who won't lie to me."

His fingers curled away from her face as he averted his gaze, staring into the darkness beyond the porch. "I need you, Amelia, and I want you happy." He shifted his gaze back to hers. "Give you my word that I won't lie to you again."

His large palm cradled her cheek, just before his lips touched hers. The kiss was tender, gentle, everything that Houston's had not been.

Her remaining nights, her remaining days, she would be kissed like this, would feel this warmth with no heat, would feel safe, secure, content. She prayed it would be enough.

He moved his mouth from hers and smiled. "Sweeter than last night's kiss."

She rubbed above her lip. "Your mustache tickled."

"Do you want me to shave it off?"

"No!" She touched her hand to his cheek. "It suits you."

"My father had a mustache." He shook his head. "I suppose Houston told you that as well."

"No, he never spoke much about your father."

"Well." Dallas stood and rubbed his hands on his thighs. "I thought we'd celebrate your arrival tomorrow evening. Kill the fatted calf. Give you a chance to get to know my men."

"I want you to invite Houston."

"He won't come."

"Invite him anyway."

He crossed his arms over his chest and leaned against the porch beam. "If it'll please you—"

"It will."

The low strains of the violin filtered through the air again. The sound almost broke Amelia's heart.

Dallas turned his head to the side. "What's that noise? Sounds like somebody dying."

"Austin is playing his violin. I think he relies on his music to help him handle things that upset him."

"Why is he upset?"

She sighed deeply. "Houston had a black stallion. Austin rode it this afternoon, and it dropped a foot in a prairie dog hole. He knew the horse was important to Houston, and I think he feels guilty because he had to shoot it."

"He shouldn't feel guilty. That's a hazard that comes from riding out here. You accept it."

"Maybe you could talk with him. You're his brother, but he sees you as his father. He wants desperately for you to notice that he's becoming a man."

"How do you do that?"

"Do what?"

"Make a man tell you what's on his mind?"

She smiled softly. "I care enough to ask."

Dallas stood within the shadows and listened, truly listened, to the music for the first time in his life. He imagined he could actually feel Austin's grief hovering around him. When Austin stopped playing, the air was still fraught with the sound, lingering on the breeze. Austin dropped his head back against the beam. Dallas could barely make out his brother's features in the darkness.

"Austin?"

Austin jumped to his feet. "I didn't know you were here. I wouldn't have been playin' if I'd known you were here."

Dallas heard the terror reflected in Austin's voice. Good Lord, Dallas expected to strike the fear of God into the men who worked for him, but not his family. He'd never wanted his brothers to fear him the way he'd feared his father.

"Well, then, I'm glad you didn't know I was here. I've never heard anything so . . . so—"

"Unmanly?"

"On the contrary. I've never heard any music that had the strength to strip emotions bare. You've got a gift there." He cursed the darkness because he couldn't tell if Austin had relaxed his stance. "Ma used to play songs that were low like that, but I don't guess you'd remember that."

"Nah, I don't."

"That's her violin."

Austin lifted the violin closer to his face. "It is?"

"Yep. It was Houston's idea to keep it. Said he thought you had Ma's long fingers. Never expected you to play better than she did."

"Never expected you to think I played good at all."

"Well, then, I reckon we both surprised each other tonight."

Austin's grin shined through the darkness. "Reckon we did at that."

Dallas stepped closer to his brother. "Amelia told me about Houston's stallion."

Austin's smile disappeared into the night. "I should have been paying closer attention."

"A man can't anticipate all that's gonna happen in life. If we always knew what the next moment would bring, we'd never look forward to it coming."

"Houston needed that horse."

"A horse can be replaced. A brother can't. We're damn grateful you didn't break your neck."

"Houston said we'd go lookin' for some more mustangs come spring."

"And you'll find them."

"Still, if I'd been paying attention—"

"Don't get into the habit of looking over your shoulder and thinking about what you should have done. Regrets make one hell of a shaky foundation on which to build a life."

With the soft light of dawn bathing the morning, Dallas dismounted and walked his horse toward Houston's corral, wishing he hadn't given Amelia his word that he wouldn't lie. He had a feeling she'd question him about inviting Houston, so he was obligated to ask, even though he knew his brother wouldn't come.

He watched as Houston led the palomino around the corral with a hackamore, a blanket thrown over its back. A saddle straddled the corral railing. Dallas had seen Houston break enough mustangs to know

Houston would get the horse accustomed to the weight of the saddle before he gave it the weight of a man. He'd just never realized his brother planned to breed them. He thought his brother would enjoy a measure of success with this venture, and he ignored the pain that came from knowing Houston hadn't wanted to share his plans.

Dallas rested his arms over the corral fence. If Houston had seen him arrive, he was doing a damn good job of pretending he hadn't. Dallas held his patience in check, although he had business to tend to and didn't have all day to stand around while his brother worked.

Houston removed the halter and blanket. He walked to the corral and slipped through the slats, presenting Dallas with his profile. Dallas stared at the horse. "Looks like a good horse."

"Will be when I'm done with her."

"How much you want for her?"

"She's not for sale."

"You can't build a business that way."

Houston crooked his elbow and placed it on the railing. "You can't build an empire that way, but then I'm not interested in empire building."

"There's nothing wrong with empire building."

"Nothing wrong with it at all if that's what you want. It's just not what I want."

Dallas shook his head, wondering why some men dreamed of great accomplishments while others were content not to dream at all. "I'm having a celebration this evening in honor of Amelia's arrival. She wanted me to invite you. Consider yourself invited."

"Tell her I appreciate the invite, but I've got other plans."

Dallas mounted his horse. "I told her you wouldn't come. Reckon we both know why."

He prodded his horse into a hard gallop. When he'd left Houston at the hospital, he'd been swathed in bandages. When he'd returned, Houston had been wearing a shirt. He'd never seen him without one since and hadn't realized how badly his body had scarred.

When Houston's place was no longer in sight, Dallas slid off his horse, dropped to his knees, and threw up.

Houston hadn't planned to come.

Celebrations and hordes of people weren't his style. Even when he helped Dallas herd his cattle north, Houston stayed on the outer fringe of the herd, circled the cattle at night, and kept his own counsel.

When he wasn't herding cattle, his evenings were spent sitting on a porch, listening to night creatures come to life: the chatter of crickets, the occasional howl of a lonesome wolf. Sometimes, he whittled.

Mostly, he just sat and sought the peace that always eluded him, taunted him just beyond reach. If he thought about the past, the nightmares would come; if he thought about the future, the loneliness eased around him. He'd learned to be content with the present, taking each day as it came.

Damn Dallas for making him yearn for a future different from the one he'd accepted as his due.

Yet, here he stood, his left shoulder pressed against the cool adobe as he watched the men milling around. He could smell the beef cooked over a mesquite fire, the coffee, and the beans.

He could hear the deep-throated guffaws of the men. He could hear the sweet, gentle laughter of a woman. She was walking beside Dallas, her arm wrapped around his. They made a pretty picture: the gallant ranchman, the genteel lady.

Dallas was smiling broadly, looking happier than Houston had ever seen him.

Amelia was as lovely as ever. Wearing the green dress they'd purchased at Mimi St. Claire's, she looked like a queen.

"Dallas said you weren't coming."

Houston jerked his head around and met Austin's gaze. "Changed my mind."

"I was afraid maybe you got to thinking about it and decided you needed to be mad at me about Black Thunder."

"I'll admit I was saddened to lose him, but he's bound to have sired a colt or two somewhere. I'll find him."

"I'll help you," he said eagerly.

"I was counting on that."

"I won't let you down this time."

"You didn't let me down before."

Austin looked away as though embarrassed. "I'm gonna get something to eat. You wanna come with me?"

"No, I won't be staying that long."

As Austin walked away, Houston turned his gaze back toward Amelia. She saw him, and her face lit up with such wondrous joy that it hurt his heart. He shoved himself away from the wall, his long strides eating up the distance between them. He told himself that he was trying to save Dallas some discomfort, but he knew in his heart that he just wanted to be near Amelia a little sooner.

He'd hurt her feelings yesterday morning, not for the first time, and probably not for the last, yet she'd comforted him when he'd lost his stallion and welcomed him now with a fierce hug before running her hands down his arms and slipping her fingers around his.

"We're so glad you came."

"I can't stay long," he said, focusing his gaze on Amelia, avoiding looking at his brother, knowing his brother was as grateful as he was that they had a woman to stare at instead of each other. Sometimes, he missed the easy camaraderie he'd shared with Dallas before the war. During the war, they had traveled side by side along different paths that had taken them away from each other.

Dallas cleared his throat. "We've got beef to eat."

"I ate before I came."

Dallas's lips thinned, and Houston knew he'd given the wrong answer. He was always giving the wrong answers, doing the wrong things. He'd never been able to please his father, and he sure as hell couldn't please his brother.

Dusk was settling in, and he thought about heading back home. He'd only have a sliver of a moon by which to travel tonight. It was a good excuse. He'd seen her. She looked happy. That was all he cared about.

A lanky cowboy, whose legs bowed out, approached and removed his hat. "Miss Carson, Cookie said he'd tune up his fiddle if you'd honor us with a dance."

Amelia blushed prettily and gave a quick glance to Houston, before looking at Dallas.

He smiled with regret. "I can't dance proper with this healing leg, but that's no reason for you not to enjoy the music."

She looked at Houston, and damn it, he knew she wanted him to step in for his brother, but if he didn't set limits for himself now, he'd forever be stepping in where he shouldn't.

"I never learned how to dance," Houston said, grateful he had an honest excuse not to hold her within his arms, wishing he didn't have any excuse.

Her face fell momentarily before she brightened and spun around. "Well, then, I'm most grateful that you asked me . . . Skinny, isn't it?"

The cowboy's face split into a grin. "No, ma'am. Slim."

"Oh, yes, Slim. You'll have to tell me how you came by that name," she said as she slipped her arm through his and followed him to an area near the corrals.

Houston could have sworn her attentions had the cowboy growing two inches. As the couple approached, the men let out a whoop and formed a big circle. Cookie climbed on a wooden box, slipped the fiddle beneath his chin, and started playing a fast little tune. Slim hooked his arm through Amelia's, skipped her around, then released her and stepped back, clapping and stomping his foot as another cowboy pranced into the circle, slipped his arm through hers, repeated Slim's previous movements, then backed out of the circle, giving another man a chance.

Houston smiled at Amelia's surprised expression and the smile of pure delight to which it quickly gave way.

"Imagine she was expecting something closer to a waltz," Dallas said, a wide grin shining beneath his mustache.

"Reckon she was."

Dallas leaned on his cane. "Thought you had other plans for the evening."

"Got to thinking about it and figured if Amelia sent the invite, I'd best come. She's not a woman you want to rile."

"So I'm learning." Dallas shifted his stance. "I'm thinking of setting aside some land for a town. A woman needs certain things. I aim to see that Amelia gets them."

A town would bring more people. Houston hated the thought, but he hated more the idea of Amelia doing without. "When I was in Fort Worth, I heard talk of them taking the railroad farther west. If it stays on the course they've set for it, I'd say it's gonna hit the southernmost portion of your spread. You'll need the railroad to bring the businessmen."

Dallas nodded slowly. "Makes sense. I'll keep that in mind. Speaking of Fort Worth, I don't think I ever thanked you proper for going to fetch Amelia for me."

Houston slipped his hand inside his duster pocket, his fingers trailing over threads that were becoming worn. "I'd planned to shoot you when I got back."

Dallas jerked his head around, then turned his attention back to the dancers. "Why didn't you?"

"Lost a case of bullets when the wagon overturned, so at the moment I don't have any to spare."

Dallas's laughter rumbled out. "Then I'd better hope that preacher gets here before the supplies. I think you care for Amelia too much to make her a widow."

Houston watched as Austin, with his gangly arms and legs, took a turn at dancing with Amelia. Dallas was right. Houston cared for her too much to make her a widow . . . too much to make her his wife.

Chapter 17

✢

"DURING THE CEREMONY tomorrow, do you think I should stress that a husband should not beat his wife?"

Amelia scrutinized the minister who had just spoken, a man who leisurely hitched up his hip and sat on the porch railing, his long black coat opening to reveal his pearl-handled revolver. "I hardly think that will be necessary," she assured him.

Reverend Preston Tucker nodded slowly. "After speaking with Dallas earlier, I didn't think so, but a wedding ceremony is more for the woman than the man. Most men I know would consider the deed done with little more than a 'Do you?' followed by 'I do' and a handshake."

"Incredibly romantic."

"Romance is seldom involved out here. I've performed several ceremonies involving mail-order brides. Some women feel more comfortable if I stress how they should be treated."

"I feel fairly confident that Dallas will treat me just fine."

He studied her as one might a bug beneath a rock, his blue eyes penetrating. Dressed all in black—black shirt, black trousers, long black coat—he appeared relaxed, and yet he left the distinct impression that he was ever alert, ever watchful. He reminded her more of a gunfighter than a preacher.

His full lips lifted into a smile that she thought could tempt any woman into sinning.

"Something's bothering you," he stated simply.

"I was just wondering if you planned to wear the gun during the ceremony."

He slowly stroked the revolver strapped to his thigh. "No, I just wear it when I'm traveling. It bothers you, though. Perhaps I bother you."

"I just never expected to see a man of God wearing a gun."

"Life is different out here, Miss Carson. It's still considered a wilderness. Renegades and outlaws run rampant. Frontier justice often becomes more of an injustice. I have no intention of meeting my Maker before I'm ready."

"Would you kill a man?" she asked.

He averted his gaze and squinted into the distance. "Somebody's coming."

Amelia followed the direction of his gaze, and her heart leapt with joy. "It's Dallas's brother."

She rushed off the porch and crossed the yard, keeping her distance as Houston brought Sorrel to a halt. He was leading the palomino beside him.

"You've tamed her," she said, a hint of question in her voice.

"Yep."

Cautiously, she approached and rubbed the horse's neck. "She's so beautiful. She'll give you a fine herd of horses to sell."

"I doubt that." He leaned down and extended the reins toward her. "She's yours."

She stared at the leather strips threaded through his long tanned fingers. She took a step back. "I can't accept her as a gift."

"She's your wedding gift. The saddle, too. It's not a woman's riding saddle, but it was the best I could find on such short notice."

She touched her fingers to the detailed etching worked into the fine leather. The saddle was as beautiful as the horse, not something he'd simply run across.

"I've grown used to riding in men's saddles," she said.

"Figured you had, what with all the riding you do with Austin."

She looked up. "I'm getting married tomorrow."

"I know. Dallas sent word to me this morning."

"That's Reverend Tucker on the porch."

He glanced toward the porch and touched a finger to the brim of his hat in acknowledgment. "He looks like a gunfighter."

Amelia laughed. "That's what I thought."

"Did I ever tell you that I like the way you laugh?" he asked, his voice low.

She placed her hand over his, slowly threading her fingers through the reins, relishing the roughness of his palm against hers. "Take me for a ride."

He straightened. "I'd best not."

"Please. I think you should be with me the first time I ride Palomino so she'll understand that she's changing owners."

He smiled as though secretly pleased with himself, and she wished she could have a lifetime of his smiles.

"I didn't name her Palomino."

"Golden?"

His smile increased. "Nope."

"Mustang?"

He shook his head. "I named her after the woman who'd be riding her."

She laughed. "Amelia?"

His smile slipped away. "Valiant."

Tears stung her eyes. "Please take me for a ride."

Whatever good sense he might have possessed must have left him because he dismounted and walked around to her. "We won't go far," he said.

She nodded. "That's fine."

"We won't stay gone for long."

"That's fine."

He cupped his hands together and bent down. She put her foot within his palms, and he hoisted her up. She settled into the saddle as Valiant sidestepped, snorted, and shook her head.

Houston grabbed the reins and spoke in a low voice near the mare's ear before moving aside and mounting Sorrel. He glanced at Amelia. "Let's test her speed and endurance, but I'll set the pace."

She could only nod as she began to hoard away all the images that would make up the memories of their last ride.

*　　*　　*

Amelia removed her socks and shoes and dipped her feet into the cold water of the springs. She hadn't expected their short trip to take them this far, but it seemed appropriate to finally have the chance to say good-bye properly and to say it here.

Houston was stretched out beside her, raised on an elbow, watching her as though he'd never again have the opportunity to look at her. And perhaps he wouldn't. At least not in the same way.

Tomorrow, she would become his sister by marriage. Leaning forward, she slipped her fingers into the water until they were wet enough, then she lifted them out and flicked them toward Houston. He turned his head aside as the water sprayed over him. Then he met her gaze.

"You didn't ask Dallas why he won't look at me, did you?"

"No." She tilted her nose slightly, daring him to ask.

"Why?"

"Because you've told me time and again that you take the easy way. Asking Dallas would have been the easy way for you. I deserve better than that."

He smiled sadly. "And I'd never give you better than that, Amelia."

"And you think he will?"

"I know he will."

She turned away, wondering why she was trying to push herself into the life of a man who obviously didn't want her. She couldn't explain why she loved him, why she wanted to be part of his life, his dreams.

"Accepting Dallas's offer of marriage seemed so right before I met you. Now, I no longer know what is right. I wanted to be a wife. I wanted to escape the memories from the war. I never expected to find love."

He gently grazed his knuckles over her cheek. "You should have expected to find love. There's so much about you to love."

She had never wanted anything as desperately in her life as she wanted to hear him voice aloud his love for her. Just three words. Three simple words. Yet, she knew he would never say them. To do so would force them to acknowledge a dream they could never possess, would condemn them to years of wondering what might have been.

She placed her hand over his and rubbed her cheek against his rough palm. "Will Dallas love me?"

She watched his throat work as he swallowed. He shifted his gaze to the waterfalls, his voice raspy when at last he spoke. "Yeah, he will."

She could hear the rush of the water as it spilled over the rocks, her moments with Houston flowing by as quickly. Never again would she be alone with him, to look upon him with a longing that should have never entered her heart. She had so much that she wanted to say to him, but she knew the words would only make their leaving this peaceful sanctuary more difficult, so she locked them away, hoping a day would come when she would forget that she'd ever thought them.

"I imagine this place is beautiful in the spring," she said softly.

"Yep. It's a lot greener then, and the flowers come up."

"Will Dallas bring me here to see it?"

"I don't know if he knows about it." He glanced at her. "I'll give him directions."

"How did you manage to find it?"

He shrugged. "Just happened upon it one day."

"Sometimes, life gives us the most unexpected gifts, doesn't it?"

Houston wanted to tell her that she had been an unexpected gift, along with her laughter, her smiles, and her courage. He didn't think he'd ever receive anything finer than the days he'd spent with her as they'd traveled from Fort Worth.

"Yeah, it does," he said quietly.

Inside Dallas's barn, Houston removed the saddle from Valiant's back and swung it over the slats of the stall. She was a good horse. She had a good temperament. She'd serve Amelia well.

He smelled Amelia's sweet scent before he heard her gentle footsteps. He'd put off saying good-bye as long as he could. Words failed him as they always did. He wanted to thank her for the sunshine she'd brought into his life, for the memories that would linger.

And he wished to God that he'd made different choices in his life.

"Take a dare or tell me the truth," she said softly behind him.

He swallowed hard, knowing he was damned either way. He turned slowly, memorizing the slant of her brow, the tip of her nose, the blush in her cheeks. "Dare," he rasped.

"Kiss me as though you loved me."

She stood valiantly . . . his heart-in-her-eyes woman. He had but to tell her the truth to put out the fire of love, to replace it with the cold ashes of disappointment. It should have been easy, but dear God, he didn't want her to hate him, to know him for the man he really was.

So he held his silence and played the game with her rules. He framed her face between his large hands, tilted her face slightly, lowered his mouth to hers, and plunged into hell.

She whimpered softly and leaned into him, her arms moving up to snake around his neck. He tried to be gentle, wanted to be tender, but all he could think about was her warm mouth greedily mating with his. His arms moved down until his hands were roaming over her slender back, pressing her closer to him, until her soft curves met the hard planes of his body.

God, he wanted her. He wanted her here in the hay beside the horses. He wanted her beneath the stars on a warm, sultry night, beneath a pile of blankets when the snow was falling. He wanted her sleepy smile in the morning, her contented smile at midnight.

He wanted to see her flesh when she took off her clothes and ran the damp cloth over her body. He wanted to see everything that existed behind the shadows.

He wanted to make her laugh. He never wanted to make her cry. He never wanted to hurt her.

He drew back, his breathing labored, his heart pounding so hard he thought surely she could feel it. But her breathing matched his and her eyes, her eyes of clover green, were searching his face, searching for what he could never let her see.

"I'll take a dare," she whispered hoarsely.

He touched his trembling thumb to her quivering lip. "Find your happiness with Dallas."

He edged past her, and without looking back, walked out of the barn. He hadn't given her the farewell she deserved, but then nothing he gave her would ever be what she deserved.

Amelia sat on the back porch and stared at the moon, incredibly large, shimmering in the night sky. Every so often, clouds slowly rolled before it with a touch that she imagined was as light as Houston's.

She wanted his love, but more she wanted his trust. She had seen the ugliest part of him and accepted it. Why couldn't he accept it?

"Amelia?"

She glanced up at the shadowed figure. The clouds waltzed past the moon, illuminating Dallas, his hands stuffed into his pockets. He ambled to the porch and leaned against the beam. "I couldn't sleep," he said. "Figured I'd better not risk a horse ride tonight."

Pressing on her skirt, she slipped her hands between her knees. "I couldn't sleep, either."

He hunkered down before her and draped his hands over his knees. "Thinking about tomorrow?" he asked.

She laughed self-consciously. "Yes. You?"

"Yep."

She squeezed her hands between her knees to stop their trembling. "I guess people have gotten married who knew each other less than we do."

"My pa met my ma the day he married her."

"I wonder if your mother was as afraid as I am now."

"I won't hurt you, Amelia."

"But I might hurt you. I don't know if I'll ever be able to give you my heart."

"I'm not asking for your heart. Just your hand, your loyalty, and your respect."

The warmth flared through her cheeks. "And a son."

"That would please me greatly."

"What will we name him?"

He smiled broadly in the moonlight. "What would you like to name him?"

Amelia shrugged. "I don't know."

"Well, we have a few months to think about it. It will be your choice, but I'd like a strong name. Sometimes, all a man needs is his name to make his mark on the world."

"Mark," she said quietly. "We could name him Mark."

"Short for Marcus?"

She nodded. He smiled. "Marcus it is. Marcus Leigh." He looked into the distance. "All of this is for him, Amelia. His legacy."

He brought himself to his feet. "I'd best let you get some sleep." Reaching down, he took her hand and pulled her to her feet.

"My pa told me once that love is something that grows over time. I think that'll be the way of it with us." He kissed her palm, his mouth warm, his mustache soft. "Until tomorrow."

Amelia wrapped her arms around the beam and watched him disappear into the night. She pressed her hand against her stomach. Marcus Leigh.

She would love the child, respect and honor his father, and forget that his uncle had the ability to curl her toes.

Houston sat on his front porch and listened to the night. The wind blew cold around him, but it wasn't nearly as cold as his heart.

He rubbed a hand over his unmarred cheek. Fate had been cruel enough to leave a portion of his face unscathed so he would forever be reminded of what he would have had . . . had he chosen differently.

Unmercifully, he pressed his fingers to his scars, slowly tracing every ridge, every valley, every section of knotted flesh. Each served as a testament to the man he was.

The man he would always be. The boy he had been.

"Dallas, I'm scared."

"Don't be. Ain't nothing to fear but fear itself. That's what Pa says."

"I don't know what that means."

"It just means don't be afraid."

But he had been afraid. Thirteen years later, the fear still hovered around him, the memories strong enough to catapult him back in time.

Houston could hear the roar of the cannons, feel the pounding of the earth. The land had been so green, so pretty at dawn. Then it became blackened, red, and torn. The air hung heavy with smoke and the shouts of angry men, brave men, scared men, dying men.

Houston Leigh buried his face in his hands and did what he'd been too afraid to do thirteen years before.

He wept.

The frigid winds whipped through near dawn. At Dallas's insistence, the men left the herd unattended on the range while they crowded inside the parlor, shoving and elbowing each other like children anxious to get outside.

A fire blazed within the hearth, but its warmth could not penetrate the chill seeping through Houston's bones. He stood beside Reverend

Tucker, waiting for the hell to end, for decisions and choices to be taken out of his hands.

The men fell into silence as Amelia walked into the room, Dallas at her side. She again wore the green silk dress. He'd never asked Dallas for payment, wouldn't have accepted it if it had been offered. Everything he'd ever given her was his way of apologizing for intruding in her life.

If the value of a gift was based upon what it meant to the giver, he was about to give her the finest gift of all: his brother as her husband.

Dallas stood on one side of Amelia, Houston on the other. Austin fidgeted beside Houston in a brown jacket he'd outgrow before he had the need to wear it again.

Outside, the wind howled and the sky turned gray.

Inside, the fire crackled, and Reverend Tucker asked one and all to bow their heads in prayer. As his voice rang out, Houston studied the woman standing beside him. She hadn't looked at him as she had walked into the room, and he couldn't blame her.

They'd traveled through hell together and survived. She'd clambered out of it. How could he drag her back into it?

Reverend Tucker ended the prayer and spoke about marriage, commitment, and duty. Houston stopped listening to the words. They weren't for him. They were for Amelia and the man standing on the other side of her.

Then Reverend Tucker's voice was pounding through his head, reverberating around his heart. "If anyone knows why these two should not be joined in holy matrimony, speak now or forever hold your peace."

Amelia turned her head slightly, caught, and held Houston's gaze. He wanted to tell her. God help him, he'd rather have the disappointment in her eyes than the hurt.

She turned away, and he knew that she'd said farewell at that moment, that there would be no turning back the hands of the clock. For her, he'd held his silence, would forever hold his peace.

As Dallas took Amelia in his arms and kissed her, Houston plunged into the darkest depths of hell.

The winds were cold as Houston stood on the back porch, his duster flapping around his calves. He should head out before it got much darker, taking Austin with him so the newly married couple could have some privacy.

He heard the door open and glanced over his shoulder to see Amelia. "It's cold out here. You'd best stay inside."

"Don't I have a say in where I stand?"

He smiled at her comment, but he had no desire to tease her back. She'd do what she wanted, just as he'd done what he had to do. He turned his attention back to the horizon.

She walked to the edge of the porch, briskly rubbing her hands up and down her arms. He wanted to take her into his embrace and warm her. Instead, he shrugged out of his duster and wrapped it around her. She closed it tightly around her.

"Marcus," she said softly.

He glanced at her. "Marcus?"

She nodded. "That's what we're going to name our first son. We'll call him Mark because Dallas expects him to make his mark on the world."

"With Dallas as his father, I imagine he will."

Her knuckles turned white as she clutched his coat. "I'm nervous about tonight. I don't have any women to talk to . . . and I . . . I always considered you . . . a dear friend. I was hoping maybe you might have some words of wisdom to share so I won't be afraid or disappoint him."

"You could never disappoint him."

"Unless I give him a daughter."

"Not even then."

Her cheeks reddened, but he didn't think it had anything to do with the cold chafing her skin.

"Will it hurt?" she asked quietly.

He felt as though he'd just been kicked in the gut by a mustang. What the hell did he know about a woman's first time? He knew whores. Their stench, their bodies that were always ready for a man, their out-stretched hands asking for more money. He looked away. "Christ, I don't know."

A thick silence built between them.

"Thank you," she finally said and turned to go.

He grabbed her arm and looked at her, really looked at her for the first time, into the green depths of her eyes. He could see the terror. He pulled her against him, wrapped his arms around her, and touched his cheek to her soft hair.

"He won't hurt you," he said quietly. "If he can help it, he won't hurt you. The women I've known were so used . . . He'll kiss you . . . and he just won't stop."

"But kissing won't make a baby."

He slipped his thumb beneath her chin and tilted her face up, wanting desperately to remove the worry from her green eyes. He swallowed hard. "He'll lay his body over yours." He cradled her face, wishing he could cradle her body. "And he'll give what he always gives: the best of himself."

She smiled then, so sweetly with so much trust that his heart ached. "I'll miss you," she said quietly.

"You know where I live. If you need—"

She shook her head with a profound sadness. "No, this at long last is our final good-bye." She stretched up on her toes and kissed him lightly on the lips.

He couldn't stand it: the betrayal reflected in her eyes, the hurt, the disappointment. He'd rather have the hate. "I killed my father."

He released his hold on her and averted his gaze. She'd hate him now, hate him as he hated himself.

"I don't believe you," she said softly.

He laughed derisively. "Believe me, Amelia. For thirteen years, I've run from it. For thirteen years, the truth has stayed as close as my shadow."

"How did you kill him?"

"You want the gory details?"

"I want to understand how the man I traveled with could have possibly killed his father."

He stared into the distance, stared through the passing years. "I was his drummer. He gave the orders and the beat of my drum told the men what those orders were. In the thick of battle, you can't hear a man's words, only his dying screams and the sound of the drum. The smoke grows so heavy that it drops like a fog, surrounding you, burning your eyes, your throat, suffocating you until you can't see the man issuing the orders.

"But you can hear the beat of the drum. So wherever my father went, I had to be. When he rode into battle, I ran by his side, beating . . . beating my drum while bullets whistled past and cannons roared."

His mouth grew dry with the familiar fear licking at his throat. He could smell the smoke and blood. He could hear the screams.

"His horse went down, kicking at the air, screaming in agony. My father scrambled to his feet and pulled his sword from his scabbard. 'Let's go, boy!' he yelled.

"Only I couldn't. The man standing beside me fell. The ground exploded in my face. My father hollered at me again. I started to run. As fast as my legs would take me, I started running back to the place where I'd slept the night before.

"He came after me, yelling, 'By God, I won't have a coward for a son!'

"He grabbed my arm, jerked me around, but I turned away from him, struggling to break free. Suddenly, there was a loud explosion, a bright light, pain . . . and he was gone. And then there was nothing but blackness."

"That's when you were so terribly wounded?"

He laughed mirthlessly. "Yeah, I should have died, too, but I didn't. I prayed for death hard enough, but some prayers just aren't meant to be answered."

"You can't really believe you killed your father?"

"If I hadn't run, he wouldn't have died. I was just what he always said I was. A coward. A weak no-account excuse for a son."

"But you were a child."

"I was old enough. At fifteen, Dallas was marching into battle with a rifle in hand and men following him."

"You're not Dallas."

He finally turned from the past and met Amelia's gaze. "That's right, Amelia, I'm not. And that's why I held my silence. Because you deserve better than me. You don't deserve a man who runs from his own shadow, who's afraid of life."

She tilted her head, that familiar gesture like a puppy who is sizing up another dog and deciding if he can outfight him for the bone. "Does Dallas know that you prefer solitude and have an aversion to towns?"

"Yeah, he knows."

"Yet he sent you to fetch me anyway."

"He didn't have a choice. As much as he trusts his men with cattle, I'm not altogether sure he'd trust them not to take advantage of a pretty lady on a long journey."

"He could have sent Austin."

"Austin?" Houston chuckled. "Austin is just a boy."

A deep sadness swept over her features, tears welling in her eyes, as she laid her palm against his scarred cheek. "He's older than you were the last time you stood on a battlefield."

Her words slammed against him, stunned him, left him paralyzed. He had to have been older than Austin. Austin . . . hell, Austin had shaved for the first time that morning.

The door opened, and Dallas stepped onto the porch, Austin in his wake. Austin crossed the porch, leaned down, and bussed a kiss against Amelia's cheek.

"What was that?" Dallas asked.

Austin flushed. "I was just practicin'."

"For what?"

"Houston's taking me to a sportin' house tonight."

Houston shoved Austin's shoulder and fought to find his voice. "That's between you and me."

"What?" Austin stumbled down the steps. "I don't understand anything anymore. We wanted a woman here so bad, and now that we've got her, we've all gotta change. It makes no sense to me at all."

Houston stepped to the ground. Austin brought up his fists. "I'm tired of getting hit, yanked, and yelled at for being me."

Houston slowly shook his head. "I'm not gonna hit you. Go get your horse."

Austin's eyes widened. "You still gonna take me?"

"Told you I would. Now go get your horse."

Austin released a whoop and started running toward the corral. Houston turned to the couple standing on the porch. "Thought I'd get him out of your way for a couple of days."

"'Preciate that," Dallas said as he removed Houston's duster from Amelia's shoulders and tossed it to him. He shrugged out of his own jacket and wrapped it and his arm around Amelia.

She glanced up at her husband and gave him a hesitant smile.

Houston wished to God she didn't look so small standing beside his brother, so small, and so damn vulnerable.

Houston backed up a step and threw his thumb over his shoulder. "Reckon we'll be goin'."

"Take care," she said quietly.

"We will." He started walking toward the corral, stopped, and looked back over his shoulder.

Dallas was escorting his wife into the house, her back straight, her chin held high.

The Queen of the Prairie.

Chapter 18

⁂

DUSTY FLATS WASN'T much more than a hole in the ground, a place for cowboys to spend energy and money when they were trailing cattle. It boasted one cantina with a bathing room in the back; a general store with so little merchandise that people simply traipsed in, picked up what they needed, and slapped their money onto the counter; and a house filled to capacity with sporting women. No church, no school, no town hall.

Houston hadn't detoured by the settlement in years. He'd forgotten how dismal the place appeared at midnight, but it had what he needed to distract him from all the unsettling thoughts running through his head, and it had what Austin wanted. It'd do.

He brought his horse to a halt in front of the two-story wooden framed house and dismounted.

"This it?" Austin asked as he slid off his bay gelding and absently wrapped the reins around the hitching rail.

"Yep."

Bending at the waist and peering through the dust coated windows, Austin paced the rattling wooden porch. "Ain't much light. What if they're closed?"

"They're not closed," Houston assured him as he stepped on the porch. He wondered if he'd ever been as young as Austin appeared now, ever held that much exuberance about anything. Houston had been eighteen the first time he had paid a woman for her services. He'd felt like an old man, with no excitement, no anticipation. Just something to do so he could say he'd done it. "You don't need much light for what we're gonna do." The door squeaked on dry hinges as he shoved it open. "Come on."

Austin bounded through like a puppy being tossed a bone. He swept his hat from his head, his eyes larger than a harvest moon as he took in the drab surroundings. The vacant seats of the wooden chairs had been polished to a shine by the backsides of all the cowboys who had sat waiting their turn over the years.

A woman with fiery red hair, violet eyes, and full lips painted blood red sauntered over and trailed her fingers from Austin's shoulder to his elbow and back up. She purred like a contented cat that had just lapped up the last of the cream, her smile one of appreciation.

"Hey, darlin'," she cooed in a voice as sultry as a summer night.

" 'Howdy," Austin croaked, his voice changing pitch three times. He'd latched his gaze onto her bountiful bosom which Houston thought might bust free of that shimmering red corset at any moment. He watched his brother's Adam's apple slide up and down and figured Austin was thinking the same thing.

"Maria still work here?" Houston asked.

The woman yelled over the din of a distant off-key piano. Maria shoved herself away from the lanky cowboy over whom she'd been draped and sauntered over, smiling when she recognized Houston.

She appeared older than he'd remembered, worn as thin as the wood on the chairs. The red paint she'd smeared on her cheeks didn't stop them from sagging and the dark circles beneath her eyes had little to do with the kohl she was wearing.

Because she knew him, had serviced him before, she placed her hand inside his thigh, embarrassingly close to his crotch. He was uncomfortable as hell blushing in front of his little brother.

"Been a long time, cowboy," Maria said in a weary voice. "I got that handsome fella over there interested in me. I don't know if double will make me forget him."

"Triple, then."

Her smile grew, but never reached her eyes as she wrapped her arm through his. "I'm yours."

He looked over his shoulder at Austin. "This is she first time. Be gentle with him."

The woman's throaty laughter spilled past her curved lips. "Ah, honey, I'm always gentle." She tugged on Austin's hand. "Come on, sweet thing."

"Shouldn't we talk first?" Austin asked, and the woman's laughter grew.

"Don't worry about him. Velvet will give him a time he won't soon forget," Maria said as she led Houston toward the stairs, leaving Austin standing and stuttering in the front parlor. "You want it the same as last time?"

The loneliness swept through him as he gave her his answer. "Yeah."

Houston stepped on the porch and drew in a long deep breath of the brisk fresh air. No smoke. No heavy perfume. No musky stench of stale bodies rutting like dogs.

The night air was clear, as clear as the stars twinkling above him. He thought he'd never again be able to look upon the night sky without thinking of Amelia curled in his arms.

He'd watched Maria undress . . . and felt nothing but a desire to leave. The woman's naked body hadn't been half as alluring as Amelia's shadow. He'd apologized for his lack of interest, paid her what he'd promised, and walked out without touching her. Since Amelia had come into his life, he was doing one hell of a lot of apologizing.

He crossed the porch and dropped to the top step where his younger brother was leaning against the porch post, gazing into the distance as though he'd fallen in love.

"Didn't take you long," Houston said as he settled against the opposite post. He chuckled low. "Course, as I recall, didn't take me long the first time, either."

"I didn't go with her," Austin said quietly. "I was thinking about Dallas and Amelia—"

"Well, don't," Houston snapped.

Austin turned his head slightly. "I wasn't thinking nothing personal or anything. I just thought all women were like Amelia, all clean and sweet smelling and smiling like they were glad to see me."

"There's a hell of a lot of difference between a sporting woman and a woman like Amelia."

"How come?"

Houston sighed with frustration. He didn't need or want this conversation tonight. Dallas was the one who had the vast experience with women. He should have done a better job of educating the boy. "Sporting women, well, they can be had for a price. A woman like Amelia . . . doesn't give herself lightly. Men don't fall in love with sporting women. But a woman like Amelia . . . when a man falls in love with a woman like Amelia . . . he does what's best for her, no matter what the cost to him."

"You ever fall in love with a woman like Amelia?"

"Once."

"When?"

He dug his elbows unmercifully into his thighs, welcoming the distraction of the pain. "Forever. Reckon I'll love her forever, till the day I die."

"What happened to her?"

"She married someone else."

"You loved her, but you let her marry some other fella? Why'd you do a fool thing like that?"

"Because it was best for her."

"How do you know it was best for her?"

Houston swiveled his head and captured his brother's gaze. "What?"

Austin shrugged. "What if what you thought was best for her wasn't what she wanted?"

"What are you talking about?"

Austin slid his backside across the porch. "I'm not learned in these matters so I don't understand how you know what you did was best for her."

"I just know, that's all. I just know." He surged to his feet, leapt off the porch, and began pacing across the lantern-lit path, into the darkness, then back into the light. Darkness. Light. His life before Amelia. His life after he'd come to know her. Darkness. Light.

He *had* done what was best for Amelia. She didn't need to wake up each morning next to a man who was afraid of the dark, afraid of the dawn, afraid of what the day might hold. She deserved better. He'd given her better.

Dallas feared no man, feared nothing. He hadn't run when the cannons were roaring and the lets were whizzing past. He'd stood his and led the Confederate forces through the charge . . . over and over . . . in battle after battle.

Dallas was the kind of man Amelia deserved. Amelia with her courageous heart that had seen them through disaster after disaster. Amelia with the tears shimmering in her eyes, along with understanding.

Why had she looked at him with no judgment in her eyes, no revulsion after his confession?

He wasn't the hero Dallas had been. He never would be. He had run like a frightened jackrabbit and paid a heavy price: his father's life.

He had never talked with Dallas about that day. Sometimes, Houston would wonder if the battle had happened at all. Then he'd stop to water his horse at a pond. Within the clear still waters, he'd see his reflection, a constant memento of how his father had died.

He knew his face served as a reminder for Dallas as well. For months after Houston had been wounded, Dallas had preferred to stare at his mud-covered boots rather than meet Houston's gaze.

Amelia should have averted her gaze as well. She should have been appalled and horrified. The woman kept her heart in her eyes and that was all he'd seen reflected there: her love for him.

He skidded to a dead halt and stared hard at Austin. The boy's chin carried so many nicks from his first shave that it was a wonder he hadn't bled to death. He was a year older than Houston had been when he'd last stood on a battlefield. Sweet Lord, Houston had never had the opportunity to shave his whole face; he'd never flirted with girls, wooed women, or danced through the night. He'd never loved.

Not until Amelia.

And he'd given her up because he'd thought it was best for her. Because he had nothing to offer her but a one-roomed log cabin, a few horses, a dream so small that it wouldn't cover the palm of her hand.

And his heart. His wounded heart.

He yanked the reins off the hitching post and mounted his horse.

Austin came to his feet. "Where you goin'?"

"Back to the ranch."

*　　*　　*

They rode hard through the night. Houston wasn't at all certain what he would say to Amelia, what explanation he could give Dallas.

He'd held his silence, sacrificing his right to say anything. She had pledged herself to Dallas, had become his wife. Vows Houston thought he'd ignored thrummed through his head with the rhythm of the pounding hooves: to love, honor, and obey . . . until death parted them.

He only knew that he had to see her, had to talk to her, and had to understand why she hadn't turned away from him, repulsed by his confession. Good Lord, if he didn't know better, he'd swear she had looked as though she loved him more.

Would a night in Dallas's arms sway her heart away from Houston? And if it didn't, what difference would it make? She could already be carrying the son that Dallas wanted so desperately.

Black smoke billowed in the distance, darkening the brilliance of the dawn. The familiar panic and the accustomed fear settled into Houston's gut. He urged his horse into a faster gallop, with Austin following him like a shadow.

"What is it?" Austin yelled behind him.

"Trouble!"

His horse tore up the ground with the intensity of the gallop. Houston leaned low, pressing Sorrel to ride with all her heart. Good judgment told him to slow as he neared Dallas's home, but the eerie silence urged him on.

Someone had reduced the barn to smoldering embers and the corral to broken planks of wood. With black soot and sweat smeared over their faces and clothes, the men milled around in front of the house as though lost.

Houston jerked his horse to a halt. "What happened?"

Slim lifted a shoulder and a vacant gaze. "Don't know. We were all in the bunkhouse drunk as skunks after celebrating the wedding. We heard a gunshot. Got outside, but it was too late to do any good. Barn was on fire, horses gone. The boss is still out cold. Cookie's with him. Jackson took off at a run to find some help, but on foot, it'll take him a week to reach another ranch. The rest of us ain't no good without a horse beneath us."

"Amelia? What about Amelia?"

Slim dropped his gaze. Houston dismounted and grabbed the man by the shirtfront, pulling him up to eye level. "Where's Amelia?"

Slim shifted his gaze to the other men. They stepped back. Houston shook him. "Goddamn it! Is she hurt?"

Slim swallowed. "We don't know where she is."

Roughly, Houston released his hold on Slim, his heart pounding so hard, he was certain every man in the state could hear it. "She has to be here. Find her! Now!"

"She's not here," a seething voice echoed from the doorway.

Dallas stumbled down the steps and leaned against the beam for support, breathing heavily, blood trailing near his temple.

Houston placed a steadying hand on his brother's shoulder. "You've been shot."

"It's just a crease. That's the least of my worries right now. God damn horse thieves took Amelia." Dallas pushed away from the porch. "I'm going to get her back. Nobody takes what belongs to me, by God. Nobody. Austin, I'm taking your horse."

Austin scrambled off his horse so quickly that he lost his footing and his backside hit the dirt. In an unsteady gait, Dallas headed toward the gelding. Houston knew it was determination alone that got his brother up into the saddle.

"I'm coming with you," Houston said as he mounted Sorrel.

"Suit yourself. Austin, you're in charge here till we get back."

Austin's eyes widened. "Me?"

"You got a problem with that?" Dallas asked.

Austin shook his head vigorously. "No, sir."

"Good. Any orders you give are coming from me, so don't give any orders I wouldn't give."

"Yes, sir. We'll get the corral rebuilt. Reckon you'll be bringin' the horses back."

"Damn right I will. Along with my wife."

Dallas had a reputation for protecting what was his. In his wildest dreams, Houston never would have thought anyone would be fool enough to try and take what belonged to Dallas Leigh, but as he was discovering, the men who had taken Amelia were fools. They left a trail that a blind man could have followed.

"They're not too cautious," Houston observed.

"Since they took all the horses, I don't imagine they expected anyone to come after them for a day or so. That mistake will cost them dearly."

They caught up with the horse thieves near dusk. They were ensconced in a canyon, smoke spiraling from their campfire. Houston and Dallas climbed the bluff and crawled on their bellies to its edge.

"I count six," Dallas said. "We could pick them off from up here."

Houston took Dallas's word for the number. His gaze was trained on Amelia. From this distance it was difficult to measure, but he didn't think she looked hurt.

"They might take it into their heads to use Amelia as a shield," Houston said.

"True enough, but it looks like there's only one way in. We'd make easy targets if we went that route," Dallas said.

"And we'd put Amelia at risk if we go in there with our guns firing. She's sure to get hurt."

"Then what would you suggest?"

"I go in alone."

Dallas jerked his head around.

"If I can get close to her," Houston continued, "I could at least protect her while you fire from up here. If I can get my horse close enough to her, maybe I can get her up on it, and we can ride out."

Dallas clenched his jaw. "She's my wife."

"But they know what you look like. Besides, you're a better shot than I am and my horse is faster. Figure I can go in there claiming to be an outlaw looking for a place to hide." He lifted a corner of his mouth. "My face ought to convince them I'm telling the truth."

Dallas flinched and gazed back into the canyon. "I don't want the two of you trapped in there. I won't start shooting until you can get your horse close to her. Use the diversion to get her on the horse and get her out of there. I'll take care of the thieves."

"See that you do."

"It'll be night soon. We need to work fast. If anything goes wrong . . ." Dallas's voice trailed off.

Houston grabbed Dallas's coat and jerked him around. "Just make sure Amelia comes first. No matter what happens, she gets out of there alive."

*　　*　　*

Amelia had never been so terrified in her entire life. She hugged the rocky canyon wall wishing she could melt into it and disappear. If she survived, she didn't think she would cherish her green wedding dress or its memories.

The ropes chafed her wrists, her jaw still ached. When she didn't think anyone was looking, she'd tried to gnaw the knots loose. Her attempt had earned her a flat-handed slap and tighter knots.

She saw a man, his arms raised, walking into the canyon leading a horse. Two men sauntered behind him, rifles trained on him giving them the advantage and a false arrogance. She recognized the weathered hat, the dusty black coat, and the horse. Houston didn't look at her or call out to her with reassurances. Perhaps he had no reassurances to give. Or perhaps he was simply biding his time. He seemed remarkably calm for a man who had just walked into a nest of vipers. She kept her gaze locked on him, watching for any small signal that would indicate he had a plan to rescue her.

"What have we got here?" the man she knew to be leader said as he came to his feet, his hand resting easily on the butt of his gun.

Houston walked farther into the camp, hoping to give Dallas sight of the two men behind him. He didn't know how to signal to him that another man was guarding the entrance.

"He was just ridin' in, pretty as you please, whistlin' some song like he owned the place," one of the men who had been tailing him said as they both stopped walking sooner than Houston would have liked. He didn't know if Dallas could see them from his vantage point at the top of the bluff.

"I do own the place," Houston said, trying to imitate the authority Dallas always carried in his voice. "Or at least I do when I'm lookin' for a place to hide out for a couple of days." He squatted, lowered his arms, and warmed his hands before the fire, praying no one could see how badly they were shaking. "I don't mind sharin' the place, though."

The man he assumed was the leader narrowed his eyes. "You hidin' from the law?"

"I'm hiding from anyone who's looking for me."

The man scratched his scraggly beard and chuckled. "Know that feeling. You got a name?"

"Dare."

"Dare?" the man asked, incredulously.

Houston came slowly to his feet, used his thumb to push his hat up off his brow, and met the man's gaze. "You got a problem with that?"

"Nah, ain't got no problem with it at all." He held out his hand. "I'm Colson. These here are my men."

Ignoring the outstretched hand, Houston glanced quickly around the canyon. A makeshift corral held the stolen horses. The other horses were saddled and lightly tethered to the brush growing out of the rocks. They could be mounted in the blink of an eye and riding west a half-blink later. "You seem to have a lot more horses than you do men."

"We collect 'em whenever fortune smiles on us. Can always find a man willing to pay for good horseflesh."

"And the woman?"

Colson laughed knowingly. "Reckon men are willing to pay for that, too."

"Reckon they are. Mind if I have a look-see?"

Colson rubbed his chin. "Not as long as all you do is look. She'll be keeping me warm tonight."

"Understood," Houston said as he fought the urge to plow his fist into that ugly face. He damned the men for taking his revolver. Thank God, they'd left his rifle in the scabbard, although he didn't know if it would do him much good in these close quarters. An idea came to him. He turned back to Colson, hoping the smile he gave the man looked as mean as it felt. "Mind if I have me a little innocent fun? I like to hear women scream."

Colson narrowed his eyes. "What do you mean by innocent?"

Houston jerked his head toward Amelia. "The way she's worked her way into that crack, I figured she ain't given any thought as to what's in there with her. Women hate things with tiny legs. Just thought I'd mention them to her."

Colson squatted before the fire. "I don't think she's the type to scream over a little bug, but it don't bother me none if you have your fun."

Houston walked as calmly as he could toward the far corner of the canyon, grateful no one objected when Sorrel followed him. He was going to reward the horse with a whole basket of apples if they lived through this night.

Amelia had wedged herself into a large crack in the canyon wall. She carried a fresh bruise on her cheek, and it was all he could do not to turn around right then, yank his rifle out of the scabbard, and start shooting.

As he neared, he called out, "Little lady, scorpions and snakes sure do love to hide in the cool cracks." He mouthed "scream," and bless her heart, she did.

She released an ear-splitting scream as she catapulted out of the crack and lunged into his arms. The men surrounding them guffawed. A shot rang out.

As the thieves scrambled for cover, Houston wrapped his hands around Amelia's waist and hoisted her into the saddle. She grabbed the horn. He mounted behind her and urged Sorrel into a gallop as a second shot ricocheted off the rocks.

"What the hell?" someone shouted.

Houston heard several more shots ring out. Particles of rock flew through the air, showering over them as they raced toward the entrance. Men hollered. Horses whinnied. All hell was breaking loose behind them, but he rode on without looking back.

He held Amelia as close as he could, using his body as a shield around her as much as possible as they tore through the mouth of the canyon. He heard a bullet whisper past his ear.

He kicked Sorrel's sides, prodding her into a faster gallop. He saw the setting sun glint off a rifle and he kept riding. He heard the retort of more gunfire. He didn't know how much time Dallas could buy them. He feared it wouldn't be enough.

He felt a sharp bite in his arm. He glanced back. Three riders were galloping fast and furious from the mouth of the canyon. Leaning forward, he pulled his rifle from the scabbard. He looked back over his shoulder. The three riders were gaining on them. A horse with two riders couldn't outrun a horse with one, no matter how fast he was.

"Take the reins!" he yelled.

Awkward as it was with her hands still bound, Amelia did as he instructed. His thighs hugging the horse, he pulled Amelia flush against him. " 'Keep riding!"

He took one last breath filled with her faint sweet scent. "I love you."

With fluid motions, he released her, grabbed the back of the saddle, shoved hard, and propelled himself off the galloping horse, away from the pounding hooves. He hit the ground, rolled into a kneeling position, brought his rifle up, and fired.

Amelia had heard Houston's words as though he'd whispered them in a field of flowers instead of on the open plains as they were riding hell-bent to get away. And then she had felt him leaving her . . . forever.

Against his wishes, she jerked back on the reins, fighting to bring the galloping horse to a staggering halt. She whirled Sorrel around just in time to see Houston shoot the second of three riders. The remaining rider fired his rifle. Houston jerked back, his arms flailing out to the side.

"No!" she cried, her heart screamed.

Another retort of gunfire filled the air, and the last rider slumped forward before tumbling from his saddle. Amelia urged Sorrel into a gallop, a litany of prayers rushing through her mind. She drew the horse to a halt where Houston had fallen. She scrambled out of the saddle and fell to her knees beside him.

Bright red blood soaked through his shirt. "No," she whispered, tears welling in her eyes. "No, no, no." Ignoring the pain as the rope bit into her wrists, she ripped off a portion of her petticoat and pressed it against the wound, desperately trying to staunch the flow of crimson. The white cotton rapidly became red.

Houston opened his eye. She touched her palm to his cheek. "Don't you die on me. I'll never forgive you if you die on me."

"I didn't run," he rasped.

"But you should have, you fool! You should have stayed with me!"

A corner of his mouth tilted up. "That would have been the easy way. You deserve better than that."

He sank into oblivion, his breathing shallow. A shadow crossed over his face. Amelia jerked her head up as Dallas dropped to his knees, knife in hand, and began to cut away Houston's shirt.

"Why in the hell didn't he stay on the horse? I wasn't that far be-hind—"

"He had something to prove to himself," she said quietly, the tears coursing down her cheeks.

Chapter 19

❧

$\mathcal{I}$N HIS ENTIRE life, Dallas had never met the next moment without a plan of action, had never known what it was to feel useless, without a purpose. He sure as hell felt useless now, and he didn't know what to do about it.

He'd gathered up the stolen horses and had left the men he and Houston had killed to the buzzards and coyotes. He hadn't been cruel out of vengeance, but he had recognized that time was rapidly becoming his bitter enemy. The bullet had entered and exited through Houston's shoulder, leaving a relatively clean wound, but two gaping holes through which the blood could flow. And flow it did.

As much as Dallas had hated to do it, he'd wrapped a rope around Houston to keep him from falling out of his saddle. They'd ridden through the night, keeping the horses at a slow, steady walk, their planned destination the ranch. Near dawn, when Houston's cabin had come into view, Dallas had decided not to push his luck.

He had carried Houston, unconscious, into his log cabin and laid him as gently as he could in the bed. He'd helped Amelia clean, sew, and dress the wound, his admiration for her growing as her competent hands handled each task with efficiency. She'd grown pale, her hands had trembled from time to time, but her jaw had been clenched with determination, her eyes challenging death.

She was one hell of a woman.

When Dallas had decided he'd done all he could for the moment, he had left his brother in Amelia's care while he'd raced to the ranch, horses in tow, to give orders to his men, sending four men in opposite directions to scour the countryside for a doctor. He'd sent another man to find Reverend Tucker, praying harder than he'd ever prayed in his life that he wouldn't need the preacher's services.

Austin had returned to the cabin with him. They would have taken turns relieving Amelia as she tended to Houston's needs if she had let them. As it was, they simply sat in the shadows and worried.

It hurt. It hurt to watch his brother lying so still as though he were simply waiting for death's arrival. It hurt to watch Amelia hovering over Houston, wiping the fevered sweat from his brow, his throat, his chest, talking to him constantly, softly, gently. Always talking to him about his horses, his dream of raising them, and how she didn't want to be part of a dream that died.

Amelia Carson was everything Dallas had wanted in a wife. A survivor, someone with an appreciation for the South as it had been, a willingness to reach out to the future. She was full of grit, determination, and courage.

He thought he'd never forget the way she'd looked riding back for Houston: fearless, angry, terrified. Or the depth of despair he'd seen reflected in her eyes as she'd knelt beside Houston and tried to stop his blood from spilling into the earth.

Dallas rose to his feet, stretched the ache and tightness out of his back, and walked to the hearth. He took a wooden bowl off the mantel, bent down, and ladled the simmering stew out of the pot. Houston's house was about as simple as a man could make it: a table with one chair, a bed, a wardrobe, a chest, a small table by the bed, and a stack of books. No mirrors. Not one goddamn mirror.

Straightening, he glanced over his shoulder at Austin, who was sitting on the table since Dallas had confiscated the chair. He was surprised the boy's elbows hadn't created holes in his thighs. He looked as though he was awaiting a hangman's noose. "You want to check on his horses?"

Austin shot to his feet and bobbed his head. "Yes, sir." He headed out the door.

Dallas crossed the room and knelt beside the bed. "You need to eat."

Amelia gave him a weak smile. "I can't get his fever to break. Where's the doctor?"

"I sent my men to find one. It's as hard to find a doctor as it is to find a wife." He spooned out a bit of stew and lifted it up. "Come on. Eat for me."

"I'm not hungry."

"Then eat for him." He tilted his head toward Houston. "'You won't do him any good if you get sick."

She opened her mouth, and he shoveled in the stew. Licking her lips, she took the bowl from him. "I am hungry after all."

He watched her eat, this woman he'd married, this woman who wasn't fully his wife. She had been as skittish as a newborn filly on their wedding night. He'd decided to take her for a walk, hoping to help her relax. Instead, he'd lost her.

Or maybe he'd just failed to acknowledge that he'd never had her.

When he'd confronted Houston with his accusations weeks ago, he'd convinced himself that Houston had felt nothing more than lust for Amelia. He'd closed his mind to the possibility that Houston might have fallen deeply in love with Amelia.

That she might have fallen deeply in love with Houston.

He had measured their love against what he knew of love . . . which was nothing at all. He understood loyalty, honor, and the value of keeping one's word.

Regardless of his feelings for her, Houston had never claimed Amelia. For whatever reason, he had held his silence as she and Dallas had exchanged vows. And with his silence, he had forsaken Amelia and given his own vow to forever hold his peace.

Amelia handed the empty bowl back to Dallas, her brow furrowed so deeply that he thought her face would always reflect the strain of the past few days. "Thank you."

He unfolded his body. "I'm going to step outside for some fresh air. Holler if you need me."

He set the bowl on the table, crossed the room, opened the door, and stepped into the night. He'd never felt so damn useless in his entire life. At least when Houston had been wounded during the war, Dallas had been able to take some action, he'd been able to do something.

He bowed his head. For thirteen years, he'd been fighting the guilt, never knowing if the decision he'd made that fateful night had been the right one. Every time he looked at Houston, he was reminded of the actions he'd taken and questioned his own motives for doing what he had done.

Dallas had always assumed Houston was self-conscious about his disfigurement, had distanced himself from Dallas because Dallas had kept his word. He hadn't let him die.

Now, he wondered if whatever demons had forced Houston off his horse to face those outlaws alone were also responsible for his preferring solitude over the company of others.

From his pocket, Dallas removed the watch Amelia had given him, held it to his ear, and shook it vigorously. He could hear the water swirling inside. He couldn't repair the token of her affection, he couldn't force Houston to claim her, but he could do all in his power to love her as she should be loved.

Deep, gut-wrenching sobs interrupted Dallas's thoughts. He walked to the edge of the porch and glanced around the side of the house.

Austin sat on the ground, his arms folded over his drawn-up knees, his head resting on his arms, his shoulders shaking with the force of his grief.

Dallas had never seen a man cry. His father had raised him to believe that tears were the domain of women, certainly not something a man ever let slide down his face. Awkward and out of his element, he approached Austin. "Austin?"

Austin jerked his head up. In the moonlight, Dallas could see tears streaming along Austin's cheeks, pooling around his mouth.

"Houston is gonna die, ain't he?"

Dallas dropped to his haunches. "I doubt it. He doesn't like to get on Amelia's bad side, and he'd certainly do that if he died."

Roughly, Austin rubbed his hand beneath his nose. "It's my fault."

"Don't go thinking that."

Austin scrambled to his feet. "But it's true. If you look through those horses you brought back, you'll find Houston's stallion. They stole him from me."

Dallas slowly brought himself to his feet. "But you said—"

"I lied! They snuck up on me, and I was ashamed that I let them do it, that I didn't try and stop them from taking the horse. If I'd a-told the truth—"

"Stop it!" Dallas roared. "Stop it. You don't know what would have happened if you'd told the truth. It might have made no difference at all." He held up a hand to stop his brother's protest. "I'm not gonna say that you should have lied because, by God, you should have told us the truth. But you can't let what happened eat at you. It's done." He sliced his hand through the air. "It's done."

Just like his marriage to Amelia. It was done.

Austin sniffed. "Shouldn't you punish me or something?"

Dallas shook his head. "You're nearly a man now. No man goes through life doing everything right. A man who wallows in his mistakes is destined to have a miserable life. Learn from what you did and become a better man because of it."

Austin straightened his shoulders. "I will. I won't let you or Houston down again."

"Good. Now see after those horses."

"Yes, sir."

"Dallas!"

Amelia's cry had Dallas charging around the corner of the house and bursting through the door, Austin hot on his heels. His heart slammed against his ribs at the panic reflected in her eyes.

"Houston started thrashing, calling for you. He's going to tear open his wound."

"God damn it. Austin, fetch me a rope." He strode to the bed and grabbed one of Houston's flailing arms. "Be still, God damn it."

Houston latched onto his shirt, pulling him down. "Dallas, I'm scared."

Dallas would have sworn he was meeting the gaze of a fifteen-year-old boy. "Don't be," he rasped. "I won't let nothing happen to you."

"Swear?"

Dallas swallowed hard. "Give you my word."

Houston loosened his hold and sank back into oblivion.

Austin burst through the door. "I got the rope."

"We don't need it now," Dallas said quietly. He lifted his gaze to Amelia's.

"You were both back at the war," she said softly.

"The night before he was wounded. You think he would have asked for my word if he had known my keeping it would give him the life he's had all these years?"

"You should ask him. You might be surprised by what he thinks."

"I'd rather not know."

It was near midnight when Amelia shook Dallas's shoulder to wake him. "He's shaking, and I can't find any more blankets."

Dallas looked toward the bed. Shaking? Houston was trembling as though someone had thrown him into an icy river. "Hell, he hasn't a goddamn thing around here."

He bolted out of the chair and nudged Austin's foot. Disoriented, Austin opened his eyes and stared at him.

" 'Ride home and gather up all the blankets you can. I'll get some wood, build up the fire, and see if we can warm him that way."

He followed Austin out the door and headed for the wood pile. Thank God, Houston had wood. The man's Spartan life was starting to wear thin.

He gathered into his arms as much wood as he could carry and stormed back toward the house. He shoved open the door, stepped inside, and came to a dead stop.

Houston was no longer trembling. He lay perfectly still, his face a reflection of contentment.

He no longer needed a fire or blankets for warmth. Amelia, curled against his side asleep, was giving him all the warmth he needed.

Amelia awoke drenched in sweat, Houston's sweat. A blanket had been tucked around her. Lifting her head, she searched the room until her gaze fell on Dallas as he sat in the shadows beside the bed.

"He was cold," she stammered. "I couldn't get him to stop trembling."

"I know."

She moved the blanket aside and climbed out of the bed. "I think his fever's breaking."

"Good. I'll get you some fresh water. He'll be thirsty."

Ignoring her own sweaty discomfort, Amelia began to wipe the beaded sweat from Houston's body. Not until he grabbed her wrist did she realize he was awake. She smiled softly. "You gave us quite a scare."

"Dallas?"

"He's fine."

"Horses?"

"Austin's been taking care of them."

"I . . ."

She watched him swallow. "Let me get you some water."

He nodded slightly. Turning, she took the tin cup Dallas was holding, slipped her hand beneath Houston's head, and touched the cup to his lips. "Drink slowly," she ordered although in his weakened state, she didn't know if he had much of a choice.

When he had drained the cup dry, she set it aside and took his hand. His Adam's apple bobbed. "I can smell you," he croaked.

She trailed her fingers along his brow. "Austin brought the blankets from my bed."

"What do you wear that makes you smell so sweet?"

"Magnolias. They grew on our plantation."

A corner of his mouth crooked up. "Maggie. That's a good name for a girl. Name your daughter Maggie." His eye drifted closed.

"I will," she whispered in a broken voice.

She felt a strong hand with long fingers come to rest on her shoulder. She glanced up at Dallas. He shifted his hand slightly and squeezed her neck. She rubbed her cheek against his roughened hand. "I think the worst is over," she said.

"He'll be weak for a while and probably ornery as a bear. I'm tired of feeling useless. I need to get back to the ranch and take care of business."

She rose from the bed. "You weren't useless. I couldn't have managed without you and Austin."

He touched her cheek. "I think you would have managed just fine. If you want to stay here until he regains his strength, I'll come by and check on you from time to time."

"I'd like to do that, if you don't mind."

He brushed his lips across her forehead. "Just get him strong enough to realize those dreams he has. I didn't even know he had any."

Houston lay in that damn bed for two long days trying to regain his strength just enough so he could crawl to the table. He wished to God he hadn't told Amelia that he loved her before he'd jumped off the horse, but at the time he'd figured it was safe to reveal his heart because he didn't think he had a snowball's chance in hell of surviving.

He wished to God he'd kept his mouth shut when Amelia shaved

him without meeting his gaze and fed him without asking him one goddamn question.

He wished he'd kept the words to himself when she prepared herself
for bed each evening in silence. She'd perch her hand mirror against a
bowl on the table, separate the strands of her braid, and slowly brush
her hair until it glistened in the firelight from the hearth. She'd weave
the strands back together, then check the flame in the lantern, and without so much as a "sleep well," she'd retire for the night . . . curling up on
a pallet on the floor.

He'd watch her in the hours past midnight and listen to her soft,
even breathing. He wanted her in his bed, beside him, in his arms.

But he'd given up the right to ever hold her again—forever. Because
he'd been afraid. As always, because he'd been afraid.

And now she hated him. Not for the cowardice he'd shown thirteen
years before when he'd been a boy, but for the cowardice he'd shown
now, as a man.

Ignoring the pain in his shoulder, the weakness in his knees, Houston crawled out of bed and reached for the clothes Amelia had left on
the table. He'd slipped into his trousers and was awkwardly buttoning
his shirt when she stepped into his house, carrying a bucket of water.
She set the bucket down, walked across the room, brushed his hands
aside, and buttoned his shirt.

"You ever gonna look at me or talk to me again?" he asked.

"It's harder now. I wish you hadn't said what you did before you
leapt from the horse."

"Yeah, so do I, but I didn't think a man should die without ever having said the words."

"So it's only because I was there that you spoke the words to me.
Any woman would have done," she said softly, meeting his gaze only for
the instant that a flame might flicker.

He slipped his finger beneath her chin and tilted her face. "No. I was
more afraid that I wouldn't be able to stop the men, and you'd die without ever knowing that I loved you."

She balled up her fists, tears welling in her eyes. "Damn you. Damn
you for telling me now, when it's too late."

"It was always too late for us, Amelia. You promised yourself to Dallas. He's not a man who gives up what belongs to him."

"What belongs to him? You think if I lift up my skirt, you'll find his brand on my backside? I'm not a possession, Houston. I'm not something to be owned."

"You're his wife."

"Yes, now I'm his wife. And do you know what I discovered? That you lied to me. You told me that my needs were based on lust. I won't deny that a part of that was true, but the greater part of my needs came from the love I held for you. I don't feel those needs when Dallas touches me. I just feel empty."

Her words tore through him. He knew the emptiness that came from being with someone you didn't love. He had thought Dallas would have the power to hold the emptiness at bay for her.

She suddenly laughed mirthlessly. "On the other hand, I suppose I should be grateful. I would have hated being married to a man as vain as you are."

"Vain? You think I'm vain?"

She spun around, waving her hand in a circle. "You don't have a single mirror in this whole house. You hide your face beneath the shadows of your hat."

"You think I don't have mirrors because of this?" he asked, dragging his hand down the left side of his face.

She nodded, her movements jerky.

He pointed to his right eye. " 'It's this I don't want to see. When I meet my gaze, I see the man who lives inside here." He hit his chest, grimacing as the pain shot through his shoulder. "What's inside here is uglier than anything you're looking at right now."

"You don't know the man who lives inside of you," she said angrily. "You only know the boy, the fifteen-year-old boy who ran. You won't let him go; you won't let him grow up! You see yourself as a coward because you don't meet your reflection in the mirror. You don't see the man you've become, you only see the boy you were. You jumped off the back of that horse because you thought you had something to prove—"

"I jumped off that horse because I was afraid. Afraid Dallas couldn't stop those men, afraid you'd be killed. Every decision I make in life is based on fear. The thought of you dying scared me more than the thought of me dying. That's why I jumped. I always take the coward's way."

She shook her head sadly. "The coward's way. You held me through a storm that could have easily killed us both; we fought a raging river; we captured wild mustangs—"

"I wouldn't have done any of those things if you hadn't been by my side."

"Yes, you would have. Because that's the man you've become. You just don't know yourself as I do. *Dare* to look in a mirror sometime, and you'll see the man I grew to love."

The door opened. Amelia jumped back, swiping the tears from her cheeks. Houston met Dallas's gaze as he walked into the house, Austin in his wake.

"You're out of bed," Dallas said, his gaze shifting between Houston and Amelia.

Houston nodded, searching for his voice. "Yeah, I'm feeling stronger."

"Then you won't mind if I take Amelia home."

"No, no, I don't mind at all. She's your wife. You should take her home."

"Then I'll do that." He held out his hand.

Amelia slipped her hand into Dallas's, and Houston felt as though a herd of mustangs had stampeded over his heart.

When the couple closed the door behind them, Houston sank to the bed.

"You sure you're feeling all right?" Austin asked.

"Yeah."

Austin scraped the chair across the floor, turned it, and straddled it, crossing his arms over the back. "I owe you an apology for Black Thunder."

"We've already discussed this. We'll get a new stallion in the spring."

Austin shook his head. "You must not have taken a good look at those horses in the canyon, the ones those horse thieves had."

"No, I was only thinking about Amelia and getting her out of there."

"Black Thunder was there. Dallas brought him back. I put him in his pen."

Houston rubbed his shoulder, the ache intensifying. "What do you mean he was there and now he's here? You shot him."

"Nope, I lied."

Houston stared at his brother, wondering when he'd stopped being a boy. Austin swallowed.

'The thieves took me by surprise and stole Black Thunder. I was ashamed that I didn't try and stop them. It didn't matter that there was six of them and only one of me or that they had their guns out and I didn't. I thought I'd let you down. Figured you'd never trust me again if you knew what had happened. So I lied. And because I lied, you got shot."

"I didn't get shot because you lied—"

"If I'd told the truth, you would have gone after them. They never would have taken Amelia."

"We don't know that. You can't start second-guessing what might have happened."

"Dallas said the same thing, but I needed to hear it from you."

"Well, now you've heard it, so take Black Thunder and head on back to the ranch."

"Take Black Thunder?"

"Yep, he's yours. I'd like to borrow him from time to time, of course, but he belongs to you."

"Why?"

Houston leaned forward. "Because I don't want you spending the rest of your life thinking I blame you for what happened. It wasn't your fault."

Austin laughed. "You don't have to give me the horse. Dallas told me that a man who wallows in his regrets lives a miserable life. I got a dream that I want to hold in my hand. I ain't planning on doing any wallowing."

"Take the horse, anyway."

Austin stood. "All right, I will." He walked to the door and stopped, his hand on the latch. He gazed back over his shoulder. "That woman you love . . . Do I know her?"

Houston forced himself to meet his brother's gaze. The boy only knew one woman, if he didn't count the whores in Dusty Flats. "Yeah, you do."

"She never left your side, not for one minute."

"She should have."

"Well, I'm not learned in these matters, but I'd like to think if a woman ever loved me as much as that one loves you . . . I'd crawl through hell to be by her side."

Chapter 20

❧

HOUSTON SAT AT his table, running his fingers back and forth over the cloth Amelia had embroidered for Dallas, a gift he'd kept for himself.

He'd tried to sleep after Austin left, but Amelia was still here with him. He could smell her sweet magnolia scent filling his house, filling his bed.

He wondered how long it would be before her fragrance faded, before he became like Cookie, living on memories until they became so worn with the years that they would be discarded carelessly as hand-me-downs. Houston had already spent thirteen years wallowing in the regrets of his youth. He had a lifetime ahead of him to flounder in his latest regrets.

Whether intentional or not, she'd left her mirror on the table, glass side down.

He could see her so clearly, holding the mirror, smiling at her reflection. How simple an action, how difficult a step after all these years. The rippling waters of a pond always gave a distorted image with no depth, no clarity.

A mirror would give a clearer reflection and if he looked deeply enough, it would drag him back into the past. If he looked long enough, perhaps it would set him free.

Houston's mouth grew dry as his gaze shifted between the mirror and the flowers she had sewn with delicate stitches and pink thread.

With a trembling hand, he wrapped his fingers around the handle of the mirror, lifted it from the table, and held it before him.

In the fading evening light, Amelia stood on the balcony and pulled her shawl more closely around her. Somewhere, out there, where the wind blew free and wild mustangs surrendered their freedom, lived a man with the heart of a fifteen-year-old boy.

How in God's name had Houston's mother allowed her husband to take her sons off to war? How did any woman let her son go off to war, regardless of his age?

The war had claimed so many boys, even those it hadn't killed. She wondered how differently her journey with Houston might have ended if he hadn't marched onto a field of battle before he'd ever shaved.

The hairs on the nape of her neck prickled as the cool breeze rushed past. She heard a small hushed movement and turned to see Dallas leaning against the wall, studying her, his gaze intense, penetrating.

He needed only one step to span the distance separating them. He touched his knuckles to her cheek, and she couldn't stop herself from stiffening. His hand fell to his side. "I've never forced a woman. I'm not going to start with my wife."

Reaching out, she wrapped her hand around his and shook her head slightly. "You won't have to force me."

He eased closer until only a whisper's breath separated their bodies. "Do you love Houston?"

"I'm your wife."

"I know whose wife you are. I'm asking if you love Houston."

The tears flooded her eyes. She squeezed them shut, battling the river of sorrow. "Once." She opened her eyes and met his gaze.

"Why did you marry me?"

She took a deep breath. "I had nothing in Georgia. No home, no family. You offered me a chance to have a home, a family, and a dream."

"In other words, I asked and Houston didn't."

She gave him a tremulous smile. "You asked. He didn't."

He held out his arms. With quiet acceptance, she laid her head against his chest as he enfolded her in his strong embrace. She cared for him. She liked him. Perhaps, in time, her heart would flutter when he neared, her skin would tingle when he touched her, and her toes would curl when he kissed her.

He slipped his finger beneath her chin, tilted her face, and brushed his lips over hers before lifting her into his arms and carrying her into their bedroom.

Dallas's warm mouth settled over hers as she sank into the bed. His kiss was . . . nice. His hand cradled her breast. Nice. He groaned and laid his body over hers. Lean, strong . . . nice.

The door burst open and banged against the wall. Dallas came off her like a fired bullet. He grabbed his revolver out of the holster dangling from the bedpost and put himself between her and the door, his breathing heavy. "What is it?"

Amelia scooted back against the headboard, pressing her hand above her beating heart, her breath catching in her throat.

She peered around Dallas. Houston stood in the doorway, his legs spread wide. He stared at his brother. "I need to talk to you."

Dallas slipped his gun back into his holster and wrapped his hand around the bedpost, his knuckles turning white as he faced his brother. "Can't it wait until morning?"

"No." Houston's gaze shot to Amelia, then back to Dallas. "No, it can't."

Dallas tunneled his fingers through his hair and glanced at Amelia. "Will you excuse me?"

She could do little more than nod.

Dallas stood before the window in his office, the whiskey he'd poured himself forgotten as he watched the woman standing beside the corral Austin had made the men rebuild. Dallas had known she'd slip out of the house and go to the corral. He wondered how long it would be before he knew her as well as Houston did. The palomino approached, nudged her arm, and she pressed her face against the mare's neck.

He could hear Houston pacing behind him. For a man who had wanted to talk so desperately, he'd suddenly grown eerily quiet.

Dallas turned and, for the first time in years, didn't flinch when he met his brother's gaze. "You should sit down before you fall down."

Houston brought his pacing to a halt and held onto the back of a chair. "I can stand."

"You wanted to talk?"

Houston nodded, his fingers tightening their hold on the leather. "I'm in love with Amelia."

"And when did you decide this?"

"It just came over me somewhere between Fort Worth and here."

Dallas strode across the room and threw his glass of whiskey into the hearth. The shattering glass did nothing to improve his mood. "Then we've got ourselves one hell of a situation here." He spun around. "Why in God's name didn't you say something before we were married?"

"Because I thought she deserved better than a coward."

Dallas felt as though Houston had just punched him in the gut. "What?"

"She's got more courage in her little finger than I've got in my whole body. I figured she deserved someone who didn't run from his own shadow."

"What are you talking about?"

Houston surged across the room and slapped his hands on the desk. "What? After all these years, you want me to say to your face what you know in your heart? I'm a coward. A worthless, no-account excuse for a man. You know it, I know it. That's why you can't stomach the sight of me. If I could undo what I did, I would. But I can't. God knows I try every night when I go to sleep, reliving that day, wishing I'd followed like I should have, but when I wake up the past remains as it was."

"You sound like Pa."

Houston dropped into the chair, closed his eye, and rubbed his brow. "I don't expect you to ever forgive me for killing him. Hell, I haven't forgiven myself."

"You think I hold you accountable for Pa's death?"

Houston lifted his despair-filled gaze. "Figured that was why you couldn't stand to look at me. Because you knew I'd killed him. If I'd had any backbone, I'd have struck out on my own, spared you the sight of me—"

"Oh, Jesus." Dallas sank into his chair and buried his face in his hands. "Oh, dear Lord." Then he threw his head back and laughed, a dry humorless laugh. "I thought you avoided me because you regretted what I'd done."

"What in the hell did you do?"

"I played God."

The night following a battle was always the worst. The cries of wounded men echoed through the darkness, the stench of blood thickened the air.

Dallas stepped over a corpse and knelt beside a young soldier who was holding nothing but the torso of his best friend. "Jimmy?"

Jimmy looked at him blankly. "Can't find his legs. He'd a hated bein' buried without his legs."

"I'll help you look for his legs after I find Houston. You seen him?"

Jimmy wiped a bloody hand over his tear streaked face before pointing his finger. "They're putting the dead over yonder."

Stacking them like cords of wood, one body on top of the other. Dallas had found his pa there, but he couldn't think about that now, had to ignore the pain knifing through his heart.

"Houston's not there."

"Did you check the hospital tent?"

"Yep, he wasn't there, either."

Jimmy pointed a finger. "They left the dying over there."

Dallas's stomach tightened, and his jaw tingled. Lord, he wanted to throw up, but not here, not in front of a soldier. He placed his hand on the man's shoulder. "We'll whip them Yankees tomorrow."

He struggled to his feet and wove his way among the dead who had yet to be moved, until the moaning hovering around him grew louder. So many men lay in the clearing. He might have never found Houston if he hadn't spotted the battered drum.

He knelt beside his brother. Houston was a bloody mess, lying so still, so pale even in the moonlight. Dallas worked the drum away from his brother and threw it with all his strength and pent-up anger into the nearby brush. He slipped his arms beneath Houston's still form and struggled to his feet. He ignored the cries of men wanting water, wanting help as he wended his way toward the hospital tent.

No light burned inside. Using his shoulder, he nudged the tent flap back. The moonlight spilled inside. He judged the distance to the table, walked inside, and laid his brother on the table in the darkness as the tent flap fell back into place.

Houston made no sound. Dallas went outside and quickly returned carrying a lantern. He hung it on a beam and studied his brother in its golden haze. Houston's breathing was shallow, his bloodied chest barely rising as he took in air. The anger swelled within Dallas, and he stormed out of the tent.

He raced across the compound, and without ceremony, barged into a physician's tent. "Dr. Barnes, I got a man that needs tending." He shook the sleeping man. "I got a man that needs tending!"

The doctor opened his eyes and released a weary sigh. He was still dressed, blood splattered over his clothes. Sitting up, he dropped his feet to the ground. "Where is he?"

"In the hospital tent. We need to hurry."

Dr. Barnes rubbed his face before rising to his feet. "Let's go."

He didn't walk fast enough to suit Dallas, but at least he was coming. Dallas threw back the tent flap and hurried to his brother's side. Houston hadn't moved, but he was still breathing. Dr. Barnes moved around to the other side of the table.

"Dear God."

"I need you to fix him," Dallas said.

Dr. Barnes lifted his weary gaze. "Son, he's better off dead."

"I gave him my word I wouldn't let him die."

Dr. Barnes shook his head, regret filling his eyes. "I've spent my time saving men with facial wounds like this, only to have them kill themselves once they're strong enough. Those that don't kill themselves end up living alone, not wanting people to see them." He placed his hand on Houston's brow. "I won't be doing him a favor if I tend his other wounds. My time would be better spent sleeping so I'll have the strength to save those worth saving tomorrow."

Dallas pulled his revolver from its holster.

"I gave him my word that I wouldn't let him die. I've never gone back on my word." He leveled his gun at the center of the doctor's chest. "I'm givin' you my word now that if he dies, you'll be keepin' him company in heaven."

"Don't do this, son."

"I ain't your son."

"I know it's hard to let go of those we love, especially when they're so young, but I give you my word that death is better for him."

"I ain't interested in your word. I'm only interested in mine. Now, fix him."

In resignation, the doctor sighed, reached behind him, picked up a pair of scissors, and began to cut away what remained of Houston's gray jacket. Stoically, Dallas stood and watched as the doctor worked. Two hours. Two long torturous hours of staring at his brother's mutilated flesh.

"I've done all I can do," Dr. Barnes said as he finished wrapping the last bandage around Houston's' head. "It's up to him now whether he lives or dies."

Dallas lowered his shaking hand. "I appreciate what you did."

"I guarantee you that he won't appreciate it at all. In years to come when you look at his face, you remember the night you played God."

"He was right," Dallas said with a heavy sigh. "I had to leave, go with my company, but when I came back, you weren't smiling. You wouldn't talk to me. When we were traveling home, you kept to yourself, hugging the shadows if we stopped in a town. I figured you wished I'd let you die. When I built the house for Amelia, you didn't want to live here, built yourself your own place. Figured you wanted nothing to do with me."

Houston could barely speak for the emotions clogging his throat. "I thought you wouldn't look at me because you knew I was a coward. I ran. If I hadn't run, Pa wouldn't have been killed."

"Sweet Lord, Houston, you didn't even have a gun to defend yourself, just a drum. If a soldier couldn't kill the man giving the orders, he'd do all in his power to silence the messenger. You were the messenger. I told Pa to give you a rifle, but he wanted someone to beat out his orders. You were a boy. Pa had no right to enlist you. I told him not to, but he wouldn't listen."

"You weren't much older."

"Not in years, but in temperament. I wanted to go. I wanted the glory that came with war. Only I discovered glory doesn't come with destruction. I thought I'd find it here, taming the land, building an empire, creating a legacy that I could hand down to my son."

Dallas's son. The foundation of his dream. Dallas had saved Houston's life—twice—and now Houston was asking him to sacrifice a portion of his dream so Houston could find happiness. "That brings us back to Amelia," Houston said quietly.

"Yeah, it does." Dallas shoved himself away from the desk and walked to the window.

Houston's chest ached more than it had when shrapnel had cut through it. He rose and joined his brother. "I owe you for keeping your word and not letting me die. The doctor was wrong. I never regretted that I'd lived. I only regretted that Pa didn't."

Dallas shook his head. "He had no right going after you. He had men to command. His place was to lead them. He wanted to shape you into the man he thought you ought to be. A battlefield wasn't the place to do it."

"You don't blame me at all?"

Dallas glanced at him. "It was his decision to run after you, stupid as it was. I loved him, Houston. I admired his strengths, but he wasn't perfect."

"I loved him, too," Houston said, for the first time realizing that he had indeed loved his father. "I just couldn't be what he wanted me to be."

"No fault in that. God help me, I'm his mirror image." Dallas looked back toward the corral at the woman still standing with the moonlight wreathed around her. He had never expected her to love him. He was too much like his father, a hard man to love, not truly appreciated until he was gone. Neither did he relish the thought of taking a woman to his bed, knowing she was thinking of another. Especially if that man was Houston.

"Give her a divorce," Houston said. "I swear to God I won't touch her for a month, not until she knows for sure whether or not she's carrying your son."

Dallas raised a brow. "It's highly unlikely that she's carrying my son, since we are constantly interrupted."

"Then give her an annulment."

"What in God's name makes you think she wants to marry you? You stood in my parlor and held your peace. You don't think that might have broken her heart?"

"She has every right to hate me, but at least let me ask her."

Guilt, misunderstandings, and regrets had given Houston thirteen years of solitude. Now, Houston had the opportunity to receive the love of a woman, something Dallas would never have. Any woman could give Dallas the son he wanted, but only Amelia had returned to Houston his smiles and laughter.

"I'll leave the decision up to Amelia," Dallas said quietly. "Let me talk to her. If she wants an annulment, I'll give her one. If she wants to marry you . . . I'll hold my peace."

A full moon graced the heavens, its light illuminating Dallas's way as he approached the corral. Valiant skittered away to the other side, but the woman remained, gazing into the darkness beyond the corral.

Dallas crossed his arms over the railing. "That's a beautiful horse."

"Yes, she is."

"Houston has the patience of Job when it comes to horses."

"Yes, he does."

"You know what I was thinking about when I was walking out here?"

Shaking her head, she glanced at him.

"I was thinking about the last time I heard Houston laugh. We'd been swimming in the creek. I told him to get out, and while I was dressing, he hid in the shadows. When I looked up, I couldn't see him. I thought he'd drowned. Made a fool of myself, thrashing through that water, looking for him. He laughed so hard I thought he'd bust a gut."

She smiled softly. "I can't imagine that."

"No, I don't imagine you can. The next day, our pa went to war, dragging us along with him. I never heard Houston laugh again until the first night you were here. Fifteen years is a hell of a long time for a man not to laugh."

He trailed his finger along her cheek. "I don't need love, Amelia, but I think you do, and if you find it with a man who dreams of raising horses, know that you do so with my blessing."

Tears welled in her eyes, and a tremulous smile curved her lips. "I think if you'd come to Fort Worth to fetch me, I might have fallen in love with you."

He smiled warmly. "I'd think the fates had conspired against us if I didn't believe that we shape our own destiny. In my office is a man who wants to make you part of his destiny. I think it would be worth your time to listen to what he has to say."

Houston sat in the chair, his elbows on his thighs, his shoulder aching unmercifully. He ran Amelia's cloth through his fingers, over and over. He knew every silken strand, every knot, every loop. It was all he'd have of her if she didn't come, and he had a feeling she wasn't going to come.

"Dallas said you wanted to talk with me."

He shot out of the chair at the sound of her gentle voice. He wadded up her cloth and stuffed it into his duster pocket. "Yeah, I did." He pulled her mirror out of his other pocket. "You left your mirror on my table." He extended it toward her.

"You can keep it," she said quietly. "We have lots of mirrors here."

"I'll keep it, then."

"Good. I'm glad."

He'd never rushed headlong into a battle, but he figured this time, it might be the best approach. "I spent a lot of time studying it. The back is real pretty with all the gold carving. Took me about an hour to gather up the courage to turn it over and look at the other side."

"And what did you see?"

"A man who loves you more than life itself."

Closing her eyes, she dropped her chin to her chest.

"I wouldn't blame you if you hated me. I haven't held your feelings as precious as I should have."

"I don't hate you," she whispered hoarsely. "I tried to, but I can't."

"Dallas is willing to give you an annulment."

Damn, the words were as ugly as his face, not at all what she deserved. He'd consider himself the wealthiest man in the world if he only possessed the words he thought she longed to hear, words worthy of her. He thought he could see a tear glistening in the corner of her eye. "Damn it, woman, look at me."

Slowly, she lifted her head. The sight of the tears welling in her eyes hurt more than the wound healing in his shoulder.

"I've had plenty of moments in my life when I've been scared, but I swear to you that I've never been as scared as I am right now. I'm afraid you won't take Dallas up on his offer for an annulment . . . and I'll have nothing in my life but the emptiness that was there before you stepped off that train in Fort Worth. I wouldn't blame you for staying with him. God knows I haven't done right by you—" He slammed his eye shut. "Ah, hell, this isn't what I wanted to say."

He slipped the mirror back into his pocket and sank down into the chair. He'd never felt so tired in his life. She rushed forward and knelt beside him.

"Are you bleeding?"

"No. Just need a moment to gather my strength."

"You shouldn't have come here tonight. You should have stayed in bed—"

"I couldn't. Every time I took a breath, I smelled you." He wrapped his hand around hers, pressed a kiss to the heart of her palm, and held her gaze. "I've got a one-room cabin, a few horses, and a dream that's so small it won't even cover your palm. But it sure seems a lot bigger when you're beside me."

The moonlight streaming through the window shimmered off the tears trailing along her cheeks. "I've always wanted a dream that I could hold in the palm of my hand," she said quietly.

His heart slammed against his chest, and all the things he'd feared melted away. "I want you beside me until the day I die, Amelia. If you'll have me . . . as your husband."

She smiled softly. "I'll take a question."

"What?"

She raised a delicate brow. "A question."

He swallowed hard, took her hands, and brought them to his lips. "Will you marry me?"

"Yes."

Joy overflowed within his heart, creating a sunrise bathed in love. "I'll take a dare," he rasped.

"Kiss me as though you love me."

"Woman, don't you know that I've always kissed you that way?"

Guiding her onto his lap, he took her into his arms and lowered his mouth to hers, kissing her tenderly, this woman of courage who would soon become his wife.

Chapter 21

⁓

THEY WAITED UNTIL spring, when the wildflowers formed a bright multicolored carpet over the plains.

Amelia stood beside the springs, listening to the babble of the water as it flowed over the moss covered rocks. Her dress of white lace and silk whispered in the breeze, a gift from Houston, one of many he'd brought her from Fort Worth. A gift to capture her memories.

In the years to come, she knew she would take it from the cedar chest, look upon it with fondness, and remember the first of the happiest days of her life.

She had intertwined her arm through Houston's, just as their lives would forever be joined. No brand would emblazon their union. Only the words they exchanged today.

She couldn't take her eyes off Houston as he stood beside her in his new brown jacket and woolen trousers. She thought he more closely resembled a banker than a man who spent the best part of his day with horses . . . and soon she hoped, the best part of his night with her.

The even, straight brim of his new broad-brimmed hat made her smile, and she wondered how long it would be before old habits crumpled it. Around the brim, he wore her linen of long ago, with its delicate embroidered flowers, faded and frayed. Through the eyes of her heart, she knew she'd never seen a more handsome man.

Reverend Tucker's melodious voice rang out as he once again spoke the words he'd said the previous autumn. Dallas stood solemnly beside her, and she wondered briefly if he was remembering the day she had become his wife or if he was mentally designing the layout of the town he planned to build. She hoped he was thinking of his town, and that it would bring him a wife.

Austin stood on the other side of Houston, smiling broadly, his sparkling blue eyes competing in beauty with the pond as the sun reflected off the rippling waters.

"If anyone knows of any reason why these two should not be joined in holy matrimony, let him speak now or forever"—Reverend Tucker held the gazes of the three men in attendance for the space of a heartbeat—"and I do mean *forever* hold his peace."

Amelia caught her breath and waited. She knew Dallas had the right to object. A part of her was saddened with the knowledge that she would not give him the son he desperately longed for; a corner of her heart would always be reserved for the memories of the short time that she had been his fiancée, and then his wife. And her love for him would grow over the years as he'd predicted, only it would be the love of a sister toward her brother.

Reverend Tucker cleared his throat. Amelia released her breath and repeated the vows she'd said once before, her gaze never leaving Houston's.

Reverend Tucker shifted his attention to Houston. "And if you'll repeat after me—"

"She's had those words given to her before," Houston said gruffly. "She deserves better than hand-me-downs. I've got my own words to say."

Lifting a brow, Reverend Tucker chuckled low. "Well, I've never heard my words referred to as hand-me-downs, but I suppose they are. I have no objection to you giving your own vows as long as your bride doesn't. Amelia?"

"I have no objections," she said, her heart thrumming with the rhythm of the falls. She imagined that they still carried the sound of Houston's laughter mingling with hers, and after today they would forever echo their vows.

Reaching around her, Houston cupped her elbow, tugging slightly until she faced him completely. He swept his hat from his head, the shadows retreating to reveal the craggy left side, the perfect right side that came together to form the face she loved.

He took the hand that wasn't holding the bouquet of wildflowers and stared at it, holding it so tightly that she thought he might crack her bones. Then his hold gentled. He slipped a gold ring onto her finger and lifted his gaze to hers.

"I'm not a brave man; I'll never be a hero, but I love you more than life itself, and I will until the day I die. With you by my side, I'm a better man than I've ever been alone. I'm scared to death that I'll let you down, but I won't run this time. I'll stand firm and face the challenge and work hard to see that you never have any regrets. You told me once that you wanted to share a corner of my dream. Without you, Amelia, I have no dream. With you, I have everything I could ever dream of wanting."

Tears burned her eyes as he glanced back at the preacher. "I'm done."

Reverend Tucker smiled. "In that case, I pronounce you husband and wife. With my blessing, you may kiss the bride."

Houston cradled her cheek, his gaze lovingly roaming over her features. "I love you, Amelia Carson Leigh," he said huskily as he lowered his lips to hers, sealing the vows with a sweet tender kiss, filled with the promise of tomorrow.

When he ended the kiss, she pressed her cheek against his chest, listening to the steady rhythm of his heart, gathering her happiness around her before she stepped away to face her brother by marriage.

Taking her hand in his, Dallas smiled warmly. "I never thought you'd look prettier than you did the day you married me, but you sure look prettier today. You wear love well, Amelia."

"I hope to say the same to you someday."

"That I look pretty?"

Standing on the tips of her toes, she brushed her lips over his. "That you wear love well."

"Don't hold your breath on that one," he teased.

"You could always order another bride," Houston suggested.

"Hell, no. I'll get my town built, and women will start flocking out here. Then I'll make a selection."

"Love isn't always that practical," Houston said.

"I'm not looking for love. I'm looking for a wife who'll give me a son." He glanced over Amelia's shoulder. "I'll build you a church in my town, Preacher, so I don't have to send my men chasing after you every time I need you."

"You do that, Mr. Leigh," Reverend Tucker said as he slipped his Bible into his coat pocket. "Meanwhile, I think my job is done here so I'm gonna get back to looking for a lost soul." He shook hands with the men and brushed a kiss against Amelia's cheek. "You be happy, now."

"I will."

He mounted a black stallion, and with little more than a gentle kick to the horse's sides, sent it into a flying gallop.

Dallas cleared his throat. "Well, reckon Austin and I ought to head back to the ranch."

"I need to give Amelia her gift first," Austin said. He walked over to his horse and returned carrying his violin. He sat on a boulder, stretched out one leg, worked the heel of his other boot into a crack in the rock, and rested the violin on his shoulder. "The first time I ever saw you, Amelia . . . well, this is what I heard in my heart."

The music began softly, little more than a soughing sigh. Amelia felt a touch on her shoulder and glanced up at her husband.

"Your wedding gift from me," he said as he stepped back and held out his arms. "A waltz."

Her eyes widened. "I didn't think you danced."

"Mimi St. Claire, proprietor and expert dressmaker, happens to give dancin' lessons." He reddened. "They cost more than the wedding dress."

"I love the wedding dress." She smiled as she stepped into his embrace, and they began to sway in rhythm to the music.

The lyrical strains of the violin wove around the falls, through the breeze, kissing the petals of wildflowers. They rose in crescendo, grand, beautiful, and bold, before drifting into silence.

Amelia and Houston waltzed while Austin tucked his violin under his arm. They waltzed after Dallas and Austin mounted their horses and rode away.

They waltzed until twilight, until it was time to go home.

The cabin was dark except for the fire burning lazily in the hearth. Houston had shoved the table to one side of the room and moved the bed closer to the hearth.

Amelia had imagined this night a hundred times since the evening Houston had asked her to marry him. She'd anticipated it, longed for it, but as she gazed at her full reflection in the cheval glass, she had a feeling her imaginings would pale in comparison to all this night would bring.

Her husband stood behind her, slowly releasing the buttons of her wedding dress. He parted the material and placed a kiss on her nape.

He met and held her gaze in the mirror, his knuckles brushing along either side of her throat. "You haven't asked me a question all evening."

"I can't think of anything I need answered right now."

"You can't think of anything?"

She rubbed her cheek against his hand. "I'm having a hard time thinking of anything to say, much less to ask."

"I have a lot of questions that need answering."

He nibbled on her earlobe and trailed his tongue along the shell of her ear. She thought she might melt to the floor. "You do?"

"Mmmm-huh. I'd like to watch a shadow show without the canvas between us."

"It wouldn't be a shadow show without the canvas."

He smiled, one side of his mouth moving more than the other. "Exactly, but a lot of my questions sure would be answered without me having to ask them."

He stepped back and sat on the edge of the bed. She pivoted slowly and angled her chin. "What's good for the goose—"

"Understood."

Smiling serenely, she tugged first on one sleeve and then the other, watching as her husband's gaze darkened. The gown pooled at her feet, and she stepped over it, stepped nearer to him. Slowly she removed her undergarments. Her husband swallowed hard, his lips parted slightly, and he leaned forward.

Standing before him with nothing but the air surrounding her flesh, she was surprised she felt no self-consciousness. She cupped her breasts. "You must have thought me terribly wanton the first time you saw me do this."

"I didn't think anything at all," he rasped as he came to his feet. He shrugged out of his jacket, tore his shirt over his head, and removed his trousers in one fluid movement. Then he was standing before her, cradling her cheek. "If you hadn't asked me questions, I think I might have made that whole journey without a clear thought in my head. The first time I saw you, I couldn't think of anything to say."

She trailed her fingers over his chest, admiring every aspect of his hard lean body. " 'And now?"

"A question?" He smiled warmly. "God, I hope you like my answer."

His lips swept down to cover hers, his mouth hot, his tongue exploring hers as though he'd never kissed her before when he'd actually kissed her through the winter and the beginning of spring. She had come to know his kisses intimately, but they'd never promised all that he seemed to be promising her now. The kiss promised no end . . . only a beginning.

Groaning deeply, he trailed his mouth along her chin, nibbling as he went until he pressed his mouth against her ear. "Remember how I wanted to touch you?"

"As my husband, you have that right."

"Only if it's what you want."

"How could you possibly think I wouldn't want you to touch me?"

"Good, 'cuz I'm gonna touch all of you."

He moved his large hands up her sides and cupped her breasts, his thumbs circling the sensitive flesh until her nipples hardened. Moaning, she collapsed against his broad chest. He slipped his arm beneath her knees and lifted her against his chest. She had never felt more at home than she did as he carried her to the bed and gently laid her on the thick feather mattress, stretching his body alongside hers.

She loved the length of his body, the breadth of his shoulders. She trailed her fingers over the scars that ran along his face. "Can you feel that?"

"Barely." He took her hand and placed it over his beating heart. "But I feel that."

Then his body was covering hers, flesh against flesh, warmth against warmth. His mouth blazed a trail of kisses along her throat, traveling lower to circle the crest of each breast. She scraped her fingers through his hair until a leather strip barred further exploration. "Do you mind if I remove this?" she asked.

He lifted his gaze, and she watched as his Adam's apple slowly slid up and down. "If you want," he said in a strangled voice.

"I love everything about you, Houston. Everything."

"Even the ugliness."

"That's just it. I don't see any ugliness when I look at you."

He closed his eye as she untied the leather strip and gently removed the patch covering his face. He released a ragged breath before lifting his gaze back to hers.

"I think you're handsome as sin," she said softly.

He buried his face between her breasts. "You can't love me that much."

"I love you more."

"Oh, Lord." Houston thought he might weep. That'd be one hell of a manly action on his wedding night. His father would tan his hide—

Only his father wasn't here, and he wasn't the man his father had wanted him to become. But he was the man this woman loved.

She accepted his weaknesses and his scars, inside and out. The tears burned his throat, burned his eye as he raised his face from the soft pillow of her flesh. "I haven't got the words to tell you how much I love you, but I'm hoping I can show you."

He called on the skills he'd acquired while working with horses, hoping to tame her passions, bend them to his will, to her desires. He skimmed his hands along her body, from her shoulder to her tiny bare toes. Shadows waltzed over her flesh in rhythm to the dancing flames within the hearth. He relished the sight of her skin glowing beneath his fingers.

Years ago, he'd stopped dreaming, and when he began to dream again, all his dreams revolved around her. The feel of her beside him, beneath him, around him.

He fought against rushing to have all that he wanted, forcing himself to gift her with the patience he gave his horses. She meant so much more to him than his horses. Without her, they were nothing more than animals. With her, they were a dream waiting on the horizon, a dream they would touch together.

He kissed her deeply, inhaling the scent of magnolias that would forever remain in his bed. Then he began to trail his mouth over her flesh, following the path his hands had blazed earlier.

He heard her sigh like the soughing of the wind. He took his time, allowing her to grow accustomed to the feel of his mouth on her breasts, suckling, taunting, before he trailed down to her thighs.

Slowly, leisurely, he kissed her intimately, passionately until she quivered beneath him.

"Houston? I need—"

He swirled his tongue along her sensitive flesh. "I want you to buck for me."

"Buck for you?" Amelia rasped, her fingers pressing against his face. "Oh, God." Sensations she'd never known existed swept through her: lightning flashed and thunder rumbled as he created a tempest within her body. Her entire body curled as tightly as her toes, and then the storm exploded, raining pleasure and rapture throughout until she did buck like a wild mustang.

She opened her eyes to find him gazing at her, a smile of pure joy etched across his face. "You know there are some mustangs that can't be broken, but they're always worth the ride."

"I think you just broke me," she confessed breathlessly.

"Nope. You have too much spirit, Amelia. I'd never try to break you, but I always want you to enjoy the ride as much as I do."

With one long smooth stroke, he joined his body to hers. The pain was fleeting as her body instinctively tightened around him. Then he was riding her, she was riding him, two people with one destination.

The journey was like none she'd ever taken, none she'd ever dreamed of taking. She ran her hands along the taut muscles of his chest and back, kissed the dew from his throat, relished the sight of his clenched jaw.

His mouth swooped down, covering hers, kissing her, mating their tongues just as he'd mated their bodies. She whimpered, he groaned. Her breathing became shallow, his harsh.

His thrusts grew swifter, and she kept pace as the sensations stampeded through her until her body hurled her into an abyss of pleasure, and he arched and shuddered above her.

In awe, she languorously trailed her fingers over his glistening back.

He rubbed his cheek against hers. "I love you," he whispered on a tried breath.

"Those whores were fools for charging you double."

He chuckled low, lifted his head, and brushed a strand of hair away from her cheek. "I never gave them this. I never gave anyone this. I didn't know I had it to give." He held her gaze. "I wanted you to know that when I took Austin to Dusty Flats, I didn't touch a woman."

She pressed a kiss to the center of his chest. "I'm glad. Even though you weren't married to me at the time, I'm glad."

He rolled to his side and brought her up against him. She nestled against his shoulder, relishing the day's memories and the night's wonders before drifting off to sleep.

Amelia awoke several hours later, her body sore, her heart content. Houston's body was draped over hers, his leg slung over her thigh, his large palm cradling her breast, his breath blowing across her nape like the constant West Texas breeze. It took her a moment to recognize that she was not only surrounded by him, but by darkness as well. "Houston?"

"Mmmm?" he mumbled in a sleepy voice.

"The fire went out."

"Are you cold?"

"No, but there's no light."

"Want me to find the lantern?"

"Just hold me a little tighter."

"I can do better than that," he promised as he gently rolled her over and kissed her deeply, giving her what he would always give her from that night forward . . . the best of himself.

Texas Glory

❧

For Mom and Dad N.

When your son asked me to become his wife, you welcomed me as
your daughter.

No finer gift could have been given.

Chapter 1

꙳

May, 1881

*D*REAMS. GOSSAMER IMAGES that most people carried with them into their sleep, but for Dallas Leigh, they were the incentive that woke him before dawn, the impetus that pushed him toward midnight.

Dreams were the stepping stones to glory.

By pursuing them, he had attained a level of success that exceeded most men's reach and acquired all that he had set out to gain: Land, cattle, and wealth beyond his highest expectations.

Yet, desperation gnawed at him like a starving dog that had just discovered a buried bone, and as he gazed at the stars that blanketed the velvety sky, he felt as though he had achieved nothing.

He was a man with a solitary dream that remained untouched, the one that had served as the guiding beacon for every goal that he had fulfilled. Without the realization of his greatest desire, his other accomplishments meant little, and he feared that they might mean nothing at all—if he never gained a son with whom to share them.

The lingering warmth of the parched earth seeped through his backside as he worked the ridge of his spine into a comfortable position against the gnarled and crooked post that served as one of a thousand anchors for his barbed-wire fence.

He hated the fencing with a passion, but he knew it was destined to become essential to every rancher's survival in the same manner that the railroad had wended its way into their lives. Workers continued to lay the tracks that brought more people farther west. The days of knowing one's neighbor and where his land ended and a man's own land began were dwindling. The barbed wire cut through the questions, marked a man's domain, and left no doubts as to his ownership.

Unfortunately, it was an aspect of the future that only a few men could envision, and those blinded by the traditions of the past were determined that the barbed wire would not stand.

Dallas Leigh intended to make damn sure that it did.

"Dallas?" The hoarse whisper momentarily silenced the nightly serenade of the crickets, frogs, and katydids.

He glanced at his youngest brother, who was stretched along the ground, his arms folded beneath his dark head, his tall, lanky body running the length of the fence. "What?"

"How long we gonna stay?" Austin asked.

"All night if we have to."

"What makes you think they'll come?"

"Full moon. The McQueen brothers like to do their thieving and destroying by the light of a full moon."

"I don't know how you can be sure that they're gonna cut the wire right here," Austin said, exasperation laced through his youthful voice. At twenty-one, he had little patience when it came to waiting for the next moment.

"I don't know where they will cut it, but if you shut your mouth, we'll hear the tinny sound of the cut traveling along the wire, and we'll know in which direction to ride. Just close your eyes and imagine that you're listening for that first twang to come from your violin when you slap your bow on it."

"I don't slap my bow onto anything. I place it on the strings as gently as I'd touch my fingers to a woman's soft cheek or press my lips against her warm mouth. Then I stroke it slow and long, the way I'd stroke—"

"Will you shut up?" a deeper voice growled.

Dallas didn't need to lean forward to see the disgruntled expression he knew he'd find on Houston's face. His middle brother was the only one among them to have a wife, and Dallas imagined right now he'd rather be curled up in bed with her nestled against his side. He appreciated the fact that Houston was guarding the fence instead.

Austin snickered. "You're just aggravated 'cuz you ain't home doing your own stroking."

"Watch your mouth, boy," Houston warned. "You're gonna cross into dangerous territory if you bring my wife into this conversation."

"You know I wouldn't say nothing bad about Amelia. I just figure you'd rather be at home making another baby instead of sittin' out here waitin' on something that might not happen."

"We've already made another baby," Houston said, pride and a great deal of affection reflected in his voice.

Dallas shot forward so he could see his brother's face limned by the moonlight. Despite the heavy scarring on the left side of his face and the black eye patch that hid the worst of it, Houston looked to be a man who had realized every dream he'd ever dared to hope for. Dallas sometimes envied him that contentment, especially since he'd accomplished it all by stealing Dallas's wife from him.

"When did this happen?" Dallas asked.

Houston tugged on the brim of his hat. "Hell, I don't know. Sometime in the last month or so, I reckon. Amelia just told me tonight before I rode out."

"So Maggie May is gonna have a little brother or sister," Austin said, his wide grin shining in the moonbeams that passed through the clouds. "You ain't planning to name all your young'uns after the month they were born in, are you?"

Houston shrugged. "I'll name them whatever Amelia wants to name them."

Dallas leaned back against the post. "I sure as hell am glad you took that woman off my hands. I wouldn't like living my life around a woman's wants and needs."

"If you loved her as much as I love Amelia, you'd like it just fine," Houston said.

Dallas had to admit that he probably would, but finding a woman to love in a land populated mostly by cowboys and prairie dogs was no easy task.

Hell, he couldn't even find a woman to marry and bear his son, let alone a woman to love.

The absence of decent women in this portion of West Texas was a sharp thorn in his side, a nagging ache in his heart, and a steadfast barrier to the fulfillment of his final glory: a son to whom he could pass down the legacy he had worked so hard to carve from a land known for its disappointments and broken promises.

He had hoped founding a town would attract women to the area, but Leighton was growing slowly. The banker, Lester Henderson, had a wife who easily occupied the entire width of the boardwalk when she strolled to the general store. Perry Oliver, the owner of the general store, was a widower with a lovely daughter. Dallas had considered asking the merchant for his daughter's hand. At sixteen, his mother had married his father, but Dallas couldn't bring himself to marry a woman younger than half his age. Besides, he had a suspicion. Austin had set his sights on the young woman. Why else would his brother find an excuse to ride into town every day to purchase some useless contraption from the general store?

Neither the sheriff nor the saloon keeper nor the doctor had brought women with them. The town's seamstress, Mimi St. Claire, was unmarried, but she was on the far side of forty if she was a day.

With resignation Dallas was coming to the conclusion that, once again, he would need to search beyond his town, beyond the prairie, in order to find a woman who could give birth to his son. At thirty-five, he was beginning to feel the weight of the years pressing in on him. He needed a son.

He wanted a son sitting beside him at this very moment, sharing the anticipation of the night. He wanted to count the stars with his son. He needed to feel the breeze blow over their faces and know that when it no longer touched his face—when Dallas was dead and buried—the breeze would continue to caress his son's face.

The nearby river flowed to the rhythm of Nature's lullaby: the mating call of insects mingled with the occasional swoosh of an owl's wings and the howl of a stalking coyote. Dallas wanted his son to hear that song, to appreciate the magnificence of nature, to tame it, to own it. He imagined his son standing here years from now, looking out over all that they had accomplished, listening to the water lap at the muddy shore, listening to the—

Ping!

The tune of destruction broke into the night. Dallas jumped to his feet as the high-pitched whine came again. "They're to the south."

He and his brothers mounted their horses with an agility that came from years of chasing after stampeding cattle. The moon's silver glow lighted their path along the river's edge.

With a firm grip, Dallas removed the coiled rope from his saddle. He needed only the sure pressure of his thighs to guide the stallion that had helped him herd cattle north. When the shadows of three men emerged from the darkness, the horse didn't falter.

The tallest of the men fired his gun while the two other men scrambled for their horses. Dallas heard shouts and yells. Horses snorted, neighed, and reared up, their hooves slicing at the air.

Raising his arm, Dallas snapped his wrist and threw a loop that whistled through the muggy air and circled Boyd McQueen. Dallas yanked hard on the rope. The gun flew from McQueen's hand as he stumbled to the ground. Without hesitation, Dallas secured his end of the rope around the saddle horn, set his heels to his horse's sides, and galloped toward the precious river.

Dallas glanced over his shoulder. The moonlight glinted off Boyd McQueen's angry face. Dallas took satisfaction in the man's fury and guided his racing horse into the shallow water that more closely resembled a babbling brook than a full-fledged river.

"Damn you, Leigh!" McQueen yelled just before the horse splashed into the center of the stream.

Water sprayed Dallas's legs. He looked back to make certain McQueen's head was above the surface. He didn't want the man to drown, but he intended to give him a rough ride.

Dallas heard the echo of three rapid gunshots. No responding gunfire sounded. The eerie silence that followed signaled a warning.

Dallas jerked his horse to a staggering halt. His brothers weren't behind him. Three more steady shots bellowed.

Groaning, McQueen struggled to his feet, sputtering obscenities that Dallas didn't wait to address. Releasing the rope from the saddle horn, he urged his horse back toward the fence.

Alarm skittered along his spine when he saw the silhouettes of two men standing and one man kneeling. He dismounted before his horse halted.

He dropped to his knees beside the man sprawled over the ground. "What happened?" Dallas asked.

"Austin took the bullet Boyd fired, and it doesn't look good," Houston said.

"Where in the hell is the damn doctor!" Dallas growled as he stared through the bedroom window. He'd sent his foreman into town to fetch the physician, but that had been over two hours ago.

"He'll be here," Amelia said softly. While Dallas had brought Austin home, with no help from the McQueen brothers, Houston had ridden to his house and fetched his wife and daughter. With the innocence of a child, Maggie had viewed coming to her uncle's house in the dead of night as an adventure.

Dallas stalked to the bed where his brother lay, his eyes closed, his breathing shallow. He watched as Amelia wiped a damp cloth over Austin's face. She'd stanched the flow of blood, but they needed the doctor to remove the bullet from Austin's shoulder. It hadn't come out the other side so Dallas could only assume it was embedded in his bone. He was lucky the bullet hadn't dropped lower and gone through his heart. "He looks too pale."

Amelia lifted her gaze to his. She had the prettiest green eyes he'd ever seen. He remembered a time when he'd thought he could easily fall in love with those eyes. Perhaps he had.

"I don't think it's as bad as when Houston got shot," she said quietly.

"I'd feel a hell of a lot better if he'd wake up."

She returned to her task of running the cloth over Austin's brow. "He'd only feel the pain then."

Better the pain than death. Dallas glanced at Houston who sat in a nearby chair, holding his own silent vigil, his daughter curled in his lap, asleep.

"I guess you think I should have handled this differently," Dallas said.

"It makes no sense to me to build a town, hire a sheriff, and then *not* use him when you've got trouble."

"I hired him to protect the citizens. I can handle my own trouble."

"You can't have it both ways, Dallas. If you bring the law out here, then you can't be your own law."

"I can be anything I damn well want to be. It's my land. McQueen is going to learn to stay the hell off it, and I'll teach him the lesson myself."

"But at what cost?"

The words rang out loudly with concern. Dallas turned his attention back to his wounded brother. "Why don't you tuck your daughter into my bed?" he suggested quietly to Houston.

"I'll do that," Houston replied as he easily brought himself to his feet, without waking Maggie. He walked from the room.

Dallas wrapped his hand tightly around the bedpost, searching for answers to his unfortunate dilemma. The McQueens had moved to the area three years ago, thinking they had purchased the land that ran along both sides of the river. Dallas suspected that the person who had sold them the land had been a land grabber. Land grabbing had been a common practice following the war. A man would buy a parcel of land and extend the boundaries as far as he wanted, often posting a notice in a newspaper to validate his claim. Although the practice usually worked, the notice was not legally binding. Dallas had filed claims with the land office for every acre of land he owned. Unfortunately, the McQueens seemed to believe—as many ranchers did—that a gun spoke louder than the law. They had refused to acknowledge Dallas's deed to the acreage and had blatantly prodded their inferior stock into grazing over Dallas's spread.

He wouldn't have minded sharing his water or his grass if he didn't need to control the breeding of his cattle so he could improve the quality of beef his cows produced.

He'd begun to put up his barbed-wire fence. If the McQueens had accepted that, Dallas would have left a portion of the river open to them. But they had torn down the fence before Dallas's men had completed it. Irritating, but harmless. Dallas had paid a visit to Angus McQueen and demanded that he keep his sons tethered. Then Dallas had ordered his men to finish building the fence and to carry it beyond the river.

Two months ago, Angus McQueen's sons had again destroyed a section of the fence, cutting the wire, burning the posts, and killing almost forty head of cattle, most on the verge of calving. Dallas had given Angus McQueen a bill for the damages that the man had refused to pay because Dallas couldn't prove his sons had torn down the fence and murdered the cattle.

Dallas could certainly prove McQueens had cut his wire tonight, but as Houston had stated—at what cost?

Dallas held his thoughts and his silence when Houston returned to the room and took up his vigil in the chair beside the bed.

Dallas swung around as soft footfalls sounded along the hallway. Relief washed over him when Dr. Freeman shuffled into the room. The tall, thin man looked as though he were hovering on death's doorstep himself. His bones creaked as he crossed the room without a word. He set his black bag on the bedside table and began to examine Austin's wound.

"Where in the hell have you been?" Dallas demanded.

"Had to set Boyd McQueen's arm." Dr. Freeman glanced over his shoulder at Dallas and raised a thinning white brow, his steely gray eyes accusing. "Boyd said you broke it."

Twin emotions twisted through Dallas's gut: rage because McQueen had selfishly had the doctor tend to his needs, knowing all along that his bullet had slammed into Austin; and guilt because he hadn't realized he'd broken Boyd's arm when he'd dragged him through the river.

"Did McQueen tell you that he shot Austin?"

Dr. Freeman sighed. "No, I didn't learn that bit of information until I returned home and found your foreman waiting for me." Shaking his head, he began poking his fingers around Austin's ravaged flesh. "You and the McQueens need to settle your differences before this whole area erupts into a range war."

"Is Mr. McQueen going to be all right?" Amelia asked.

"Yes, ma'am. It was a clean break, and I left him in his sister's care."

Dallas stared at the doctor as though he'd just spoken in a foreign language. "Sister? Boyd McQueen has a sister?"

"Yep. Shy little thing," Dr. Freeman said absently as he opened his black bag. "Hear tell, she spent most of her growing-up years tending to her ailing mother. Reckon she spent so much time being forced to stay at home that she never thinks to leave now that she's grown.

"How grown?" Dallas asked.

"What?"

"I mean how old is she?"

"Twenty-six."

"Twenty-six?" Dallas repeated.

Dr. Freeman jerked around and glared at Dallas. "Do I need to check your hearing before I leave?"

"I just didn't know McQueen had a sister."

"Well, now you know. Go get some more lanterns and lamps so I can have enough light in here to dig this bullet out."

A few hours later Dallas watched his youngest brother as he lay sleeping, his shoulder swathed in bandages. Dr. Freeman had assured Dallas that Austin was in no danger. He'd be sore, weak, and cranky, but he would survive. Still, Dallas decided he'd feel a lot more confident with the doctor's prognosis if Austin would awaken.

Dallas assumed Houston held the same concerns. Houston had convinced Amelia to sleep with Maggie while he sat on the opposite side of the bed, never taking his gaze off Austin.

When dawn's feathery fingers eased into the room, Austin slowly opened his eyes. With a low groan, he grimaced. Dallas eased forward. "You in much pain?"

"That worthless bastard shot me in the shoulder," Austin croaked. "How am I gonna play my violin?"

"You'll find a way," Dallas assured him.

"When . . . I'm strong enough . . . I say we run 'em off their land." Austin's eyes drifted closed.

"Dallas?"

Dallas met Houston's troubled gaze.

"Dallas, you've got to do something to stop this feuding. Dr. Freeman is right. Next time, we might not be so lucky, and I don't want my family caught in the middle." Houston shifted uncomfortably in the chair. "I *won't* have my family caught in the middle. If I have to choose—"

"You won't have to choose. I've been pondering the situation, and I think I might have a solution to our problem. I'll schedule a meeting with Angus McQueen and see if we can come to some sort of compromise."

"Good." Houston stood, planted his hands against the small of his back, and stretched backward. "I'm going to get a little sleep." He started walking across the room.

"Houston?"

Houston stopped and turned.

Dallas weighed his words. "Do you think McQueen's sister is as mean-spirited as he is?"

"What difference does it make?" Houston asked.

Dallas glanced at Austin's pale face. "No difference. No difference at all."

"By God, you have no right!" Angus bellowed.

Leaning back, Dallas planted his elbows on the wooden arms of his leather chair. He steepled his long fingers and pressed them against his taut lips. Narrowing his dark brown eyes, he glared at the spittle that had flown from McQueen's mouth and plopped onto the edge of his mahogany desk. He could imagine it sliding along the front of his desk like a slug slipping out at night to coat the land in slime.

Slowly, he raised his eyes to his adversary's. "I have every right to fence in my land," he said calmly.

"But you fenced in the river!"

"It's on my land. Any rancher of sound reputation would side with me. None would blame me for stringing up your sons from the nearest tree. We have an unwritten code that most cattlemen honor. Once a man has a valid claim to a river or a water hole, another cowman won't come within twenty-five miles of it—with or without a fence. No one would have questioned my right to take the fence back farther, but I graciously left miles of land open to grazing."

"To taunt us. I don't need grassland, damn you! I need water!"

"You have creeks and rivers on your land."

"I've got nothing but dry creek beds."

Dallas shook his head in sympathy. "I can't help that Nature chose to dry up your water supply and left mine flowing, but I don't part with anything of mine freely."

McQueen's face turned a mottled shade of red. It occurred to Dallas that the man might have an apoplexy fit right here in his office. Then Dallas would never get what he wanted.

"Freely," Angus muttered. "You won't part with your water freely, but you will part with it for a price. Is that what this meeting is about? Is that why you fenced in the river? So you could get something for the water? Isn't it enough that you stole my land?"

"I've owned that stretch of land since 1868."

Angus snorted. "So you say."

"The law backs my claim," Dallas reminded him.

Angus released a harsh breath. "Then name your price for the water, and I'll pay it. What do you want? Money? Cattle? More land?"

Dallas lowered his hands to his lap, the fingers of his right hand stroking the ivory handle of the gun strapped to his thigh. He should have insisted this meeting be held without weapons in tow.

"I have money. I have cattle. I have land. I want something that I don't have. Something as *precious* as the cool water. Something as *beautiful* as the flowing river." Giving his words a moment to echo inside McQueen's head, he tightened his hand around the gun. "Something as *pure* as the sun-glistened water."

Angus shook his head. "You're talking in riddles. I don't have anything that's pure or precious or beautiful."

"I've heard you have a daughter," Dallas said, wishing he hadn't needed to be quite so blunt.

The furrows that ran across McQueen's brow deepened. "Yes, I have a daughter, but I don't see what that has to do with anything."

Dallas was beginning to question the wisdom of holding his meeting with Angus, wondering if it might have been better to discuss the particulars of his compromise with Boyd. "Maybe you haven't noticed, but women are scarce. I need a w—"

"My God! You can't be serious!" McQueen yelled, his eyes bulging from their sockets.

"I'm dead serious."

Angus slumped in his chair. "You'll give me access to your water if I give you access to my daughter?"

With a speed Dallas never would have expected of the rotund man, Angus lunged across the desk and grabbed Dallas's shirt. Dallas brought the gun from his holster and jabbed it into the folds of Angus's neck, but the man was apparently too angry to notice. Spittle spewed into Dallas's face.

"I'll see you dead first," Angus growled.

"That won't get you the water," Dallas said in an even voice.

"I won't give you my daughter as a whore!"

"I don't want her as a whore. I want her as my wife."

Angus McQueen blinked. "You want to marry her?"

"Is there a reason that I shouldn't?"

Angus dropped into the chair. "You want to marry Cordelia?"

Cordelia? He was going to pull his fence back for a woman named Cordelia? Where in the hell had McQueen come up with that name?

"You don't even know her," McQueen said.

Dallas leaned forward. "Look, McQueen, we've been arguing over that strip of land for three years now. The law says it's mine and gives me the right to fence in and protect what's mine. Your sons killed my cattle—"

"You can't prove it—"

"Two nights ago, they damn near killed my brother. I went to war when I was fourteen. I've fought Yankees, Indians, renegades, outlaws, and now I'm fighting my neighbors." Dallas sank into his chair. "I'm tired of fighting. Angus, I need a son to whom I can pass my legacy. I need a wife to give me a legitimate heir. The pickin's around here are slim—"

Angus came out of the chair and pounded a fist on the desk. "The pickin's? If I were ten years younger I'd pound you into the dirt for thinking so lowly of my daughter."

"I think very highly of her because I respect her father. We're both working hard to carve an empire from desolate land, and we're both on the verge of destroying all we've attained. Barbed wire is part of the future. I put it up, you tear it down. I'm going to keep putting it up." He took a deep breath, ready to play his final hand. "But tomorrow at dawn, I'm giving my men orders to shoot to kill anyone who touches my wire or trespasses on my land."

"You are a son of a bitch," Angus snarled.

"Maybe, but I've poured my heart and soul into this ranch. I'm not going to let you destroy it. Marrying your daughter will give us a common bond."

"You don't even know her," Angus repeated, bowing his head. "She's—"

Dallas had his first sense of foreboding. "She's what?"

"Frail, delicate, like her mother." He lifted his gaze. "I honest to God don't know if she could survive being married to you."

"I'd never hurt her. I give you my word on that."

Angus walked to the window. Beyond the paned glass, the land stretched into eternity. "You'll pull your fence back?"

"The morning after we're married."

Angus nodded slowly. "Deed the land that runs for twenty-five miles along both sides of the river to me, and I'll have her on your doorstep tomorrow afternoon."

Damn! Dallas wondered if Angus had read the desperation in his voice or in his eyes. Either way, Dallas had lost his edge, and staring at the cocky tilt of his neighbor's chin and the gleam in his eyes, he knew that Angus understood he had the upper hand. "When she gives my a son, I'll deed the land over to you."

Angus pointed a shaking finger at him. "All the land that I thought I owned when I came here."

"Every acre."

"Are you out of your mind?" Houston roared.

Fighting not to squirm, Dallas stared into the writhing flames burning low in the hearth. Houston of all people should understand his brother's desire to have a wife. Hell, he'd taken Dallas's wife from him. Houston could at least support Dallas in his quest to find a replacement.

"Maybe I am, but the town we're building hasn't done a whole hell of a lot to get women out here. Eligible women, anyway."

"You don't even know her!"

Dallas spun around and met his brother's gaze. "I didn't know Amelia either when I married her."

"You knew her a lot better than you know Angus's daughter. At least you wrote letters to each other. What in the hell do you know about this woman?"

"She's twenty-six . . . and delicate."

"From what I hear, I don't imagine she's much to look at either."

Dallas snapped his head around to stare at Austin. He sat in a chair rubbing his shoulder, his face still masked with pain.

"What have you heard?" Dallas asked.

"Cameron McQueen told me she doesn't have a nose."

"What do you mean she doesn't have a nose?"

Austin lifted his uninjured shoulder. "He said Indians cut it off. Nearly broke her heart so her pa fashioned her one out of wax. He took the wire off some spectacles and hooked it to the wax so she has a nose to wear . . . like someone might wear spectacles."

Dallas's stomach roiled over. Why hadn't Angus revealed that little flaw in his daughter? Because he hadn't wanted to lose the chance to obtain the water and the land. He imagined the McQueen men were having a good laugh right about now.

"Call it off," Houston said.

"No. I gave my word, and by God, I'm gonna keep my word."

"At least go meet her—"

Dallas slashed his hand through the air. "It makes no difference to me. I want a son, goddammit! She doesn't need a nose to give me a son."

Houston picked his hat off a nearby table and settled it low over his brow. "You know, until this moment, I always felt guilty for taking Amelia from you. Now, I'm damn glad that I did. She was a gift you never would have learned to appreciate."

"What the hell does that mean?" Dallas asked.

"It means for all your empire building, big brother, you'll never be a wealthy man."

Chapter 2

✒

$\mathcal{J}$T WAS A woman's lot in life to live within the shadows cast by men.

Cordelia McQueen knew that unfortunate truth and understood its ramifications only too well.

With her hands folded primly within her lap, she gazed out the window toward the horizon where the sun boldly retreated. She had never blamed her mother for wanting to run toward the majestic blues and lavenders that unfurled across the sky. Her mother had called it an adventure, but even at the age of twelve, Cordelia had recognized it for what it was: an escape.

Her mother packed one carpetbag and told Cordelia and Cameron to bundle up their most precious possessions. She explained that Boyd and Duncan were too old to go on the journey, Cordelia and Cameron too young to stay behind.

They were walking down the hallway when her father trudged up the stairs, his face flushed with fury.

Cordelia pulled Cameron into a far corner, hiding his face within the crook of her shoulder while her father ranted and raved that Joe Armstrong wouldn't be taking his wife—his property—anywhere.

Horror swept over her mother's face. She turned for the stairs, and her father jerked her back. "That's right! I know! I know everything!" He backhanded her across the face and sent her tumbling down the stairs.

Her mother's scream echoed clearly through Cordelia's mind as though she had heard it this afternoon. For ten long years she had cared for the woman who had once cared for her. The accidental fall—as her father referred to it—had left her mother an invalid, with woeful eyes housed within an immobile body, her thoughts trapped by a mouth that could no longer speak. Only when her mother's eyes had welled with tears, did Cordelia know for certain that her mother lived within the withering shell that held her prisoner.

Her mother had simply exchanged one prison for another, and now it seemed as though Cordelia would do the same.

"Goddammit, Pa! There are other ways to get the water we need," Cameron said. Six years younger than she was, Cameron had always been her champion. Often his blond hair and pale blue eyes reminded her of the foreman who had disappeared the day her mother was injured. "You don't have to give Cordelia to that man!"

That man. Cordelia had only seen Dallas Leigh once, and then only from a distance. He was taller than she was, broader than she was, and when he'd announced that the land he'd roped off was to be used for a town, the wind had been gracious enough to carry his deep voice to everyone who had gathered around him. She didn't think he was a man who would have accepted less.

Now he was demanding that she become his wife. The thought terrified her.

"This matter isn't open to discussion, Cameron," Boyd said. A tall dark sentinel, he stood behind his father's chair. Since they had moved to Texas from Kansas following her mother's death, her father's health had diminished considerably. Within the family, Boyd blatantly wielded the power. Only his love and respect for his father allowed him to let outsiders think his father remained in charge.

"When I want your opinion on a matter, Cameron, I'll ask for it," her father said.

"I'm only saying—"

"I know what you're saying, and I'm not interested in hearing it. I've already given him my word."

"Well now, you won't be breaking your word if he happens to die tonight, and we can certainly arrange that," Duncan said.

Cordelia kept her gaze focused on the pink hues sweeping across the horizon. She had no desire to see the depth of their hatred for this one man. She had seen hatred that deep once before: when her father had confronted her mother. She knew of no way to stop it. As a child, she'd hidden from it in a shadowed corner.

As a woman she had a strong desire to hide again, in her room, deep within one of her books. She feared Duncan was not in a mood to jest. As her father continued to hold his silence, she became concerned that he thought murder might have some merit.

"Killing him won't get us the water!" her father finally bellowed. "That's what this is all about. The water!"

"Leigh will treat her no better than a whore!" Duncan roared.

Flinching, Cordelia clenched her hands in her lap. She hated the anger and rage, hated the way it distorted faces that she loved—for she did love her brothers—into faces that she feared.

"Cordelia, go to your room. Your brothers and I obviously have a few details to work out," her father barked.

She rose to her feet, her hands aching as her fingers tightened around them. She had considered weeping. She had considered dropping to her knees and begging, but she had learned long ago that when her father and Boyd set upon a path, nothing would deter them. She salvaged what little pride remained, angled her chin, and met her father's glare. "Father, I'm not opposed to this marriage."

Cameron looked as though she'd just pulled a gun on him. "You can't be serious."

She took a tentative step forward. "Try and understand. Father's dream is to raise cattle, and you have always been part of it. I've only ever been able to watch from the window. Now, I have an opportunity to be part of his dream. I am the means by which he can gain the water he needs."

"You've no idea what goes on between a man and woman, Cordelia," Cameron said, his voice low. He abhorred violence as much as she did, and she knew he followed Boyd's orders so his brothers would never question his manhood.

She looked at her father, remembering when she had been six and a nightmare had sent her scurrying to her parents' room. Her mother had been weeping. Her father had sounded like a hog grunting as slop was poured into the trough. He had called her mother a damn cold bitch, and although Cordelia had not known what the words had meant at the time, the force with which her father had spat them had seared them within her mind. "I do know, Cameron," she said quietly.

"Then you should understand why Duncan and I are opposed to this. Dallas Leigh hates us all, and he'll show you no mercy."

"Surely, he's not that unkind."

"Then why did his first wife leave him within a week of their marriage?" Duncan asked.

He stood like a pillar of strength, watching her as though he truly expected her to know that answer. Dark hair, dark eyes, it was only his usually sedate temperament that distinguished him from Boyd.

"I want to do this," she lied, for Cameron's benefit and peace of mind if for no one else's.

Her father slapped his hand down on the table. "Then, by God, it will be done."

For as long as she could remember, Cordelia had wanted to be a man, to enjoy the freedoms that men took for granted. She pulled the curtain away from the small window of her traveling coach and gazed at the barren, flat land. How anyone could deem this desolate place a paradise was beyond her. Why men would fight to own it was incomprehensible to her.

But fight they had. Boyd's broken arm served as a testament to one of the battles, and tonight the man who had harmed her brother would come to her bed. She prayed for the fortitude to suffer through his touch in silence, without tears.

A huge adobe house came into view. She could only stare at the massive rectangular structure. A balcony surrounded each window that she could see on the second floor. The crenellated design of the roof reminded her of a castle she'd once read about.

Riding on his horse beside the coach, Cameron leaned down and tipped his hat off his brow. "That's where you'll be living, Dee."

"Are those turrets on the corners?"

"Yep. Hear tell Leigh designed the house himself."

"Maybe after today, you and Austin can be a bit more open with your friendship."

Cameron shook his head. "Not for a while yet. Be grateful you're not riding out here, Dee. The hatred is thick enough to slice with a knife."

"I thought today was supposed to make the hatred go away."

"What you're doing today is like the waves of the ocean washing over the shore. No matter how strong it is, it only takes a little of the sand away at a time."

She smiled shyly. "You're such a poet, Cameron."

He blushed as he always did when she complimented him.

"Listen, Dee, Dallas scares the holy hell out of me—I won't deny that—but I'll try and find a moment alone with him to ask him to show you some gentleness tonight."

She reached through the window and laid her hand over his where it rested on his thigh. "He'll either be gentle or he won't be, Cameron, and I don't think your words will change him, so spare yourself the confrontation. I'll be fine."

She settled back against the seat of the coach and drew the veil forward to cover her face.

Standing on the front veranda, with his brothers flanking him on either side, Dallas watched the approaching procession. It looked like the cavalry, as though McQueen had every man who worked for him coming for the ceremony.

Good. Dallas had all his men here as well as everyone from town. He wanted witnesses, plenty of witnesses.

He'd even managed to locate the circuit preacher. Fate was on his side.

He squinted at the red coach traveling in the center of the procession. He'd seen it once before: the day he had set aside the land upon which he planned to build Leighton.

"Do you think she's inside that red coach?" he asked.

Austin leaned against the beam. "Yeah, that's what she travels in when she's allowed to travel, which isn't often, according to Cameron."

"If you know so much about her why didn't you tell me she was in the area?" Dallas asked.

Austin shrugged. "Didn't figure you'd want a woman who didn't have a nose."

Dallas pointed his finger at each of his brothers. "Don't go gaping at her. Dr. Freeman said she was shy. That's probably why, so don't stare at her."

"I'm hardly in a position to gape at anyone with a disfigurement," Houston said, scraping his thumb over the heavy scars that trailed along his cheek below his eye patch.

Dallas nodded and turned his attention back toward the caravan. "A nose isn't important." Eyes. Eyes were important. God, he hoped she had pretty eyes.

The horses and coach came to a halt. All the men sat in their saddles, glaring, not a smile to be seen.

"Where's your father?" Dallas asked Boyd McQueen.

"He was feeling poorly this afternoon, so I'll be acting in his stead, and I'll be wanting a word with you in private before the ceremony."

"Fine."

Dallas watched as Cameron dismounted and opened the door of the coach. A white gloved hand slipped into Cameron's tanned one. A slender hand. Long fingers. A white slipper-covered foot came into view, followed by a white silk skirt, a silk and lace bodice, and a white veil. The veil covered her face, but beyond it, Dallas could see she had swept up her black hair.

"Stop gaping," Houston whispered beside him, but Dallas couldn't help himself.

The woman was tall. Dr. Freeman had said she was a "shy little thing," and Dallas had expected a woman along the lines of Amelia, a woman who came no higher than the center of his chest. But Cordelia McQueen was as tall as her brothers. He thought the top of her head might be level with the tip of his nose. Slender, she was a fine figure of a woman.

Dallas took a deep breath and stepped off the veranda. He noticed the subtle tightening of the woman's fingers on her brother's hand. The thick veil hid her features from him, but he thought she might have dark eyes. He could live with a woman who had dark eyes. He could tell by the slight jutting of the veil that her father had carved her a tiny nose. He wondered if it melted in summer when the stifling heat dried the land. Maybe he'd whittle her a nose of wood, small like the one she had of wax.

Dallas swept off his hat. "Miss McQueen, it's a pleasure to have you here."

"I hope it will be, Mr. Leigh."

Her voice was as soft as falling snow.

"I'll do all in my power to see that it is, Miss McQueen. Give you my word on that."

It was impossible to tell with the veil covering her eyes, but he had a feeling in his gut that she was staring at him.

"Stay here, Cordelia," Boyd said as he dismounted. "We need a few minutes alone with your future husband."

Turning, Dallas glared at Boyd. Of all the McQueens, Dallas had taken an instant dislike to Boyd the moment their paths had first crossed. "I imagine what you have to say concerns her, so she'll come with us."

"Fine," Boyd said through gritted teeth. "We'll need the preacher as a witness."

Dallas crooked his arm and tilted his head toward Cordelia. "Shall we go inside?"

She glanced at Cameron who gave her a smile and a nod. Then she released her hold on her brother and wrapped her fingers around Dallas's forearm. He wished he couldn't feel through the sleeve of his jacket that she was shaking worse than a leaf in the wind.

Cordelia had never seen a house with such cavernous rooms. Their footsteps had echoed over the stone floors as they walked to Dallas Leigh's office.

She wondered if he would allow her to spend time in this room. She was in awe of the floor-to-ceiling shelves that lined three of the walls. Empty shelves—save one—but shelves all the same. She imagined all her books could have found a home in here.

Cameron had convinced her to bring only a few of her belongings in the event she decided not to stay. As though she would have a choice in the matter. Watching the man sitting behind the large mahogany desk, she had a feeling that leaving him would not be an option for her once she became his wife.

Just as leaving had not been an option for her mother.

When Dallas Leigh had removed his hat and the shadows had retreated, she had been unprepared for the perfection of his chiseled features. She tried not to stare at him now, but she seemed unable to stop herself. A thick black mustache framed lips that looked too soft to belong to a man.

Over the years, the wind and sun had carved lines into a face that reflected pride and confidence. And possession. Dallas Leigh was a man who not only owned all that surrounded him, but he owned himself as well.

Soon he would own her, just as her father had owned her mother.

His brothers sat at the back of the room as though none of this arrangement concerned them, and yet, she was left with the distinct impression that they were poised to change their minds in the blink of an eye.

Boyd stood before the desk, Cameron and Duncan standing just a little behind him. She had always found her brothers a trifle intimidating. It looked as though Dallas Leigh only found them irritating.

Reverend Preston Tucker had kindly introduced himself before they'd entered the room. Appearing amused, he stood near the windows that lined the remaining wall.

Boyd withdrew a sheet of paper from inside his jacket. "Before Cordelia signs the marriage certificate, we want your signature on this contract we've had drawn up. It spells out the two conditions under which my father agreed to give you permission to marry his daughter. We've added a third condition."

Dallas lifted an eyebrow, and she was reminded of a raven's wing in flight. "And that condition would be?"

"If fate should be kind enough to make her a widow, she inherits all you possess on this day and all that you gain from this day forward."

Cordelia watched Dallas's jaw clench. She couldn't say that she blamed him. Had her family lost their minds to think he'd agree—

"It goes without saying that if she's my wife, all that I have goes to her upon my death."

"You don't think those two sitting back there would object?" Boyd asked.

"Not if I tell them not to."

"Not good enough," Boyd said. "We want it in writing and signed."

"My word is good enough for the bank, good enough for the state, good enough for any man who has ever had to depend on it. It had damn well better be good enough for you."

Cameron and Duncan cast furtive glances at each other. Boyd simply pulled his shoulders back. "Well, it's not good enough. If you don't sign the document, we go home, and Cordelia goes with us."

Cordelia thought it would be difficult enough to build a marriage on a foundation of hatred, but to begin it knowing no trust existed . . . She eased forward in the chair. "Boyd, surely this isn't necessary—"

"Shut your mouth, Cordelia," Boyd growled.

Cordelia shrank against her chair as Dallas Leigh planted his hands on the desk and slowly came to his feet. Cameron and Duncan stepped back, and she thought given the choice, they'd gladly leave the room. She wanted to leave herself.

Dallas's brown eyes darkened, and she imagined Satan would look like an angel standing next to this man when he was consumed with rage.

"Never use that tone of voice in my presence when you're talking to a woman and, by God, never talk to the woman I'm going to marry in that manner."

"You won't be marrying her if you don't sign the paper," Boyd said.

Dallas narrowed his eyes until they resembled the sharp edge of a knife. She knew pride kept him from applying his signature to the document. Pride would keep her from becoming a wife today.

Cordelia heard the patter of tiny feet and saw the flash of a blue dress and blond curls as a little girl raced past her. Jostling the small kitten she held securely in her arms, she rushed toward the man standing behind the desk. The woman who walked behind her was obviously ignorant of the seething hatred and anger filling the room. Houston stood, but he seemed hesitant to interfere.

"Unca Dalls?" the little girl said as she tugged on Dallas's trousers.

Cordelia slowly rose from her chair, fearful for the child's well-being, uncertain as to what she could do to prevent Dallas from turning his rage on the child.

Then it was too late.

He glanced down, and the girl pointed her finger toward his nose. "Kitty bit me."

The anger in Dallas's eyes faded into concern. His brow furrowed. "He did?"

She bobbed her head, the blond curls bouncing with her enthusiasm.

"Where?"

She stretched up on her toes, taking her finger higher. "There."

"Ah, Maggie," Dallas said as he reached into his pocket. "Looks bad."

Maggie nodded, although Cordelia could see no blood, and the child had yet to release her hold on the offending animal. Dallas knelt, kissed Maggie's finger, and wrapped his handkerchief around it, giving her a bandage almost as big as her hand. She giggled. He touched his finger to the tip of her nose. "Run along now."

As she hurried across the room and found additional comfort in Houston's arms, Dallas stood, picked up a pen, dipped it in the inkwell, and scrawled his name over Boyd's document. "Let's get this goddamn thing started."

Cordelia wished Boyd had bene gracious enough not to smile triumphantly.

"I'm sorry I wasn't outside to greet you when you arrived."

Cordelia swiveled her head at the soft voice. The woman who had followed the little girl into the room smiled at her. "I'm Amelia, Houston's wife. I put Maggie down for a nap and ended up falling asleep myself. I hope you'll forgive me."

"There's nothing to forgive. I truly didn't expect you to be here."

"Why ever not?"

Cordelia felt the warmth suffuse her face. She couldn't very well explain that she hadn't expected Dallas to welcome the woman who had abandoned him back into his house nor had she imagined that the woman would remain friends with a man who had been such a poor husband. "I just . . . well, this arrangement just came about so quickly I didn't expect anyone to be here."

Amelia smiled warmly. "Between all the ranch hands and the people from town, we have quite a gathering. Dallas believes in doing everything in a grand fashion."

Cordelia felt as though a swarm of bees had suddenly invaded her stomach. She had hoped for a small, quiet ceremony, but it appeared her future husband was a man of bold preferences.

She glanced toward Dallas. He wore impatience as easily as she wore her gloves.

Boyd was explaining to Reverend Tucker that he needed his signature to serve as a witness. Reverend Tucker didn't seem inclined to want to give it.

"Goddammit! Just sign the paper," Dallas said, irritation heavily laced through his voice.

Reverend Tucker tightened his jaw and slowly nodded. "If this is what you want." He dipped the pen into the inkwell. "Revenge is mine sayeth the Lord." With a piercing blue gaze, he glared at Boyd. "Keep that in mind."

Signing the document had been a damn stupid thing to do, Dallas decided in retrospect as Reverend Tucker performed the ceremony. Boyd McQueen had given him an honorable way to get out of marrying his sister, and Dallas had been too stubborn to take it.

For her sake, he wished he hadn't insisted she come to his office, wished he'd left her outside so she wouldn't have had to witness all that had transpired. Her hand rested on his arm as they stood before the preacher with everyone they knew standing behind them, and he could feel that she was shaking worse than she had been earlier when he'd first met her.

He'd told Reverend Tucker to use words that had to do with trust, honor, and respect and steer clear of love. He didn't want to make the woman aware of what she wasn't getting.

Reverend Tucker finished his opening remarks. "Would you two face each other and join hands?" he asked quietly.

As Dallas took Cordelia's hands, her trembling increased until he thought it rivaled the shaking of the ground during a stampede.

"Do you, Cordelia Jane McQueen, take this man to be your lawfully wedded husband, for better or worse, through sickness and through health, to honor and to cherish from this day forward?"

A hush settled around them. Dallas resisted the urge to peer beneath the veil and assure his bride that everything would be all right.

Why was she wearing a veil anyway? Dallas never closed a business deal without looking a man straight in the eye. A marriage was just as important. It seemed to him that this moment was the one time when a woman shouldn't be shielding her gaze from a man.

The silence became suffocating. Dallas was grateful that Reverend Tucker spoke low enough that only those standing nearby could hear. He was even more grateful that only family stood nearby.

Reverend Tucker leaned forward slightly. "If you're inclined to marry Dallas, simply say, 'I do.'"

"She does," Boyd said.

"Goddamm it, McQueen, let her say it," Dallas snarled.

"What the hell difference does it make?" Boyd asked.

"Years from now, it might make a difference to her."

Reverend Tucker cleared his throat. "Could we possibly refrain from using the Lord's name in vain during the ceremony?"

Dallas felt the heat rise in his face. "Sorry, Reverend. Why don't you leave out that part about cherish?"

"That doesn't leave much," Reverend Tucker said.

"Leaves enough."

"Very well. Do you, Cordelia Jane McQueen, take this man to be your lawfully wedded husband, to honor from this day forward?"

She held her silence, and Dallas damned his impatient nature. He should have taken a few minutes to put her at ease, to talk with her. He'd been so worried that he'd lose this opportunity to have a wife that he had rushed into it without considering her feelings. He'd call the whole thing off if he didn't think he'd lose the respect of every person standing in his front parlor.

Reverend Tucker rubbed the side of his nose. "I've had dealings with Dallas off and on for over five years now. I can assure you that it won't be difficult to honor him."

"I do," she said quietly.

Dallas worked hard not to let the relief show in his face.

Reverend Tucker turned to him. "And do you, Dallas Leigh, take this woman to be your lawfully wedded wife to have and to hold, through sickness and through health, to honor and to cherish from this day forward?"

"I do."

"You have a ring?"

Nodding, Dallas reached into his pocket and pulled out the ring that had once belonged to his mother, had once been worn by Amelia. Awkwardly, he tugged off the glove that covered Cordelia's left hand. Her hand was almost as white as the glove . . . and as cold as a river in winter. He'd heard once that if a woman had cold hands, she had a warm heart. He latched on to that small hopeful thought as he slipped the ring onto her finger. "With this ring, I thee wed."

He glanced at Reverend Tucker. "Sorry, Reverend, I got ahead of you."

Reverend Tucker smiled. "That's all right. We've been here before, haven't we? I now pronounce you man and wife. You may kiss the bride."

Dallas's mouth went dry, and now his fingers trembled worse than hers as he slowly lifted the veil.

She had a cute little chin and the reddest lips he'd ever seen. Perhaps the red seemed more brilliant because her skin was incredibly pale, as though it had never known the touch of the sun. Her mouth reminded him of a ripe strawberry, shaped to torment a man. He could live with that.

He whipped the veil up and against his will, his gaze latched on to her nose. Her tiny, perfect nose.

He narrowed his eyes and glared at Austin. Austin's mouth had dropped open. Austin jerked his gaze to Cameron, who looked as stunned as Dallas felt.

"Your brother has a strange sense of humor," Dallas said quietly as he turned his attention back to the perusal of his new bride. She had brown eyes that reminded him of a fawn he'd once seen. They were shaped like almonds, large . . . frightened.

He hated the fear reflected there and decided if he could make her relax, could fill those eyes with happiness, they would be her most striking feature.

Dallas smiled. "Let's see if your brother likes my sense of humor."

He'd planned all along to give her a quick kiss and be done with it, but he understood that sometimes the circumstances demanded that he change the plans. He decided a long, slow, enjoyable kiss was in order, might even make her brothers squirm.

He cradled her face in his large hands, lowered his mouth the short distance to hers, and discovered what he should have known: she'd never been kissed. She'd puckered her lips as though she'd just bitten into a lemon.

He drew back because he had no desire to initiate her into the proper way to kiss in front of the whole town.

"Ladies and gentlemen," Reverend Tucker's voice boomed. "I present to you Mr. and Mrs. Dallas Leigh."

Chapter 3

ॐ

SHE WAS MARRIED.

Cordelia stared at the wide band of filigreed silver on her finger. She wasn't surprised to discover that it didn't fit properly. Bending her finger to keep the ring from slipping off, she feared nothing in her life would ever feel right again.

People she had never met introduced themselves, the men smiling broadly as though their happiness for her husband knew no bounds, the few women wiping tears from their eyes as though they knew she was doomed to unhappiness. All called her Mrs. Leigh. She wasn't comfortable with the name, but she couldn't dredge up the courage to ask them to call her Cordelia.

Pumping Dallas's hand, men congratulated him. While women kissed his cheek, he never let his eyes stray from her. Her mind had turned into a freshly painted blackboard, erased clean of all previous thoughts and shared knowledge. She seemed unable to remember the simplest of statements. He was her husband, and she had no idea how to uphold her end of the vows they had exchanged—how to honor him.

When her mother had become incapacitated, Cordelia's world had shrunk until it encompassed little more than her mother's bedroom, her family, and works of fiction. Until this moment, she didn't realize how ill-prepared she was to become a wife.

Like vultures anticipating their prey's final breath, her brothers stood on the other side of the unfurnished parlor, their arms folded over their chests, their gazes locked on to Dallas as though they were waiting for him to make a mistake. She prayed that he wouldn't.

Music began to slowly drift across the room. People shuffled back, leaving an empty space in the center of the floor. At the far edge of the circle, a white-haired man played a fiddle.

Dallas extended his hand toward her. "Would you honor me with a dance?"

She lifted her gaze to his and quickly lowered it. "No. I mean . . . I don't know how to dance."

"It's not hard. I'll guide you."

She shook her head briskly. "Please, not in front of all these people."

"Give me your hand."

Wishing the floor would suddenly crack open and swallow her, she curled her fingers until her nails dug into her palms.

"Trust me," he said quietly.

She thought she heard an edge of desperation in his voice, and only then did she realize how he must appear to his friends, his family—holding his hand toward her while she blatantly ignored it. Since no one else was dancing, she assumed everyone expected that the bride and groom would dance first, no doubt alone, the center of attention. Without looking at him, she took a deep ragged breath and slipped her trembling hand into his. Strong and coarse, his fingers closed around hers.

"We're going to step outside for some fresh air," he announced in an authoritative voice as he addressed the gathering. "Enjoy the music."

Cordelia feared she might weep with relief as he guided her through the doors. As soon as she stepped onto the veranda, she released his hand and walked to the far corner. "Thank you."

The music floated through the open door, laughter and voices mingling with the soft strains. Her husband's footsteps echoed around her as he neared. Her husband. Dear God, what had she done?

"I suppose your father told you that I was a mean-hearted bastard."

Cordelia spun around, her eyes wide. Dallas Leigh studied her, his face grim.

"Yes, as a matter of fact he did."

"What else has he called me?"

"A thief."

He raised a dark brow as though amused, and she was unable to stop herself from throwing the rest at him. "And a cheat."

"Yet he gave his blessing for your marriage."

Humiliation swamped her as tears sprang to her eyes. "Because you offered him something that he valued more than he valued me." She turned away, squeezing her eyes shut, fighting back the burning river of shame. "I'm not certain I can forgive you for that."

"I don't need your forgiveness. You can hate me, for all I care, but it won't change the fact that you are now my wife."

She flinched at the cold, ruthless reminder. He cursed harshly, and she wondered if he might strike her. With his large, powerful hands, he would be able to inflict a great deal of damage in a very short time.

"I don't imagine you ever expected your wedding to go exactly as it did today," he said, his resonant voice enveloping her like a mist at dawn. "I'm sorry for that."

She dared to look at him. "Sorry enough to let me leave?"

"No."

She wouldn't beg, but dear God she wanted to fall to her knees and plead with this man for mercy and freedom.

His gaze dropped to her lips, his brown eyes smoldering with an emotion she couldn't identify. She didn't think he was angry, but her wariness increased.

"Where did you learn to kiss?" he asked.

She ran her tongue over her tingling lips, and his eyes darkened further. "Books. I read a lot of books."

He nodded slightly. "I reckon the women in those books always pucker up to kiss."

"Yes, they do," she answered, wondering how he had drawn that conclusion from her simple statement, only one answer quickly coming to her mind. "Perhaps we've read the same books."

"I doubt it," he said, his voice low. He cradled her cheek. "Don't pucker."

Before she could protest, he covered her mouth with his. She'd barely noticed when he'd kissed her before, but now she realized his lips were warm, pliant. She hadn't expected that of a man as hard as he was rumored to be.

His mustache was soft, reminding her of the fur of a puppy she had once owned, a puppy Boyd had killed.

Dallas slowly rubbed his thumb along the tender flesh beneath her chin. "Relax your jaw," he whispered against her mouth, his breath strangely sweet and warm as it fanned over her cheek. Another thing about him that she had not expected.

"Wh—" She learned the answer before she'd fully formed the question.

His questing tongue slipped between her parted lips and waltzed in rhythm to the lilting music she still heard in the background.

Bold. Strong. Like the wind before a storm, a tempest sweeping across the horizon—

"You couldn't even wait until your guests left to taste her again," Boyd said, his voice rife with disgust.

Dallas drew away from the kiss. Mortified, Cordelia would have stepped away from him but his hand tightened on her neck.

With anger blazing within his eyes, Dallas looked at Boyd. "I don't think anyone would find fault with a husband stealing a kiss from his new bride."

"Well now, you'd be the one to know about stealing, wouldn't you?" Boyd asked.

Cordelia was close enough to see Dallas's nostrils flare. He reminded her of a raging bull. For a moment, when his lips had touched hers, she'd almost forgotten that he was the man her family hated, the man who had broken Boyd's arm, the man who had revealed exactly what she was worth to her father. She started shaking, suddenly feeling cold where she had only moments before felt warmth.

"Please let me go," she whispered, wishing she didn't sound like a starving beggar willing to settle for crumbs.

Dallas looked at her, no anger shining in his eyes, and she wondered how he changed his emotions so quickly. His callused hand slid away from her neck.

When he returned his attention to Boyd, the anger accompanied him. "Because your sister deserves fonder memories of her wedding day than we've given her so far, I'll overlook that remark. You wanted something?"

"A private moment with my sister."

Dallas shifted his gaze between the two of them as though he trusted neither of them. Cordelia didn't know why that knowledge hurt.

"I need to tell our guests to move the celebration outside so they can enjoy the beef my men prepared. If your sister isn't standing in this spot when I get back, my fence will remain where it is."

"Then you'd be going back on your word."

Dallas took a menacing step toward Boyd. Boyd flinched.

"Man to man," Dallas said, his voice low, "you know I want more than words exchanged before I'll pull my fence back. Don't try to cheat me out of what is now mine by right."

He shouldered his way past Boyd and disappeared into the house. Cordelia wrapped her arms around herself and pressed her back against the cool adobe wall. "I can't stay here, Boyd," she whispered.

He crossed the small distance separating them, his eyes hard. "You've got no choice, Cordelia."

She longed for someone to put his arms around her, to hold her close, to comfort her, but her family consisted of men who never expressed themselves with anything but their voices.

Boyd clamped his fingers around the veranda railing instead of holding her trembling hand. "Believe it or not, I did come out here to talk to you."

He appeared to be on the verge of delivering bad tidings, and she wondered if her father was more ill than she realized. "Is it Father?" she asked.

"No, but since he's not here and Mother is dead, the chore falls to me, and I don't want you going to Leigh's bed not knowing what to expect."

A scalding heat rushed through her body, her heart thundering. "Boyd—"

"It's gotta be said, Cordelia, for your sake. It'll go a lot easier on you if you don't fight him. Just crawl into his bed, lift up your nightgown, and lie as still as you can."

She squeezed her eyes shut to block out the images his words brought to mind. "I can't do this," she whispered hoarsely.

"If you don't, you'll kill Father's dream, and probably him along with it. Is that what you want?"

She opened her eyes. "We've moved before. Why not find land that has more water?"

"Goddammit! We thought we had the land and water when we moved here, but that bastard you married stole it from us. Now we have a chance to get it back if you do your duty."

Her duty. She forced herself to nod and wondered where she would find the strength.

Dallas decided that today was quickly becoming a day in his life that he'd prefer to forget.

Nothing had gone as he'd hoped.

Clutching his arm, his wife spoke only when spoken to. She never offered her opinion on anything, and he couldn't figure out how to make the fear leave her eyes. Everything he said only seemed to deepen it.

He cursed Boyd McQueen for whatever he had told his sister to terrify her.

She seldom raised her gaze to his, but preferred to stare at a button on his shirt. He'd considered yanking it off, but figured she'd just find another button to stare at. He didn't think it would be seemly for a man of his position to greet his neighbors with no buttons on his shirt.

People had wandered outside. He could hear their laughter and the drone of their voices as they ambled to the cookhouse he'd built near the bunkhouse.

Plenty of food and drink awaited them on the planked tables inside. Cookie continued to play his fiddle. The half-dozen women who lived in the area were going to wear out their shoes by the end of the evening.

He watched Amelia waltz with Houston, remembering the first time he'd seen her dance. She hadn't feared him, but then considering the hell she'd gone through to get to him, he didn't think she'd ever feared anything.

He glanced over at his present wife. She looked more nervous than a cat in a room filled with rocking chairs.

"Do you want something to eat?" he asked.

Her gaze darted to him briefly. "No, thank you."

"Something to drink?"

"No."

"Well, just standing here is about to drive me crazy. Let me show you around."

She nodded. "All right."

Turning away from the people who were dancing, Dallas pointed. "That's the house."

Cordelia wondered if perhaps he was teasing her. It had never occurred to her that he would have a sense of humor. She could think of nothing significant to say. "It's big."

"I designed it myself. Hired a fella from Austin to come build it for me when Amelia . . . uh, a few years back."

He began to walk away before she could respond. She tightened her grip on his arm so she could keep up with his long strides.

"It reminds me of a castle," she said, searching for anything to distract her from Boyd's earlier words.

He shortened his strides. "It's supposed to. When I moved here, there was nothing. I wanted something—" he held out his hands as though he thought the words might appear in them—"something glorious."

He shifted his gaze away from her as though embarrassed by his words. "That's the cookhouse."

He pointed to a small stone building. Smoke, carrying the scent of mesquite, spiraled from the chimney.

"During roundup, the cook takes the chuck wagon out to the men. Other times, he just stays here. They either take something with them or come back in to eat. Cookie brings our meals to the house."

She remembered the name "Cookie." He was the gentleman playing the fiddle.

"The bunkhouse. I've got twelve men hired on right now. Come roundup, I'll hire twelve more."

She wished she knew what to say. She didn't know if twelve was a lot. She had no idea how many men worked for her father.

"Corral, barn."

She walked with him until they passed the barn. He stopped and jerked his head toward a wooden lean-to. "Blacksmith works there."

"Dallas?"

They turned together as Reverend Tucker approached, his long black coat flapping with his movements, revealing the gun he wore strapped to his thigh.

"Dallas, if you've no further need of my services, I need to get about the business of searching for a lost soul."

Dallas smiled warmly, the humor shining in his eyes mesmerizing. For a moment he wasn't the man her family despised, but a man she thought any woman would happily call husband.

"Did you get something to eat?" Dallas asked.

Reverend Tucker rubbed his stomach. "More than I should have, I'm afraid. Gluttony is a sin."

"I know of worse sins."

"Reckon we both do," Reverend Tucker said.

"You know, Reverend, I was serious about building a church in my town where you could preach."

"I know you were, and I wish I could take you up on the offer, but I can't."

Dallas shook his head, his smile widening. "I imagine we have plenty of lost souls around here."

"But I'm looking for one in particular."

Dallas extended his hand. "Then I hope you find him."

"Her," Reverend Tucker said as he shook Dallas's hand. "And trust me, I will. Sooner or later, I will find her."

He tipped his head toward Cordelia. "Mrs. Leigh, I wish you all the best."

Cordelia envied him the freedom to leave. "Thank you, Reverend."

"Would you mind if I had a moment alone with your husband?"

She welcomed the opportunity to escape from her husband's side. If she could just find Cameron, talk with him, she knew he could lay her fears to rest. "No, of course not. I want to talk with Cameron. Excuse me."

Dallas watched his wife practically gallop away. He hoped she wasn't entertaining any notions of leaving with Cameron.

"Things seem a bit awkward," Reverend Tucker said.

Dallas blew out a quick gust of air. "I can count the number of decent woman I've known in my life on one hand. I'm not skilled when it comes to talking to them."

"You never seemed to have a problem talking to Amelia."

"Hell, a fence post could talk to Amelia. She has a way about her of making you say things."

Reverend Tucker smiled. "She does at that."

"I can't seem to find the right wording when I'm talking to . . . Cordelia." He grimaced. "Where do you think her father got that name?"

"Jewel of the sea."

Dallas lifted a brow.

Reverend Tucker blushed. "I used to have an interest in names and their meanings. Maybe she'll become your jewel of the prairie."

"She's pretty enough. Hell, she's beautiful. I wasn't expecting that. Maybe that's why I get tongue-tied around her."

"Sometimes you don't need words if the actions are right."

"Still, I'd like to give her words. Hell, I'll give her anything she wants if she'll give me a son."

"You think a son is what is missing from your life?"

"I know it is," Dallas said with conviction.

Reverend Tucker gazed toward the setting sun. "I used to think I knew what was missing from my life." He smiled sadly. "But I discovered too late that I was wrong."

"I'm not wrong."

Reverend Tucker met Dallas's gaze. "You know you signed your death warrant today."

"Boyd McQueen wouldn't be that stupid."

"I know his type. He's a man without scruples. Watch your back."

"I always do."

Sitting with his back pressed against the side of the house, Austin watched the sun sinking below the horizon. He moved the bottle of whiskey from his mouth and took a moment to enjoy the burning in his gut before passing the pleasure on to his best friend.

Cameron took the bottle and downed his share before handing it back. "I can't believe you told Dallas that story about Cordelia's nose."

"I didn't know you'd lied to me when I asked you why she never came to town."

"I was only funning with you. I didn't think you'd believe it."

Austin took another gulp of whiskey. All the colors of the sunset seemed to be running together. "Why not? You're my friend. You ain't supposed to lie to me."

Cameron grabbed the bottle and took a long swallow. Then he wiped the back of his hand across his mouth. "You know what really bothers me, though?"

Austin shrugged and winced as the pain rolled through his shoulder. They'd already finished one bottle of whiskey. He didn't see how Cameron could be bothered by anything with the world spinning around them the way that it was.

Cameron grabbed his shirt, and they both wavered. "He married her anyway."

Austin snatched the bottle. "Hell, yeah, he married her. She coulda come to him without a face, and he woulda married her." He held up the bottle. "'A woman don't need a face to give me a son,' he woulda said. That's all he wants. A son. Reckon he woulda married her if she didn't have a head."

Cameron chuckled. "She'd a been dead without a head." His eyes brightened. "That rhymes!"

"You're such a poet, Cameron."

Austin jerked his gaze around at the sound of the sad feminine voice. Two women swam before him, then they bumped into each other and became his newest sister-by-marriage.

"Ah, hell," he groaned, feeling a sickness in his stomach that had little to do with the whiskey churning inside him.

"What are you doing, Dee?" Cameron asked, his words slurred.

"I was looking for you. I wish now that I hadn't found you." She spun around and quickly walked away.

Cameron struggled to his feet. "Hell, I'd better . . . go after her."

"Think she heard everything?" Austin asked.

Cameron nodded, stumbled to the ground, and started to snore.

Damn! Austin decided that he needed to go after his best friend's sister and figured as soon as he found his legs he would. Meanwhile, he downed the remaining amber brew. Unfortunately, the burning in his throat didn't ease the ache in his heart.

"There you are."

Austin heard a voice sweeter than any sound his violin could make. Dusk was easing in around him as he squinted at the girl standing before him.

Becky Oliver. Sweet Becky Oliver. With eyes the color of a summer sky. The setting sun turned her auburn hair a shade of red. Her father owned the general store. Austin started to smile at her and then remembered she was the reason he was trying to get drunk. He tipped back the bottle. Two drops were hardly enough to satisfy him.

She knelt beside him, and he could smell vanilla. She always smelled like something he'd like to run his tongue over.

"You're angry at me," she said softly.

He shook his head, then nodded. "You were dancing with Duncan McQueen."

"I would have danced with you, but you didn't ask."

"Only got one good arm," he said as he tapped his shoulder and grimaced.

"You could dance with one arm."

He shook his head. "Like to hold my women close. Need two arms to do that."

She worked the empty bottle from his grip and tossed it aside. "How many women do you have?"

He smiled crookedly. "One. Just one." He touched her cheek. It was softer than a cloud billowing in the sky. "I wanted to play my violin for you, but I can't do that either."

She lowered her gaze to her lap. "Do you need two arms to kiss me?"

"To do it proper." He slid down the adobe wall. He deserved to have his head slam into the hard ground. Instead, she scooted nearer, and he found his head nestled in her lap, a pillow softer than any he'd ever known. He closed his eyes. "Gotta kiss you proper the first time."

She combed her fingers through his hair. The darkness swirled around him. He moved his good arm around her backside, and promised himself that as soon as his shoulder healed, he'd kiss her proper.

Cordelia wanted to hide, to be alone with her thoughts, her sorrow. She wanted to be in her own room, curled in her bed, with a book in her lap.

But here, in this huge house, she had no room that belonged only to her. She had no private sanctuary. No place to call her own.

She closed the heavy front door behind her and held her breath. She heard no voices, no footsteps. Everyone was outside, celebrating her marriage, a marriage she didn't want, a marriage that family obligations forced her to accept.

She tiptoed down the hallway, retracing the steps she'd taken earlier in the day until she reached Dallas's office.

Quietly, she opened the door and peered inside. Early evening shadows lurked in the corners. Slipping into the room, she closed the door. She walked to the chair and sat, pulling her legs onto the soft cushion.

And gave the silent tears the freedom to fall.

Dallas Leigh didn't want a wife. He wanted a son.

She felt like a prized mare chosen for the offspring she could produce. Dallas Leigh cared nothing for her appearance, her wants, her needs, her dreams. She wasn't the person he wanted by his side as he journeyed through life. She was simply the means to an end.

Her thoughts drifted back to the kiss Dallas had begun on the veranda. She wondered where it might have led. She supposed that Boyd had interrupted them because he knew exactly where it would have taken them.

Boyd's horrid words slammed into her, terrifying her . . . unless she held on to the memory of Dallas's kiss. When he had looked at her, before he had kissed her, she had felt . . . touched, as though his hands were on her when they weren't. Perhaps if he kissed her again . . .

She buried her face in her hands. She didn't want to be here. She didn't want to be a wife. She didn't want to give him a son.

She heard a soft crackling. She tensed, her heart beating at a rapid tempo. She lowered her hands and gazed around the room.

She was alone.

The sound came again as though someone were crumpling paper. Slowly, she eased her feet to the floor and stood.

She heard a thump come from his desk, a bump too loud to have come from a mouse. She held her breath, waiting, wondering what sort of animals Dallas kept, wondering if she should find him and let him know that one of his creatures had escaped.

Another bump and crackle.

She studied his desk. Someone had shoved the chair away. The front of the desk spanned its width and nearly reached the floor, where she saw a scrap of blue.

Hadn't the little girl been wearing blue?

Quietly, she sneaked across the room and peered around the desk. A tiny black shoe tapped the air, the foot moving in rhythm to no music Cordelia could hear.

Cordelia knelt and looked into the alcove where Dallas would normally sit. The little girl sat with sacks wadded within her lap. Her eyes widened to form huge circles of green.

Cordelia smiled softly. "Hello. You're Maggie, aren't you?"

The girl nodded, scooted forward, and touched her tiny finger to Cordelia's damp cheek. "You got a sad."

Cordelia swiped at the tears that lingered on her lashes. "No, not really."

"Yes, you do. I can make the sad go away."

"You can?"

Maggie nodded enthusiastically. She crawled out from beneath the desk and struggled to pull open a drawer.

Cordelia eased a little closer to her. "I don't think you should play in your uncle's desk."

Maggie pressed her finger to her lips. "Shh." She pulled out a sack and shoved the drawer back into place.

Smiling brightly, she crawled into her previous hiding place and crooked her finger. "Come 'n."

Folding her body, Cordelia worked her way under the huge desk, wondering if everything in Dallas's life was big.

"Close your eyes," Maggie said.

"Why?"

"Unca Dalls says so."

Dallas had taught the little girl how to make sadness go away? Cordelia lowered her lashes.

"Open your mouth."

Hesitantly, Cordelia obeyed. She heard paper crackle. Then something hard skipped across her teeth and hit her tongue. She tasted sweet and bitter before she spit it into her hand. She stared at the lemon drop.

"When it's gone, so is your sad," Maggie said. "Unca Dalls says so." She reached into the bag. "I gotta sad, too." She popped a lemon drop into her mouth and snuggled against Cordelia's side.

Holding the child close, Cordelia popped the confection back into her mouth. She heard Maggie smacking as she sucked on the candy.

She was surprised to discover that a little of the sadness did melt away.

Chapter 4

*I*T HAD BEEN a mistake to leave his new wife alone, but then it seemed to be a day for making mistakes.

After Reverend Tucker left him, Dallas decided to carry her belongings to the house. She had only brought one small trunk, and it didn't take Dallas long to haul it to his bedroom, but apparently it was long enough to lose her.

Darkness was settling in, and people were beginning to take their leave. Without his wife by his side, Dallas thanked them for coming and refused to answer the questions he saw reflected in their eyes.

When the last wagon filled with townspeople rolled into the night, the tension within him increased. He was beginning to think he might know how a length of rope felt when it was being made: stretched taut and wound.

He needed to find his wife, give her the opportunity to say farewell to her brothers, send them on their way, and get to the business of realizing his final dream.

He saw Houston leaning against the corral and didn't waste any time in crossing the space separating them.

"You seen my wife lately?" he asked.

"Nope."

"I took her trunk up to my bedroom, and now I can't find her."

Turning, Houston scanned the dwindling crowd that consisted of the lingering ranch hands. "She has to be here."

"I've looked everywhere. Even in that gaudy thing she travels in."

"I know what you're thinking. Nobody stole her."

"But she might have left."

Houston nodded sagely as though he thought she probably had. "Let's find Austin—"

"Houston!"

Both men turned at the sound of Amelia's frantic voice.

"I can't find Maggie," she said as she skidded to a stop and dug her fingers into Houston's arms.

"What do you mean you can't find her?" Houston asked, panic threaded through his voice.

"I mean she's lost. The men were supposed to take turns watching her, and they lost track of whose turn it was. I should have kept my eye on her. I shouldn't have started dancing—"

Houston leaned down and pressed his mouth to hers to silence her. "We'll find her."

"But what if—"

"I know where she is," Dallas said.

Relief washed over Amelia's face. "You've seen her?"

"No, but I know where she likes to hide out. If I'm right, she's gonna go home with a big bellyache."

He started walking toward the house, Amelia's peace of mind taking precedence over his own.

"Have you seen my wife?" he asked Amelia as they neared the house.

"Not since you took her walking. Why?"

"I think she's left."

He shoved open the front door.

"Surely not," Amelia said softly.

"I can't find her, and I don't imagine she's hiding under my desk with Maggie."

Dallas walked down the hallway. He quietly opened the door to his office and peered inside. He didn't want to startle his niece if she had a lemon drop in her mouth.

He heard paper rattle and smiled. He so loved that little girl.

With Houston and Amelia following in his wake, he crept across the room and waited beside his desk until her heard the paper crackle again, a sign that she'd finished one lemon drop and was reaching for another. He'd taught her not to put more than one in her mouth at a time.

He quickly moved behind his desk and dropped to his haunches. "Caught you!"

A piercing scream ricocheted through the room. Dallas stared at his wife, hunched over beneath his desk. She screamed again.

Maggie yelled, her tiny hands waving frantically. The kitten hissed and slashed a paw through the air.

Dallas reached for his wife. Drawing back, screaming again, she kicked him in the shin. He grunted. Maggie started to cry. The cat made a puddle on the floor.

Houston shoved him aside, and Dallas landed hard on his backside. "Shh. Shh. It's all right," Houston cooed in a voice that Dallas had often heard him use to calm horses. "It's all right. No one is in trouble. No one is going to get hurt. Shh. Shh."

Maggie crawled out from beneath the desk and into Houston's arms. Houston passed her up to Amelia.

With tears streaming her face, Maggie looked at Dallas with accusation in her green eyes. "We had a sad!"

Dallas felt like a monster as he brought himself to his feet. Houston was holding his hand out to Cordelia. "Come on, Cordelia. It's all right. Dallas doesn't mind that you ate his lemon drops."

He watched as his wife cautiously peeked out from beneath the desk. It didn't ease his conscience to see that she'd been crying, too. She allowed Houston to help her to her feet.

"I'm sorry," she whispered as she swiped at the tears glistening on her cheeks.

"It was my fault," Dallas said. "I shouldn't have . . ." He shouldn't have what? Tried to tease his niece? How in the hell was he to know his wife would crawl—

Thundering footsteps echoed down the hallway and Cordelia's three brothers burst into the room, Cameron waving a gun through the air. "Get the hell away from her, you bastard!" Cameron yelled.

"Cameron—" Cordelia began but Dallas held up a hand to silence her.

He moved around the desk and slowly walked toward her brother, putting himself between those behind the desk and the gun, since neither Boyd nor Duncan seemed inclined to try to take the weapon from Cameron.

"Give me the gun, Cameron," Dallas said in a low, calm voice.

He shook his head. "I'm not gonna let you hurt my sister."

"I'm not going to hurt her."

"I heard her scream. I know the sound of her scream."

He waved the gun to his right, and Dallas stepped in front of it. "I frightened her," Dallas said. "It won't happen again."

Cameron turned a sickly shade of green and sweat popped out on his brow. Dallas reached for the gun.

"I won't hurt her," he repeated.

"Give me your word," Cameron rasped, the shaking of his hand increasing.

"I give you my word," Dallas said as he snatched the gun from Cameron's grasp.

Cameron doubled over and brought up his dinner.

As the others in the room gagged and moaned, Dallas leapt back and ground his teeth together. Wonderful. Now he had vomit *and* piss to clean up.

Cordelia rushed past him and pressed her fingers to Cameron's brow. "Oh, Cameron."

"I'm all right, Dee," he said, wiping his sleeve across his mouth and averting his gaze from Dallas.

Dallas glared at Boyd. "McQueen, wish your sister well, gather up your brothers, and get the hell out of my sight."

Cordelia eyed him as though he were a snake. "Cameron can't leave. He's sick."

"He can throw up outside as easily as he can inside."

"You're heartless," she said.

"I'm all right now, Dee," Cameron repeated. He extended his hand toward Dallas. "Can I have my gun back?"

"I'll bring it to you in a couple of days after tempers have cooled," Dallas said. "Right now, it would be best if you left."

Cameron nodded and looked at his sister. "Night, Dee," He eased his way past her.

"Do you have to leave?" she asked.

"Your husband's demanding it," Boyd said. "Let's go."

He spun on his heel and stomped out, with his brothers following like dogs with their tails tucked between their legs.

Not exactly the way Dallas had planned to end the evening.

Maggie padded across the room, placed her tiny hands on Dallas's thighs, and tilted her head back. "We had a bunch of sads," she said. "A bunch of sads."

He lifted her into his arms. "Are they all gone now?" he asked her, although he focused his gaze on his wife who watched him as though she thought he might harm the child.

Maggie nodded and laid her head on his shoulder. "Only now my tummy hurts."

"I'm not surprised." He looked at his brother. "Why don't you take your daughter, and I'll show my wife to her room? Then I'll deal with this mess."

He handed his niece over to Houston and held his arm out to his wife.

"Mrs. Leigh," he said, knowing his voice sounded too stern, but unable to stop it. He'd lost one wife on his wedding night. He didn't intend to lose another.

She stepped toward him hesitantly as though he'd just said he was going to take her to the gallows instead of to her room. Her fingers dug into his forearm, and dammit, she was still trembling.

"This way."

Cordelia followed him from the room, down the hallway, and up a wide flight of stairs. He walked to the last room on the right—the corner room where the door was closed.

"This is our bedroom. I moved your trunk into it earlier so it's waiting for you."

Their bedroom. Not hers, but theirs. She knew he fully intended to share it with her tonight. "I'm sorry we ate all your lemon drops," she said inanely, wishing the sun had never set, night had never fallen.

"Did it work?"

"I beg your pardon?"

"Did it make the sadness go away?"

"Not entirely."

"I'm sorry to hear that."

"I'm sorry I screamed."

"I knew Maggie was hiding beneath my desk. I wouldn't have tried to startle her if I'd known you were there as well."

"I'm sorry I said you were heartless."

A corner of his mouth tipped up. "We could probably stand here all night apologizing for things we said or did throughout the day. Let's just acknowledge we got off on the wrong foot, and we'll go from there."

He put his hand on the doorknob.

"The first two conditions—" she said quickly.

He removed his hand from the door, straightened, and looked at her. She licked her lips.

"The first two conditions that my father agreed to . . . what were they?"

"Didn't he tell you?"

"He said you would share your water with him if I married you. Without the water, he would lose his cattle."

"That was the first condition. I promised to pull my fence back the morning after we were married."

"Was that your idea?" she asked.

"It was my offer."

"And the second condition?"

"When you give me a son, I'll deed a portion of my land over to your father."

"Was that your idea as well?"

He hesitated. "No."

Cordelia felt as though someone had just pulled her heart through her chest.

"Isn't there a name for a woman who trades her favors for gain?" she asked.

"There's also a name for a woman who takes a husband. You're my wife, not my whore."

"In this case, Mr. Leigh, it seems to be a fine line. May I have a few moments alone?"

He nodded and opened the door to their bedroom. "I'll see my brother and his family off, and then I'll come back."

She slipped inside the room, closed the door, and pressed her back against it.

Her father knew the fears she harbored, knew what she had seen as a child. She had been standing in the doorway, terrified, when he'd finally rolled off her mother.

He had promised her that no man would ever touch her. He had traded his promise for a strip of land, knowing full well that what Dallas Leigh expected of his wife was what her father had sworn she would never have to give.

Dallas leaned against the veranda beam and watched as Houston tucked Maggie into the back of the wagon. Amelia had been kind enough to help him clean up his office. He wished she had the power to wipe away his doubts as easily as she had wiped away the kitten's puddle.

Was a son such a terrible thing for a man to wish for?

"Have a safe journey home," he said.

Houston looked up from his task. "We will."

"If you need anything—"

"We'll be fine," Amelia said. "Get back to your wife."

Walking into the house, Dallas closed the door behind him. After a day filled with guests, the house seemed unbearably empty. His footsteps echoed down the hallway. He began climbing the stairs.

His wife was waiting for him. His wife. He'd planned to dance with her, toast her happiness, and charm her.

Instead, she'd seen his temper flare up more than once, and he'd frightened her. Her scream had been one of pure terror.

He stopped outside the door to his room. A pale light slipped into the hallway. She was inside waiting on him.

Tonight he'd have someone beside him, and with any luck, nine months from now, he'd have someone in his heart.

He'd vowed for better or worse. He'd do all he could to make everything better for her, but he'd live with worse if he had to.

He put his hand on the knob, turned it, and discovered she had locked him out.

By God, he had been challenged at every turn today, and he was damn tired of it. With a burst of rage that sent the blood rushing through his temples, he kicked in the door.

She screamed and flew out of the chair by the fire he'd built earlier in the hearth, clutching her brush to her breast.

"Never lock the door against me," he said in a low menacing voice. "Not in my house."

She shook her head and took a step back. "No, no, I wouldn't. I know my duty. I . . . I was just preparing myself for you."

Her duty. The words sounded incredibly harsh, but then what had he expected? She knew less about him than he knew of her because all she knew of him had come from her brothers, and it was obvious after the confrontation in his office and conversations held throughout the day that they had few kind words to say about him.

Her eyes were as large as a harvest moon, and he could see now that her brush was tangled in her hair. Tangled in her thick black hair that cascaded down to her narrow hips like a still waterfall.

She wore a white cotton shift with lace at the throat and tiny pearl buttons running down the front. Something a woman might sleep in.

As he took a step forward, he saw her bare toes curl. For some inexplicable reason, that small action touched him as nothing had all day. He glanced over at the door, hanging at an awkward angle, torn from the top hinges. He looked back at Cordelia. "I'll send someone up to repair the door."

She gave him a jerky nod. He walked from the room, rushed down the stairs, and stormed into the night. He saw Houston, standing by the wagon, kissing Amelia as though he hadn't spent the whole day with her, wasn't sharing the rest of his life with her. "Houston!"

Houston lifted his head and drew Amelia closer to him.

Dallas felt like a fool. A damn fool. "I need you to . . . to fix the door to my bedroom."

"Fix it? What happened to it?"

"A little misunderstanding. I kicked it in, and now it's hanging off the hinges. I thought it might be better if someone else repaired it."

Dallas grunted when Amelia hit him in the stomach.

"Watch our daughter," she ordered.

Amelia and Houston hurried into the house. Dallas walked to the back of the wagon and glanced inside. Maggie lay on a bundle of blankets, the kitten Dallas had given her curled within the curve of her stomach. "Wouldn't you like to have a little boy to play with?" he asked quietly.

He caught sight of a movement out of the corner of his eye. Austin was weaving toward the wagon. "Austin?"

Austin stumbled to a stop. "What?"

"Watch Maggie. I need a drink."

He ignored Austin's groan as he headed into the house.

Cordelia was shaking so badly that she didn't think she'd ever be warm. Amelia had added wood to the fire, but Cordelia still felt cold, so cold. Amelia had draped a blanket around Cordelia's shoulders but that hadn't brought any warmth with it either.

"I can't stay here," she whispered.

Amelia knelt before her and took her hands. "It'll be all right."

Cordelia shook her head. "My brother Duncan told me that you had married Dallas and that he had been so cruel that you left after only a week."

Cordelia saw a spark of anger ignite within the green depths of Amelia's eyes.

"Is that what he said?"

Cordelia nodded. "I can understand why you left him."

Amelia began to work the brush free of Cordelia's hair and smiled softly. "No, I don't think you do understand. I was promised to Dallas. A few days after we were married, he realized that I loved Houston, and that Houston loved me, so he gave me an annulment."

"I wish he'd give me one."

Amelia began to brush her hair. "I'll never forget what he said to me that night . . . when he let me go."

Cordelia didn't want to know anything more about the man she'd married, certain she knew all she needed to know. He had a temper worse than any she'd ever seen, that ignited like a piece of kindling.

Yet she remembered earlier in the day how he'd banked his temper when his niece had tugged on his trousers. The lemon drops. His unwillingness to let Boyd speak for her during the ceremony. Against her will, she heard herself ask, "What did he say?"

" 'I don't need love, Amelia, but I think you do, and if you find it with a man who dreams of raising horses, know you do so with my blessing.' " Amelia stood and handed Cordelia the brush. "I'll leave you with a little secret. Dallas does need love—more than any of us. I know your marriage hasn't begun under the best of circumstances, but I think if you give him a chance, he will worship the ground you walk on."

His elbows digging into his thighs, Dallas stared blankly at the low fire flickering within the hearth in his office. He remembered the day he'd married Amelia. He'd seen disappointment in her eyes, a touch of sadness, but there had also been hope and trust.

He thought about the day she had married Houston. She had glowed with love and happiness.

He hadn't expected the woman he married today to glow, but neither had he planned to fill her with raw fear. What had he been thinking to marry a woman he'd never met? He'd arranged to marry her as though she were little more than a carefully selected brood mare. He couldn't blame her for being offended, wary, and frightened.

"I fixed the door," Houston said.

Without turning his attention away from the fire, Dallas merely nodded. " 'Preciate it."

"You scared the hell out of Cordelia . . . again."

Dallas grimaced. "I know." He sighed deeply. "I know how to bed a whore. I've got no earthly idea how to go about bedding a wife."

"You didn't seem to have any problem when you were married to Amelia."

Dallas glanced up at the anger reflected in his brother's voice. He'd offended someone else without trying. "You know as well as I do that we never got that far. With Amelia getting kidnapped on our wedding night and you getting shot when we rescued her, I barely had the opportunity to kiss her. I never saw her standing in front of the fire in some flimsy gown that was little more than shadows. Cordelia has legs that go clear up to her shoulders."

Houston gave him an understanding smile. "I know all about shadows." He cleared his throat. "Look, Dallas, this is none of my business, but there's no law that says you gotta bed her tonight. Knowing her pa, she probably didn't have much say in this marriage. What would it hurt to give her a couple of days to get used to it?"

Dallas stood. "Yeah, I've been thinking the same thing. It's getting late. Did you and your family want to stay here tonight?"

" 'Preciate the offer, but there's a good moon tonight and a clear sky. We'll be fine."

Dallas followed his brother from his office and stood at the stairs, waiting while Houston walked through the front door. Dallas glanced up. The stairs had never before seemed so high. As he began to climb them, he started running apologies through his mind, trying to find the right one, the one that would undo all the damage he'd unwittingly inflicted on his wife's peace of mind.

When he reached his bedroom, he tapped lightly on the door and waited an eternity for her to open it.

Cordelia peered out at the formidable man standing in the hallway. She opened the door farther, giving him access to the room, offering him access to her. She watched as his Adam's apple slowly slid up and down.

"Be ready to ride before dawn," he said gruffly and turned toward the stairs.

Stunned, Cordelia stepped into the hallway. "You mean to ride a horse?"

He stopped walking and stared at her. "What the hell else do you think we ride? Cows?"

She shook her head. "No . . . I just . . . I have something to wear. I've just never . . . ridden a horse."

She thought if she released a deep breath, he'd fall over and tumble down the stairs.

"You've never ridden a horse?"

"Father said it was too dangerous. I always traveled in my coach."

"There is no way in hell my wife is going to travel around the countryside in that red contraption. I had your brothers take it with them."

"Oh." She pressed her hand to her throat, trying to think of something to say.

"I've got a gentle horse you can ride, and if you don't want her, you can ride with me."

Quickly she shook her head. "The gentle horse is fine."

"Good. Then I'll see you before dawn."

He spun on his heel and stomped down the stairs. Cordelia slipped back into her room, closed the door, and leaned against it. She pressed her fingers against her mouth. He had made her brothers take the hideous coach away!

Tomorrow, she was going to start riding a horse around the countryside.

She wrapped her arms around herself. He had said he'd see her in the morning. Did that mean she would be safe tonight? She could sleep alone?

She walked to the bed. It wasn't until she reached up to pull the blankets down that she noticed the flowers resting between the pillows.

Wilted now, their fragrance still wafted over the bed. She picked up a yellow flower and trailed her finger over the fragile petal. They grew over the prairie. Easy enough to find. Not much trouble to pick.

Yet tears welled in her eyes. So simple a gesture. She wanted to believe Amelia had left them for her, but somehow she knew they had been a gift from Dallas.

She walked to the far side of the room, drew the heavy draperies aside, opened a door of windows, and stepped onto the balcony.

In the distance, she saw the silhouette of her husband sitting on the top railing of the corral, his shoulders hunched, as he gazed in the direction of the moon.

Chapter 5

୬

CORDELIA LAY IN the massive oak bed listening for her husband's footsteps. Several minutes past midnight, she finally heard them on the stairs. She followed the sound along the hallway until she heard him stop outside her door. She held her breath, waiting for the click of the turning doorknob, the echo that would announce he was coming to claim her as his wife.

But all she heard was the fading tread of his boots as he walked away.

She rolled to her side and watched as the shadows played around the room. Her room.

She wondered how long he would give her before he insisted on making it "their" room.

She slept fitfully through the night and finally crawled from the bed in the early hours of the morning to prepare herself for her first ride on a horse. It was then, in the quietness before dawn, that she noticed the many things she'd overlooked the night before.

She washed her face using the water that filled the heavy oak washstand. She gazed at her reflection in the oval mirror that hung on the wall. She imagined Dallas usually shaved here. His shaving equipment rested on a small table beside the washstand. She knew he was skilled with a razor. His chin and cheeks had been smooth and carried no nicks or scars, save one small one just below his left eye, but she didn't think a careless razor had created it. His mustache had been evenly trimmed.

Using one of the two towels he had set beside the washstand, she patted the moisture from her face. Then she walked to the mirrored dresser, sat in the straight-backed chair, and unraveled her braid.

On the dresser, he had placed a small bottle of bay rum. Her brothers often doused themselves with it, yet it had smelled different on Dallas's tanned skin. He owned this ranch, but she didn't think he spent nearly as much time in his office as her father did. Dallas's features were too brown, too weathered.

She swept up her hair, then quickly donned her red riding habit. She'd only worn it once. The day Mimi St. Claire had delivered it to her, a gift from Cameron in hopes he could convince their father to let her ride. She had admired the woman for traveling to the ranch, unescorted, in a buggy. She had envied the woman the freedom she had to come and go as she pleased because she was not shackled to a man.

Cordelia had asked her father if perhaps she could do the same, but he had forbidden her to travel unescorted, as though he didn't quite trust her to return. No one had found the time to escort her to town after the day Dallas had set aside the land.

She had devoted so many years to caring for her mother that staying at home had become a way of life that she had seldom questioned. She had grown up with her father's adage, "A woman's place is in the home, tending her menfolk."

Cordelia jumped at the rapid-fire knock. Taking a deep breath, she crossed the room and opened the door. She was struck once again with the handsome shape of Dallas's chiseled features. His gaze slowly traveled from the tip of her hat to the tips of her toes.

"We need to go," he said in a voice that sounded as though he were strangling.

She followed him down the stairs and into the early morning darkness. He had tethered two horses to the front veranda.

"This is Beauty," Dallas said as he placed his hand on the mare's chestnut rump. "She's about as docile a horse as you'll ever find. Pull back on the reins to stop her. Give her a gentle nudge in the sides to make her go. For the most part, she'll just follow my horse."

"Sounds easy enough," Cordelia said.

Dallas looked at her and squinted. "You've never ridden?" he asked as though he thought he'd misunderstood her the night before.

She shook her head. "My father considered it unseemly and danger-ous for a woman to ride a horse."

He walked backward until he stood by the horse's shoulder. "You just grab the saddle horn, put a foot in the stirrup, pull up, and swing your other leg over."

Although she was tall, she still found the horn to be exceptionally high as she wrapped her hands around it. Dallas grabbed the stirrup and held it steady after her foot missed it twice. She slipped her booted foot into the stirrup, took a deep breath, and bounced up. Dallas grabbed her waist with one hand, pressed his other hand to her backside, and hoisted her over. Heat flaming her cheeks, Cordelia settled into the sad-dle. No one had ever touched her so intimately.

As the horse shied to the side, Cordelia dug her fingers into the sad-dle horn. Dallas grabbed the bridle, and the horse calmed.

"Take these," he said, holding the reins up to her.

Cordelia stared at the strips of leather threaded through his fingers. Long fingers that had easily spanned half her waist. She reached out and took the reins. "Thank you."

"You don't have to thank me," he grumbled as he stalked around to his horse and mounted in one fluid movement. "Come on. Give Beauty a gentle kick."

She did as he instructed, and Beauty followed Dallas's horse at a slow pace. She wondered how it would feel to gallop across the plains, the wind blowing in her face. She could feel the breeze now, just a slight breath over her cheeks.

The man riding beside her looked as though he'd been born to the saddle, as though he and his horse were one.

Cordelia glanced around, expecting others to join them. "Where's the escort?"

Dallas stared at her. "What escort?"

"My father always insisted that I travel with at least six men to guard me. I just assumed your men—"

"I protect what's mine," he said in a taut voice.

He didn't have to move his hand to the gun resting along his thigh or the rifle housed in his saddle to convince her that he spoke truthfully.

"What . . . what is your horse's name?" she asked.

"Satan."

The black devil rode Satan. It somehow seemed appropriate.

"I had a devil of a time breaking him," Dallas explained. "In the end, I had to let Houston handle him."

"You sound disappointed."

He shrugged. "That's where Houston's talent lies, taming horses."

"What is your talent?"

He held her gaze. "I build empires."

They rode west for over an hour with nothing but silence and a soft breeze between them.

Dallas fought to keep his gaze focused on the far horizon instead of on his new wife. He'd thought she had looked lovely dressed in white yesterday. In red, she was devastatingly beautiful. The deep shade brought out the richness of her porcelain skin, black hair, and brown eyes.

The combination was almost enough to make him change his mind about what he'd decided to do this morning. But the hesitancy in her voice when she spoke to him and the fear that still resided in her eyes kept him from altering his plans.

He drew Satan to a halt at the top of the small rise and turned the horse slightly. Beauty stopped beside him.

"Why did we stop?" Cordelia asked.

"To watch the sunrise."

He couldn't explain why he wanted to watch the sun ease over the horizon with this woman by his side. Dawn wasn't his favorite time of day. He preferred the night, when the clouds faded away to reveal the stars. The stars had guided him home countless times. As a boy, he'd even wished on them.

He had thought about asking Cordelia to ride with him last night when he couldn't sleep, but he'd needed time alone to think, to wade through the quagmire he'd inadvertently created. He didn't know if he could untangle the mess, but he was hoping he could give them a smoother trail to follow.

He heard her small intake of breath as the sun began to wash away the darkness. He wondered if she'd ever watched the start of a new day. He knew so little about her. It had all seemed unimportant until last night.

"It's beautiful," she said quietly.

So are you hung on the tip of his tongue, but he couldn't bring himself to say the words, not knowing how the morning would end.

Barely turning her face in his direction, she gave him a hesitant smile. "Thank you."

He grimaced. "I didn't make the sunrise. I just brought you to see it."

She nodded slightly and averted her gaze. He would have taken back the gruffness in his voice if he could. He didn't know why he always sounded angry when he spoke to her. Perhaps because the fulfillment of his final dream rested on her willingness to give it to him.

Reaching out, he grabbed Beauty's reins and turned both horses away from the rising sun.

Cordelia stared at the river, the men lining its far bank, and the barbed-wire fence that stretched along the length of the stream. In the distance, beyond the fence, a cloud of dust rose toward the sky as cattle tromped toward the fence.

She recognized her brothers leading the herd, Boyd with his arm still in a white sling, Duncan and Cameron on either side of him. They brought their horses to a halt, and the cattle wandered to a stop behind them as the men flanking each side cut off the cows that wanted to keep moving.

She heard the babbling of the river and low bawling of the cattle. Her heart tightened in her chest as she realized why Dallas had brought her here: to see exactly what her family had traded her for.

She wished she were skilled enough with a horse that she could simply gallop away.

Beside her, Dallas removed his hat and draped his wrist over his saddle horn. "I've always considered myself easy on the eyes. I've got more land than I know what to do with and enough money that my family will never do without. I assumed any woman would be pleased to have me for a husband.

"Your family and I have been feuding over this strip of land every since the day you arrived. I want a son. I want the feuding to stop. Marrying you seemed a way to have both. Unfortunately, I failed to take your feelings on the matter into consideration."

He shifted his gaze away from her. "See that man standing by the fence?"

She saw a tall, lean-boned man positioned next to the barbed wire, his horse tethered to a post. "Yes?"

"That's Slim, my foreman. You ride down there, and he'll cut the fence for you, let you go through so you can meet up with your brothers on the other side."

"And you'll still pull your fence back?"

He turned his dark unwavering gaze on her. "This land has soaked up my sweat and blood . . . and that of my brothers. I won't give an inch of it away if I receive nothing in return."

Her hopes plummeted. "And if I stay here?"

"Raise your hand and lower it. Then my men will pull the fence back. Today I'm giving you what your family and I failed to give you yesterday: a choice. Stay or go. It's your decision."

"But we're already married."

"It can be undone easy enough."

"My father and brothers will be furious.'

He held her gaze. "I'm prepared to deal with that."

"You broke Boyd's arm before. What will you do this time? Kill him?"

His gaze never faltered. "If I have to."

Her stomach lurched. She certainly couldn't accuse Dallas Leigh of being dishonest. Her mouth grew as dry as the wind. "You've only given me the illusion of a choice."

"Sometimes, that's all life gives any of us."

A few moments ago, she had marveled at the beauty of the sunrise, and now she was seeing the ugliness of men and their greed.

"Do you want to be married to a woman who hates you?" she asked, realizing with sickening dread that she could very well grow to hate this man.

He settled his hat on his head, throwing shadows over his face. "I don't need your love, but I need your decision. My men have work they need to get to."

She felt the anger seething through her. "My father was right. You are a coldhearted bastard."

He turned his head sharply as though he were as surprised by the vehemence in her voice as she was. She'd never in her life dared to speak so sharply to anyone. She expected him to give her what her father gave her brothers when they used that harsh tone on him: a backhand across the face.

"I'm giving you a choice he wasn't willing to give you," he said.

Hearing the tautness in his voice, she marveled at his restraint.

"I'll gladly take it," she said as she kicked the sides of her horse. She allowed the mare to take a half-dozen steps before she pulled back on the reins. She glanced over her shoulder. Dallas hadn't moved. Not a muscle. She remembered him as she had seen him last night: sitting on the corral, staring at the moon.

What choice had life given him for a wife? She hadn't counted, but she had seen fewer than a dozen women at her wedding. Her brothers were always discussing the absence of women, speculating as to where they might find a wife, going so far as to answer advertisements in magazines.

Perhaps an illusion of choice was all any of them truly had.

Her true choices were limited to living within the shadows cast by her father and brothers or living within the shadow cast by this man. Shadows when she longed for sunshine.

Prison was prison, but at least her current jailer gave her the freedom to ride, an inane reason to raise and lower her hand, but she did, never taking her eyes off her husband. The air suddenly filled with shrill whistles, whoops, and yells.

Dallas urged his horse forward until it was even with hers. "You might as well watch what you've given them," he said, his voice low.

She turned her gaze from him as his men lassoed the crooked posts and began pulling them back across the river. Her brothers removed their hats, waved them in a circle over their heads, and urged their horses forward, the cattle following.

"I want a son," Dallas said quietly.

Cordelia's heart thudded madly in her chest. "I'm aware of that. My family gets the land they want. And what do I get?"

He removed his hat and met her gaze. "Anything you want."

Cordelia considered asking for her freedom, but she knew in her heart that she would never abandon a child she brought into the world. His son would bind her to Dallas more strongly than any vows she had spoken yesterday.

She had never known what it was to hate anyone, but she felt the uncomfortable stirrings now. Her father had sheltered her, protected her, until she had become little more than a possession to be bartered away.

"Love?" she asked.

His eyes darkened. "Give me a son and I'll find a way to give it to you."

Austin dearly wanted to kill the little men who were building a town inside his head. Their constant pounding reverberated between his temples.

He forced himself to sit up and swing his legs over the side of the bed. The pounding grew louder, and he realized a good deal of it wasn't in his head at all.

"Breakfast is ready!"

He groaned at Dallas's booming voice.

"I'm coming," he mumbled. He bowed his head and hoped to God Dallas had let Cordelia sleep late. He didn't know how in the world he was going to be able to look her in the eye.

He shoved himself to his feet, washed up as quickly as he could, changed into a clean shirt, and headed down to breakfast.

Dallas and Cordelia were already sitting across from each other, Dallas chewing his food, Cordelia scraping the eggs from one side of her plate to the other. Austin took the chair between them.

"You look like hell," Dallas said.

"I feel like hell."

Dallas shoved a plate of fried eggs toward him. The yellow yolks quivered, and Austin's stomach roiled.

"Get something into your belly," Dallas ordered.

Austin reached for the coffeepot and poured the steaming black brew into his cup. "I just want coffee."

He planted his elbow on the table and set his chin on his palm to keep his face from falling to the table.

"'Preciate you hauling me to bed last night," Austin said.

"Couldn't very well leave you in the back of Houston's wagon."

He remembered thinking how comfortable Maggie looked curled up in the wagon, and he'd climbed in beside her. His mouth felt as though he'd swallowed the cat's tail.

"What time you gonna pull your fence back?"

"I've already pulled it back."

Grimacing at the censure in his brother's voice, Austin forced himself to meet Dallas's gaze. "Reckon I should have been there."

"Reckon you should have been, but it's done now. You planning to go into town today?"

"I don't think I could sit in a saddle for more than five minutes without puking."

Dallas shook his head. "What in the hell were you and Cameron thinking?"

"We were trying not to think."

Dallas leaned back in his chair. "I'm going to work on my books for a while, and then I need to check on the herd. Will you be able to take care of my wife if she needs anything?"

Austin glanced quickly at Cordelia and nodded.

"Good." Dallas scraped his chair back and picked up his plate.

"I'll clean that for you," Cordelia said softly.

Austin had never seen Dallas look as though he didn't know what to do, but he sure looked hesitant now. They weren't accustomed to having a woman around to see after their needs.

"I don't mind cleaning up after the meals," Cordelia said.

Dallas set the plate on the table. "Fine, then. I appreciate the gesture."

He strode from the room, and Austin wished he could have left with him, but he knew too many things remained unsaid between him and Cordelia, and living in the same house would be hell until everything was settled.

He took a long drag on his coffee, hoping to clear his head. Then he leaned toward her. "Do you mind if I call you Dee? I know Cameron does."

She glanced up, then back down. "That's fine."

"No, it ain't fine, and we both know why." He put his hand over hers, and she snapped her gaze up to his. He gave her a sad smile. "You heard something last night that you were never supposed to hear."

She lowered her gaze. "It doesn't matter."

He squeezed her hand until she looked at him again. "It does matter. When men get drunk, they say things they shouldn't. I won't deny that Dallas wants a son . . . bad. But I also know he'll treat you right, the way a man ought to treat a woman."

"Cameron told you I didn't have a nose?"

Austin grimaced. "Yeah, I don't know why he did that."

"And you told Dallas."

"Yep, and I don't know why I did that."

"And he still married me. He must be desperate indeed."

He took her hand between both of his. "You have to understand our family. You've seen Houston. Men don't come much more scarred than he is. Amelia fell in love with him. After seeing that, I reckon we just don't put much stock in looks."

"What in God's name did you think you were doing this morning?"

Dallas glanced up from the spittle that had landed on his desk and met Angus McQueen's fiery gaze.

"Moving my fence back."

"With my daughter on a horse, on a rise where she could have easily fallen and been killed. I told you she was delicate."

"Your daughter sits a horse well, McQueen. The horse is gentle enough that my three-year-old niece rides her. Your daughter was safe."

"So you say. You've got to protect her—"

"I'll protect her, but I'll do it my way."

Angus dropped into the chair. His sons continued to stand, their arms crossed, although Dallas thought Cameron looked as though he might bring up his latest meal at any moment, a thought he didn't find particularly reassuring.

"You just don't understand," Angus said. "Women can't protect themselves. You've got to keep them close or they'll harm themselves, just as my dear wife did."

Dallas rubbed his brow, trying to ease his headache. He'd wanted an end to the strife, and he'd only managed to reshape it. "Look, McQueen, she's my wife now. I'll take care of her."

"It's not easy to hand your daughter over to another man's keeping."

"Seemed easy enough yesterday. You couldn't even bother to drag yourself over here to be with her when the very devil himself took her as his wife."

McQueen narrowed his eyes. "I wasn't feeling well—"

"My guess is you'd spent the night before drowning your guilt, and a hangover kept you at home." When the man started to rise from his chair, Dallas held up a hand. "I don't want to hear it, McQueen. Your excuses, your worries, your concerns. I don't give a damn about any of them. You want to visit with your daughter, fine. Visit with her. But don't lecture me on how to care for her. You gave that right up when you traded her for my water. She can ride bareback, buck naked across the plains for all I care."

Dallas was certain the man was going to keel over from heart failure, his face turned so red, his mouth worked, but no words spewed forth.

Dallas stood. "I'll let her know you're here."

He walked from the room and up the stairs. Austin had told him Cordelia had retired to her room after they had finished breakfast. He had a feeling he hadn't accomplished all he'd planned to this morning. She was still too wary of him.

He knocked lightly on her door. He heard her quiet footsteps on the other side. She opened the door and peered out as though she expected to find a monster on the other side.

"Your family is in my office. They'd like to visit with you . . . if you want to see them."

"Yes, I'd like to see them."

"I need to check on my herd. I won't be back until after dark. Austin will be here if you need anything."

"Thank you," she said softly.

Not exactly what he wanted to hear. *Be careful. Hurry back. I'll wait up for you.* Any of those would have pleased him.

He slapped his gloves against his palm. She flinched.

Not caring much for the sting in his chest that her reaction caused, he turned to leave, stopped, and glanced over his shoulder. "Do you want me to stay while you visit with them?"

"No. I prefer to see them alone."

He headed down the stairs, knowing he hadn't accomplished a damn thing that morning.

*   *   *

Cordelia stood outside Dallas's office, gathering her courage. She had hoped her family would wait to visit, would wait until the ache in her heart had lessened. Taking a ragged breath, she walked into the room.

Cameron sat in a chair holding his head. She supposed the whiskey, and not illness, was responsible for that. Austin had looked much the same when he'd joined them for breakfast that morning.

Boyd and Duncan flanked her father. Her father brought himself out of the chair. She wished he didn't look so old.

"How are you, daughter?"

She eased farther into the room and sat in a nearby chair. "Fine. I'm fine."

Her father lowered himself into his chair and leaned forward. "Did the bastard hurt you last night?"

It suddenly occurred to her that she had never heard Dallas refer to any member of her family with such loathing. He never called them derogatory names. He never hinted that their parentage might be questionable or that they might not be men of honor.

"No, Father, my husband did not harm me."

"He didn't hurt you at all?" Boyd asked.

She glanced up and met Boyd's baffled gaze. "No, Boyd. Did you expect him to?"

"Did he bed you?" Boyd asked.

Cameron snapped his head up. "I don't see where that's any of our business."

"She came to him a virgin," Boyd said. "A virgin always feels pain. Did he or did he not bed you last night?"

Cordelia could not believe the words Boyd threw at her as though she had no feelings, no privacy. She had thought her heart would break last night when she'd heard the conditions of her marriage. At this moment, she felt her heart shatter. She wished she had the courage to ask them all to leave.

"Answer him, girl," her father said.

She stared at these men, wondering if she knew them at all. She didn't think she could have answered them if her life depended on it.

"Sweet Lord, you better not have denied him his rights last night," Boyd said.

"Do you think he would have pulled the fence back if she had denied him?" Cameron asked.

"I just want a simple answer, Cordelia. Yes or no." Boyd demanded. "Did he bed you?"

"That is absolutely none of your business."

Cordelia jerked her head around. Houston stood in the doorway, his hand resting on the gun housed in his holster. He tilted his head toward Cordelia. "Didn't mean to barge in. I was looking for Dallas."

"He . . . he had to check on the herd," Cordelia said.

"Well, then, I feel confident in speaking for him. You *gentlemen* need to be headin' out."

The way he said "gentlemen" made Cordelia realize he didn't consider them gentlemen at all.

Boyd glared at Houston. "That sounded like an order. This ain't your house."

"I'm gonna do you a favor, McQueen. I'm not gonna tell Dallas what I just heard in this room. Now bid your sister good day and head home."

Her father stood. "We were leaving anyway." He patted her head as though she were a trained dog. "We'll keep in touch."

Her father shuffled toward the door. Houston moved aside, leaving ample room for her father and brothers to file past.

Cameron stopped at the doorway and glanced at her before leaving. She thought he looked miserable.

Houston crossed the room and took the chair her father had vacated. "Are you all right?" he asked.

Nodding, she pressed her trembling fingers to her lips, fighting to hold back the tears.

"Think there are any lemon drops left in Dallas's desk?" he asked.

She shook her head. "I don't think they could take away a sad this big."

She didn't know how it happened, but suddenly his arms were around her and her face was pressed against his shoulder.

"Go ahead and cry," he said quietly.

The sobs came hard and heavy. "They don't care about me. They only want the land. Dallas only wants a son."

His arms tightened around her. "I can't deny it looks that way, but sometimes things aren't always the way they seem."

Stifling her sorrow, she worked her way out of his embrace. He handed her a handkerchief, and she wiped the tears from her face. She took a deep shuddering breath. "How is Maggie this morning? Is her tummy all right?"

"She's right as rain."

She handed his damp handkerchief back to him. "Thank you."

"You're more than welcome. I take it things aren't much better this morning."

She shook her head. "Dallas frightens me."

"I know. He frightens me, too, sometimes."

His words startled her. If Dallas scared his brother, what chance did she have of ever feeling comfortable around him? "Yesterday, when we were all in here, and Maggie ran to him, I was so afraid . . ." She sniffed. "You were here. You knew how angry he was, but you let her approach him anyway." She studied him, remembering how slowly, calmly he had come to his feet. "You knew he wouldn't harm her."

"With the exception of doors, Dallas isn't one to direct his anger at the innocent."

He wrapped his hands around hers, just as Austin had earlier. The small gesture was incredibly comforting. What she would have given if her father or brothers had done the same for her instead of badgering her for knowledge about her wedding night.

"It's probably not my place to say this," Houston said quietly, "but it might help you to understand Dallas a little better if you know . . ." He lowered his gaze.

Alarm rushed through her, and she scooted up in the chair. "Know what?"

He gave her an awkward smile. "I can talk to Amelia about the war, but I'd forgotten how hard it is to talk to others about it."

"The War Between the States?"

"The War of Northern Aggression is how Dallas refers to it. I was twelve, he was fourteen when our pa enlisted us."

"Fourteen?"

"Yep. I was Pa's drummer, and Dallas . . . Dallas was his second in command. A lot of the men resented that a boy was giving them orders. In the beginning they gave him a hard time, seemed to take delight in doing the opposite of what he told them to do. It bothered him, bothered him a lot. One night, I heard Pa giving him a dressing down because he'd discovered some men hadn't followed the orders Dallas had given. Pa told Dallas, 'They don't have to like you, but they gotta respect you and they gotta obey you.'"

Houston shook his head. "Dallas stopped caring whether or not they liked him. He stopped asking them to do things, and he started telling them. The habit stayed with him, even after the war ended."

He leaned forward. "I guess what I'm trying to say is that he doesn't mean to sound angry or hard, but a lot of people depend on him . . . and he's simply forgotten how to ask."

He released her hands and stood. "Well, I need to find Dallas and head back home. Will you be all right now?"

She liked the way he said "home." As though he knew of no finer place in the whole world.

"I'll be fine."

For long moments after he left, she simply sat in the chair and remembered the comfort of his touch, the calming resonance of his voice. She could certainly understand why Amelia had overlooked his scars and fallen in love with him.

Chapter 6

ॐ

As a clock downstairs chimed twelve times, Cordelia eased from the bed. Dallas hadn't come to her room. She wasn't even certain if he was home.

She wished she had brought her books. She had expected to be busy as a wife. She'd thought she would have no time for reading, but she found she had nothing but time.

She remembered the half-filled shelf in Dallas's office. She slipped on her night wrapper, increased the flame in the lamp, and headed into the dark, quiet hallway.

She crept toward the stairs, holding the lamp high. Careful of her step, she descended the stairs, walked to Dallas's study, and opened the door.

Her breath caught at the sight of Dallas sitting behind his desk. His head came up, and like a doe that scented danger, she couldn't move. The lamp on his desk burned low, so low that much of the room remained in shadow. He had the drapes drawn aside so the wide windows gave her a view of a thousand stars twinkling in the night sky.

He scraped his chair across the floor and stood.

She waved her hand. "No. Don't get up. I'm sorry. I didn't mean to disturb you. I didn't know you were here."

He angled his head. "You needed something?"

"I couldn't sleep. I remembered that I saw some books on your shelves. I thought I might borrow one."

"Help yourself."

She licked her dry lips. "Houston was looking for you this afternoon."

"He found me. His lumber came in. I'll be going to his place on Sunday to help him build an addition onto his house. You're welcome to come."

She thought of Maggie, Houston, and Amelia. She thought she would enjoy spending the day in their company, with people who weren't always angry. "I'd like that."

"Good. How was the visit with your family?"

"It was fine. Just fine." She walked quickly to the bookshelf. "I'll just be a minute."

"Take your time."

Only a half-dozen books stood at attention on the shelf. The covers were frayed and worn. She lifted the lamp higher until she could make out the title of the first book: *Whole Art of Husbandry*. The book nestled beside it was entitled *The Practical Husbandman*.

She trailed her fingers over the spines. Out of the corner of her eye, she saw her husband move in beside her. "Have you read these?" she asked.

"Every word," he said, his voice low, his breath skimming along her neck.

"You read books on how to be a husband?" she asked in awe.

She turned her head to find him staring at her. "I didn't know," she explained. "I didn't know books had been written on this subject. Do you think someone has written a book on wifery that I could read?"

He laughed. Deeply, richly. Smiling broadly, he touched his fingers to her cheek. The warmth that swirled through her body startled her, and she shrank back, her heart beating hard, her breath lodged in her throat.

His smile withered away, and he returned to his chair behind his desk. "Feel free to read any of my books."

She grabbed *The Practical Husbandman*. Surely the advice offered to a husband would apply to a wife. Clutching the book to her breast, she scurried across the room and stopped at the door. She swallowed hard before looking over her shoulder at her husband. He was watching her, but no humor remained in his dark eyes. "Will . . . will you be coming to bed soon?"

"Do you want me to?" he asked.

She tightened her fingers around the book. Was he giving her a real choice or only another illusion? "I'd rather you didn't."

"Then I won't." He dipped his pen into the inkwell and began to scrawl in his ledgers, dismissing her in the process.

"Thank you."

She hurried into the hallway and rushed up the stairs to her room. Setting the lamp on the bedside table, she removed her wrapper and slipped beneath the blankets. She put the pillows behind her back, brought her knees up, and opened the book, anticipating all the secrets it would unlock.

It was not the key she had hoped for.

With the early morning sunlight streaming through the window at the end of the hall, Dallas stood outside the door to his bedroom, knowing he had the right to simply walk into the room, knowing it was a right he wouldn't exercise. Not yet anyway.

He hated the fear he saw in his wife's eyes every time she looked at him. The few times he'd touched her, the fear had intensified. What the hell did she think he was going to do: ravage her?

He despised the way she opened the door and peered out as though fearful of what she might find on the other side, but he knocked anyway. She opened the door, and he bit back his frustration at the apprehension reflected in her eyes.

"I'm sending one of my men into town this morning to pick up some supplies. If you'll give me a list of things you need, I'll have him pick them up for you."

"Oh, thank you. I'll only be a moment."

He stepped into the doorway as she hurried to the bureau and tore a piece of paper from a book. He supposed she kept a journal. He knew so little about her, but he discovered he liked the shape of her backside when she bent over and began to write on the piece of paper. She straightened and turned sooner than he would have preferred. Hesitantly, she held the paper toward him. He took it from her.

"Thank you," she said softly.

He hated her gratitude as well. He stalked from the house and crossed the yard to where a young man was waiting beside the wagon.

He extended the slip of paper toward Pete. "Need you to pick these up for my wife."

Pete dropped his gaze and started kicking the ground with the toe of his boot.

"Come on, boy, I ain't got all day." Dallas shook the list under his nose. "Take the list and git."

Pete looked up, his freckled face redder than the hair that his hat covered. "I can't read."

"What do you mean you can't read? I give you a list every week, and you take it into town and pick up my supplies."

Pete shifted his stance. "Nah, sir. Cookie reads the list to me. I remember everything on the list, but I didn't know you were gonna have another list for me, and Cookie's gone out with the herd today, but you can tell me what she wrote and I'll remember it. I got a good memory."

Dallas figured over half his men probably couldn't read. They were smart men he could depend on to get the job done, and that job seldom required reading. His son would need a tutor if the town didn't have a school in a few years. Dallas would see to it that the tutor also taught any of his men who wanted to learn. Meanwhile, they'd do the best job they could with what they had.

Dallas unfolded Cordelia's list and stared at the singe word she'd written.

Pete cleared his throat. "You don't read neither?"

Dallas met the young man's earnest gaze. "No, I read just fine, but this is something I'll need to take care of myself. You go on to town and get the supplies I need."

"Yes, sir."

Not until Pete had climbed on the wagon and started to roll toward town did Dallas dare to look at his wife's list again. He shook his head in bewilderment, wondering if he'd ever understand how a woman's mind worked, convinced he'd never understand his wife.

He headed into the house, searching through every room, certain she wouldn't still be in her bedroom. She'd been dressed when he'd knocked on her door earlier. Surely she didn't stay in the bedroom all day.

But when he knocked on her bedroom door, she opened it as hesitantly as she always did. He held up her list. "Flowers? You wanted my man to go into town and purchase you some flowers?"

She blinked, clutching her hands before her. "I was thinking he could pick them on his way back to the ranch."

"Why can't you pick them?"

Her brown eyes widened with alarm. "They're outside."

"I know where flowers are."

"I'm not allowed outside. The dangers—"

"Jesus Christ! Were you a prisoner in your father's house?"

Tears welled in her eyes. "In Kansas, I cared for my mother. Here . . . here, my father thought it was in my best interest to stay inside. He said there were dangers. Renegades. Outlaws. A woman wasn't safe."

Dallas repeatedly swept his thumb and forefinger over his mustache, trying to make sense out of what she had just said. "Have you been staying in this room all day?"

She nodded. "Is there another room I should stay in?"

He slammed his eyes closed. She wasn't just afraid of him. She was afraid of everything. Good Lord, could he have married a woman who was more opposite than he was?

Heaving a sigh, he opened his eyes. "You don't have to stay in any room. You don't have to stay in the house. If you want flowers, go out and pick them."

She looked aghast. "But the dangers—"

"I'm not leaving you alone here. My men are about. If you need them all you have to do is holler. They'll be by your side before your mouth closes, so go get your flowers."

He turned to walk away.

"Where will you be?" she asked.

"Checking on my herd." He wished he hadn't seen relief plunge into her eyes.

Cordelia stood on the front veranda, enjoying the feel of the warm breeze as it riffled through her hair, gently working the strands free from her bun. She inhaled deeply and imagined that she could smell freedom. The freedom to roam from the house to the barn, to walk in the fields that lay beyond the house.

She could hear the steady clanking of iron on iron. She stepped off the porch and walked toward the lean-to on the other side of the barn. A man worked bellows to heat the coals.

"Hello," she said softly.

He turned his dark gaze toward her. He was powerfully built, his black skin glistening with his labors. "Ma'am."

"I was just taking a stroll," she told him.

"Nice day for it. 'Nother month or so and it'll be too hot to enjoy."

She gnawed on her lower lip. "I think I saw you at my wedding, but I don't remember your name."

"Samson."

She blushed self-consciously at the sight of his muscles straining against his shirt, the arm hanging at his side that still looked as if it were gripping something. "Samson? The name suits you."

"Yes, ma'am, that's what my master thought when he named me."

"You were a slave?"

"Yes, ma'am, surely was."

She allowed her gaze to roam past him to the open land that stretched toward the horizon. "Freedom is a little frightening, isn't it, Samson?"

"Yes, ma'am, it surely is, but it brings with it a measure of glory. I remember the first breath of air that I took as a free man. I thought it smelled so much sweeter than anything I'd ever breathed before."

She linked her fingers together. "I was thinking of picking some flowers."

"You do that, and when you get out where the flowers are the brightest, you just stop a minute and take a deep breath."

She smiled shyly. "I will."

She walked around the side of the barn just as another man was walking out of the barn. She remembered his name because it described him so well and because he had been waiting at the barbed-wire fence for her decision.

"Hello, Slim," she said hesitantly.

He came to a quick halt and doffed his hat. "Mrs. Leigh."

Cordelia's stomach tightened. She thought she might never get used to having that name directed her way. "Is Beauty inside the barn?"

"No, ma'am. I took her back to Houston."

Disappointment reeled through her. She had so liked the horse.

"You want me to saddle up another horse for you?" Slim asked.

Cordelia shook her head. "No, I'm just going to walk today."

"Well, you let me know if you want to ride, and I'll find you a horse."

"Are you married?"

Beneath his dark tan, his face flushed. "No, ma'am."

"Is anyone around here married?"

"Dallas is married, but then I reckon you knew that."

He smiled as though they were sharing a private joke.

"Yes, I knew that." She waved her hand before her. "I was just going to walk out there and pick some flowers. Do you think it's safe?"

"Oh, yes, ma'am. Just watch out for prairie dog holes. Wouldn't want you to turn your ankle."

"Thank you for the warning."

She walked through the tall prairie grasses, enjoying the feel of the sun warming her face.

Before her accident, her mother had tended a flower garden, the only time she had seemed truly at peace. Years had passed since Cordelia had thought about her mother's garden, the sweet lilt of her mother's voice as she had hummed while she tended the flowers, the sharp fragrance of freshly turned soil on her mother's hands, and the beautiful blossoms that had always adorned each room.

Cordelia bent and plucked a wildflower. She wondered if Dallas would mind if she planted flowers near the veranda. Surely not, if he didn't mind if she walked beyond the house.

She glanced over her shoulder. The house wasn't so far away that she couldn't see it. She could still hear the steady pounding of the blacksmith as he worked.

As though she were a child, she sat on the ground, tilting her head back, and closed her eyes. She had spent long hours reading books to her mother. They had taken Cordelia everywhere that she wasn't allowed to go while taking her mother to places where she could no longer go.

After her mother had died, Cordelia had continued to retreat into her books. It had been easier than trying to step beyond the boundaries her father had established over the years.

Until she had married Dallas, she had been content with a life that revolved more around fiction than reality. But now she wondered what she may have missed, what did lie beyond her small world.

She only knew that she had no skills when it came to talking to a husband. Each time she looked into his dark brown eyes, her heart sped up, her palms grew damp, and her breath would slowly dwindle away to nothing.

If only he didn't always seem so angry.

"Well, now, what are you doing?"

She opened her eyes and was greeted with Austin's smiling face as he hunkered down beside her. He had the most beautiful blue eyes she'd ever seen, eyes the shade of the hottest flames that writhed within a fire.

She held up her solitary flower. "I was picking flowers."

"There are prettier ones farther out." He stood and held his hand toward her. "Come on."

She slipped her hand into his, and he pulled her to her feet. As they began to walk, her hand remained nestled within his. She wished she could feel this comfortable around her husband.

Cordelia heard a small bark. She glanced around, but couldn't see any sign of a dog. The bark came again, a tiny yip.

Austin released her hand and withdrew his gun from its holster.

"What is it?" she asked.

"A prairie dog," he said as he picked up his pace. "You stay here."

She had never disobeyed a man's order before, and she didn't know what possessed her to disobey now . . . perhaps it was the pitiful cry that sounded so much like a hurt child or the fact that Austin reminded her of Cameron and she had yet to think of him as a man.

She saw the small brown animal before Austin did, whimpering as its tongue darted out beneath its long snout to lick its paw.

"Oh, no," she whispered as she rushed forward, knelt beside the small creature, and studied the iron trap that had captured its paw. "Who would do such a thing?"

Austin crouched beside her. "Head on back to the house. I'll put it out of its misery."

She snapped her head around. "I don't think her leg is broken. Her bone isn't sticking out like Boyd's did when Dallas broke his arm."

"What's that got to do with anything?" Austin asked.

Cordelia furrowed her brow. "If you can pull the metal sides apart, I could remove her paw from the trap. Then I could take her to the house and tend her wound."

Austin could do little more than stare at the woman. "It's a prairie dog," he reminded her.

Cautiously, she brushed her fingers over its head. "It's just a baby. Please help her."

Dee was looking at him with so much hope in her big brown eyes that he couldn't do what he knew needed to be done. He slipped his gun into his holster. Thank God, she was married to his brother and not to him. Dallas could break her heart. Austin wouldn't.

Near dusk, Dallas brought his horse to a halt in front of the corral. The flowers he'd pulled from the ground along the way had wilted in his hand. He dismounted, trying to decide if his wife would want them anyway.

"Boss?"

He turned at Slim's irritated voice.

"We got trouble," the lanky man said.

Dallas sighed, not at all surprised. One of his wells had run dry, and he had cattle dying on the north end. "What kind of trouble?"

"Prairie dog. Austin took your wife walking, and they found a prairie dog. He let her keep it."

"He what?"

"He let her take it into the house to doctor it up. Said she was gonna feed it some milk. You ever hear of anything like that? I dadgum guarantee that ain't gonna sit well with the men. Thought you oughta know."

The flowers fell from Dallas's hand. "See after Satan, will you?"

"You'll get rid of that prairie dog, won't you?" Slim asked.

"I'll get rid of it."

Marrying a woman he didn't know hadn't sounded like such a bad idea until he'd done it. What in the hell could she want with a prairie dog?

Dallas strode toward the house. Austin sat on the steps, one long leg stretched out before him, the other serving as a resting place for his violin as he plucked the strings.

Dallas ground to a halt, and Austin tilted his head back, his blue eyes looking as innocent as a newborn babe's.

"Tell me that we're having prairie-dog stew for supper," Dallas commanded.

Austin smiled. "I'd be lying if I said that. Learned long ago that lying only brings trouble."

"Then what in the hell were you thinking to let her take a prairie dog into the house?" Dallas bellowed.

Austin lifted a shoulder in a careless shrug. "She ain't my wife. Didn't think it was my place to tell her she couldn't keep it. Figured that decision was yours to make."

"There's no decision to make. A prairie dog isn't a pet. It's a varmint."

"You gonna tell her that?"

"Damn right I am."

"You gonna tell her she can't keep it?"

"Hell, yes, I'm going to tell her she can't keep it."

Austin shook his head. "I sure wouldn't want to walk into that house wearing your boots."

"You couldn't if you wanted. Your feet are too big. Where is she?"

"Last I saw her, she was in the kitchen."

He marched through the house and strode into the kitchen. With the creature squirming in her lap, Cordelia fidgeted in a straight-backed chair. She jerked her head up.

"Oh, thank goodness," she said on a rushed sigh with obvious relief.

The anger drained right out of him at the sight of her lovely face with no fear in her eyes.

"Here," she said as she stood and held the varmint toward him. "Hold her."

"What?"

"Hold her," she repeated as she shoved the animal into his hands, grabbed his arm, and pulled him to the chair. "Sit down."

Stunned by the urgency in her voice, Dallas sat.

"I cleaned her wound and put some salve on it, but I was having a terrible time trying to wrap her leg," she explained as she picked a strip of white linen off the floor. "Hold her paw for me so I can dress it. Otherwise, she'll lick off the salve."

Dallas fought to hold the animal motionless while Cordelia wound a piece of good clean linen around its wound.

Her hands suddenly stilled, and she looked at him. "Someone set a trap on your land. What sort of cruel person would do that?"

Guilt had him clearing his throat. "Someone who recognized that a prairie dog is dangerous."

Her hands once again stilled. "How is she dangerous?"

"Because it lives underground and burrows holes across the prairie. A horse drops a leg into that hole, he usually breaks his leg and has to be shot."

"Then the hole is dangerous, not the prairie dog."

"That's like saying a gun is dangerous, not the man holding it."

"It's not the same at all." She finished wrapping the bandage around its paw. "Austin thought I should name her Trouble, but I like the name Precious. What do you think?"

He thought he could get used to carrying on a conversation with her that wasn't guided by fear, but he had to deal with this unpleasant task first. "Prairie dogs are a cowboy's worst enemy. You can't keep it."

"Why? I'll keep Precious with me. I won't let her dig any holes."

"I need to take the prairie dog outta here."

She grabbed the animal from his hands and scurried to the corner, hunching her shoulders as though to protect herself and the animal. "What are you going to do with her?" she asked, the apprehension plunging into her eyes.

The dog released a high-pitched yelp. Dallas couldn't tell the woman he was going to shoot the varmint. He shoved himself to his feet with such force that the chair teetered and toppled to its side. His wife flinched.

"I'll make it a damn leash, but if it gets off the leash I won't be responsible for it."

Dallas stormed through the kitchen door at the back of the house and headed into the barn. He jerked the reins off the wall and stalked to the workroom at the back of the building. He set the leather strips on the scarred table, unsheathed his knife, and started cutting.

If he ever had any daughters, he was going to teach them how to deal with a rough world. They could cuss, chew tobacco, and drink like a man for all he cared, but they sure as hell weren't going to be docile creatures afraid of their own shadows or their husbands' voices.

He heard the muffled footsteps and carved more deeply into the tanned hide.

"So did you break the news to her?" Austin asked as he leaned against the doorway.

"Yep," Dallas ground out through his clenched teeth as he drilled a ragged hole into the leather with the point of his knife.

"How did she take the news?" Austin asked.

"She took it just fine."

Austin shook his head. "Sure wish I had your skill with people. I couldn't think of a way to tell her without breaking her heart."

He ambled into the room and looked over Dallas's shoulder. "What are you doing?"

"Working."

"I can see that. What are you making?"

Dallas tightened his jaw until it ached. "A leash."

"A leash? For what? That's so tiny . . . Good Lord! You're letting her keep it."

Dallas spun around and brandished the knife in front of his brother's face. "Don't say another word. Not one word. If you value your hide, you'll wipe that stupid grin off your face and get the hell out of here."

Holding up his hands, Austin began to back away. "I wouldn't dream of saying anything."

But when he was out of sight, his laughter echoed throughout the barn.

Chapter 7

༚

*A*IN'T NEVER SEEN a prairie dog on a leash before," Houston said.

Dallas slammed a nail into the fresh lumber, hoping that his brother would choke on his strangled laughter.

"A man of vision would open himself up a store in Leighton that sold leashes especially designed for prairie dogs," Austin added, grinning.

Dallas stopped his hammering and glared at his youngest brother. "If you don't want *your vision* hampered by two swollen eyes, you'll discuss something else."

"I think Austin has a valid point," Houston said. "With all the prairie dogs around here, selling leashes could be a booming business, particularly for a man interested in building empires."

"No doubt about that," Austin said, "and it doesn't take Dallas long to put a leash together. The one he made Dee only took about ten minutes, and he wouldn't have needed that much time if he hadn't carved the dog's name into it."

Houston started to chuckle. "You gotta have the dog's name on it just in case he loses it. How else would you know who it belongs to?" The laughter he'd been holding in exploded around them.

Austin's guffaws filled what little space remained for noise. Dallas failed to see the humor in the situation.

"Thought you wanted to add onto your house?" he asked.

He could see Houston struggling to stifle his laughter. He had a strong desire to come to his brother's aid and hit him up side the head with his hammer.

"I do," Houston finally managed to say.

"Then we need to stop jawing and get the frame up."

"You're right," Houston admitted, his face growing serious a brief moment before his laughter erupted again. "Good Lord, Dallas, a prairie dog on a leash. I never thought you'd let a woman wrap you around her finger."

"I'm not wrapped around her finger, and I liked you a lot better when you never laughed."

Houston's laughter dwindled. "But I didn't like me. Didn't like me at all."

Dallas knew Houston had held himself in low esteem until Amelia had wrapped herself around his heart. He also knew no wrapping would take place between him and Cordelia . . . not around his heart, not around her finger. It wasn't his way.

He unfolded his body. "Let's get this frame up."

"It's so good to hear them laughing, to know they're enjoying each other's company," Amelia said.

Cordelia glanced at the woman standing beside her, her fingers splayed across her stomach, a contented smile on her face.

"When I first came here, they seldom spoke to each other and they never laughed," Amelia confided quietly.

"Why?" Cordelia asked.

"Guilt and misunderstandings mostly." As though drawn to painful memories of another time, Amelia released a long, slow sigh before walking to the open mesquite fire where the beef was cooking.

Cordelia watched as the men began to raise the frame that would serve as the structure for the addition to Houston's house. She was rapidly discovering that Dallas did everything as though he were on a quest for success.

Along with Austin, they had begun their trek long before dawn and had arrived at Houston's homestead just as dawn whispered over the horizon. Dallas helped her dismount before taking the cup of coffee that Amelia offered him as she stepped onto the porch.

"You know what you want?" he asked Houston as his brother slipped his arm around Amelia and kissed her cheek.

"Yep," Houston said, handing Dallas a scroll.

Dallas unrolled the parchment and held it up so the day's new light could shine on it. "Looks like you want to add two rooms to the back and put a loft above them."

"That's what Amelia wants."

"Then let's get to it."

And they had. The measuring, the sawing, the pounding of hammers against nails, nails into wood, had echoed over the prairie.

When they finished setting the frame in place, Dallas took his first break. Cordelia held Precious more securely within her arms and watched as Dallas jerked off his hat, pulled his sweat-soaked shirt over his head, and shook like a dog that had just come out of a river. He tossed his shirt over a nearby bush, settled his hat into place, and returned to work. Although he had not spared her a glance since their arrival, she could not take her eyes off him.

His bronzed back glistened, his muscles bunching and stretching as he hefted a board. His long legs made short work of the distance between the pile of lumber and the newly erected frame. He laid the board against the frame and crouched, one hand holding the board in place while the other searched through the grass for his hammer. His trousers pulled tight across his backside. She didn't think she'd ever noticed how lean his hips were. He reminded her of the top portion of an hour glass: his broad shoulders fanning out, his back tapering down to a narrow waist—

"I wish they hadn't done that," Amelia said on a sigh.

Her cheeks flushed, Cordelia glanced at Amelia. "What?"

"Taken off their shirts. I'm trying to prepare dinner, and all I want to do now is watch them work."

Cordelia turned her attention back to the men. She didn't know when Houston and Austin had removed their shirts, but their backs didn't draw her attention the way Dallas's did, didn't make her wonder if his skin was as warm as it looked.

She watched as Maggie ran toward the men, her blond curls bouncing as much as the ladle she carried. Water sloshed over the sides.

Cordelia didn't think more than a few drops could have remained in the ladle when the little girl came to an abrupt stop beside Dallas and held it out to him.

A warm smile spread beneath his mustache as he took the ladle, tipped his head back, and took a long, slow swallow. As Maggie clasped her hands together and widened her green eyes, Cordelia had a feeling Dallas was putting on a show for his niece. When he moved the ladle from his mouth, he touched his finger to the tip of her nose and said something Cordelia couldn't hear. Maggie smiled brightly, grabbed the ladle, and ran back to the bucket of water.

Breathless, she looked up at her mother. "Unca Dalls said it was the sweetes' water he ever had the pleasure of drinkin'. I'm gonna git him some more." She dunked the dipper into the bucket before running back to her uncle, the water splashing over her skirt.

"Poor Dallas. She adores him. He won't get any work done now," Amelia said.

"The feeling seems to be mutual," Cordelia said, wishing he would bestow that warm smile on her.

"You're right. He spoils her. I shudder to think how he will spoil his own children."

The heat fanned Cordelia's cheeks at the reminder of her wifely duties. "I . . . I meant to thank you earlier for the flowers you placed on my bed the day I was married."

Amelia smiled. "I didn't place any flowers on your bed."

"Oh." Cordelia looked back toward Dallas. They had finished raising the frame and securing it in place. The men had begun to lay the wooden planks for the floor. Dallas was holding a nail while Maggie tapped it with a hammer. After a few gentle taps, Dallas took the hammer from her and slammed the nail into place.

She didn't know what to make of Dallas Leigh. He seemed as hard as the nails protruding from his smiling mouth, hardly the type of man to pick flowers . . .

Knowing for certain that he was the one who had placed the flowers on her—their—bed made it difficult for her to dislike him, much less to hate him. Yet still she did not relish the thought of the marriage act.

Maggie scrambled over the frame they had laid across the ground— the frame that would support the floor—and began to hold nails for

Austin. Although he carried his arm in a sling, he was managing to pull his share of the load. Something Cordelia had to admit she wasn't doing. "Amelia, what can I do to help?"

"I left several quilts on the porch. Why don't you place them around the tree so we can sit under the shade?"

Cordelia set Precious on the ground, and with her pet tagging along on her leash, hurried to the porch, grateful to have a task, although she didn't think it would stop her mind from wandering to thoughts of her husband.

From the corner of his eye, Dallas watched his wife scurry toward the front of the house. He was having a hell of a time keeping his mind focused on the task at hand—building Houston's house.

He kept finding his thoughts drifting toward his wife. It hadn't helped that during the week she had laundered his clothes and when he had begun to sweat earlier, her lavender scent had risen up around him. He'd thought he might go insane, having her fragrance surround him while she stood incredibly far away.

He had made a mistake not exercising his husbandly rights on their wedding night. Now, he had no idea how to approach her and let her know that her reprieve was over.

He knew if he knocked on her door, she'd open it with terror in her eyes, and he couldn't stand the thought. She reminded him of the way too many soldiers had looked at him during the war. They'd followed his orders and gone into battle, fearing him more than they had feared the enemy or death.

He didn't believe in living with regrets, but sometimes he wondered how many men his hard nature had sent to their deaths.

He didn't want his wife looking at him with that same fear in her eyes when he came to her bed. Only he didn't know how to erase it. For a short time while they had tended the prairie dog, the fear had left her eyes, but Dallas couldn't see himself bringing her a wounded prairie dog every night.

He brought himself to his feet and went to fetch more boards and nails. When he neared the pile of lumber, he stopped long enough to admire his wife's backside as she bent over and laid quilts on the ground.

He wished he knew how to keep the fear out of her eyes—permanently.

They ate their meals in silence except for the conversation Austin provided. Dallas could never think of a single thing to say to his wife. It reminded him of when he had first started writing to Amelia. His first letter had only been a few lines. By the end of the year, he had been sharing whole pages of his life with her. He'd thought about writing a letter to Cordelia, but that seemed the coward's way out. He needed to learn how to say the kind of words that put a softness in a woman's eyes, the kind of softness Amelia wore every time she looked at Houston.

He carried several boards to the frame structure, set them in place, knelt beside one, and removed the nails from his mouth. "Houston, when you and Amelia were traveling here . . . what did you talk about?"

Houston pounded a nail into a board that would serve as flooring and shrugged. "Whatever she wanted to talk about."

Dallas clamped down on his frustration. "What did she want to talk about?"

Houston tipped his hat up off his brow. "You, mostly. She was always asking questions about the ranch, the kind of man you were, the house."

"You must not have told her the truth about the house if she came anyway," Austin said.

Dallas swung his gaze around. "What's wrong with my house?"

Austin wiped the smile from his face and looked at Houston. Houston shook his head and gave him a "you should have kept your mouth shut this time" look. Then he started pounding a nail into the board.

"What's wrong with my house?" Dallas asked again.

"Uh, well, uh . . . it's big," Austin explained.

"Of course it's big. I intend to have a large family."

"Well, then, there's nothing wrong with it," Austin said. He handed Maggie a nail. "Maggie May, hold it right here for your Uncle Austin."

Dallas glared at his brother, trying to make sense out of what he'd just heard. "Your comment had nothing to do with the size of my house. I want to know what you meant."

Austin slammed his eyes closed and blew out a quick breath before meeting Dallas's gaze. "It doesn't look like a house. It's . . . it's . . ." He shifted his gaze to Houston, who had stopped his hammering.

Dallas thought his brother might be searching for courage. He knew his house was unusual.

Austin looked back at Dallas. "I think it's downright ugly. There, I said it, but that's just what I think. Houston might think otherwise."

Houston narrowed his eye. "Keep me outta this conversation, boy."

Dallas felt as though a herd of cattle had just trampled him. "Do you agree with him?" he asked Houston.

Houston clenched his jaw. "It's different. That's all. It's just different. It's not what I'd want to live in—"

"Food's ready!" Amelia called.

"Thank God," Houston said as he stood. "I'm starving. How about you, pumpkin?" Maggie squealed as he swung her into the air.

Dallas unfolded his body and grabbed Austin's arm before he could escape. "Why didn't you ever say anything before?"

Austin's face burned bright red. "You were just so proud of it, and what we think isn't important. What matters is what Dee thinks of it. Maybe you ought to ask her."

Ask her if she hated the house as much as she hated her husband? Not if he lived to be a hundred would he ask her.

"I like the house," he stated flatly.

Austin gave him a weak smile. "Then there's no problem. Let's go eat."

After tethering Precious to a nearby bush, Cordelia watched with growing trepidation as the men approached. Each had quickly washed at the water pump before slipping back into his shirt. For that small act, she was extremely grateful. She didn't think she could eat if Dallas's chest had remained bare.

She had laid three quilts around a wooden box. Amelia had set platters of beefsteak strips and potatoes on the box, plates and utensils on the quilts.

Amelia sat on one quilt. Houston dropped beside her, Maggie nestled in his arms. "Looks good," he said.

Cordelia knew it was pointless to hope that Austin would sit on the quilt beside her, but she found herself wishing anyway. He gave her a smile before he took his place on the opposite quilt.

On the small quilt, Dallas seemed incredibly large as he sat beside her.

"This isn't one of my cows, is it?" Dallas asked.

Houston smiled. "Probably. He wandered onto my land. What was I supposed to do?"

"Send him home."

"Not on your life."

Austin held out his arm. "Will you lookee here? I'm the only one without a woman to share my quilt. Maggie May, come sit with me."

Her face bright with excitement, Maggie jumped up, crossed the small area, and rammed into Austin. Hissing sharply, Austin moved her aside with his good arm.

Houston snatched his daughter back into his arms. "You all right?" he asked Austin.

Austin had paled considerably, but he nodded. "I'm fine."

"Sorry," Maggie said, her bottom lip trembling.

He smiled. "It's all right, sweetie. I'm still a little sore." He patted his thigh. "Just come sit beside me, not on me, all right?"

Ever so carefully and slowly, she crawled over the quilt and sat beside him.

"What happened to your arm?" Cordelia asked.

A hush fell over the gathering as everyone looked at Cordelia. The heat rushed to her face. "I'm sorry. I didn't think to ask before."

Austin appeared uncomfortable as he answered, "I got shot."

"Dear Lord. Outlaws?" she asked, horrified at the thought.

"Cattle rustlers," Dallas said as he slapped potatoes onto his plate. "But they won't be bothering us anymore."

"I'm grateful to hear that," Cordelia said. She cut her meat into tiny pieces, eating sparingly.

"You don't eat enough to keep a bird alive," Dallas said.

She glanced up to find him glaring at her plate, his brow deeply furrowed. She couldn't very well tell him that whenever he was around her stomach knotted up so tightly that she could barely swallow.

"I've never been a big eater," she said quietly and dropped her gaze to her plate.

"Guess I'm just used to watching men eat," Dallas said gruffly.

"I never eat as much as my brothers," she said.

A desperate silence surrounded them. Cordelia wished she could think of something—anything—to say.

"When do you think the railroad will get here?" Amelia asked.

Dallas reached for more potatoes. "Sometime next year."

"Things should change then," Amelia said quietly.

"Reckon they will. With any luck, Leighton will start growing as fast as Abilene. I'll be wanting to build a school. Do you want to be in charge of finding a good teacher?" Dallas asked.

Amelia smiled. "I'd love to. Besides, I have experience at placing advertisements, and we'll definitely want someone from the East."

"Give me a list of everything you'll need so I can tally up the costs before I go talk to Mr. Henderson at the bank."

Amelia leaned forward and took Cordelia's hand. "Dee, would you like to help me?"

Cordelia glanced at Dallas. He was studying her as though waiting for her answer. Surely if he had wanted her to help, he would have suggested it.

"I don't know anything about schools. I had a tutor."

"Then we'll learn together," Amelia said.

Cordelia shook her head. "No, I don't think I can—"

"Our son will do his learning at this school," Dallas said. "You ought to have a say in it."

Cordelia nodded quickly. "All right, then, I will."

"Good," Dallas said brusquely.

Amelia squeezed Cordelia's hand. "It'll be fun."

Yes, she imagined it would be, and it would give her something to do besides wash dishes and clothes. Dallas and Austin were seldom inside the house and maintaining it required so little of her time that she thought she could quite possibly go insane.

The conversation turned to other aspects of Leighton, but it made little sense to Cordelia. She had not visited the town since the day the land had been set aside. She'd asked several times for someone to take her, but none of her brothers had ever had time. She had always thought it would be exciting to watch something grow from nothing . . . like watching a child grow into an adult.

Her husband had planted the seeds for the town the day he had set aside the land. She remembered that Boyd had called him a greedy bastard that day . . . one of the nicer names he had for Dallas. She knew little about business, but she didn't see how a school or the church he'd offered to build for Reverend Tucker would bring him much money.

As a matter of fact, in the short time she had been his wife, she had seen no evidence of his greed except for the morning he'd refused to pull his fence back if she left him. But even then, he had gained nothing but a reluctant wife while her family gained access to the river. Eventually, he would gain a son while her family would gain land.

She was beginning to think that Dallas hid his greedy nature well . . . so well that she wondered how Boyd had ever discovered it to begin with.

"The new addition to the house seems to be coming along fine," Amelia said, shifting the conversation away from talk of Leighton.

"Ought to have the first floor and most of the walls in place before nightfall," Dallas said.

"It means a lot to me that you and Austin would give up your day of rest to build onto our house."

"That's what family is for," Dallas said.

"But we won't be able to return the favor. I can't imagine that you'll ever need to add onto your house."

"Speaking of Dallas's house," Austin said. "Dee, what do you think of it?"

Cordelia snapped her gaze to Austin, then to Dallas who watched her with such intensity that her breath almost stopped. Meaningless words scrambled through her mind.

"We need to get back to work," Dallas said, setting his empty plate on the quilt.

Houston groaned and rubbed his stomach. "I'm too full. I intend to sit back and relax for a while."

"Thought you wanted these rooms," Dallas said.

"We do, but we can finish them up next Sunday."

"It'll be that much hotter next Sunday," Dallas said as he stood. "I'm going back to work."

Cordelia watched her husband jerk his shirt over his head as he stomped back toward the house.

"One day, Austin, you're gonna learn when to keep your mouth shut," Houston said.

*   *   *

Dallas hefted a board and carried it to the far side of the house. He'd grown tired of hammering the floor into place. Houston and Austin could finish it when they woke from their naps. They'd both fallen asleep beneath the scraggly boughs of the tree—Houston with his head nestled in Amelia's lap, Austin with Maggie curled up against him.

Cordelia simply sat in the shade, her hands folded in her lap—looking beautiful.

He wondered if she'd given everyone, except him, permission to call her Dee. Not that he had asked . . . nor would he, but Dee sure rolled off his tongue a lot easier than Cordelia. He thought Dee suited her better, was softer.

He set the board upright against the side of the house and nailed it into place. Sweat rolled along either side of his spine. He was looking forward to a good hot bath this evening.

He set another board into place and began to pound the nails into the wood.

A good hot bath in his house. In his big house.

He spun around and froze. Cordelia stood beside him, holding a ladle of water. Fear plunged into her eyes.

"Amelia thought you might be thirsty."

"Not very neighborly of her to send you into the lion's den, but I appreciate the water."

He took the dipper from her trembling hand and downed the clear liquid in one long swallow. His gaze riveted on hers, he wiped the back of his hand across his mouth before handing the dipper back to her. "Thanks."

He lifted another board and set it against the frame.

"About your house—" she began.

"I'll build you another one," he said as he lined up the board. "Makes no difference to me."

"Actually, I rather like it."

He glanced over his shoulder. She was gripping the ladle tightly enough to make her knuckles turn white. "You do?"

She nodded jerkily. "Uh, I think it's a bit stark . . . uh, I mean, I think it would seem more friendly if you had some decorations—"

"You mean like knickknacks?"

"And perhaps some paintings or wall hangings. Maybe a flower bed in the front. I could give you a list of ideas—"

"No need. Just do it." He crouched and set a nail against the board.

"What if you don't like what I do?"

"Apparently my taste in things isn't to everyone's liking." He hit the nail. "I'll trust your judgment. I've got a Montgomery Ward catalogue in my office. Order what you need from there or go to Oliver's general store and get it from him."

Standing to position another nail, he looked over his shoulder, expecting her to comment, but she was staring, eyes wide, at the area where they'd eaten their meal. Dallas peered around the edge of the board. Houston had apparently woken from his nap, angled his body over his wife's, and was enjoying his dessert: Amelia's sweet lips.

"It's not polite to stare," Dallas said as he pounded another nail into place.

"But they're . . . they're . . ."

"Kissing," Dallas said. "They're just kissing."

Cordelia turned away, her face red. "But they're so close to each other."

"It's more fun that way. Didn't that book you borrowed tell you that?"

He didn't think her blush could grow any deeper, but it did.

"That book is misnamed," she said in a hushed whisper as though afraid someone might hear. "It has nothing at all to do with being a husband."

He couldn't stop himself from smiling. "But it has everything to do with husbandry."

Confusion clouded her eyes. "I don't understand."

"Husbandry is a polite word for breeding and taking care of livestock."

"You might have explained that to me before I took it."

He shrugged. "You married a rancher. Figured it wouldn't hurt for you to read the book. It'll give us something to discuss at dinner."

Her eyes widened. "We wouldn't!"

His smile thinned until it disappeared into a hardened line. "Not if you can think of something else to talk about during our meals. I'm getting tired of eating in silence. If I wanted that, I'd stay out on the range and eat."

"I didn't realize you wanted to talk while we ate. At home, I wasn't allowed to speak during meals."

"Seems your pa and mine had the same attitude: children were to be seen and not heard, but you're not a child any longer."

"No, women . . . women were to be seen and not heard."

Dallas shook his head in disbelief. "I spend all day listening to bawling cattle and the rough voices of men. In the evening, I'd like to hear the soft voice of a woman."

"I'll . . . I'll try to think of something we can discuss during meals."

"Good." He turned back to his task. "Before we leave, you need to tell Houston to let you pick out a horse. Beauty belongs to Maggie. Reckon it's time we stopped borrowing her."

With the early evening shadows moving in, Dallas leaned against the wooden beam of Houston's front porch and stared at Cordelia, standing at the corral, talking with his brother. Talking, smiling, occasionally laughing.

He'd never before heard her sweet laughter. It sounded as innocent as she was.

"Would you like something to drink?" Amelia asked him.

Without taking his eyes off his wife, Dallas wrapped his fingers around the glass of lemonade Amelia offered. "My brother seems to have become quite the ladies' man."

"He's not a threat to her," Amelia said softly.

Dallas jerked his head around. "And you think I am?"

"*She* thinks you are."

"Christ, I don't know how she can think that. I haven't touched her since the day I married her."

"How often have you called her by name since you were married?"

"What's that got to do with anything?"

"You've been here since dawn, and never once did I hear you speak her name. A woman likes to hear her name from time to time."

"Her name gets tangled in my tongue."

"Her name isn't that much different from mine, and you never have any trouble with it."

"It's a hell of a lot different. Your name is soft. Her name is . . . hard . . . like a stack of wood."

"I like her name."

"Well, I don't."

She hit his arm, and the lemonade sloshed over the glass onto his hand. He stepped back. "Goddamm it!"

She hit him again. "Then call her something else."

"Like what?"

"Sugar bunch."

He grimaced.

"Sweetheart, darlin'."

"I can't see words like that rolling off my tongue."

"Then find a word that will, but call her something."

"Why? She's never said my name either."

"You're acting like a two-year-old."

He felt like a fool, watching his wife with another man, looking as though she was enjoying herself when she'd never enjoyed a single moment of his company.

Amelia rubbed his arm. "I'm sorry. It's really none of my business. I just want to see you happy."

"I will be as soon as I get my son."

A sadness washed over her features. "Is a son so important to you?"

"Yes. It's the only unfulfilled dream I have left."

"Why did you have love and cherish removed from your marriage vows?"

He shifted his gaze to the glass of lemonade, the truth as bitter as the drink in his hand. "I'm not an easy man, Amelia. I know that. Love isn't something she's likely to give me. Didn't see any point in asking her to take a vow she couldn't keep." He handed the glass back to her. "We need to get going before darkness settles in." He stepped off the porch.

"You don't give yourself enough credit," she said softly.

With a sad smile, he glanced back at her. "Seems I gave myself too much. If I told her she could leave and I'd still keep my fence pulled back, she'd be gone before the first star came out."

Chapter 8

*D*ALLAS CROSSED HIS arms over the top railing and stared at the stars. Spending the day with his brother's family had sharply brought home just how much was missing from his own life: not only his son, but the warm glances Houston and Amelia had exchanged throughout the day that had revealed the depth of their love for each other without a single word being spoken.

He didn't expect Cordelia to ever look at him the way Amelia looked at Houston: as though he hung the moon and stars. If he were a kind man, he'd set Cordelia free, send her back to her father without ever knowing the complete taste of her mouth, the feel of her flesh within his palms, the sound of her cries as he poured his seed into her.

But he wasn't a kind man. He wanted to kiss her again, more deeply than before, his mouth devouring hers. He wanted to skim his hands over her breasts, across her narrow waist, and along her slender hips. He wanted to hear her gasps, sighs, and moans.

He wanted her in his bed—he groaned in frustration. She was already in his bed. His problem was that he didn't know how to get himself back into his bed without knocking on her door and seeing the fear reflected in her eyes.

He'd thought about slipping into her room in the dead of night, nuzzling her awake, trailing kisses—

"Dallas?"

He swung around at the hesitant lilt of Cordelia's soft voice. She had come to his study shortly after they had returned home to get his catalogue. He had hoped she would browse through it in his office, but she'd just grabbed it and scurried out like a frightened rabbit. He hadn't seen her since, had assumed she'd gone to bed—without him once again.

He crossed his arms over his bare chest and wished to God his feet weren't bare. He felt naked and chose to clothe himself in anger. "What are you doing out here?"

"Austin told me to come talk to you."

First Amelia. Now Austin. It seemed his whole family was intent on nudging the woman toward him. Unfortunately, he wanted her to come of her own accord.

Cautiously, she eased closer to the corral and ran her finger along the railing. "I see you out here often. Do you have trouble sleeping?"

"I've just got a lot on my mind."

"Like what?"

How pretty your eyes are. How soft your skin looks. How sweet you smell. How much I want to hold you.

"My brand. I need to change it."

"Why?"

Because I haven't held a woman in years, not since Amelia.

"Because the symbol isn't right anymore."

"What happened to change it, to make it wrong?"

Destiny.

"When I first bought this land, I used a *D* for Dallas. When Amelia agreed to marry me, I added an *A*. I made it lean against the side of the *D* so the letters were joined. Only she and I aren't joined. You and I are, so I need to change the symbol, but your name doesn't lend itself well to leaning against the D. A *C* and *D* just look like two *D*'s back to back so I'm trying to figure out how to put the *C* and *D* together so they look like themselves and not other letters." *And rambling like an idiot in the process.*

She held his gaze in the moonlight. "Did you love her?"

"Who?"

She lowered her lashes. "Amelia. Did you love her?"

He brushed his thumb and forefinger over his mustache. He'd never stopped to ask himself that question. Maybe he should have. "I was fond of her. She added a grace to my life while she was here, but no, I didn't love her. Not the way Houston did then; not as deeply as he does now."

"They seem happy."

"I reckon they are."

She stepped on the bottom rung of the fence. Her toes curled around the wood. He thought about touching his bare foot to hers, rubbing his sole along her delicate ankle.

Pulling herself up, she leaned against the corral. Within the shadows of the night, he could see the curve of her breasts pressing against her wrapper. He ached to slip her wrapper off her shoulders, cup her breasts, and feel her satiny skin against his roughened palms. He dug his fingers into his arms to keep them from reaching for her when she looked so serene.

"I think back to back would work," she said softly.

Back to back? The woman was incredibly innocent. Back to front might work, although he'd prefer front to front. He'd never known a woman as tall as she was. Pressed against her, he imagined he would find very little of himself not warmed by her flesh. Thigh to thigh. Hip to hip. Chest to breasts. His shoulders might come a little higher than hers, but he could live with that.

She glanced over at him. "Cameron calls me Dee. I prefer it to Cordelia, so you see, two *D*'s back to back might work."

"Two *D*'s? Back to back?" He snapped his head back, gasping for breath. "My brand. You're talking about my brand."

"What did you think I was talking about?"

He gave her a jerky nod. "My brand. I thought you were talking about my brand."

She angled her head as though she didn't quite believe him and wanted to figure out exactly what he had been thinking. He shoved his sweating hands into his trouser pockets. "Why does he call you Dee?"

"When he was a baby, Cordelia was too hard for him, so he just started calling me Dee. I never liked Cordelia but we don't get to choose our names . . . or our families."

He imagined in the last week, she'd learned more about her family than she'd care to know. Houston had told him what he'd overheard in Dallas's office, and it had taken every bit of restraint Dallas could muster not to pay the McQueens a visit. He'd cursed Houston long and hard for making him give his word he'd pretend he didn't know what had transpired before Houston had ever told him what had.

"I heard Austin and Amelia call you Dee. I could call you that if you want."

"I'd like that."

"Fine. I'll see about putting two *D*'s on our brand."

She tilted her face toward the stars. "What happens to your men when they get married?"

Like the length of her body, her throat was long and slender. He stepped closer to the corral and rested his elbow on the top railing so he could see her more clearly. "They don't get married."

"Never?"

"Not a ranch hand. If a man wants a family, he's gotta save up his pay, purchase some land, and start his own spread so he's got a place for his family to live."

"Doesn't that seem sad to you?"

"Never thought much about it. That's just the way it is. A cowboy knows that from the beginning."

She seemed to contemplate his answer. He wished he knew what she was thinking, wished he knew what she would do if he put a foot on the railing, cupped her fragile face in his wide hands, and kissed her.

He had the right—

She diverted her attention away from the stars. "Austin is going to town in the morning. Can I go with him?"

He ignored the jab to his pride because she preferred to travel into town with his brother. He would have happily taken her if he'd known she wanted to go. "You're not a prisoner here. You can do anything you want. You don't have to ask my permission."

"I can do *anything?*" she asked.

"You can't move back home," he quickly answered, certain her thoughts were about to head in that direction.

She jerked her chin up slightly, almost defiantly. "You claim to give me freedom, but then you limit the choices, which takes away the freedom."

She stepped off the railing. "Thank you for giving me permission to leave with Austin tomorrow."

She strolled away. He wanted to grab her braid, wrap it around his hand until he'd brought her face even with his . . . and kiss her until neither one of them had any choices.

Studying the words she'd written before she'd gone to sleep last night, Cordelia slowly chewed on the biscuit. She knew freedom was an illusion. She could come and go as she pleased as long as she didn't go where she wanted—someplace where she could cast her own shadow.

Still, she intended to enjoy the day. Even Dallas's apparent lack of interest in her topics wasn't going to spoil her mood. She glanced up from her notes. "Why do you suppose the leaves change color in autumn?"

With his egg-laden fork halfway to his mouth, Dallas stilled. "Because they die."

"I see." She looked at Austin. "Are you of the same sentiment?"

Peering at her over the brim of his cup, steam rising from the coffee, humor in his eyes, he nodded.

She returned her attention to her list. She had been incredibly pleased with herself last night for walking to the corral to ask Dallas for permission to ride to town with Austin. Of course, Austin had shoved her out the door and locked it, forcing her to find the courage to face her husband, but still she had found it..eventually.

"What is your favorite color?"

"Brown."

She lifted her gaze. "Brown? Of all the colors in the world, why do you like brown?"

Dallas couldn't bring himself to tell her the truth. He favored brown because her eyes were brown. The one time he had seen them without fear or wariness clouding them, they had mesmerized him. "I just do."

"Oh."

She looked at her scrap of paper, and Dallas bit back a scathing expletive. He had threatened her with a discussion on husbandry if she didn't talk, and she had brought a list of topics to the table this morning and kept running her finger over it, looking for things to discuss.

Wind. Rain. The shape of clouds. The entire time she prattled about things, he discovered that he wanted to talk about her. What she had feared as a little girl. Her dreams. If she was lonely.

He shoved his chair back, and she jerked her head up. He stood, walked to her end of the table, and set an envelope beside her plate.

"What's this?" she asked.

"Spending money." For over an hour, he had contemplated how much to give her, fearing too little or too much might offend her. He had no idea how much money ladies needed and had settled on twenty dollars. "If it's not enough, you can put your purchases on my account, and I'll take care of it the next time I go to town."

She trailed her fingers over the envelope, and he wondered what it would feel like to have her slender fingers skim over his chest.

She peered up at him. "Thank you."

"You're my wife. I'm supposed to see that you don't do without." He glared at Austin. "Take care of her, or I'll hang your hide out to dry."

He stalked from the room, wondering why he couldn't have simply leaned down, kissed her on the cheek, and told her to enjoy the day.

Cordelia took great delight in riding with Austin. He possessed much more patience than his older brother. He had already taught her how to send Lemon Drop into a trot. She loved the feel of the wind brushing across her face, the movement of the golden mare beneath her, and the knowledge that she was in control of the beast.

If only she could control her husband as easily. If only he would set her free.

She slowed her horse to a walk. Beside her, Austin did the same.

"You did that real well," he said, smiling broadly.

She felt the warmth fan her cheeks. "She's a good horse."

"That's the only kind Houston raises."

"Do you think we'll go back and work on their house this Sunday?"

"I'm sure we will. Dallas ain't one to leave a job half-done."

"No, I don't imagine he is at that." She shifted her backside over the saddle. "Why did your parents name you and your brothers after towns in Texas?"

"According to Houston, our pa had a wandering streak in him and named us after the town he was living in at the time we were born. I don't remember our pa, but Houston says Dallas is a lot like him, says that's the reason Dallas purchased so much land. He could wander far and wide and still be at home."

His answer gave her pause for thought. She wondered if Dallas had longed for roots while he was growing up as much as she'd longed to leave. She brushed a fleck of dirt off her riding skirt. "I was wondering . . ."

Austin tipped his hat off his brow. "Yes, ma'am?"

"My father sends someone into town every week for supplies. Wouldn't it save you considerable time if you brought a wagon so you wouldn't have to go into town every day for supplies?"

Austin's face turned beet red as he tugged his hat down. "I ain't goin' into town for supplies. Dallas sends Pete in to get the supplies."

"Then why do you go every day?"

He cleared his throat. "I just like to."

"Dallas doesn't mind?"

"Long as I get my work done, he don't mind at all."

She contemplated his answer. Her days were long, her nights even longer. She wondered if she could find something in town to help her pass the time.

Tightening her hold on the reins, Cordelia stared as Leighton came into view. Half a dozen wooden buildings checkered the wide dusty street. On the outskirts of town, it looked as though people had haphazardly thrown up tents.

Workers were hammering on the frame of a building. The scent of sawdust filled the air. She had never seen anything like it.

The day Dallas had announced that he was setting aside the land for a town, she had seen nothing but open prairie. She hadn't returned since.

She had known the town had acquired a dressmaker and a general store. She hadn't known about the saloon or the bank or the jail.

"What are they building?" she asked Austin as he led their horses down the center of town.

"A livery and a blacksmith shop."

"It really is going to be a town," she said in awe. "Boyd had said it would never happen. That Dallas was a fool."

"Boyd's the fool," Austin said. "I've never seen Dallas fail at anything."

Austin brought their horses to a stop in front of a false-fronted building that proclaimed OLIVER'S GENERAL STORE. He dismounted, tethered both horses, then reached up and helped Cordelia dismount.

A whole town to walk through. Well, not quite a whole town, but it would be someday, and her husband was responsible. An empire builder.

Perhaps he was more. A builder of dreams.

How did one even go about knowing where to begin?

Austin opened the door that led into the general store. As soon as he entered the building, he swept his hat from his head and an easy smile played at the corners of his mouth.

Becky Oliver stood on a ladder, placing canned goods on a shelf. She glanced over her shoulder, her blue eyes growing warm.

Cordelia thought she might have discovered Austin's interest in coming to town every day.

"What can I do you for?" asked a balding man standing behind the counter.

Cordelia remembered being introduced to Perry Oliver at her wedding.

Becky rolled her eyes and climbed down from the ladder. "Oh, Pa, you got the words all mixed up again."

He winked at Cordelia. "Young'uns. They ain't never happy with what their parents do." He looked at Austin. "Well, young man, what brings you into town today?"

"Dee needs something so I just brought her into town."

Cordelia fought to keep the surprise off her face. She didn't need anything, but Austin gave her an imploring look that begged her to play along. How could she resist the plea in those blue eyes?

"What do you need then, Mrs. Leigh?" Mr. Oliver asked.

Mrs. Leigh? She thought she'd never get used to that name. "I..uh . . . books . . . I need some books."

Mr. Oliver's eyes widened. "You already read those books your husband came in and purchased last week?"

Cordelia glanced at Austin. He simply shrugged. She had no idea what books her husband had bought. No doubt more on husbandry. "No, he didn't share them with me," she finally confessed.

Mr Oliver rubbed his palm over his shining bald pate. "That's odd. He said they were for you. Said you liked to read." He squinted his pale blue eyes and puckered his lips. "Let's see. I had *A Tale of Two Cities* and *Silas Marner*. He bought them both."

Words failed her. If Dallas had purchased the books for her, wouldn't he have told her? If he hadn't purchased them for her, why had he told Mr. Oliver that he had?

"They were all I had in stock," Mr. Oliver continued. "He told me when I got more books in, I was to set them aside until he'd had a chance to look at them."

The bell above the door tinkled as a young boy walked hesitantly into the store. His black hair was in dire need of a cut and his face a good scrubbing. His bare feet shuffled over the wooden floor as he neared the counter and dug his hand into the pocket of his coveralls. One strap trailed down his backside since he had no button on the front of the coveralls to hold it in place. It looked as though the button on the other side wasn't going to stay with him much longer.

Perry Oliver leaned over the counter. "Well, Mr. Rawley Cooper. What can I do you for today?"

The boy slapped some coins on the counter. "My pa's needin' some cig'rette makin's."

"I've got some right back here," Mr. Oliver said as he disappeared behind the counter.

The boy gazed at the jars of colorful candy that lined the counter. Cordelia didn't think he could be much older than eight. His black eyes shot back to Mr. Oliver when the man set a pouch of tobacco and some papers on the counter.

"Obliged," the boy said as he slipped the supplies into his pocket and turned to leave.

"Hold on there a minute, Rawley. You gave me too much," Mr. Oliver said as he placed a pudgy finger on a copper penny and slid it across the counter.

Rawley looked doubtful as his gaze darted between Mr. Oliver and the penny. Hesitantly, he placed his grubby hand over the penny.

"I'm selling licorice for a penny today," Mr. Oliver said. "Don't reckon your pa would miss a penny."

Rawley shook his head, grabbed the penny, and hurried out the door.

"You should have told him it was free," Austin said.

Mr. Oliver shook his head. "Tried that. The boy has too much pride to take something for nothing. Beats anything I've ever seen. Considering who his pa is, I don't know how he managed to latch on to any pride."

"Who is his father?" Cordelia asked.

"One of the workers putting up the buildings, although calling him a worker is giving him the benefit of the doubt. Mostly he just draws his pay and gets drunk."

"Where is Rawley's mother?" Cordelia asked.

"Dead, I reckon."

Austin pulled two sarsaparilla sticks out of a jar. "Put these on my account," he said as he headed toward the door.

"He won't take them," Mr. Oliver called after him.

Austin flashed a disarming grin. "I can be quite charmin' when I want to be."

As the door closed behind him, Cordelia backed away from the counter, feeling self-conscious without Austin by her side. "I'm going to look around."

Mr. Oliver nodded. "You let us know if you need anything."

Cordelia walked to the far side of the store, not certain what she should do if she did find something she wanted to purchase. She felt vulnerable and lost, like a child who had let go of her mother's hand in a crowd of people.

She was twenty-six years old, and she had no idea how to purchase a ribbon for her hair. Her father and her brothers had gotten into the habit of bringing everything to her while she had tended to her mother. The habit had remained long after her mother had passed away.

Where once she had felt pampered, she now felt afraid.

She had allowed herself to become dependent on the kindness of her family, and they had pulled that kindness out from under her. She turned toward the soft footfalls.

Becky smiled at her. "Did you find something that you wanted?"

Cordelia wrung her hands together. She supposed she should begin turning Dallas's house into a home. "I was looking for some rugs."

"We have some over here," Becky said.

Cordelia skirted barrels and boxes as she followed Becky to the other side of the store. Becky patted a stack of rugs.

"This is all we have. Just look through them and let me know if you want one."

Careful not to disturb the pile, Cordelia removed one rug at a time and examined it. She wanted something with brown woven through it, Dallas's favorite color.

"I sure was surprised when I heard Dallas was going to marry you," Becky said.

Cordelia glanced up from the selections and smiled. "I guess you didn't know my brothers had a sister."

"Oh, I'd heard the rumors," Becky said. "I was just surprised Dallas would marry you after Boyd shot Austin."

Cordelia's heart rammed against her ribs, and she could feel the blood draining from her face.

Becky's eyes widened. "Oh, my goodness. Didn't you know?"

Cordelia lowered her gaze to the floor. Why wouldn't it crack open and swallow her whole?

"I'm sure Dallas has forgiven him, otherwise he wouldn't have married you."

The door swung open, and Austin sauntered into the store, a sarsaparilla stick jutting from his mouth. "Well, I did it. Got the boy to take one of the sticks."

He strolled over to Cordelia, confidence in his step. "What you got there, Dee?"

"R-rugs. I thought . . . I thought I'd purchase one for the house."

"That'd be fine," Austin said, talking around the sarsaparilla stick. "Which one?"

Cordelia quickly searched through the stack and pulled out a brown rug. "This one."

Becky took it from her. "I'll wrap it for you and put it on Dallas's account. You can pick it up on your way out of town."

"Can we go home now?" she asked Austin.

"Thought you wanted to see the rest of the town?"

"Oh, yes, I forgot." She couldn't bring herself to look at Austin, knowing her brother had shot him.

Austin took her arm. "Come on, Dee, you're looking pale. Let's get some air."

She allowed him to lead her outside. Then she broke away from him, crossed the small boardwalk, and wrapped her trembling hands around the railing.

Austin studied the woman clinging to the railing as though she were afraid she'd drown in the dust without it. He took the sarsaparilla stick out of his mouth. "What happened, Dee?"

She looked at him, with hurt and anger mixed in her eyes. His stomach dropped clear to the ground, and he fought the urge to reach out and touch her, to wipe the hurt and anger away. "What did I do?" he said, his voice low.

"Boyd shot you."

He furrowed his brow. "Yeah?"

"You said it was cattle rustlers."

"Dallas said it was cattle rustlers."

"Why?"

Austin shrugged. "Maybe he didn't think you'd believe him, or maybe he was trying to spare you some hurt. Sitting in that shade, eating our meal, it just didn't feel right to me to say Boyd had shot me. I reckon Dallas felt the same way."

"But Boyd did shoot you."

"Becky tell you that?"

She nodded.

"Dang, that girl has a big mouth."

"Why did he shoot you?"

"Don't think he meant to. He was just shooting, and I got in the way."

Tears welled in her eyes. "I don't have any friends, Austin. I need a friend right now. Be my friend."

"Sure. Whatever you want."

"Friends never lie to each other," she said.

With his thumb, Austin pushed his hat off his brow, wishing he'd been a little slower in agreeing to be her friend. "What do you want to know?"

"Do you know what happened the night that Dallas broke Boyd's arm?"

"Yep. That's the night I got shot."

"Was Boyd guarding his cattle? Did you, Dallas, and Houston attack him?"

Austin jerked off his hat and looked at the sky, wondering where wisdom came from.

"I want the truth," she said. "Am I married to a man who sneaked up on my brother in the dead of night and broke his arm?"

He lowered his gaze to hers. Within her brown eyes, he saw a sparkle of hope, and he wondered which would hurt her the least—the truth or a lie.

"The truth," she whispered as though understanding his hesitancy.

"No, you're not married to a man who'd sneak up on anyone. It's not Dallas's way. It never has been. He meets every problem head-on. Your brothers were gettin' into the habit of cutting through Dallas's fence and killing off his cattle. That night, we were waiting for them. When the pain ripped through my shoulder, everything went black, but Houston told me that Dallas had dragged Boyd through the river. I reckon his arm must have hit a rock or something and got busted, but I do know Dallas didn't do it on purpose."

"Dallas frightens me, Austin."

Austin couldn't stop himself from stepping closer and wrapping his arms around her. "I know. I see it in your eyes every time you look at him. He sees it, too, and it makes him mad, which scares you more and makes him furious. It's a circle you can't seem to get out of."

"The things Boyd told me . . . I don't know what to believe anymore."

Austin leaned back and cupped her chin. "Well, you might try by not looking at him through Boyd's eyes, but look at him through your own. Pretend you just met him and had never heard anything about him."

"I think he'd still frighten me."

Austin laughed. "He scares the hell out of me. Out of Houston, too." He grew somber. "But he'd never hurt you, Dee. I know that."

"But he won't set me free."

"If he did, what would you do? Was living with your family better than what you have now?"

"I need something more, Austin. I don't know what, but I know I need something more than what Dallas or my family has the power to give me."

He drew her close, pressing his cheek against the top of her head. "Then I hope you find it, Dee. I truly do."

Chapter 9

*D*ALLAS STEPPED OUT of the bank and wished to God that he hadn't desperately searched for an excuse to come into town. He'd hoped to casually cross his wife's path, perhaps walk through the town with her.

He hadn't expected to see her on the boardwalk wrapped tightly within his brother's arms.

Austin looked up and his blue eyes widened. "Dallas!" Like a snake wrapped around a low-lying tree branch, Austin slowly uncoiled himself from around Cordelia. "Didn't know you had plans to come to town."

"Obviously." Dallas balled his hands into fists and clenched his jaws, his gaze darting between his brother and his wife. The terror had returned to her eyes, and he imagined right now she had good reason to fear him.

With a loose-jointed walk, Austin approached him. "Dee found out that Boyd shot me. She was a little angry at us for not telling her outright, for saying it was cattle rustlers. I was just trying to cool her temper."

Dallas glared at his brother. "You don't hug me when I'm angry."

Austin barked out his laughter. "I will if you want me to because I can sure tell that you're fit to be tied right now." Stretching out his arms and tilting his head, he flashed an infectious grin that Dallas was certain he would use to charm the ladies if there were any ladies around. "Want a hug?"

Dallas stepped back. "Hell, no." Dallas shifted his attention at Dee. She was studying him as though he were a stranger, which he realized he was. What did she really know about him? What did he know about her?

"How did she find out?" he asked.

Austin jerked his head toward the general store. "Becky." He rubbed his hands on his thighs. "Listen, Dee's never visited Leighton. Would you show her the town while I talk with Becky for a while?" Austin swiveled his head around. "You don't mind going with Dallas, do you, Dee?"

Dallas watched his wife grow pale before she finally nodded. "That would be fine."

"Thanks. I'll catch up with you."

Austin disappeared into the general store. Dallas wished he had been the one to whom Dee had turned, the one who had held her when she'd learned the truth.

"You've never been to town?" he asked.

She shook her head. "Not this town. Not after the day you set the land aside. My brothers never had time to bring me."

"Well . . ." He stepped off the boardwalk, suddenly self-conscious with all that remained undone. "It's nowhere near finished." He pointed straight ahead. "The general store." He moved his hand to the left. "The bank."

"What were you doing at the bank?" she asked as she walked to his side.

"I wanted to talk with Mr. Henderson about a loan for another building."

"What sort of building?"

He cleared his throat. "A man—cabinetmaker—wrote to me. He wants to move here, but he hasn't the means to finance his own business. I think he would be a good investment."

"Do you have the means to finance him?"

"With the assistance of the bank, I'll help him get his start. Eventually, he'll own his business outright, but the more people I can get to Leighton, the more we'll grow."

"How do you determine which businesses would be a good investment?"

He studied her, not expecting the questions she was asking, but pleased that she knew enough to ask them. He crooked his elbow and watched as she swallowed before placing her hand on his arm. Together they walked slowly along the street.

"I try and figure out what people need," he explained to her. He pointed toward the clothing store. "Houston was always going to Fort Worth to purchase clothing for Amelia. He'd visit Miss St. Claire's dress shop. The idea of a new town intrigued her, so she moved her business here, hoping the town would prosper and more women would come. Until then, she sews clothing for men and women."

"There aren't many women from what I've seen."

"A half dozen if that many. I haven't figured out how to attract them to Leighton. I've been thinking of running an advertisement for brides, similar to the one Amelia placed for a husband. Only I'd want a whole passel of women to come, and I'd need to have husbands waiting for them. I've got to give some thought to the best way to handle that. I don't particularly relish the thought of being a marriage broker."

She slowly nodded, and Dallas almost imagined that he could see wheels spinning in her mind. He wanted to ask her what she thought of the town. He wanted Leighton to be more than just a town . . . he wanted it to be a place that drew people in and gave them a reason to stay.

They neared the saloon. Hesitantly, she glanced at him. "Can I look inside the saloon?" '

"Sure."

Cautiously, Cordelia neared the swinging doors and peered inside. The smoke was thick. The odors not entirely pleasant. She could see a few men sitting at a table playing cards. One of the men was her brother.

"What is Duncan doing here?" she asked.

Dallas glanced over her shoulder. "Playing cards."

"I mean why isn't he out working with the cattle?"

"I guess he's just taking some time off."

Stepping back, she studied her husband. "When do you take time off?"

He led her away from the saloon. "Saloons don't appeal to me. I never could bring myself to let the draw of a card take away the money I'd worked so hard to earn."

"But you must relax sometime."

"When I need to relax, I ride out at night and visit one of my ladies."

Cordelia was unprepared for the pain that slashed through her. Why had she expected him to remain faithful to her just because they had exchanged vows? Incensed for reasons she could not begin to fathom, she strode off the boardwalk. "I think I've seen all I want to see of the town."

He grabbed her arm, and she jerked free. "Please don't touch me. Not after you've just thrown your mistresses into my face."

"My mistresses?" He drew his brows together over eyes mired with confusion, then he started to laugh. "My ladies."

"I don't see that it's funny."

"I wasn't thinking."

"Obviously not. A gentleman doesn't mention his other women to his wife. I think we'd both be a good deal happier if you'd married one of them instead of me." She spun on her heel and started to walk away.

"Dee?"

She wanted to keep walking, but a longing in his voice touched her, reached for her, forced her to turn around. No longer smiling or laughing, he watched her as though searching for something.

"The ladies are my windmills," he said quietly. "I enjoy listening to them in the quiet of the night. It brings me peace. I'd like to share that with you sometime."

Incredibly embarrassed, she slammed her eyes closed. "I'm sorry. I acted like a shrew."

"You should get angry more often."

Her eyes flew open. The one time her mother had gotten angry her father had struck her down. "Why?"

"Anger puts a fire in your eyes. I'd rather have the fire than the fear."

"Dallas!" a man yelled.

Cordelia watched as a slender man rushed toward Dallas.

"Tyler, you got a problem?" Dallas asked.

The man skidded to a stop. "Not a problem."

As though he suddenly noticed her, Tyler jerked his hat from his head. He swept the blond locks from his brow and smiled at Cordelia. "Mrs. Leigh, we met at your wedding although you probably don't remember me. Tyler Curtiss."

"I'm not very good with names," she confessed.

"I'm not very good with faces except when they're beautiful like

371

yours." He blushed as though unaccustomed to flirting, and Dallas scowled.

"Tyler designs the buildings and manages the construction," Dallas said, his voice taut.

She smiled with interest. "So you're building the town?"

"With a great deal of help. I'd like to get your husband's opinion on a few things if you can spare him."

"Yes, that's fine."

Dallas seemed to hesitate. "Can you find Austin?"

She nodded. "I'm sure he's still at the general store."

"I'll see you at home then."

She watched him walk away. She could tell from his stance that he was listening intently as Tyler prattled.

Why had it hurt so much when he'd mentioned his ladies with such affection? Why was she relieved to discover he had been visiting windmills?

She began strolling toward the horses tethered to the hitching post in front of the general store. She had erupted with anger and instead of retaliating, he had told her to get mad more often. She decided his suggestion might have some merit. She had found the burst of fury . . . emancipating.

Standing on the balcony outside her bedroom, Cordelia stared at the night. She heard the steady clack of the nearby windmill—one of Dallas's ladies.

He was so unlike her father, her brothers. He angered easily, the rage flashing within his dark eyes, but he kept his temper tethered.

Where the men in her family concerned themselves only with their wants and needs, Dallas broadened his horizons to include others. People were coming to his town because he gave them a chance to share in a corner of his dream, and in sharing, his dream would grow.

She was certain Boyd would have referred to his actions as selfish and greedy, but how could she fault Dallas Leigh with wanting to build a future for his sons . . . a future grander than anything she had ever dared to dream?

A town. A community. A community of men.

She frowned, surprised to discover that she wanted a part of his dream as well. She wanted to accomplish what he had yet to achieve. She wanted to find a way to lure women to Leighton.

She didn't see her husband standing by the corral. She hadn't heard his footsteps echoing along the hallway.

She wondered where he was—if he was in his office. If the two books he'd purchased were waiting there as well.

She didn't want to fear Dallas, but more she didn't want to be dependent on him. She had once coveted freedom, but now she realized without independence, freedom didn't exist. The first step toward independence was conquering her fear.

She walked into her bedroom and retrieved the book she had borrowed from him—*The Practical Husbandman.*

She remembered the depth of his laughter, that night and this afternoon. The spontaneity of it. The way it had reached out and struck a corresponding chord deep within her.

Holding the lamp, she made her way to Dallas's office. She saw the light spilling out from beneath the door and almost changed her mind. Instead, she forced herself to knock.

"Come in," boomed from the other side.

Her heart quickened. She took a trembling breath and opened the door. Dallas sat at his desk, the ledgers spread out before him. He came to his feet.

"Oh, no, don't get up," she said as she slipped into the room. "I just wanted to return your book."

"Fine."

She took a step closer to the shelves. "Do you always work on your ledgers late at night?"

"Usually."

She licked her lips, her mouth suddenly dry, her determination withering. "My father . . . my father works on his books during the afternoon."

"He has three sons to watch his spread. I only have me."

"And Austin."

"It's not his responsibility. Someday, he'll figure out what he wants from life and he'll leave."

When Austin left, she'd be alone with this man. This man who wanted sons.

"Please don't let me disturb you." She held up the book. "I'll just put this back."

He sat and she hurried across the room. She slipped the book into place, then she trailed her fingers over one of the new books on the shelf: *A Tale of Two Cities*.

She glanced at Dallas. He was writing in his ledger as though her presence made no difference to him . . . and yet, he also seemed to be waiting.

She took the book off the shelf. "I've never read *A Tale of Two Cities*," she said quietly.

"It's yours," he said gruffly. "Along with the other one. Just don't thank me for them. Should have put books in here a long time back. Not much point in having shelves if you don't put books on them."

"That's what I thought the first time I saw this room. I fell in love with it."

He snapped his head up and stared at her, his eyes incredibly dark.

"I thought—" She cleared her throat. "I thought these shelves might hold a thousand books."

He leaned back in his chair. "A thousand?"

She nodded. "Or more."

"Let me know what the tally is when you get the shelves filled up." He went back to writing in his ledgers.

Holding the book tightly, she began to walk across the room, then she stopped. The room was quiet except for the occasional scratch of his pen across the paper.

"I used to read to my mother before she died," she said softly.

He lifted his head and looked at her.

"I miss reading to her," she added. "I miss her."

He propped his elbow on the desk and rubbed his thumb and forefinger over his mustache. She remembered its softness as he had kissed her.

"Dr. Freeman mentioned something about your mother being an invalid."

She had never spoken the words. After all these years, acknowledging the truth was still painful. "She and my father had an argument. In the scuffle, she lost her balance and fell down the stairs. She couldn't move after that, but she wasn't dead. So I cared for her."

"The scuffle? You mean your father struck her?"

She nodded, wishing she'd kept the incident locked away. It sounded incredibly ugly spoken aloud. Had he risen from his chair, had he come toward her, she thought she might have taken flight and rushed back to her room.

Instead, he remained perfectly still. "No matter how angry I get, Dee, I would never hit you. I give you my word on that."

Filled with conviction, the quietly spoken words left her no choice but to believe him.

"Can I read to you?" she asked.

She almost laughed at the startled expression that crossed his features, as though she had spoken the very last words he had ever expected to hear. He looked as though she'd thrown a bucket of cold water on him.

"I know you don't have a lot of spare time. I could read while you work on your ledgers."

As though unable to determine her motive, he nodded slowly. "That'd be fine."

She set the lamp on a small table and sat in the stuffed chair beside it. Bringing up her feet, she tucked them beneath her. She felt him watching her and tried not to be bothered by his scrutiny.

She turned back the cover and several pages before clearing her throat. " 'It was the best of times, it was the worst of times . . .' "

She glanced up. His pen was poised above the ledger, his ink dripping onto the paper.

"Can you work while I read?" she asked.

He nodded and dipped the pen into the inkwell again. When he began to write in his ledgers, she filled the shadowed room with the story.

Dallas wasn't certain of the exact moment when his wife had come to regret her decision to read to him, but he thought it might have been sometime after midnight.

Her eyes had been drifting closed, her words becoming softer, less frequent. He had asked her if she wanted to go to bed. She'd snapped her head up and claimed she wasn't tired.

He figured she just didn't know how to stop reading and announce she was going to bed without leaving the door open for him to join her.

So she had read for two more hours, her voice growing hoarse, her eyes crossing from time to time until eventually they had closed and her head had dropped back.

She looked damned uncomfortable propped up in the chair, her head tilted at an awkward angle, and incredibly lovely with all the worry and fear slipping away for the night.

He wished he knew how to keep the worry and fear out of her eyes when she was awake. He'd considered being blunt and simply explaining to her what he expected and what he would settle for.

But he imagined that a woman needed more than a man's view on the subject. She probably wanted tender words that he didn't know how to give.

As quietly as he could, he pushed his chair back, rose to his feet, and walked to the chair where she was slumped. Gingerly, he eased the book from her grasp and set it on the table beside the chair.

Then he slipped one arm around her back, the other beneath her knees, and cradled her against his chest. Sighing, she snuggled her cheek into the crook of his shoulder.

He hadn't expected her to be as light as a summer breeze, to feel so dainty in his arms. As tall as she was, he had expected her to weigh more. She was little more than soft curves and warmth.

He carried her to her bedroom and gently laid her on the bed. She rolled onto her side, drew her knees up toward her chest, and slipped her hand beneath her cheek. He brought the blankets over her, crouched beside the bed, and watched as she slept.

He had enjoyed the spark of temper that his reference to his ladies had ignited in her eyes that afternoon.

Knowing what he now knew about her mother's ailment, he realized that her outburst, small as it was, had been a form of trust. Perhaps she was beginning to test her boundaries, to see how far he would allow her to go.

He thought about telling her, but he didn't think she'd believe him. He'd simply have to show her.

Cordelia awoke with a start. A faint glimmer of sunlight shadowed the room. She pulled the blankets up to her chin trying to remember when she had come to bed.

Dallas had been in her room. Somehow she was certain of it. His presence lingered like a forgotten scent. Had he brought her to bed and then left her alone to sleep?

She thought she might never understand him.

He had wanted a wife to give him a son, and yet, with the exception of their first night, he had made no overtures toward her. She wondered if he regretted marrying her, if perhaps he would never truly become her husband.

She eased out of bed, walked to the balcony doors, and drew the curtain aside. She could see Dallas standing by the corral talking with his foreman. When Slim walked away, Dallas mounted his black horse and looked up. His gaze locked with hers.

Her breath caught and her heart pounded. His mouth moved, forming words she couldn't hear.

She unlatched the door and stepped onto the balcony. "What?" she asked.

"Get dressed to ride!"

"Now?"

"Yep."

As he dismounted, she hurried back into her room, closed the balcony door, drew the curtains together, and wished she'd never ventured from her bed.

Dallas wasn't certain what had possessed him to invite his wife to ride with him, although he had to admit that she probably hadn't considered his words an invitation.

It wasn't in his nature to ask. Perhaps it had been when he was a boy, but the war had driven it from him. At fourteen, he'd issued his first order. When the war had ended, he'd continued to issue orders. It was the easiest way to accomplish what needed to be done. Tell a man. If he didn't like it, he could move on.

Unfortunately for Cordelia, if she didn't like the way he issued orders, she had no freedom to move on. A marriage contract bound her to him, whether she liked it or not.

He'd hoped they were making progress toward an amicable relationship when she'd offered to read to him last night, but now she rode beside him with her back as stiff as the rod of a branding iron, her eyes trained straight ahead, and her knuckles turning white as she held the saddle horn.

The horses plodded along as though they had all day to get to where they were going.

"How good are you at keeping your word?" he asked.

She swiveled her head toward him, her brow furrowed. "I don't lie, if that's what you're implying."

"My pa taught me that a man is only as good as his word. I've never in my life gone back on my word. I'm just wondering if your pa taught you the same."

Cordelia was at a loss for words. She couldn't recall her father teaching her much of anything except her place within a man's world, a place she had never questioned until she had discovered that it didn't fit very well within her husband's world. "I know how to keep a promise," she finally admitted. "I suppose it's the same thing."

He nodded. "Then I need you to give me a promise."

"What sort of promise?"

He drew his horse to a halt. She did the same. Removing his hat, he captured her gaze.

"I want you to promise that if something should happen to me you won't give my land to your brothers."

"What would happen to you?"

"Anything could happen to a man out here. I just don't want your brothers to benefit from my death."

His death? The words echoed through her mind, through her heart. "Why would you die?"

His lips curved into a slight smile. "I'm not planning to. I just want your word that if we have a son, you'll hold on to the land for him."

"And if we don't have a son?"

"Then hold on to the land for yourself or sell it. Just don't give it to your brothers."

"I wouldn't know what to do with the land," she confessed.

He looked toward the distant horizon. "Give me your word that you won't give the land to your brothers, and I'll teach you how to manage it."

She swept her gaze over the land. He was entrusting her with his legacy. She realized that if something did happen to him, she would need to know how to manage the ranch so she could teach their son. She glanced at him as he steadfastly watched her. "I could destroy everything you've built."

"If I thought there was the slightest chance in hell of that happening, I wouldn't have made the offer."

The force of his words slammed into her. He trusted her with the empire he had built, trusted her to honor her word, just as she had vowed to honor him.

He was giving her the opportunity to level the shaky foundation upon which they had begun to build their marriage. "I give you my word."

A slow smile spread beneath his mustache. "Good."

In the days that followed, she came to know his men and their respective jobs. She had assumed that they simply watched the cattle. She could not have been more wrong. Men constantly rode the fence line, mending the cut or broken wire, replacing posts. The mill rider visited the windmills to grease the bearings and repair anything that had broken. Bog riders searched for cattle that had become tangled in the brush or trapped in mud. The numerous types of riders and their various tasks astounded her.

It seemed everything always needed to be checked and checked again: the fence, the windmills, the cattle, the water supply, the grazing land. Decisions had to be made as to when and where to move the cattle.

By the end of the week, Cordelia was overwhelmed with the knowledge she had attained.

She also had a greater respect and understanding of her husband and his achievements.

Dallas pounded the nail into the floorboard. This Sunday was turning out to be much the same as last Sunday.

He worked on the loft while his brothers lollygagged. He was surprised they'd managed to get the walls put in on the first floor.

He heard the deep rumble of laughter, followed by the gentler giggles. Against his better judgment, he unfolded his body and carefully walked across the beams until he got to the edge of the second floor. He leaned against the open frame.

Cordelia stood at one end of the yard. Everyone else was positioned in different places. She turned her back to them, and everyone moved up. Houston took one big step and stopped. Amelia took three tiny steps. Maggie skipped and fell to her knees. Austin ran.

Cordelia spun around. Austin staggered to a stop. She pointed a finger at him. "I saw you running."

"The heck you did!" he yelled while everyone else laughed.

She wagged her finger at him. "Go back to the beginning."

He stomped to a rope stretched along the ground several yards away from Cordelia. Cordelia pivoted, giving them her back, and everyone started moving again.

Dallas shook his head. No doubt another one of Amelia's games. The woman had more games than a tree had leaves.

Dallas smiled as Maggie and Houston got sent back to the rope. Houston lifted his daughter onto his shoulders.

Cordelia turned her back, and Austin's legs churned faster than the blades of a windmill when a norther blew through. Dallas clamped his teeth together to stop himself from yelling a warning.

Cordelia spun around too late. Austin scooped her off the ground. Dallas's chest tightened as she threw her arms around Austin's neck and laughed. Austin twirled her around, his laughter mingling with hers.

Maggie yelled that she wanted to play again. Austin set Cordelia on her feet. She glanced toward the house and her gaze slammed into Dallas's, her smile withering like all the flowers he'd pulled for her over the week and never given her. Dallas turned away and walked to the other side of the room, wondering when he'd grown so old.

A few minutes later he heard the footsteps on the stairs—the stairs he'd built that morning. He couldn't fault Houston. If he had a wife who looked at him the way Amelia did and a daughter who adored him, he wouldn't be up here pounding nails into wood either.

"I thought you might like some lemonade."

He glanced up at Cordelia. She stood uncertainly in the doorway, holding a glass. He crossed the short space separating them, took the glass, and downed the drink in one long swallow. He handed the glass back to her. "Thanks."

He walked back to his corner, lined up the board, and hammered the nail into place.

"You put me to shame," she said softly.

Furrowing his brow, he glanced over his shoulder. "Why?"

She walked across the floorboards he'd already nailed into place and knelt beside him. "I have a clearer understanding of how you spend your days now. All week long you manage a ranch, you oversee the building of a town, and on what should be a day of rest, you're building an addition onto your brother's house while I'm playing silly games and purchasing rugs—"

"I like the rugs."

She tilted her head sideways. "Do you?"

He regretted that he hadn't mentioned it earlier. "Yeah, I do. I like the quilt you hung on the wall in the parlor and those curtains."

"I thought they made the room seem more cozy. I've ordered some furniture for the parlor."

"Good."

Since the night she had first begun to read to him and the day he had first started explaining the managing of the ranch to her, the wariness had slowed faded from her eyes. She watched him now with no fear. He considered leaning over and kissing her, but he discovered that it wasn't enough that the fear had left. He wanted to see a warmth reflected in her gaze when she looked at him. He wanted her to want him as much as he wanted her.

A damn foolish thing to desire.

She dropped her gaze and scraped her fingernail over the nail he had just hammered into place. "Is it hard to build a floor?" she asked.

"Nope." He extended the hammer toward her. "Do you want to do it?"

A sparkle lit her eyes. "Can I?"

"Sure."

She took the hammer, and he handed her a nail.

"You want the nail to go through the top board and dig into the beam running lengthwise. That holds it in place. Keep your eye on the nail and tap gently."

"It always sounds like you hit the nail hard."

"I have experience behind me so I'm less likely to hit my thumb."

"Oh."

He watched with amusement as she set the nail in place and gripped the hammer. Her brows came together to form a deep furrow. She pulled her bottom lip between her teeth.

He swallowed, remembering the feel of that lip against his.

Her eyes darkened with concentration. He wanted to see them darken with passion.

Gently, she tapped the nail, the furrow deepening, her teeth digging into her lip, her knuckles turning white. He thought about giving her some more instruction, but some things in life were better learned through trial and error. After a dozen hits, the nail had settled into its new home.

She rubbed her fingers over the nail. "Is that what building a town feels like?" she asked.

He'd never thought about it, didn't know how to answer her question.

She looked at him with wonder in her eyes. "Children will crawl over this floor. Then they'll walk over it and run across it. If this house remains for a hundred years, what you have done today might touch children you'll never meet. It's the same with your town and your ranch. Everything that you do reaches out to touch so many people. The things I do touch no one."

She laid the hammer on the floor and rose quietly to her feet.

He fought the urge to grab her ankle and halt her steps away from him.

"I could use some help," he growled. "Tell Houston to get his butt up here."

She disappeared through the doorway. He pressed his thumb against the nail she had embedded in the wood, and damned his pride. He hadn't wanted her to leave. He didn't want to hear her laughter and not be part of it. He didn't want to witness her smiles from a distance.

He hadn't been able to bring himself to ask her to stay, to share the task with him, to lighten his load with her presence.

If he couldn't ask her for something as small as that, how in the hell did he think he was going to ask her to welcome him into her bed?

Chapter 10

༄

WITH THE FLOWERS wilting in his hand, Dallas walked through the house. Every room was empty. Every room except the kitchen, and there, he only found the prairie dog.

He'd come in from the range early with the thought of asking his wife to take a ride with him, and he couldn't find her.

He stalked out of the house and headed to the barn. It didn't ease his mind any to see the empty stall where Cordelia's mare should have been.

"Slim!"

His foreman came out of the back room. "Yes, sir?"

"Do you know where my wife is?"

"Yes, sir. She went to town with Austin."

"Thought she went to town with him yesterday."

"Yes, sir, she did, and the day before that as well."

Trepidation sliced through Dallas as remembered moments rushed through his mind: Austin holding Cordelia outside the general store. Austin lifting Cordelia into his arms and spinning her around at Houston's house.

Cordelia talking to Austin during meals without the aid of her topic list.

In the evening, Austin had begun to come into Dallas's office and listen to Cordelia read. Dallas would occasionally look up from his ledgers to find Austin gazing at Cordelia as though she were the most wonderful woman in the world.

Dallas hated himself for resenting Austin's intrusion. Austin had been five when their mother had died, and he'd grown up with no other women in his life. Dallas knew he shouldn't begrudge Austin the pleasure he found in Cordelia's soft voice—but he did.

"You want me to stop saddling her horse?" Slim asked.

"No," Dallas answered quickly. "No, she's free to come and go as she pleases." He tossed the flowers into the empty stall and strode back to the house.

Dusk had settled over the land before they returned.

Sitting at the head of the table in the dining room, Dallas heard their hushed laughter in the hallway. His gut clenched at the delightful sound she never made in his presence.

He forced himself to his feet when they entered the dining room, looking as guilty as two children who had sneaked away to go fishing before they'd finished their chores.

"Sorry we're late," Austin said as he pulled Cordelia's chair out for her.

Smiling shyly at Austin, she sat. Austin took his place beside her and began to ladle stew into both their bowls. "We lost track of the time."

"I figured that," Dallas said as he took his seat. "I fed your damn prairie dog."

Cordelia glanced up, then quickly lowered-her gaze to her bowl of stew. "Thank you."

"It was yapping so loud I couldn't concentrate on my work," Dallas said.

"I'm sorry. I'll take her with us next time."

With us next time. The words hung heavy in the air. Dallas's stomach tightened. "How was your trip into town?"

Cordelia snapped her head up. She looked at Austin. Austin opened and closed his mouth.

"Fine," Cordelia said. "Just fine."

Dallas scraped his chair across the floor. As though consumed with guilt, Cordelia and Austin jerked back from the table.

"I'll leave you to enjoy your meal," Dallas said.

He wasn't surprised that neither of them protested.

He walked to the corral, knowing himself to be a fool. He'd asked

Amelia to marry him, then he'd sent Houston to fetch her, and she'd fallen in love with his brother.

He'd married Cordelia, and he'd told Austin to keep her company. What in the hell had he expected to happen?

Reaching into his pocket, he withdrew the watch Amelia had given him as a sign of her affection when she had first arrived at his ranch. He didn't expect Cordelia to give him anything as a symbol of her affection, but he was certain she was going to leave him.

He considered arguing that too many years separated Cordelia from Austin, but he figured love didn't put a lot of stock in the passage of years. Besides, he was several years older than Cordelia and his heart didn't seem to notice.

He'd build them a house on a distant corner of his land because he didn't think his pride could tolerate seeing the two of them together knowing at one time she was supposed to be his. Then he'd see about finding himself another wife. He could run an advertisement in the newspapers back East or maybe he could—

"Dallas?" Austin's voice came from behind him. "Dallas, I need to talk to you."

He jammed the watch back into his pocket and wrapped a wall of indifference around himself. Shoving the part of himself that could be hurt back into a dark hole, he turned to face his youngest brother.

"Figured you did," he said as he crooked an elbow onto the railing of the corral.

Austin looked down and scuffed the toe of his boot into the dirt. "I don't rightly know how to say it."

"Just come straight out with it. That's usually the best way."

Austin nodded and met his brother's gaze. "Dee asked me not to say anything to you, but I figured you ought to know."

Dallas swallowed past the knot that had formed in his throat. "I appreciate that."

Austin shoved his hands into his pockets. "Remember when you took me to that circus when I was seven?"

If Austin had hoped to lessen Dallas's anger, he had succeeded. Christmas, 1867. The Haight and Chambers New Orleans Colossal Circus and Menagerie had pitched tents in San Antonio. Dallas and Houston were still recovering from the war, with little spare change clinking in their pockets, but they had wanted to give Austin a Christmas he wouldn't soon forget. Dallas couldn't stop himself from smiling at the fond memories. "Yeah, and you pestered me all day with questions. I threatened to pay that sword swallower to stick one of his swords down your throat just to shut you up."

Austin chuckled and rubbed the side of his nose. "I thought you were serious."

"The threat didn't work, though, did it?"

Austin shook his head. "Nope, and that's the way Dee is when I take her to town. She's got so many questions and everything amazes her. They never took her into town, Dallas. Never."

"But you did, and I reckon she's grateful for that."

Austin took a step closer. "I wasn't paying any attention to the questions she was asking. I was just answering them. The whole while I'm answering the questions, she's working this idea up in her head. Today, she finally gets the courage to do something about it . . . and Mr. Henderson laughed at her. What made it worse is that Boyd was there and the bastard—"

"Whoa. Hold your horses." Dallas held up his hand. "What are you talking about?"

"I'm trying to tell you what happened in town today. See, Dee figured when the railroad comes through here, people are gonna need a place to sleep. So she was thinking of building a hotel. She knew you had talked to Mr. Henderson about a loan for the cabinetmaker so she figured that was where she needed to start—by getting a loan. Yesterday she stood outside the bank all day. Couldn't get up the courage to go inside.

"Today she reaches deep down, gathers up that courage, and heads into the bank. Only Boyd is inside, and he tells her the saloon has all the spare rooms this town is ever gonna need. Then he and Mr. Henderson start to laugh. Boyd tells her that your bed is the only bed she needs to be concerned with."

"What did she do?" Dallas asked through clenched teeth.

Austin smiled. "You woulda been proud. She just thanked Mr. Henderson for his time and walked out with her head held high."

"Who else was in the bank?"

"A couple of ranchers and the teller. Anyway, she's feeling lower than a snail's belly. I've been trying to tell her funny stories to make her laugh, but that ain't what she needs. I thought maybe tonight you could sweet-talk her, make her feel special."

"Sweet-talk her?"

"Yeah, you know, say those words women like to hear. The words that make them shine brighter than a full moon."

Dallas nodded. "I'll do that."

Austin's face split into a wide grin. "I'm glad I told you. She was afraid you'd be mad at her for wanting to do something on her own."

"I'm not mad at her."

"I knew you wouldn't be." Austin backed up a step. "Reckon we ought to get to the house. She'll be wanting to read soon. I sure do like listening to her read." He turned toward the house.

"Austin?"

Austin stopped and looked back over his shoulder.

Dallas weighed his words. "Don't ever tell her that you told me what happened today."

"Oh, I won't. You just be sure you give her some good sweet-talkin'."

Dallas nodded. "I will."

Sweet-talking. What did he know about sweet-talking?

Not one damn thing.

Dallas pounded on the door until the hinges rattled. He heard the hesitant footsteps on the other side.

"It's Dallas! Open up!"

The door opened a crack. Dallas reined in his temper.

Lester Henderson opened the door wider. "Dallas, good Lord, you scared me to death. Is something wrong?"

"I don't know, Lester. I heard a rumor, and it's keeping me from sleeping. I'm just hoping it's not true."

Always eager for gossip, Lester Henderson stepped onto the back porch of the second floor. Like most of the newcomers to Leighton, he lived above his business and his business was the bank. "What rumor?" he asked.

"I heard my wife came into the bank and asked for a loan today."

Lester laughed with a high-pitched squeal that grated on Dallas's nerves. "Oh, that. Don't worry, Dallas, I turned her down. Boyd was there, and he explained to her the foolishness of her request. She's supposed to be giving you a son, and Boyd spelled that out loud and clear."

Dallas balled his hands into fists to keep them from circling the little weasel's throat. "Could you come out a little farther, Lester?" Dallas asked.

"Sure."

Lester walked to the edge of the porch. Dallas pointed to the far horizon. "What do you see out there, Lester?"

Lester shrugged. "Moon. Stars. Land."

"My land," Dallas said. "As far as you can see, I own it. I don't have a son, Lester. If I get gored by a bull tomorrow and die, all that land goes to my wife." Dallas tilted his head. "Come to think of it, the land already belongs to her because she honored me by becoming my wife."

He tore his hat from his head and lowered his face until he and Henderson were staring eye to eye. Lester backed up, and Dallas stalked him until the man had nowhere else to go and no choice but to bend over the railing like a sapling in the wind.

"If my wife comes into your bank, I don't want her to have to ask for a damn thing. I want you to jump out of your chair and ask her what you can do for her. If she wants a loan, then by God, you give her a loan."

"But . . . but collateral," Henderson stammered.

"I just showed you her goddamn collateral!"

"But Boyd said—"

"I don't give a damn what Boyd said or what any other member of her family says. If she wants the moon, by God I'll find a way to give it to her. Right now all she wants is a loan from you, and I'd appreciate it greatly if you'd think on her request tonight and decide in the morning that it would be in this town's best interest to give it to her."

Dallas stepped back. Henderson straightened and puffed out his chest. "Are you threatening me?"

"No, Henderson, I'm not," Dallas said in a voice that rang out as deceptively mild. "I never threaten, but I'll give you my word that if you ever embarrass my wife like you did today, I'll build a bank next to yours and put you out of business. Wherever you go, I'll follow until the day I die, and you'll never again work in a bank, much less own one."

Dallas spun on his heel and started down the steps. He stopped and turned. "Henderson, I never want my wife to know of this conversation." Henderson nodded mutely, and Dallas stomped down the steps. He didn't figure Lester Henderson would ever accuse him of sweet-talking.

The following morning at breakfast, Dallas watched as his wife slowly trailed her finger over her list of topics.

"Dee?"

She looked up, disappointment etched over her features.

"You don't have to talk to me if you don't want to. I won't discuss husbandry at the table."

She nodded grimly, glanced quickly at Austin, then looked back at her notes.

Dallas could feel Austin's blue glare boring into him. Apparently, Austin had figured out that Dallas had not sweet-talked his wife last night, and it didn't sit well with him.

Cordelia shifted her gaze back to Dallas and gnawed on her bottom lip. "What would you have done if Mr. Henderson hadn't given you the loan for the cabinetmaker?"

Dallas leaned back in his chair, incredibly pleased with her question, more pleased that she wasn't planning to let Henderson or her brother stop her from reaching for her dream. He wondered what other questions she'd written on her list. "I'd go to a bank in another town, convince them to give me the loan."

"What town?"

"Fort Worth would probably be best."

"How far away is—"

A pounding on the door interrupted her question, but he had a good idea where she was headed with the questions, and he hoped she wouldn't have to travel there. "Austin, why don't you go see who's at the door?" Dallas asked.

Austin shoved his chair back and stalked from the room. A few minutes later, disbelief mirrored on his young face, he escorted Lester Henderson into the dining room.

Cordelia gracefully swept out of her chair. "Mr. Henderson, what a pleasure it is to have you in our home. Would you like me to get you some coffee while you speak with my husband?"

Dallas didn't know if he'd ever met anyone as gracious as his wife, and at that moment he was damn proud she was married to him.

Henderson turned his hat in his hand. "Actually, Mrs. Leigh, I'm here to speak with you."

Dallas scraped his chair across the floor. Henderson looked as though he'd almost come out of his skin. Dallas stood. "You can use my office. I need to check on the herd."

He walked out of the house, headed to the barn, and saddled Satan. By the time he rode the horse out of the barn, Henderson was climbing into his buggy.

"I hope you know what you're doing," Henderson snapped, his lips pursed.

Dallas smiled with satisfaction. "I wouldn't be as successful as I am today if I didn't know the value of a good investment."

"Women know nothing about business," Henderson said.

Dallas tipped his hat off his brow. "They know how to manage a home. They know how to manage a family. Why in the hell don't you think they can manage a business?"

Sputtering, Henderson slapped the reins and sent the horse into a trot, the buggy rolling back to town.

Dallas heard his wife's excited squeal as she called Austin's name.

He ignored the ache in his chest because she hadn't chosen to share her joy with him, and he pretended that it didn't matter because sooner or later, she'd have no choice.

She would have to come to him.

When she did, she'd learn that nothing in life came without a price. In order to have what she wanted, Dallas would have to get what he wanted.

At the gentle tap on his office door, Dallas turned from the window and the night sky. "Come in."

Cordelia opened the door and peered inside. "Can I talk to you for a minute?"

He heard the tremble in her voice. "Sure."

Like someone about to confront an executioner, she walked into the room and stood before his desk. She waved her hand toward his chair. "You can sit."

"Is that what you prefer?"

She gave him a jerky nod.

In long strides, he crossed the room and dropped into his chair. He planted his elbow on the desk and slowly rubbed his thumb and fore-finger over his mustache. He lifted a brow.

She dropped her gaze to the floor. "I . . . uh." She cleared her throat. "I thought it would be nice if your town had a hotel. I managed to get a loan and Mr. Curtiss is drawing up the plans for the building—"

"Dee?"

She glanced up.

"You should always look a man in the eye when you're discussing business."

She visibly swallowed. "It makes it harder."

"The man you're doing business with knows that. He'll respect you for it, and he's more likely to give you what you're asking for."

"Do you know why I'm here?"

"I've got a good idea."

"And you're still going to make me ask?"

"Everything in life worth having comes with a price."

"And your price?"

Distrust and fear lurked within the dark depths of her eyes. He hated them both. "Ask."

She took a deep breath and balled her hands into fists at her sides.

"I have the money. I have someone to build it." She clenched her jaw and angled her chin. "But I need the land. When you announced that you had set aside land for a town, in my ignorance, I assumed that meant it was free for the taking. This afternoon, Mr. Curtiss explained to me that you still own the land, and that merchants must purchase the lots before he can build on them." Resignation ripped through her voice. "Without the land, I can't build the hotel."

Dallas shoved his chair back. She jumped. If he had to tie her down, he was going to make her stop jumping every time he moved.

He went to a corner and picked up a scroll. He placed it on the desk and gave it a gentle push. It rolled across the flat surface, revealing the layout of his town: the planned streets, the building lots. He set his inkwell on one end of the scroll to hold it in position and placed the lamp on the other end.

"Where do you want your hotel?" he asked.

Curiosity replaced the fear as she leaned over the map. She trailed her finger along the widest street.

"Main Street," she said quietly. "I suppose I'd want it on the same street as the bank and general store. Where will the railroad be?"

"I'm expecting it to come through at this end of town," he said, touching the southernmost point.

"What are these smaller blocks of land for?" she asked, touching a section set back from the town.

"Houses, if we get enough people moving in."

She gnawed on her lower lip. "The hotel should be near the railroad." She lifted her gaze to his. "Don't you think?"

He wasn't prepared for the shaft of pleasure that speared him. She wanted his opinion. He swallowed hard. "That's where I'd put it."

She nodded and placed her finger on a parcel of land just down from where he'd said the railroad would be. "How much would this piece of land cost me?"

He felt the glory of success surge through him. Her dream was to build a hotel. He understood dreams. His dream was to have a son. A simple trade: one dream for another. They could both have what they wanted. But without trust, without affection, the price suddenly seemed too high.

"A smile," he said quietly.

She jerked her gaze up. "I beg your pardon?"

"The price is a smile . . . like the ones you give Austin or Houston . . . or that damn prairie dog of yours."

She blinked her eyes and straightened. Then she pulled her lips back to reveal a tortured grin that more closely resembled a grimace.

The lesson learned was a painful one: he couldn't force affection. He couldn't force a smile. And he imagined if he crawled into her bed and took what was his by right, he'd feel emptier than he did now.

He dipped his pen into the inkwell and scrawled "Dee's Hotel" across the blank square on the map of his town. Then he walked to the window, placed his hands behind his back, and gazed at the moonless sky, trying to fill a void that only seemed to deepen with each passing moment.

"That's it?" she asked behind him.

"That's it."

"That block of land is mine?"

"It's yours."

"Oh, Dallas."

He turned from the window. In obvious awe, she touched the words he'd written on the map. Tears glistened in her eyes as she looked at him and smiled . . . a glorious smile that stole his breath away.

"I've never owned anything in my whole life, and now I own this little piece of land—"

"You own a lot more than that. In truth, you didn't even have to give me a smile. It was yours all along."

"I don't understand."

"When you married me, you became my partner not only in my life, but in everything—my ranch, the town . . . everything, and I became your partner."

As he'd known it would, her smile retreated like the sun before a storm.

"Then the hotel . . . it will be yours as well?"

"Ours. But I'll be a silent partner."

"What does that mean?"

"You're free to do whatever you want with the hotel. Make it into whatever you want it to be, and I'll keep my mouth shut. But if you ever want an opinion on something, I'll be here."

She folded her hands in her lap and stared at them.

"Nothing has changed, Dee."

"Everything has changed," she said quietly. She lifted her gaze to his. "What if I want the hotel to take up two of these spaces on the map?"

He raised a brow. "Two spaces?"

She nodded. "I want it to be a grand hotel. When people pass through here, I want them to talk about it."

He walked back to the desk. "Then mark off another block."

Smiling, she dipped the pen into the inkwell and with deliberate strokes, wrote her name in a space on the map. She peered up at him. "What if I want three?"

"I have some plans for the town, too."

She leaned forward. "What are your plans?"

Her question echoed through his heart. He'd felt slighted when she hadn't shared her plans with him before, and what had he shared with her? Not one damn thing.

He sat, placed his elbow on the wooden arm of the chair, and brushed his mustache. He'd only ever told people what they needed to know in order to get the job done. He couldn't recall ever telling anyone everything he hoped for.

"Uh, well, I've got a newspaperman interested in coming to Leighton."

Her eyes widened. "A newspaper? We'll have a newspaper?"

He liked the way she'd said "we."

"Yeah, we'll have a newspaper. He'll be able to do announcements and post bulletins for people."

"What will the paper be called?"

"*The Leighton Leader.*"

"What else?"

"A mortician."

She visibly shuddered.

"People die," he said.

She looked back at the map and traced her finger along the lines that represented streets.

"McGirk, Tipton, Phillipy . . ." Her voice trailed off, leaving the names of so many other streets unspoken. "Who did you name these streets after?"

He stopped stroking his mustache. His mind suddenly filled with the sounds of cannons, explosions, and gunfire. "Men I sent to their deaths," he said quietly. "They were boys really, more afraid of me than they were of the enemy." He lifted a shoulder. "Naming the streets after them is my way of remembering them, honoring them."

"You weren't very old during the war."

"Few soldiers were."

She scooted up in her chair. "I know so little about you."

"What do you want to know?"

"Everything." She averted her gaze as though embarrassed. "Did you know I wanted to build a hotel?"

"I'd heard the rumor."

She peered at him. "Do you think it will be successful?"

"Absolutely."

She placed her hands on the desk, fear etched within the dark depths of her eyes, but he didn't think it was fear of him.

"Dallas, I want to do something different with the hotel."

She stood and began to pace. So graceful. So elegant. He wondered if he'd ever truly watched her walk.

"What do you want to do?" he asked.

She stopped and grabbed the back of her chair. 'I want to use the hotel to bring women to Leighton."

He furrowed his brow. "What?"

She scurried around the chair, sat, and leaned forward, an excitement in her eyes, the likes of which he'd never seen. "You mentioned placing an ad to get women to come to Leighton as brides, which seems so unfair to me. A woman has to promise herself to a man she's never met—just as Amelia promised herself to you. What happens if she falls in love with someone else? Not every man will be as generous as you were. Not every man will give up his claim. Or what happens if she meets the man and doesn't like him?"

She hopped out of the chair and began pacing again. Dallas was fascinated watching her, as though he could actually see her thoughts forming.

"I want to give women a reason to come to Leighton that has nothing to do with marriage. I want to have a nice restaurant inside the hotel where men will meet to discuss business. I want women to manage the hotel and work in the restaurant. We'll bring women from all over the country here. Train them. Give them the skills they need to work in our hotel. If they happen to meet a man and get married, it won't be because they had no choice."

Her words rammed into him with the force of a stampeding bull. She'd had no choice. He wondered who she might have chosen to marry if she'd been given the choice.

She stopped pacing, placed her palms on his desk, and met his gaze. "What do you think?"

That you should have had a choice.

He held his thoughts, stood, and walked to the window. In the distance, he could hear his windmill. Behind him, he could feel Dee's tenseness as she waited for his answer.

He had not given her a choice when the decision was made that they would marry, but he could give her a choice now. He would stay out of her bedroom until she wanted him there.

Turning, he captured her gaze. "I think you're about to build an empire."

Chapter 11

✥

W ITHIN DALLAS'S OFFICE, Cordelia shifted in the chair and scribbled more notes across what had once been an unmarred sheet
of paper. She was quickly discovering that building an empire was no
easy task. Details abounded.

In the morning she worked quickly to clean away any evidence that
they had eaten breakfast. She tidied the house and made beds.

It occurred to her one morning that if Dallas would truly become
her husband, sleep in her bed, she would only have to spend time making two beds, instead of three, washing sheets for two beds, instead of
three.

She'd considered discussing the arrangement with him, but she
couldn't quite gather enough courage. She was certain he would want to
do more than sleep in her bed, and she wasn't altogether ready for what
the "more" might entail.

Although with each passing day, she found herself thinking of Dallas with increasing frequency.

After she finished her chores around the house, Austin would escort
her to town. She constantly thought about Dallas as she viewed the
plans that Mr. Curtiss was drawing up. She would wonder if Dallas was
tending his cattle. She would hope that a reason would surface for him
to come into town as well.

It seemed their paths continually crossed. She enjoyed walking
through the town with him, listening as he explained the strengths and
weaknesses in the buildings or discussed the other businesses that were

coming to Leighton: the sign maker, the baker, the cobbler, and the barber.

But she anticipated the evenings most of all. She would curl up in the stuffed chair in Dallas's office and discuss her plans with him: the wording of her advertisements that would bring women to Leighton to work in her hotel, the type of furniture she wanted to place in the hotel rooms, the variety of meals she wanted to serve in the restaurant.

He had offered to give her a discount on beef. She had reminded him that she didn't need a discount. As his partner, she could simply take the cattle she wanted.

He'd laughed, deeply, richly, and she had realized that she loved his laughter, loved the way he listened to her, loved the approval of her suggestions that she saw reflected in his brown gaze.

"What's bothering you?"

Cordelia looked up from the notes she'd been making regarding the restaurant. She tucked her feet more securely beneath her. "Nothing. Everything is fine."

Sitting behind his desk, Dallas narrowed his eyes. "Have you got a problem with the hotel?"

She gnawed on her lower lip. "It's not a problem really. Mr. Curtiss finished the design of the hotel . . . and it's just not exactly what I had in mind."

"Then tell him."

She shifted in the chair. "He worked so hard on the design that I hate to hurt his feelings."

"But it's not what you want. You're paying him to give you what you want. You are paying him, aren't you?"

"Yes."

"Then go into town tomorrow and tell him."

She drew Dallas's latest brand at the edge of the paper. It reminded her of a heart more than it did two *D*'s back to back. All it needed was Cupid's arrow. She drew his brand again, biding her time, wanting to ask him to go with her—

"Do you want me to go with you?"

She glanced up, drawn by the intensity of his gaze. Once she had been uncomfortable with his scrutiny. Now she recognized it for what it was: simply his way of looking at everyone, everything.

She smiled softly. "No, I can handle this matter on my own."

His gaze grew warm, and her heart fluttered like butterflies in the spring. Her answer had pleased him, and she wondered when it was that she had begun to care whether or not she pleased him.

The next morning, with the sun barely easing over the horizon, Dallas guided his horse through the village of tents. Someday they'd all be gone and nothing but wooden buildings would remain. People would come. His town would grow. His son would have a good future here.

He saw Tyler Curtiss standing outside his tent, his suspenders dangling as he shaved in front of a mirror strapped to the tent pole. Dallas drew Satan to a halt.

"Tyler?"

Tyler turned from the mirror and smiled broadly. "Dallas, you're out and about kinda early this morning."

Nodding, Dallas leaned on the saddle horn. "You're making good progress on the town."

"Every time I think my job is nearing completion, I get a request to design and construct another building. I have a feeling this town will be forever growing."

Dallas smiled. "I hope so. Things should boom once the railroad gets here." The saddle creaked in the predawn stillness as he shifted his weight. "Tyler, my wife is going to come by this morning. She's not happy with the plans you drew up for the hotel."

Tyler furrowed his brow. "Yesterday, she said they were fine."

Removing his hat, Dallas studied the distant horizon. With feath erlight touches, the sun stroked the dawn with soft hues, much as his wife gently brought sunshine to his days. "You ever been married?"

"No, sir, can't say I've had the pleasure."

"I don't know how much of a pleasure it is. Women are contrary. When Dee says something is fine, it's not fine at all. When it's fine, she gives you a smile . . . a smile that will steal your breath away." Dallas settled his hat on his head. "When she comes to see you today, make certain you do whatever it takes to give her that smile."

Tyler nodded. "I'll do that."

"I'd appreciate it." He turned his horse.

"Dallas?"

He glanced over his shoulder.

"What should I do with the plans I drew up a few months back for the hotel you wanted to build?"

Dallas shrugged. "Do whatever you want with them. This town only needs one hotel."

Cordelia had never in her life been as nervous as she was now. She stood back and watched as the surveyor team pounded markers into the ground and roped off the lots where the hotel would one day stand.

Mr. Curtiss had finished the blacksmith shop and the livery. He was ready to begin construction on the hotel.

She squeezed Dallas's arm as he stood beside her, dressed much as he had been the day she married him: brown trousers, brown jacket, a brown satiny vest. He looked like a successful businessman, not the cowboy who rode in at dusk, covered in sweat and dust. He glanced at her.

"It's really going to happen, isn't it?" she asked.

His lips spread into a warm smile, a smile that touched his deep brown eyes. "Yep."

Holding Precious close within the nook of her arm, she looked over her shoulder. People were gathering behind them, watching the surveyors with interest. She could see all of Dallas's ranch hands.

She saw Houston weaving his way through the crowd, holding Maggie, her arms looped around his neck. Amelia trudged along beside him, her arm entwined through his. As they neared, Amelia released her hold on Houston and hugged Cordelia close. Precious barked. Amelia laughed.

"This is so exciting," Amelia said.

Cordelia couldn't contain her smile. "Mr. Curtiss thinks he can have the hotel completed by October."

"Four months?" Houston asked. "He thinks he'll need that much time?"

Cordelia nodded. "It's going to be a large hotel, a grand hotel." She squeezed Amelia's hand. "That's what we're going to call it. The Grand Hotel." She glanced at Dallas. "Aren't we?"

"We'll call it whatever you want to call it," he said.

Houston chuckled. "Sounds like naming a hotel is sorta like naming children."

Dallas scowled at his brother. "Ain't nothing like it at all."

In long strides, Austin walked up to Dallas and whispered something in his ear. Dallas nodded. "Good."

Austin smiled at Cordelia. "Hard to believe it's been less than three weeks since you walked into Henderson's bank. I think you work faster than Dallas when you get an idea burning."

She blushed and lowered her gaze. "I think this will help the town grow. It will give people a nice place to stay when they visit Leighton." She glanced at Amelia. "We thought we'd have a special room where the schoolteacher could live."

"That would be wonderful," Amelia said, "although much to my shame I haven't done anything to see about securing one for the town."

"I haven't helped you either."

"That'll have to be our next order of business," Dallas said.

Cordelia's breath caught when she saw her brothers striding toward her. Only Cameron smiled at her. He reached out and took her hand. "Hi, Dee, you're looking well."

She felt well, felt happy. "I wasn't expecting to see you today."

"Dallas sent word that he had an announcement to make," Boyd said. He dropped his gaze to her stomach. "Reckon we all know what that announcement is since your husband seems to think everyone cares about his business."

The animosity surprised her. She hadn't realized until this moment that she'd grown accustomed to living in a house where anger didn't always reign supreme. "Where's Father?"

"He couldn't make the trip," Boyd said.

"Is he ill?" she asked.

"Age just catching up with him."

She looked at Dallas. "I really should go see him soon."

"I'll make the arrangements."

One of the surveyors approached. "We're done."

Dallas nodded and turned his attention to Cordelia. "Do you want to walk around the edge of the property before the ceremony begins?"

"The ceremony?" Boyd asked.

With obvious satisfaction, Dallas smiled at her brother. "The groundbreaking ceremony. Our announcement involves the hotel Dee plans to build in Leighton."

Boyd visibly paled. "Hotel? You're not announcing that she's carrying your child?"

"Nope."

Boyd's eyes narrowed. "What's the matter, Leigh? Aren't you man enough to get her with child?"

Cameron shoved his oldest brother back. "That's uncalled for, Boyd."

Boyd held his shaking finger in front of Cameron's nose. "Never do that again. Never."

Cameron shook his head. "This is Dee's moment. Don't ruin it for her."

"You knew she was building a hotel?"

Cameron's gaze darted to Austin before returning to his brother. "Yeah, I knew."

"I don't give a damn about any hotel. All I care about is the land that bastard stole from us." Boyd stormed away.

Cordelia looked at her two remaining brothers. They shifted from one foot to the other as though uncomfortable.

Duncan finally grinned. "I hear there's gonna be dancing, free food, and free whiskey. I plan to stay."

"Me, too," Cameron said with less enthusiasm.

"We're glad to hear that," Dallas said. He turned to Cordelia. "A quick walk around the edge? People are getting anxious for us to begin."

She was anxious for it to end. It always came back to the land, to her giving Dallas a son.

Yet, the man who wanted the son, the man who should be angry because she had not shared her bed with him, was the one standing beside her now, walking around the property that had cost her little more than a smile.

The day she had met him, she had deemed him to be a man of little patience. Yet in the past month, he had never badgered her for what was his by right. He had patiently listened to her plans for the hotel, offered advice, and given her the chance to reach for something that she wanted.

He had asked for nothing in exchange.

"What do you get out of all this?" she asked as they rounded the first corner and walked along the side that would be the back of the hotel.

He seemed surprised as he glanced over at her. "I like to see you smile. Building the hotel seemed to give you plenty of reasons to smile."

"It's that simple?" she asked.

"It's that simple."

They walked around the next corner. "It's going to be big, isn't it?" she asked as her gaze stretched from one taut rope to the other.

"Biggest building in town."

They returned to where they had begun. Mr. Curtiss was standing at the corner, holding a shovel. Dallas and Mr. Curtiss stepped over the rope and walked to the center of the property.

Cordelia felt Amelia slip her hand around hers and squeeze gently. Houston stood behind Amelia. Maggie wrapped herself around Cordelia's legs. Austin moved in beside Cordelia and put his arm around her shoulder.

Cameron and Duncan stood off to the side. With a mixture of sadness for the family she seemed to have lost and resounding happiness for the family she had gained, she turned her attention to her husband.

He swept his hat from his head and a hush descended over the gathering. Pride rang through her heart at the sight of the man she had married standing so tall, so bold before the crowd.

She wanted the women who came to Leighton to have a choice. As for herself, she was no longer certain if she would have chosen differently if she had been given a choice.

"A little over a month ago," Dallas began, the deep timbre of his voice reverberating around him, "I had the pleasure of sharing with you—our friends and neighbors—my joy as Dee became my wife. To-day, we want to share with you the beginning of what will be a landmark building in Leighton. Dee's vision for her hotel will set the standard by which all future buildings in Leighton will be judged." He held his hand toward her. "Dee, the dream is yours. The land is yours to break."

Cordelia's breath caught, her heart pounded, and her knees shook. Surely he didn't mean for her to join him in front of all these people. She stepped back and rammed into Houston's hard body.

"Go on, Dee," Houston urged her quietly, gently.

Austin squeezed her shoulder and smiled broadly. "If you can walk into the bank and ask for a loan, you can walk into your own hotel."

Her own hotel.

She looked at Amelia, whose eyes were filling with tears. "I told you," she whispered, "that given the chance, he'd worship the ground you walked on."

Cordelia snapped her gaze back to her husband. His hand was outstretched as he waited for her. She clutched Precious more closely, took a deep breath, and stepped over the rope.

The crowd clapped and cheered, Dallas's smile grew, and her shaking increased. She walked across the plot as quickly as she could and slipped her hand into her husband's, surprised to find his trembling as well.

Mr. Curtiss held the shovel toward her. "You'll need this," he said, grinning brightly.

"Give me the damn prairie dog," Dallas grumbled past his smile as he released her hand.

She handed Precious off to him and took the shovel. Mr. Curtiss helped her to position it. She tightened her hold on the handle, pressed her foot on the shovel as he instructed, and flipped aside a small portion of dirt.

She glanced at Dallas. "How big should I make the hole?"

Shaking his head, he took the shovel and handed it to Mr. Curtiss. "That's all you need to do." He crooked his elbow. She placed her hand on his arm, and he led her toward the waiting crowd.

She clung to Dallas's arm as people surrounded her, asking her questions.

"I won't leave you," Dallas whispered near her ear.

She relaxed her fingers. No, he wouldn't leave her. Had she ever noticed how often he was there when she needed him?

"How many rooms will the hotel have?" someone asked.

Cordelia smiled. "Fifty."

"I hear it's gonna have a restaurant."

"A very nice restaurant," Cordelia assured them. "The finest food in town."

"Speaking of fine food," Dallas interjected, "we've got beef cooking near the saloon. You're all invited to enjoy it."

As people wandered away, Cordelia turned her attention to Dallas.

"Why didn't you tell me I was going to have to dig a hole in front of all these people?"

"Figured it would just make you nervous, and you might decide not to come. I didn't want you to miss your moment."

Her moment.

"Mrs. Leigh?"

She turned. A young man stood before her, holding a pad of paper. "Mrs. Leigh, I'm a reporter with the Fort Worth *Daily Democrat*. Since the same railroad that touches our town will eventually touch yours, I was hoping you could spare a few minutes to answer a few questions about your hotel."

Cordelia looked at Dallas. He smiled. "Your moment."

As he walked away, she began to answer the earnest young man's questions about The Grand Hotel. She explained the fact that women would manage the hotel and work in the restaurant. When she answered his final question, she began to walk toward the other end of town where people were congregating. She could hear the sweet strains of a waltz. She saw Austin standing in the back of a wagon, playing his violin. Houston and Amelia danced, as did Becky and Duncan. Several men danced together.

"Dee?"

She stumbled to a stop and smiled at her youngest brother as she took his hand. "Cameron, I'm so glad you were here today."

"You look happy, Dee. Is Dallas treating you right?"

She glanced toward the saloon. She could see her husband leaning against the wall, Precious nestled within the crook of his arm as he talked to Mr. Curtiss.

"He treats me very well." She squeezed his hand. "You should come visit us. I think you would like Dallas if you stopped looking at him through Boyd's eyes."

Out of the corner of her eye, she caught a flash of black streaking by. "Excuse me," she said to her brother as she scurried away. "Rawley! Rawley Cooper!"

The boy staggered to a grinding halt and dropped his gaze to the dirt. She knelt in front of him.

"Hello, Rawley. I don't know if you remember me. I saw you at the general store one day."

"I 'member."

"I was wondering if you could do a favor for me."

His black gaze darted up, then down. He started digging his big toe into the dirt. She wanted to wrap her arms around him and hug him fiercely. She wondered if anyone ever had.

"I'll pay you," she said softly.

His gaze came up and stayed focused on her, but she could see the doubt and distrust swimming in his eyes.

"How much?" he asked.

"A dollar."

He bit into his bottom lip. "What I gotta do?"

"Take care of my prairie dog so I can dance with my husband."

"Fer how long?"

"Until tomorrow morning."

He narrowed his eyes. "You gotta pay me first."

"All right." She rose and held out her hand. "Let's go talk to my husband."

With his fingers curled, he reached for her hand, then quickly drew it back. "Holding hands is fer sissies."

She wondered briefly if her brothers were of the same opinion. As far back as she could remember, Cameron was the only one who had ever touched her, and then his touch had always been hesitant. She didn't want that for her children.

She walked toward the saloon with Rawley shuffling along behind her. She knew the exact moment Dallas saw her. His attention veered away from Mr. Curtiss, and although the architect and builder continued to talk, she felt as though she had Dallas's undivided attention.

As she stopped in front of her husband, Precious yipped and Dallas shifted her in his arms.

"If you'll excuse me, I want to talk with Miss St. Claire," Mr. Curtiss said. "She's thinking of expanding her business into an emporium."

"Appreciate your help today," Dallas said.

"My pleasure." He tipped his hat toward Cordelia before walking away.

"How did the interview go?" Dallas asked.

"If I didn't sound knowledgeable, I think it's safe to say I was at least enthusiastic about the new hotel."

Precious barked again and began to squirm. Cordelia touched Rawley's shoulder, and he jerked away. She hoped she wasn't making a mistake.

"This is Rawley Cooper. He's going to watch Precious for us."

Dallas lifted a brow. "Is that so?"

Rawley jerked a nod. "But you gotta pay me. A dollar. Up front."

"That's a bargain," Dallas mumbled as he reached into his pocket and withdrew a dollar. He laid it in Rawley's palm.

Rawley looked at the coin as though he hadn't really expected to receive a dollar. He pocketed the money, held out his dirt-covered hands, and took Precious. He glanced at Cordelia. "Where you want me to meet ya tomorrow?"

"Where do you live?"

He dropped his gaze. "Around."

"We'll find you," Dallas said.

Rawley nodded and slowly scuffled away as though he carried something fragile.

"Now, why did you do that?" Dallas asked.

Cordelia turned her attention to her husband. "Precious was in the way." She stepped onto the boardwalk. Her gaze was nearly level with Dallas's. She could hear the gentle strains of another song fill the air. Her heart began to pound, her stomach to quiver. "The day we were married, you told me that it wasn't hard to dance, and that you would guide me. I was wondering if your offer was still open."

He shoved away from the wall and held out his hand. "It's always open for you."

She placed her hand in his. His palm was rough, his pads callused, his fingers long, his skin warm as his hand closed around hers. She walked with him to an area where only a few others danced.

When he placed his hand on her waist, it seemed the most natural movement in the world to place her hand on his shoulder. He held her gaze. When he stepped in rhythm to the music, she followed.

The melody swirled around her. Beyond Dallas's shoulder, the muted hues of the sky began to darken, lengthening the shadows of evening. He guided her through the waltz as easily as he had guided her toward this day.

"How did you know that I wanted to build a hotel?"

His gaze never faltered. "Austin told me about your visit to the bank."

"Did you tell Mr. Henderson to give me the loan?"

"I simply explained to him that you had collateral—"

"Your land."

"Our land. He had no reason not to give you a loan."

"And if the hotel fails?"

"It won't."

"How can you be so sure?"

His hold on her tightened as he drew her closer. Her thighs brushed against his.

"I've seen you terrified. You stayed when I have little doubt that you desperately wanted to leave. A woman with that much fortitude isn't about to let a business flounder."

"I was a fool to fear you."

He shook his head slightly. "I was the greater fool. I never should have forced our marriage. I should have taken the time to court you."

She watched as he swallowed.

"I should have given you the choice that you want to give other women."

She swayed within his arms, now knowing beyond a doubt that if he had courted her, if she had been given the choice, she would not have chosen differently.

Dallas was not a man prone to doubts, but this evening as Dee rode beside him back toward the ranch, doubts plagued him.

Her lips were curved into a soft smile, her face serene as the moon guided them home. She seemed happy and content, more so than he'd ever seen her.

Like a hopeful litany, her words echoed through his mind: *I was a fool to fear you.*

A warm breeze blew gently over the land, and in the distance, he could hear the constant clatter of his newest windmill. He held his silence until the windmill came into view, a dark silhouette against the prairie sky.

"I want to show you something," he said quietly, hoping none of his actions tonight would put the fear back into her eyes.

She glanced over at him. "What do you want to show me?"

He brought his horse to a halt beneath the windmill. She drew her horse to a stop and smiled. "Oh, one of your ladies."

Dallas dismounted and wiped his sweating palms on his jacket before helping her off her horse.

"I've never been so far from home at night," she whispered as though someone might be lurking nearby to overhear her words.

"This is my favorite time of day," Dallas said. "I like to view it from up there."

He pointed to the top of the windmill and her eyes widened.

"How do you get up there?"

"This windmill has a ladder and a small platform." A platform he had built in anticipation of this night. He held out his hand. A warm jolt of pleasure shot through him when she placed her hand in his.

He led her to the windmill. "Just one foot at a time," he said. "Hold onto the railing. The ladder will take you to the platform at the top."

He followed closely behind her until she crawled on the platform. He climbed on after her. The platform was small, barely enough room for the two of them to stand.

Dallas had thought about this moment a hundred times, all the things he would tell her: the things he felt, the things he wanted, the dreams left unfulfilled.

He wanted her to see all that he saw: the vastness of the sky. The canopy of stars. The land that stretched out before them. In the far-off distance, he could hear the lowing of cattle. He could smell the soil, the grass, the flowers that had bloomed throughout the day

He could smell the night. He could smell her sweet fragrance.

And he knew that no words he could utter would do justice to the magnificence that lay before them, to the future they might share. If she couldn't envision it of her own accord, he couldn't describe it so she would. If she didn't understand it, he couldn't explain it.

"It's beautiful."

Her soft voice, laced with reverence, wrapped around him, increased tenfold the majesty of all he'd acquired, all he had worked so hard to attain.

He had never felt as close to anyone as he felt to her right now, standing high above the earth, with the night surrounding them, and he somehow knew that if he had misjudged the moment, his dream would crumble into dust.

"I want a son, Dee."

She turned her head and met his gaze, and he prayed that it wasn't a trick of the moonlight that made it seem as though she harbored no fear in her eyes.

"I want a son that I can share this with. I want to bring him up here at dawn, at sunset, at midnight. As grand as all this is, I want him to know that it pales in comparison to all that he will be." He swallowed hard. "But I won't take what you're unwilling to give."

He watched her gaze slowly sweep over the land as though she were measuring its worth.

"I want to give you a son," she said softly.

His heart was thudding with such force that he was afraid he might not have heard her correctly. "You do?"

She nodded, and he could have sworn she blushed in the moonlight.

"So if I come to your room tonight, you won't be afraid?"

She shook her head. "Nervous, but not frightened."

He thought about kissing her. He thought about making love to her beneath the windmill, but he wanted everything perfect.

He wanted to give her in one night the courtship he should have given her before he ever married her.

Chapter 12

꒦

B ECKY OLIVER HAD never known terror, but she found herself fearing everything now: the rough hands, the fetid breath that stank of too much whiskey, the strong fingers clamped around her wrists holding them behind her back. His mouth missed its mark and skid across her cheek, leaving a slobbery trail.

"Duncan, stop!"

He shoved his thigh between hers. "Come on, Becky, you know you want a little kiss."

She wanted nothing of the kind, at least not from him. She wanted to scream, but she thought she might die if anyone saw her like this: pressed against the back wall of the general store with this man wrapped around her.

"Duncan, please let me go," she pleaded.

"Kiss me first."

She felt the tears threaten to surface. Somehow, she knew that he would enjoy watching the tears fall, so she held them back. "Duncan—"

"She's not interested."

She heard Austin's voice and relief swamped her. Duncan grunted and she was suddenly free of his hold. She cowered beside the boxes that lined a portion of the back wall and watched as Austin slammed his fist into Duncan's face. Duncan cried out and stumbled back.

Oh, she was glad, so glad, even though she knew whiskey had made him mean, had made him frighten her.

Austin stood with legs akimbo, his hands balled by his side, wait-ing . . . waiting.

"Come on, McQueen, get your ass up out of the dirt so I can hit you again."

Groaning, Duncan rolled over and came to his knees. "You broke my nose!"

Duncan looked over his shoulder, and Becky could see his blood glistening in the moonlight. She rushed from her hiding place and wrapped her fingers around Austin's arms. "Don't hit him again."

Austin snapped his gaze to hers. The anger burning in his blue eyes frightened her almost as much as Duncan had. She'd never seen Austin angry.

"He hurt you."

"No, he didn't. Not really. He just scared me."

Austin pointed his finger at Duncan. "Stay away from Becky or next time I'll kill you."

She knew without a doubt that he meant it, and that knowledge ter-rified her. He turned to her then, and she could see the worry etched in his face, along with the anger.

"Let me take you home," he said.

Leaving Duncan struggling to his feet, Austin walked with her to the side of the general store and followed her up the stairs. On the land-ing, he said quietly, "Are you all right, Becky?"

She wasn't and she had hoped to slip into the house without his ever knowing, but his voice was filled with so much concern that she couldn't stop herself from turning to him, with the tears slipping past her defenses.

"Ah, Becky," he said softly as he welcomed her into his embrace and pressed her cheek against his shoulder.

"He said he wanted to show me something," she rasped through the thick knot in her throat. "I didn't know—"

"Shh. How could you know, sweet thing?"

"You're angry with me."

"No, I'm not." He cupped her face and tilted her head back slightly. "Well, maybe a little. Why couldn't you have danced with Cameron?"

"Duncan asked." She lifted her shoulder. "I really wanted to dance with you."

412

He stroked her cheek with his thumb, over and over, the anger fading from his eyes, leaving them the blue of a flame writhing within a fire. "I can't dance and make the music. Did you like the music?"

"I thought you played lovely. I would have been happy to just sit and listen to you all evening."

"You looked beautiful dancing, Becky, even if it was with Duncan. I couldn't take my eyes off you." A corner of his mouth curved up. "I could sit and look at you all night." He dipped his head slightly, and her heart sped up. "Tell me to stop, Becky, and I will. Otherwise, I aim to kiss you."

"You gonna do it proper?"

"Proper, the way you deserve."

She had dreamed about his kiss at night while she slept, beneath the blankets, and during the day while she worked, on top of a ladder stacking canned goods. But none of her dream kisses were as wonderful as the reality.

He touched his mouth tentatively to hers, briefly, then brushed his lips over hers, reminding her of the way he had tuned his violin before he had ever begun to play the first song. Testing, teasing, searching for the right sounds.

Waiting for the right moment.

Then the moment came when he settled his mouth over hers and struck a resonant chord within her heart.

Dallas cringed when he looked in the mirror. Like some young buck shaving for the first time, he had three tiny nicks embedded in his chin. Squinting he leaned closer, wondering if he should even out the sides on his mustache a little more.

He'd bathed and trimmed everything on him that could be trimmed: his hair, his nails, his mustache.

He'd never been so damn nervous in his entire life.

Wearing only his trousers—new trousers, never before worn—he examined himself, wondering if Dee would find him lacking. He fought the urge to squirm as his reflection glared back at him.

He jerked his shirt off the bed and slipped it over his head. He started to button it and stopped. Dee would only have to unbutton it— or he would—and his fingers were shaking so badly he didn't know if he'd be able to release the buttons without sending them flying across the room.

Better to leave it unbuttoned.

He yanked his shirt over his head and threw it on the bed. Better not to wear it at all.

They both knew why he was coming to her room. No need to pretend otherwise.

Taking a deep breath, he grabbed the bottle of wine and two glasses. He'd never gotten to open the bottle when he was married to Amelia. He had begun to fear he'd never get a chance to open it.

Only this evening Dee had told him she wanted to give him a son.

The odd thing was as much as her words had thrilled him, they'd also left him wanting. He just wasn't sure exactly what it was he wanted from her anymore.

Her smiles. Her laughter. Her feet tucked beneath her as she considered business decisions.

Her body curled against his.

He opened the door to his bedroom and the sound echoed down the hallway. Had he ever noticed how everything echoed in this house?

In bare feet, he crept toward her room, his heart thundering harder than it had when a bull had stampeded after him in his youth. He wanted to smooth down his hair and run his fingers across his mustache, but his hands were full so he simply took another deep breath and rapped his knuckles on her door.

Immediately the door opened a crack, and he wondered if she'd been waiting for him on the other side. She peered out, her brown eyes large, her smile tremulous. Then she opened the door wider and stepped back.

He walked into the room. Her lavender fragrance permeated the air, along with the lingering scent of her bath.

She clicked the door closed, and his mouth went dry. Sweet Lord, he hadn't been this nervous when he had visited a whorehouse for the first time, not really certain what to expect.

And he realized with sudden clarity that he had no idea what to expect tonight. He only knew that he wanted to give to her as much as he had to give, wanted to ease the way for her, wanted to keep the fear out of her eyes.

He turned and looked at her. She was wearing the white gown she'd been wearing that first night. Every tiny button was captured snugly within its corresponding loop, clear up to her throat where the lace rested beneath her chin. Why did he find that bit of innocence more alluring than any half-clothed woman he'd known in his youth?

He held up the bottle and glasses. "I brought some wine. I thought it might help you relax."

She smiled timidly. "I'm incredibly nervous."

"Yeah, me, too."

Her eyes widened in awe. "Are you?"

He nodded and walked to the dresser, setting his offering down before the bottle and glasses slipped from his sweating hands. He wiped his palms on his trousers and pulled the cork. Then he filled each glass halfway.

He picked up the glasses, turned, and handed one to her. He clinked his glass against hers. "To our son."

Her cheeks turned a lovely hue of crimson, reminding him of the sunset. Staring at his chest, she touched the glass to her lips and took a small sip. She released a tiny gasp and lowered her gaze to his bare feet.

"Dee, look at me."

She lifted her eyes to his. "I'm sorry. I forgot this is business."

He took the glass from her hand and set their glasses on the dresser.

"It's hardly business." Threading his fingers through the black hair she had brushed to a velvety sheen, he braced the heel of his palms on either side of her face and lowered his mouth to hers.

He skimmed his tongue over her lips. So soft. He tasted the wine that lingered and felt the tiny quivering of her mouth beneath his, wondering if she could feel the tremors racing through him. Like a cowboy with a trick rope, he swirled his tongue over hers in a figure eight.

She took a step nearer, her gown brushing against his chest. An unexpected pleasure shot through him with a gesture that coming from her was as bold as brass.

He angled her head, running his tongue along the seam of her lips, teasing her mouth until it parted slightly. The he plunged his tongue into the welcoming abyss of warmth and flavor unique to her.

He felt her hands moving between them. He continued to plunder her mouth, waiting for the moment when her hands would touch him, his breath locked in his chest, his body straining for her touch.

But all he felt was the strange knotting and unknotting of her hands.

He drew away from the kiss and glanced down. Raised above her knees, her gown was bunched in her fists.

"What are you doing?" he asked.

Confusion plunged into her eyes. "Boyd told me I was supposed to lift my nightgown for you. I . . . I wanted to do this right."

He slammed his eyes closed and hurled silent curses at her brother.

"I've made you angry," she said quietly.

Opening his eyes, he brushed his knuckles along her reddened cheeks. "No, you haven't made me angry, but your brother is a fool. I want you to forget everything he ever told you."

Reaching down, he pulled her gown free of her clutched fingers, watched as the white linen fell back toward her bare ankles, and wished he were a man of tender words.

He lifted his gaze to hers and could see that she was fighting the fear lurking in the corner of her heart. He cupped her face in hands that were too rough for her smooth skin. "Dee, when a man and woman come to-gether . . . there is no right, no wrong. It's simply a matter of doing what each of us is comfortable with." He stroked his thumbs beneath her chin. "If I do something you don't like, all you have to do is tell me and I'll stop."

"And if you do something I like?"

He smiled warmly. "Then you can tell me that, too."

"How will I know what you like?"

His smile deepened. "You'll figure it out." He trailed his mouth along her throat, up her neck, until his lips were near her ear. "But I guarantee I don't want you lifting your gown for me. When I truly make you my wife, I don't want you wearing anything at all."

She gasped and stiffened. He ran his tongue along the delicate shell of her ear. "I've spent a month wondering if your body is as lovely as your face. Tonight I intend to find out."

"Are you going to be wearing anything?" she asked breathlessly.

He dipped his tongue inside her ear before taking a quick nibble on her earlobe. "I wasn't planning on it."

416

"Is that the way it's done?" she asked.

He lifted his head and met her gaze. "That's the way we're gonna do it. And if it takes me all night to get you comfortable with the idea, then we'll take all night."

She smiled warmly, her large brown eyes aglow like a thousand candles burning in the night. She placed her palm on his chest, her fingers splayed just above his heart, her hand steady. The only tremors he felt were those running through his body as he held his urges in check, not wanting to frighten her. He never again wanted to see fear of him reflected in her eyes.

"I don't think it'll take all night," she whispered.

"Thank God for that," he rasped as he again took possession of her mouth.

She ran her hands up his chest, and twined them around his neck. Groaning, he wrapped his arms around her and pressed her body flush against his. Their bodies met exactly as he'd imagined it a hundred times: perfectly, the way the sky dipped down to touch the land at the horizon, blue against green, soft against hard.

He thought he could feel her heart pounding in rhythm with his, beating against the cloth that separated her body from his. Slowly, he moved his hands around to the lace that decorated her throat.

With a patience he hadn't known he possessed, he worked the first tiny button free and trailed his mouth down to press a kiss to the newly exposed flesh.

Her arms fell away from him as he worked another button free and then another, his lips following the virgin trail that the parted material revealed. Her breath hitched as his knuckles skimmed the inside swells of her breasts. He planted a fervent kiss in the valley between her breasts as his fingers gave freedom to the last of the buttons.

He straightened and slipped his hands beneath the material at her throat. He could feel the slight tremors cascading through her, and feared they had little to do with passion.

"Look at me. Dee."

Her eyes met his. "I think Boyd's way was easier," she whispered.

"His way would have cheated us both. I give you my word on that." He raised his hands to cup her cheeks. "But I won't force you to share your body with me."

She pressed her fingers to her lips, tears welled in her eyes, and his heart sank. Boyd's way may have been easier but he'd be damned before he'd only know a portion of her when he wanted to know all of her, from the top of her head to the tips of her toes, inside and out.

"Share?" she asked. "I never thought of this as sharing." She lowered her hands and smiled softly. "It's not so frightening when I think of it as sharing."

"I want to know all of you, Dee. Not just your face and the shape of your toes, but all of you." He glided his hands down her face, her neck, and along her shoulders. Then he slipped the parted material off her shoulders.

The gown slid down her body and pooled at her feet, taking his breath with it. He scooped her into his arms and carried her to the bed.

Gently he laid her down. He began to unbutton his trousers. Her almond-shaped eyes rounded.

"Don't be afraid, Dee."

"I won't be," she said.

"You can close your eyes if you want."

"Don't you think I've wondered what you look like?"

He suddenly wished he'd doused the flame in the lamp, that the room was clothed in darkness. Being self-conscious wasn't something he was accustomed to feeling, but after putting her through the ordeal of baring her body, he couldn't very well deny her the chance to see him. Holding her gaze, taking a deep breath, he dropped his trousers.

"I won't hurt you," he said, his voice low.

"I know."

Her gaze dipped down, then shot back up to his.

"Don't be afraid," he pleaded gently.

"I'm not afraid."

He eased onto the bed. She jumped when his thigh touched hers.

Cupping her face with his palm, he placed his mouth near her ear. "I can't stand it when you're afraid of me, Dee."

"I'm just nervous."

He trailed his mouth along her neck and dipped his tongue into the hollow at the base of her throat. She tasted fresh, pure, and unused— unlike any woman he'd ever tasted.

"Don't be nervous," he said.

He lowered his face until his mouth touched the swell of her breast. She gasped. Without moving his mouth, he glanced up to find her watching him. He moved lower. His tongue circled her nipple.

"Dallas?"

"Shh. Every night I dreamed of tasting you." He closed his mouth around the taut bud and suckled gently.

Closing her eyes, she moaned. He skimmed his mouth over the valley between her breasts and swept his tongue over her. He glided his hand along her stomach, a stomach as flat as the prairie. Months from now, it would swell, swell with the son he might give her tonight.

He nestled his hand between her thighs, and when she might have protested, he covered her mouth with his, his tongue delving deeply, devouring her sighs, her moans.

Not until she twisted her body toward his, did he give himself the freedom to move his body between her thighs. Then as gently as the wind blew across the plains, he eased his body into hers.

She stiffened and he held still, knowing as fact what he'd only before known as rumor. He had no choice but to hurt her.

"I'm sorry, Dee," he rasped as he blanketed her mouth with his, plunged deeply, and swallowed her cry.

Cordelia wrapped her arms more tightly around him, the plea for forgiveness she heard in his voice bringing tears to her eyes. He stilled above her, his body taut. He continued to kiss her, only to kiss her, as though he couldn't get enough of her.

His mouth blazed a scorching trail along her throat. "It'll get better, Dee."

She plowed her fingers through his hair, cradling his head, turning his gaze toward hers. "I want this," she whispered. "I want to give you a son."

He released a guttural sound low in his throat, and she felt his chest vibrate against her breasts. He returned his mouth to hers, kissing her deeply, his tongue plunging, sweeping, caressing.

He moved against her, slowly, almost hesitantly. The pain receded, and a warmth deep inside her began to unfurl.

He slid his hand beneath her and lifted her hips. "Follow me, Dee," he pleaded in a ragged voice near her ear.

As though she had any other choice. He raised himself above her, his thrusts growing deeper, faster. She watched the shadows within the room play over his chiseled features.

And then as he had done from the beginning, he began to guide her toward the sunlight. To a place where no shadows hovered. She cried out his name as a myriad of sensations exploded within her.

Dallas felt Dee's body tighten around him as she arched beneath him. Pressing deeply, he followed where she had gone.

Glory had never felt so sweet.

Dallas awoke. He had turned down the flame in the lamp before he'd fallen asleep beside Dee. Now only moonlight spilled in through the parted drapes. He rolled to his side and reached for her.

All he found was the fading warmth of her body. Squinting through the shadows, he saw her standing beside the window, peering into the night, her arms wrapped around herself.

He eased out of bed and joined her. "Dee, are you all right?"

She glanced at him and smiled timidly. "I just wanted to hold it."

"Hold what?"

"The baby you gave me tonight."

He trailed his fingers along the curve of her cheek. "I might not have given you a baby."

She furrowed her brow. "But we—"

"It doesn't always happen the first time."

"Then what do we do?"

"Well, we have two choices. We can wait and see if you have your woman's time or"—he smiled warmly—"we can assume you're not carrying my son and we can keep trying. The choice is yours."

She averted her gaze, and his heart sank. "You shouldn't feel any pain the next time. It hurt tonight because you were a virgin."

She nodded quickly. "I think we should wait and see."

He'd given her the choice and she'd taken it. He didn't know which hurt worse, his pride or his heart.

"Fine, then."

He walked to the bed and snatched his trousers off the floor. "You just let me know."

He strode from the room, closed the door, and headed for his cold empty bed. He wished he'd bedded her as Boyd had suggested.

It'd be a hell of a lot easier to stay away from her if he didn't know how perfectly her body aligned with his, how snugly she fit around him, how wonderful she felt.

Chapter 13

≫

CORDELIA WONDERED HOW in the world a wife looked at her husband the morning following the night that they had made love.

How did she meet his gaze without remembering the hint of wine that had lingered on his lips, the bronzed shade of his skin, the muscles that had tensed as he'd risen above her, the sweat that had beaded his throat and chest as he'd rocked against her, the groans, moans . . .

She splashed more cold water on her face, trying to drown the images of Dallas's clenched jaw and his smoldering gaze.

She couldn't face him. She would simply stay in her room until she knew if she was carrying his son. She would . . . miss out on so much of life.

Last night had been an unexpected gift. It had been unlike anything she had witnessed between her parents. It had not resembled anything Boyd had hinted at.

The knock resounded against her door. She hoped it was Austin, but even as she strolled across the room, she recognized the steady staccato rap as belonging to her husband.

She bundled more snugly within her wrapper and opened the door. His gaze darted around the door frame before finally settling on her, and she wondered if he found it as difficult as she did to speak of mundane, inconsequential things after the intimacy they had shared.

"You didn't come down to eat breakfast," he said gruffly. "I just wanted to make sure you were all right."

She couldn't bring herself to admit that she experienced a slight tenderness when she walked. "I'm fine. Just fine."

He narrowed his eyes. "Are you hurting?"

The heat flamed over her cheeks as she lowered her lashes. "A little."

"I'm sorry for that. I'll . . . I'll do what I can to make it better next time."

She dared to lift her gaze. "If there is a next time. Maybe we were lucky last night."

If she didn't know him as well as she did, she would have thought she'd hurt his feelings from the expression that had flitted across his face.

"Yeah, maybe so," he said. He shifted his stance. "Are you going into town to get your damn prairie dog or do you want me to fetch her?"

The brusqueness in his voice hurt more than a dullbladed knife plunged through her heart. After his abrupt departure last night, she had feared that she had somehow disappointed him. Now, she knew without a doubt that she had. She swallowed her tears. "I'll fetch her."

"Fine."

He turned on his heel, took two long steps, halted, and glanced over his shoulder. "I need to talk with Tyler today. I'll ride into town with you if you have no objection."

Like a pebble thrown onto still waters, the joy rippled through her. "I'd like that. It'll just take me a few moments to get ready."

"Take your time. I'll saddle our horses."

She slipped into her room, pressed her back against the closed door, and splayed her fingers over her stomach. She wanted to give to Dallas as much as he'd given her. If only fortune had smiled on them last night.

Dallas had shared so much of himself with her, had given her such immense gratification, that she didn't see how he could not have given her a child as well.

As Dallas rode beside Dee, he took pleasure in the smallest of things: the graceful slant of her back as she sat her horse, the loose strands of hair that toyed with the wind, the anticipation that sparkled within her eyes as they neared town.

Dallas had decided in the early hours of the morning, as sleep eluded him, that he would steer clear of his wife until she knew whether or not they had *gotten lucky.*

That resolution had lasted until dawn's fingers crept into his room, and he awoke alone with the thought of a day not shared with Dee stretching out before him.

He couldn't deny that he wanted to be in her bed every night, buried deeply inside her, but he also recognized that he wanted more than that.

He wanted her warm smiles at breakfast, her laughter as she galloped across the prairie on Lemon Drop, the squeeze of her hand, the joy in her eyes, her soft voice when she spoke to him.

If he couldn't share her nights, he had decided sitting at the breakfast table with no one but Austin for company that he would content himself with sharing her days and evenings.

She fairly stood in the saddle as the site for the hotel came into view. "Oh, Dallas, they've started building it."

"Of course they have. That's why you broke the ground for them yesterday."

"Still, I didn't think it would happen so fast."

She turned to him with such a radiant smile that it was all he could do not to reach across and plant a sound kiss on her mouth.

"Can we go in closer and watch?"

"It's your hotel, Dee. You can hammer the nails into the wood if you want."

"Can I?"

"Sure."

As they brought their horses to a halt, Tyler Curtiss left the throng of workers, smiling broadly. "Morning!"

Before Dallas could dismount and assist his wife, Tyler was enjoying the privilege, his hands resting easily on Dee's waist.

Jealousy, hot and blinding, shot through Dallas like molten lead, catching him off guard. Even when he'd suspected Houston had harbored feelings for Amelia, he'd never felt jealous. Anger, certainly, but nothing that made him want to snatch a man's arm off simply because he'd helped his wife dismount.

Tyler stepped away from Dee and waved his hand in a wide circle. "What do you think?"

"It's wonderful. I can't believe you already have a portion of the frame up."

"The bonus Dallas offered the men if they get the hotel finished within three months had the men sawing and hammering at daybreak," Tyler explained.

Dee turned her attention to Dallas. He shifted his stance, uncomfortable with her scrutiny.

"You're paying them a bonus?" she asked.

"Figured the sooner they finished, the sooner you could get your ladies here, get them trained."

Tyler looked as though a good strong wind might blow him over. "What ladies?"

"Dee plans to have women managing her hotel and lady waiters serving food in the restaurant."

"Lady waiters?" He grinned crookedly. "You wouldn't have had to pay a bonus if you'd told the men that."

"These are respectable women," Dallas said, "not whores. Any man who doesn't treat them properly will answer to me."

"Marriageable women?" Tyler asked.

Dee glanced quickly at Dallas, then at Tyler. "They're not coming with the express purpose to marry, but I expect a few of them might decide marriage is in order."

"Where are they going to live?"

"In the rooms we're putting above the restaurant."

"Then I need to get the men back to work and get this hotel finished." Dee stepped forward. "Mr. Curtiss?"

He spun around. "Yes, ma'am."

"Can I hammer a nail into place?"

"Yes, ma'am. You can do anything you want. Women waiters. Who would have thought . . ."

Standing back, Dallas watched as his wife confidently walked around the construction site, greeting each man individually. She hardly resembled the woman who had stood in his parlor, hesitant to pledge herself to him.

He wondered if she ever looked at the men she was coming to know and wished she had been given the opportunity to choose the man who would be her husband.

A man handed her a hammer while another gave her a nail. Two other men held a board in place. She pounded the nail into the wood, satisfaction spreading over her lovely features.

He wondered if she might have invited another man to return to her bed last night, if once with Dallas was enough; if once with another man might have never been enough.

He despised the doubts that plagued him because he would never know if given the choice, she would have chosen another.

Squatting in the tall prairie grasses, Rawley Cooper held the prairie dog close and watched as the lady walked through the skeleton of the newest building.

She was the most beautiful thing he'd ever seen. He figured she looked like an angel—if angels existed. He harbored a lot of doubts about things like angels and heaven . . . and goodness. But the lady made him want to believe.

She stepped through a hole in the frame and backed up a few steps, holding her arms out, as though she couldn't believe how big it was.

Then she turned, smiled softly, and began walking toward him.

His heart started beating so hard that he could hear it between his ears, and it hurt to take anything other than a little breath. He stood, clutching the critter close against him. It yelped and struggled to get free, but he held it tight.

"Hello, Rawley Cooper."

She had the sweetest voice. He wished he had a hat so he could tip it at her like he'd seen some men do yesterday.

She knelt in front of him. She smelled like she'd brought a whole passel of flowers with her, but he couldn't see that she was holding or wearing any. She took the prairie dog out of his arms. "How's Precious?"

"Fine."

Her smile grew. "I appreciate your watching her for me."

He wanted her to hug him the way she was hugging the prairie dog, but he knew she wouldn't, knew no one ever would. He backed up a step. "I gotta go."

As fast as his legs would churn, he ran toward the buildings where he could hide in the shadows.

Sitting in a rocking chair on the veranda, Cordelia closed her eyes and listened as the music circled her on the wind. The crescendo rose, grew bolder, louder until she could envision a man galloping across the plains, dust billowing up behind him . . .

"Dallas," she said softly and peered through one eye at Austin.

Smiling broadly, he stilled the bow. "Yep."

She closed her eye. "Give me another one."

Dallas had escorted her home and then gone to check on his herd. Austin had joined her on the veranda, the violin tucked beneath his chin as he played tunes of his own creation, melodies that he based on the characteristics of people whom he knew.

She had guessed every song correctly so far—Houston, Amelia, Maggie, Dallas—but this melody was different. It carried no pattern. Strong for one moment, weak, weak, growing weaker with each note.

She opened her eyes, jumped to her feet, rushed to the edge of the veranda, and waved at her brother as he approached. "Cameron!"

"That's right," Austin said as he stopped playing.

Cordelia jerked her head around. "What?"

"That worthless song was Cameron." He shot to his feet and turned toward the house.

"Austin!" Cameron cried as he brought his horse to a halt and dismounted.

Austin swung around. "What?"

Cameron placed a foot on the step, then returned it to the dirt as though he wasn't certain if he was welcome. His gaze darted to Dee, then back to Austin. "I know you're angry."

"Damn right, I'm angry. When I can't be with Becky, you're supposed to take care of her for me. That's what friends are for."

Cameron blushed beneath his hat. "She was dancing with my brother. How was I supposed to know—"

"You should have known, that's all. The minute he took her off to the shadows you should have known. She won't be seventeen until next month. Duncan has to be on the far side of thirty—too old and too experienced for her."

Cordelia stepped cautiously across the porch. "What happened?"

"Nothing happened," Austin said, "because I stopped it." He pointed his bow at Cameron. "And you can tell your sorry excuse for a brother that if he touches her again, I'll kill him."

"Think he figured that out when you broke his nose."

"You broke Duncan's nose?" Cordelia asked in shock.

"I would have broken his whole face, but Becky stopped me." Austin stalked into the house.

Cameron plopped onto the step, planted his elbow onto his thigh and his chin against his fist. Cordelia sat beside him and took his hand.

He turned his palm over and threaded his fingers through hers before looking at her with such a baleful expression that she nearly wept.

"You ever wonder how our family came to be the way it is? Pa ain't feeling poorly. He's drunk most of the time. Boyd's got so much hatred in him that he gets downright ugly for no reason. I think Duncan's straddling a fence. He can't decide whether to set out on his own or follow Boyd."

"What did he do last night?"

"Took Becky out behind the general store and tried to force his affections on her. Austin was playing music for folks—" Cameron shook his head. "And I was a girl."

"A girl?"

"Yeah, there ain't enough girls around so we had to draw bandannas out of a hat. If we pulled a red one, we had to tie it around our sleeve and be the woman. I nearly got my boots danced off."

She pressed her cheek against his shoulder. "Is that why you weren't watching Becky? Too busy dancing?"

"Maybe."

She rubbed the back of his hand, remembering the many times she'd done so as a child, wondering now when he had acquired the hand of a man. Even relaxed the veins bulged, the muscles appeared strong.

"Are you happy, Dee?"

Sighing, she closed her hand around his. "Yes, I am. Dallas is . . . fair."

He jerked his head back. "Fair?"

"I don't know if I can explain it. He never expects more of his men—of anyone—than he's willing to give. He's up before dawn, working, and he labors into the night. He talks to me, but more he listens. I don't know if I've ever had anyone truly listen to what I had to say."

"Do you love him?"

She shrugged and spoke as wistfully as her brother had only moments before. "Maybe."

She glanced up at the pounding hooves of an approaching rider. Dallas drew his horse to a halt beside Cameron's.

Cameron leapt off the steps. "I need to go," he said, bussing a quick kiss across Dee's cheek.

"Can't you stay for supper?" she asked.

"No, I—"

"Your sister wants you to stay," Dallas said, his voice echoing over the veranda.

Cameron nodded quickly. "Then I'll stay."

"Doesn't anyone in your family eat?" Dallas asked as he watched Cameron and Austin ride away from the ranch, heading for the saloon in town. The hostility between the two that he'd first noticed when they'd sat for dinner had abated during the meal. "Your damn prairie dog eats more than he does."

"He was just a little uncomfortable—"

Dallas turned toward her and raised a dark brow.

She dropped into the rocking chair and folded her hands in her lap. "You terrify him."

Dallas hitched a hip onto the railing. He needed a porch swing with a bench that wasn't too wide so he could sit next to Dee and enjoy the evening breeze as night moved in. As soon as the cabinet maker set up shop, Dallas would order one, specially made with his new brand carved into the back.

"Reckon you understand that feeling."

She smiled. "I also know what it is *not* to fear you."

He couldn't argue with that. If she still feared him, maybe she wouldn't have been so quick to kick him out of her bed.

He liked the sight of her sitting on his veranda. It felt right, like the breeze that turned his windmill. The gentle wind that blew her little chimes.

Reaching up, he touched the various lengths of barbed wire that Dee had strung together and hung from the eaves of the veranda, the eaves of the various balconies. They clinked in the wind. She had touched his life with an abundance of small gestures.

"Walk with me," he said.

She rose and followed him down the steps. In companionable silence, they strolled toward the setting sun.

He thought about taking her hand, but after last night, he wasn't exactly sure where he stood, and it would gouge his pride if she didn't welcome his touch.

He had spent thirty-five years sleeping alone, and suddenly he desperately wanted something that he couldn't even put a name to: the filling of an emptiness that he'd discovered within himself last night only after it had overflowed with contentment as he'd lain in her bed, holding her within his arms, listening to her soft breathing.

He almost found himself hoping that he hadn't given her a son.

"I'm not carrying your son."

Dallas snapped his head up and looked across the table at his wife, her gaze locked on her cold eggs. Austin had left only a few moments before, leaving a heavy silence in his wake, a reticence shattered by her words.

"Are you sure?"

She gave a brisk nod. "I knew several days ago. I just thought it would be better to wait until . . . until now to tell you." Her gaze darted up, then down, and her cheeks flamed red.

He stood and walked to her end of the table, a thousand sentiments thundering through his mind like stampeding cattle. He wanted to kneel beside her, take her hand, kiss her brow, her nose, her chin. He wanted her to look at him, but she just stared at the damn eggs so he spoke words that conveyed little of what he was feeling.

"I'll come to your bed this evening then, if that's agreeable to you." She nodded brusquely. "I'm sorry."

"Maybe we'll have better luck tonight."

"I hope so."

With a purpose to his stride, Dallas stormed from the house, yanked Satan's reins off the corral post, mounted the black stallion, and kicked him into a gallop. He rode fast and hard over the plains until his brother's house came into view. The past ten days had been hell: wanting to hold Dee, knowing she had no interest in his touch.

It was strange but he had to admit he wasn't disappointed that Dee wasn't yet carrying his son.

He still desired a son, but the urgency of his dream had lessened. What he wanted now was a few more nights stretched out in Dee's bed, with her nestled against him.

Houston was working with a mustang in the corral when Dallas drew his horse to a halt at the house and dismounted.

Amelia sat on the porch, churning butter. Maggie scrambled to her feet and ran down the steps. She squealed as Dallas lifted her toward the clouds.

"I see freckles popping out," he said.

"No!" she cried as she rubbed her nose. "Kiss 'em off! Kiss 'em off!"

He obliged her by quickly raining kisses over her face until she giggled. Lord, he loved her fragrance. She smelled of flowers dug from the earth, kittens, and sweet milk. Her innocence always humbled him.

She crinkled her nose. "Did you git me a boy to play with?"

"Not yet. I'm still working on it."

"Where's he gonna come from?"

Dallas jerked his gaze to Amelia. Shaking her head, she smiled.

Dallas slipped a lemon drop out of his pocket and handed it to his niece. "Why don't you go suck on this for a while?"

"I don't got a sad."

"I do and I need to talk to your ma about it."

He set Maggie on the porch. She plopped the candy into her mouth and began to suck vigorously. Dallas removed his hat, draped an arm over the porch railing, and studied Amelia. He thought she looked pale.

"How are you feeling?" he asked.

"Just a little sick in the mornings, but it'll pass."

"You gonna give Houston a son this time?"

"He's partial to daughters."

"It's a wonder to me that the two of us are related."

"You and Houston are more alike than you think."

He shook his head. "With his skill with horses, he could have himself a thriving business. I'd never settle for less."

"It's not a question of settling for less. It's a matter of knowing what you want and finding contentment in that," she said softly.

"Do you have all you want?"

"As a matter of fact, I think we do. Would you like to tell me about your sad?"

"It's not a sad really. I just said that for Maggie's benefit."

Amelia angled her head as though she didn't believe him. Damn the woman, she'd always seen and figured out too much. He turned his hat in his hands, studying it, searching for the right words.

"Do you remember when we were married?" he asked.

Amelia smiled warmly. "A woman isn't likely to forget her first marriage."

"When I kissed you . . . did you like it?" he asked gruffly.

She glanced up quickly as though the answer rested within the eaves of the porch before returning her gaze to his. "I thought it was nice."

"Nice? The weather is *nice*. A kiss should be—" He stopped abruptly at the flush racing up her cheeks. "What about when Houston kisses you?"

Her blush deepened. "My toes curl."

"Is that why you chose him over me?" The words were spoken before he could take them back. Amelia had always had a way of making a man say what was on his mind. It had charmed and aggravated him at the same time.

She rose to her feet, crossed the porch, and wrapped her hand around his. "When it comes to the heart, choice is seldom involved. I don't know why I fell in love with Houston and not with you. I only know that I did."

"I don't begrudge you that," he said.

She squeezed his hand. "I know you don't."

"I just . . . damn." He forced the bitter words past his tight throat. "I don't know how to please Dee in bed . . . and I want to."

"That's the first step, isn't it? Wanting to please her?"

"Apparently, it's a damn little first step. What does Houston do when he kisses you?"

"I don't know. He just kisses me. Maybe you should ask him."

He glanced over his shoulder. Houston was slipping through the slats of the corral. Dallas had never in his life asked another man's opinion on anything. It stuck in his craw that he was having to ask now—especially about something as intimate and personal as bedding his wife.

"I appreciate your being honest with me," he told Amelia.

She patted his shoulder. "Go talk to Houston."

His stomach reeling worse than the blades of a windmill when the sucker rod had snapped in two, Dallas approached his brother.

"What brings you out today?" Houston asked as he buttoned his shirt.

Dallas shoved down his pride. "How do you kiss Amelia?"

Houston's fingers stilled over the last button, and he furrowed his brow. "What?"

Dallas heaved a deep sigh of frustration. "Amelia says when you kiss her, you make her toes curl."

Houston's mouth split into a distorted grin that moved one side of his face while leaving the scarred side immobile. "She said that, did she?" He peered around Dallas and looked in the direction of the porch where his wife had taken up churning butter again.

Irritated, Dallas stepped in front of him. "Yeah, she said that. So how do you kiss her?"

Houston shrugged. "I just sorta latch my mouth on to hers like there's no tomorrow."

"That's it? Don't you do something special?"

"Like what?"

"If I knew I wouldn't be asking!"

Houston narrowed his eye. "I learned how to kiss watching you. How could you forget how to do it?"

"I didn't forget, but I only ever kissed whores except for Amelia." He grimaced as her description of his kiss resounded through his head. "She says I kiss nice." He stepped forward and crossed his arms over the top rail of the corral. "Nice, for God's sake. I'm surprised Dee didn't gag."

Houston eased up alongside him. "Maybe it has nothing to do with the way you kiss her. Maybe it has everything to do with what you're feeling when you kiss her."

Dallas shifted his gaze to his brother. "What do you mean?"

Houston rubbed the scarred side of his face, his fingers grazing his eye patch. "You'll get angry if I tell you."

"No, I won't."

"Give me your word."

"You got it."

Houston released a deep breath. "The first time I kissed Amelia, we had just crossed that flooded river—"

"You kissed her before you got to the ranch?"

"You said you wouldn't get angry."

"I'm not angry, I'm aggravated. I trusted you—" Dallas reined in his temper. Five years ago, he'd made a decision that had left him without a wife. He didn't plan to repeat his mistake. "Finish your explanation."

Houston gave his throat a sound clearing as though contemplating the wisdom of his words. "Well . . . I was furious because she'd jumped into the river to save me, I was damn grateful she hadn't drowned, and it hit me harder than a bucking mustang that I loved her. I couldn't tell her so I tried to show her. I poured everything I felt into that kiss, and I've been kissing her that way ever since."

"And making her toes curl."

Houston smiled broadly. "Apparently so."

Dallas shoved himself away from the corral. "Thanks for the advice."

"Maybe in time, once your feelings for Dee deepen—"

"That's my problem, Houston. I think I've fallen in love with her and I've got no earthly idea how to make her love me."

Chapter 14

༁

ALLAS STOOD OUTSIDE Dee's room. He had decided that if he was
only going to have one night with her each month, he was going
to make the best of it.

He wouldn't leave her bed this time until dawn eased over the horizon, and if she didn't want him to make love to her again, he'd content
himself with simply holding her within his arms through the night.

He knocked on the door and waited an eternity for her to open it.
He stepped into the room and slammed the door.

"You're early," she said as she drew the brush through her silken
black hair.

"Didn't see any point in waiting." He took her in his arms and
latched his mouth onto hers like there was no tomorrow, wishing to God
that there would be, that her toes would curl, and she would want him
in her bed every night.

Her brush clattered to the floor, and she wound her arms around his
neck tighter than the noose on an escaping calf. She pressed her body
flush against his, and her soles crept over his toes.

He groaned, she moaned, and need rushed through him like a raging river. Holding her close with one hand, his mouth devouring hers,
he used his other hand to release the buttons on her gown, hearing several clink as they hit the floor.

He pulled down her gown and bathed in the glorious sight of her
bared body as he yanked off his trousers. He lifted her into his arms and

carried her to the bed. He laid her down, then draped his body over hers, raining kisses over her face, her throat, her breasts.

He touched her with his hands, his mouth, his eyes, all the while marveling at her beauty, the pink glow of her skin, the deep brown of her eyes.

When he joined his body to hers, he heard no sharp intake of breath, no cry of pain, only a sigh of wonder. He rocked his hips until her sighs became gasps and her body writhed beneath his. He thrust harder, deeper, reveling in the moment when her soft voice echoed his name and she shuddered within his arms.

With a guttural groan, he threw his head back, clenched his teeth, and with a final thrust hurled himself into an abyss of pleasure.

Breathing heavily, he sank onto her quivering body. He could still feel her body pulsing around him. He pressed a kiss to her throat, her chin, her cheek . . . and tasted the salt of her tears.

Self-loathing replaced the blissful replete. He hadn't given her any of the tenderness he'd planned. He'd charged into this room like a rampaging bull, with one thought, one purpose on his mind: burying himself as deeply and as swiftly as he could into her glorious warmth until they were so close that a shadow couldn't have slipped between them.

She would share her body with him once a month. Instead of savoring the moment, he had taken her offering and used it as quickly as lightning flashed against the sky.

He pressed his lips against the corner of her eye where her tears glistened, fresh and warm. "I'm sorry, Dee," he rasped. "I didn't mean to hurt you."

"You didn't hurt me," she whispered.

He lifted his head and met her gaze. He could see the pain he'd caused swirling within the dark depths of her eyes. He might not have harmed her physically, but he had little doubt he'd bruised her woman's heart, the part that longed for more than a man satisfying his lust. He threaded his fingers through her hair. "I did hurt you, and I regret that."

She shook her head. "No, you didn't hurt me. It was wonderful."

Wonderful? She thought that hasty mating was wonderful? "Then why are you crying?"

She touched her trembling fingers to his jaw. "Because it always hurts you so much."

He stared at her, unable to make sense of her words. "What?"

Her cheeks flamed red as she lowered her lashes. "I watch you," she confessed, her voice barely above a whisper. "You grunt and groan. Your muscles tense and strain. You clench your teeth." She lifted her lashes. "The agony must be unbearable. Is that how Nature evens things out? Since childbirth is excruciating, women receive a gift of pleasure while making the baby and men only receive pain?"

"You thought I was in pain?"

She nodded shyly. Hope flared within him like the crude skyrockets he and Houston had made out of carpet scraps as boys.

"Is that why you wanted to wait and see if you were carrying my son? To spare me the suffering of trying when it might not be necessary?"

She trailed her fingers along his cheek, her thumb brushing over his mustache. "I can't stand to see you hurting like that."

"Oh, God." He flopped onto his back, dropped one arm over his eyes, and burst out laughing. His shoulders shook forcefully, and the bed trembled with his outburst.

"What's so funny?"

Fighting to stop his laughter, he peered at Dee's concerned face. She had risen on an elbow, her black hair a silken curtain draped over her shoulders. Wearing a broad smile, he reached out, wove his fingers through her hair, and brought her sweet lips closer to his. "You're precious, you know that? So damn precious."

He brushed a light kiss over her tantalizing mouth. "I wasn't in pain."

Her dark brown eyes widened until they were larger than any full moon that had ever guided his journey through the night. "Not at all?"

"No, quite the opposite in fact."

He eased her onto her back, tucking her body beneath his, unable to wipe the grin off his face. "So Nature gave you no trade-offs."

"That hardly seems fair." She smiled warmly, her blush creeping beneath the sheets she'd drawn up to cover her breasts. "But I'm glad."

His grin slipped away as he swallowed. "Does that mean you wouldn't mind trying again? Just in case we didn't get lucky?"

Burying her face against his throat, she nodded and pressed a kiss just below his Adam's apple.

Joy shot through him. He leaned back, cupped her cheek, and lowered his mouth to hers, kissing her deeply as he worked the sheet aside so he could feel the length of her limbs pressed against his.

Several long minutes later, he dared to peer down at her feet. Distracted, he slid his mouth across her chin.

"What are you doing?" she asked.

Grimacing, he considered returning his mouth to hers and kissing her until she forgot the question and his strange behavior, but he had to know the truth. Dammit, he had to know. "Amelia told me that her toes curl when Houston kisses her. I was just trying to see if your toes curl when I kiss you."

She turned a lovely shade of rose and rolled her shoulders toward her chin. "My whole body curls when you kiss me."

"Your whole body?"

She nodded quickly. "Every inch."

"Well, hell," he said as he settled his mouth greedily over hers with plans to keep her body tightly curled for the remainder of the night.

"Susan Redd," Dee said.

Dallas glanced up from his ledgers. Dee was sitting in his office, curled in her chair, a stack of letters on the table beside her. "Susan read what?" he asked.

She threw her head back and laughed. Lord, he loved her laugh, the ivory column of her throat, the glimmer of joy in her eyes.

"Susan Redd, R-E-D-D. That's the name of the woman I'm thinking of hiring to manage the hotel. She runs a boardinghouse back East which I think gives her wonderful experience. Don't you agree?"

He planted his elbow on the desk and ran his thumb and forefinger over his mustache. A small thrill always raced through him when she asked his opinion, when she shared a corner of her dreams with him. "What I think . . . is that we need to go to bed."

Her eyes widened, not with fear but with wonder and anticipation. "Dallas, it's not even dark yet."

He scraped his chair across the floor, brought himself to his feet, and stalked toward her. "I made love to you this morning, and it wasn't dark then either."

"That was different. We hadn't gotten out of bed yet."

"A mistake I can remedy." He took the letter from her fingers, tossed it onto the table, and scooped her into his arms.

Laughing, she nuzzled her nose against his neck as he carried her out of his office. The front door opened and Austin sauntered into the house.

"Where are you going?" Austin asked.

"To bed," Dallas said as he started up the stairs.

"What about supper?"

"Go see the cook."

"Go see the cook," Austin said. "That's what Dallas said. Then he and Dee start giggling like a couple of coyotes drunk on corn whiskey."

Houston looked across the table at Amelia and smiled. "So you decided to come help yourself to our meal?"

Austin shrugged. "Better than waiting on those two. They might never come back downstairs." He winked at Amelia. "Besides, Amelia's meals taste better than the cook's."

Reaching around the pot of beans, Amelia patted his hand. "I appreciate the compliment. It sounds as though things are better between Dallas and Dee."

"Strange is what they are," Austin said as he cut into the beefsteak.

"In what way?" Houston asked.

Austin planted his elbow on the table and pointed his fork at Houston. "Dee reads to us every evening. Dallas is supposed to be working in his ledgers. Only he ends up watching her. Then she'll look up and forget all about reading. They'll just stare at each other for a few minutes, then Dallas will say it's time for bed, and they'll leave, and I'm left to wonder what's going on in the story. Dee started reading *Silas Marner* to us over a week ago and she hasn't finished the first chapter yet."

"You might have to start reading to yourself," Amelia suggested.

"It isn't the same hearing the story in my voice." Austin continued to cut his steak. "I just need to be patient. I reckon things will get back to normal once Dallas gets his son."

"I wouldn't count on it," Houston said, meeting his wife's gaze. He knew from experience that when the woman a man loved brought his child into the world, the bond only deepened and grew stronger.

*   *   *

"Mr. Curtiss?"

Cordelia stuck her head inside the tent where Tyler Curtiss worked. She had awoken at two in the morning with a thought about the hotel that she wanted to share with him, but she couldn't find him anywhere.

Stepping into the tent, she decided to wait.

Large sheets of paper littered his desk, and she couldn't stop herself from looking at them. She saw the new plans for the newspaper office and the apothecary. Small businesses. Large businesses. They would find a home in Leighton.

Moving the papers aside, she saw a drawing of a building with a great many rooms. Bold letters across the top proclaimed it to be a hotel.

Sinking into a chair, she studied the drawing. It wasn't her hotel, and yet the layout seemed incredibly familiar, reminded her of Dallas. Bold. Daring. The rooms were large, designed for comfort not convenience. Not practical for a town where a great many people would simply be passing through. Yet a portion of it appealed to her, particularly if—as she suspected—her husband had been responsible for the plans.

"Mrs. Leigh. What a pleasure!"

She jumped out of the chair with a start. "Mr. Curtiss, I wanted to speak with you." Her gaze drifted back to the drawing. "Whose hotel is this?"

"Oh, that." He gave her a guilty grin. "Uh, well . . . uh." He swept his blond hair off his brow.

"Dallas asked you to draw up plans for a hotel, didn't he?"

"Yes, ma'am. Some months back, as a matter of fact."

"What are you going to do with the plans now?"

"He told me to ignore them. Said this town only needed one hotel."

"Thank you, Mr. Curtiss." She began to walk out of the tent.

"I thought you came to discuss something."

She smiled. "I just realized that I need to discuss it with my husband first."

As she rode into the ranch, she saw Dallas standing by the corral. A broad smile spread beneath his mustache as she drew Lemon Drop to a halt and dismounted.

She strode to him, entwined her arms around his neck, and kissed him, deeply, soundly. From the moment he had made her his wife, he had been secretly placing gifts within reach, gifts that came without wrapping or bows, gifts whose worth could only be measured by the heart.

He drew back, his brow furrowed. "What was that for?"

"I saw the plans for your hotel."

He grimaced. "Oh, that. It was just an idea I was toying with. It never took hold, not like your plans."

She combed her fingers through the hair that curled at the nape of his neck. "I woke up this morning with a thought. I want one of the rooms to be special, but I wasn't exactly sure what I wanted. I was going to talk with Mr. Curtiss about it, and then I saw your drawings. Your rooms were so much larger than mine."

"I wanted to give a man room to stretch out."

"I want to give a man and woman a place to make love."

She broke away and began pacing, the idea little more than a seed. "I truly believe that many of the women who come to work at The Grand Hotel will eventually marry. Some will marry men like Slim, and you'll have to provide your men with a different type of living quarters."

"Is that so?" Dallas asked, intrigued as always with the way Dee set the wheels of an idea spinning inside her head, like a windmill built in the path of a constant breeze.

Her steps grew quicker as the excitement burned brightly within her eyes. "For the most part, they'll marry men of modest means, men who are content to let others dream. They'll get married in the church that you'll one day build, and then they'll go to the house where they'll probably live for the remainder of their life.

"Most won't be able to take a wedding trip, but I want to give them a place where they can go for one night and feel special. A room as beautiful as their love, as grand as their hopes for the future, where a man can make love to his wife for the first time in a huge bed with flowers surrounding them." She stopped pacing. "What do you think?"

That I should have taken you someplace special. He had never stopped to consider exactly what a wedding meant to a woman, what the first night of her marriage should have heralded.

Certainly not her husband kicking in the door as she prepared herself to please him.

He couldn't undo the mistakes he'd made in the past, but he could ensure he didn't repeat them in the future.

She stood on the tips of her toes, her hands clasped tightly before her, waiting on his answer. He could do little more than share the truth with her.

"Think you might need more than one special room."

She grabbed his hand. "Two rooms, then. Will you help me design and furnish them? I want a room where a cowboy would feel comfortable taking off his boots, and a woman could feel beautiful slipping out of her wedding dress."

"Then you should definitely have a bootjack in the room."

A faraway look crept into her eyes. "I should have a bootjack in every room." She shook her head. "I've completely ignored the details."

"I don't think you've ignored anything. I'm the one who has overlooked things." He brushed the errant strands of her hair back from her face. "I don't think I ever bothered to tell you that you're beautiful."

A lovely blush rose high over her cheeks, her eyes warmed, and her lips parted.

He lifted her into his arms. "Slim, see after my wife's horse."

She snuggled against him as he carried her toward the house.

Life was a series of changes, and Cordelia knew that after tonight her life would forever be different. She could no longer put off the inevitable.

Joy and sorrow wove themselves around her heart as she read the final words of the story and closed the book.

"I liked that story," Austin said. "What are you gonna read next?"

"I'll find something," she said quietly as she turned the ring on her finger. She could feel Dallas's gaze boring into her, but she couldn't bring herself to look at him—not yet.

She would gain so much tonight . . . and lose even more.

Austin unfolded his body and stood. "Reckon I'll head on to bed."

"We'll see you in the morning," Dallas said.

She listened as Austin's footsteps echoed through the room and the door closed.

"You haven't looked at me all evening," Dallas said.

"I know." She set the book aside and lifted her gaze to his. "I went to see Dr. Freeman today."

Deep furrows marring his brow, he came out of his chair. "Are you sick?"

She smiled uneasily. "No."

He walked around his desk and knelt before her. "Then what's wrong?"

I'll be sleeping alone again when I've grown accustomed to sleeping with you.

"We finally got lucky. I'm carrying your child."

He dropped his gaze to her stomach. "Are you sure?"

She splayed her fingers across her waist where their child was growing. She had suspected for two months, but she had wanted to be certain before she told him, before she gave him hope and took away his reason for coming to her bed. "Your son should be here in the spring."

He intertwined his fingers with hers until their joined hands resembled a butterfly spreading its wings. "My son." He lifted his gaze to hers. "Our son." He touched his free hand to her cheek. "How are you feeling?"

"Fine. Just Fine." Tears welled in her eyes. "Except that I want to cry all the time, but Dr. Freeman said that was normal."

With his thumb, he captured a tear before it fell from the corner of her eye. "I've wanted this for so long, Dee, I don't hardly know what to say. Thank you doesn't seem like enough."

"For God's sake, don't thank me." She shoved hard on his shoulders, and he tumbled over, his backside slamming against the stone floor. She rose to her feet and glared at him. "This is why you married me, isn't it? Why my family gave me to you? I'm just doing what I was brought here to do!"

Ignoring his stricken expression, she hurried from the room before he could see the tears streaming down her face. She wanted to give him a son, a chance to realize his dreams, but she didn't want his gratitude.

She wanted his love.

A son.

He was going to have a son.

Standing at the corral, Dallas grinned like an idiot while the winds of change circled him, bringing the cooler weather that heralded the arrival of autumn. When the warmer winds arrived in the late spring, he'd be holding his son in his arms.

And until then . . . he'd be sleeping alone.

Dee had made that painfully clear.

The smile eased off his face. She'd been letting him into her bed because she'd felt an obligation. He'd begun to think he slept there because she wanted him there.

He shivered as the wind howled and drove all the warmth from his flesh. He'd been looking forward to winter for the first time in years. He'd imagined waking up with Dee nestled beside him, the warmth they shared beneath the blankets growing.

He'd miss so many things. The way she burrowed her nose into his shoulder. The way she rubbed the sole of her foot over the top of his. The way she smelled before he made love to her; the way she smelled afterward.

He groaned deep within his throat.

At one time, he'd thought he had only one dream left: to have a son. A sad thing indeed when a man his age realized he'd settled for a small dream when he might have possessed a larger dream: to have a woman who loved him give him a son.

He pounded his fist against the corral railing. He didn't need love, but damn, he suddenly wanted it desperately. How in the hell could he make her love him, a man who knew nothing of tenderness or soft words or any of the gentle things women needed?

He didn't know how to ask. He only knew how to command. His father had taught him that.

He turned from the corral and walked slowly back to the house. He had no desire to sleep in his cold bed alone. He'd work on his books for a while. Then he'd ride out to look at his herd, to check his windmills, to search for something he might never find.

He opened the door that led into the kitchen and stumbled to a stop. Dee was holding a log in one arm, bending over to retrieve another one.

"What the hell do you think you're doing?" he roared.

"The fire in my room is almost gone, and I could hear the wind. I thought it would be colder in the morning."

"Give me that," he said, taking the log from her arm. He crouched and stacked more logs into the crook of his arm. "You don't need to be hauling stuff."

"I'm not helpless," she said, hands on her narrow hips.

He wondered if he'd ever noticed how slim she was. He knew he had, he just hadn't considered how that might affect her when it came time to deliver his son.

"I didn't say you were," he said gruffly as he stood. "But I don't want you carting wood or anything else that's heavy. If you need something, you let me know."

"You weren't here."

"Then get Austin."

She looked like she wanted to argue more, but she simply stalked past him. When did she get so darn ornery? He'd have to go see Houston tomorrow and find out what other little surprises were waiting for him in the next few months.

He followed her to her room. She sat on the edge of the bed while he rekindled the fire in her hearth. He stood and brushed his hands over his trousers. "There. I'll come in every couple of hours or so and check on the fire. No need for you to get out of bed."

"Fine."

He glanced at her. Her hands were balled in her lap, her bare feet crossed one on top of the other.

"You didn't even have sense enough to wear shoes while walking over these cold stone floors?" he asked as he knelt before her and planted her heels on his thighs. "Your feet are like ice."

She shoved the balls of her feet against his chest and sent him sprawling over the floor.

"They're fine," she said.

He narrowed his eyes and slowly, deliberately came to his full height. "Get under those blankets and get under them now," he said in a low even voice.

She opened her mouth as though to protest. When he took a menacing step toward the bed, she snapped her mouth closed and scrambled under the blankets. He jerked his shirt over his head.

"What are you doing?" she asked.

He dropped to the edge of the bed and yanked off his boots. "I'm gonna warm your feet."

Standing, he pulled off his trousers before slipping into her bed with one quick fluid movement. "Put your feet between my thighs."

445

Her eyes widened. "But they're freezing."

"I know that. Now, do it, dammit!"

She pressed her lips together and shoved her feet between his bare thighs. He sucked in a deep breath between his teeth.

"Is that what you wanted?" she asked, glaring at him.

"No, but I want you warm," he answered, glaring back.

Tears welled in her eyes, and she averted her gaze. "It wasn't supposed to be like this when I told you. We were supposed to be happy."

Cradling her cheek, he gently guided her gaze back to his. "I am happy, Dee. Happier than I've ever been in my life."

She placed her hand on his chest and he jumped.

"Sweet Lord! Even your hand is cold." He took her other hand and pressed her palms against his chest, laying his hands over hers. "How can you be so cold?"

"You were outside. How can you be so warm?" she asked.

"I've got more meat on my bones."

She ran her tongue along her lower lip. "I'm sorry that I shoved you before—in your office and in here. I don't know what came over me—"

"It doesn't matter. I want a son, Dee, more than I've ever wanted anything."

"I know. I want to give you this child. I hope he'll look like you."

He touched her cheek. "I never gave any thought to what he might look like. I reckon he'll have no choice but to have black hair and brown eyes."

"He'll be tall," she said.

"Slender."

She nodded slightly and gave him a soft smile. "It'll be a while before he has a mustache."

"I reckon it will be at that." His thumb drifted back and forth over her cheek. "I know you don't want my gratitude, and I know you're not helpless, but I want to take care of you while you're carrying my son."

She didn't protest when he reached down, fisted his hand around the hem of her gown, and slowly lifted it over her head. She didn't move when he pressed his mouth against her stomach.

"Our son is growing here," he said in awe, wondering why he had ever thought he would be content to let just any woman bring his son into the world, why he hadn't realized that he needed a woman he could respect and cherish, a woman like Dee.

She threaded her fingers through his hair. He swallowed the lump in his throat and peered up at her. "I'm glad you'll be his mother."

Fresh tears shimmered within her eyes. Easing up, he kissed her as gently as he knew how. Then he drew back and smiled at her. "Your nose is cold. I might have to sleep in here just to keep you warm."

"I wish you would."

"If you want me to, I will. I'll give you anything you want, Dee."

Because she was carrying his son. Cordelia's heart ached with longing as much as with joy. The bond that joined them would forever be a wall that separated them.

But walls could be breached, and tonight, she wanted—she needed—him to scale the wall for her.

"Make love to me. I know there's no reason to now that I'm carrying your—"

He stroked his thumb over her lips as a wealth of tenderness filled his eyes. "I'm thinking there might be more of a reason to now."

He lowered his lips to hers, and with a whispered sigh, she welcomed him, his warmth, his flavor, his gentleness as his tongue slowly swept through her mouth.

The urgency that had seemed to accompany all their lovemaking before melted away like frost upon the windowpane as the sun reached out to touch it.

The goal that had once brought him to her bed was now a spark of life growing inside her. Her breasts had already begun to grow tender, and soon her belly would swell.

With their purpose achieved, she had expected a chasm to widen between them as they waited for the birth. She hadn't expected to bask in the glory of his appreciation.

With infinite tenderness, he touched her as though she were a rare gift, his fingers trailing over her flesh, taunting, teasing until his mouth moved in to satisfy.

She felt as though her body had turned to warm liquid, the sensations a swirling mist as they traveled from the top of her head to the tips of her toes. No matter where his mouth lighted, it felt as though he touched all of her.

She glided her palms over his shoulders, pressed her hands along his back, threaded her fingers through his hair, relishing the different textures of his body: the light sprinkling of hair that covered his chest, the hard muscles that rippled each time he moved, the warm breath that left a trail of dew over her flesh as his mouth continued its sojourn over her body.

Nothing they had shared before had prepared her for this: the ultimate joy of being wanted, of feeling cherished.

When he lifted himself above her and captured her gaze, her breath caught. When he entered her with one long, slow stroke, her body curled tightly around him.

She moved in rhythm to his sure, swift thrusts: giving, taking, sharing. His power. His strength. Her determination. Her courage. The life they had created.

Where once she had feared him, now she understood that she loved him.

Her body arched against his, and in his eyes, she saw reflected the glory and the triumph, and welcomed it as her own when he shuddered and buried his face within the abundance of her hair, his breath skimming along her neck and shoulder.

Lethargically, she lay and listened to his deep breathing.

Had he loved her in return, she didn't think he could have given her more.

With his child growing within her, hope spiraled anew within her heart that one day he would come to love her.

Chapter 15

ॐ

THE COLD WINDS whipped down Main Street as Cordelia hurried along the boardwalk, drawing Dallas's sheepskin jacket more closely around her. He had given it to her when he'd noticed her two middle buttons were undone on her coat to accommodate her swelling stomach. He had pulled an older jacket out of a trunk for himself.

Lifting the collar, she inhaled Dallas's bay rum scent. A definite advantage to borrowing his coat was that she always felt as though he were near.

She went into the general store, removed her gloves, and rushed to the potbellied stove to warm her hands.

"Thought you had one of them in your hotel," Mr. Oliver said.

Cordelia smiled. "I do. I was warm when I left the hotel, but I got cold so I thought I'd drop in here. Besides, I need to see if my order arrived."

"Sure did. Set of Shakespeare. Twelve dollars."

Her Christmas gift for Austin, not only the books, but the reading of them to him through the next year. "I'll pick it up when we're ready to leave town."

She began to slip her hands back into her gloves. Mr. Oliver motioned her over.

"This has been my best year yet, what with them women waiters you got working in the restaurant. You better plan on putting a Christmas tree up in that hotel so them cowboys have a place to put all the presents they've purchased for them gals."

The first group of women had arrived in October. When they had completed their training, Cordelia had opened the restaurant and the first and second floor of the hotel. She was still furnishing the third floor, but business was good. Leighton was expanding. She squeezed Mr. Oliver's hand. "Wait until next year. I'll have another group of women arriving in the spring."

"Lordy, we're gonna be a real town. I had some doubts in the beginning—"

"Faith, Mr. Oliver. You had faith in Dallas's judgment or you wouldn't be here."

She swept out of the general store. The wind buffeted her as she walked across the street to the clothing store. Bells tinkled over her head when she opened the door and stepped into the shop.

A robust woman with flaming red hair, Mimi St. Claire thrust aside the curtains that led to her sewing room, making a grand entrance into her own establishment.

"You are here for zee beautiful red dress with zee big belly. Yes?"

Cordelia laughed at the description of the dress. She was rapidly losing her waistline and cared not one whit. "Yes. Is it ready?"

"Of course, madam. Your husband pays me too well to make certain your clothes are ready on time."

"He wasn't supposed to know about this."

"He does not know." She lifted a shoulder. "Still, he would expect me to add a little extra to his bill."

"We wouldn't want to disappoint him, would we?" Cordelia teased.

"Of course not. I finished zee coat for Rawley, too. I gave it to him yesterday when zee winds began to blow. It is too cold for a little boy who has no meat on his bones."

Reaching out, Cordelia squeezed her arm. "Thank you. Double the extra that you add to our bill."

Mimi waved her hand in the air. "Zat I do for nothing except zee cost of zee materials which you can afford and I cannot."

"Fair enough. Wrap up the dress. We'll be taking it with us when we leave."

Mimi wagged her finger at Cordelia. "But you cannot wear it until Christmas, no matter how tempting it becomes to please your husband before zen—because zis will please him."

"I know it will. Thank you for having it ready."

Bracing herself for the onslaught of cold, she opened the door, rushed outside, and scurried along the boardwalk until she reached the tanner's. She slipped inside. Dallas turned away from the counter.

Smiling, he opened his coat. She burrowed against him as closely as she could, hampered by the child growing within her.

"Glad you dropped by," he said. "I need to know what we're going to name our son."

"You need to know right this minute?"

"Yep. I'm gonna have his initials put right here on this saddle."

In disbelief she stared at his blunt-tipped finger pressing into the corner of a small saddle resting on the counter. "Tell me you did not purchase that saddle."

"My son's gonna need it."

"Not for years."

He kissed the tip of her nose, a habit he'd acquired when he wanted to distract her from pointing out the purchases he was making too soon. Pint-size boots with intricate stitching and a tiny black Stetson hat were already waiting in the nursery.

"Your nose is cold. There's a hotel up the street. We could get ourselves a room. I could warm you—"

"Dallas, we're not visitors here. We live—"

"An hour away in the cold. It would only take us a minute to get to the hotel. Come on, Dee. Let me warm you."

She caught a movement out of the corner of her eye and turned her head slightly. A heavyset man leaned against the door frame that led into his work area. "Hello, Mr. Mason."

"Mrs. Leigh."

"We're gonna go discuss names, Mason. I'll come back and tell you what initials to put on that saddle."

The man's face broke into a hearty grin as he shook his head in obvious amusement. "You do that, Dallas."

With his arm snugly wrapped around her, his body protecting her from the wind, Dallas escorted Cordelia outside. They walked briskly up the boardwalk and to the far end of town where the red-brick hotel stood.

Dallas shoved open one of the doors, and Cordelia rushed inside.

She took a moment to enjoy the aromas filtering out from the restaurant, the scent of fresh wood, the sight of new red carpet, the candles flickering in the chandeliers in anticipation of dusk.

She looked at Dallas. "You aren't really going to register us for a room are you?"

His eyes grew warmer than the fire blazing within the hearth at the far side of the lobby. "Let's stay the night."

"I didn't bring any clothes."

"You won't need any."

Anticipation and joy spiraled through her. She had never expected him to lavish as much attention on her as he did: his touch was seldom far away, his gaze constantly seeking hers as though he needed her as much as she needed him. Every night she slept within his arms. Every morning she awoke to his kiss.

"I want to check on the restaurant while you get the room," she said.

With a smile that promised no regrets, he kissed her lightly on the lips before he strode to the front desk. The child within her kicked. She slipped her hand within the coat and stroked the small mound. If only Dallas would love her as much as he already loved this child.

Turning, she walked into the restaurant.

"Mrs. Leigh!"

She smiled warmly at the restaurant manager. "Hello, Carolyn."

With rosy cheeks, Carolyn James carried excitement within her hazel eyes. "I was wondering if you would mind if we held a Christmas celebration here Christmas Eve. I thought it might be nice for the girls, ease the loneliness of being away from family."

"I think it would be lovely."

She blushed prettily. "Perhaps your brothers would like to come."

"I'm sure they would. Is everything else going well?"

Carolyn nodded. "Very well, although I'll be glad when additional girls arrive in the spring. Some of these cowboys eat four and five meals a day."

Cordelia smiled, knowing their appetites had little to do with the need for food, but with the desire to simply watch a woman. "We'll discuss the details of the Christmas celebration next time I come to town."

"Don't leave it too long. Christmas will be here in two weeks."

Two weeks. As Cordelia walked back into the lobby, she thought it hardly seemed possible that she had been with Dallas for seven months, carrying his child for almost five. She hadn't decided what to give him for Christmas. He had everything he wanted. Maybe she would simply tie a big ribbon around her belly.

At the absurd thought, she bit back her laughter as she approached the front desk where Tyler Curtiss was talking with Dallas. Dallas slipped his arm around her. "This is the woman you need to talk to."

"About what?" Cordelia asked.

Tyler looked at Susan Redd as she stood behind the counter, her chin angled.

"Red, here—"

"It's Miss Redd to you," she said, her voice smoky.

The moment Cordelia had met her hotel manager, she had liked her. Her auburn hair was swept up, curling strands left to frame her face.

"Miss Redd," Tyler said, "isn't inclined to give my workers a discount on the rooms. With this cold spell blowing through, I thought they might enjoy a few nights in the warmth of the hotel, sleeping in a real bed instead of on a cot. Since they built the hotel, it only seemed fair to offer them a special rate."

"I've seen your workers. Most are filthy. No telling what sort of bugs they'll bring with them," Susan said.

Cordelia placed her hand on the counter. "Offer them a discount, half the normal rate, on the condition that they visit the bathhouse before they register. That should satisfy both of you."

Tyler smiled warmly. "Thank you, Mrs. Leigh. I'll work out the details with Miss Redd and let the men know."

She patted his arm. "See that you get one of the nicer rooms."

Dallas secured her against his side and began walking toward the stairs. "I think working out the details with her is what he intended all along," he said in a low voice near her ear.

Cordelia jerked her head back. "You think he has an interest in Susan?"

"Yep."

Before she could turn around to observe that interest, Dallas was escorting her up the stairs. At the landing, she stepped into the hallway. "Which room?"

He scooped her into his arms and carried her up the next flight of stairs.

"Dallas, this floor isn't ready."

"You sure? Thought it was."

"Only the bridal—" Her voice knotted around the tears forming in her throat.

In long strides, he walked to the end of the hallway, bent his knees, and inserted the key into the lock. "Seemed right that you should be the first to use your special room." He gave a gentle push and the door swung open.

A fire was already burning lazily in the hearth, and she realized his real reason for coming into town was not to talk with the tanner as he'd told her that afternoon, but to bring her to this room.

"You deserved something better than what you got on our wedding night so this is a little late in coming."

"What does it matter when you've given me so many special moments since then?"

"I plan to give you more . . . a lot more."

Because she carried his son. What did the reasons behind his thoughtfulness and kindness matter? His generosity was directed toward her.

But the reasons did matter. In a shadowed corner of her heart, they did matter.

Contentment swept through Dallas as gently as dew greeting the dawn. He'd never before experienced this immense satisfaction, not only with himself, but with his life, because always before, no matter how much he had—something was always missing.

That something was now draped over half his body, her breathing slowly returning to normal, a glow to her warm skin that spoke of her enjoyment as eloquently as her gasps had only moments before.

He combed his fingers through the ebony hair fanned out over his chest. He loved the silken strands. He loved the brown of her eyes and the tilt of her nose. He loved the tips of her toes, even though they were growing cold.

She started rubbing them along his instep. He loved that as well.

He loved her.

And he didn't know how to tell her. Sometimes, he would mention that he was happy, and she would smile at him, but something in her eyes made her look sad, as though she didn't quite believe him.

He thought all his contentment might seep out like a hole in the bottom of a well if he told her what was in his heart and the silent disbelief filled her eyes.

He'd brought her here to tell her, to share his feelings in the special room she had envisioned for women to spend their wedding night, but she'd given him that look before he'd ever spoken the words, so he'd shoved them back and tried to show her his feelings instead.

He smiled with satisfaction. If her moaning and shuddering were any indication, he'd successfully shown her.

Still, he'd like for her to hear the words . . .

Where her stomach was pressed against his belly, he felt the slight rolling of his son. His contentment increased. He slipped his hand beneath Dee's curtain of hair and splayed his fingers over her small mound.

Dee wasn't growing as round as Amelia was. He figured it was because Amelia was short, and her baby had nowhere to go but out. Dee was tall, giving their child a lengthier area in which to grow.

He enjoyed watching the changes to her body. The darkening of her nipples where his son would nurse, the slightest widening of her hips, the hint of an ungainly walk.

Sighing, she wriggled against him, opened an eye, and peered up at him. "Mmmm. I knew this room was a good idea. It'll be hard to let people I don't know sleep in here now."

"Then don't."

Her other eye popped open, and she lifted her head. "That's the purpose of a hotel."

He trailed his thumb along the side of her face. "Nothing wrong with the owners having a private room that they can use at their convenience, anytime they want."

She narrowed her eyes in suspicion. "Is that why you told me I'd need two rooms—"

Leaning up, he began to nibble on her lips. She shoved him back down. "You planned to use this room all along, didn't you?"

He shrugged. "Seemed like a good idea at the time, an even better one now that we've tried it out."

Laughing, she snuggled into the crook of his shoulder, trailing her fingers over his chest, each stroke going a little higher, a little lower. "Maybe I'll give you this room as a Christmas present."

"Give me something I already own for Christmas? What kind of gift is that?"

She lifted her face. "You have everything."

"No, I don't."

"What else could you possibly need?"

Your love. He swallowed hard. "Something that can only be given if it isn't asked for."

She stared at him. "What does that mean?"

"Hell if I know. Get me a new saddle."

"Oh!" She rolled off him.

He came up on an elbow. "What?"

She looked over her shoulder as she began to gather her clothes off the floor. "I just thought of something."

"Something to get me?"

She waved her hand dismissively through the air. "No, silly. I just thought of something I need to tell Carolyn."

"Can't it wait?"

"No, she wants to have a Christmas celebration here. I want her to go ahead and have Mr. Stewart at the newspaper office make up invitations and announcements that we can send out over the area."

Dallas flopped back onto the pillow. "That can wait until the morning. Come to bed."

She was hastily donning her clothes. When she got an idea she was like a dust devil kicked up by the wind.

"It'll just take me a few minutes." She hurried to the door. "Besides, I'll no doubt get cold when I get downstairs, and you can warm me up all over again."

"Count on it!" he called out to her as she slipped from the room.

Good Lord, she was more obsessed with empire building than he'd ever thought about being, or maybe she simply enjoyed it more.

He'd be content these days to do nothing more than sit on the veranda in their bench swing. That gift had pleased her so much that he'd had a smaller one made—one that he'd hung on the balcony outside their bedroom.

He shoved his hands beneath his head and stared at the ceiling. He'd tell her that he loved her when she got back, whisper the words in her ear just before he joined his body to hers. If she didn't distract him with all those glorious sounds she made and the way her body moved in rhythm to his.

Smiling, he let his eyes drift closed and began to plan his seduction. Seducing her was so easy. Pleasuring her carried rewards he'd never known existed.

A scream shattered his thoughts. A scream of terror that he'd heard once before—on his wedding night.

He leapt from the bed and jerked on his trousers, buttoning them as he rushed down the stairs, his heart pounding, his blood throbbing through his temples.

On his way down, he met Susan Redd on her way up, her brown eyes frightened. "There's been an accident."

"Dear God." He tore past her.

"She's behind the restaurant!" Susan called after him.

He raced through the lobby, the restaurant, and out the kitchen. Wooden crates that had once been stacked outside now lay helter-skelter. Tyler Curtiss was lifting one off Dee's sprawled body.

Oblivious to the cold winds hitting his bare chest and feet, Dallas knelt beside his wife and touched his trembling fingers to her pale cheek. The cold numbed his senses. He couldn't feel her warmth or smell her sweet scent. "Dee?"

She looked like a rag doll a child had grown tired of playing with and thrown aside.

"She swore she heard a child cry," Carolyn wailed, her voice catching. "I didn't hear anything . . . but she came outside . . . I heard a crash, her scream . . . is she dead?"

"Go find the goddamn doctor!" Dallas roared and the people surrounding him ran off in all directions.

He needed to get her warm, needed to get her inside. Gently, he slipped one arm beneath her shoulders, the other beneath her knees.

It was then that he felt it, and fear unlike any he'd ever known surged through him. He'd carried too many dying men off battlefields not to recognize the slick feel of fresh blood.

*　　*　　*

He had brought her home, thinking he could somehow protect her better, keep her safe.

But as she lay beneath the blankets, bathed in sweat, her face as white as a cloud on a summer day, her hand trembling within his, he feared nothing he did, nothing anyone did, would keep her with him.

With a warm cloth, he wiped the glistening dew beading her brow. He didn't want her to be cold.

If she died, she'd be cold forever. He couldn't bear the thought, but it lurked in a distant corner of his mind like an unwanted nightmare, keeping company with the sound of her scream.

He would forever hear her scream.

She moaned and whimpered, a pitiful little sound, that tore his hear into shreds.

Where was the damn doctor when he needed him? He was going to find another doctor for Leighton, a doctor who knew how to keep his butt at home so he was there when he was needed, not a doctor who gallivanted around the countryside caring for people Dallas didn't even know.

Dee released a tiny cry and tightened her hold on his hand. He'd never in his life felt so utterly useless.

He had money, land, and cattle. He'd bathed in the glory of success and what the hell good was it doing him now? He'd trade it all for a chance to turn the clock back, to keep her in that room with him.

"Dallas?" Amelia placed her hand on his shoulder. "Dallas, she's losing the baby."

"Oh, God." Pain ripped through him so intensely, so deeply, that he thought he might keel over. He bowed his head and wrapped his fingers more firmly around Dee's hand. He'd never known what it was to need, but he needed now, he needed Dee's quiet strength.

"Just don't let me lose her," he rasped.

"I'll do what I can. If you want to leave—"

"No. I won't leave her."

And he didn't. He stayed by her side, wiping her brow when she released a tortured cry, holding her hand while her body twisted in agony.

Words failed him, became insignificant. He considered telling her that the loss didn't matter, that they would have other children, but he couldn't bring himself to lie to her, and he knew she'd know his words for the lie they were.

No other child, no matter how special, how precious, would replace this first child.

So he did all that he knew how to do. He remained stoic, held her, and wished to God that somehow the pain could be his and not hers.

And he watched as she wept silently when Amelia wrapped the tiny lifeless body in a blanket. Dallas forced himself to his feet. "I'll take him."

Amelia glanced up, despair sweeping over her face. "Dallas—"

"I'll see after him while you finish taking care of Dee."

He took the small bundle and left the room. It was the dead of night, but he did what needed to be done.

He built a small coffin and padded it with the delicate blankets Dee had bought to keep the child warm. Then he laid his tiny son inside the wooden box.

With the cold winter winds howling around him, he dug a grave near the windmill beside the house and laid his son to rest.

As gentle as an angel's soft tears, snowflakes began to cascade from the heavens.

A shudder of despair racking his body, Dallas dropped to his knees, dug his fingers into the freshly turned soil, and wept.

Cordelia forced herself through the fog of exhaustion and pain. Every inch of her body protested, her heart protesting most of all for it remembered the loss and the grief on Dallas's face as he'd taken his child from Amelia.

She bit back a cry as fingers poked and prodded. She opened her eyes. Hadn't she suffered enough? Why was Dr. Freeman torturing her now?

He pulled down her gown and brought the blankets over her, seemingly unaware that she had awakened. Through half-closed eyes she watched him walk across the room to the window where Dallas stood gazing out through the paned glass.

"She gonna live?" Dallas asked.

"She should," Dr. Freeman said, "but she's going to need a lot of rest. Pamper her for a while." Dr. Freeman put his hand on Dallas's shoulder. "And find a way to tell her gently that she's not going to be able to have any more children."

Cordelia's heart constricted, and she pressed her hand against her mouth, biting her knuckles to keep herself from crying out. Dallas jerked his head around and stared at the doctor.

"Are you sure she can't have any more children?"

Dr. Freeman sighed heavily. "She's lucky to be alive. She got hurt inside and out. Her injuries were extensive, and there's going to be a lot of scarring. Based on my experience, I don't see how she could possibly get pregnant."

He walked quietly from the room. Dallas placed a balled fist on the window and bowed his head.

Cordelia's heart shattered with the knowledge that he'd lost his dream.

Chapter 16

᷍

BEFORE SHE WAS fully awake, before she'd opened her eyes, she was aware of his warm fingers threaded through hers. Her eyelids fluttered, and she could see Dallas sitting in a chair beside the bed, his dark head bent, his face unshaven.

Tears clogged her throat and burned behind her eyes. He looked to be a man in mourning. She used what little strength she had to squeeze his fingers.

He snapped his head up and leaned forward. His eyes were blood-shot and red-rimmed. Gently he brushed wisps of hair from her face. "How are you feeling?" he asked in a voice that sounded as rough as sandpaper.

He became blurred as her tears surfaced. "Was our baby a boy?" she asked.

He squeezed his eyes shut and pressed his lips against the back of her hand. Then he opened his eyes and held her gaze. She watched his throat work as he swallowed.

"Yeah, yeah he was. I, uh, I laid him to rest near the windmill. I . . . I always liked the way the blades clack when the wind comes through, and I didn't know what else to do."

She wished she had the strength to sit up and wrap her arms around him, to comfort him. The tears welled. "I overheard what Dr. Freeman said—that I won't be able to have other children. Dallas, I'm so sorry—"

"Shh. You're gonna be all right and that's what matters. I thought I was gonna lose you, too."

At that moment she didn't think she could love him more—for the lie he had spoken with such sincerity. She knew the truth. If she had died as well, he could remarry—any of the women who had recently moved to Leighton—and have the son he so desperately wanted.

He eased up in the chair. "Dee, I want to know what happened."

Sniffing, she furrowed her brow. "What happened?"

"You left the room. I heard you scream—"

She squeezed his hand, pieces of images racing through her mind. "Oh, Dallas. Rawley."

"Rawley?"

"The little boy. I heard a child cry. I went behind the hotel, and I saw him pressed into a corner. Then someone shoved me and the boxes fell . . . Oh, Dallas, he could have gotten hurt, too. Did you see him?"

"I only saw you."

"Dallas, we have to find him." She tried to sit, and he placed his hands on her shoulders.

"You've got no business getting out of bed. I'll send Austin to find him."

"Have him bring Rawley back here so I can see that he's all right."

Rawley Cooper knew he was in a heap of trouble. Had known it for days and knew sooner or later his mistake would catch up with him.

He would have preferred later.

He sat staring at the red and orange flames as they danced and warmed the room. The man who had brought him to this big house sat with his feet propped on the desk, his spurs dangling over the edge.

The man had told him his name was Austin. Once Rawley had gone through a town named Austin. He figured this man was pretty important since he had a town named after him.

Important men scared Rawley. They could do anything they wanted and nobody would stop them.

Rawley nearly jumped out of his skin when Austin pulled open a drawer.

"Dallas has some lemon drops in here. You want one?"

He peered over at Austin, saw the bag he held in his hand, the yellow ball he was rolling between his fingers. He remembered the man had given him a sarsaparilla stick once and hadn't hurt him when he'd taken it. But that was a long time back. He shook his head and turned his attention back to the fire.

He knew all he wanted to know about taking gifts. Sooner or later, they always came with a heavy price.

"You don't talk much, do you?" Austin said.

Rawley wondered if he ran into the fire if it would swallow him up. He thought about that sometimes. Finding a way to disappear so no one could touch him, no one could hurt him.

"Where's your ma?" Austin asked.

"Dead I reckon."

"Don't you know?"

Rawley lifted a shoulder.

The door opened. Austin dropped his feet to the floor and stood. Rawley stood, too, his legs trembling. Better to face the man who wanted him.

"You found him," the man said.

The man was big. Rawley had seen him with the pretty lady.

"Yep. His pa was passed out in the saloon. I told the barkeep to tell him the boy was here when he woke up."

"Good."

The man sat in his chair at the desk. Austin hitched up a hip and planted his butt on the corner of the desk. Rawley tried not to look scared but he had a feeling he wasn't having much success at it.

The man leaned forward. "Do you know who I am?"

Rawley nodded. "Yes, sir. You belong to the pretty lady."

A corner of the man's mustache lifted as he smiled slightly. "I reckon I do at that. My name is Dallas Leigh. The pretty lady is Mrs. Leigh." His smile quickly disappeared, leaving his mouth looking hard. "She got hurt a few nights back."

Rawley's heart started pounding so fast he thought it might escape through his chest. "Did she die?"

"No, but she's hurt . . . bad. She said someone pushed her. Do you know who pushed her?"

Rawley shook his head quickly and dropped his gaze to the floor so Dallas Leigh couldn't see that he was lying. Silence stretched out between them. Rawley heard the logs crackle as the flames devoured them. Soon they'd be nothing but ashes. He wished something would turn him into ashes.

"Would you like to see her?"

His gaze shot up. Dallas Leigh was looking at him like he could see right through him. He figured anyone who lied to Mr. Leigh came away with a blistered backside.

He nodded hesitantly, wondering what it would cost him to see the pretty lady, hoping she wasn't hurt so badly that she wouldn't be able to smile at him. He dearly loved her smiles. Her smiles weren't like the smiles most people gave him, smiles that hid something ugly behind them.

Mr. Leigh came to his feet and looked at Austin. "Dr. Freeman is getting a bite to eat in the kitchen. Fetch him upstairs."

Austin walked out of the room with his arms swinging. Mr. Leigh put his hand on Rawley's shoulder. Rawley shrank back.

Mr. Leigh studied him for a minute, his brown eyes penetrating. Rawley figured he could see clear through to his backbone.

"Follow me," Mr. Leigh said and walked in long strides toward the door.

Rawley would have swallowed if he'd had any spit, but his mouth had gone dryer than the cotton he'd picked one summer.

He followed Mr. Leigh into the hallway. He'd never seen a house so big nor stairs so wide. He figured ten men could walk side by side down those stairs without bumping into each other. At the top of the stairs, he wanted to take a moment to look down, to pretend he was the king of the world, but he didn't dare. He didn't think Mr. Leigh was a man of patience and would understand his desire to look down at a world that always looked down on him.

Mr. Leigh opened a door. "In here."

Rawley's heart jumped into a rapid-fire beat. The pretty lady would smile at him, maybe hold his hand, and talk to him in a voice that sounded as soft as the wind. He wiped his hands on his britches, not wanting her to feel his sweat, and stepped into the room.

His heart dropped to the floor.

His gaze darted around the room, searching for a sign that he hadn't been tricked, but with a knowledge a boy his age shouldn't possess, he understood all too well the truth of his situation.

He knew better than to trust, better than to hope, better than to want.

He heard a shuffling and turned. A man who looked like he ought to be lying in a coffin stood in the doorway.

"This is Dr. Freeman," Mr. Leigh said. "He's gonna have a look at you."

Rawley swallowed the bile burning his throat. "The pretty lady—"

"You can see her as soon as Dr. Freeman is done with you."

"Does she want me to do this?" he asked.

"Yep." Mr. Leigh nodded slightly at the doctor and stepped into the hallway, closing the door.

Rawley fought off the bitter disappointment of betrayal and began to carry himself away to a place where the sun kept him warm, the grass was soft beneath his feet, and the breeze always smelled like flowers.

Dallas had little doubt that the boy knew who had pushed Dee, who was responsible for the harm that had taken away their child.

But he'd also seen what he was too familiar with plunge more deeply into the boy's eyes: fear.

The boy wouldn't tell Dallas what he wanted to know because the boy feared whoever had been behind the hotel more than he feared Dallas.

"It seems to be taking Dr. Freeman a long time," Dee said softly.

Dallas turned from the window and looked at his wife. He had propped pillows behind her back so she could sit up in bed. He was bringing her meals, making certain she had plenty to drink, and had started reading to her in the evenings. She seemed to have little interest in anything but the welfare of the boy, and it had taken Austin two days to find him.

"It just seems that way because we're waiting. Time passes differently when you're waiting." She still looked so pale. "Want me to brush your hair again?"

"No." She studied her clasped hands.

She'd barely looked at him since she had lost the baby. He couldn't blame her. He hadn't listened to her father, hadn't believed she was delicate. He had let her walk out of the hotel room unescorted while he had lain in that bed thinking about what he wanted to do with her body when she returned.

Shame rose within him. He hadn't held her as precious as he should have, and his lack had cost them both, not only a son, but a chance at a future together. She had wanted to give him a son, and for a short time it had appeared that she had wanted him as well. She had laughed so easily while she carried his son, glowed with anticipation, and smiled constantly.

Late into the night, they had whispered silly things: the books she would read to him, the ranching skills Dallas would teach him, the building skills Dee would share with him. They would take him to the top of a windmill and teach him how to dream—big dreams.

So many planned moments that in one night had crumbled into dust to be blown over the prairie and lost.

The door opened, and Dr. Freeman poked his skeletal face into the room. "Dallas, I need to speak to you for a moment."

Dee furrowed her brow. "Is Rawley hurt?"

"He's fine," Dr. Freeman said. "I just need to talk to Dallas."

He disappeared into the hallway. Dallas walked out of the room and closed the door.

Dr. Freeman was standing beside a window, looking out, his hands balled into tight fists at his side. "There are times when I regret taking an oath to cause no harm," he said through clenched teeth. "That boy has more scars than the parched earth has cracks. Do you know what he thought I wanted to do?" Dr. Freeman shook his head fiercely. "No, of course you don't."

When he turned, Dallas was surprised to see tears shimmering in the man's eyes.

"I think that sorry excuse of a man who calls himself the boy's father has been selling him."

Dallas jerked his head back. "Selling him? To whom?"

"Men. Men who prefer boys to women."

Dallas's stomach roiled. "Are you sure?"

"I can't swear to it, but I'd stake my life on it."

"In Leighton?"

"Perversion doesn't come garbed any differently than you or me. You can't look at a man and tell what's in his head or on his mind. I have seen the most upstanding men in other communities do things that would turn your stomach, and I only learned about them because they went too far and needed my services."

Dallas felt the impotent anger swell within him. "Is there anything you can do for the boy?"

Dr. Freeman shook his head. "The hurt he's had on the outside is healing, but it's the deep pain that he's gotta be feeling on the inside that concerns me, the scars he'll carry with him for the rest of his life."

"I won't be taking him back to town," Dallas said with determination.

"I'll let his father know—"

"You leave his father to me."

Rawley Cooper knew he had made a big mistake. All the doctor had wanted to do was look at him.

Rawley couldn't remember what he'd said, but he knew the exact moment that the doctor figured out what Rawley thought he wanted to do to him.

He'd thought the skinny man was going to puke on the floor, and Rawley knew they wouldn't let him see the pretty lady now. They knew he was dirty on the inside and out.

He heard the door open. He bundled up his shame the same way that he'd bundled up his clothes. He turned from the window.

Mr. Leigh filled the doorway. "Put on your clothes, boy."

Rawley nodded and did as he was told. He'd thought about putting them on before, but the doctor hadn't told him to so he'd decided to wait. He was forever doing what he wasn't supposed to do.

When his fingers had skipped over the two buttonholes in his shirt that no longer had buttons belonging to them, and he had buttoned the top button at his throat, the button that nearly gagged him but made him feel protected, he lifted his gaze back to the towering man.

Mr. Leigh stepped into the hallway. "Come with me, boy."

Taking one last look at all the fine and pretty things in the room, he slowly walked into the hallway. Mr. Leigh was standing beside an open door that led into a corner room.

"Stop dragging your feet. My wife is anxious to see you."

Rawley's heart felt like the fluttering wings of a butterfly he'd once cupped in his hands. Mr. Leigh knew the truth about him—he could see it in his eyes—and he was still going to let him see the pretty lady. He hurried into the room before Mr. Leigh could change his mind.

Then he stumbled to a stop.

The lady was sitting in the bed, looking like an angel. She smiled softly and held out her hand. "Rawley, I'm so glad you could come visit me."

He edged closer to the bed, and she waved her hand. "Give me your hand."

He shook his head. "I ain't clean."

"That doesn't matter."

He knew she thought he was talking about dirt, but he was talking about something so filthy it touched his soul. Tears burned his eyes when he shook his head this time.

Mr. Leigh walked to the other side of the bed and stood near his wife. "It's all right, Rawley."

Rawley dared to lift his gaze. Mr. Leigh nodded.

He took a step closer and touched his fingers to the lady's hand. She closed her hand around his. Her hand was warm and soft and swallowed his. He wondered if his ma's hand had been like this.

The lady tugged gently and he moved closer. She brushed her fingers over his brow. He'd never been touched with such gentleness.

"Are you all right?" she asked.

He nodded. "The boxes didn't fall on me."

"I'm glad."

He suddenly remembered all the screaming that had been going on, all the blood, all the yelling about the baby. "Where's your baby?"

Tears welled in her eyes, and Mr. Leigh dropped his gaze to the floor.

"He's in heaven," she said quietly.

"I'm sorry," Rawley croaked as the tears he'd been fighting to hold back burst through. "I'm sorry."

She drew him close and pressed his head against her bosom. "It wasn't your fault."

But he knew it was. If only he hadn't cried out. He knew better than to cry out.

468

The lady rocked him back and forth while he cried. He didn't know he had so many tears. When he stopped crying, her gown was wet but she didn't seem to care.

For the longest time, he simply stood beside her and let her hold his hand.

When the lady fell asleep, he helped Mr. Leigh bring the blankets up to her chin. Through the window, he could see that night had fallen. He followed Mr. Leigh through the house, through big rooms, until they came to the kitchen.

Austin sat at a small table, slurping stew.

"Sit down, boy," Mr. Leigh said.

Rawley slid into the chair. He was embarrassed when his belly growled like an angry dog. Austin smiled at him. Mr. Leigh put some stew into a bowl and placed it in front of him.

"Go on, boy, eat," Mr. Leigh said.

Rawley squirmed. "Ain't got no way to pay for it."

"What happened to that dollar I gave you?"

"I buried it. They built a hotel on top of it. Didn't know they were gonna do that till it was too late."

Mr. Leigh rubbed his mustache. "That must be why the hotel is such a success. Maybe we ought to change the name to the Lucky Dollar Hotel."

Rawley shrugged.

"Go on and eat, boy. You made my wife smile. That's worth more than a dollar to me."

Cautiously, Rawley brought a spoonful of stew to his mouth. Normally he ate whatever his pa left behind, which usually wasn't much. He'd never had his own bowl before. His own food. His mouth and belly wanted him to eat fast, but he forced himself to eat slow, to pretend he had his own food every night and could eat as much as he wanted.

When he finished eating, Mr. Leigh made him take a bath and put on some of Austin's old clothes. He told Rawley that Austin had been eight years old when he'd worn the clothes. Since the clothes fit him, Rawley wondered if that meant he was eight years old. He wondered if it meant that he'd grow to be as tall as Austin.

Because he knew he couldn't outrun or outfight Mr. Leigh, Rawley followed him back up the stairs to the room where he had been earlier, where the doctor had looked at him. Mr. Leigh stopped and held something toward Rawley.

"Do you know what this is?" Mr. Leigh asked.

"A key."

"Do you know what it's used for?"

"You lock the door so I can't get out."

Mr. Leigh walked into the room and inserted the key in a hole on the other side of the door. "From now on, this is going to be your room. You close the door and turn the key so no one can come in this room unless you want them to."

"Not even you?" he asked suspiciously.

"Not even me. Give you my word."

Mr. Leigh walked out of the room and closed the door. Rawley shoved the key farther into the hole and turned it. He heard the echo of a click.

He waited and listened hard. He heard Mr. Leigh's boots hitting the floor of the hallway. He heard them on the stairs. Then he heard them not at all.

Moonlight streamed in through the window, guiding him. He walked to the bed, removed his boots, and crawled beneath the blankets.

They smelled clean and fresh, just like he did, and crackled beneath him.

He stared at the door for the longest time, at the shadow of the key in the lock. When his eyes drifted closed, for the first time in his life, he slept without fear.

Dallas walked through the swinging wooden doors of the saloon. The scent of freshly poured whiskey and stale cigarette smoke assailed his nostrils.

Come Saturday night, he wouldn't be able to walk through the saloon without bumping into someone, but tonight only the dregs of his town were here.

Several men played cards at a table. A man sat alone at a corner table nursing a whiskey. Another man stood at the bar, his arms folded across the top.

"Come on, barkeep, give me a whiskey," he said, his voice raspy.

"I don't sell liquor on credit," Beau said as he dried a glass, then held it up so the candles in his chandelier could dance over the glass. "Why don't you head on home, Cooper?"

" 'Cuz I ain't drunk enough."

Dallas strode to the bar and slapped a coin on the counter. "Whiskey."

Beau set a glass in front of him and poured a long drink, then walked to the other end of the bar. Cooper's black gaze darted to the glass. He ran his tongue over his chapped lips.

"Wouldn't consider buying me a drink, would ya?"

"Nope, but I want to talk to you about your son."

"Rawley?" His lips spread into a distorted grin. "You don't hardly look the type to be interested in Rawley, but then what a man is on the inside don't always show on the outside." He leaned closer and his rancid breath billowed out like a cloud of dust. "Five dollars for twenty minutes. Twenty dollars you can have him all night."

Dallas had hoped, prayed, that Dr. Freeman had been wrong. He made no attempt to keep the loathing out of his voice. "Can we discuss this outside?"

Cooper sneered. "Sure. You don't want people knowing your pleasures. I can respect that. Know how to keep my mouth shut, too."

He staggered out of the saloon. Dallas found him beside the building. A lantern hanging from a pole sent a pale glow over the man as he held out his hand.

Dallas had never hit a man. He'd never used anything but his voice to make a man listen and obey, to make a man squirm when necessary, to make a man regret he'd chosen differently.

But tonight, his voice just didn't seem to be enough. He brought his arm back and slammed his knotted fist into Cooper's nose.

Cooper squealed like a wild hog and reeled back, blood spurting through his fingers as he covered his face. He hit the ground and cursed as he staggered to his knees.

Dallas waited until Cooper was again on his feet before burying his fist in the man's paunchy gut. When Cooper bent over with a grunt, Dallas drove his fist into the man's chin.

He heard the satisfying sound of bone cracking. Cooper landed flat on his back, moaning and crying. "Don't hit me! Don't hit me again!"

Dallas crouched beside the pitiful excuse for a father, grabbed his shirt, and jerked him upright. Cooper cried out. "No more!"

Dallas glared at the bloody carnage. "Stay the hell away from Rawley or the next time I'll use my gun."

"He's my boy!"

"Not anymore," Dallas said as he shoved the man back to the ground. "Not anymore."

Dallas watched as Rawley shoveled the eggs and biscuits into his mouth. It had taken Dallas ten minutes to convince the boy the food was for him, that he was being given another meal.

Once convinced, Rawley had plowed through a plate of eggs and four biscuits, as though afraid the offer would be rescinded. Dallas had little doubt the boy had been offered a lot in his life that was quickly taken back.

Dallas planted his elbows on the table and slowly sipped the black coffee from his cup. That morning, when he'd taken Dee her breakfast, he had told her that the boy was going to be staying.

"I want him to stay, Dallas, but we can't go about deciding what's best for people. Rawley might have been happy where he was. I don't think he was, but you can't take him away from it without knowing."

She was right, of course. Dallas had taken her away from her home without knowing—or caring—if she wanted to leave. He seemed to have a habit of deciding what people should do with their lives. Asking never entered his head.

When Rawley had shoved the last bite of biscuit into his mouth and downed his glass of milk, Dallas set his cup aside. He glanced at Austin before shifting his gaze to Rawley. "Rawley, I have an offer for you."

Distrust plunged into the boy's eyes, and he looked like he might bring up his breakfast.

"I need a helper," Dallas hastily added.

Rawley furrowed his brow. "A helper?"

"Yep. I've got a big ranch, a lot of responsibilities. Sometimes, I don't have time to do everything. I need someone who can help me take care of things."

"Like what?" he asked.

Dallas's stomach knotted. A boy Rawley's age shouldn't know enough about life to have suspicion marking his gaze.

"Take care of the damn prairie dog, for one thing."

"I'm good at that."

"I know you are. I also need someone who can oil my saddle, brush my horse, someone to keep my wife company while I'm checking on the ranch. For your trouble, you get to sleep in that room upstairs, eat all the food your belly will hold, and you get a dollar a week."

Rawley's black eyes widened in wonder. "You mean a dollar a week to keep?"

"To keep, to spend. It's up to you. Just don't bury it. If you want to save it, we'll put it in the bank."

Rawley's brow furrowed, and he gnawed on his bottom lip. "My pa—"

"I talked with your pa last night. He said it's fine if you want to stay here and work for me."

Rawley nodded vigorously, his black hair slapping his forehead. "I do. I can work hard."

"I know you can, son." A sharp pain stabbed through Dallas's chest. He hadn't meant to call the boy that. His son was lying in the cold ground. He shoved the chair back and stood. "When you've finished eating, you go on upstairs and ask Mrs. Leigh to read to you. She likes reading out loud."

In long strides, he left the house before he changed his mind about letting the boy stay. The boy couldn't replace his son—no one, nothing could.

Chapter 17

❧

STANDING AT HER bedroom window, Cordelia gazed at the land that looked as cold as her heart, as empty as the place inside her where a child had once grown.

Sometimes, she imagined that she could still feel him kicking. She would press her hand to her stomach, remembering all the times Dallas had laid his large hand beneath her navel and waited, his breath held, for the moment that would join the three of them. The tender smile he had bestowed upon her when the movement came. The warmth of his lips against her flesh as his mouth replaced his hand, kissing her gently, making her feel precious.

Precious because his dream was growing inside of her.

The tears surfaced and she forced them back. She was tired of crying, tired of the ache in her chest that she knew would never leave, tired of longing for the dreams that would never be.

With the baby, she'd held hope that Dallas would come to love her—if not for herself, for the fact that she had given him a son, through her he had acquired his dream.

But the hope had died with their son.

Dallas came to her room each evening to ask after her health, but he never came to her bed. He never held her. He no longer looked at her as though she hung the stars.

And she missed that most of all.

A knock sounded on her door, and she turned from the gray skies. "Come in."

Dallas stepped into the room. "You're not ready."

She glanced at the red dress he'd brought her from town. How could she wear red when she was in mourning? Or did a child who had never lived receive no mourning period?

"I'm just not up to seeing people."

"You've been in this room for two weeks, Dee. If you can't walk down the stairs, I'll carry you, but Christmas Eve has always been a special time for my family. It's about the only tradition we have." His Adam's apple slowly slid up and down. "It'd mean a great deal to me if you'd join us—if not for me, then for Rawley. I'm not sure the boy even knows what Christmas is."

Rawley. She thought of the way he sat as still as stone and listened, barely breathing, when she read to him. "I'll be downstairs in ten minutes."

He nodded and left the room. Quickly she washed up in the warm water he'd brought her earlier. She brushed her hair and swept it up off her neck. Then she donned the red dress—for Dallas—a small inconsequential gift to him because she knew he preferred her in red.

She stepped into the hallway, surprised to find Dallas leaning against the wall, his head bowed. She had noticed so little about him before, but she noticed everything now.

The shine on his boots, the red vest beneath his black jacket, a red that matched her gown, the black tie at his throat.

Slowly, he lifted his gaze. At one time, she knew he would have smiled at her. Now, he only looked at her with uncertainty, a woman to whom marriage vows had chained him, a woman who couldn't fulfill his heart's solitary desire.

He stepped away from the wall and crooked his elbow.

Always the gentleman . . . even now honoring his word when she could no longer honor hers.

She braved a smile and placed her arm through his. Slowly they descended the stairs, a wall of silence shimmering between them. How could a child that she had never held in her arms, patted on the head, or kissed good night leave such an aching chasm in her soul?

They walked into the parlor and the world was transformed into gaiety. In a far corner, with red ribbons, strung popcorn and raisins, and brightly painted horseshoes decorating its branches, an expansive cedar tree brushed the ceiling.

Austin sat Indian style beside the tree, Maggie curled against his side. He took a package from beneath the tree, placed it between their ears, and shook it. Maggie's smile grew as the rattle bounced around them.

"What do you think?" he asked.

"A puppy!"

Austin chuckled. "I don't think so." He put the package down and reached for another.

Houston and Amelia sat on the sofa, their fingers intertwined, whispering to each other without taking their eyes off their daughter.

Rawley stood beside an empty chair, wearing a miniature version of Dallas's jacket, vest, and tie. With his black hair slicked down, his face scrubbed almost raw, and his hands knotted at his sides, she wondered if he knew Christmas came with gifts.

Maggie squealed. "Aunt Dee, you came!" She hopped up, ran across the room, and wrapped her small arms around Cordelia's knees. "I'm so glad." She looked up at Dallas. "Now?"

He touched the tip of her nose. "In a minute."

Awkwardly, Amelia brought herself to her feet with assistance from Houston. Pressing a hand to her protruding stomach, smiling softly, she waddled across the room. With tears in her eyes, she hugged Cordelia. "Merry Christmas," she whispered.

Cordelia fought back her own tears. She had expected a Christmas filled with joy, not sorrow. As Amelia drew back, Cordelia squeezed her hands and gave her a quivering smile. "How are you feeling?"

Amelia smiled brightly. "I woke up this morning and wanted to clean the house from top to bottom. I'm so glad Christmas Eve is today when I'm not tired."

"Me, too," Houston said. "She wanted me to help her clean." He leaned over and pressed a kiss to Dee's cheek. "Merry Christmas, Dee."

"Why don't you sit over here?" Dallas said as he escorted her to the chair where Rawley stood, a silent sentinel.

Sitting in the chair, she smiled at Rawley and touched a finger to the lapel of his jacket. "You certainly look handsome."

Twin spots of red colored his cheeks. He looked down at his boots—new boots, as shiny as Dallas's. She had been so wrapped up in her grief that she hadn't considered the child might need—might want—new clothes. She glanced up, wanting to thank Dallas for making certain the child was dressed as nicely as everyone else on this special day.

But he had moved away and was standing by the tree. He cleared his throat. "Our mother believed in tradition. She didn't have many, but the ones she had always seemed special." He met Houston's gaze. "Austin didn't remember the traditions because he was so young when our mother died, but Houston and I remembered them. We gave our word that we'd share them with Austin, and in time with our families. It always makes us feel as though our mother is still with us." He cleared his throat again. "Anyway, she always sang a song before we opened the gifts."

Houston stepped up beside him. Austin picked up his violin, placed it beneath his chin, and set his bow upon the strings. With one long, slow stroke, he brought the beautiful music into the room.

Then Dallas and Houston added their deep voices to the lyrical strains of the violin.

"Silent night, holy night . . ."

Dallas's voice was a rich resonance that seemed to reach out and touch every corner of the room. Houston sounded as though cattle had taught him to sing, but it didn't matter. The words journeyed from their hearts and their memories. Cordelia sat in awe, listening as three men, three brothers, paid their special homage to the woman who had brought each of them into the world.

Dallas faltered at the words "mother and child," and fell into silence. He looked at her, and for a brief moment she saw the raw pain he'd been hiding from her. Then Amelia's voice filled the room as she nestled against Houston's side and he wrapped his arm around her.

Cordelia wanted to get out of the chair, cross the room, wrap her arms around Dallas, and tell him that everything would be all right. She would find a way to make it right again, but she saw a family standing before the tree, four people who loved each other. She couldn't find the courage to walk into their midst, to ask them to accept her as she was— broken.

A small hand found its way into hers. Smiling softly at Rawley, she wondered if he felt as though he didn't belong as much as she did.

The voices rang out with the final words of the hymn, and as they died away, Austin took his time, allowing the last strains of music to fade.

Maggie walked up to Dallas and tilted her head back. "Now?"

He smiled warmly. "Now."

She squealed and dropped to the floor, clapping her hands. "Now, Unca Austin, now."

Austin set aside his violin and pointed a finger at her. "No peeking, no opening anything until they are all passed out."

Nodding her head, she scooted up. Houston and Amelia returned to their places on the sofa, and Dallas leaned against the wall, his arms crossed over his chest.

Cordelia squeezed Rawley's hand. "Don't you want to move closer to the tree?"

He shook his bowed head, but she could see him peering beneath his lashes at the tree.

Austin dropped to his knees and reached for a gift. "All right, let's see what we've got here." He turned the wrapped box over and over, frowning. "Mmmm . . . oh, wait, I see it." He smiled broadly. "Maggie May."

She clapped, took the gift, and shuffled her bottom over the floor.

Austin reached for another box and lifted a brow. "Maggie May."

Maggie had six gifts beside her before Austin furrowed his brow and glared at her. "How come you're gettin' all the presents?"

She smiled brightly. "I was too good." She glanced over her shoulder at Rawley. "Wasn't you good?"

Cordelia felt Rawley's hand flinch within hers and saw his jaw tighten. "He was very good," she said in his defense, wishing she'd been well enough to travel to town to purchase him a gift, wondering what she might have in her room that she could give him.

"Well, I reckon he was," Austin said. "Lookee—here. This one's for Rawley." He handed the gift to Maggie. "Run it over to him, Maggie May."

Maggie popped up and brought Rawley the gift. She held it out to him, but he only stared at the small oblong box.

"Don't you want it?" Maggie asked.

"I'll take it," Cordelia said and set the gift at his feet. She read the tag, grateful to Austin for remembering the child.

"I'll be darned," Austin said. "Rawley again."

"Oh!" Maggie cried as she took the large flat gift from Austin and ran it back to Rawley.

"And here's one for me," Austin said as he started to untie the ribbon that held the paper in place.

Maggie screeched and grabbed his hand, her brow deeply furrowed. "Gotta wait."

"Then let's get the rest passed out fast."

She helped him, laying presents at the grown-ups' feet. Cordelia looked at her two gifts. One from Austin. One from Houston and Amelia. She had lost her enthusiasm for the season when she'd lost her child, but judging by the number of gifts appearing, she assumed Dallas hadn't. Watching him as he stood apart from the gathering, she thought she could tell when a gift from him was handed off to someone. A warmth touched his eyes, as though he were pleased that he could give abundantly to those he loved.

Yet she received no gift from him.

"What in the heck is this?" Austin asked as he pulled a large wrapped box from behind the tree. Maggie's eyes widened and her mouth formed a large circle. "Goodness gracious, it's for Rawley," Austin said. "Help me shove it over to him, Maggie May."

They both made a great show of pushing the package across the room. When they stopped, Maggie planted her hands on the box and leaned toward Rawley, tipping her head back. "You musta been gooder than me."

Austin clasped his hands together. "That's it. Let's see what we got."

Austin hurried across the room and began to tear into his presents as though he were the same age as Maggie.

Cordelia heard quiet footsteps and glanced up. Dallas stood before her, holding a small wrapped box with a tiny red bow on it.

"It's just a little something," he said. "I was afraid it might get lost under the tree."

With trembling fingers, she took the gift, carefully untied the red ribbon, peeled back the paper, and opened the box. A heart-shaped locket was nestled between cotton. Tiny flowers had been engraved over the gold. Tears burned the back of her throat as she looked up at Dallas. "I . . . I didn't get anything for you," she whispered.

"Under the circumstances, I didn't expect you to." He crouched in front of Rawley. "You gonna open your presents?"

Rawley stared at Mr. Leigh, and then dropped his gaze to the wrapped boxes, trying to believe they were really for him, wondering if it wouldn't be better to leave them as they were, carefully wrapped with his name on them, the only true gifts he'd ever received in his life.

"I always start with the smallest," Mr. Leigh said as he picked up the first gift Rawley had received and held it toward him.

Rawley's mouth went dry. He had to confess first. They'd take the presents away, but he had to tell Mr. Leigh the truth. "I wasn't good."

Mr. Leigh rubbed his thumb and forefinger over his black mustache. Rawley had figured out that he did that when he was thinking hard.

"There's a difference between being good and doing bad things. Sometimes, a person does something because he doesn't have a choice. He might not like what he did . . . but it doesn't make him bad."

Rawley had done a lot that he didn't like. Mr. Leigh shook the box beneath his nose. It rattled something fierce. "Austin, did you put a rattlesnake in here?" Mr. Leigh asked.

Austin was shoving his hand into a new glove. He looked up. "Don't tell him. It'll ruin the surprise."

Mr. Leigh lifted a brow. "What do you think?"

Rawley wrinkled his nose. "Thought rattlers slept in winter."

"Maybe you'd better open it and see."

Rawley nodded and took the gift. His fingers were shaking so badly that he could barely grab the tiny piece of string. He pulled the bow free and moved the paper aside. Then holding his breath, he lifted the lid and peered inside. "Holy cow," he whispered.

He'd never seen so many sarsaparilla sticks in his whole life— except at the general store. He didn't know much about counting but he knew a hundred was a big number so he figured he had at least a hundred sticks in that box. He'd be an old man before he finished eating them.

"You can eat them anytime you want, Rawley," Austin said, wearing a big grin.

"Can I eat one now?" he asked.

"You don't have to ask," Mr. Leigh said. "They're yours to do with as you want."

His. A hundred sarsaparilla sticks. Maybe more. His mouth watered as he took one from the box and slipped it into his mouth. The tangy flavor washed through him. He looked at the lady. She had tears in her eyes. He figured she wanted a sarsaparilla stick, too, but it didn't look like her boxes were the right size to hold one. He knew what it was to want—and to never have. He held the box toward her. "Want one?"

More tears filled her eyes along with the glorious smile she gave him as she reached into his box. "Thank you."

He'd done that. Made her smile. He'd never in his life had anything but misery to share with people. He felt warm inside knowing he had something good he could share, even if it meant he wouldn't get to eat them all. He shoved the box toward Mr. Leigh. "Want one?"

Mr. Leigh smiled, too, as he took a stick and put it in his mouth. Rawley wondered if Mr. Leigh's mustache would smell like sarsaparilla after he'd eaten the candy.

Gathering his courage, he went around the room, offering to share his gift with everyone, even the bratty girl, watching their smiles grow, wishing he had more to give them. When he returned to his place, he glanced at the two unopened boxes. He didn't figure they could hold anything better than what he'd already gotten.

He set his box of candy aside and opened the next present, saving the biggest for last. His heart plummeted when he looked inside the box. A blanket. A blanket he could use when they took him back to town, and he was sleeping beside buildings again. He'd been working so hard, hoping they'd keep him forever, but he hadn't worked hard enough.

"Gonna open the last one?" Mr. Leigh asked.

Rawley nodded, even though he didn't want to open it, to see what else they'd given him. He pulled the bow apart and peeled back the paper, opened the box, and stared.

Stared at the fine brown leather that shone like someone had spit on it over and over. Mr. Leigh reached into the box and pulled out the saddle.

Mrs. Leigh touched her fingers to a corner of the saddle. "Those are your initials."

He didn't know what his initials were but he sure knew good carving when he saw it, and someone had carved little designs all along the saddle, except for the place where he'd put his backside.

"Well, now, if that ain't the stupidest gift I've ever seen," Austin said as he walked over for a closer look. "What were you thinking, Dallas?"

Cordelia wondered what Dallas had been thinking. He'd planned to give that saddle to his son, a son he would never have.

"What good does a saddle do him, if he ain't got a horse?" Austin asked.

"But we brung him a horse!" Maggie slapped her hand over her mouth and turned round green eyes to her father.

Houston scooped her into the air, and she squealed. "You kept that secret longer than I thought you would," he said, grinning.

Dallas unfolded his body. "Let's go outside."

He held his callused hand out for Cordelia. She slipped her hand into his, relishing the strength she felt, the warmth, remembering the feel of his hands touching her intimately as they would never touch her again.

He pulled her to her feet. Austin tossed Dallas a coat from a nearby chair. He draped it around Cordelia. The others shrugged into their coats before walking through the doors that led onto the veranda.

Rawley had put on his jacket, but now he stood like a statue, staring at the door, gasping for breath. Cordelia extended her hand toward him. "Come on, Rawley. It sounds as though this last gift was too big to wrap."

He shook his head vigorously. "I don't want a horse. I don't want to have to leave."

"You don't have to leave, son," Dallas said.

Cordelia's heart lurched at the word—*son*—spoken with such ease.

"Then why you givin' me a horse if you don't want me to ride it outta here?"

"How else are you gonna ride over my range and count my cattle for me?"

Panic delved into Rawley's dark eyes. "I don't know how to count."

"Can you tie a knot in a rope?"

Rawley nodded vigorously.

"Then I can teach you to count."

Cordelia slammed her eyes closed. Dallas would teach Rawley as he'd once planned to teach his own son. She wondered if he was even aware that he was saying to Rawley things that he'd planned to say to his own son.

But Rawley didn't carry Dallas's blood; he wasn't a Leigh. Yet, she couldn't help but wonder if this child of misfortune could possibly fill the gaping hole in their hearts.

Opening her eyes, she wrapped her hand around Rawley's. "We'd better look this horse over before you start making plans. You might not even want to keep him."

Rawley nodded enthusiastically. "Oh, I wanna keep him. Even if he's butt ugly."

Dallas cleared his throat and a smile tugged at the corner of his mouth. "You're too easy to please, Rawley."

They walked to the porch, hand in hand, a family that might have been, a bittersweet reminder of what would never be.

Tethered to the veranda railing, a brown and white spotted horse nickered.

Rawley released Cordelia's hand and walked to the edge of the veranda. Dallas continued to hold her hand tightly. She ached to have his arm come around her, to find again the intimacy they had shared as they had anticipated the birth of their child.

Rawley spun around, disbelief in his eyes. "He's mine?"

"He's yours," the three brothers said at once.

They exchanged looks, and Cordelia saw a bond between them that didn't exist between her brothers.

"Because he looks like someone splashed paint on him, he's known as a paint or pinto," Amelia explained. "You'll need to give him a name."

"Spot!" Maggie cried as she wrapped her hands around the veranda beam and leaned back. "Spot's a good name."

Rawley looked at her as though she'd lost her mind. "Spot? That ain't no name for a horse."

She crinkled her nose and stuck out her tongue. "What then?"

Rawley furrowed his brow. "My ma was Shawnee. Could I call him Shawnee?"

Amelia released a small cry and stumbled against Houston, her hand pressed against her stomach.

"I don't got to call him that!" Rawley yelled. "You can name him!"

Houston wrapped his arms around his wife as she began gasping for air. Dallas's hand tightened around Cordelia's.

"What's wrong?" Houston asked, a thread of panic in his normally calm voice.

"Ma? Ma?" Maggie said weakly, tears welling in her eyes as she reached for her mother. Austin snatched her into his arms, the blood draining from his face.

Amelia's breathing began to even out. She glanced around the stunned crowd, her smile quivering, her hand pressed below her throat. "I'm sorry, but we're going to have to go home now."

Houston stared at her incredulously. "Are you having the baby?"

"I think so. We need to go home."

"The hell with that," Houston said as he scooped her into his arms. He looked at Dallas. "Which room?"

"Dee's room. The corner room."

"I don't want to have the baby here," Amelia said.

"Too damn bad," Houston said gruffly. "Austin, fetch Dr. Freeman."

Houston swept into the house, his protesting wife in his arms. Austin handed Maggie off to Dallas.

"Hell," Austin grumbled. "December. Could she have picked a worse month? I refuse to call any relation of mine Something December."

"Just go get the doctor, and we'll worry about what we're gonna call the baby later," Dallas told him.

Without another word, Austin ran toward the barn. Dallas touched his finger to Maggie's nose. "Your ma's gonna be all right."

"Promise?" she asked in a shaky voice.

"Give you my word." He looked at Cordelia. "Houston can probably manage until the doctor gets here, but why don't you go see if they need anything? We'll put Shawnee in the barn, then we'll come inside."

She gave him a shaky nod and walked into the house, praying that everything would be all right. Outside her room, she took a deep breath of fortitude before opening the door.

Houston had a fire burning low in the hearth, the drapes pulled back on the windows, and his wife lying in the bed. Her outer clothing was draped over a chair.

Cordelia gave them both a tremulous smile. "Would you like to borrow a nightgown?"

"Yes," he said.

"No," she said.

With a sadness in her eyes, Amelia held her hand toward Cordelia. Cordelia rushed across the room and wrapped both her hands around Amelia's.

"I'm so sorry," Amelia said. "I've been having little twinges all day, but I thought they'd pass. I know this is hard on you. I didn't want to have my baby here."

Cordelia brushed a wisp of blond hair from Amelia's brow. "Don't be ridiculous. You can't stop having babies just because I can't have them. Let me get you a nightgown. It'll probably swallow you up, but you'll be more comfortable."

Amelia nodded slightly in acquiescence. Cordelia walked to the bureau. She heard a gasp and spun around.

Amelia's face was contorted in pain, her hand squeezing Houston's, her breathing ragged.

"Try and relax," he said in a soothing voice.

"You try and relax," she snapped. She fell against the pillows, breathing heavily. She smiled at her husband. "Don't take anything I say from this room." She released a long slow breath. "This baby is going to be here too quickly."

Too quickly turned out to be not soon enough as far as Cordelia was concerned. She felt as though the hours dragged by while she helped Dr. Freeman, wiping Amelia's brow, holding her hand, reassuring her that everything would be all right—until she heard that first lustful cry a few minutes after midnight. Tears filled Cordelia's eyes as Dr. Freeman placed the baby in Amelia's arms.

"Oh, isn't she beautiful?" Amelia asked in a hushed voice.

Cordelia patted the glistening sheen of sweat from Amelia's throat. "Yes, she is."

Amelia looked at her. "Go get Houston."

"Not yet, girl," Dr. Freeman said. "We're not through yet. Don't know why it is you women think we're finished the minute you're holding that baby."

"Maybe because that one minute is the one we've been waiting for,"

Amelia said as she brushed her fingers over her daughter's dark hair.

"Hand her over to Cordelia for a minute," Dr. Freeman ordered, "while you and I finish up here."

Cordelia took the precious child and wrapped her in a soft blue blanket she had planned to wrap around her own child. So tiny. With deep blue eyes, the child stared up at her. "Should I wash her?" Cordelia asked.

"Give her some time to get used to being outside," Dr. Freeman said. "You can wash her while Amelia sleeps."

"I want to see Houston first," Amelia said.

Dr. Freeman brought the blankets over her. "Then I'll fetch him. My job is done tonight so I'm gonna head on home, but I'll see you tomorrow afternoon." He pointed a gnarled bony finger at her. "You stay here until I say you can go home."

She smiled softly. "Thank you."

"Don't thank me, girl. This is the part of being a doctor that I enjoy the most." He wrinkled his brow. "Come to think of it, it might be the only part I enjoy." He patted her head. "See you tomorrow."

Cordelia placed the baby back into Amelia's arms. "You'll want to show Houston his daughter."

Amelia grabbed her hand. "Thank you. I know it was difficult for you—"

Cordelia squeezed her hand. "I didn't want to be anywhere else."

She stepped back as Dr. Freeman shuffled across the room and opened the door.

"Reckon you're waiting to get inside here," Dr. Freeman said.

"She all right?" Houston asked as he made his way past Dr. Freeman.

"Course she is."

Houston crossed the room and knelt beside the bed, his gaze focused solely on his wife. Smiling, she folded the blanket back. "We have a daughter."

"A daughter," Houston said in awe as he touched a large finger to the tiny fisted hand. "She's as beautiful as her mother." He lifted his gaze to his wife's. "I'm never gonna touch you again."

Amelia looked at Cordelia. "Will you take her now?"

Gingerly, Cordelia wrapped the child within her arms.

"I mean it this time," Houston said.

"I know you do," Amelia said as she touched his cheek. "Now, come hold me."

Carefully, he climbed on the bed, lay beside his wife, put his arms around her, and pressed his cheek to the top of her head. "I love you."

"I think that's our signal to leave."

Cordelia snapped her head around. She hadn't heard Dallas come into the room, but he was looking at her with an intensity that had her heart beating faster than thundering hooves. "I need to wash the baby."

He nodded. "I've warmed up the kitchen."

She followed him from the room, and he closed the door quietly.

"Are you all right?" he asked as they walked down the stairs.

"Just tired."

"Houston figured they had a couple more weeks, or he wouldn't have brought them over today."

"I'm glad they came. I'd like to think they needed us."

They walked through the dining room. "Where are the children?" she asked.

"I put them to bed shortly after sundown." He opened the door into the kitchen.

A warm cozy feeling settled around Cordelia, and she held the child closer to her bosom. Dallas removed a kettle from the low fire and poured water into a bowl. He'd already set towels and blankets on the table. "You've done this before," Cordelia said quietly.

He glanced up at her. "When Maggie was born. Houston is pretty useless worrying about Amelia the way he does."

"And when your son was born?"

She watched as his Adam's apple slowly slid up and down. "Yeah, I bathed him, too." He set the kettle down. "Why don't you lay her on the towels there. I'll hold her while you wash her."

She laid the child down. Dallas slipped his large hand beneath the child's dark head.

"We'll wash her hair first. She won't like it, but it's gotta be done," he said.

As Cordelia sprinkled the first drops of warm water over the child's head, the baby scrunched up her face and released a wail.

"Do you think I'm hurting her?" Cordelia asked as the wail intensified.

"Nah, she's just exercising her lungs." Gently, he turned the child, cradling her on her side so Cordelia could wash the back of her head.

"She's so tiny," Cordelia said.

"Yep, but that won't last."

As Dallas helped her clean the child, an ache settled deep within her chest for all the children Dallas would care for in the future, all the children who would not belong to him. Houston's children. Austin's children. But never his.

How unfair of Fate to give Rawley's father a son he would never appreciate while Dallas would live the remainder of his life with no hope of ever acquiring a son.

Dallas, whose large hands cradled and comforted the child.

Dallas, who looked upon a child barely an hour old, with love in his eyes.

While Rawley's father gave his son nothing but pain, Dallas would have seen to it that his son had all that his heart desired.

When she finished washing the baby, she watched as Dallas patted his niece dry and slipped a blue gown over her head. A gown his son would have worn.

He brought a dry blanket around the baby and cradled her within the crook of his arm. A corner of his mustache lifted as he smiled. "Hello, little December. Aren't you a beauty? You ready to see your ma? Get something to eat?"

He looked at Cordelia, a sadness in his eyes. "Did you want to take her upstairs?"

At that moment she knew she loved him more deeply than she thought possible. "No, you go ahead."

When he'd left, she glanced around the kitchen. Together they had cared for Houston's daughter. They worked well together, they always had. "We would have made good parents," she whispered to the shadows in the corner. "It's not fair that we were denied the chance."

Without knowing her destination, she walked out of the house, her slippered feet leaving a trail in the thin blanket of snow.

The wind whipped around her, and she heard the rapid clackety-clack of the windmill. Then she was standing beside her son's grave—for the first time.

His wooden marker was simple:

LEIGH

SON

1881

She wanted to hold him. She wanted to bathe him and comb his hair and watch him grow. She wanted his tears to dampen her shoulder, his laughter to fill her heart.

She wanted all that she could never have—and she wanted it desperately.

The anguish ripped through her chest for all they had lost: their son and the foundation for a love that he might have given them. Dallas would never love her now as she loved him.

She heard muted footfalls, but couldn't bring herself to turn around. She tried to wipe the tears from her cheeks, but others surfaced. She wrapped her arms around herself, trying to hold in the pain, but it only increased.

Dallas placed his sheepskin jacket on her shoulders. His arms circled her, and he brought her back against his chest.

To her mortification, she released a small wail and his hold tightened.

"I never even saw him," she said, her voice ragged.

"He was so tiny, it was hard to tell . . . but I like to think he would have looked like you."

"It hurts. God, it hurts."

"I know," he said in a raw voice.

"We lost so much when we lost him."

"Everything," he said quietly. "We lost everything."

His words circled her on the wind.

Everything.

Chapter 18

❧

CORDELIA WALKED INTO the entryway and stumbled to a stop at the sight of Cameron and Duncan standing just inside the doorway. Joy swelled within her as Cameron looked up and smiled.

She rushed forward, taking his hands. He brushed a kiss against her cheek. Then she reached for Duncan.

"It's so good to see you," she said.

"Christmas isn't the same without you," Cameron said, and Duncan nodded his agreement.

"I'd hoped to come by today, but"—she pointed toward the stairs—"Amelia had her baby last night, and everything has been so hectic."

Sadness filled Cameron's eyes as he dropped his gaze to her waist. "We heard you lost your baby."

The tears came suddenly, without warning, burning her eyes, clogging her throat until she could do little more than nod.

"I'm sorry, Dee," Cameron said.

She pressed her hand to her lips, wishing she could control the overwhelming grief.

"Actually, that's why we're here," Duncan said. "Boyd wanted to meet with Dallas."

Cordelia swallowed back the tears. "Boyd is here?"

"Yeah, he's in the office talking to Dallas."

"About what?"

Her brothers averted their gazes, one staring at his boots, the other

490

at the ceiling. Foreboding ripped through her. She rushed down the hallway and eased her way past the partially opened door.

Dallas stood before the window, gazing out. Boyd stood beside the desk, a scroll in his hand.

"So that's the way I see it," Boyd said. "The contract says if she gave you a son, you'd deed the land over to us. She gave you a son. It's unfortunate he died, but that doesn't change the fact that she upheld her end of the bargain. Now, I expect you to uphold your end—"

"The hell he will," Cordelia said.

Dallas spun around, agony reflected in his gaze, just before he threw on a mask of indifference. "Dee—"

"This doesn't concern you, Cordelia," Boyd said.

"The hell it doesn't. You and Father bartered me away for a strip of land, and now you have the gall to say it doesn't concern me? How dare you! How dare you come into our home and demand anything of us, anything of Dallas. There isn't a court in the state that will side with you, that will say a dead son is the same as a live son—"

"Dee—" Dallas began.

"No!" she said, hurting for him, the pain twisting inside her for all that they had lost. They would lose no more. She turned her hardened gaze on her brother and pressed a hand to her chest. "We hurt, damn you! We lost something that we desperately wanted, something we can never regain. Where was my family when I was suffering? Where was my family when I thought I might die? Marking off the land they wanted to claim!" She trembled with rage, hurt with disappointment. "I never again want you to step foot in this house. You will never acquire the land because I am now unable to give Dallas a living son. I have a strong need to hit something, Boyd, and if you don't get out of my sight right this minute, there's a good chance you'll be the thing I hit."

Boyd glared at Dallas. "You gonna let her do the talking for you?"

Dallas nodded sagely. "I'll even hold you for her if she wants to hit you."

"You'll regret going back on your word," Boyd spat out just before he stalked from the room.

Cordelia sank into a chair, shaking as though she'd been thrown into an icy river. Dallas knelt beside her.

"I've never gone back on my word, Dee, but for you, I will. I'll move my fence back across the river if you want."

She shook her head. "I don't know what I want right now. Just hold me."

He wrapped his arms around her. She pressed her face to his shoulder and wept: for the family named McQueen that she had lost, for the family named Leigh that she would never have.

Sauntering from the back room in the barn, Austin heard the faint harsh breathing, like someone running, fighting for air. He halted and listened carefully. Then very cautiously and quietly, he climbed to the loft.

Rawley was crammed into a corner, his arms wrapped tightly around his drawn-up knees, rocking, rocking back and forth.

Austin eased over the straw-covered floor. "Rawley?"

Austin had never seen raw terror, but he knew he was looking at it now. He touched the boy's shoulder and could feel the tremors racing through him.

"He's here," Rawley whispered.

"Who's here?"

"The man what hurt Miz Dee."

Austin crawled on his belly to the open window in the loft and gazed out. He recognized the three horses tied to the railing, but he couldn't believe one of the McQueen brothers was responsible for hurting Dee. He glanced over his shoulder. "You sure he's here?"

Like a frightened turtle, Rawley drew his shoulders up as though he thought he could hide his head. "He paid my pa."

"What he'd pay your pa for?"

Rawley rolled his shoulders forward. "To hurt me," he whispered in a voice that echoed shame.

Rage surged through Austin. "Can you point him out to me when he leaves?"

Rawley shook his head vigorously. "Said he'd kill me if I ever told."

"Give you my word, Rawley, that he'll never touch you again." He held out his hand. "But I gotta know who it is before I can deal with him. Come on. Help me."

Slower than a snail, looking as though he'd retreat back to the corner at any second, Rawley crawled toward Austin. Austin pulled him down beside him until they lay flat on the floor, their eyes just above the straw.

Austin saw the three McQueen brothers leave the house and mount up. "Which one?"

Rawley pointed a shaking finger. "The one in the middle."

"You sure?" Austin asked.

"Yes, sir."

Austin turned his head and smiled at the boy. "You done good, Rawley. You just leave the rest to me."

Two hours later Austin swaggered into the saloon. The smoke was thick, the noise thicker. He slapped a nickel on the counter and eyed his quarry. "Beer."

He took the glass and downed the bitter brew in one swallow. He was the youngest, the baby, the one everyone else always watched out for.

Not this time.

He removed his gun from the holster, took careful aim, and fired a bullet in the wall of the saloon . . . just above Boyd McQueen's head.

Boyd tipped over in his chair and hit the floor with a resounding thud. He came up sputtering.

Austin couldn't believe the calmness that settled over him as he strode across the room. Men jumped out of his way. Men who had been sitting at Boyd's table hastened to move to other tables.

Austin planted his hands on the table and glowered at Boyd. "I know the truth—everything. You stay away from me, mine, and anyone I consider mine or my next bullet goes through your heart."

He spun on his heel.

"You don't have the guts to kill," Boyd taunted.

Austin slowly turned and faced his adversary. "Mark my words, McQueen. Nothing would bring me greater pleasure than to rid the ground of your shadow."

Spring came as though winter had held no sorrow, blanketing the earth in an abundance of assorted reds, yellows, and greens.

Cordelia sat on the front porch of Amelia's house, watching as Amelia nursed Laurel Joy. The child kicked her chubby arms and legs in rhythm to her sucking mouth. Cordelia did not resent that Amelia held the child to her breast, but she could not help but ache for the children she would never nourish.

Cordelia turned her attention to a lean-to where the men and Rawley were working to help a mare deliver a foal. Always births would abound. Always the pain inside her would deepen, for what she could not have, for what she could not give Dallas.

"You look as though you have something on your mind," Amelia said.

Cordelia averted her gaze from those she loved. She gnawed on her lower lip. "You told me that you and Dallas had acquired an annulment. How did you go about it?"

Amelia shifted Laurel to her shoulder, buttoned her blouse, and studied her as though trying to understand the reason behind the question. "It was really rather simple. We never consummated our marriage."

"Oh." Cordelia felt her heart sink. "That wouldn't work for us, would it?"

"No, you were obviously intimate at one time."

At one time. Dallas hadn't come to her bed since the afternoon they'd shared in the hotel. He watched her with wariness as though he wasn't quite certain what to do with her.

"Then what would a woman do if she no longer wanted to be married?" Cordelia asked.

"Have you talked with Dallas about this?"

"No, we don't talk at all anymore. We are more like strangers now than we were before we got married."

"He's hurting—"

"So am I. But I can end his hurting."

Laurel Joy burped and Amelia scooted up in her chair. "How?"

"By leaving him. By giving him the opportunity to marry someone who can give him a son."

Amelia shook her head. "I don't think he wants that, Dee. When you were losing the baby, he begged me not to let him lose you, too."

"Words easily spoken—"

"Not for Dallas. He's never been one to speak what he feels."

"He didn't know what it would cost him to say them because he didn't know I'd never be able to give him the son he so desperately wants."

Sympathy filled Amelia's eyes. "You love him."

Tears clogged Cordelia's throat. "Help me, Amelia. Help me to give him what he wants."

Amelia sighed with resignation. "You should probably talk with Mr. Thomaston."

"The lawyer?"

Amelia nodded. "There's something called a divorce. I don't know much about how it's done, but I know a divorced woman is looked down upon, so think hard on this before you do it, Dee."

She looked back toward the lean-to. Dallas was hunkered down beside Rawley, pointing toward the mare, his mouth moving, instructing, explaining as she knew he'd always wanted to teach his own son. He deserved that opportunity to teach a child who carried his blood.

"I don't have to think about it," she said softly.

Standing inside Shawnee's stall, Rawley noticed the stench first, liked boiled eggs he'd hidden once so he wouldn't have to eat them. Then the cold of dawn crept over him much as he imagined a skeleton's bony fingers would feel as they skittered over his neck.

He swallowed what spit he had and crept out of the stall. A barn owl swooped down with a swoosh that nearly stopped Rawley's heart from beating.

Shadows quivered in the corners. He could see sunlight hovering between the crack where the doors to the barn met.

He smiled. The first light of dawn. Mr. Leigh would be waiting on the back steps—

The pain ripping through his chest caught him unaware as something slammed into him and knocked him to the ground. Someone straddled him and wrapped a large hand around his throat. He didn't know why. He couldn't have breathed if he'd needed to . . . and he needed to. He needed to bad.

A face hovered within inches of his, a face that he'd once known. The face now looked like a wooden puzzle that someone had put together wrong.

Black and white dots fought each other in front of his eyes. The black was winning.

"I'm gonna move my hand away. If you yell, I'll snap your neck in two," his pa rasped.

His pa. His insides recoiled at the thought.

The hand moved away. Rawley dragged in a deep breath, swallowing the bile that rose as the stench of his father filled his nostrils.

His pa got off him and pulled him to his feet as though he were little more than Maggie's rag doll. He slung him against the wall, and Rawley wished he were a doll so he wouldn't feel the pain fixing to come his way.

"Living fancy, ain't you, boy?" his pa rasped.

Rawley shook his head.

His pa smiled. He didn't have as many teeth as he'd once had and those that remained were black at the top of his smile. "Well, I'm gonna be living fancy, too, and you're gonna help me."

Rawley listened to the words. He wanted to take himself away to that place inside his head where nothing could hurt him.

But he knew if he did . . . his pa would kill the lady.

The picnic had been Rawley's idea.

"A way to make you happy," he'd said shyly, eyes downcast.

Cordelia should have known then that something was wrong, but she was too wrapped up with thoughts of leaving Dallas. Rawley had told her that he knew of a perfect place for a picnic, a place Dallas had shown him.

That should have tipped her off as well. Rawley always referred to Dallas as Mr. Leigh.

In retrospect, she could see that he had given her clues, small hints that something was amiss.

But it wasn't until they had sat on the quilt to enjoy the food—not until the riders arrived and Rawley's eyes brimmed with tears and he refused to look at her—that she came to understand the true reason behind his suggestion for a picnic.

Dear Leigh,
I am Mr. Cooper's prisoner. You got until noon tomorrow to

bring $1,000.00 to the dried well on the north end of your ranch.
Wait there alone, without any guns or knives.
I ain't hurt, but if you don't follow his orders, he'll kill me.

Mrs. Leigh

Cordelia glared at her captor. He snatched the paper from beneath her hands and held it toward the light of the lantern. "Good, good, you wrote just what I said."

She wondered if he could read, if he did indeed know that she had written his words exactly as he'd spoken them. She wished she hadn't written them at all.

She glanced at Rawley, her sole reason for doing as Cooper instructed.

Within the shed, he sat on a wooden crate. Unmoving. His hands folded in his lap, a grown-up posture out of place on a little boy. He seemed to be staring at the flame quivering in the lantern, only the flame, nothing else . . . as though he wished there were nothing else.

As though staring at the lantern, holding himself perfectly still, would make the gun pressed against his temple go away.

"Well?" the man holding the gun asked.

Rawley's father nodded. "Go ahead."

Before Cordelia could react, the man pulled the trigger. She screamed as a resounding click echoed around the room.

Rawley's father laughed. "You lucked out again, Rawley."

He drew his hand back and slapped Rawley across the face. Rawley staggered off the box and hit the floor.

"No!" Cordelia cried as she hurried to the corner and took Rawley into her arms. He was shaking as though he'd been dunked into an icy river.

"He didn't feel it," his father cackled. "He's tetched in the head; goes someplace far away. He ain't smart like me." He pointed to his temple. "Now, me, I'm a thinkin' man. Always thinkin'." He knelt and brought his abhorrent body odor with him. "Know what I'm thinkin'?"

Cordelia gathered her strength around her as she tucked Rawley more closely against her. "It doesn't matter what you're thinking."

"He'll come, and when he does I'll kill him."

"Why? You'll have the money—"

"I told you I'm a thinkin' man. Your brother paid me to kill him, but I'm thinkin'—Dallas Leigh ain't gonna be an easy man to kill. He'll fight.

"Then I get to thinkin', Dallas Leigh thinks he's smart. Thinks I'm dumb. So I think to myself, I'll kidnap his wife. Make him bring me money. Then I'll kill him. I get money from him. I get money from your brother."

"Dallas won't come. He's not a man to trade something for nothing. He wants a son which I can't give him. With my death, he will gain an opportunity to marry a woman who can give him a son."

Rawley's father stood. "You'd better pray he does come 'cuz if he don't come"—he raked his gaze over her body and Cordelia forced herself not to shudder—"I know lots of men what would pay to spend time with you, just like they paid me to spend time with that boy's ma."

"That boy? You mean Rawley? You sold your wife—"

"She weren't my wife. She was a squaw I found." He tapped his temple. "Told you I'm a thinkin' man. Took her in, made a lot of money off her till she died. Give her boy my name, but I don't imagine I'm his pa. He ain't nearly as good-looking as I used to be. And you'll be better than she was 'cuz I won't have to worry about you leaving me any worthless brats."

Chapter 19

❧

$\mathcal{D}$ALLAS STARED THROUGH the window of his office as darkness settled around him . . . along with the loneliness. He'd never before experienced loneliness, perhaps because he'd never understood companionship: the comfort of knowing someone was willing to listen to his thoughts, the joy of sharing something as simple as watching the stars appear within the velvety sky.

He wanted Dee to be in his office now, curled up in her chair discussing her ideas, her plans. But she hadn't come to his office since she'd had the confrontation with Boyd.

He crumpled the note she'd left him on the dining-room table.

Rawley and I have gone on a picnic.

Only a few months before, she might have invited him to join them. Now, she didn't even want his company when she rode into town to check on her hotel.

They had become strangers.

After her accident, he had been afraid to sleep in her bed, fearful of hurting her. With each passing day, a chasm had widened between them, a chasm he had no earthly idea how to close.

He wondered if she would even come home tonight. She had begun to spend more nights at the hotel. He bent his head until his chin touched his chest. Damn, he missed her, and he didn't know how to get her back.

Her smiles for him had disappeared, along with her laughter. Sometimes, he would hear her chuckle at something Rawley said. He'd hoard the moment as though it were for him, knowing full well that it wasn't.

It seemed that the night they had lost their son, whatever tender feelings she might have had for Dallas had perished as well. How could he blame her? He hadn't been there to protect her. He had been as useless as a dry well.

He heard the galloping hooves and looked up in time to see the rider bring his arm back. The window shattered as a rock sailed through it.

What the hell?

He found the rock, untied the string that surrounded it, and unfolded the note. He recognized Dee's flowing script long before he saw her signature.

Sitting at his desk, he turned up the flame in the lamp. He read the note a dozen times. The words remained the same, chilling him to the bone.

He planted his elbows on the desk and buried his face in his hands, digging his fingers into his brow. Christ, he didn't know what to do.

The well on the north end was visible for miles—as was everything around it. If anyone followed him to offer assistance, whoever waited at the well would see him.

If Dallas held his silence, told no one about the ransom note, brought no one with him . . .

He sighed heavily. He'd probably viewed his last sunset, already regretting that he hadn't taken the time to appreciate it, for he had little doubt that a bullet would be waiting for him beside the well.

Dallas pounded on the door until the hinges rattled.

The door opened slightly, and Henderson peered out into the darkness. "Good God, Dallas, your wife didn't ask for a loan today."

"I know that. I need a thousand dollars—cash."

"Come see me at eight when I open the bank."

He started to close the door, and Dallas slammed his hand against it. "Now. I need it now."

"For what?"

"Business. You can charge me double the interest on it."

Henderson scurried outside, and Dallas followed him down the steps. As Henderson fumbled with the keys, Dallas refrained from grabbing them and shoving them into the locks himself.

When Henderson turned the key on the last lock, he glanced over his shoulder at Dallas. "You stay here while I get the money."

Nodding, Dallas handed him the saddlebag. "Make sure it's exact."

As Henderson disappeared into the building, Dallas walked to the edge of the boardwalk and gazed toward the end of town where Dee's hotel stood before turning his attention to the sheriff's office. He toyed with the idea of waking the sheriff as well, of explaining the situation to him in case Dee didn't return home tomorrow. But if Cooper didn't release Dee, what difference would anyone knowing make? None at all.

He glanced back at the hotel, and the pride swelled within him. The Grand Hotel. She had envisioned it and turned it into reality. He couldn't remember if he'd ever told her how proud he was to have had her at his side.

For a man who thought he'd lived his life by sidestepping regrets, he suddenly discovered that he had left a great many things undone.

Dallas arrived at the well an hour before the sun shone directly overhead. The windmill clattered as the slight breeze blew across the plains. He shifted his backside over his saddle and waited.

He loved the land, the openness of it, the way it beckoned to a man. If treated right, the land returned the favor, but it couldn't curl against a man in the dead of night. It wouldn't warm his feet in the middle of winter.

He saw the solitary rider approaching. He wasn't surprised that the exchange wasn't going to take place here. Still he had hoped.

The man who neared wasn't Cooper. Dallas had never seen the burly man before, and he hoped to never see him again.

"You got the money?" the man asked through a mouth of missing and rotting teeth.

"Yep. Where's my wife?"

"At the camp." The man held out a black cloth. "Put this on."

Dallas snatched the cloth from the grimy fingers and bound it over his eyes. He wasn't a man accustomed to playing by another's rules, but he had no choice. He'd do whatever it took to keep Dee alive.

She'd lost their child because he'd thrown caution to the wind. He didn't intend to be as careless this time.

The dark material muted the afternoon sun's blinding rays, but Dallas used the intensity of the light to measure the passing of the day, to gauge the direction that they traveled: west, toward the sunset.

After what seemed hours, Satan stumbled to a stop.

"You can remove the mask now," his captor said.

Dallas jerked off the foul-smelling cloth. His eyes needed little time to adjust as dusk was settling inside the small canyon.

His gaze quickly swept the area, registering the dangers, the risks . . . the terror in Dee's eyes as she stood with her back against a tree, her arms raised, her hands tied with coarse rope to the branch hanging over her head.

Dallas dismounted, grabbed the saddlebags, and strode toward Cooper, ignoring the man's knowing smirk, unable to ignore the whip he was trailing in the dust like the limp tail of a rattlesnake.

"Cut her loose," Dallas ordered as he neared the loathsome man who called himself Rawley's father, sorry to discover that he'd left too much of the man's face intact.

Cooper spit out a stream of tobacco juice. "Not till I got the money."

Dallas slung the bags at Cooper's feet and stalked toward Dee.

"Stop right there or Tobias will shoot her," Cooper snarled.

Dallas spun around. A man standing to the right of Cooper had a rifle trained on Dee. The man who had brought Dallas to the camp had dismounted and snaked an arm around Rawley, holding him close against his side, a gun pressed to the boy's temple. Dallas would have expected fear to be hovering within Rawley's dark eyes. Instead they only held quiet resignation. Dallas tamped down his anger. "You've got the money. Let them go."

Cooper chuckled. "This ain't just about the money. This is about what I owe you." He snapped the whip and the crack echoed through the canyon. "My face can't even attract a whore after what you done to it. Hurts something fierce. Figure you could do with a little hurt yourself." His lips spread into a smile that lit his eyes with anticipation. "How many lashes you think it would take to kill her?"

Dallas took a menacing step forward.

A rifle fired.

Dee screamed.

Dallas froze. He slowly glanced over his shoulder. Dee vigorously shook her head. He could see no blood, no pain etched over her face.

"Next time, Tobias won't miss," Cooper said.

Swallowing hard, Dallas turned his attention back to Cooper, deciding it was time to risk everything in order to gain all. "Kill her and you'll never get the money."

Cooper's laughter echoed around the canyon as he kicked the saddlebags. "You damn fool. I've got the money."

"Do you?" Dallas asked.

The laughter abruptly died as Cooper dropped to his knees and flung back the flaps on the saddlebags. Frantically, he pulled out paper. Pieces and pieces of blank paper. Fury reddened his face as he glared at the man who had escorted Dallas to the camp.

"Quinn, you fool, didn't you look in the saddlebags before you brung him out here?"

"You didn't tell me to look in the saddlebags. You just told me to bring him."

Cooper glowered at Dallas. "Where's the money?"

"In a safe place. All one thousand dollars, but you don't get it until I know Dee is safe. She leaves with me now, and I'll bring the money back to you. Give you my word."

"Your word. You think I'm some kinda idiot? I ain't letting her out of my sight until I've got the money, and you ain't never leaving here alive."

"Then we can handle this another way. Take her to town, let her check into the hotel. A man is waiting there, watching for her return. When he knows she's safe, he'll give you the money. Meanwhile, you'll have me as insurance."

Cooper narrowed his eyes. "Who is it? One of your brothers?" He rubbed his jaw. "Austin. It's gotta be Austin."

Dallas shook his head. "Nope. Figured you'd expect it to be one of my brothers. You'd never suspect this man."

Cooper struggled to his feet, his knuckles turning white as he clenched the whip. "You'll tell me who has the money, by God. You'll tell me!"

With a quick flick of his wrist, he brought the whip back and snapped it. It whistled through the air. Dee gasped as it sliced through her skirt.

"Damn you!" Dallas roared.

"Tell me who it is," Cooper yelled, "or I'll whip her to death."

When Cooper brought his arm back, Dallas raced across the expanse separating him from Dee. He pressed his body flush against hers, drawing in a hissing breath through his teeth as the whip bit into his back.

Reaching up, he fumbled with the knots in the rope.

"If you untie them ropes, Tobias will shoot her!"

Dallas stilled his hands. He'd never in his life asked or begged for anything. "Christ! You want me on my knees, crawling on my belly? I'll do anything you want, just take her into town. Let her register for a room at the hotel. The man and the money are waiting for you."

"So you say," Cooper yelled. "The law's probably waiting on me."

Dallas heard the whistle and clenched his teeth, but he couldn't stop his body from jerking when the whip sliced across his back. His shirt offered little protection against the razor-sharp tip, and he realized with sickening dread that he had lost his gamble. He'd hoped his change in the plans would have forced Cooper to honor his end of the bargain.

He wrapped his hands around Dee's trembling fists, gasping when the lash hit him again.

"Move away," she whispered hoarsely.

"No." He slammed his eyes closed when the pain ripped through him. When he opened his eyes, tears hovered within hers. "Don't you dare cry," he growled through clenched teeth. "Don't you dare give him that satisfaction."

She nodded bravely, and he could see her blinking back her tears. Dear God, but he couldn't have asked for a finer wife.

"You have to get away from here," she said in a low voice as the whip tore into him. "One of my brothers paid him to kill you."

"Figured it was something like that. That's why . . . tried to force him to take you to town." He lowered his trembling fingers to her soft cheek. "Keep the promise you made to me . . . my land . . ."

The pain intensified, drowning out his thoughts, his muscles quivering as the onslaught continued. He buried his face against her neck, her warmth, her sweet fragrance. He wanted to tell her something else, something important, but it hovered at the edge of the agony.

"I'm sorry," slipped past his lips before the blackness engulfed him.

With the sputtering flame from the stub of a candle casting a fluttering glow over Dallas's back, Cordelia tried to asses the damage.

She had removed what remained of his shirt, the blood-soaked strips that could not even serve as a bandage. Crimson rivulets of torn flesh and seeping blood criss-crossed his broad back. His trousers had grown black and stiff as the blood had flowed more freely with each strike of the lash.

Although unconscious, he groaned and clenched his fists. Her trembling fingers hovered over his tortured flesh. She didn't know how to ease his pain, how to stop infection from settling in, although infection was the least of her worries. They intended to kill him, and with a sickening dread, she knew they intended for his death to be a slow, agonizing affair.

"Why did you come?" she whispered hoarsely as she brushed the black hair from his furrowed brow.

She stiffened as she heard a key go into the lock of the shed's door. It opened and Cooper burst into the room. "He awake yet?"

Cordelia moved so her body partially covered the sight of Dallas's back. "No."

Cooper lumbered across the room and squatted beside Dallas. He grabbed his hair and jerked his head up. Dallas moaned, his eyes opening to narrow slits.

"Who has the money?" Cooper demanded.

"Go to hell."

Cooper slammed Dallas's head against the dirt floor. "I'm gonna take her into town tomorrow. If I don't come back with the money, you're gonna die a slow death. I spent time with the Indians, and I know how to keep a dead man screaming for days."

He shoved himself to his feet.

"And if the money's there," Cordelia said, hating the plea she heard in her voice, "you'll let him go."

Cooper sneered at her. "If I get the money, then I'll kill him quick. Like I said before, your brother paid me to kill him. I ain't got no choice in the matter except to decide if he dies fast or slow. Now that decision is in his hands."

He left the shack, slamming the door into place. Cordelia heard him lock the door. She leaned close to Dallas's ear. "Does someone have the money?" she asked.

"Yes."

"Who?"

"You're safer . . . not knowing."

"I won't leave you here."

Grunting and groaning, he struggled to sit up, sweat beading his body, his muscles quivering with the strain. Roughly, he cradled her cheek and brought her face closer to his. "You will leave, dammit."

"He's going to kill you," she whispered brokenly.

"Maybe." He dropped his hand to the dirt. "Look, I think we're here."

In the dim light of the candle's glow, she could see his hand trembling as he drew an X in the dirt.

"Well on north end." Another X.

"The house." X.

"Town." He lifted his pain-filled gaze to hers. "Once you get into the hotel, wait in our room with the door locked until a man comes for you. He'll say, 'You hold my heart.' Draw him a map. Go with him to the sheriff. There's a chance they could get back here . . . in time."

She knew from the resignation in his eyes that he thought the chances were slim. His face was a mask of agony as she laid her palm against his cheek. "Lie down. You need to save your strength. I'll see if I can stop some of this bleeding."

His breathing shallow, he stretched out beside her. She imagined each intake of breath was agony as his back expanded. She had no way to cauterize the gaping slashes. She tore off a strip of her petticoat and pressed it against the worst of his wounds, trying to stanch the seepage of glistening blood. The air hissed through his teeth.

"I'm sorry. I don't know what else to do." She glanced at his face. His eyes were closed, his jaw clenched. She touched his cheek, realizing with gratitude that he had lost consciousness.

She trailed her fingers along his sides where the whip had sometimes slithered. The cuts were shallow and had stopped bleeding. She wanted to curl beside him, wrap her arms around him, and take away his pain.

She hadn't planned to fall asleep, wasn't certain when she had, but she awoke to a scratching at the door. The candle had gutted and the small shed was wrapped in darkness.

The scratching intensified, then she heard a click, and the door squeaked open on dry hinges. A small silhouette stood in the doorway.

"Miz Dee?"

Cordelia rose to her knees. "Rawley?"

He took a small step forward. "We gotta go."

"Where's your father?"

"They're all passed out, drunk as skunks, but we gotta hurry."

Cordelia shook Dallas's shoulder. He groaned. She slapped his cheek, alarmed to find it so warm. "Dallas?" She slapped him again. "Dallas, wake up."

Moaning, he grabbed her hand before she could hit him again.

"Rawley unlocked the door. We need to go." She slipped her hands underneath his arms. "Help me. Come on. Get up."

Slowly, laboriously, she got him to his feet. He draped an arm over her shoulder, and she wrapped her arm below his waist, trying to give him some support.

"Horses?" he whispered.

"They never took off the saddles," Rawley rasped into the darkness. "But we gotta hurry. They'll whip my butt if they wake up."

They staggered into the night Cordelia didn't know how Dallas managed to pull himself into the saddle, but he did.

Then they were galloping, galloping toward freedom.

Cordelia kept the map Dallas had drawn emblazoned in her mind, her gaze focused on the North Star he had shown her one night. She knew they were heading in the right direction, away from their captors, but she didn't know exactly where the house was, or the town, or Houston's home. They could all easily be missed with the vast expanse of land stretching out before them.

She had no way to gauge the time as the steady pounding of the hooves echoed over the plains. Rawley kept glancing back over his shoulder. She didn't blame him. She had little doubt his punishment would be severe if they were caught.

"Dee!"

She jerked her gaze around. Dallas was slouched over the saddle horn, his horse slowing to a trot. She brought her own horse to a stop and circled back as Satan staggered to a halt.

"Dallas?"

His breathing was shallow, his knuckles white as he gripped the saddle horn. "Tie me."

"What?"

"I'm close to passing out. If I fall, you won't have the strength to get

507

me back on this horse." He struggled to loosen the rope from its place on his saddle. "I want you to tie me to the saddle so I can't lose my seat."

She glanced around. "Surely you can hold on a little while longer. We can't be that far from home."

"We have hours yet to ride." A corner of his mouth tilted up. "That's the problem with owning so much land. It takes forever to get home."

Rawley had sidled his horse up against hers, his young face etched in worry.

Cordelia reached out, took his hand, and squeezed gently. "You keep a look out while I help Mr. Leigh. If you see riders coming, you ride fast and hard for town."

He gave a quick nod and settled his anxious gaze in the direction from which they'd ridden. Cordelia dismounted, worked the rope free from the saddle, and glanced up at Dallas, the pain carved deeply into the creases of his face.

"What do I do?" she asked.

"Slip the rope beneath the legging of the saddle . . . wrap it around my leg . . . bring the rope up . . . loop it around my waist and the horn in a figure eight . . . take it to the other side, wrap it . . . secure my hands to the saddle horn . . . give me your word if something happens and I can't ride . . . you'll keep going."

"No."

"Dee—"

"No," she insisted as she wound the rope around his leg and knotted it. "If you want me safe, then you'd best find a way to keep riding."

"When did you . . . get so ornery?"

She knew it was unfair to ask so much of him when he was suffering as he was, but she'd be damned before she'd let him give up. She brought the rope up to his waist, careful not to let the rough hemp touch his bare back.

When she had finished following his instructions, she mounted Lemon Drop and took Satan's reins. "Am I going in the right direction?"

He gazed at the stars before looking out over the land. "Head south . . . east."

She kicked her horse into a lope, ignoring her husband's strangled groans, hoping that home lay just beyond dawn.

Chapter 20

ᔖ

CAMERON JERKED AWAKE, his neck stiff, his arm numb from using it as his pillow. His gaze darted around the lobby of The Grand Hotel.

It was empty, silent. Even the low fire that had been burning within the hearth had died quietly. Through the windows, he could see the darkness of night. It had been night when last he'd looked.

When was that?

He thrust himself to his feet and shoved his hand into his pocket, pulling out his watch. Two-thirty.

Dallas would kill him if he'd been sleeping . . .

He rushed across the lobby and pounded the little bell on the registration desk.

Bleary-eyed, Susan Redd peered out from the room behind the desk. "What do you need?"

"Has Mrs. Leigh registered?" he asked, unable to keep the alarm out of his voice.

Susan sighed and shook her head. "No, but she has a key to one of the rooms upstairs. She could have come in without me knowing."

"What room?"

"Three-oh-one."

"Thanks." Cameron dashed up the stairs and pounded on the door. "Dee?"

With an unexpected burst of panic, he kicked in the door. The room was empty.

Dread filled him. She should have been here by now. Christ, why had Dallas laid this burden on his shoulders? Should he wait . . . or should he leave?

He took a coin from his pocket and tossed it into the air. Heads he'd leave.

It landed with a thump on the floor.

Heads it was.

The fiery flames licked at Dallas's back unmercifully. He searched for the peaceful cocoon of oblivion, but it hovered beyond reach as the pain shot through his back and his whole body jerked in rebellion.

"Damn!"

"Sorry, son, but I have to get these wounds cleaned."

Dr. Freeman.

Dallas forced his eyes open, only then realizing that he was lying in a bed, his hands fisted into the mattress.

"Dee?"

"I'm here," she said softly as she laid her palm over his hand.

He wanted to turn his hand and intertwine his fingers with hers, but he was afraid he'd crush her bones. He didn't seem to have any control over his body as it flinched with Dr. Freeman's not-so-gentle ministrations.

"Home?"

She placed her cool fingers against his fevered brow. "Yes, we're home. When I didn't show up at the hotel, Cameron came here and told Austin what had happened. Austin had the men out searching for us. Our paths crossed near dawn." She brushed his hair up off his brow. "Why did you trust Cameron with the money?"

"The day you married me . . . he was the only one who cared about you . . . enough to threaten me. What about Cooper?"

"Austin went to town to get the sheriff so they can go arrest them. I drew them a map like the one you drew for me."

"Good. Your . . . other brothers?"

When Cameron had heard the whole story, he'd paled considerably. She'd told him to check into a room at the hotel until the matter was resolved. She knew he didn't have the stomach for the harsh conflict about to erupt. "I'll take care of them. I'll take care of everything. You just need to get well."

510

"Put out the fire."

She brushed her lips along his ear. "There is no fire. You have a fever and your back . . . your back is a mess."

He thought he felt rain falling along his cheek, soft gentle rain. Then he thought nothing at all as the pain carried him under to the darkest recesses of hell.

Cordelia carefully wiped her tears from Dallas's face, then swiped them from her own. "Is he going to live?"

"Hell, if I know," Dr. Freeman answered, the frustration evident in his voice. "He's lost a lot of blood, he's fighting infection, and there's not a whole hell of a lot left for me to sew up." He turned his wizened gaze her way. "But then he's a fighter. Always has been so I reckon he'll fight this, too."

He went back to work and Cordelia averted her gaze from the sight of Dallas's ravaged back. A gentle hand closed over her shoulder.

"I fed and bathed Rawley. He's sleeping now. Let me take care of you," Amelia said.

Cordelia shook her head. "Not until Dallas's fever breaks."

"That could be a while."

"I know."

After Dr. Freeman left, she stayed by Dallas's side, wiping the sweat from his brow, his throat, rubbing ointment over his chaffed wrists, fighting back the tears that threatened to surface every time she gazed at his back.

He was so undeserving of the suffering. Even unconscious, his jaw remained clenched, his brow furrowed, his fists balled around the sheets. His body jerked from time to time. He moaned low in his throat, the sound like the bawl of a lonesome calf lost on the prairie.

It was late afternoon before footsteps thundered up the stairs. She came to her feet as Austin and Houston stormed into the room, the sheriff in their wake.

"How is he?" Houston asked as he ran his gaze over his brother's back.

"Fighting. Did you find the men—"

"We found them," Austin said as he slung himself into a chair beside the bed.

She looked at the sheriff. He seemed ill at ease standing in the room, holding his hat in his hand. "Did you arrest them?"

"No, ma'am. They're dead."

Cordelia stumbled back. "Dead?"

"Yes, ma'am. Somebody got to them before we did. Looks like whoever it was slit their throats while they were sleeping."

Cordelia slammed her eyes closed. "Then you have no way of knowing which of my brothers paid them to kill Dallas."

"No, ma'am."

"Boyd," Austin said.

"Why Boyd?" Sheriff Larkin asked. "Because he's the oldest? Because he shot you? I gotta have a better reason than that to arrest a man."

Austin bolted to his feet. "I can give you a good reason to arrest him."

Houston harshly cleared his throat. Austin dropped his gaze. "Dallas wouldn't want you to arrest him anyway. He takes care of his own problems."

Houston stepped between Austin and the sheriff. "We're all tired and bickering among ourselves isn't going to help anything."

Sheriff Larkin settled his hat into place. "Let me know when Dallas is up to talking. Maybe he knows something else." He pointed his finger at Austin. "Don't go breaking the law thinking it'll even things out. Two men breaking the law is just two men breaking the law."

"I ain't gonna break the law, but I'm not going to let them get away with it either."

Cordelia put her hand on Austin's arm to restrain him. "I'll handle this." She shifted her gaze to the sheriff. "Thank you, Sheriff. If we should gather any other information, we'll let you know."

"You do that, ma'am. I'm sorry I can't do more."

He walked from the room. Cordelia turned to Austin. "What were you going to say before Houston stopped you?"

Austin looked at Houston, and Houston shook his head. Cordelia dug her fingers into Austin's arm. "You promised to be my friend. What do you know that I don't?"

Austin sighed heavily, his blue eyes filled with sadness as he touched his fingers to her cheek. "Boyd was behind the hotel the night you got hurt."

Cordelia felt the blood drain from her face. "No."

She watched Austin swallow. "Yeah, Dee. Apparently, he enjoyed hurting Rawley, paid his pa to let him do it."

She staggered back and fell into the chair, her hand covering her mouth.

"I'm sorry, Dee, I never meant for you to find out."

"Does Dallas know?"

"No. Houston and I talked about it. We figured Dallas would kill Boyd if he knew."

"That doesn't mean Boyd is responsible for this," Houston pointed out. "We just know he's got a mean streak . . . and apparently no conscience."

Cordelia rose from the chair and took a deep breath. "If one of you can watch Dallas, I need to go speak with my family this afternoon."

"I'm going with you," Austin said.

Cordelia captured his gaze. "I'm taking the men with me. You're welcome to come, but understand that I want no interference."

"Amelia will watch Dallas. We'll both come with you," Houston said.

"All right. Let me make the arrangements."

She walked out of the house to the barn where she found Slim brushing Satan's coat to a velvety sheen. She supposed everyone felt a need to do something for Dallas in their own way. "Slim?"

He turned and gave her a lopsided grin. "Yes, ma'am."

"I need you to gather up the men. I want to go talk with my family this afternoon, and I have no desire to go alone. Be sure every man is carrying a rifle and a side arm, and that they are prepared to use them if necessary—but only on my orders."

"Yes, ma'am."

"Austin and Houston are coming along as well. I'm certain they'll go into the house with me. I'd like you there as well."

"Yes, ma'am. I'll saddle your horse."

"Thank you, Slim." She walked from the barn, across Dallas's domain, grateful her name was no longer McQueen.

She didn't bother to knock when she arrived at her father's house. She simply walked through the door, Houston, Austin, and Slim in tow.

The house was shaped like an H. One story with three bedrooms on each side, the main living quarters arranged in the center. She walked through the front parlor, straight into her father's study.

Her father sat behind his desk, nursing what she supposed was a whiskey, Duncan was slouched in a chair, and Boyd was staring out a window.

Boyd turned. Blinding white-hot rage swept through her as she crossed the room, brought her hand back, and slapped Boyd as hard as she could.

He grabbed her wrist, his fingers digging into her flesh. "What the hell?"

Three guns were drawn and cocked.

"Let her go," Austin snarled, "or I'll put a bullet through you where you stand."

Boyd released her.

"What's going on, Dee?" Duncan asked as he came to his feet.

"Boyd murdered my child. How could you? How could you leave me there? And then to demand that Dallas give you his land—" Bile rose in her throat as she turned away from him. She had never felt such revulsion.

"Well, after that little dramatic display—"

She spun around so quickly that Boyd stepped back. "You haven't seen my dramatic display yet."

He smiled condescendingly. "Calm down, Cordelia. This behavior isn't like you."

"It's exactly like me . . . now that I'm free of the oppression I lived under in this house."

Boyd walked across the room and took his place behind her father's chair. "You've made your point, Cordelia. You didn't need to air our dirty laundry in front of others."

"My point, Boyd?" Cordelia asked, the quivering in her stomach intensifying, but not yet spreading into her voice. "I haven't begun to make my point. You need to move your cattle away from Dallas's river. In the morning, our men will take the fence back to where it stood the day Dallas married me. Any of your cattle that remain will be confiscated."

Her father struggled to his feet. "Have you lost your mind? Your husband gave his word—"

"Yes, he gave his word that he would pull the fence back if I married him. He kept his word. I just watched him flayed to within an inch of his life because one of my brothers paid Cooper to kill him."

Boyd remained motionless, Duncan lowered his gaze. Her heart sank.

"Oh, Duncan, tell me it wasn't you."

"I don't know what you're talking about, Dee."

He lifted his gaze, and she saw the truth within his eyes. The plan had been Boyd's, and Duncan had known of it.

"You knew," she whispered. "You knew what Boyd planned, and you went along with it."

"I don't know what you're talking about," he repeated. "Cooper was a drunk. Whatever he said was a lie."

"Duncan's right," Boyd said. "It's our word against Cooper's. Who are you going to believe? Family or a drunk?"

"Cooper and his associates are dead," she said with resignation, "so the sheriff won't make any arrests because we have no proof. But let me make something perfectly clear. If Dallas dies, I inherit his land, and unless a blizzard blows through hell, you will never possess that property. So you gained nothing, and lost everything. Get your cattle off our land."

She spun around.

"Cordelia!"

She staggered to a stop and slowly turned as her father's voice reverberated around the room.

"You just accused your brothers of trying to commit murder."

"No, Father. From this day forward, Cameron is the only brother I have. If you allow these two to remain in your home after what I have just told you, then I also have no father."

"You're as high-spirited and stubborn as your mother. I warned Leigh that he needed to keep a tight rein on you, but he wouldn't listen."

"Dallas isn't one to follow in other men's footsteps. Giving him permission to marry me was the finest gift you could have ever given me."

Dallas grew warmer with each passing hour. When he shivered, Cordelia didn't dare bring the blankets up to cover him. Dr. Freeman had told her Dallas's raw back needed air. Even if that weren't true, she didn't think he could have survived anything touching him.

Night had fallen by the time they returned from the McQueen spread. Houston had taken Amelia and the children home. Austin had ridden to town. Rawley slept soundly, not even stirring when she'd brushed the hair back from his brow.

She had taken up her vigil beside Dallas, placing her hand over his. Such a strong hand, with a gentle touch. Such a strong man, with a tender heart.

He would deny it, of course, but she had seen too much evidence not to recognize the truth. For all his gruffness, he had a heart as big as Texas.

She heard shuffling and turned to see Rawley standing in the doorway, his black hair sticking straight up on one side. She held out her hand. "Come sit with me."

He hurried across the room and stopped just short of her reach. "I can't, Miz Dee. I tricked you. He said he'd kill you if I didn't. I didn't know he was gonna hurt Mr. Leigh. Honest to God, I didn't know. I won't do what he says no more. I swear to God I'll let him kill me before I do what he says."

She reached out for him, and although he was resistant, she finally managed to work him into her embrace, onto her lap. She began to rock back and forth, her heart breaking for the life this child had endured.

"He won't hurt you, Rawley," she whispered, stroking her fingers through his hair. "He's gone away. He's gone to heaven."

Rawley jerked back, studying her. "You mean he's dead?"

She hadn't wanted to put it so bluntly, and in all honesty, she didn't think he had gone to heaven either. Although she didn't think Rawley had any affections for the man, Cooper had been his father. "Someone killed him."

"I'm glad," Rawley said with vehemence. "I'm glad he'd dead so he can't hurt nobody no more."

She pressed his face against her breast and soon felt his warm tears soak through her clothing. She knew he needed to grieve. Even though his father had never loved him, he had still been Rawley's father. Just as she needed to grieve for the family she had said farewell to that afternoon.

She had finally come to realize that with the exception of Cameron, she had never truly known their love, but still it hurt to say good-bye.

The heavy pounding on the door awoke Cordelia at dawn. She had put Rawley back in bed and returned to Dallas's side, only to fall asleep in the chair. She placed her palm on his cheek. His fever had risen.

The pounding continued, and she wondered why Austin didn't attend to it.

She rushed into the hallway and began her own pounding. "Austin, can you answer the door?" When he failed to respond, she opened his door. His bed was empty and looked as though he hadn't slept in it. Had he come home?

She hurried down the stairs and flung open the door. Sheriff Larkin filled the doorway. She pushed her way past him. "Slim?"

The foreman turned from the group of men. "Yes, ma'am?"

"Send someone into town to fetch Dr. Freeman. Right away."

"Yes, ma'am."

She turned to the sheriff. "I'm sorry, Sheriff. Did you need something?"

"I need to talk to Austin."

With her fingers, she brushed the stray strands from her face and tried to remember when she'd last taken a comb to her hair. Too long. "I don't think he's here," she said as weariness settled in. "He went into town yesterday evening, but it doesn't look as though his bed has been slept in so you might check the hotel."

"I've already made inquiries around town. No one saw him yesterday evening. He didn't check into the hotel."

Alarm skittered along her spine. "He said he was going into town. Do you think he's hurt?"

Beyond the sheriff's shoulder, she saw Rawley shuffling out of the barn. "Rawley!" She motioned for him and he ran to the house.

"Rawley, have you seen Austin?" she asked.

He shook his head. "Not since I told him 'bout the man."

Cordelia knelt in front of him. "What man?"

"The man what paid my pa to kill Mr. Leigh."

Her heart started pounding.

"Who would that be, boy?" Sheriff Larkin asked.

Rawley didn't take his eyes off Cordelia as he answered, "The man what hurt you."

"Boyd?"

"Don't know his name. Pa always called him 'my special friend.' Only I never thought he was special at all."

Cordelia agreed with Rawley's assessment of her brother. He had not been special, only cruel.

"How do you know that he's the one who paid your father to kill Mr. Leigh?" she asked.

"Pa told me that once he'd killed Mr. Leigh for my special friend, he was gonna give me to him for keeps."

Imagining the terror that the child must have felt upon hearing his father's words and the fate that might have awaited him had they not escaped, she drew him into her embrace.

"And you told this to Austin?" she whispered.

He nodded. "Said he'd take care of everything."

She rose to her feet as the vague outline of a rider on a black horse emerged in the distance. Out of the corner of her eye, she saw Sheriff Larkin rest his hand on the butt of his gun. "There's Austin."

Austin brought his horse to a halt and dismounted, eyeing Sheriff Larkin warily. "What's going on, Dee?"

It suddenly occurred to her that she had no idea what was going on, what exactly had brought the sheriff out to the house. "I'm not—"

"You got blood on your shirt," Sheriff Larkin pointed out.

Austin glanced down and touched his fingers to the slender trail of blood that ran along the side of his shirt. He looked up and met the sheriff's gaze. "Must have scratched myself."

"You got somebody that can vouch for your whereabouts last night?" Sheriff Larkin asked.

Austin took a step back, his gaze darting between Cordelia and Sheriff Larkin. "What in the hell is going on?"

Sheriff Larkin blew out a big gust of air. "Mrs. Leigh, I didn't want to break the news to you like this, but Boyd was murdered last night. We found him out on the prairie. Gut shot."

Cordelia staggered back and wrapped her arms around the beam. She'd been angry at him, quite possibly had come to hate him, but she hadn't wanted that for him. No one deserved that slow agonizing death. "Who do you—" Her heart slammed against her ribs as Sheriff Larkin turned his full attention on Austin.

"Now, then, boy, you got someone who can swear you were with them last night?"

Austin looked at Cordelia, a silent appeal for forgiveness in his eyes, before he quietly spoke. "No."

"That's too bad," Sheriff Larkin said as he stepped off the porch, jangling the manacles. "Because Boyd wrote your name in the dirt before he died."

While Dallas's fever raged, Cordelia constantly rained cool water over his body and worried about Austin.

A circuit judge had arrived that morning, and he saw no point in putting off the inevitable until Dallas had recovered.

"Dee?"

She moved up at the sound of Dallas's raspy voice and laid her hand over his where it was tied to the bedpost. They had been forced to bind him, spread-eagle, to stop his thrashing at the height of his delirium.

She brushed her lips over his fevered brow, his eyes glazed with pain.

"You have . . . to get away," he rasped.

"No, we're safe now. We're home."

"Home?"

She laid her cheek against his bristly one. "Yes, we're home."

"Bury me beside our son."

The rage exploded through her. "You are not going to die!" She clamped her hand beneath his chin, digging her fingers into his jaw. "Do you hear me? You are going to have a son, but only if you live. Do you hear me? You're going to get what you want."

He looked at her through a pained gaze. "Not . . . what . . . I want."

His eyes closed, and she felt his tensed body relax. She wondered if the fever was damaging his brain. A son was what he wanted. All he'd ever wanted. Why was he denying that now?

Near dusk, she heard footsteps along the hallway just before Houston walked into the room. His face told her the verdict long before he was able to speak the words.

"They found him guilty."

Her heart plummeted. "How could they find him guilty? I should have gone to the trial. I should have testified—"

Houston wrapped his hands around the bedpost and leaned his forehead against the scrolled wood. "It wouldn't have made any difference. Not after it came out that he had threatened to kill both Boyd and Duncan. Damn it all, he even went so far as to shoot a bullet into the saloon wall right above Boyd's head and announce that he wanted to rid the ground of Boyd's shadow."

Cordelia slammed her eyes closed.

"I wanted to shake him when I heard that testimony," Houston added.

"This is going to kill Dallas when he's well enough to understand what happened."

"Yep. The sheriff is escorting Austin to the prison in Huntsville tomorrow."

"So soon?"

Houston nodded. "Think the sheriff is afraid that if he waits until Dallas is well, Dallas will interfere." Houston laughed derisively. "He's right."

"I need to talk to Austin."

"I'll watch Dallas. Amelia's cooking supper. Thought we'd stay here tonight, do what we can to help you because we sure as hell can't help Austin."

The jail was built of brick, but it didn't look as grand or as lovely as her hotel. It looked cold, hard, and depressing.

The sheriff's office was small. He sat at his desk, his legs crossed over papers scattered on top. A door at the back stood ajar.

"Reckon you're here to see Austin," he said as he brought himself to his feet.

She nodded, her voice knotting in her throat. She had to be brave, she had to be strong.

He pointed. "You'll find him through that door."

Cautiously, she walked through the door, not certain what to expect. Bars stretching from the floor to the ceiling ran along both sides of the corridor. Other bars divided each side into two. Four jail cells altogether.

Austin was in the last one, leaning against the brick wall, his hands cupping Becky Oliver's face while her fingers clutched his shirt through the bars.

He turned his head slightly and gave Cordelia a halfhearted smile. "Hey, Dee."

The truth of his situation hit her hard. "I'll come back."

"That's all right. Becky was just leaving."

Tears streaming along her cheeks, Becky tilted her head back to look at Austin. "Let me tell them, Austin."

"Shh." He touched his thumbs to her lips. "You just wait for me, sweet thing. Like we talked about."

With a sob, she released her hold on him and skirted past Cordelia. Austin turned his face toward the wall. Cordelia could see his throat muscles straining, working. She gave him time to compose himself before she quietly approached.

"I didn't kill him, Dee," Austin said as he met her gaze.

Reaching out, she trailed her fingers over his bristly cheek. "I know that, Austin. That's the one thing I've never doubted in this whole mess."

He looked as though she had just lifted a weight from his shoulders. "How's Dallas?"

"His fever hasn't broken, but I just left Dr. Freeman. He's going to see what more he can do."

They looked at each other—with so much to be said—but here, with the words traveling between iron bars, too much remained unsaid. Taking a deep breath, Cordelia finally ventured, "You're protecting someone, aren't you?"

Austin dropped his gaze to his boots, the toes sticking through the bars as though searching for freedom.

"Cameron?"

"No."

"If it's the person who killed Boyd—"

"It's not."

"But you were with someone that night, weren't you?"

He continued to stare at the floor, and the truth dawned on her so clearly that she wondered why no one else had thought of it. "Becky," she whispered hoarsely. "You were with Becky."

He lifted his gaze.

She wrapped her hands around the cold bars. "That's what she meant when she said, 'Let me tell them.' Austin, she can vouch for you—"

He shook his head sadly. "It's just five years, Dee. It's not worth ruining her reputation. It's not worth bringing her shame. We want to live here. Raise our children here. I won't have people whispering behind her back."

"But you've been accused of murder. You don't think people will whisper about that?"

"When I get out, I'll figure out who did it, and I'll handle it."

"But, Austin . . . five years."

"Houston married Amelia five years ago, and it seems like yesterday. It's not that long."

"It's an eternity when you have no freedom."

He wrapped his hand around hers. "You tell Dallas to stay clear of this."

Reaching through the bars, she hugged him as fiercely as she could. "You take care of yourself."

"Take care of my violin and my horse. I'll need them both when I come home."

Chapter 21

꒰

CORDELIA WEPT WITH relief when Dallas's fever finally broke near dawn. The pain hadn't gone away with the fever, but they were able to untie him. He was incredibly weak, too weak to sit, but he managed to slurp broth from a spoon that she held to his lips ... over and over ... off and on throughout the day whenever he wasn't sleeping.

While he ate, she prattled, explaining things that had happened since they'd returned to the ranch, carefully avoiding any mention of Austin. She told him about moving the fence back beyond the river, the death of Rawley's father, her plans to add a theater to Leighton.

Talk of the theater made him smile.

Houston and his family remained at the house and took turns seeing to Dallas's needs. To say he was a difficult patient was an understatement.

The third morning after his fever broke, Cordelia walked in the room to find Dallas sitting on the edge of the bed taking short gasps of air, his hands knotted around the mattress, sweat beading his body.

"You shouldn't be up," she scolded as she hurried into the room and set his breakfast tray on the foot of the bed.

"Where's Austin?"

The moment she'd dreaded had finally arrived. All the words she'd practiced saying suddenly seemed trite, insignificant. She knelt in front of him and placed her hands over his. She could see the pain etched in his features, the strain in his muscles. How she hated to add to his pain.

"He's in the prison in Huntsville."

He blanched as though she'd struck the whip against his back again. She tightened her hold on his hands.

"Boyd was murdered. Apparently, before he died, he scrawled Austin's name in the dirt. They sentenced Austin to five years in prison because he had threatened to kill Boyd. And Austin wouldn't say who he was with the night Boyd died."

"Who was he with?" Dallas said through clenched teeth.

Cordelia pressed her forehead to his knee. "He doesn't want anyone to know." She looked up, her eyes pleading. "Give me your word that if I tell you, you won't betray his trust."

He averted his gaze, and she watched him swallow. "Give you my word," he said with resignation.

"Becky Oliver."

"Get my horse saddled."

Cordelia fell to her backside as Dallas stood. "You gave me your word."

"I'm not gonna break my word, but I'll be damned if I'm gonna let him give up five years of his life for a woman."

He took a step, faltered, reached for the bedside table for support, and sent the table and himself crashing to the floor.

He cried out in pain, rolling to his stomach. Cordelia yelled for Houston. He stormed into the room and dropped to his knees beside Dallas, slipping his hands beneath Dallas's arms, trying to help him get to his feet.

"What happened?" Houston asked.

"I told him about Austin," Cordelia said.

Dallas glared at his brother. "Why in the hell didn't you do something?"

"I did all I could do. The evidence was stacked against him, and he wouldn't open his goddamn mouth. The one time he should have opened it, and he kept it closed."

Struggling, Houston finally got Dallas to his feet. Dallas shoved away from him, staggered, and regained his balance.

"Austin told me to tell you to stay out of this. It's his problem and he'll take care of it," Cordelia said.

"He has a hell of a way of taking care of it. Prison, for God's sake."

Dallas walked stiffly across the room, jerked the drapes down, shoved open the door, and stepped onto the balcony. He took a breath of fresh air, fighting off the pain and nausea. He thought his back had been in agony, but the hurt didn't compare to the anguish ripping through his heart.

"There really was nothing we could do," Houston said quietly from behind him. "The judge was lenient with his sentence because of the antagonism that existed between the two families."

Dallas flung his arm in a wide circle. "Look out there. I own it. Every goddamn acre, but it didn't stop my son from dying. It didn't stop someone from abducting my wife. It didn't stop Austin from going to prison for a murder he didn't commit. What the hell good is it?" He bowed his head. "I want to see him, Houston."

"I know you do, but he'd rather you didn't. I know we raised him, and it's hard to see him as anything but our baby brother, but he's a man now. He knew what it would cost him if he held his silence, and he was willing to pay the price. All we can do now is give him a place to come home to."

"What in the hell did he think he was doing?"

"Reckon he thought he was following in our footsteps, doing whatever it took to protect the woman he loves."

Cordelia waited until Dallas's strength returned, until his wounds had healed enough that he could wear a shirt and effectively manage the affairs of his ranch.

Taking a deep breath of fortitude, Cordelia rapped her knuckles on the door to Dallas's office. Her courage faltered when his voice rang out, bidding her to enter.

She would never again step into this room, never again hear his voice booming on the other side. Even as she opened the door, he smiled as he came to his feet. Always the gentleman. Always the man she would love.

She crossed the room as quickly as she could, clutching her hands together. Dallas tapped his pencil on her meticulous notes.

"You took care of a lot of loose ends while I was . . . recovering."

"I tried to manage things as I thought you might. Your men were most helpful." She took a step closer. "Dallas, I've given our situation a great deal of thought—"

"Our situation?"

Her mouth went dry, and she wished she had brought a glass of water into the room with her. "Yes, our situation. Our marriage was one of convenience. The reasons holding it together no longer exist. My family does not deserve, nor will they gain the right to hold your land as their own. And I can't give you a son."

He tossed his pencil onto his ledgers. "Dee—"

"I think we should petition for a divorce," she stated quickly, flatly, before her resolve melted away like a solitary snowflake.

"A divorce? Is that what you want?"

She forced herself to keep her gaze focused on the disbelief mirrored in his eyes, knowing it was the only way he would believe her. "I think it would be best for both of us."

He walked to the window and gazed out over his land. "Do you know what life is like for a grass widow?" he asked, his voice low. Turning, he met her gaze. "No matter what reasons we give, people will question your morals, not mine. They'll blame the failure of our marriage on you, not me. Your prospects for building another business, for finding another husband, will dwindle—"

"Then I'll move to another town, where no one knows me. As long as men continue to lay rails for the trains, towns will flourish along the tracks and hotels will be in demand."

"You're looking at years of hardship—"

"A year ago the thought would have terrified me." Tears rose, and she fought them back. "But I'm a stronger person for having been your wife."

A corner of his mouth lifted. "You were always strong, Dee. You just didn't know it."

At this moment she felt incredibly weak. She wanted to cross the expanse separating them and let him enfold her in his embrace. Instead, she tilted her chin. "I'll leave in the morning."

"Fine." He turned away from her. "If that's what you want."

She didn't want it, but life gave her no choice, not even the illusion of a choice. She wanted Dallas to be happy, and he would never be happy if she stayed by his side.

"About Rawley. I thought it would be best for him if he could stay here."

"I've got no problem with that. He's already drawing wages."

"I'll explain things to him then before I leave. Will I see you in the morning?"

"Probably not. I need to check on my herd."

"Then I'll say good-bye. In spite of the heartache we've suffered, I'll take some cherished memories with me, and I thank you for that."

"Goddammit! I don't want your gratitude." He spun around, anger flaring in his eyes. "I never wanted your gratitude."

"That's too bad because you have it."

A ghost of a smile flitted over his face. "Whatever happened to the shy woman I married, the woman who cowered when I kicked in the bedroom door? You'd probably throw your brush at me now."

"Yes, I think I would." If her fingers hadn't been trembling, she might have gone with her instincts and reached out to comb the wayward lock of hair off his brow. "On your next wedding night, don't kick in the door."

"I won't."

His quietly spoken words hurt far more than she had expected them to. He would have another wedding night, another wife . . . the son he desired—all that she wanted him to have. The knowledge should have filled her with joy, not pain.

"I need to start packing." She walked halfway across the office, stopped, and glanced over her shoulder. "Dallas, next time hand your wife the flowers instead of leaving them on the bed. She might discover them too late."

She strolled out of the room while everything inside her screamed to stay.

Rawley Cooper knew too much about sadness not to recognize it when he saw it.

Miz Dee was about the saddest-looking person he'd ever seen. He thought she might even be sadder than she'd been the night they whipped Mr. Leigh.

She sat on the edge of his bed, wearing a smile that looked like she'd drawn it on a piece of paper and slapped it over her lips. It wasn't warm like her smiles usually were. It didn't reach up and touch her eyes.

At any moment, he expected her to cry, and she was holding his hand so tightly that he was surprised he hadn't heard a bone crack. With trembling fingers, she brushed the hair off his brow. It fell back into place, and she brushed it again, over and over.

"I love you, Rawley," she finally said quietly.

Those were the prettiest words he'd ever heard, and he was afraid he'd be the one who cried. He wished he could say them back to her because he did love her, but the words couldn't get past the pain in his chest.

"I wanted you to know that because I'm going to be leaving, and it has nothing to do with you."

"Leaving?" he croaked.

"Yes, I'm going to build hotels in other towns."

"What about Mr. Leigh?"

"He's going to stay here and take care of you."

"You gonna come back?"

She bit her bottom lip. "No. So I need you to do two very special things for me. I need you to take care of Precious, and I need you to take care of Mr. Leigh. When he has a new wife, I know she will love you as much as I do."

She stood and pulled back the covers. "Now get into bed."

He crawled beneath the blankets. She tucked the ends around his shoulders. Then as always, she leaned down to kiss his forehead. He threw his arms around her neck.

"I love you, Miz Dee. Please don't go."

She hugged him close. "I have to, Rawley. Because I love you and Mr. Leigh, I have to leave."

"He won't let you go. Mr. Leigh won't let you go."

She pulled back, and her gaze roamed over his face as though she were trying to etch it in her mind. "Yes, he will. He always gives me what I want, but I can't give him what he wants."

She pressed a quick kiss to his forehead—a final kiss, the last one he would ever receive—and walked out of the room, closing the door behind her.

A glimmer of moonlight filtered through the window. Rawley could see the key in the lock. He no longer felt a need to turn it.

He rolled to his side, curled into a ball, and watched the shadows dance over the walls. He thought about slipping out of the room, finding

Mr. Leigh, and talking to him man to man about Miz Dee leaving, but he didn't see the point.

Mr. Leigh was a man who knew how to fight for what he wanted. Rawley figured sooner or later, Mr. Leigh would decide on his own that he wanted Miz Dee to stay with him.

The clock downstairs chimed midnight as Cordelia placed the last of her belongings into a box.

Heaving a deep sigh, she stretched to work the ache out of her back. She was incredibly tired, but she knew sleep would elude her. It had ever since Dallas had stopped sleeping in her bed, his body draped over hers.

She had thought about asking him to sleep with her tonight, just to hold her, but she feared it would make her leaving that much harder on them both. The memories of what had been, what might have been, would have been rekindled. As it was, they were slowly fading into glowing embers.

She walked across the room, drew back the drapes, opened the door, and stepped onto the balcony. A million stars twinkled in the black velvety sky. From the top of a windmill, she had viewed the land through Dallas's eyes.

She wondered why she had ever thought it desolate.

She heard a horse whinny and glanced toward the corral. Her heart pounding, she eased closer to the edge of the balcony.

She could see her husband sitting on the corral railing, his shoulders slumped, his head bent.

If she didn't know how strong a man Dallas Leigh was . . . she would have thought he was weeping.

With a painful knot forming in her chest, Cordelia watched as Slim loaded the last of her boxes into the wagon.

She held close to her heart the farewell Rawley had given her last night. It had been so hard to release him, to leave him alone in his room, but her leaving was for the best.

She didn't know what the future held for her, where she would go, what exactly she would do, but she knew Rawley needed stability and he would find it here with Dallas.

Dallas was part of the land, his roots buried deep within the soil.

The bump of the last box hitting the floor of the wagon echoed around her. Her chest tightened in response. Her mouth grew dry, her eyes stinging as she searched for fortitude.

Slim turned and wiped his hands on his trousers. "Well, that's it. You taking your horse?"

Lemon Drop. She had ridden the horse beside Dallas. She nodded.

"I'll get her and your gear, then."

In long strides, Slim began to walk toward the barn. Cordelia heard the front door slam and heavy footsteps resound from the veranda. She had hoped Dallas had gone to check on his herd as he'd said he would last night. She didn't know if she could survive one more farewell.

She pivoted and met Dallas's unflinching gaze. He leaned against the beam, his hands stationed behind his back, his eyes dark, his expression hard. He reminded her of a predatory animal, waiting, waiting to strike.

She intertwined her fingers, searching for the words that would lessen the pain of her departure, but the words remained hidden. She cleared her throat. "Everything is packed. Slim is getting Lemon Drop. I suppose it's all right if I take the horse."

Dallas only glared at her, like a wooden statue in front of a store. If a muscle in his jaw hadn't jerked, she might have thought he'd turned to stone. She took his silence as approval. "Do you want to contact the lawyer or should I?" she asked.

His stare intensified.

"I suppose I should talk with him," she said into the silence permeating the air. "I'll tell him to send word to you regarding the best way to handle this matter. I'm going to stay in our room at the hotel until I decide exactly where I'm going to go. I'm fairly certain that I won't stay in Leighton. I think it would be easier on us if I left. I'll let you know what I decide." The words were running out of her mouth now, and she seemed unable to stop them. She knew the tears would not be far behind. "I wish you all the happiness you deserve."

She spun around and hurried toward the front of the wagon.

"Stay."

The strangled word, spoken in anguish, tore at her heart, ripped through her resolve. She swiped at the tears raining over her cheeks and slowly turned, forcing the painful truth past her lips. "I can't stay. I can no longer give you what you want. I can't give you a son."

Dallas stepped off the veranda and extended a bouquet of wildflowers toward her. "Then stay and give me what I need."

Her heart lurched at the abundance of flowers wilting within his smothering grasp. She shook her head vigorously. "You don't need me. There are a dozen eligible women in Leighton who would happily give you a son and within the month there will be at least a dozen more—"

"I'll never love any of them as much as I love you. I know that as surely as I know the sun will come up in the morning."

Her breath caught, her trembling increased, words lodged in her throat. He loved her? She watched as he swallowed.

"I know I'm not an easy man. I don't expect you to ever love me, but if you'll tolerate me, I give you my word that I'll do whatever it takes to make you happy—"

Quickly stepping forward, she pressed her shaking fingers against his warm lips. "My God, don't you know that I love you? Why do you think I'm leaving? I'm leaving because I do love you—so much. Dallas, I want you to have your dream, I want you to have your son."

Closing his eyes, he laid his roughened hand over hers where it quivered against his lips and pressed a kiss against the heart of her palm.

"I can't promise that I won't have days when I'll look toward the horizon and feel the aching emptiness that comes from knowing we'll never have a child to pass our legacy on to . . ." Opening his eyes, he captured her gaze. "But I know the emptiness you'll leave behind will eat away at me every minute of every day."

"When I was a boy, I went to war searching for glory. I didn't find it. I came here, thinking I'd find glory if I built a ranching empire or a thriving town." He trailed his thumb over her lips. "Instead I discovered that I didn't even know what glory was, not until you smiled at me for the first time with no fear in your eyes."

His gaze swept beyond her, to encompass all that surrounded them. "A hundred years from now, everything I've worked so hard to build will be nothing more than dust blowing in the wind, but if I can spend my life loving you, I'll die a wealthy man, a contented man."

Tears overflowed and spilled onto her cheeks.

"Stay with me," he said.

Nodding mutely, she wrapped her arms around his neck. The flowers floated to the ground as he lifted her into his arms and carried her into the house.

"Your back," she said as he started up the stairs. "You shouldn't be carrying me."

"My back's fine."

It wasn't fine. It would forever carry the scars he'd earned trying to protect her. A hundred times she'd wondered what she might have done differently to prevent his suffering. A hundred times, she could think of nothing.

Inside their room, she slid along his body until her feet touched the floor.

With infinite patience and tenderness, as though they had a lifetime to fill, he removed her clothing, pooling them at her feet. His knuckles skimmed the inside swell of her breast as he gathered the heart-shaped locket he'd given her for Christmas within the palm of his hand.

"I didn't know you were wearing my gift," he said huskily.

"I thought wearing it was the closest I'd come to ever holding your heart."

"You've held my heart for so long that I can't remember when you didn't, but I didn't know how to tell you. I thought if I gave you this, you'd figure it out. Discovered today that the words aren't that hard to say. I love you."

His mouth swooped down to covers hers, kissing her deeply, warmly. He had kissed her before, so many times before, but never like this . . as though her mouth were the only one he'd ever known, as though her lips were the only ones he'd ever teased, as though her kiss were the only one that would ever satisfy him.

He loved her, and as he carried her to the bed, she wondered why she'd never realized it before. He had shown her in so many different ways, enticing her into the sunlight until she cast her own shadow.

He shrugged out of his clothes and lay beside her. She trailed her fingers over his chest and his eyes darkened. She guided her hands to his back and felt the uneven ridges that he would forever carry. Tears welled in her eyes.

He cupped her cheek. "Don't cry."

"I hate that they did this to you."

He kissed her cheek. "You have scars, too. I'd take them away if I could."

But he couldn't. They both knew it. His scars on the outside. Hers on the inside. They had both hovered near death. The scars would serve as a reminder of their triumph.

She braced her palms on either side of his face and held his unwavering gaze. "Dallas, are you sure you can give up your dream without coming to hate me?"

"You were my dream, Dee. I just didn't know it. The part of me that I was always searching for."

His lips found hers, hot and vibrant, full of life, desire. His hands touched and fondled, stoking the dying embers of her passion to a roaring blaze.

She kissed his neck, his chest, running her hands over his chest and lower, boldly stroking, relishing the deep guttural sounds that vibrated within his throat.

They had made love, trying to fulfill a dream. They had made love to celebrate the promise of the dream.

Now, at long last, they were celebrating what they should have gloried in all along: their love for each other.

He captured her gaze as he sank his body into hers. She marveled at the perfection of their joining. Then he began to rock, the brown depths of his eyes smoldering, the fire raging through her, burning brightly until it exploded with a glorious burst of sensations, colors, and sounds, unlike any she'd ever known.

Dallas shuddered above her before collapsing on top of her, his breathing harsh near her ear, his fingers threaded through her hair, gently scraping her scalp.

"I love you," she whispered.

" 'Bout time you gave me my Christmas present," he whispered low, in a tired voice.

"Your Christmas present?"

"That's all I wanted for Christmas. Your love."

She closed her eyes, remembering his words in the hotel room that night so long ago. "Something that could only be given it if wasn't asked for."

Something she would gift him with for the remainder of her life.

Epilogue

May, 1884

*D*ALLAS HEARD HIS wife's scream and bolted out of the chair.
"Sit down!"

With panic raging through him, he stumbled to a stop and glared at his brother.

"Sit down!" Houston ordered again.

Dallas balled his hands into tight fists. "A husband should be with his wife at a time like this."

"You'd just drive her crazy. Hell, you're driving me crazy."

Dallas dropped back into the chair, dug his elbows into his thighs, and buried his face in his hands. "Dr. Freeman said she couldn't have children. Christ, I'll never touch her again."

"You'll touch her," Houston said.

Dallas looked up, determination etched deeply in the lines of his face. "No, I won't."

"Yes, you will. One night, she'll curl up against you, all innocent-like—" Compassion, understanding, and a wealth of sympathy filled Houston's gaze. "You'll touch her."

The door to the office opened, and Rawley slipped into the room as quietly as a shadow. "I thought I heard Ma yell."

Dallas smiled at the boy. His black hair was neatly trimmed, his face scrubbed clean. The dirt and grass stains on his newest coveralls were the only evidence in sight that he wasn't as grown-up as he tried to pretend he was.

They had adopted him in their hearts long before the documents

534

made it legal. Against Dallas's preference, Rawley had kept his last name, mumbling something about not deserving the Leigh name. Dallas hoped with time and patience, the boy would someday change his mind.

Rawley had quickly fallen into the habit of calling Dee "Ma." He had yet to call Dallas anything other than Mr. Leigh. Dallas had a feeling that the boy had a long way to go before he'd trust men.

"Why don't you take Precious for a walk?" Dallas suggested.

Rawley eased farther into the room. "I already took her to play with her friends for a while."

Dallas furrowed his brow. "Her friends?"

Rawley nodded. "Yep. She's got a whole passel of friends out in the meadow. They like to play leapfrog. Only they don't jump over her. They just sorta jump on her. Looks like they keep trying to jump over her, but they just ain't strong enough, I reckon."

"Good God, is she in heat?"

Rawley shrugged. "Reckon she gets hot out there. I do and I ain't got all that fur."

Houston's laughter reverberated around the room. "I'd say before too long, you're gonna be making a whole lot of leashes."

Dallas was on the verge of issuing a threat to silence his brother when Cordelia's scream resounded through the house. Rawley visibly paled and backed into a corner.

Dallas shot out of the chair. "Take care of Rawley."

He rushed out of his office and bounded up the stairs, taking them two at a time. As he neared his room, he could hear a small wail. He staggered to a halt, his heart pounding. He placed his forehead on the door and listened to the lustful cries of his son. A miracle he'd never expected. A child born of the love he shared with Cordelia.

The door opened and Dallas nearly tumbled into the room. He caught his balance as Amelia smiled at him.

"Hello, Papa."

"How is she?" he asked.

"Oh, she's fine."

He peered into his bedroom. Late-afternoon shadows graced the corners. At least his son had the good sense to be born at a decent hour.

"Can I see her?"

"Dr. Freeman is finishing up now."

She took his arm and led him into the room. He felt awkward

standing at the foot of his bed, watching his wife run her fingers over their son's head.

Dr. Freeman snapped his black leather bag closed. He gave Dallas a hard state. "Enjoy this child because you aren't getting any more. I guarantee it. I don't know how she managed to give you this one."

He shuffled from the room, Amelia in his wake. She closed the door behind them, leaving Dallas alone to gaze in wonder at his wife.

She cast a glance his way and smiled shyly. Dallas walked around the bed and knelt beside her. He brushed back a loose strand of her hair. "How are you feeling?"

"Tired, but happy. So happy." Joy lit her face, warmed her eyes.

Dallas gazed at the tiny bundle nestled snugly within her arms. A small head, a scrunched-up face that looked as though it belonged on an old man, and black, black hair. "He sure has a lot of hair."

He shifted his gaze to Dee. Her smile withered, and she brought the child closer to her breast as though to protect it.

"What?" he asked. "What's wrong with him?"

She ran her tongue slowly around her lips. "He's fine. Just fine."

Dallas narrowed his gaze. "No, he's not. I've never known anything to be fine when you say it's fine."

She took a deep breath before blurting, "He's a girl."

"What do you mean he's a girl?"

She gingerly folded back the sides of the blanket. "You have a daughter."

He stared at the spindly legs, the tiny toes, the small chest rapidly taking in air and releasing it. Quickly he covered the child to prevent her from getting chilled. His fingers inadvertently brushed against the child's taut fist. She unfurled her hand and tightly wrapped it around Dallas's finger.

She may as well have flung her arms around his heart.

"I'm sorry," Dee said quietly.

"Sorry?" Dallas croaked.

"I know you wanted a son—"

"I have a son, and now I have a daughter." He trailed his fingers along Dee's cheek. "We have a daughter, and she's beautiful, just like her mother."

Tears welled in her eyes as she laid her palm against his bristled cheek. "I love you so much."

Leaning over his daughter, he pressed his lips to Dee's, kissing her deeply, bringing forth all the love he held for her.

"Will you hit me if I thank you for giving me a daughter?" he asked quietly.

She buried her face against his neck. "No. I was so afraid you'd be disappointed."

"Nothing you give me could ever disappoint me."

A soft rap sounded on the door before it slowly opened. Houston stuck his head into the room. "Rawley's been worried."

Dee waved her hand. "Bring him in."

Rawley shuffled into the room, cautiously approaching until he stood beside Dallas.

"Heard ya scream."

Reaching out, Dee took his hand. "Sometimes, things hurt, but we get wonderful things in return." She turned the baby slightly. "You have a sister."

Rawley scrunched up his face. "A sister?"

"What do you think of her?" Dallas asked.

Rawley glanced up. "Think she's butt ugly."

Dallas grinned. "Give her a few years, and you'll no doubt feel differently."

"What are you gonna call her?"

Dee met Dallas's gaze. "I was thinking of Faith," she said quietly, "to remind us that we should never lose faith in our dreams."

Dallas awoke to the sound of a small cry. The flame burned low in the lamp as he carefully eased away from Dee. He slipped out of bed and, in bare feet, padded to the cradle where he had laid his daughter earlier—after he had bathed her and marveled at her perfection.

Gingerly, he lifted her into his arms. "Hello, sweetheart," he whispered. She stared at him with deep blue eyes, and he wondered if the color would change to brown.

He glanced toward the bed. Dee was curled on her side, her eyes closed, her breathing even.

Quietly, he crossed the room, pulled the curtain back, unlatched the door, and stepped onto the balcony. The warm night air greeted him.

Holding his daughter close with one arm, he pointed toward the distant horizon. "As far as you can see—it all belongs to you, Faith. Someday, I'll take you to the top of a windmill and teach you to dream. When you reach for some of those dreams, you might fall . . . but your mother and I will be there to catch you because that's what love means: always being there. I love you, little girl." He pressed a kiss to his daughter's cheek. "So much . . . it hurts. But I reckon that's part of love, too."

He stood for the longest time, holding his daughter, remembering a time when he'd been a man of small dreams, a man who measured wealth in terms of gold.

"What are you doing?" a sleepy voice asked.

He glanced over his shoulder as Dee sidled against him. "Just showing her the stars and wishing Austin were here."

Dee slipped her arm around his waist and nestled her cheek within the crook of his shoulder. Carefully balancing his daughter within his embrace, he hugged his wife closer against him.

"He should have been here," he whispered through the knot building in his throat. He still didn't understand all that had happened, but in his heart, he knew his brother was innocent.

And there wasn't a damn thing he could do about it. The detective he'd hired had been unable to find any evidence to prove Austin's innocence or another's guilt.

Dee laid her palm against his cheek and turned his head, until their gazes locked. "He chose to hold his silence for whatever reason—"

"It was a damn stupid thing to do, whatever the reason."

She smiled softly. "You'd never do something stupid to protect the woman you love?"

He recognized from the warmth in her eyes that she knew she had cornered him. He had done something stupid: going after her alone, knowing death waited for him. And he knew beyond a doubt that he'd do it again, would risk anything for her. How could he condemn his brother for sacrificing five years of freedom when Dallas would gladly give his life to keep Dee from experiencing any sort of suffering?

Shaking his head, he gazed at the canopy of stars. His daughter would be walking by the time Austin came home. His son would be herding cattle. His wife would be building a theater in Leighton . . . and anything else that struck her fancy.

Drawing Dee more closely against him, falling into the depths of her dark gaze, he allowed himself to be lured into the glory of her love.

Texas Splendor

For my dear niece Terri

The roads we travel in our youth
are seldom smooth.
You traveled a difficult road.
When you could have turned back,
you forged ahead with courage.

May all your future journeys lead you
down roads paved with gold.

Chapter 1

✣

April 1887

MOMENTS STOLEN . . . NEVER to be regained. Memories not worth remembering lingering at the edge of his awareness, unwilling to be forgotten.

Five years of slowly dying.

Austin Leigh stared at the gates of Huntsville Prison, knowing that the remainder of his life waited on the other side, just as he'd left it five years earlier when twelve men he had trusted found him guilty of murder.

After surviving one thousand eight hundred and twenty-five days as a "slave of the state," he once again wore his own clothes. The blue cambric shirt hung loosely from his wide shoulders, and his denim britches threatened to slip past his narrow hips. But they were his, clothes he'd worn at twenty-one when he'd been filled with the vibrancy of youth, when he had foolishly believed that a person had only to reach for a dream in order to obtain it.

In the passing years, no one had laundered the clothes, and when he closed his eyes, he imagined that he smelled a woman's fading vanilla fragrance, felt her slender fingers clutch his shirt one last time, tasted her tears as his lips brushed over hers during an agonizing farewell.

Becky. Sweet Becky Oliver. Within his heart, the distant memories waltzed and he saw her clearly—smiling at him, laughing with him, loving him beneath the stars on a moon-shadowed night. A night when they had given so much to each other, not knowing that another's actions would snatch everything away.

Clanging chains jarred him from his reverie. With loathing, he glared at the guard unlocking the iron cuffs that circled his wrists. The shackles fell away and Austin rubbed the pink scars that had formed over the years.

"Now, then, boy," the guard began, "don't do anything out there that will land you back in here. I might not be so understanding next time."

"Just open the goddamn gate," Austin snarled through clenched teeth.

The guard narrowed his eyes as though contemplating the consequences of striking a man on the verge of regaining his freedom. Then he shoved open the gate. Its creaking hinges echoed in the stillness of dawn.

Austin latched his gaze onto the brightening sky that lay beyond the walls. It appeared untouched by the filth and degradation that existed within the prison. With long strides, he walked into freedom, relishing his first breath of unfetid air. His heart tightened when he caught sight of his two brothers standing in front of three horses.

"You look like hell," Dallas said, his voice strangled with emotions.

Austin wondered when the silver had streaked through Dallas's black hair. The furrows in his brow had deepened and bits of white peppered his thick mustache. "I feel like hell," he said, forcing his mouth to shape a grin.

Dallas jerked him against his chest. "Damn you, boy, what in the hell did you think you were doing?"

Austin worked his way out of his brother's strong grip. The last time he had seen Dallas, his older brother had been fighting for his life. Austin had dreaded the moment when he'd have to face Dallas's uncompromising brown gaze and explain his actions. "What I thought was best."

Turning, he found it easier to meet Houston's gaze. His middle brother had sat behind him during his trial. The war had ravaged Houston's face, but the passing years had treated him more kindly. Or perhaps it was simply that the black leather eye patch remained unchanged so it seemed all else had stayed the same.

Austin had intended to give Houston nothing more than a handshake, but as soon as their roughened palms met, he found himself pulled into a fierce hug. Houston had always been a man of few words, and right now Austin was grateful for his brother's silence. "See you brought Black Thunder."

He freed himself from Houston's hold and mounted the ebony stallion in one lithe, smooth movement, relishing the feel of a horse beneath him. Certain his brothers would follow, he set his heels to Black Thunder's flanks, sending him into a hard gallop.

The road opened up before him, but he feared no matter how fast or far he rode, he'd never truly escape the walls that had surrounded him . . . not until he'd seen Becky. Touched her. Held her. Made her his wife.

Austin's heart swelled as he caught sight of the massive adobe house. He carried the dust of several days' travel, but at this moment, it seemed unimportant.

He was home.

As they neared Dallas's house, Austin saw a girl jump up from the veranda steps and run inside. He drew his horse to a halt and dismounted, his brothers doing the same.

The girl bounded back outside, her blond curls bouncing around her tiny shoulders, her arms flung open wide. "Uncle Austin! You're back!"

She leapt for him, and he swung her up into his arms.

"I'm so glad!" she cried. "I missed you so much!" Her soft rounded cheek brushed against his bristly one, her arms tightly wound around his neck.

He tipped back his head, taking joy in the green glint of her eyes. Houston's oldest daughter had been three years old when he'd left. "Maggie May, when did you grow up?"

"A long time ago. Me and Rawley go to school now."

"Is that so?" He looked past her to the tall boy leaning against the veranda beam, his black hair neatly trimmed, his clothes showing little wear.

"Uh-huh," she assured him.

He set her down and slowly approached Rawley Cooper. It hadn't surprised Austin when Dallas had written to inform him that he and Dee had adopted the boy. "Hear tell that I'm your uncle now."

"You don't gotta be, on account we ain't got the same blood. Only if you wanna be."

Austin pulled the boy close. "Oh, I wanna be."

Why hadn't he realized these children would continue to grow without him around, leaving him to miss out on so much?

He heard the rapid patter of tiny feet as four small girls stampeded through the doorway, their high-pitched voices reminding him of chirping birds. "Pa! Pa! Pa!"

Kneeling, Houston cradled three blond girls against his chest. Amelia had given birth to Laurel the Christmas before Austin went to prison. Amanda and A. J. had been little more than words scrawled in a letter until this moment. The same as Faith, the dark-haired beauty Dallas lifted into his arms.

"You're home!" Dee cried.

Tall and slender, she was a sight for sore eyes as she gracefully glided across the veranda, her smile bright enough to blind a man.

"You've gotten skinny," she said as she embraced Austin and thumped his back.

"They don't cook like you do."

She laughed. Lord, he'd forgotten how true uninhibited laughter washed over a man and filled him with unrestrained joy.

"I don't cook," she reminded him. "Amelia cooks."

She stepped aside. Before he caught his breath, Amelia wrapped her arms around him, hugging him closely. The first woman to come into their lives. God, he loved her . . . almost as much as he loved Becky.

When Amelia moved away, Austin smiled. "I know one of those girls has to be Laurel Joy. She couldn't even crawl when I left. The others weren't even here."

"You'll have plenty of opportunity to get to know them and catch up," Amelia assured him. "Right now, we've got supper waiting."

"Sounds like heaven. I haven't had a decent meal . . . in years."

Amelia and Dee slipped their arms through his and led him into the house. Like a man lost in the wilderness, Austin searched for recognizable sights to guide him toward the welcome haven of familiarity, but he found none. A portrait of Dallas and his family hung on the wall. A new rug ran the length of the hallway.

The girls rushed past him as they entered the dining room. The old oak table was gone, replaced by a longer one that could accommodate the growing family. Dallas and Houston lowered the girls onto tall chairs before taking their places. Maggie patted the empty chair between her and Rawley. "Sit by us, Uncle Austin."

Unexpectedly feeling awkward and out of place, he dropped into the chair. The bowl set before him brimmed with stew, steam spiraling upward. His mouth watered. He hadn't realized how hungry he was. He picked up the spoon, bent forward, and placed his elbows on the table, allowing his arms to circle the bowl, forming a protective barrier around his dinner. He'd slurped two spoonfuls before the hairs on the back of his neck prickled and he realized everyone was staring at him.

He shifted his gaze to Maggie. With wide green eyes, she watched him as though he were a stranger.

"Don't reckon you'll steal my food, will you?" he asked, his voice low, afraid he'd failed miserably at making light of his strange behavior.

She pressed her lips together, her brow creasing as she slowly moved her head from side to side.

Austin straightened and glanced around the table, wondering why he felt so isolated when surrounded by family. "My apologies. I seem to have forgotten how to eat around decent folk."

"No need to apologize," Amelia said. "We're family, for God's sake. You should have eaten at this table for the past five years anyway."

He shifted his gaze to Dallas. They had journeyed to the ranch much as they had traveled through life before Amelia—asking no questions, sharing no sorrows. "Reckon you'll want to talk about that."

Dallas shook his head. "It was your life, your decision. But you should know I hired a detective to find Boyd's killer. Unfortunately he hasn't had any luck."

"He still looking?"

"He's not devoting himself to it any longer, but he keeps an ear to the ground. Whoever killed Boyd knew what he was doing. He didn't leave any evidence."

"Why don't we discuss this after dinner?" Dee suggested.

Reaching out, Dallas covered Dee's hand. "Sorry. Sometimes, it's difficult to remember that Boyd was your brother."

Dallas could not have spoken truer words. Boyd McQueen had possessed a temperament that hinted the devil had spawned him, while Dee had the disposition of an angel.

"I have marble cake waiting in the kitchen," Amelia announced. "We need to eat up so we can enjoy it while it's still warm."

Warm cake and stew, the constant smiles and innocent ways of children. Austin had taken them for granted in his youth, but he was determined to appreciate them from this moment on.

Night had fallen by the time Austin stood on the veranda and watched the wagon filled with Houston's family lumber north. A crescent moon smiled in the black sky, stars winking on either side of it. "I can't believe Houston has a whole passel of girls," Austin said.

Turning his gaze in the direction of the retreating wagon, Dallas leaned against the beam. "I think another one might be on the way. Amelia didn't eat much tonight."

"What about you and Dee? You gonna have any more?"

Dallas slowly shook his head. "Nope. Faith was a miracle we weren't expecting. Reckon a man should consider himself the luckiest of men if he has one miracle in his life."

Austin understood miracles. He had one of his own waiting for him. "Think I'm gonna ride into town."

A silence permeated the air, thick, hovering, as though something needed to be said. Permission, Austin decided. He was waiting for Dallas to give him permission to leave only he didn't require his brother's consent any longer. He was a grown man, free to come and go as he chose. He stepped off the veranda.

"Becky's married," Dallas said quietly.

Austin felt as though someone had plowed a tightly balled fist into his gut. Unable to draw air into his lungs, he feared his knees might buckle. He wrapped his arm around the beam to keep from stumbling down the remaining steps. Swallowing hard, he forced the words past the painful knot that had formed in his throat. "Becky Oliver?"

Dallas faced him squarely. "Yeah."

"Who'd she marry?"

"Cameron."

Cameron McQueen? Dee's brother? Austin swallowed the burning bile that had risen in his throat. "When?"

"About two years ago."

Austin glared at his brother. "Why in the hell didn't you mention that little bit of news in your letters?"

"I didn't figure prison was the best place for you to learn about it."

"You could have told me at any time during the past few days."

"Didn't see any reason to ruin your homecoming."

His homecoming? Without Becky he had no homecoming. He leapt off the porch and hit the ground with a purpose to his stride.

"Where are you going?" Dallas called after him.

"Wherever I damn well want to go," Austin threw over his shoulder as he stalked toward the barn.

He'd never saddled a horse more quickly nor ridden as hard as he rode now. Black Thunder's pounding hooves ate up the distance between Austin . . . and Becky.

As the dim lantern lights of Leighton came into view, burning into the night, Austin jerked back on the reins. The stallion protested the rough treatment and reared up, his neigh echoing over the vast plains. Austin regained control and patted the horse's sweating neck. "Sorry, old man."

He shifted his gaze toward the town. He could make out the silhouette of Dee's Grand Hotel. And the train depot. The railroad tracks had reached the town while he'd been in prison. He saw the outline of buildings he didn't recognize, streets, houses, a town . . . a town he'd once known . . . a town that was now achingly unfamiliar.

And somewhere within that town, beneath the shadows of the night, Becky was lying within the arms of another man.

The pain slashed through him, intense, overpowering.

And the tears he'd held at bay for five long, torturous years finally broke free. Bowing his head, he dug his fingers into his thighs as the sobs wrenched his body.

Becky had deserted him when he had needed her the most . . . and he hadn't even known it.

Memories drew Austin to the general store. Businesses had sprung up on either side of the false-fronted building where Becky Oliver had worked with her father. He resented every structure that smelled of new wood, resented that little had remained the same.

He halted his horse and glared at the sign that still read OLIVER'S GENERAL STORE. Becky had lived in the rooms above. Pale light spilled through the upstairs windows so Austin figured she still lived there— with Cameron.

He dismounted, tethered his horse to the railing, and walked along the alley between the two buildings. He spotted the landing where he'd kissed Becky for the first time. Had Cameron kissed her there? His gut clenched with the thought.

He heard the bump of a crate hitting the ground. As he rounded the corner, within the light cast by the lantern hanging on the back wall of the store, he saw Cameron McQueen heft a wooden crate from the wagon, stack it next to the back door, and reach for another one. If he and Cameron were still friends, he would have given him a hard time about the starched white apron he wore over his crisp white shirt.

Cameron reached for another box, then stilled as though sensing another's presence. He glanced over his shoulder, his blond hair falling across his brow. With his gaze wary, he approached slowly. "Austin, it's good to see you."

"I'll just bet." Austin slammed his knotted fist into Cameron's face. Cameron staggered back and hit the ground with a sickening thud that sounded like a crate of tomatoes bursting open.

"Get up, you sorry son of a bitch!"

Working his jaw back and forth, Cameron rolled over. "I'm not gonna fight you."

"You don't have to fight me, but at least give me the satisfaction of pounding you into the ground."

Cameron pushed himself to his knees, close enough to standing as far as Austin was concerned. He hit him again and sent him sprawling back to the ground. "You were my best friend, damn you! I trusted you!"

Cameron squinted at him, blood trailing along his cheek. "Honest to God, I tried not to love her."

"Not good enough. Stand up."

Cameron struggled to his feet and stood, his arms dangling at his sides like the useless broken blades on a windmill.

"At least put your hands up, give me some satisfaction," Austin commanded.

Cameron shook his head. "You wanna beat the crap out of me, go ahead. I won't stop you."

Impotent rage surged through Austin. He'd beat the crap out of him, all right—and then some. He brought his arm back—

"Cameron!" the sweetest voice called.

Austin snapped his head around. The light from the lantern illuminated Becky as she stood in the doorway, holding a tow-headed boy close against her breast.

She was the prettiest thing he'd ever set eyes on. The stolen years began melting away, just as he'd known they would.

"Pa!" the boy cried, squirming in his mother's arms.

The years came crashing back with a vengeance. She wasn't Becky Oliver, his girl. She was Becky McQueen, his best friend's wife.

"Cameron, aren't you finished yet?" she asked softly.

Austin realized then that the shadows hid him, that the lantern light wasn't touching him. From where she stood, Becky couldn't see him or the blood trailing down Cameron's face.

"I'll be there in a minute," Cameron said quietly, keeping his profile to her.

"Well, don't take too long. Supper's getting cold." She disappeared into the store, and Austin knew she was probably climbing the indoor stairs that led to the second floor, to the home she shared with Cameron.

"Honest to God, Austin, I didn't mean for things to turn out this way," Cameron said, his voice low.

Austin took a menacing step toward him. Cameron flinched but didn't back away. "Think on this," Austin said, his voice seething with the pain of betrayal. "She loved me first."

"Believe me, that thought haunts me night and day."

Austin wished he'd just hit Cameron again and kept his mouth shut. He'd wanted to hurt the man, and he knew by the despair that had plunged into Cameron's blue eyes that he had succeeded. He didn't know why that knowledge brought him no satisfaction but only served to increase his anger over a situation that he was unable to change.

He nodded briskly. "Well, I'm glad to hear it." Abruptly, he spun on his heel and strode through the alley until he reached the boardwalk. He'd never felt more lost in his life.

Although the family had welcomed him home with open arms, he no longer felt a part of them. His brothers had wives, children, and successful businesses. And what did Austin have? Nothing but a tarnished reputation that he should have never possessed.

Stalking down the boardwalk, he was surprised his feet didn't split the boards with the weight of his anger as he headed toward the far end of town where the saloon beckoned.

Smoke thickened the air as he stormed through the swinging doors of the saloon. A huge gilded mirror hanging on the wall behind the bar reflected the patrons who occupied the chairs or stood against the walls.

He felt gazes boring into him, and even in the din of male voices and raucous laughter, he thought he heard people harshly whispering his name. He ambled toward the crowded bar and hooked the heel of his boot on the brass railing that ran the length of the bar. The men closest to him sidled away like he had festering sores covering him. He slapped a coin on the counter. "Whiskey."

The bartender picked up a glass and poured the amber brew, his gaze never leaving Austin. It had always amazed Austin that Beau could serve drinks and never once look to see what he was doing.

"Heard you'd be home soon," Beau said as he eyed Austin warily.

"Well, you heard right." Austin crossed his arms on the bar and leaned forward slightly.

Beau set the full glass in front of him. "I don't want no trouble in here."

"I don't plan to start any," Austin assured him.

With a brusque nod, Beau ambled to the far end of the counter, wiping the shining wood as he went. An icy shiver skittered along Austin's spine. He despised the sensation of being watched and judged. In prison, guards had glared at him, dogs had followed his every movement, other prisoners had scrutinized him and measured him against their own low standards.

He jerked his head around and locked his blue glare onto Lester Henderson. The portly banker stood at the bar, his dark eyes set in a face that greatly resembled bread dough. Averting his gaze, Lester downed the remainder of his beer. He wiped a pudgy hand across his mouth, straightened his shoulders, and approached Austin.

"I had no choice but to vote guilty," Henderson said, his voice hitching. "The evidence—"

"I know what the evidence was. I was at the goddamn trial."

"Can't give a loan to a man fresh out of prison—"

"Did I ask for a loan?"

"No, but I just wanted to save you from asking." Henderson scurried away like a squirrel that had spotted the last pecan on the ground.

Austin wrapped his fingers around the glass of whiskey and studied the contents. As soon as he finished the whiskey, he'd set about clearing his name. He didn't anticipate that it would take long. He had always known that Duncan McQueen had pinned the blame on him.

He brought the glass to his lips, tipped his head back, and caught the reflection of a raised knife in the mirror.

He moved swiftly, but not quickly enough. Agonizing pain tore through his back. He darted to the side, spun around, and plowed his fist into Duncan McQueen's face before the man could strike again. As Duncan staggered back, Austin grabbed the hand holding the knife and slammed it hard against the wooden counter. The knife clattered to the floor.

Austin caught an unexpected fist just below his jaw. Pain ricocheted through his head as his knees buckled. He hit the floor hard, blackness encroaching on his vision. He scrambled to his knees, struggling to get to his feet, the bitter taste of blood filling his mouth.

"You bastard!" Duncan roared before lunging for Austin.

Austin reversed his efforts, dropped to his side, and kicked Duncan in the knee. Grunting, Duncan fell to the floor and grabbed the knife. Hatred burned brightly within his dark eyes as he jumped to his feet. "Five years! That's all they gave you for murdering my brother because Dallas owns this part of the state. They should have hanged you!" He brandished the bloodied knife in the air. "I reckon it's up to me to deliver the justice you deserve."

"Not in my saloon!" Beau said as he rounded the corner of the bar, gun in hand. He shoved Duncan on the shoulder. "Back up."

His head pounding, his back throbbing, Austin struggled to his feet and glared at Duncan. "What the hell are you ranting about, Duncan? You killed Boyd and made it look like I did it."

"Don't see how that could be," Beau said in a slow drawl. "Duncan showed up here in the late afternoon and sat in that corner right over there until dawn, getting drunk."

"Why would I kill my brother?" Duncan asked, loathing laced through his voice.

That was the one answer Austin didn't have.

"Everyone knows you murdered him," Duncan snarled.

Austin scrutinized the men who had gathered around the bar. The knowledge in their eyes spoke louder than Duncan's words. He saw no doubts. Not one questioning look. He saw nothing but absolute certainty staring back at him. They all thought he had murdered Boyd McQueen.

"Why the hell else would my brother have written your name in the dirt before he died?" Duncan demanded.

Why indeed?

Austin sat on the back steps of Dallas's house and stared at the moon. He rolled his shoulders, grimacing at the pain caused by the movement. After leaving the saloon, he had stopped at the doctor's house, but the man hadn't been there. By the time Austin had arrived home, the bleeding had stopped so he'd simply changed shirts. No need to alarm his family. They'd had enough worry the past five years. Besides, he'd survived worse in prison.

He heard the door open and the echo of soft footfalls. Looking over his shoulder, he watched Dee sit beside him on the step.

"You were right. You told me five years was an eternity when a person has no freedom," he said into the stillness of the evening.

Using her fingers, she brushed the dark strands of hair off his brow. "Not all prisons come with walls. Dallas was the key that unlocked mine."

Austin shifted his gaze to the canopy of stars, allowing a companionable silence to ease in around them.

"What's their son's name?"

"Andrew. We call him Drew," Dee said quietly.

"I hit his father this evening."

"I'm not altogether certain Cameron didn't deserve that." She placed her hand over his. "But I know how much he loves Becky. I think he may have loved her before you went to prison."

"That doesn't make what he did right."

She sighed. "I know this is difficult for you, but Dallas forgave Houston for taking Amelia from him. Maybe in time, you can forgive Cameron—"

"My situation is completely different from Dallas's. All he gave Amelia was a train ticket. I gave Becky my heart and five years of my life."

"Becky offered to testify that she was with you the night Boyd was killed, but you wouldn't allow it. You can't blame her now for the years you spent in prison. That's not fair."

"Life *is never* fair, Dee. Having Houston and Dallas for brothers should have taught me that a long time ago, but I had to learn it on my own." He looked toward the distance. "So much has changed. Everything is different from what I expected it to be."

"Not everything. Your violin is the same. I kept it for you just like you asked. I was hoping you'd play something for me tonight."

He glanced at the silhouette of the instrument resting in her lap. "I don't hear the music anymore, Dee. While I was in prison, it just shriveled up and died."

He shoved himself to his feet and walked to the barn. He needed to ride, to feel the wind rushing against his face. He had finished saddling Black Thunder when he heard a thump and grunt come from the back of the barn. He strode to the back room and peered inside. Rawley struggled to move a box. "Shouldn't you be in bed?" Austin asked.

Rawley spun around, his face burning bright red. "I wanted to get this room cleaned first. Gotta earn my keep."

Austin leaned against the door frame. "Rawley, you always worked harder than I ever did, and Dallas never kicked me out."

"You're blood, I ain't." Rawley walked to the worktable and began to put away tools someone else had left out.

"That doesn't matter to Dallas—"

"Matters to me."

Austin studied the boy as he straightened the room. "Is that why you didn't take Dallas's name when he adopted you?"

Rawley stilled. "I just figured it was best is all." He peered at Austin. "I've always wondered . . . what did you do to get a town named after you?"

Austin smiled. "I don't have a town named after me."

"Sure you do. I went through a town named Austin once."

"The capital? It's the other way around. I'm named after it. Our pa named us after towns—" Austin's mind reeled with possibilities. "Sweet Lord."

"What?" Rawley asked.

"I gotta go." Austin raced through the barn, mounted Black Thunder, and galloped into the night.

An hour later, he pounded on the door of the second floor landing over the general store. When it opened, his voice lodged in his throat. Why hadn't he considered that he might see Becky if he came here? Why did the pain have to slice through his heart, ripping open the fresh wound?

God Almighty, he wished he could hate her. He wanted to shake her. He wanted to yell at her. But most of all, he wanted to hold her, her body flush against his, her warmth thawing the chill that permeated his soul.

"I need to talk to Cameron," he croaked.

The shock reflected in her blue eyes quickly gave way to anger. Becky planted her hands firmly on his chest and shoved hard, causing him to stumble backward. "Well, he doesn't need to talk to you. How dare you hit—"

"Becky!"

She pivoted around. Cameron stood in the doorway, one eye discolored and swollen. "Drew's calling you. I'll take care of this."

Austin watched her jaw tighten before she gave him a scathing glare and shouldered her way past Cameron to go inside.

"Did you want to come in?" Cameron asked.

Austin shook his head, wondering why he'd come to the man who had betrayed him. He walked to the railing and stared at the town, light from the lanterns fighting the darkness. Cameron's quiet, hesitant footsteps as he came to stand beside Austin brought back memories of confidences shared.

"All these years I thought Duncan had shot Boyd and arranged the evidence to put the blame on me." He glanced sideways at the friend from his youth, suddenly realizing that losing Cameron's friendship hurt almost as much as losing Becky's love. "But our paths crossed this evening and I realized I was wrong. Rawley said something, though, that got me to thinking. What if Boyd didn't write my name in the dirt—"

"He did. Sheriff Larkin took me to the place where he found Boyd. He'd written your name in the dirt as plain as day."

"What if he didn't mean me, but meant the town? What if he didn't know the name of the man who killed him, but he knew that he came from Austin?"

"That's grasping at straws, isn't it?"

"That's all I've got," Austin said. "People avoid me like I have tick fever or something worse. I knew the men on the jury had voted guilty because of the evidence, but I never thought they actually believed deep down that I murdered Boyd. I've got to prove I'm innocent, and I can only do that if I figure out who killed him. Did he have any business in Austin?"

"Boyd never confided in me. Sometimes he'd leave for a few days, but he never divulged where he went."

Austin took a few steps back. "Reckon it won't hurt to ride into Austin and see if I can find out anything."

"Guess I'd do the same if I were in your boots, but watch your back. If the man who killed Boyd *is* in Austin, I don't imagine he's going to welcome the prospect of being found."

Austin turned for the stairs, halted, and glanced over his shoulder. "If I ever hear that Becky isn't happy, I'll finish what I started out back this evening."

Cameron held his gaze. "Fair enough."

Austin hurried down the remaining steps. Some bastard had stolen five years of his life. Austin intended to make damn sure he paid dearly for every moment.

Chapter 2

❧

S WEARING VICIOUSLY, AUSTIN glared at the jagged cut on the underside of Black Thunder's hoof. He released the horse's foreleg, unfolded his aching body, and jerked his dusty black Stetson from his head. Exhausted, resenting the dirt working its way into every crease of his body, he stood beneath the April sun feeling as though he'd stepped into the middle of August.

Using the sleeve of his cambric shirt, he wiped the sweat beading his brow, grimacing as pain erupted across his back—from the middle of his left shoulder to just below his ribs. He had expected the gash he'd received during the brawl with Duncan to have healed by now, but he supposed riding all day, late into the night, and sleeping on the ground hadn't been the best treatment for the wound. When he had ridden out of Leighton several days before, he hadn't considered that he'd have no way to clean or tend the injury. Only one thought had preyed on his mind: The city of Austin might hold the key that would lead him to Boyd's killer, the man whose guilt would prove Austin's innocence.

Slipping his fingers into the pocket of his vest, he pulled out the map Dallas had given him. Wearily he studied the lines that marked the start of his journey and his final destination. He stuffed the wrinkled paper back into his pocket. He wouldn't reach the town tonight.

Settling his hat low over his brow, he sighed heavily. He was in no mood to walk, but the stallion's injury left him no choice. Gazing toward the distance, he saw smoke spiraling up through the trees. He threaded the reins through his fingers and trudged into the woods.

Shafts of sunlight and lengthening shadows wove through the branches, offering him some respite from the damnable heat. With a sense of loss, he remembered a time when he would have appreciated the simple beauty surrounding him. Now he just wanted to get to where he was going.

He heard an occasional thwack as though someone were splitting wood. With the abundance of trees and bushes, he didn't imagine anyone had to depend on cow chips for a fire.

A wide clearing opened up before him. Lacy white curtains billowed through the open windows of a small white clapboard house. The weathered door stood ajar. Near the house, a scrawny boy wearing a battered hat, threadbare jacket, and worn britches struggled to chop the wood. A large dog napped beneath the shade of a nearby tree. The varying hues of his brown and white fur reminded Austin of a patchwork quilt. As Austin cautiously approached, the dog snapped open its eyes, snarled, and rose slowly to its full height, curling back its lips and deepening its growl.

Moving quickly, the boy dipped down, swung around, and pointed a rifle at Austin. Austin threw his hands in the air. "Whoa! I'm not looking for trouble."

"What are you lookin' for?"

"Austin. How far is it from here?"

"Half a day's ride on a good horse." The boy angled his head, the rumpled brim of his hat casting shadows over his face. "Your horse looks to be favoring his right leg."

The boy's insight caught Austin off-guard, although he certainly admired it. "Yep. He cut his hoof on a rock. Your folks around?"

The boy gave a brisk nod. "And my brother. I'd feel a sight better if you'd take off the gun."

Austin untied the strip of leather at his thigh and slowly unbuckled the gunbelt. Cautiously removing the holster, he laid the weapon on the ground, his gaze circling the area. He wondered where the rest of the family was working. He saw no fields that needed tending or cattle that needed watching. The aroma of fresh baked bread and simmering meat wafted through the open door of the house. "Something sure smells good."

"Son-of-a-gun stew."

"Think you could sneak me a bowl if I finish chopping that wood for you?"

The boy shifted his gaze to the wood scattered around an old tree stump, then looked back at Austin. "What's your business in Austin?"

"Looking for someone."

"You a lawman?"

"Nope. My horse is hurt. I've been walking longer than I care to think about. I'm tired, hot, and hungry. I can chop that wood twice as fast as you can, and I'm willing to do it for one bowl of stew. Then I'll be on my way."

Slowly, the boy relaxed his fingers and lowered the rifle. "Sounds like a fair trade."

Rolling his sleeves past his elbows, Austin strode to the tree stump. Ignoring the snarling dog that lumbered in for a closer inspection of his boots, Austin picked up the ax, hefted a log onto the stump, and slammed the ax into the dry wood. He stifled a moan as fiery pain burst across his back. When he reached his destination, his first order of business would be to find a doctor.

"I'm gonna take your gun," the boy said hesitantly. "And your rifle."

"Fine. There's a Bowie knife in the saddlebags." He didn't begrudge the boy his cautions, but he longed for the absolute trust he'd once taken for granted. Hearing the boy's bare feet fall softly over the ground as he walked to the house, Austin glanced over his shoulder. The boy had grabbed his saddlebags as well.

Austin glared at the dog. "Your master ain't too trusting, is he?"

The dog barked. Austin glanced to his left and spotted a hen house and a three-sided wooden structure that offered protection to a milk cow. He found that odd since the property had a huge barn.

He heaved the ax down into the wood, wondering if he was wasting his time traveling to the capital city. If he had any sense, he'd head home and try to rebuild a life that never should have been torn down. But stubborn pride wouldn't allow him the luxury of turning back. His family believed he was innocent. Becky knew he was innocent. But the doubts would forever linger in everyone else's minds.

When he had split and stacked enough wood to last the family a week, he ambled to the house, dropped to the porch, and leaned against the beam that supported the eve running the width of the house. The dog strolled over, stretched, yawned, and worked its way to the ground near Austin's feet.

"Changed your mind about me, did you?"

Lifting its head, the dog released a small whine before settling back into place. Austin was sorely tempted to curl up beside the dog and sleep. Instead, he looked toward the horizon where the sun was gradually sinking behind the trees. While serving his time, he'd hated to see the sun go down. He had despised the night. Loneliness had always accompanied the darkness.

"Here's your meal," the boy said from behind him.

Austin glanced over his shoulder, his outstretched hand stopping halfway to its destination. The air backing up in his lungs, he slowly brought himself to his feet. The britches and bare feet were the same, but everything else had changed. The crumpled hat and shabby jacket were gone. So was the boy.

"What are you staring at?" an indignant voice asked.

Austin could have named a hundred things. The long, thick braid of pale blond hair draped over the narrow shoulder. The starched white apron that cinched the tiniest waist he'd ever seen. Or her eyes. Without the shadow of the hat, they glittered a tawny gold.

He tore his Stetson from his head and backed up a step. "My apologies, ma'am. I thought you were a boy."

A tentative smile played across her lips. "It's easier to get the work done when I'm wearing my brother's britches. Besides no one's usually around to notice."

"What about your family?"

A wealth of sadness plunged into the golden depths of her eyes. "Buried out back."

So they were *around* as she'd told him, but not in a position to help her. She extended the bowl toward him.

"Here. Take it."

He reached for the offering, his roughened fingers touching hers. They both jerked away, then scrambled to recapture the bowl, their heads knocking together. Cursing as pain ricocheted through his head, Austin snaked out his hand and snatched the bowl, effectively halting its descent. The stew sloshed over the sides, burning the inside of his thumb.

"Damn!" He shifted the bowl to his other hand and pressed his thumb against his mouth. He peered at the woman. Her eyes had grown wide, and she was wiping her hands on her apron. He remembered the many times Houston had scolded him for swearing in front of Amelia, and he felt the heat suffuse his face. "My apologies for the swearing," he offered.

She shook her head. "I should have warned you that the stew is hot. I'll get a cool cloth."

Before he could stop her, she'd disappeared into the house. Austin dropped onto the porch, wondering if he had a fever. How could he have possibly mistaken that tiny slip of a woman for a boy?

He thought if he pressed her flush against him, the top of her head would fit against the center of his chest. Incredibly delicate, she reminded him of the fine china Dee now set on her table. One careless thump would shatter it into a thousand fragments.

He saw a flash of dung colored britches just before the woman knelt in front of him. She took his hand without asking and pressed a damp cloth to the red area. "I put a little oil on the cloth. That should draw out the pain."

Her voice was as soft as a cloud floating in the sky, and again he wondered how he had mistaken her for a boy. Lightly, her hand held his, but he still felt the calluses across her palm. Her fingernails were short, chipped in a place or two, but clean. And her touch was the sweetest thing he'd known in five years.

She peered beneath the cloth. "I don't think it's gonna blister." She touched her finger to the pink scar that circled his wrist. "What happened here?"

Austin stiffened, his throat knotting, and he wished he'd taken the time to roll down his sleeves after he'd finished chopping the wood. He considered lying, but he'd learned long ago the foolishness of lies. "Shackles."

She lifted her gaze to his, her delicate brow furrowing, anxiety darkening her eyes, imploring him to answer a question she seemed hesitant to voice aloud.

He swallowed hard. "I spent some time in prison."

"For what?" she whispered.

"Murder."

He had expected horror to sweep across her face, would not have blamed her if she had run into the house to fetch her rifle. Instead, she continued to hold his gaze, silently studying him as though she sought some secret long buried. He considered telling her that he hadn't killed anyone, but he'd learned that the voices of twelve men spoke louder than one. Unfortunately, until he proved someone else had killed Boyd McQueen, he was the man who had.

"How long were you in prison?" she finally asked.

"Five years."

"That's not very long for murder."

"It's long enough."

Releasing his hand and his gaze, she eased away from him. "You should eat. You earned it."

He gave a brusque nod before delving into the stew. She sat on the bottom step of the porch and put one foot on top of the other. She had the cutest toes he'd ever seen. The second toe was crooked and pointed away from the big toe like a broken sign giving directions to a town.

She hit her thigh. "Come here, Digger."

The dog trotted over and nestled his head in her lap. With doleful eyes, he looked at Austin.

"Digger?" Austin asked.

She buried her fingers in the animal's thick brown and white fur. "Yeah, he's always digging things up. Do you have a name?"

"Austin Leigh."

"I thought that's where you were headed."

"It is. I was born near here. My parents named me after the town."

"Must get confusing."

"Not really. Haven't been back in over twenty years." He returned his attention to the stew, remembering a time when talking had come easy, when smiling at women had brought such pleasures.

"I'm Loree Grant."

"I appreciate the hospitality, Miss Grant." He scraped the last of the stew from his bowl.

"Do you want more stew?" she asked.

"If you've got some to spare."

She rose, took his bowl, and walked into the house. The dog released a little whimper. Austin reached out to stroke the animal. A wave of dizziness assaulted him. He grabbed the edge of the porch and breathed deeply.

"Are you all right?"

He glanced over his shoulder. Loree stood uncertainly on the porch, the bowl of fresh stew in her hand. He brought himself to his feet, afraid what he'd already eaten wasn't going to stay put. "Reckon one bowl was plenty. Sorry to have troubled you for the second. I was wondering . . . with night closing in . . . if you'd mind if I bedded down in your barn."

Wariness flitted through her golden eyes, but she gave him a jerky nod.

"'Preciate it. You can hold on to the saddlebags and guns until morning if it'll help ease your fears about my staying. Before I head out, let me know what chores I can do as payment for the roof over my head."

He strode toward Black Thunder, hoping he could get the horse settled before he collapsed from exhaustion.

He didn't have the eyes of a killer. Loree repeated that thought like a comforting litany as she sat crossed-legged on her bed, the loaded rifle resting across her lap, her gaze trained on the door.

Five years ago, she'd looked into the eyes of a killer. She knew them to be ruthless and cold. Austin Leigh's eyes were neither. She shifted her attention to the fire burning in the hearth. In the center, where the heat burned the hottest, the writhing blue flames reflected the color of his eyes. Eyes that mirrored sorrow and pain. She wondered if any of the creases that fanned out from the corners of his eyes had been carved by laughter.

Hearing thunder rumble in the distance, she hoped the storm would hold off until he'd left, but she thought it unlikely. The clock on the mantel had only just struck midnight.

The barn roof had more holes than the night sky had stars. Still it would offer him more protection than the trees. And he probably had a slicker. All cowboys did, and he certainly looked to be a cowboy. Tall and rangy with a loose-jointed walk that spoke of no hurry to be anywhere.

The rain began to pelt the roof with a steady staccato beat. She cringed. The nights were still cool, but he hadn't asked for additional blankets or a pillow, and he couldn't build a fire inside the barn. She cursed under her breath. He wasn't her worry. He was a murderer, for God's sake.

If only he had the eyes of a murderer. Then she could stop worrying about him and worry more about herself. If only his eyes hadn't held a bleakness as he'd spoken of prison. She wondered whom he had killed. If he'd had good reason to murder someone.

She tightened her fingers around the rifle. Did any reason justify murder? She had asked herself that question countless times since the night the killer had swooped down on them. The answer always eluded her. Or perhaps only the answer she wanted eluded her.

She slid off the bed and walked to her hope chest. She knelt before it and set the rifle on the floor. She ran her hand over the cedar that her father had sanded and varnished to a shine for her fourteenth birthday. For three years she had carefully folded and placed her dreams inside . . . until the night when the killer had dragged her to the barn. Her dreams had died that night, along with her mother, father, and brother.

The rain pounded harder. The wind scraped the tree branches across the windows. The thunder roared.

She lifted the lid on the chest for the first time since that fateful night. Forgotten dreams beckoned her. She trailed her fingers over the soft flannel of a nightgown. She had wanted to feel delicate on her wedding night so she had embroidered flowers down the front and around the cuffs. She had tatted the edges of her linens and sewn a birthing gown for a child that she now knew would never be.

The killer had charged into her life with the force of a tornado. He had stolen everything, and when she'd tried to regain a measure of what he'd taken—he had delivered his final vengeance. With one laugh, one hideous laugh that had echoed through the night, he had shattered her soul.

She slammed down the lid and dug her fingers into her thighs. She had no future because the past kept a tight hold on her present.

She rose to her feet, walked to the hearth, and grabbed the lantern off the mantel. Using the flame from the lamp, she lit the lantern. She jerked her slicker off the wall and slipped into it, calling herself a fool.

Then she walked to the corner and pulled two quilts from the stack of linens. Digger struggled to his feet, his body quivering from his shoulders to his tail.

"Stay!" she ordered. His whine tore at her heart. The dog got his feelings hurt more easily than the town spinster. Loree softened her voice. "If you get wet and muddy, I won't be able to let you back in. I won't be long." She stepped outside. Lightning streaked across the obsidian sky. Rain pelted the earth. The barn was as black as a tomb. She couldn't remember if a lantern still hung in the barn. She shivered as memories assailed her.

Satan had risen from the bowels of Hell and made their barn his domain. It had been raining that night as well, and the water had washed their blood into the earth.

She pressed her back against the door. She hadn't gone into the barn since. Her mouth grew dry, her flesh cold. So cold. As cold as the death that had almost claimed her.

Austin Leigh wasn't her worry, but the words rang hollow. Her mother would have invited him into the house and provided him with shelter and warmth. Her mother's innocent words flowed through her. "There are no strangers in this world, Loree. Only friends we haven't yet met."

Reaching deep down, she gathered her courage. Clutching the quilts, with the lantern swinging at her side, Loree darted to the barn, hopping over puddles, landing in others. She stumbled to a stop in the doorway of the barn. "Mr. Leigh?"

She raised the lantern. The shadows retreated slightly, hovering just beyond the lantern's pale glow. With all the holes in the roof, the barn resembled a cavern filled with waterfalls. Bracing herself against the memories, she took a step. "Mr. Leigh?"

She had sold all her animals except for one cow and a few chickens. She heard his horse snort and saw it standing in the distant stall. Using the lantern to light her way, she peered in the stalls she passed until she reached the stallion, secured in the driest area of the barn. How could a man who placed his horse above himself be a murderer?

Holding the lantern higher, she gazed inside the stall. The horse nudged her shoulder. "Where is your owner?"

The animal shook his head.

"You're a big help." She turned at the sound of a low moan. The glow from the lantern fanned out to the opposite stall, revealing a man curled against the corner, lying on his side, knees drawn up, arms pressed in close against his body. She eased toward the stall. "Mr. Leigh, I brought you some quilts."

His only response was a groan. Stepping inside the stall, she noticed that his clothes were soaked and he was visibly trembling. Hugging the quilts, she knelt beside him. Tiny rivulets of water ran down his face. He had removed the vest that he'd been wearing earlier and tucked it beneath his head. His drenched shirt hugged his body, outlined the curve of his spine, the narrowness of his back. "Mr. Leigh?"

Slowly he opened his eyes. "Miss Grant, I wouldn't hurt you."

"I realize that."

"Do you?" He released a short laugh. "You don't trust me because I've been in prison. A man makes choices in his life, and he's gotta learn to live with them. But he doesn't always know what those choices are gonna cost. It'd help if we knew the price before we made the decision."

The anguish reflected on his face, limned by the lantern light, made her want to draw him within her arms, to comfort him as she had her brother when he was a boy. It had never occurred to her that he would be offended if she took his weapons. She wished she could have overlooked them, but he had worn the gun so easily. "I'm sorry."

His lips curled into a sardonic smile. "You didn't send me to prison. Did that to myself." He raised up on an elbow and leaned toward her, the smile easing into oblivion. "You know the worst part? The loneliness. You ever get lonely, Miss Grant?"

"All the time," she whispered as she set the lantern aside, shook out a quilt, and draped it over his back. Shaking as he was, the warmth of his body surprised her. She pressed her hand against his forehead. "My God, you're hot. Are you ill?"

"A man didn't think my five years in prison was a just punishment. He thought I should pay with my life. He cut me across my back. I think it might be festering."

"We need to get you into the house so I can look at it."

"Wouldn't be . . . proper."

Curiosity sparked within her, making her wonder at the circumstances that had caused a man who worried about her respectability to commit murder. People appeared to kill with little provocation: a card skimmed from the bottom of the deck instead of the top, a small half-truth that blossomed into an ugly lie.

"I thank you for your concern over my reputation, but no one's around to notice." Grabbing his arms, she struggled to get him to his feet. Groaning, he staggered forward before catching his balance. She picked up the lantern. "Lean on me," she ordered.

"I'll crush you."

"I'm stronger than I look."

He slung an arm over her shoulders, and she locked her knees into place.

"I'm heavier than I look," he said, his voice low, but she almost thought she heard a smile hidden within it.

She slipped her arm around his waist. "Come on."

The quilt fell from his shoulders, wedged between their bodies, and trailed in the mud as they trudged toward the house. The wind howled, slinging the stinging rain sideways. The porch eaves couldn't protect them from the merciless storm. She let go of the man and released the latch on the door. The wind shoved the door open, nearly taking her arm with it. She pulled on Austin Leigh. "Get inside!"

He stumbled into the house. She followed him, slammed the door, and jammed the bolt into place, imagining she heard the wind howl its protest. Digger lifted his head, released a small whine, and settled back down to sleep.

Loree stared at the man standing in her house, wondering what in the world she thought she was going to do with him now. He looked ready to collapse at any moment. She set the lantern on the table and pulled out a chair. "Sit down."

He obeyed, hunching his shoulders and wrapping his arms around himself. She stepped behind him and cringed when she saw the brown stain on the back of his shirt. She might have noticed it earlier if he hadn't been wearing a vest.

"Let's get your shirt off." With trembling fingers, she unbuttoned his shirt, pulled the ends free of his trousers, and worked the clinging shirt off his body. Then she studied the long jagged pus-filled gash. Red irritated flesh surrounded it, and she wondered briefly how he had managed to chop her wood. "I'm going to have to lance it. Let's get you into bed."

She helped him to his feet. He followed without complaint as she led him into her bedroom. "Can you finish undressing yourself?" He stood, enfolded in silence. She cradled his roughened bristled cheeks between her hands. Images of doing the same thing to her father just before she had kissed him good night as a child swamped her. "Listen to me. You have to get out of these wet clothes and into bed. Can you do that?"

He gave a short nod as though even that was too much effort.

"Good." She hurried to the closet, pulled out a towel, and tossed it on the bed. "You can use that to dry off. I'm going to prepare some hot salt water to draw out the infection after I've lanced it. I'll be back in a few minutes." She slipped out of the room, clicking the door closed.

Austin dropped onto the edge of the bed and tugged off his boots, grimacing as the pain assaulted him. He should have realized his back was festering and sought out a doctor before now, but clearing his name had made everything else seem insignificant.

He struggled out of his soaked trousers, discarding them on the floor. Ignoring the towel, he crawled into the bed, drew the blankets up to his waist, and rolled onto his stomach. The next few minutes were going to be unpleasant, but at least he'd be in the company of a pretty lady.

A soft tap sounded against the door before it opened a crack. "Are you in bed?" she asked quietly.

He forced the word past his thick tongue. "Yep."

She walked into the room and set the bowl and a knife on the bedside table. Frowning, she eased onto the bed and touched his cheek. "You didn't dry yourself."

He thought about telling her he was lucky to have made it to the bed, but he didn't think it was worth the effort. She reached for the towel and gently patted the moisture from his face, the furrows in her brow deepening. The towel kept catching on the stubble covering his jaw, and he wished he'd taken the time to shave that morning. She leaned closer, the soft swell of her small breast pressing against his shoulder as she wrapped the towel around strands of his hair and squeezed out the rain. Closing his eyes, he inhaled her sweet scent and was reminded of the blue-flower-coated hills he'd been traveling.

Her touch was gentle, careful as though she thought she might hurt him. How many times in the past five years had he thought of Becky touching him like this? When he'd longed for a hot bath that he knew was years away, he'd think of taking it with her, drying her off afterward, standing still as she dried him. Then they would make love until dawn, slowly, leisurely, the way they should have done it the first time.

He opened his eyes, the burning behind them increasing, and he feared it had little to do with his fever. Tenderly, the woman touched his cheek, the concern in her eyes drawing the words from his ravaged heart. "Why didn't she wait?"

She leaned closer until he saw the black rings that circled the gold of her eyes. "Who?"

"Becky. She promised to wait till I got out of prison . . . but she married Cameron." He squeezed his eyes shut, wishing she'd left the rain on his face so his tears would have a place to hide.

Loree had never seen a man cry. She didn't think this man usually gave in to tears. His fever, his pain were lowering walls she would have preferred remain in place. The woman inside her who would never know so deep a love ached for this man, and she found herself wishing that a woman she knew nothing about had waited for him.

He buried his face in the pillow. "Just do what you gotta do and be done with it," he croaked.

She wondered if he realized she had taken the time to dry his face and hair so she could put off the unpleasant task that awaited her. She didn't relish the thought of cutting into his flesh. She allowed her gaze to roam the length of his bare back. A few scars indicated he was no stranger to pain. She wondered what he had done to deserve the beating, if the woman who had abandoned him knew all that he had suffered.

Her gaze came to an abrupt halt where the sheet met his narrow hips. She swallowed hard. Beneath the sheet was nothing but flesh. She grabbed a quilt and draped it over the outline of his legs and buttocks, as though doing so would clothe him. She pressed her hands together to stop their trembling. "I'll be as gentle as I can. I know it's going to hurt, but try not to move."

He bunched his fists around the pillow, the corded muscles of his back tightening. Taking a deep breath of fortitude, she picked up the knife and pricked his wound. He flinched. "I'm sorry," she whispered repeatedly as she lanced the long gash. Then she took the cloth she had left to soak in the hot salt water and applied it to the injury.

She heard his breath hiss between his teeth. "I'm sorry, I know it hurts. My brother's scrapes and cuts were forever festering. He'd holler so loud when Ma cleaned them. At least you don't holler."

She knew she was rambling, trying to distract herself from the task as much as him from the pain. His muscles were firm, and she knew he had worked hard in his life. But even with all the work, he managed to have the most beautiful hands she'd ever seen. Although his fingers were bunched in the sheets, she remembered noticing how long they were when she'd watched him eat earlier.

She couldn't imagine that such handsome hands had killed. Instead she imagined them stroking the strings of a violin. Her father had possessed long fingers and with them he had created the most magical music.

No, a killer should not have beautiful hands. They should be ugly, like hers, with short stubby fingers, stained and roughened.

And a killer should not possess deep blue eyes that filled with tears.

After repeatedly applying the hot wet cloth to the wound, she brought the lamp nearer and scrutinized the gash. It still looked red and tender, but it was clean. "I think that's all I need to do tonight."

He released a shuddering breath and his hands relaxed their hold on the pillow. Turning his head slightly, he looked at her. "Sorry for the trouble."

She didn't know if she'd ever heard anyone sound so tired. She combed her fingers through his black hair. "Try and sleep. We want your fever to break."

She draped additional blankets over his arms and a portion of his back, leaving the wound exposed to the air. Slowly, gently she trailed her hand back and forth over his broad shoulders, above the wound. She began to sing the ballad that had caused her father to desert and brought him home from the war, while so many others had perished. He had named her in honor of the song, and she often wondered if she owed her existence to someone's gift with lyrics.

She sang until she felt the tenseness leave Austin's body, until she heard his quiet even breathing. She moved to a rocking chair and watched him through the night, wiping the beading sweat from his brow, keeping the blankets tucked around him, wondering what sort of man would go to prison for murder . . . then weep because a woman hadn't waited for his return.

Chapter 3

◦◦◦

*L*OREE HADN'T MEANT to pry. She'd retrieved Austin Leigh's saddle-bags with the intent of discovering if he had other clothes to wear. Her search stopped the moment she found his treasured keepsake. Sitting cross-legged on the floor beside the tub of steaming water, she stroked the locks of auburn hair he had bound together with a white velveteen ribbon. She had little doubt the silken strands had once belonged to his beloved Becky. When she held them up to the early morning sunlight filtering through the window, they turned a warm shade of red, unlike her own hair, which held no color at all.

She reasoned that he had possessed the precious memento before he went to prison. She could not envision him requesting the hair of a woman who had married another. When she brought the hair beneath her nose, she smelled the fading fragrance of vanilla mingling with a scent that she recognized as belonging to the man lying in her bed. After tending him through the night, she had become familiar with many aspects of his person.

She wondered how long he had possessed the token of his heart's desire and marveled at so great a love that even now he would not part with a portion of the woman who had betrayed him.

"What are you doing?"

Loree released a tiny screech at the rumble of the angry voice and shoved the lock of hair back into the saddlebag before glancing over her shoulder. Austin Leigh had risen up on an elbow, his blue penetrating gaze pinning her to the spot.

"Nothing. I . . . I washed your clothes this morning and then it occurred to me that you wouldn't have anything to wear. Since your fever broke near dawn, I thought you might want a bath." She slapped her trembling hand against the wooden tub to emphasize her good intentions. She held up his saddlebag. "I was looking to see if you had some clean clothes."

His eyes narrowed with suspicion. "I do."

"Oh, good." She shoved herself to her feet and set the saddlebag on the foot of the bed, certain he wouldn't appreciate knowing what she'd found. "Do you feel strong enough to manage on your own?"

"I'm willing to give it a try."

"I'll start cooking breakfast."

Austin watched the woman scurry from the room like a frightened rabbit. He didn't have anything in his possession worth stealing, and even if he did, he didn't think Loree Grant was one to steal. In spite of her wariness, she had been generous toward him—offering him food, shelter, and aid when she could just as easily have left him to suffer alone. Still, he'd had little privacy in the past few years and he coveted it now.

He felt like a man who had downed three bottles of cheap whiskey without taking a breath in between. He rolled to a sitting position, every muscle and bone he possessed protesting the movement. He swung his legs over the side of the bed and took a moment to catch his breath. His gaze fell on his boots—polished to a shine—standing at attention beside the rocking chair. Good Lord, how was he going to pay the woman back for all she'd done since his arrival?

He shoved himself to his feet. A wave of weakness assailed him and he closed his eyes, willing himself to stand.

With the movements of an old man who had been thrown off a horse one too many times, he padded to the bathtub. The woman thought of everything. He sank into the heavenly warmth, letting it soak days of dirt and grime from his body. Leaning back, he closed his eyes. Moments woven through the night filled his mind like an elaborate tapestry. Soft touches over his fevered brow. Cool water gliding down his scorched throat. A gentle voice offering reassurance.

And tears. His tears. He groaned. Whatever had possessed him to ask the woman about Becky? Bowing his head, he dug his fingers into the sides of the tub. Thoughts of Becky had filled his mind, his heart from the first moment his gaze had fallen upon her seven years before. She was as much a part of him as his name.

A name that might have cost him her love.

Using the hard lye soap, he scrubbed unmercifully at his face and body and washed his hair. The pain still throbbed through his back, but not nearly as much as it had the day before. He'd been a fool to leave home without seeing that it was properly tended by a physician, but then he seemed to have gained a knack for being a fool.

He brought himself to his feet and dried off. Wrapping the towel around his waist, he walked to the bed and removed his shaving equipment from his saddlebag. He ambled to the woman's dresser and studied his reflection in the mirror. He hadn't really taken the time to look at himself since he'd left prison. He was suddenly hit with the hard realization that he had aged more than either of his brothers. Deep crevices fanned out from the corners of his eyes. The wind, rain, and sun had worked together to wear away, shape, and mold the face of a boy into the hardened visage of a man. He hardly recognized himself and he missed the laughing blue eyes that had always looked back at him.

He dropped his chin to his chest and released a heavy sigh. Of all the things that had changed, he hated most of all that he had changed— inside and out. He was as much a stranger to himself as he was to the woman preparing him breakfast.

Moving her hairbrush, comb, and hand mirror aside, he set his shaving box on the dresser. Using the warm water she'd left in the bowl, he stirred up some lather for his face, his gaze lighting upon all the little gew gaws scattered over her dresser. He stopped stirring and trailed his fingers over a smooth wooden box. Embedded in the wood was a silhouette of a violin. He shifted his gaze to the door. She'd pried into his belongings . . .

Gingerly he touched the lid of the box and slowly lifted it. Music tinkled out. He slammed the lid closed. A music box.

Shaking his head, Austin set about shaving several days growth of beard from his face. Then he pulled fresh clothes from his saddlebags, stepped into his trousers, and pulled on his boots. Grabbing his shirt and a towel, he walked to the door and quietly opened it.

The aromas of freshly baked biscuits and brewed coffee wafted toward him. He leaned against the doorjamb and watched Loree stir something in a pot on the cast iron stove. She wore a dress the shade of daisies and the same white apron she'd worn the day before cinched at her waist. Her narrow hips swayed in a circular motion as though following the path of the spoon. The lilt of her soft voice filled the room with a song.

"What are you singing?"

She spun around, her eyes wide, her hand pressed just below her throat. "Oh, you startled me."

"I'm sorry."

She shook her head. "That's all right. I'm just not used to having company. I was singing *Lorena*. My pa told me that they sang it around the campfires during the war. It made him so homesick that one night he just got up and started walking home." She turned back to the stove. "I didn't mean to disturb you with my caterwauling."

"I'd hardly call it caterwauling."

She glanced over her shoulder. "Did you find everything you needed?"

"Yes, ma'am." He held up the towel. "I was wondering if you'd make sure my back was dry."

"Oh, yes." She wiped her hands on her apron before pulling a chair out from the table and turning it. "Why don't you sit down?"

Austin crossed the short distance separating them, handed her the towel, straddled the chair, and folded his arms over its straight back. She pressed the towel against his wound. He closed his eyes, relishing her touch, as gentle as the first breath of spring. He'd been too long without a woman, without the peacefulness a woman's presence offered a man. It was more than the actual touch. It was the lilt of her voice, her flowery fragrance. The smile she was hesitant to give. The gold of her eyes.

Lightly, she pressed her fingers around the wound. "I don't see any signs of infection brewing, but it's still red and angry-looking. I wonder if I should sew it."

"Is it bleeding?"

"No."

"Then just leave it. I've been enough trouble."

"It's going to leave an ugly scar."

"Won't be the first."

Reaching around him, she picked up a brown bottle that had been set near some cloths. He suspected that she'd anticipated he would need further care this morning. It galled him to need her help. Why couldn't Duncan have cut him someplace that he could have reached and treated himself? He supposed he should just be grateful that he'd moved soon enough to avoid giving Duncan the opportunity to slice any deeper.

"I thought I'd put some tincture of iodine on it this morning," she offered.

"Fine."

She pulled the stopper and the acrid odor assailed his nostrils. She drenched the cloth with the reddish-brown liquid. Dallas had always had a fondness for the medication, pouring it on every cut and scrape Austin had ever had. He supposed it was because his brother had seen too many men die from infection during the war. He probably wouldn't be sitting here now if he'd told Dallas about the cut.

"This is going to sting," she said quietly.

Austin gritted his teeth and dug his fingers into the back of the chair. When she touched the saturated cloth to his back, he sucked in air with a harsh hiss.

"I'm sorry, so sorry," she whispered, and he thought he heard tears in her voice.

He focused his attention on the man he hoped to find in Austin. Each day, the man owed him more. He wouldn't be sitting here fighting back the pain if the man hadn't run off after killing Boyd.

She removed the cloth, and Austin released a long slow breath. He eased away from the chair as she wrapped a bandage around his chest and across his back.

"You'll want to keep it clean and have a doctor look at it when you get to Austin."

"Yes, ma'am."

Her fingers strayed to an old wound on his shoulder.

"Someone shot you," she said quietly.

"Yes, ma'am. A little over six years ago."

She jerked her hand back as though he'd bitten her. She placed the bottle of iodine on a shelf, scrubbed her hands at the sink, and wiped them on her apron, over and over, until he thought she might remove her skin.

"Is something wrong?" he asked as he stood and shrugged into his shirt.

"I just didn't expect you to clean up so nice."

Her blush pleased him more than her words. "I . . . I've got some porridge going here if you'd like some."

He swung the chair around and dropped onto the seat. "Just some coffee."

She slapped the porridge into a bowl and set it in front of her place at the table before pouring the coffee into a cup and handing it to him. "I've got milk and—"

"Just black."

He wrapped his hands around the cup, absorbing its warmth, waiting as she poured herself some coffee and took her seat. While she dumped six heaping spoons of sugar into her coffee, he watched with amusement. He hadn't been amused in a long time. She was incredibly innocent. Living out here alone, away from town, away from the influence of people, how could she be otherwise?

Maybe not completely innocent. Even as she offered him food and shelter, a wariness remained in her eyes, a caution as though at any moment she feared he might turn on her like a rabid dog.

She glanced up and blushed again. "I like a little coffee with my sugar."

"Is what why you're so sweet?"

Her blush deepened as she lowered her gaze. Austin cursed himself and wondered what the hell he thought he was doing. He had no business flirting with a woman, especially one as innocent as she was. "I appreciate all that you did for me last night."

"You should never let a wound go unattended so long."

"I had other things on my mind." He brought the cup to his lips and peered over the rim at the woman sitting across from him. She was sprinkling sugar over her porridge. A corner of his mouth curved up. He thought she might save time if she simply poured the porridge into the sugar bowl.

Having known so few women in his life, he'd developed an appreciation for them, an appreciation that even Becky's betrayal couldn't diminish. He had no memory of his mother. Houston's wife— Amelia—was the first woman to whom he'd ever really spoken.

He'd always liked the way she listened, as though she truly thought he had something of importance to share. He'd even played his violin for her when he'd never dared to play it for anyone else. Then Becky Oliver had moved to town, and Austin had thought she was an angel—his angel. As much as he wanted to hate her, he only seemed capable of missing her.

"Other than building you a new barn, what can I do to repay your kindness?" he asked abruptly, more harshly than he'd intended, memories of Becky tainting his mood.

Her head shot up, her delicate brows drawn together over eyes mired with confusion. "I think you ought to spend the day resting and gathering your strength."

"I need to see to my horse."

"I fed and brushed him this morning."

"And washed my clothes and polished my boots. Good Lord, don't you ever stop doing?"

She dropped her gaze to the remaining porridge. "I like to keep busy." She rose to her feet, picked up the bowl and cup, and carried them to the sink.

"My apologies, Miss Grant. I had no cause to take out my frustration on you."

"It doesn't matter."

But it did matter, more so because she thought it didn't. Austin scraped his chair back and stood. She spun around, the wariness back in her eyes.

"I don't doubt you took good care of my horse, but I want to check on him anyway." He walked out of the house. The dog bounded across the yard and leapt up on Austin's chest, his huge paws wet and muddy. Austin scratched him behind the ears. "If you're her protector, you need to do a better job of protecting her from me."

The dog fell to all fours and gazed up at him as though measuring his worth. Then he barked and scampered away to chase a butterfly.

Austin strode into the barn. Sunlight streamed through the holes. Black Thunder knickered. He rubbed the stallion's nose. "So she's taking good care of you, too, is she?"

He glanced around the run-down structure. Severed and ragged at the end, a rope hung from a beam. He wondered what kept a lone woman living here. Why didn't she pack up and move into town? He had been teasing her when he'd mentioned repairing the barn, but he wasn't certain he could chop enough wood to repay his debt.

He retrieved a rope halter that was hanging on the wall and slipped it onto Black Thunder before leading the stallion into the sunshine. At the corral, he bent and brought the horse's foreleg up between his knees. He studied the festering wound and wondered if his back had looked this nasty when Miss Grant had tended it.

Releasing the foreleg, he knew he wouldn't be traveling today. He looked toward the house. The dog had either captured the butterfly or given up because he was stretched out beneath the shade of a distant tree. A weakness settled in Austin's legs. It galled him to have to admit Loree may have been right—he wasn't quite recovered.

He ambled to the tree. Always watchful, the dog opened an eye and closed it. A flash of yellow caught Austin's attention and he shifted his gaze. He leaned against the rough tree trunk. A strange sense of contentment stole over him as he watched Loree stand in the middle of a vegetable garden with a fawn nibbling something out of her cupped palm. Three other deer tore up the growing foliage. A family, he mused, and discontentment edged the peacefulness aside.

"I could string up some barbed wire for you," he said.

The deer bounded into the thick grove of trees. Loree turned, her lightly golden brows drawn tightly together. "Why would I need barbed wire?"

"To protect your garden. Keep the pesky critters away."

She looked toward the trees where the deer had disappeared. "They aren't pesky, and I always grow more than I need." She walked toward him, eyeing him suspiciously. "How are you feeling?"

Like he'd fallen from his horse, caught his foot in the stirrup, and been dragged across the state.

"A little tired. Do you have any kerosene? My horse's hoof is festering. I need to tend it."

"I'm sorry. I didn't even think to check his hoof."

"You shouldn't have to be concerned with my horse at all."

Or with me. He'd shown her far more of himself than he wanted her to see. She was a stranger, but he had disconcerting memories of telling her things . . .

He followed her into the house and retrieved his knife from his saddlebag while she found the kerosene. By the time he returned outside, she was waiting beside Black Thunder, stroking the horse's mane.

Stepping away from the stallion, she dropped her gaze to the knife Austin held. "Do you want me to hold his head?"

"It's not necessary. He's trained." Giving the horse his backside, he brought the hoof up between his knees and dug the knife into the wound. He heard a whinny just before the sharp pain ricocheted through his butt. He dropped the hoof and jumped away from the horse. "Son of a—! Damn!"

He rubbed his backside while glaring at the horse that tossed its head like a woman might tilt her nose with indignation. Then he heard the laughter.

Light and airy, like a star drifting down from the heavens. He turned his attention to the woman. She had pressed her fingers against her lips, but he saw the corners of her mouth tilting up, carrying her smile to her eyes, shining like a golden coin. "You think it's funny, Miss Grant?"

She shook her head vigorously. "No, Mr. Leigh. It's just not what I would have *trained* him to do."

A bubble of laughter escaped from between her lips and it touched a chord of warmth deep within his chest. "Believe me, he picked that trick up while I was gone."

She dropped her hand, and he watched as she fought to contain her smile. "You just don't seem to have any luck."

"Oh, I have luck, Miss Grant. Unfortunately, it's all bad."

Her smile withered. "I'm sorry."

"You aren't the cause of it." He jerked his thumb toward the horse. "I'll hold his head if you'll rub the kerosene into his hoof."

He grabbed the halter on either side of Black Thunder's head. When Loree bent to grab the hoof, Austin almost thanked the horse for nipping him. Her skirt lifted to reveal her bare ankles and pulled taut across her backside. How in the hell had he mistaken her for a boy the day before? His fever must have addled his brain.

Loree Grant was a tiny bundle of delicate femininity. Just as she had at the stove, she swayed her hips slightly with the motion of her hand, rubbing the kerosene into the horse's hoof. Sweet Lord, it was pure torture to watch, to imagine that backside pressed against him, circling—

She dropped the hoof, straightened, and faced him. "Is there anything else I need to do for the horse?"

He swallowed hard and unclenched his fingers from around the halter. "Nope."

She lowered her gaze and drew a wiggly line in the dirt with her big toe. "I should probably"—she glanced up quickly, then down—"check your backside, make sure he didn't break the skin." She lifted her gaze. "You don't want to get an infection"—she waved her hand limply in the air—"back there."

He smiled warmly. "No, ma'am, I surely don't. I swear, Miss Grant, when I stopped here yesterday, I had no intention of putting you to all this trouble."

"It's no trouble, Mr. Leigh. Besides, I'll put the tincture of iodine on it to begin with so it shouldn't fester at all."

He watched her hurry to the house and decided it was a good thing that the medication burned hotter than hell. Otherwise, he didn't know how he'd endure her gentle fingers touching his backside without his body reacting and making a fool of him.

Loree pumped the water into the sink, then set about scrubbing her trembling hands. What in the world had possessed her to offer to look at Austin Leigh's backside? She wondered if the tincture of iodine would be as effective if she simply poured it into a pan and told him to sit in it and soak his wound. If there was even a wound to soak.

She heard his boots hit the porch. She inhaled deeply, grabbed a towel, and dried her hands. She glanced over her shoulder. He stood in the room, looking as uncomfortable as she felt.

She'd drawn the curtains aside allowing the late morning sun to pour inside. She pointed to a chair opposite the one he'd used that morning. "I can probably use the sun best if you stand there."

He gave her a long slow nod, but she thought she saw worry reflected in his blue eyes.

"I'll be gentle," she assured him.

"That's not what concerns me," he grumbled as he moved to stand behind the chair.

She grabbed the bottle of iodine and a cloth. She hurried to the table, but once she arrived she wished she'd walked more slowly. She pulled the stopper and soaked the cloth. She only wanted to do this once, really didn't want to do it at all. She glanced up. He was staring hard at something on the far wall.

"I . . . I guess you need to lower . . . your britches," she said hesitantly.

She saw a muscle in his cheek jerk.

"Why don't you get behind me?" he suggested.

She stepped around him and tried not to think about the buttons his fingers were releasing. Her breath came in short little gasps. She watched as he grabbed the back of his britches and struggled to lower one side while keeping the other raised. He bent over slightly.

"Can you lift your shirt?" she asked.

She stared in amazement as his skin came into view. So incredibly white that it reminded her of clouds on a summer day, but just above his hip, his skin turned as brown as soil. He must have often worked without a shirt, and she realized with sudden uneasiness that she was about to touch a part of him that the sun had never seen.

"Is the skin broken?"

She flinched at the harshness in his voice and dropped her gaze to the area where he had halted his britches' downward journey. Torn flesh and blood marred his otherwise smooth backside. "Yes."

Gingerly she touched his britches, the tip of her finger skimming over him. He jumped as though she'd pressed a red-hot brand to his flesh.

"I'm sorry. I just . . . I just need to lower these a little more." She brought them down as far as she dared, grateful the horse had nipped him high on the cheek.

She pressed the iodine to the wound, heard his sharp intake of breath, and saw his fingers tighten around his shirt. "I'm so sorry."

"Trust me. The more it stings, the better."

She heard the strain in his voice and worked as fast as she could, pressing the cloth to the wound—

"Good God Almighty! What are you doing, Loree?"

Loree spun around at the unexpected voice, lost her balance, and toppled into Austin as he was turning, struggling to pull up his britches. He reached out to steady her, swore harshly, and released her to grab his britches before they slipped any lower.

Loree would have laughed if it weren't for the young man standing in her doorway, glaring at her. Her heart was pounding so hard that it sounded like a herd of horses stampeding between her ears. "Dewayne, what are you doing here?"

Dewayne Thomas removed his hat, his blond hair glinting in the sunlight, his brown eyes narrowing as he scrutinized Austin. "Come to check on you after last night's storm. Heard there were tornadoes about. Wanted to make sure you were all right." He jutted out his chin. "Who's this?"

"Mr. Leigh. He was traveling to Austin, but his horse came up lame—"

"So how come he's taking off his clothes in your house?"

"He wasn't taking off his clothes. He was treating his horse and it nipped his backside." She held up the stained cloth as evidence. "I was just applying some tincture of iodine to his wound so he wouldn't get an infection."

"Good God, Loree, I'd think you'd have more sense than to let a stranger into your house after that man murdered your family."

Out of the corner of her eye, she saw Austin Leigh jerk his head around, his gaze boring into her.

"What do you know about this here fella?" Dewayne asked.

"I know all I need to know."

"You know what a man can do once his britches is undone?"

"That's enough, Dewayne!" she yelled. She hurried to the sink, threw the cloth into it, and began frantically pumping water and washing her hands. Tears stung her eyes, and she felt the heavy silence permeating the room. She heard the hesitant footsteps.

"I meant no harm, Loree, but I was Mark's best friend. He'd want me watching out for his sister."

She grabbed a towel, began to dry her hands, slowly turned, and forced herself to smile. "I know, Dewayne."

As though her words reinforced his position, he turned to Austin. "What's your business in Austin?"

"My business in Austin is my business," Austin said, his eyes hard, his mouth a firm line. "But I'm no threat to Miss Grant. As soon as my horse is healed, I'll be on my way."

Dewayne snorted. "I'm supposed to believe that just 'cuz you say so."

"I've lied once in my life and it nearly cost my brother his life. I'd need a damn good reason before I'd lie again." He tilted his head toward Loree. "I appreciate your gentle ministrations, Miss Grant. I'll finish tending to my horse now."

She watched him walk through the door, his back stiff, and she somehow knew that Dewayne's distrust had wounded Austin more than his horse or some man in a saloon had.

"I don't like him being here," Dewayne said, the inflection in his voice reminding her of a petulant three year old. "What if he finds out what we did?"

"How's he gonna find out?"

Dewayne pushed out his bottom lip. "You might tell him."

"Why would I do that?"

"You trust him enough to drop his britches, you might trust him with our secret."

"He has no interest in anything around here. He just wants to get his horse healed so he can move on. He's been a perfect gentleman. He chopped wood for me—"

"I coulda chopped wood for you."

Smiling softly, she touched the nick on his chin, remembering when he'd ridden over after his first shave, wanting to show it off. "You can't always watch out for me."

Dewayne blushed and ducked his head. At moments like this she found it difficult to look at him and not see what her brother might have been as a man. He had only been fourteen when the killer had hanged him from the rafters. Only fourteen. How often had she wished she had been the one to die, and he the one to live?

"Then why don't you move to town, Loree?"

"I like living here." In her self-imposed exile, her punishment for what had happened that night and all that had followed.

"But what if some fella stops by who ain't a gentleman?"

"I have my rifle and Digger. Remember how he attacked you the first time you showed up after I'd found him?"

Dewayne laughed. "I still got the scars on my calf. You sure it was the man's horse and not Digger that bit him?"

Loree tilted her head in thought. "Oddly enough, he only growled at Mr. Leigh. He didn't attack him."

"Maybe Digger is getting to be like you. Too trusting."

Smiling, she shook her head. "No, he chased away a man in a medicine show wagon last week. I think Digger would attack anyone he thought would harm me."

"Well, if the storm didn't do any damage here, then I reckon I'll head home. If that fella's still around tonight, you bolt the door."

Simply to appease him, she said, "I will."

She walked outside with him, hugged him as she always did—the way she had hugged her brother—and watched him mount his horse and ride away. Then she strolled over to the man who was brushing his stallion near the corral.

"Dewayne meant no offense," she said quietly.

"None taken." He stopped brushing his horse and met her gaze. "Why didn't you tell me someone had murdered your family?"

"Why didn't you tell me you'd lied?"

"It's not the same."

"How is it different?"

"It just is." He walked around his horse and began brushing the other side as though he needed to put distance between them. "I told you I served time in prison for murder." His hand stilled, his blue gaze capturing hers. "I'm not a murderer."

Her throat tightened. She knew he spoke the truth. He wasn't a cold-blooded murderer. Remembering the puckered flesh on his shoulder—a scar similar to the one she possessed—the kind of scar a healing bullet wound left behind, she imagined he had killed in self-defense, shooting the man who had shot him. "I know that. You don't have the eyes of a murderer."

He seemed to relax as though she'd lifted a burden from his shoulders. "Who did he hang?" he asked, his voice low.

Loree stumbled back, her heart racing. "What?"

"There's a rope dangling from the rafters in the barn."

She had to give Austin Leigh credit. He didn't miss much. Dewayne had cut her brother down. Until last night, she'd never found the courage to return to the barn, much less remove the rope that had taken her brother's life. "My brother. He dragged us to the barn, tied us up, and hanged my brother before shooting the rest of us."

Horror delved into the depths of his eyes. "He shot you?"

Oddly enough, his reaction told her more about him than anything else. He wasn't a man who would hurt a woman.

"Yes, but he didn't check to make certain I was dead. I guess since I'm so small, he assumed one bullet would be sufficient."

"Did the law find him?"

"No."

He laughed derisively. "Ain't that the way of it. They send me to prison, and they let a man who murdered three people go free. You gotta wonder about the justice system sometimes."

She had wondered about justice a lot in the passing years, wondered if it even existed.

"Is that why you let the barn go to ruin?"

Once again, his insight surprised her. She nodded. "I can't stand to go inside."

"You went inside last night, looking for me."

She felt the warmth suffuse her cheeks. "Because I was worried about you. My mother always got after me because I worry more about others than I do about myself. She said it would get me into trouble someday. I've thought about burning the barn, but I'm afraid I'd set the whole hillside ablaze."

"Imagine your brother's friend would have helped you with that."

"Dewayne is sweet and he means well, but sometimes he does or says things without thinking of the consequences."

"He seems to care for you."

"He was the one who found us. I'd probably be dead if not for him." She turned away, the bitter memories bringing forth images of soul-searing pain. A warm, gentle hand came to rest on her shoulder.

"I'm sorry."

She looked into blue eyes that reflected not only a pain equal to hers, but an absence of dreams. Each had suffered as the result of a killing, and she couldn't help but believe that he was as much a victim as she was. Neither had escaped unscathed. "It wasn't your doing."

"No, it wasn't, but making you remember was." He removed his hand from her shoulder and heaved a sigh. "So now I owe you more than I did before. There's gotta be something around here that I can do for you."

"Actually I do need something done."

"Tell me what it is and I'll do it. I pay my debts."

He paid his debts. Loree wondered if that was the reason he didn't seem overly bitter that he'd spent time in prison. He had killed someone. He'd given up a portion of his life. He'd paid his debt.

Now he wanted to repay her. She didn't think his pride would accept that his company was payment enough. No, he needed a chore. Smiling, she began to walk away, trusting him to follow. She knew the perfect chore for those beautiful long fingers of his.

Chapter 4

~

$\mathcal{F}$OLLOWING THE WOMAN as she walked past the house, Austin admired more than the gentle sway of her hips. He admired the courage that had allowed her to put her fears and ugly memories aside to come to his aid last night.

More than that, she had overlooked what she knew of his past. He hadn't received so fine a gift in a good while. Little wonder he had wept in her bed. She possessed a heart that was as pure as the gold of her eyes.

Hell, once he found the man who had stolen five years of his life, maybe he'd search for the man who had killed her family and see him brought to justice.

She came to a halt and flung her arm toward the garden. "Your chore."

The chore turned out to be no chore at all: plucking red ripe strawberries from her garden and placing them gently in the bucket so they wouldn't bruise. She had told him that she couldn't abide the fruit when it was bruised. Based on the fact that she had devoted over half her garden to growing strawberries, Austin figured she had a fondness for them.

Near dusk, she set a quilt beneath a tree and brought out two large bowls. One was filled with washed strawberries. The other with sugar.

She plopped onto the quilt, took a strawberry out of the bowl, rolled it around in the sugar, and popped it into her mouth. She closed her eyes and released a low throaty moan that made Austin want to groan.

Against his better judgment, he stretched out on the quilt beside her and raised up on an elbow. She opened her eyes and smiled at him. "There is nothing finer than the first strawberry in spring."

He disagreed. He could have named a hundred things: her smile, her sun-kissed cheeks, the strands of her hair that had escaped her braid and framed her face like the petals of a dandelion. As a boy, he'd often taken a deep breath before blasting the dandelion petals onto the breeze. Right now, he wanted to blow softly, gently, his breath as quiet as a whisper while it fanned across the nape of her neck.

Digger barreled around the corner of the house. Loree grabbed a strawberry and tossed it into the air. The dog leapt up, his jaws clamping around the ripe fruit. The animal hit the ground and rolled over. Loree laughed joyfully, reminding Austin of the first time he had placed a bow on the strings of a violin. The music had sounded just as sweet because it had been unexpected: something he had created. He found himself wishing he'd been the one to make Loree laugh. Not the stupid dog.

"Help yourself to the strawberries," she said as she tossed another one to the dog before taking one for herself.

Austin brought a strawberry to his lips and bit into the succulent fruit. The sweetness filled his mouth. It didn't need sugar. It amused him to watch Loree carefully coat each strawberry with sugar before she ate it. He grew warm as her tongue darted out to slowly, meticulously capture each errant grain of sugar that clung to her lips. He imagined her kiss would taste of strawberries and sugar.

He'd been too long without a woman, and he was having one hell of a time taming his thoughts. Watching the wind whip strands of her hair around her face, he wanted to play with it as well. He wanted to touch her rounded cheeks with his fingers and the upturned tip of her nose with his lips. He'd known too few women in his life, and even though one had torn out his heart and shredded it to pieces, he couldn't bring himself to hate women.

He figured women were like men. Some good. Some bad. Some fickle. He'd latched onto a fickle one the first time and it had cost him dearly. But in spite of the steep price he'd paid, he couldn't see himself spending his remaining days without the comfort of a woman. Once he'd cleared his name, he'd take a wife. He wanted what his older brothers had. Neither had gained their wives without paying a price.

The comforting silence eased in around them as the shadows lengthened. The dog loped to the edge of the clearing, barked, and raced back to catch another strawberry. Austin was beginning to doubt the dog's ability to protect Loree. Other than last evening when the dog had growled at him, he had seen no signs of aggressiveness. The dog reminded him of an overgrown puppy.

"Why are you out here, Miss Grant?"

She jerked her head around to stare at him. "I like watching the sunset, I enjoy eating strawberries—"

"No. I mean why do you live out here alone? Why not move into town? I can't see that this is a working farm. What keeps you here?"

"Memories. We were happy here. I guess I feel that if I left, I'd be abandoning my family."

In the distance, he saw a white picket fence surrounding three granite headstones. "How old were you?"

"Seventeen. How old were you when you went to prison?"

"Twenty-one."

"That sounds so young."

"Not as young as seventeen."

She dug another strawberry into the sugar. "You mentioned a brother . . ."

He nodded. "Houston."

Her eyes widened as she bit into the strawberry. She laughed as the red juice dribbled down her chin. He clenched his hands to stop his fingers from gathering the juice and carrying it back to her lips, or better yet to his own. She wiped her face with her apron. "Another town?"

"Yep. My parents lived there for a while."

"Have you been to Houston?"

"Nah, they lived there before I was born."

She sighed wistfully and gazed toward the trees. "I used to dream of traveling the world and looking at the stars from different cities." She shifted her gaze to him. "Do you think the stars look different on the other side of the world?"

"I don't know. Never thought about it. Never dreamed that big."

"What did you dream of?"

Marrying Becky. Raising a family. But before that . . . a distant memory flickered at the back of his mind of standing at the edge of a

gorge, yelling out his dream . . . and listening as the echo carried it back
to him. Then the memory died like a flame snuffed out because there
wasn't enough air to keep it burning. "I don't recall."

"My father used to tell me that I had to put my heart into my dream
if I wanted it to come true. How do you put your heart into something?"

Austin hadn't a clue. He'd watched his brothers pour their hearts into
the women they loved, thought he'd done the same with Becky, but if he
had, she would have waited for him. He was convinced of that. Whatever
their love had been, it hadn't been strong enough to endure separation,
and he couldn't help but wonder what else it might not have endured.

The dog came charging back from the edge of twilight, dropped low
to the ground, and growled, baring his teeth. Worry etched over her
face, Loree rose to her knees. "Digger, what is it?"

The dog barked and bounded back for the trees, disappearing in the
brush. A high-pitched shriek rented the air.

"Bobcat!" Loree cried as she jumped to her feet. "Digger!"

The dog barked and the ear-splitting feline cry came again, followed by a yelp echoing pain.

"No!" Loree yelled as she began running toward the trees.

Austin surged to his feet, ran after her, and grabbed her arm, halting her frantic race to the trees. "Where's my rifle?"

"In the corner of the front room, by the hearth."

"Come with me while I get it."

She shook her head vigorously. "I'll wait here but hurry."

He didn't trust her to stay, but he heard the dog's wounded cry, the
cat's victorious screech, and knew he had no time to argue. With his
heart thundering, he raced inside the house. He grabbed his rifle, loaded
it, and shoved a handful of bullets into his pocket. Then he tore back
outside, rounded the corner, and staggered to a stop in the clearing.

The woman was gone!

"Loree!" Fear for her edged any rational thoughts aside. He stalked
toward the trees where the dog had disappeared. "Loree!"

He no longer heard the thrashing of battle. An eerie silence settled
over the woods. He tread carefully between the trees, his heart hammering. When he found the woman he planned to shake her every way but
loose for scaring the holy hell out of him. How dare she risk her life for
a stupid dog.

He found her kneeling between two mighty oak trees, rocking back and forth, silent tears streaming down her cheeks, her arms wrapped around her dog. Austin knelt beside her. "Loree?"

She opened her eyes, the golden depths revealing her ravaged grief. "He was all I had left," she whispered hoarsely. "He was just a dog, but I loved him."

"I know," he said quietly. "You take the rifle and I'll carry him to the house."

"Let me hold him for just a minute . . . while he's still warm."

She buried her face in Digger's thick fur. Austin scanned the trees, his ears alert. He didn't like the thought of Loree living out here alone with wild animals. The deer he didn't mind, but a bobcat was another story.

Gently, he touched Loree's shoulder. "We need to get back before it's too dark."

She lifted her head, sniffed, and nodded. Blood had stained the front of her dress and panic surged through him. "You're hurt."

She glanced down before lifting a vacant gaze to his. "No, it's Digger's blood. The cat was gone by the time I got here."

"You should have stayed by the house like I told you."

"I was worried about Digger. He never backs—backed—away from a fight."

"Christ, your mother was right. You put a dog before yourself—"

"I'd put anyone, anything I loved before myself. I don't see that as a fault."

He didn't mean to sound harsh, didn't want to lecture her, but the thought that she might have been the cat's next victim had him shaking clear down to his boots. "Take the rifle."

She grabbed it, and he slipped his arms beneath the dog. He ignored the pain shooting through his back as he strained to lift the heavy beast. With the darkness closing in around them, they walked in silence to the house, his boots breaking dried twigs, her feet scattering the fragile leaves that had died last autumn.

"Will you bury him near the garden? That's where he liked to dig," she said quietly as they neared the house.

"Sure will. You got a shovel?"

"In the barn."

"I'll get it. Why don't you go inside and wash up?"

Nodding, she leaned over and pressed a kiss to the top of the dog's head. "Bye, Digger."

Austin watched her run to the front of the house, leaving him feeling useless. Giving comfort had never been his strong suit, was something he hadn't even known existed until Amelia had come into their lives.

He laid the dog on the ground. He walked to the quilt where he had shared a few peaceful moments with Loree. In her rush to get to the dog, she'd knocked over the bowl, spilling sugar over the quilt. Ants were having a picnic. Austin picked up the bowl and shook out the rest of the sugar, wishing he knew how to ease Loree's grief as easily.

Loree had lit a lamp to ward off the darkness and the constant fears that surrounded her. She had warmed a bucket of water, removed her blood-stained clothes, bundled them up, and shoved them into a corner of her bedroom. Now she stood before her dresser, stripped to the waist, wearing nothing but her linen drawers, scrubbing, scrubbing the blood from her chest, her hands, her arms. So much blood.

She lifted her gaze to the mirror and caught the reflection of Austin Leigh standing in her doorway, watching her with an intensity in his gaze that she thought might have frightened her under ordinary circumstances.

But tonight wasn't ordinary. She'd just had the last bit of love she'd ever known torn from her life. She turned to face the man who had given her beloved Digger a final resting place. "I can't get his blood off."

She watched his throat muscles work as he swallowed, saw his hands clench and unclench before he quietly walked across the room in bare feet. In a distant part of her mind, she realized he must have left his soiled boots outside.

In silence, he took the cloth from her hand, dipped it into the bucket of water, wrung it out, and gently, slowly wiped the cloth over her face, his deep blue gaze touching her as sunshine greeted the dawn, warming her when only moments before she'd been chilled.

He wiped her throat, her shoulders, and brought the cloth lower. He touched his thumb to the scar just above her left breast. "Is this where he shot you?" he asked hoarsely.

She could do little more than nod, knowing he needed no answer as his mouth replaced his thumb.

"How could he have hurt you?"

Another question for which she had no answer. She felt him tremble as his knuckles skimmed the inside swell of her breast. He shook his head slightly.

"There's no more blood," he rasped as he stepped back.

She grabbed his hand. "There's blood on you."

He glanced down at his shirt. Of their own accord, her fingers began to undo his buttons. She heard his breath hitch. She had never been so bold, never bared her body to a man. The embarrassment she had anticipated was drowned out by need. A need she didn't fully understand, but knew existed because it beckoned to her from the farthest reaches of her heart and soul.

She removed his shirt and bloodstained bandage. Taking the cloth from his hand, she wiped it across his chest even though she saw no blood.

With one roughened palm, he cradled her cheek and tilted her face until their gazes met and held. She heard his uneven breathing. Beneath the hand she had rested on his chest, she felt the rapid, steady pounding of his heart.

She had long ago accepted the fact that she would live out the remaining days of her life alone. She hadn't realized how much she missed the scent, sight, sounds, and touch created by another person. She thought she had effectively warded off the loneliness.

Now, she knew it had only been in hiding, gathering strength, waiting until her defenses were down to attack. All the days of silence and nights alone suddenly loomed before her. A lifetime's worth. And she hated them. She hated every one of them and the man whose actions had condemned her to the loneliness.

She suddenly felt plain and poor, longing for things she would never know: a husband's smile, the laughter of children.

Austin's gaze drifted to her lips, the blue of his eyes darkening until she felt the warmth of a fire, burning hot and bright, creating even as it consumed. He lowered his head slightly and her lips parted.

"So sweet," he whispered, and she wondered if within the words, she heard an apology.

Then his mouth was pressed against hers, warm, soft, moist, and she had her first taste of a man. Deep inside, she smiled. He tasted of strawberries.

Then he deepened the kiss, and when his tongue sought hers, she raised up onto the tips of her toes, wrapped her arms around his neck, and gave to him all that he asked.

He groaned deep within his throat and she felt the rumble of his chest against her breasts. His arm snaked around her, pressing her closer against his body.

She had never been wanton, but then the loneliness had never been this great, this consuming. Nor had the need to be held, to be loved been so strong. She did not delude herself. He did not love her. In his eyes, she had seen the stark loneliness that mirrored hers. They were kindred hearts with a haunting past that had stolen dreams. Still, he would leave and never look back.

And with that thought, she found comfort. She could accept what he offered, knowing that he would never discover the secrets that the killer had forced her to lock away. Austin Leigh would never look upon her with revulsion. Years from now, when she brought forth the memories of this man, she would only see the desire that deepened the blue of his eyes.

His mouth trailed along her throat, pressed kisses against the sensitive flesh below her ear. "So sweet," he repeated in a ragged breath, like a litany that stirred his actions.

He guided her to the bed, skimming her remaining clothes from her body before laying her down. Holding her gaze, he slowly unbuttoned his trousers as though giving her time to tell him that what he was offering wasn't what she wanted.

But she did want, more than she had ever wanted, to be without the loneliness. When he stretched his tall lean body alongside hers, she'd never felt so tiny, so delicate. He cupped her breast, his hand shaping and molding her flesh as his mouth teased and taunted. Desire spiraled through her, strong enough to send the loneliness into oblivion. For one night, she would have what she might never have again: a man's touch, a man's whispered words, a man's strength and ability to hold the loneliness at bay.

His mouth came down on hers, hard, devouring, but his hands remained gentle, as though she were shaped from hand-blown glass. She trailed her hands over the firm muscles of his shoulders, digging her fingers into his back, careful to avoid the wound that had forged a bond between them.

When his hand skimmed along her stomach, she shivered. When he touched her intimately, she gasped as his fingers made promises she knew his body would keep.

He moved until his hips were nestled between her thighs. Then slowly, cautiously, he joined his body to hers. The pain was fleeting, the fullness of him satisfying. As he rocked against her, the past blurred into insignificance, the future that awaited her lost its importance. All that mattered was this moment, this joining. Sensations she'd never known existed wove themselves around her, through her, creating beauty where she'd only known ugliness. She reveled in the sound of his throaty groans, the feel of his sure, swift thrusts.

And then she cried out, arching beneath him as everything spilled over into ecstasy.

As he shuddered above her, she heard a name whisper raggedly past his lips. Suddenly all that had passed before meant nothing . . . and the loneliness increased tenfold.

Austin stilled, his breathing labored, sweat glistening over his trembling body, self-loathing and guilt increasing as he felt Loree stiffen beneath him.

Ironically, he'd held no thoughts of Becky until her name escaped his lips, but he didn't think it would soothe Loree's hurt if he told her that. As a matter of fact, he could think of nothing to say, nothing to do that would ease the pain he'd caused her—and hurting her was the last thing he'd intended.

He eased off her. She rolled to her side, presenting him with her back, drawing her knees toward her chest. Reaching down, he pulled up a blanket and covered her.

He got out of bed, snatched up his britches, jerked them on, and headed outside. He stormed to the corral and slammed the palm of his hand against the post. The sound of vibrating wood echoed around him. He hit the post again and again. He would have kicked it if he'd thought to pull on his boots. He dug his fingers into the top railing of the corral, squeezed his eyes shut, and bowed his head.

He could argue that he'd been too long without a woman, but the argument would have been rift with lies because he knew that if he had lain with a woman that afternoon, he still would have wanted Loree tonight.

She was so incredibly sweet, pure, and innocent . . . all the delightful aspects of youth that a man lost as he grew older. When he had kissed her, felt the tentative touch of her tongue, he was the man he had been before prison. A man who believed in goodness. She had touched the tender part of himself that he'd locked away in solitary confinement in order to survive within prison walls. With her arms circling his neck, she had sent his good intentions to perdition and unleashed desires and needs that he'd kept tightly reined.

And for those few moments of splendor, when he had held her close, the loneliness that always ate at his soul had ceased to feast.

Until he had carelessly whispered another's name.

Then the loneliness had consumed him once again and invited guilt to the banquet.

He slammed his palm against the post. Why in the hell had Becky's name escaped his lips? She hadn't been in his thoughts. Hell, he hadn't been thinking at all. He'd just been feeling, feeling with an intensity he hadn't experienced in years. Maybe that was the reason he'd spoken her name. He'd always associated deeply held emotion with Becky.

And that sure as hell hadn't been fair to Loree.

He might have been able to forgive himself if he had something to offer her—but he had nothing. What woman would want to marry a man fresh out of prison? A man who couldn't prove his innocence?

He had no job, no prospects.

Within his mind, he saw her golden eyes filled with trust. She had wanted the comfort he had to offer, and in taking it, she had given it back. He'd never wanted to taste anything as much as he'd wanted to taste her, to touch as much as he'd wanted to touch her, to know . . . He found it impossible to believe so little time had passed since he'd first set eyes on her.

Again, he slammed his palm against the post. A delicate hand covered his as it gripped the pillar.

"You're gonna bust your hand if you're not careful," she said quietly.

Austin's heart thundered so loudly that he barely heard the crickets chirping. Loree stood in the pale moonlight, her gaze watchful. She'd slipped into a nightgown and draped a blanket over her shoulders.

"Can't see that it would be any great loss."

She took his hand, turned it, and pressed a kiss to his palm. "I disagree."

"Loree—"

"It's all right. I was thinking of someone else as well."

Her words sliced across his heart like a well-honed knife cutting deeply, the pain taking him off guard. He knew he deserved them, knew she had every right to say them, but he didn't like hearing them. "Who were you thinking of?"

She angled her chin defiantly. "Jake."

He heard the slightest hesitation in her voice and knew beyond any doubt that she was lying. Whether she was hoping to hurt him or salvage her pride, it didn't matter. He'd give her back what he could.

"Then he's a damn lucky man," he said, surprised by the roughness in his voice.

She dropped her gaze to her bare feet. "Anyway, there's no reason for you to sleep out here. The barn is probably still damp."

Even now, after he'd hurt her, she was still more worried about him than herself. "Sleep doesn't come easy for me."

"For me either."

He tilted up her face, and with his thumb, he wiped a glistening tear from the corner of her eye. "We're a fine pair, aren't we?"

She gave him a hesitant smile and nodded. He cupped her cheek and lowered his mouth to hers, imparting with his kiss the apology she wouldn't accept in words. She swayed toward him and wrapped her arms around his neck.

He trailed his lips along her throat until he reached the curve of her shoulder. "Loree, know that I never meant to hurt you."

"I know."

He slipped his arm beneath her knees and lifted her into his arms.

Cradling her close, he carried her into the house. With his foot, he closed the door behind him and walked into the bedroom.

Carefully, he laid her on the bed. She curled on her side, and he draped the blanket over her. He walked to the other side of the bed. Without removing his trousers, he lay on top of the covers and wrapped his arm around her. She stiffened. He pressed his lips to the top of her head. "I'm just going to hold you, Loree. Believe it or not, that's all I'd intended to do when I came into the house looking for you earlier."

He heard her muffled sob and tightened his arms around her. Another sob came. Gingerly, he turned her toward him. "Come here, Sugar."

She rolled into the circle of his arms and pressed her face against his chest. Her warm tears dampened his flesh.

"I'm sorry, Loree. I'm so sorry."

Her sobs grew louder, her tears flowed more freely, and he could do little more than hold her closely, knowing he was the cause of her heartache.

Chapter 5

A LOUD BANG STARTLED Loree from her sleep. Her nose stuffy, her eyes stinging, she crawled out of bed. The morning sunlight filtered through the curtains.

She heard another crash. What in the world was Austin doing to himself now?

She scurried out of the house and stumbled to a stop. Raising her hand to shield her eyes from the glare of the morning sun, she stared at the man crouched on the roof of her barn. He worked a board free and tossed it to the ground. "What are you doing?" she called up to him.

His chest bare, he twisted around and shoved his hat off his brow with his thumb. "Thought you wanted to burn the barn."

"I do."

"Then I aim to burn it. Figured it would be easier to break it into piles of lumber we can manage than to cut down the trees surrounding it."

"You're gonna open that wound on your back."

"That's my worry."

"It'll be my worry if it festers."

He rubbed his thumb over the head of the hammer, studying it. Then he lifted his solemn gaze to her. "I'll be leaving as soon as I'm done with the barn."

She heard regret laced through his voice, and her heart tightened as though stretching toward a dream it could never hold. She'd always known he'd leave. Still she hadn't expected that he might take a part of her with him. "I'll fix some breakfast."

"Just coffee for me."

He returned to his chore. For several minutes she watched him work and came to the realization that although last night had caused her anguish, she had no regrets. Despite the fact that he'd been in prison, she knew he was a good man, honorable in his own way.

And she wondered if the woman he loved ever thought of him, truly knew how firm a place she held in his heart.

She strolled into the house, scrubbed her face, brushed and braided her hair, and slipped into a clean dress. She walked into the kitchen and began to prepare her morning porridge. Her life was filled with routine. She had to remind herself not to set out a bowl of food for Digger, but she couldn't stop herself from listening for his bark. She keenly felt his absence as she worked about the kitchen, never finding him underfoot. He'd never chase another butterfly or lick her hand.

The tears stinging her eyes increased when she placed a cup of coffee on the table and saw the sugar bowl she'd left outside the night before. She remembered knocking it over, spilling its contents on the quilt. She traced her finger around its rim. Now it was full.

What sort of man was Austin Leigh to go to the trouble to retrieve her bowl and fill it with sugar?

She heard his booted feet hit her front porch and step through her doorway. "Your coffee's ready," she told him, averting her gaze, turning to the stove to slap her porridge into a bowl. She listened as he pulled out his chair and took his seat, a gesture that seemed more intimate after all they'd shared last night.

She sat at the table and, with trembling fingers, lifted the spoon and sprinkled sugar over her porridge. She felt his gaze boring into her, but couldn't bring herself to look at him.

"Loree, about last night—"

"I'd rather not discuss it." She lost count of the number of spoonfuls of sugar and decided it didn't matter. She'd just pour on sugar until she no longer saw the oats.

"I've got nothing to offer you, Loree."

She snapped her gaze up to his. He'd removed his hat and put on a shirt. His black hair curled over his collar. She ached to run her fingers through it. "I don't recall asking for anything."

His eyes were somber. "You didn't, but you deserve everything—everything a man would give a woman if he could."

"You didn't force me. I knew where the trail was leading, and I was willing to follow it."

"I told you sometimes a man makes choices not knowing the cost. Did you know the cost?"

She lowered her gaze to the porridge. "No," she admitted quietly. "But I'd pay it again." Looking at him, she forced a tremulous smile. "Although I don't know how I'm going to look Dewayne in the eye the next time he comes over after what he said yesterday."

"You can't look at a woman and know whether or not she's shared herself with a man."

Shared herself. She felt as though she'd given nothing and taken everything. "Sometimes you say things in such a way that I wonder if you're a poet."

He shook his head. "I have no gift with words. Last night served as evidence of that. I appreciate the coffee. I'd best get back to the barn."

Watching him walk from house, she wondered how soon it would be before he walked out, never to return. She shoved her bowl of porridge aside, discontent rearing its ugly head. Suddenly greedy for memories that she could hoard away and bring out on the loneliest of nights, she scrambled from her chair and dashed outside, hurrying to the corral. His horse grazed nearby. A beautiful beast that belonged to a beautiful man.

She turned her attention to the barn. With a wistfulness she knew she had no business feeling, she watched Austin work. Last night she had received a sampling of what she *would* never have. She had not expected to yearn so intensely for that which she *could* not have.

"Get the kerosene!"

Loree snapped back to the present as Austin climbed lithely down from her barn.

"Fetch some old blankets, too," he told her. "I'll get some buckets of water."

"That's not very much to burn," she said, studying the meager pile of ragged lumber.

"Thought it best to start small until we figure out what we can control."

She fetched the kerosene and blankets as he'd instructed, returning to see him put the last bucket of water in place. He took the kerosene from her and doused the wood. Sweat glistened over his bronzed back, and she worried about his wound. It didn't look nearly as angry as it had the day before, but it was certain to leave him with a jagged scar.

When he finished, he held up a match. "You want the honors?"

She nodded jerkily. He lifted his foot, struck the match on the bottom of his boot, and handed it to her. She got as close as she dared and tossed the match onto the kerosene drenched wood. She watched the flame grow and spread across the pyre. The wood crackled and blackened. Smoke rose toward the clouds. She crossed her arms beneath her breasts, feeling as though she was finally doing something to put the nightmare to rest.

The barn had been a cavernous reminder of how those she loved had died. She hated the rope most of all, but she'd never been able to bring herself to touch it.

"I want to burn the rope, too," she whispered hoarsely never taking her gaze from the fiery red blaze.

He wrapped his arms around her, bringing her back against his chest. She welcomed the sturdiness of his embrace. He brushed his lips lightly across her temple. "It's already burning."

His words didn't surprise her. Somehow, he seemed capable of anticipating her needs before she knew she had them. "My brother was so young. I wish he'd hanged me instead."

Austin's arms tightened around her. "Is that why you live here alone—to punish yourself for living when they died?"

She held her silence because he had the uncanny ability to understand far more than anyone else ever had.

Gently, he turned her within his arms, tucked his knuckle beneath her chin, and tilted her head back. "Loree, I've listened to you talking about your family. I know you loved them. For you to love them as much as you do, they had to love you in return. They wouldn't want you living here alone."

Gazing into his earnest eyes, she desperately wanted to explain everything—the fear, the fury, the hatred. Surely a man who had lived his life would understand, but if he didn't understand, something far worse than living a life alone awaited her.

"I'm here because I want to be. I'm . . . content." Or at least she had been until last night.

His gaze told her that he didn't believe her. "I spent five years surrounded by men, but I was alone because there was no one I cared about, no one I trusted. You don't have to live like that, Loree. Pack up your belongings and I'll move you to Austin—"

She jerked away from him. "I can't."

"Why?"

"Because that night still lives inside me! You don't know what I did!"

"You survived."

Tears burned her eyes. "If only it was that simple. I'm here because I deserve to be. Call it a punishment. Call it a life sentence. Call it whatever you want. I made my decision and I'm not leaving." The tears rolled over onto her cheeks. "Despite what you thought, I knew *exactly* what you meant when you said a person makes decisions not knowing the cost—but regardless, once you act on the decision, you still have to pay the price." Five years ago, the price had been her dreams.

"Even if it costs you your life? Loree, your friend Dewayne was right. You didn't know anything about me when you accepted my offer to chop your wood for a bowl of stew. I could have been intent on hurting you."

"I took your weapons."

He released a mirthless laugh. "You think that would have stopped me?"

"Digger would have stopped you."

"You don't have Digger anymore."

She flinched at the reminder. He cursed harshly and reached for her. "Come here."

She tried to resist, but he was insistent, drawing her into his arms and pressing her face against his chest. "I'm sorry. I shouldn't have said that, but I'm worried about you, Sugar. I don't like the idea of you living out here alone."

"I'll be all right," she assured him, even though she knew it wasn't the absolute truth. After he left, she'd be lonelier than she'd ever been in her life.

He held her, his hands gliding up and down her back, comforting and strong, the silence broken only by the snap and crackle of the fire. It seemed an eternity passed before he finally spoke, and when he did, it was as though their argument had never taken place.

"I think we'll be all right if we keep the fire small like this. I could go back to tearing down the barn, tossing the planks down, and you can feed them to the fire."

Releasing her, he met her gaze. "Holler if things get out of hand."

She nodded mutely, knowing that by working with him, she would hasten his departure. Knowing that every time she gazed into the deepest depths of a fire, she would see the blue of his eyes.

By nightfall Loree was exhausted, but she felt a measure of peace. Over half the barn was smoldering ashes.

She lay in her bed, curled beneath the covers, listening as Austin moved around in the front room. After supper, he'd dragged in the bathtub and helped her fill it with hot water. While he had tended to his horse and drenched the ashes once more, she had enjoyed the luxurious warmth of the water and pampered herself by using some French soap she'd hoarded away in her hope chest.

When she had dried off and thrown on a clean nightgown, she had opened the door to discover him sitting on the steps.

"Would you mind if I took a bath?" he'd asked quietly, and she could no more ignore that plea in his eyes imploring her to trust him than she could ignore the sun rising over the horizon.

So now he was bathing, and all she could think about was the water gliding over a chest that she had touched. She imagined him shaving, combing his hair, and slipping on his britches.

She wondered where he would bed down tonight, and continually asked herself where she wanted him to sleep. She heard several bumps followed by a scrape and knew that he was emptying the tub and taking it outside. She held her breath, waiting, listening, wondering.

The house grew silent. Rolling over, she pressed her face to the pillow in an effort to hide her disappointment. He had left her alone.

Austin walked around the house numerous times, searching for the ever elusive sleep. He knew from experience that it would be long after midnight before he'd find it.

Besides he needed to air out. Loree had used some fancy smelling bath salts, and although they smelled sweet on her, they reeked to high heaven on him. Lord, if his brothers caught a whiff of him now, he'd never hear the end of it.

That thought had him turning northwest, staring at a part of Texas that rested beyond his vision. He wondered what his brothers were doing. No doubt, whatever it was, they were doing it with their wives. He didn't begrudge them the love they had in their lives, but he did envy that they had the joy of sleeping with a woman every night—simply sleeping with her.

He'd never slept with a woman through the night until last night. He'd found it incredibly comforting to listen to Loree's soft even breathing once her tears had subsided.

He wished he'd never caused the tears. He looked at the silhouette of the remaining barn. At least he could repay her by taking away some of her painful memories—memories he wished she had never possessed.

With a deep sigh, he headed for the porch where he'd stored his gear earlier before he'd begun tearing down the barn. He thought about laying his pallet out beneath the stars, but prison had taught him to appreciate fine moments when they came along. And it had been a long time since he'd known anything finer than Loree Grant.

Loree heard the door open and held her breath. She'd long ago given up on Austin joining her and had extinguished the flame in the lamp. Now only pale moonlight spilled into the room. She listened to the soft tread of his bare feet growing nearer. She felt the bed dip beneath his weight.

He lay on top of the covers as he had last night. His arm came around her, firm and heavy. She felt his bare chest warming her back through her nightgown. He pressed his cheek against the top of her head. She heard what she thought was a quiet sigh of contentment followed by a soft snore.

For a man who claimed sleep didn't come easily, he'd fallen asleep incredibly quickly. Contented, she closed her eyes and drifted into sleep.

Austin awoke near dawn. Sometime during the night, Loree had rolled over. Her cheek was pressed against his chest, her hand curled over his side. Her warm breath fanned over his skin. This morning her face wasn't splotchy from crying and her nose wasn't red. The temptation to awaken her with a kiss and make love to her was almost more than he could resist.

But he had hurt her once. He wouldn't risk doing it again. She deserved a man whose heart wasn't tethered to the past.

She'd never find a man like that if she continued to live here alone. What had the bastard who murdered her family done to her? Austin knew he hadn't raped her but he had made her do something that haunted her. Dee had been right when she told him that not all prisons came with walls. Austin deeply wished he possessed the key that would set Loree free from the past.

She sighed and snuggled closer against him. He was tempted to stay here all day, just holding her, listening to the little noises she made, enjoying the scent of flowers that was part of her, but he knew himself well enough to know his resistance was weakening.

And if he made love to her again, he'd have to stay. The first time, a shared need for comfort had propelled them. The guilt still gnawed at him, but in some strange way, he could justify walking away. But if his needs alone drove him to bury himself deeply inside her . . .

He pressed his lips to her temple. He needed to be gone by nightfall.

Loree watched Austin work as though the hounds of hell nipped at his heels. The planks of wood fell to the ground with a steady rhythm. And with each thud, she knew he was that much closer to leaving.

Near dusk, they stood and watched the glowing embers slowly die. Loree wrapped her arms around her middle. "I should have done this a long time ago." She turned and met his gaze. "Thank you."

He touched her cheek. Smiling wryly, he dropped his hand to his side. "You had a bit of soot on your cheek. Thought I could clean it off, but I just made it worse. Seems to be a habit of mine where you're concerned."

"Guess a bath is in order then."

He tapped his hat against his thigh. "Not for me. Not tonight."

He strode past her to the porch. Her heart tightened as he lifted his saddle and with long sure strides, approached the stallion.

"Surely, you'll want to eat before you leave," she said even though she knew the longer he stayed, the harder it would be to watch him go.

"I'll get something in town."

She wrung her hands together. "It'll be midnight before you get there."

"I'll find something." He cinched the saddle and dropped the stirrup. He slung the saddlebags over the horse's rump.

"Promise me you'll have a doctor look at your back."

He stilled. "I'm not worth your worry, Loree."

"Promise me," she repeated obstinately.

He glanced over his shoulder and smiled, the first genuine smile she'd seen cross his face, and it very nearly stole her breath away. She wished he'd given it to her at noon instead of in the fading twilight where it would be nothing but a shadowed memory.

"I promise," he said.

"You keep your promises, don't you?"

"Every one I've ever made."

"Then promise me that you'll take care of yourself as well."

"Only if you promise to do the same."

She nodded, her throat constricting with all that remained unsaid. How could she have been intimate with a man and not know how to tell him everything that she wanted him to know?

"Think about moving to town," he said quietly.

"I can't."

"A woman like you deserves more than memories in her life—"

"You need to get going before it gets much darker," she whispered, the tears stinging the backs of her eyes.

"When I'm finished with my business in Austin, I could stop back by here—"

"No." She shook her head emphatically. "It'd be best if you didn't."

"I'm going to worry about you, Sugar," he said in a low voice as though he wasn't comfortable admitting his concern.

"I'll be fine," she assured him.

He gave a brusque nod and, with one lithe movement, swung up into his saddle. "If you need to get in touch with me—for any reason—I'll be staying at the Driskill Hotel."

"That's a fancy hotel."

"So I hear."

He touched the tip of his finger to the brim of his hat. "Miss Grant, you are without a doubt, the sweetest woman I've ever known."

He sent his black stallion into a gallop.

Loree watched until he disappeared in the fading twilight. Then she dropped to her knees and wept. He was wrong. A woman like her didn't deserve more than memories in her life.

She deserved to hang.

Austin walked the streets of the state capital wondering just what in the hell he thought he was doing. His tracking experience was limited to finding cow dung over the plains of West Texas. Dallas had taught him to use a rifle, gun, and knife but even those skills were useless here. He'd left his gun in his saddlebag in his room at the hotel.

He'd arrived near midnight, anxious to register for a room and bed down for the night. He'd been bone weary and had expected to fall asleep as soon as his head hit the pillow.

But the pillow didn't smell like the one that graced Loree's bed. As comfortable as the bed was, it didn't have the one thing he wanted: a tiny lady who had somehow managed to slip beneath the gates that surrounded his heart.

It was ludicrous to care for her as much as he did after knowing her such a short time, but he couldn't get her out of his mind. Every time he heard soft laughter, he turned to see if it was hers. When he passed women on the street, he compared them to the woman who had tended his wound—and he found them all lacking. None carried her guileless smile. None walked without pretense. He couldn't see bare toes, smudged cheeks, or golden eyes filled with tears.

And he wanted what he couldn't have: to see those eyes filled with happiness. But even the thought of going to her had no place in his heart when he had nothing to offer her. He'd only bring her more pain until he cleared his name. If he took her to Leighton, she'd have to endure the suspicious stares that followed his every step. The shadow of his past would touch her, and he couldn't stand the thought. With that realization, his determination to find Boyd McQueen's killer increased.

He walked through the doors of a saloon and began to feel more in his element. Saloons didn't differ that much from town to town.

Wiping a glass, the bartender raised a dark brow. "What can I do for you?"

Austin tilted his head toward the sign above the bar that boasted BARTON SPRINGS HIGH GRADE WHISKIES.

"I'll take a whiskey."

The bartender smiled. "Good choice."

He poured the amber brew into a glass and set it in front of Austin. Austin leaned forward, placed his elbows on the counter, and wrapped his hands around the glass. "You get a lot of business in here?"

The bartender nodded. "At night mostly. Not that much during the day."

"Could you get word out that I'm paying fifty dollars to anyone who knows anything about a man named Boyd McQueen?"

The bartender sucked one end of his mustache into the corner of his mouth and began to chew, his eyes narrowing in thought. "Other fella's paying five hundred."

Austin's stomach tightened into a hard ball. "What fella?"

The bartender nodded toward the back. "The fella at that table in the corner."

Austin turned and studied the man sitting at a distant table. Dressed in a black jacket and red brocade vest, he reminded Austin of a gambler. His fingers nimbly set one card after another on the table.

"Just sits there and plays cards by himself all day," the bartender offered.

"I'll take the bottle of whiskey," Austin said as he laid down his money and grabbed the neck of the bottle along with his glass. He ambled across the hardwood floor, his spurs jangling. He found comfort in the sound he'd been without for five years. "Hear you're looking for information on Boyd McQueen."

The man raised his eyes from the cards, pinning Austin with his dark gaze. "Yep."

"Found out anything so far?"

"Nope."

Not appreciating the man's brief answers, Austin tethered his temper. "Five hundred dollars is a lot of money—"

"Ain't coming out of my pocket."

Suspicion lurked in the back of Austin's mind. "Whose pocket is it coming out of?"

"Your brother's." With the toe of his boot, the man shoved a chair away from the table. "Have a seat."

"You're the detective Dallas hired?"

"Yep."

Cautiously Austin settled into the chair. "How did you know who I was?"

"You've got your brother's eyes."

Austin released a breath of disgust. "No wonder you haven't located the person who murdered Boyd. Dallas has brown eyes." He leaned forward, opening his eyes wide. "Mine are blue."

"They're shaped the same, and they both show a man of little patience. You've got his thick brows, his square chin, and a jaw that tightens when you're angry." With one hand, he swept up the cards spread over the table and rearranged them with a quiet shuffle. "And you walk like a man who just spent five years in prison and doesn't know if he can trust anyone."

Austin downed his whiskey, refilled his glass, and poured the amber liquid into the empty glass resting beside the man's arm. He didn't particularly like that the man had summed him up so easily and precisely. Between the town folk actually thinking him capable of murder and Becky's betrayal, he'd lost a great deal of his faith in his fellow man. Although Loree's touch had certainly made him want to believe in the worth of people. "Dallas didn't tell me your name."

"Wylan Alexander."

"What brought you to this town?"

"Your brother sent me a telegram."

Austin leaned forward. "What do you think of my theory that Boyd meant this town and not me when he wrote 'Austin' in the dirt?"

Wylan slapped the cards down on the table and swallowed all the whiskey in his glass before meeting Austin's gaze. "I'm here, ain't I?"

"But you think it's hogwash."

Wylan shook his head and patiently began laying the cards one face up, six face down. "I'll admit when I got your brother's telegram telling me what you thought, I laughed out loud, but I'm as desperate as you are and just as angry. It's never taken me more than six weeks to solve a case. This one's been hanging around too long and it's ruining my reputation, not to mention being hard on my pride. If McQueen hadn't written your name in the dirt, I'd say he was in the wrong place at the wrong time and some drifter got lucky."

Austin rubbed his hands up and down his face. "But he did write my name. Damn, I wish my parents had been living in Galveston when I was born."

Wylan chuckled. "Yep, might have saved us all some grief."

Austin took a sip of the whiskey. "You haven't learned anything at all?"

"Unfortunately, no."

"So what do we do?"

Wylan began to turn up cards and rearrange the ones on the table. "We wait."

Waiting had never been Austin's strong suit. He had thought prison guards had beat patience into him, but now that he was once again his own man—no longer a slave of the state—impatience had become his companion.

He had spent three days walking the streets, talking to people in saloons. The seedier the saloon, the more hopeful he had been that he would glean some information. Although Boyd McQueen had appeared upstanding to many in the community, he had possessed a darker side that curdled Austin's gut. He had to admit that it didn't bother him that the man had come to an untimely end. His only regret was that he had been the one to pay for it.

He had hoped by now that he would have had a glimmer of information. He walked past the post office and approached the Griedenweiss stables. He had a need to ride fast and hard over the hills, to feel Black Thunder's hooves pounding the ground beneath him, taking him away from an elusive quest toward . . . an unknown future.

Out of the corner of his eye, he saw a slight movement and shifted his gaze. A boy no older than seven was pulling a wooden wagon along the boardwalk. A sign hung over the side of the wagon.

PUPYS 4 SALE

2 BITS

Austin changed directions, ambled across the street, and easily caught up with the boy. "What you got here?" he asked.

The boy ground to a halt and furrowed his brow. "Don't you read?"

Austin smiled. "Yeah, I do. What kind of dogs are these?"

Confusion filled the boy's brown eyes as he swiped his nose with his sleeve. "The kind that's got four legs and a tail."

Smothering a grin, Austin hunkered down beside the wagon. The boy obviously didn't know a lot about breeding. Austin peered at the two puppies tumbling over each other. The tiny brown and white one caught his fancy. He scooped it up and studied it from all angles.

"That one's a boy," the child told him.

"Yeah, I can see that. How big was his mama?"

The boy held his hand level with his waist. " 'Bout this big."

"Think he'll be a good hunting dog?"

The boy nodded his head briskly. Austin figured he didn't know if the dog would be good at hunting, but he needed to get rid of him. The puppy squirmed, yipped, and gnawed on his thumb. A fighter. He liked that. "I'll take this one."

"The other's one better," the boy said.

"Why is that?"

"On account of the other one's a girl. If you git her, some day you can git more dogs that won't cost you nothing."

Grinning, Austin unfolded his body and reached into his pocket for a quarter. "I only need one."

He handed the silver coin to the boy. "Don't spend it all in one place," Austin said, tucking the dog beneath his arm.

Feeling more content than he had in days, Austin ambled to the livery and had one of the workers saddle Black Thunder. He mounted the horse and settled the dog into the crook of his thigh. Then he turned the stallion west and prodded him into an easy lope.

He reached his destination just as the sun began to paint its farewell across the sky. It had been a long time since he'd thought of the sunset as anything but the sun going down, yet he almost imagined he heard the fiery ball announcing the end of its daily journey.

His heart pounding as the weathered house came into view, he brought Black Thunder to a walk. He saw Loree sitting on the porch, her elbows on her knees, her chin cradled in her palms as she gazed into the distance. Her braid was draped over her shoulder, the bottom curling near her waist. As though sensing his presence, she straightened and looked in his direction. Slowly, she rose to her feet, a tentative smile playing across her lips. "Hello."

His heart felt as though someone had just closed a meaty fist around it. He drew the horse to a halt near the porch. "Howdy."

She crossed one bare foot over the other and put her hands behind her back, causing the worn material of her dress to stretch taut across her breasts. Austin's mouth went as dry as the West Texas wind in August.

"Did you find the man you were looking for?"

"No."

She peered around Black Thunder, obvious curiosity furrowing her delicate brow. "What are you holding?"

Austin glanced at his thigh. "Dog."

Dismounting, he remembered a time when he could have spoken more than one word without his throat closing off. She'd urged him not to return, and he had been leery of the welcome she'd bestow upon him. He wouldn't have blamed her for leveling her rifle at him and pulling the trigger this time. Cradling the animal in his palm, he extended it toward her. "It's for you."

Tears welled in her eyes, and her smile faltered before returning brighter than before. She took the puppy and rubbed it against her cheek. "He's beautiful."

She dropped to the porch and set the dog on her lap, running her small hands over the brown and white fur, and Austin knew a pang of envy.

She leaned close to the dog. "Do you have a name?"

His pink tongue snaked out and licked her chin, her nose. Loree laughed and Austin felt a shaft of pure joy pierce his soul. She looked up at him. "Does he have a name?"

Austin eased down to the porch, keeping a respectful distance, knowing it was ludicrous to even worry about respectability after all they'd shared. "Between town and here, I was calling him Two-bits. That's what he cost me."

"Two-bits," she repeated as she scratched behind the dog's short ears. The dog's body visibly quivered, and it released a little sound deep in its throat that had Austin shifting his butt on the porch, wondering what it would take to get Loree to rub her hands over him.

She peered at him. "Thank you."

"My pleasure." It truly was his pleasure to see her eyes shining like gold touched by the sun, and he wished he had more to offer her. She turned her attention back to the dog, and Austin shifted his gaze to the sunset, realizing why he'd come here. In town, surrounded by people, the loneliness had sharpened and grown. But here on this porch, sitting beside this woman, the loneliness eased away.

"Were you and Becky engaged?"

He snapped his head around and met her hesitant gaze. She licked her lips. "I was just curious. I always thought I'd know everything there was to know about a man before I . . ."

Even in the fading light, he saw the embarrassment flaming her cheeks. He watched her swallow.

"It just seems to me that we . . . we got ahead of ourselves," she said softly.

She struggled to hold his gaze, and his heart went out to her. He owed her. More than he could ever pay. Leaning forward, he planted his elbows on his thighs and clasped his hands tightly together. "No, we weren't engaged. We'd talked about getting married, but we never announced it. Guess I thought the talking about it etched it in stone, and that wasn't the way of it."

"Did you know the man she married?"

"He was my best friend."

Sympathy filled her eyes. "That must have been so hard—to lose Becky and your best friend."

He shrugged. "I always told Cameron that he needed to take care of Becky if I couldn't. Reckon he took my instructions to heart." He worked his jaw back and forth, knowing he should stop there, but this woman had a way about her that made him want to continue. "They've got a son. That hurt, seeing him for the first time. Until then, I thought . . ."

She leaned toward him. "What did you think?"

His mouth grew dry, and he stared at the scuffed toes of his boots. "That maybe she wasn't lying in Cameron's arms at night." He unclasped his hands, afraid the tension radiating through him would snap a bone.

"Do you think she's happy?"

He wiped his sweating hands on his thighs. "I hope she is." Peering over at her, he gave her a sad smile. "Truly I hope she is."

Reaching out, she threaded her fingers through his. "I imagine she wishes the same for you."

Strangely, he thought she was probably right. He closed his fingers gently around hers and rubbed the thumb of his free hand back and forth across her knuckles. "So tell me about Jake."

She drew her brows together. "Jake?"

Unwarranted joy shot through him, and he had to fight like the devil to keep the smile buried deep within his chest, to keep his face serious. He'd suspected that there had been no Jake in her life. "Yeah, Jake. Remember? You were thinking about him—"

Her eyes widened. "Oh, Jake."

She tried to pull her hand from his, but Austin tightened his grip. "So tell me about him."

The dog tumbled out of her lap, hit the ground with a yip, and pounced after a bug. Loree stopped struggling and lowered her gaze to her bare toes. "There is no Jake."

Austin slipped his finger beneath her chin and tilted her face back until her gaze met his. "I suspected as much."

"Why? Because I'm so plain?"

"You're not plain, Loree. There's something about you—a sweetness that just bubbles up from deep inside you. It touches your eyes, your lips. Once a man had gained your affections, he'd be a fool to leave you." He grazed his thumb over her full lower lip. "I have been known to be a fool."

"You say that as though you had gained my affections. If you believe that, you assume too much. I don't even know you. I was hurting and needed comfort. You offered, and as wrong as it was, I took. That's all."

"Was it wrong, Loree?"

In the encroaching darkness, he still saw the tears welling in her eyes as she nodded briskly.

"Why did you have to say her name?" she rasped. "Now, I can't even pretend you wanted me. I *know* you were thinking of someone else." She shot off the porch like a bullet fired from a rifle. She waved her hand dismissively in the air. "It doesn't matter. You used me. I used you." She scooped up the dog and hugged it close against her breast. "You don't owe me anything."

But it did matter, and he did owe her because he didn't think Loree

Grant could *use* someone if her life depended on it. He came slowly to his feet, his gaze never leaving hers. "Maybe I owe me something."

"What does that mean?" she asked.

"I'm not sure." He mounted Black Thunder and touched his finger to the brim of his hat. "Take care, Miss Grant."

He set his heels to his horse's sides and sent him into a lope. Austin had spent five years thinking about an auburn haired blue-eyed beauty. He didn't intend to spend the rest of his life thinking about a golden-eyed blond haired woman who had touched him one night and sent all his common sense to perdition.

He'd given her the damn dog. He had nothing else to offer her. And she was right. Even his heart wasn't free.

Chapter 6

❧

AUSTIN LEIGH OWNED her nothing. Loree repeated that litany in the following days as she watched Two-bits romp through her garden. He was a fierce protector. As she watched him attack the worms he uncovered, she couldn't remember when she'd laughed so hard.

Two-bits would never replace Digger in her heart, but he was slowly earning his own place, different but just as precious. She wondered if any woman would ever replace the woman Austin held in his heart. She thought it unlikely. She doubted that his heart even held room for another.

She wished she had kept her hurt buried deep inside and hadn't shown it to him when he visited her. She had driven him away with her accusations. He'd never return now. She knew it was for the best, but the loneliness increased because for some unfathomable reason when she had seen him sitting astride his horse, it felt as though a part of her had come home.

Standing in her garden, she heard the rapid clop of horses' hooves and the whirl of wheels. She spun around, her heart imitating the rapid motion of the buggy as it approached, two matching bay horses trotting before it. Austin pulled back on the reins, jumped out of the black buggy, and swept his hat from his head. "Morning, Miss Grant."

Her breath hitched at the warm smile he bestowed upon her. "What are you doing?"

"Well . . ." He turned his hat in his hands as he walked toward her. "I told you my parents had lived near Austin. My brother drew a map of the area for me before I left. I woke up this morning with a hankering to see the old homestead. I was hoping you'd give me the pleasure of your company."

He halted his steps and his fingers tightened around the brim of his hat. "But I'm not courting you, Loree. I've got nothing to offer you so I want to make that clear at the outset, but since you'd mentioned not knowing me well . . . and thinking that you should, I just thought you might like to come." His smile lessened. "And I'd like for you to be there with me."

"I could pack some food and we could have a picnic."

His smile returned, deeper than before. "I had the kitchen staff at the hotel fix us something and I bundled up the blankets from my bed . . ." His gaze slowly roamed over her. "So you wouldn't have to get your britches dirty."

"Oh." She glanced down at her brother's clothes. "Do you have time for me to change into a dress?"

He settled his hat into place. "I have time for you to do anything you want."

"I won't be long," she assured him as she hurried past him and scurried into the house, her heart beating so hard she was certain he'd been able to hear it. He had come back. His reasons didn't matter, and she didn't care that he wasn't courting her. She would spend the day without the loneliness eating at her.

She washed up quickly before donning the faded yellow dress. She rolled the stockings over her callused feet and up her calves before reaching beneath the bed and dragging out her black shoes. She worked her feet into the hated leather, reached for the button hook, and sealed her feet into what she'd always considered an instrument of torture.

But for reasons she couldn't understand, today, she was glad she'd kept them. She almost twisted her ankle with the first step she took toward the mirror. She gazed at her reflection, wishing the dress were a bit more fashionable, her hair more colorful. She wasn't a beauty. Yet Austin had rented a buggy and two horses and driven out here, seeking her company, when surely he had met women in town.

She tossed the braid over her shoulder, hating the way it made her look like a little girl. But she had never tried to sweep it up into a womanly fashion and had no idea where to begin. With a sigh, she grabbed a ragged shawl just in case they didn't get back before nightfall and headed out the door.

Austin shoved himself away from the porch beam as she closed the door, the shawl draped over her arm. She hadn't noticed before how his shirt appeared to be freshly laundered, recently ironed. His hair no longer curled around his collar, but was slightly shorter, cut even along the edges, and when the breeze blew by him and traveled to her, she smelled soap and a scent that was uniquely his. For a man who wasn't courting, he'd gone to a lot of trouble. When she had finished her slow perusal, she lifted her gaze to his sparkling blue eyes.

"You're wearing shoes," he said quietly, but she heard the amusement in his voice. "I was beginning to wonder if you owned a pair."

"I wear them in winter . . . and on special occasions." The heat warmed her cheeks. "I've never taken a ride in a buggy."

"Then you're in for a treat. This buggy rides well."

She stepped off the porch, and he fell in step beside her, his hand coming to rest easily on the small of her back. The buggy had two seats. The bench in the back held two boxes.

"What's in the boxes?" she asked.

"Our lunch is in one, and your dog is in the other."

Looking up at him, she nearly tripped over her feet. He steadied her and smiled. "Didn't figure you'd want to leave him here alone. I put him in the box with some blankets and my pocket watch. He went right to sleep."

He took her hand, helped her into the carriage, and settled beside her, his thigh brushing hers. She pressed her knees together and clenched her hands in her lap. He lifted the reins and gave the horses a gentle rap on the backside. In unison, they surged forward into a trot.

They rode in silence for several moments, the countryside unfolding before them, bathed in the blue of bluebonnets.

"I love this time of year," Loree said wistfully, "when the flowers coat the hills."

"Their fragrance reminds me of you."

Peering at him, finding his gaze fastened on her, she released a self-conscious laugh. "I gather them up, dry them out, and sprinkle the petals around the house. Sometimes I put them in my bath water."

His eyes darkened and she wondered if he was thinking of the night when he'd washed her. His gaze drifted down to her lips and she knew he was.

"How far away is your old home?" she asked hastily.

"If my brother's map is accurate, I figure an hour or so."

The journey took a little over two hours, and Loree thought it was the most pleasant two hours of her life, even though they spoke little. When he finally drew the buggy to a halt, Loree felt a somberness come over him. She couldn't say that she blamed him. Weeds, overgrowth, and a dilapidated structure that might have once been a one-room cabin greeted them.

Although she had grown up with little, she knew she'd had more than he might have possessed here. The buggy rocked as he climbed out. He walked around the horses and came to her side, extending his hand. He helped her out, then reached beneath the seat and gathered up a handful of bluebonnets. She was surprised to feel the slight trembling in his hand as he wrapped it around hers.

"I don't remember much about the place," he said quietly as he led her away from the buggy.

"How old were you when you left?" she asked.

"Five."

They walked until they reached a towering oak tree, the branches spreading out gracefully, the abundant leaves whispering in the breeze. Hanging from the lowest branch, a swing made of fraying rope and weathered wood swayed slightly. On the ground to the right of it, among the weeds and briars, stood a wooden marker.

Lovita Leigh.
Wife and Mother.
Deeply Loved, Sorely Missed
1829–1865

Austin released Loree's hand, removed his hat, dropped to one knee beside the grave, pulled at the weeds until he'd made a small clearing, and placed the flowers in front of the marker. He braced his forearm on his thigh and bowed his head.

Loree knew a moment's hesitation, feeling awkward because she was familiar with every aspect of the outer man and understood so little of the man who dwelled inside. Yet from the beginning, she had been drawn to him and the anguish in his eyes that spoke when his voice didn't.

She knelt beside him and laid her hand on his forearm, squeezing gently. He turned his hand slightly and moved it back until he was able to intertwine his fingers with hers.

"I don't remember what she looked like," he said quietly. "A man should remember his mother."

"You do remember her or you wouldn't have felt a need to come here." She touched the blue petals of the flowers he'd set on the ground. "I bet you picked flowers for her."

A faraway look came into his eyes and a corner of his mouth quirked up. "Yeah, I did. She laughed. Not because she thought it was funny, but because it made her happy." He closed his eyes. "Lord, she had a pretty laugh . . . like music."

"Did she tell you stories at bedtime?"

He opened his eyes, and it gladdened her heart to see that a small portion of the sadness had melted away.

"She told me stories, but not with words. She used songs. I remember she'd sit on the edge of my bed, and I'd watch her fingers caress the violin strings as she moved the bow and the most beautiful sounds flowed from the wood through the strings. I tried so hard not to fall asleep so I could keep watching her hands. I loved watching her hands." Turning his head slightly, he smiled warmly. "I remember her hands. She had the longest fingers—"

"Like yours."

Surprise flitted across his face. He lifted the hand she wasn't holding, turned it, and studied it from all angles. "I reckon so. I never noticed before."

"You should learn to play the violin."

She felt his hand stiffen within hers.

"You have to hear the music in your heart before you can create it with a fiddle. I can't do that," he said.

"You could try—"

"I can't."

He surged to his feet, pulling her up with him, his fingers tightening around hers as he walked away from the grave. Loree stumbled as she followed. He swung around, caught, and steadied her.

"You all right?" he asked, concern clearly reflected in his eyes.

Her cheeks grew warm, and she suddenly wished she'd spent the last five years practicing to be a lady as her mother had wanted instead of a hoyden thinking no man would ever look at her the way Austin Leigh was looking at her now. She nodded jerkily and gave him a wan smile. "I'm just used to ground beneath my feet instead of leather."

As though amused, he slowly shook his head and glanced at her scuffed shoes. Unexpectedly he dropped to one knee and slapped his raised thigh. "Put your foot up here."

"What are you going to do?"

He grabbed her ankle and lifted her foot. Thrown off-balance, she clamped her fingers onto his shoulder to brace herself. She watched in amazement as he freed the buttons on her shoe. She thought about jerking her foot back, insisting the shoes stay where they were, but he dropped his head back and she fell into the depths of his blue, blue eyes. How many times during the past week had she caught herself staring into the flames of a fire, searching for the warmth of his gaze?

He worked her shoe off, and when she would have removed her stockinged foot from his thigh, he covered it with his palm and held it in place. His gaze holding hers, he slowly guided his hands over her ankle, beneath her skirt, up her calf, past her knee, until his fingers grazed the bare flesh of her thigh just above her stockings. Scalding heat shot through her, and she dug her fingers into his shoulders.

Using his thumbs, he rolled her stocking down her leg, while his fingers trailed over her skin, his gaze never leaving hers, the blue darkening until she felt as though he had ignited something within her. Her heart beat so hard that she was certain he'd be able to feel the pounding in her toes. He skimmed her stocking over her foot, and finally lowered his gaze to her bare foot. He rubbed his finger over the top of her foot.

"You've got the cutest toes."

"They're crooked," she told him as though he didn't have a clear view of her toes as he massaged each toe thoroughly before moving onto the next.

Feeling as though every bone in her body was melting, she was surprised she still had the ability to stand.

"Did you break this toe?" he asked when he reached the toe next to her biggest toe.

"No. My pa had toes like that. He called it a hammer toe. See, it looks like a hammer."

He gave her a grin that very nearly caused all the breath to leave her body. She was too aware of him. Memories of his touching her in the ways that a man touched a woman threatened to turn from cold ashes into a blazing fire. She jerked her foot off his thigh.

As though he knew exactly what she'd been remembering, he patted his thigh and his smile grew. "Other foot."

She took a deep calming breath. "I can take it off." To her embarrassment, her voice hitched, but he didn't laugh. He just turned those blue eyes on her, challenging her. "Come on, Sugar. Give me your other foot before you break your pretty neck."

She had never been able to resist a challenge. She stomped her foot onto his thigh. He laughed deeply, richly, like a man remembering what it was to enjoy life.

"So you've got a bit of a temper," he said as he attacked the buttons.

"Sometimes." She watched the deftness with which his fingers worked. "Not often."

He dropped her shoe to the ground and started gliding his hands over her leg. She wasn't certain she could survive his removing the other stocking, and when he lifted his gaze to hers, she was certain she wouldn't.

"Where's your father?" she blurted, to distract herself from the heavenly sensation of his fingers sliding beneath her skirt.

He blinked, halting his hands behind her knee. "He died at Chickamauga."

"So he fought in the war."

"Yep."

"Who raised you then?"

"My brothers."

He had mentioned the one. "How many do you have?"

"Two. They're considerably older than me. Both fought in the war alongside my pa. I don't remember my pa at all, but my oldest brother supposedly looks just like him."

He began to massage her knee.

"Aren't you getting tired of kneeling?"

He smiled warmly. "Nope."

"I'm getting tired of standing on one leg."

He barely looked contrite as he apologized and rolled down her stocking. As soon as her stocking cleared her toes, she removed her foot from his thigh. He didn't appear offended as he stuffed her stocking into her shoe.

Loree took a moment to relish the feel of the grass beneath her soles, but it somehow paled in comparison to his warm thigh against her foot. He grabbed her shoes and unfolded his long, lanky body.

"I'll put these in the carriage," he offered.

She watched him walk to the carriage, wishing she didn't have so many mixed emotions where he was concerned. Dreading the feelings his touch stirred within her, desperately wanting the easing of the loneliness that his presence caused. As often as DeWayne visited, he never managed to take the loneliness away.

Austin scooped Two-bits out of the box and set him on the ground, laughing as the dog scampered after a butterfly. She liked the rumble of his laughter, the glow in his eyes as he walked to her, the slight curving of his lips, and the warmth of his hand as he wrapped it around hers before they continued their journey into his past.

Night had fallen by the time Austin brought the buggy to a halt in front of Loree's house. He set the box containing the sleeping puppy on the table, lit a lamp, and walked through the house as though he owned it, checking all the dark corners and closets.

"Everything seems to be in order," he said, his voice low, and Loree wondered why everyone always talked quieter at night.

Her gaze drifted toward the bedroom door, and she wondered what, if anything, he expected now. Once an intimacy had been shared, how did one establish boundaries?

"I appreciate that you went with me today."

She snapped her gaze to his. "I enjoyed it."

"Did you?" he asked, turning his hat in his hands.

She smiled softly. "Yes, I did."

"Good." He glanced quickly around the room. "I'd best get back to town, get the buggy and horses turned into the livery."

With long strides he crossed the room and opened the door. Loree followed him onto the porch, the pale light from the lamp spilling through the doorway and across his face. Within the shadows, she saw his fingers working the brim of his hat.

"Loree . . ."

Her breath caught and held. She didn't know where she'd find the strength to refuse him if he asked to come back inside. He took a step nearer and rubbed his knuckles across her cheek.

"Loree, I'm not courting you," he said quietly.

"You told me that earlier today. I haven't forgotten."

"I just want to make sure that you understand that."

"I do."

"Good."

His mouth swooped down to cover hers, his arm snaking around her waist, drawing her flush against his body. Hot, moist, and hungry, his lips taunted and teased. Of their own accord, her arms wound around his neck, and she returned his kiss with equal fervor. She knew it was wrong. She had nothing of permanence to offer him.

When he finally drew away, Loree was surprised her legs were able to support her.

"Get inside before I do something we both regret," he rasped in a ragged voice.

She nodded, slipped inside, and closed the door. She pressed her ear against it. It was long moments before she heard his boots hitting the porch, carrying him away, before she heard the buggy roll into the night.

She sank to the floor and buried her face in her hands, but she couldn't hide from the truth. Had he asked, she would have invited him to stay.

Chapter 7

᠉

*A*USTIN STARED AT the five cards in his hand. The queen of hearts looked damned lonely with no other face cards to keep her company. He understood that feeling. Christ, loneliness had been his companion for most of his life. He loved his brothers, but hanging on to their shirttails, he'd found little affection and when it came, it had been little more than a quick nod of the head for a job well done. He didn't resent that. A man's world was decidedly different from a woman's.

Amelia had taught him that affection deepened with a touch: slender fingers on a clenched fist, a hand rubbing a shoulder, a hug, or a kiss on the cheek. Small things that breached the mighty wall of lonesomeness. But Amelia had belonged first to Dallas, then to Houston, never to Austin. As much as she had eased his forlorn heart, she had also left him wanting. Until he'd first set eyes on Becky.

She had been his: to look at, to smile at, to laugh with—whenever he wanted. But he'd kept his hands and lips to himself, waiting until she was old enough. She had been nearly seventeen, the first time he'd kissed her. And nine months later, he was sitting in a cold barren cell with nothing but the memories. And the loneliness had increased because he had known what it was to live without it.

He told himself that it was loneliness that had him riding out to Loree Grant's house late into the night. He'd simply sit astride Black Thunder and stare at the shadowed house. More than once he had to stop himself from dismounting and knocking on her door. He didn't imagine she'd appreciate being disturbed from her slumber at two o'clock in the morning. And what could he have said?

I can't sleep without holding you, smelling you, listening to your breath whispering into the night.

He'd gone so far as to pull bluebonnets from the fields and stuff them beneath his pillow at the hotel just so he could pretend she was near.

It had been a week since he'd taken her to the old homestead and his loneliness had increased with each passing day. He wasn't in a position to court her, had nothing to offer her, and even though he'd told her that, he had seen a measure of hope reflected in her golden eyes. He couldn't bear the thought of disappointing her, and he feared if he spent much more time with her, he might do just that.

"You in or out?"

Austin snapped his gaze up to the detective's. Wylan had lifted a brow. Austin tossed down his cards. "I feel like we're wasting our time. Or at least I am. I might as well be spitting in a high wind for all the good I'm doing here."

Wylan gathered up the cards and began his infuriating silent shuffle. "I finished visiting the last of the brothels last night. Didn't glean any information."

"You've been visiting brothels?"

"Yep. No telling what a man might say in the heat of passion."

Austin knew too well the truth of that statement. "I could have saved you the trouble."

Wylan smiled. "Oh, it was no trouble."

The man's easy attitude was beginning to wear thin. Austin planted his elbows on the table and leaned forward. "Boyd McQueen had a preference for boys."

The cards Wylan had been shuffling went flying out of his hands and disbelief swept over his face. "What?"

Austin rubbed his jaw wondering how much he could say without causing harm. He'd learned of Boyd's perversions from Rawley. Furious over a past he'd been unable to change, Austin had shot a bullet over Boyd's head in the saloon and announced that nothing would have brought him greater pleasure than to rid the ground of Boyd's shadow.

Those words had served to condemn him as much as Boyd writing "Austin" in the dirt. Austin sighed deeply. "Boyd took pleasure in hurting boys, among other things."

"Your brother's son?"

"I didn't say that."

"You didn't have to. The boy has a haunted look in his eyes. I just couldn't figure out what had put it there." Wylan poured himself a whiskey and downed it in one swallow. "I gotta tell you, the more I learn about Boyd McQueen the more I hope I don't find the man who killed him. But then there's the matter of your innocence."

Austin fingered his glass of whiskey. "I spent five years thinking someone had killed him and purposely put the blame on me. The thought of getting even burned inside me. Now, I'm beginning to think I just got unlucky. No one set out to hurt me. Someone murdered Boyd, and I got blamed for it. If it hadn't destroyed my life, I'd be applauding whoever killed him."

"Which is the reason I'll keep looking, but this gives me a different angle: an irate father, a young boy McQueen might have hurt who finally grew to manhood . . . People will be less likely to share that sort of information, but I'll keep that in mind as I'm digging."

"I'm thinking of heading home. I can't see that I'm doing any good here. Boyd stole five years of my life. I don't want him taking any more."

Wylan gathered up his scattered cards and began to play a game of solitaire. "I'm going to stay here a few more days, then head back to Kansas, see if this new information brings anything to the surface."

The McQueens had moved to Texas from Kansas several years back. If Dee hadn't brought such joy to Dallas's life, Austin would have wished they'd never left Kansas.

"Mr. Leigh?"

Austin glanced up at the hesitant voice. Recognition dawned and he slowly came to his feet. "Dewayne, isn't it?"

"Yes, sir. I was out visiting Loree today. She looks a might poorly. I have a feeling you're the cause, but she said it ain't my place to judge."

Guilt cut through him like a rusty knife. He should have honored her request that he never return. "That was mighty generous of her."

"She's a generous sort—to a fault, if you want to know the truth. I don't like to see her hurt."

"I have no intention of hurting her." It was that intention that had kept him away from her when everything inside him wanted to see her again.

"Well, see that you don't 'cuz you'd have to answer to me if you did."

Dewayne spun on his heel. Austin dropped into his chair and met Wylan's speculative gaze.

"What was all that about?"

"Personal," Austin said just before he downed his whiskey, relishing the burning in his gut. Dewayne obviously had a soft spot for Loree. Hell, who wouldn't?

"Nothing that might help me find Boyd's killer?"

"No, but what would it cost me to have you search for another killer?"

"Not a cent. Your brother is paying me enough to find ten killers."

"What information would you need?"

"Name helps. Description. Anything at all. What do you know about him?"

"Not much. He killed a family—"

"Mr. Leigh?"

Austin jerked his head around. Dewayne held out an envelope. "I forgot that Loree asked me to drop this off at the Driskill for you, but reckon I can just give it to you here."

Austin took the envelope, studying the scrawl on the paper that looked as though it had been written with a trembling hand. " 'Preciate it."

Dewayne gave him a slow nod before sauntering away.

"That from your Loree?"

"She's not *my* Loree." Austin tore open the envelope and pulled out the letter she'd written. The words had joy, fear, and dread weaving through him. He surged to his feet, knocking the chair over.

"What is it?"

"I was wrong. She is my Loree. Do whatever it takes to find Boyd's killer. I'm headin' back to Dallas's ranch."

His Loree. Austin stood in the doorway of her bedroom, watching her. She was too trusting, leaving the front door and the door to her bedroom open. And the dog wasn't a damn bit of good. It had neither heard nor smelled his approach, but just continued to gnaw on one of Loree's black shoes near the bed, growling at it as though it were a threat when the real threat was leaning against her doorjamb.

In her daisy colored dress, she sat on the floor, her legs tucked beneath her, her toes peering out from under her backside. Her thick braid was draped over her shoulder. She had opened a wooden chest and was slowly removing tiny pieces of clothing, spreading them over her lap, and pressing them flat with her fingers, as though each garment was precious—as precious as the child growing within her.

His child.

His knees felt like a couple of strawberries left too long on the vine, until they were soft and worthless. Her note had asked nothing of him. She expected nothing from him. She had simply wanted him to know that she was carrying his child.

He'd gathered up his belongings at the hotel, saddled Black Thunder, and ridden hard, every word of her letter emblazoned on his mind, echoing through his heart. He wished he could offer her more than an uncertain future and broken dreams.

He shoved himself away from the doorjamb. His boot heels echoed through the room as he walked toward her, his stomach knotted as though someone had lassoed it and given the rope a hard tug. She jerked her head around, the wariness in her golden eyes remaining as he neared. Sweeping his hat from his head, he hunkered down beside her. "Howdy."

She gave him a tentative smile, her fingers wrinkling the tiny gown she'd just smoothed across her lap. "Hello."

"Dewayne gave me your letter."

"You didn't have to come."

A shaft of deep sadness pierced his soul. "You don't know me at all, Loree, if you believe that."

Tears welled in her eyes as she dropped her gaze to the delicate clothing in her lap. Reaching out with his thumb, he captured a teardrop that slowly rolled from the corner of her eye. "I'm going home, Loree."

She snapped her gaze up to his. "You found the man you were looking for?"

"No, but I think it's unlikely that I ever will, after all this time. I spent the past five years dying. I want to start living again."

She gave him a hesitant smile. "I don't even know where your home is."

"West Texas. My brother has a ranch. For as long as I can remember, I've helped him work his spread, herd his cattle."

Her smile grew. "I guessed that you were a cowboy."

Not by choice. He'd always hated ranching, had always dreamed of leaving, but the places life had taken him weren't exactly what he'd had in mind. His gaze drifted to her stomach, flat as a board. He was about to travel another trail he hadn't knowingly chosen, but oddly, he had a feeling this one would leave him with no regrets.

"I'd be real honored if you'd marry me," he said, his voice low.

More tears filled her eyes just before she averted her gaze. He wished the blue flowers hadn't disappeared from the hills. He would have liked to have brought her some. Maybe he should have settled for the red and yellow flowers that remained. Or maybe he should have brought her a bright yellow ribbon for her hair, anything to accompany the words that sounded as cold as a river in January. He watched helplessly as she swiped the tears from her eyes, knowing he was the cause.

She peered at him and gave him the saddest smile he'd ever seen. "No."

He felt as though she'd just hit him in the chest with an iron skillet. "What do you mean no?"

"I mean I don't want to get married."

"Then why did you send me the note?"

"I just thought you had a right to know about the child."

"I have more than the right to know. I have the responsibility to care for it. I'm not gonna have him labeled a bastard."

She flinched and angled her chin. "Her."

"What?"

"I think it's a girl."

That made sense to him since it seemed the Leigh men were only capable of producing girls. "All right, fine. It's a girl. You want her whispered about 'cuz that's what'll happen." He softened his voice. "And they'll whisper about you, too, and don't tell me that there's nobody around to notice. You can't live like a hermit with a child. You can't deny her the world just because you've seen the ugliest side of it. Marry me, Loree."

"Do you love me?"

Her quietly spoken question was like a fist closing around his heart. "I like you well enough," he answered honestly. "Don't you like me?"

"I like what I know of you, but what do I really know? Until a few minutes ago, your home could have been on the moon as far as I knew."

"Well, I *don't* live on the moon. I live in West Texas, and I have the means to provide for you—not in as grand a fashion as I'd like, but I think it'd be tolerable."

"Tolerable?"

"Dammit, Loree! I wronged you and I'm willing to do whatever it takes to make it right."

"How does convincing me to marry a man who doesn't love me make it right?"

"Maybe it doesn't make it right for us, but it'll make it right for the baby. We have to put her first."

"Do you still love Becky?"

His stomach tightened, and he clenched his jaw. Wylan had certainly been right about words spoken in the heat of passion. He'd uttered one word, and this woman was going to hold it against him for the rest of his life. He surged to his feet and stormed from the house. He headed for the woodpile, worked the ax out of the stump, lifted a log, and slammed the ax into it.

He tried to put himself in Loree's place, remembering the relief he'd felt when she'd confessed there was no Jake. Only for her, there would always be a Becky. His first love.

"What are you doing?" she asked from behind him.

He tossed the split wood onto the pile and hefted another log to the stump. "Chopping you twenty years worth of wood. I'm gonna repair your house, paint it, and do anything else around here that needs to be done. You don't want to marry me? Fine. But I'll be damned before a child of mine is gonna suffer because of mistakes I made."

I'll be damned before a child of mine is gonna suffer because of mistakes I made.

Those words echoed through Loree's mind as she lay in her bed unable to sleep. They told her a lot about the man. He accepted responsibility for his actions.

But then, if she were honest with herself, she'd already known that, had learned that fact about him the first night when he'd chopped wood for a bowl of stew.

She didn't know the little things about him: his favorite foods, preferred colors. She didn't know if he danced or sang.

But she knew the important things: He was a rare man who thought more with his heart than his head. When he loved, he loved deeply and years didn't diminish his affections even when memories faded. She had seen him weep over the loss of a woman, had watched him place flowers on the twenty-year-old grave of his mother. Had welcomed his gifts of a burned barn and a puppy.

But above all else, she had welcomed the comfort of his presence, the warmth of his touch. For a while, he had eased the sorrow and the loneliness.

For the past two hours, she had heard Austin tromping around her house. He had no barn in which to sleep. She had left the front door unbolted, the door to her room ajar, a portion of her hoping that he would sleep with her—just sleep with her, his arm around her, his breath skimming over the nape of her neck.

She strained her ears for several moments, but no longer heard him stirring outside. He had probably stretched out in the wagon he'd brought along with his plans to pack her up and haul her to West Texas as his wife.

She pressed her hand to her stomach. It wasn't the first time that the actions of one night would forever change her life, but their actions were reaching out to touch an innocent child.

Austin was right. Their child would suffer because of their mistake. Born out of wedlock, she would burden the shame that rightfully belonged to them.

She threw off the blankets and scrambled out of bed. In bare feet, wearing nothing but her nightgown, she padded through the house, opened the front door, and saw Austin sitting on the porch steps. He glanced over his shoulder. She felt his gaze travel from the top of her head to the tips of her toes before he turned his attention back to the blackness stretching across the sky.

She knew that rejecting his proposal had hurt him. He hadn't joined her for supper. He'd prepared a bath for her, but hadn't indulged himself in the luxury. He seemed intent on giving all to her and taking nothing from her.

Her mouth grew as dry as cotton. She crossed the porch and sat beside him. His knees were widespread, his elbows resting on his thighs, his hands clamped together before him, his gaze trained on the distance. In the shadows of the night, she saw the slight breeze brushing his black hair over his collar.

"Lot of stars falling from the sky tonight," he said, his voice low.

She followed the direction of his gaze. A ball of light arced through the black void and disappeared like a dream that was never meant to be.

"Make a wish, Loree," he said quietly.

She closed her eyes. One wish. If she were allowed only one wish, she wished she could unburden her past on this man sitting beside her. She thought he, of all people, would understand all that she had done, the things the killer had goaded her into doing. She wished she could tell him and not risk losing any of the affection he might hold for her.

"What did you wish?" he asked.

Opening her eyes, she peered at him. He watched her, and even in the darkness, she felt the intensity of his gaze. "If I tell you, it won't come true. Did you make a wish?"

He leaned toward her, propping himself up on an elbow. "I wished that you would marry me."

Her heart beat faster, harder than the hind foot of a rabbit. He took the curling end of her braid and carried it to his lips. She almost imagined she felt his breath fanning over it, his soft lips brushing over it.

"I want you to marry me for the sake of our daughter—"

"Son."

His hand stilled, the locks of her hair resting against his chin. "Earlier you said—"

"Well, now I'm thinking it's a boy." She rolled her head to her shoulder. "I can't decide what it is."

He chuckled low. "Marry me because you make me smile when I haven't in a long time."

"Less than a week ago, you told me that you weren't courting me, that you had nothing to offer me."

"That was before I knew you needed my name." He cradled her cheek. "I'd give you the world if I could, Loree, but I made a decision five years ago that's gonna limit the things I can offer you. The only thing I have that I can give you is my name, and I hate like hell that I can't give it to you untarnished. But I'll work hard. I think I can give you—and our children—a good life. I know I can give you a better life than the one you have here. At least with me, you won't have the loneliness."

During the past month, she could count the number of days that contained a promise of happiness. The promise always arrived when he did. Her child could have a father who had been in prison or no father at all. Was the past more important than the present? And who was she to judge? Her past was as tarnished as his.

"Will you promise me something?" she asked hesitantly.

"Anything."

Her stomach quivered, and she clasped her hands tightly together. "Will you promise never to make love to me if you're thinking of Becky?"

A profound silence stretched between them. Earlier he had mentioned children, not child, and she knew he expected more than a marriage in name only. She also knew that she could easily come to care for this man, perhaps she already did more than she should. Her heart would shatter if he ever again whispered another's name while joining his body to hers.

"I promise," he rasped.

"Then I'll marry you—for the sake of the child."

A warm smile crept over his face, and he grazed his knuckles over her cheek. "I'll make it good for you, Sugar. You won't regret that you had to marry me."

He drew her face toward his and kissed her. Not with passion, not with fire. But with an apology and understanding.

She knew she'd never regret marrying him, and she hoped he would never discover what she had done, the actions that had prompted her to settle for a life of solitude. For if he did, she feared that he would deeply regret marrying her.

Chapter 8

⌇

"OH MY GOODNESS!"

As the wagon rolled along, Loree shifted Two-bits on her lap and stared at the massive adobe structure. Turrets in the corners. A crenellated roof. She'd never seen anything like it. "Is that an inn?"

Beside her on the wagon seat, Austin chuckled. "Nope. That's my brother's house."

Loree pressed her hand against her stomach as though to protect the child. "It's so big."

"I think it's god-awful ugly."

"Well, it's not exactly what I would want in a house—"

"What do you want, Loree?"

She turned at the serious tone of his voice. They had been married in Austin, with only Dewayne and his family in attendance. She had worn a white dress and new soft leather shoes that Austin had purchased for her. She'd carried a bouquet of wildflowers that he had picked for her.

As nervous as she'd been, she'd also felt a spark of happiness because he treated her with reverence and respect, and he constantly worried over her. Too many years had passed since anyone other than Dewayne had worried over her.

He had packed up her belongings, loaded them on the wagon, and traveled slower than a snail's pace for fear the jarring wagon would cause her to lose the baby. At night, they slept within each other arms, beneath the stars, but he never attempted to exercise his husbandly rights.

"Something smaller," she assured him. Then she smiled brightly. "Something much smaller."

He returned her smile. "I ought to be able to give you that."

She slipped Two-bits into his box on the floorboards. He no longer looked like a puppy and was rapidly outgrowing the box. Austin had promised to build a shelter for the dog as soon as they arrived.

"Are we going to stay with your brother?"

"For a while. Till we get settled. Decide what we want, where we want to live. I have a little money saved up, but it won't get us far."

The wagon rolled past a huge barn that bore no resemblance to the one that had sat on her property. She heard the clanging of iron from the blacksmith who worked near the barn. Horses trotted around a large corral. In the distance, she saw a long narrow clapboard house and a brick building. She felt as though she were traveling through a miniature town. Men wearing chaps and dusty hats sauntered between the buildings. Only a couple acknowledged Austin as he drove the wagon by them.

She might have thought he didn't know the others if it weren't for the tightening in his jaw. He brought the wagon to a halt in front of the veranda. A man and woman sitting on a bench swing slowly came to their feet. The man stood as tall as Austin did, and she knew from the facial features that he was Austin's brother. The woman was nearly as tall. Slender, she moved gracefully across the porch.

"You should have sent word that you were on your way home," she said as she floated down the steps.

Austin leapt from the wagon, walked briskly to her, and hugged her fiercely. "Didn't know how long we'd be. Didn't want you worrying about us."

"Did you find out anything?" his brother asked, and Loree sensed in the tone of his voice that he was a man who gave no quarter.

"Not a damn thing," Austin said as he stepped toward the wagon and held his arms up to her.

Loree wiped her sweating palms on her skirt before she placed her hands on his shoulders. He grabbed her waist, and she felt his trembling through her clothes. She met his gaze and saw the worry in his eyes. She tried to give him a smile of reassurance, but feared that she had failed miserably.

He brought her to the ground and slipped his arm around her. "This is my brother Dallas and his wife, Dee."

Dee smiled prettily and Dallas looked as though he were waiting for a clap of thunder to sound.

"Did your parents name all their sons after towns?" Loree asked.

"Yeah, they did." Austin met his brother's darkening gaze. "This is Loree. My wife."

Dallas narrowed his eyes. "Your wife?"

Shock rippled across Dee's face, before her eyes warmed, and she gave Loree a sincere smile. Stepping forward, she wrapped her arms around Loree's shoulders. "How wonderful! Welcome to the family."

As Dee released her hold, a wave of nausea hit Loree, and the world suddenly spun around her. She staggered backward. Austin reached out, steadying her. Her cheeks burned as concern swept over Dee's face.

"Are you all right?" Dee asked.

Loree nodded. "It's just the baby. I get light-headed when I go too long without eating."

"The baby?" Dallas ground out in a clipped voice. "And when is this blessed event to take place?"

From the tone of his voice, Loree wasn't certain he truly considered it to be a blessed event, but she wasn't going to let him think she was ashamed of carrying his brother's child. She angled her chin. "End of January."

"Dee, why don't you take Loree inside and get her something cool to drink?" Austin suggested. "I'm afraid I might have pushed us a little too hard trying to get here before nightfall."

Dee wrapped her arm around Loree's waist. "I'd love to get her out of this heat. Come on inside."

Loree glanced over her shoulder at Austin.

"Go on," he urged.

Austin watched Dee guide his wife into the house. Then he met Dallas's blazing glare.

"She's your wife and she didn't know your brother's name?" he asked.

"I told her I had brothers. I mentioned Houston to her. Guess I just never got around to mentioning your name. Don't take it personal." Austin stepped onto the porch. Dallas grabbed his arm and jerked him back down.

"Let me get this straight," Dallas said, his voice seething. "Five years ago, you bedded Becky Oliver and to protect her reputation, you kept your mouth shut and ended up in prison. Now, you've been gone less than four months and show up at my door with a wife—a pregnant wife at that. Do you have a problem keeping your trousers buttoned or do you just have a tendency to get involved with women who have no morals—"

Dallas's tirade ended the instant Austin's fist made contact with his jaw and sent him staggering backward. He landed hard in the dirt. It took every ounce of control Austin could muster not to pound his brother into a bloody pulp. "You don't know a goddamn thing about any of it, and until you do, keep your goddamn mouth shut!"

Austin stormed up the steps and threw open the door. "Loree, we're leaving!"

He stalked down the steps, taking deep breaths, trying to calm himself before Loree got outside. Dallas worked his way to his feet, backhanding the blood trailing from the corner of his mouth. "Where in the hell do you think you're going, boy?" Dallas demanded.

"I'm not a boy. If prison does nothing else, it beats the boy right out of you. Where I'm going is none of your damn business," Austin snarled. He spun around at the sound of footsteps and held his hand toward Loree. "Come on, Sugar."

Worry etched creases into her brow. "Is something wrong?" she asked, her gaze darting between him and Dallas.

"No, I just decided we'd be better off staying at the hotel in town." The anxiety didn't ease from her face. He squeezed her hand. "Honest."

He helped her into the wagon, then climbed up, released the brake, and slapped the reins. He'd expected coming home with a wife to be difficult. He just hadn't expected it to rip away the last bonds he had with his family.

Staring at the night sky through the window of his office, Dallas felt a need to ride across the plains, climb to the top of one of his windmills, and listen to the clatter created by the constant breeze. Instead, he quietly sipped on his whiskey and wondered where he had gone wrong.

He heard the quiet footsteps, downed the remaining whiskey, and set his glass aside.

"Are you ready to tell me why Austin hit you?" Dee asked softly.

"I questioned his wife's morals."

"Then, I'm glad he hit you. It says a lot about his feelings for the woman."

"And I questioned his ability to keep his trousers buttoned."

"Oh, Dallas, you didn't."

He spun around and faced his wife. "Dammit, Dee, by my reckoning, he must have bedded her two minutes after he met her. He's given himself a life sentence with a woman he barely knows—"

She angled her head and lifted a dark brow.

"Dammit! Our situation was different."

"I realize that. You didn't know me *at all* when we married."

He twisted around, gazing back into the night, into the past. "I raised him, Dee. From the time he was five, I was more of a father than a brother. I hate seeing him waste his life, making decisions that lead him nowhere."

She placed her hand on his shoulder, a habit she'd acquired once she realized his back had little feeling in it after the beating he'd received five years before as a result of her oldest brother's greed. "You gave him a good foundation. Now you have to give him the freedom to build on it."

He snapped his head around. "And if I don't like the life he's building on it?"

"As hard as it is, you have to learn to accept it. Someday Rawley and Faith will leave us. All we can do is hope that the foundation we give them is strong enough to sustain their dreams . . . and their failures."

He drew her into his embrace and pressed his cheek against the top of her head. "I remember coming home from the war and finding him living like an animal. I don't know how long our ma had been dead before we got there or how Austin managed to survive. It took me and Houston weeks to earn his trust. Then he looked at everything we gave him as though he were afraid we'd snatch it away. I always expected him to dream bigger dreams, go farther than I ever dared. I feel as though I've failed him."

She leaned back and cradled his face between her hands. "Do you know what Cameron's biggest fear was?"

Dallas blinked at the abrupt change of subject. "I've got no idea."

"Once Austin realized that Cameron and Becky were married, he'd post a public announcement telling the town that he had been with Becky the night Boyd was killed. Neither he nor Becky would have blamed him had he done so, but he didn't. Becky trusted him that night and he won't betray that trust. How can you have failed him when you raised him to be such a fine young man, to accept responsibility for his actions?

"Loree and I didn't have much of an opportunity to talk, but I know he met her on his way to Austin. She didn't even know where he lived until today. He could have ridden out of her life and never looked back. Instead he convinced her to marry him. You didn't fail him, Dallas. You raised him to be the kind of man you can be proud to call 'brother.'"

Dallas heaved a weary sigh. "If I didn't fail him in the twenty years I raised him, I'm afraid I may have failed him today."

"Only if you let what happened this afternoon fester between you. He needs us now more than he ever has before, and I'm sure tomorrow he'll wake up with a few regrets of his own. Go talk to him first thing in the morning."

"What in the world did I do to deserve such a wise wife?"

She smiled seductively. "Come to bed, and we'll try to figure it out."

Laughing, he scooped her into his arms and hoped his youngest brother hadn't made the biggest mistake of his life.

Holding the curtain aside, Austin gazed into the quiet street where lanterns fought to hold the darkness at bay. He'd never felt so unsure of himself in his life.

He heard his wife's movements as she changed into her nightgown behind the screen. The day they were married, they'd returned to her house and slept in her bed. Just slept. Holding each other.

They'd continued that ritual through the journey, but tonight he needed more. The only family he had left was sharing this room with him, and the memories they'd created spanned only a few weeks.

Memories of Dallas spanned years.

He wanted—needed—Loree's touch on his skin, her scent filling his nostrils, her taste on his lips. And dammit, he didn't know how to go about getting it.

He'd made love twice in his life. Neither time had been planned. He'd sought comfort, given comfort.

The one time he'd stood in a room with a woman knowing he had the right to her body, he'd walked out because no matter how much he'd paid her, he couldn't make himself want her.

"I've never been in so fine a place," Loree said quietly.

Austin released his death grip on the curtain and faced his wife. Her hands were clasped in front of her. He smiled, hoping to ease her nervousness as much as his own. "Dee would only settle for the best."

"Why didn't we stay with your brother?"

Austin plowed his hands through his hair. "Because he still sees me as a boy. He never noticed that I grew up."

"He's angry that you married me."

The sadness in her voice had him crossing the room with only one thought: to comfort her. He cradled her delicate face between his large hands. "It doesn't matter. He ain't got a dog in this fight."

She blinked, one corner of her mouth curling up. "What does that mean?"

"It means you—our marriage—is none of his business." He traced the edge of his thumbs across her brow, down her temple, across her cheek. "My reasons for marrying you are my business." Her eyes lured him the way gold lured miners, and he felt as though he were traveling into a mine, guided by light and darkness, searching for the treasures that lay within. He touched his thumbs to the corner of her mouth. He'd given her a perfunctory kiss after they'd exchanged vows. It had been less than satisfying. He wasn't certain what she expected of this marriage, but he damn sure knew what he wanted.

He lowered his mouth to hers, tasting her sweetness on his tongue. Her small hands pressed against his chest, and he wondered if she felt the heavy pounding of his heart. He guided her toward the bed and they fell together into the deep softness of the mattress. He'd have to remember to compliment Dee on her taste in furnishings.

Austin tucked Loree's finely boned body beneath his. He'd take his time tonight, go slowly, savoring every moment, every inch of her, making certain he caused her no discomfort. He trailed his lips along the slender column of her throat and dipped his tongue into the hollow at the base of her throat.

"Remember your promise," she pleaded softly.

His promise? He'd made so many of late. To find the man who murdered Boyd. To love Loree, honor, and cherish her . . .

To never touch her if he was thinking of Becky.

Groaning, he rolled off her and draped his arm over his eyes, his body aching with need and desires that would go unfulfilled. He felt the stiffness of her body as she lay beside him. She hadn't moved—not a finger, not a toe. He wasn't even certain if she was still breathing.

He peered out from beneath his arm and watched a solitary tear escape from her tightly closed eyes and trail toward her ear. Anger, sadness, guilt swamped him.

He swung his legs off the bed, sat up, and rubbed his hands up and down his face. Then he stood, jerked his hat off the bedpost, and headed for the door.

"Where are you going?"

"I need some fresh air." He yanked open the door, stopped, and looked over his shoulder at the woman who was now sitting up in the bed, her face a mask of anguish. "I wasn't thinking of her, Loree," he said, his voice low. "But I'm not going to make that announcement every time I touch you. You're gonna have to learn to trust me to keep my promises." He forced his tense body not to slam the door in his wake.

He strode from the hotel. The sultry summer night wrapped around him, offering no comfort. His boot heels echoed over the boardwalk. He stepped off the planks and allowed the dirt to muffle his passing.

He came to an abrupt halt in front of the general store. He saw a pale light glowing within a window upstairs. He wondered where the boy slept. He wondered where Becky and Cameron held each other through the night.

He started walking again, toward the far end of town. He heard the tinny sound of an off-key piano wafting out of the saloon. A bottle of whiskey appealed to him, but he'd never enjoyed drinking alone.

And the drinking companion of his youth was probably making passionate love to Becky right about now. He went to the livery, saddled Black Thunder, and rode into the night, trying to escape the invisible prison that surrounded his heart.

He felt the terror that had engulfed him when they'd put him in solitary confinement. The loneliness had been absolute, frightening. Just as it was now. Loving Becky had been so easy. They had never argued, she had never questioned.

But as he rode, it wasn't Becky who haunted his thoughts. It was Loree with golden eyes that didn't quite trust him and a heart that might never be his.

Chapter 9

❧

HOLDING HIS HAT in a tight fist, Austin leaned against the beam of Dallas's veranda and watched as dawn brought the majestic colors to the day. He remembered a time when he'd celebrated dawn with his violin. Now, more often than not, he welcomed it with a curse.

The front door opened. Dallas stepped beneath the archway and stumbled to a stop when his gaze rammed into Austin's. Austin shoved himself away from the beam. "I'm here to grovel. I've got a wife, a baby on the way, and no way to support them. Cameron is probably the only one in town who'd hire me, but I can't see me stacking cans and sweeping floors." He swallowed hard. "But I'll do it if I have to."

"Good morning to you, too," Dallas said, a corner of his mouth lifting his mustache.

Austin slumped against the beam. "Needed to spit out what I came to say before I lost the nerve to do it."

Dallas gave a slow nod as he walked to the edge of the veranda. The morning sun hit his bruised face.

"How's your jaw?" Austin asked.

"Sore. You knocked a damn tooth loose."

Austin flinched. "Sorry."

"I deserved it, and it was less painful than the dressing down my wife gave me last night." Dallas settled his black broad-brimmed Stetson on his head and stepped off the veranda. "I was just coming to look for you. Since you saved me the trouble of finding you, why don't you take a ride with me?"

Austin knew his brother well enough to know he never asked. Even words that sounded like a question were an order. Austin swung up into the saddle as Dallas mounted the horse his foreman brought him. Then as he had for most of his life, he followed the trail his brother blazed.

They rode in silence for long moments, the plains opening up before them. Austin had never appreciated the wide expanse of land as his brother did. Until recently, towns had appealed to him, the constant movement of people going places, the rumble of wagon wheels, the clop of horses' hooves.

"I never knew what your dreams were," Dallas said, his deep voice rumbling over the prairie, "but I figured they'd take you beyond this place. You always looked toward the horizon like maybe you'd inherited Pa's wandering streak."

"I thought about leaving more than once, but when I finally did, I sure as hell didn't go where I wanted to go."

"So you're figuring to make this place your home?" Dallas asked.

"I'd like to, but it depends on Loree. Her family was murdered a few years back and she's been living alone ever since. I thought she'd find it easier living here where she could get used to having people around— and I wanted to get her away from the memories."

"Sounds like I stepped knee-deep into a fool's pasture yesterday. I owe you an apology for that."

Austin had always known his brother was a big man, but he'd never seemed bigger than he did at this moment. Austin's throat tightened. "I realize now that I should have sent a telegram—"

"Might have made things a little easier on Loree. A wife and baby tie a man down whether he wants to be tied down or not."

"I accepted that before I ever asked Loree to marry me. She deserves better than the life I can give her."

Dallas looked off into the distance. "Dee taught me the only thing that matters is what you give her from your heart."

"My heart's not entirely free."

Dallas pierced him with a darkening gaze. "Then I'd say you wronged her pretty damn bad."

"You'll get no argument from me on that, but I aim to make it up to her."

Dallas gave him a long slow nod. "Well, this spread is getting too big for one man to handle. Reckon I could use some help."

"Same pay as before?"

A corner of Dallas's mouth lifted up, carrying the end of his mustache with it. "Those were a boy's wages." He rubbed the bruise on his jaw. "As you so tactfully pointed out to me yesterday, it's time I realized you were a man. Let's head back to the house, and we'll settle the particulars."

Loree stood on the boardwalk outside the hotel. The town had grown. She never would have recognized it if it weren't for the hotel. As they'd ridden in last night, the massive silhouette of the building had loomed before them, throwing her back in time to a night five years before.

"Why this town?" she whispered beneath her breath. As vast as West Texas was, why couldn't Austin have settled somewhere else?

Fate had a cruel streak running through her. No doubt about that.

The town hadn't possessed a sign when she'd been here before. She hadn't known its name. She hadn't cared. But it proudly bore a sign on the outskirts now: Leighton.

Named for her husband's family. Why had Fate chosen to bring a man to her door who lived in the one place she had never again wanted to see?

But more, she wondered if Fate would be kind enough to bring the man back to her?

He hadn't returned to the hotel room last night, and she wondered where he was, if he'd abandoned her. She wished she'd kept her insecurities to herself. What did it matter if he thought of someone else as long as he held her?

Stupid, stupid girl! she chastised herself. She had known by the pain reflected in his gaze that she'd hurt him to the core. She wanted to trust him, but life had taught her to value caution. And because of life's lessons, she knew she needed a gun.

She strolled along the boardwalk, her stomach quivering as people skirted past her. The men touched their fingers to the brim of their hats, some even smiled at her, but she refused to look any of them in the eye.

She was grateful when she saw the sign for Oliver's General Store.

She slipped inside, cringing when the cowbell above the door announced her arrival.

A woman standing behind the counter looked up and smiled warmly. "Hello. Can I help you?"

Loree wiped her damp palms on her skirt. "I'd just like to look around."

"Let me know if I can help you with anything."

Loree nodded her appreciation of the offer and strolled down the nearest aisle. Toys of all shapes and sizes greeted her. She hadn't seen many children in the town, but she'd noticed the red schoolhouse near the hotel. She supposed her child would attend school there. She and Austin might purchase toys here. Or would he carve the toys himself?

She picked up a wooden rattle. Did her husband whittle? What hidden talents did he possess? The sparse knowledge she possessed grew frustrating with each passing day. She supposed it should be enough that she didn't fear him and that he was for the most part considerate of her.

Yet she couldn't help but feel that he held a part of himself back. She wondered if he'd always been distant with people or if prison had reshaped him.

How could it have not reshaped him?

Her heart picked up its tempo, beating unsteadily with the thought of iron bars and brick walls and guards. How had he survived five years without freedom? She knew it would very likely have killed her.

Carefully, she placed the rattle back onto the shelf. She'd have to find out if he planned to make one before she purchased it. And she'd have to find out if they had the means for her to purchase it. She needed the little money she possessed for something more important.

She walked to the counter. The woman stopped dusting the shelves behind the counter and turned. Her burnished hair was pulled back into a stylish bun. The color reminded Loree of the locks she'd discovered in Austin's saddlebags. The woman had eyes the blue of a summer sky.

"Did you find what you were looking for?" she asked in a soft voice.

Loree tightened her fingers around her reticule. "I was looking for a small gun, something like a derringer."

The woman's delicate brow furrowed. "We don't carry guns anymore, not since the gunsmith came to town. You'll find his shop—"

"Becky!"

Loree's heart felt as though an iron fist had just clamped around it. How many Beckies could reside in this town? How many with hair the shade of autumn leaves?

A tall man stormed through the curtain behind the counter. With his hand he combed his blond hair off his brow. "I just saw Austin."

"He's back?"

"Yep, and it's the dangdest thing. He got married."

Loree watched the blood drain from Becky's face, and she hoped her own feelings weren't as visible.

"Married? Who in the world did he marry?" she whispered, her voice achingly low. Then as though just remembering she had a customer, she blinked several times and returned her attention to Loree. "I'm sorry. You wanted the gunsmith. You'll find him at the end of Main Street, near the saloon. I know Mr. Wesson will be able to help you." She turned back to the man. "Cameron, did he tell you about his wife?"

Loree didn't want to hear the answer. She hurried out of the general store. Once outside, she slumped against the front of the building. The woman inside the store was beautiful. How in the world could she expect Austin not to think of that woman when his wife was incredibly plain?

Then she remembered what the man had said. He'd just seen Austin. She hurried along the boardwalk, back to the hotel. She rushed inside and up the stairs, bursting through the door to their room.

Austin stood near the bed, stuffing her clothes into her suitcase on the bed. He jerked back, his brow deeply furrowed. "Where have you been?"

She closed the door more quietly than she'd opened it and eased into the room. "I needed something. I went to the general store."

He reached across the bed, grabbed her nightgown, and shoved it into the bag. "We're going back to Dallas's."

"I met a woman at the general store. A Becky." He stiffened. Her heart pounded so hard that she was sure he heard it. "Is she your Becky?"

"No, she is not *my* Becky," he replied through a clenched jaw. He grabbed her hairbrush from the bedside table and threw it into the bag.

"*Was* she your Becky?" she asked, unable to let it go for reasons she couldn't understand.

With one rapid-fire movement, he sent her bag and everything in it crashing to the floor. She stumbled back. She'd never seen him truly angry and wondered if she'd pushed him too far.

He dropped onto the bed, planted his elbows on his thighs, leaned forward, and buried his face in his hands. She heard his harsh breathing, saw the tenseness in his shoulders. He held out a hand. "Come here."

But her feet remained rooted to the spot. She knew nothing about how he acted in anger. If he gave as much of himself to anger as he did to passion . . .

He looked up, the torment in his eyes deepening as he met her gaze. "Come here, Loree. Please."

The anguish in his voice had her walking toward him, seeking to comfort him for the painful memories her constant badgering brought him. As she neared, he reached out, clamped his hand on her waist, and brought her to stand between his thighs.

He took a deep shuddering breath, staring at a button on her bodice. "Yes, she *was* my Becky." He tilted his head back, his deep blue gaze capturing hers. "But she's not anymore, and she never will be again."

He pressed a kiss to her slightly rounded stomach, to the place where their child grew. "I need you, Loree," he rasped.

She wrapped her arms around him, pressing his head against her belly. How could the woman have not waited for Austin? With demons haunting her and no family, the past five years had been an eternity, but at least she'd had the stars at night, the sunrise at dawn, and the freedom to walk wherever she wanted. "I hate her because she hurt you," she said, her voice seething.

"She doesn't deserve your hate."

"She doesn't deserve your loyalty or your love."

He tipped his head back, meeting her gaze. "Five years is a long time."

"I would have waited," she said, surprised by the conviction in her voice, more surprised to realize the words were true. If she were fortunate enough to possess his love, she'd wait forever.

A corner of his mouth quirked up and he brushed the stray strands of her hair behind her ear. "You know, I do believe you would have."

"I hate that she hurt you."

"And I hate that I've hurt you."

"You didn't hurt me on purpose. I know that."

"But I don't imagine it lessened the pain."

No, the pain had been sharp, agonizing but she was tired of letting the wound fester. She needed to lance it, clean it, and let it heal.

"She's very pretty," she admitted reluctantly.

He smiled broadly. "She is that."

He tugged her down until she sat on his lap. He cradled her cheek. "But then so are you."

She shoved his hand away and averted her gaze, the heat flaming her face. "No, I'm not. I'm uglier than the back end of a mule."

When he didn't jump to her defense, she dared to peer at him. Narrowing his eyes, he scrutinized her features. "Don't go staring at me."

"How else am I gonna find the ugly?"

"It's there for the whole world to see."

"Where?"

She pursed her lips. "My nose for one thing. The end tips up like a broken twig."

"And here I thought it looked like a petal unfurling."

His eyes grew warm, a touch of humor twinkling in the centers.

"And my lips. I don't hardly have a top lip and my bottom lip looks swollen like a bee stung it."

"It reminds me of a plump, ripe strawberry just waiting to be tasted."

She felt the heat suffuse her face as his eyes darkened.

"My hair," she said in a rush, desperate to convince him of her flaws. "It's got no color."

He took her braid and carried the end to his lips. "I always thought it looked like it had been woven from moonbeams. Reckon that's why I stole some of it."

She furrowed her brow. "What?"

He leaned back slightly, dug his hand into his pocket, and brought out several locks of her hair, tied together with a dainty ribbon.

"When did you do that?"

"That first night I slept with you, after you'd fallen asleep."

Tears stung her eyes as she pressed her hand to her mouth. "Oh, Austin. You must like me some to carry my hair around."

"I like you more than some, Loree. I wouldn't have married you otherwise."

She knew she shouldn't ask, knew she risked angering him again, but she had to know. "What about the locks of Becky's hair that you carried around?"

"I know words can't undo actions, but I'm hoping actions can undo the harm caused by a careless word." She watched his Adam's apply slowly slide up and down as he swallowed. "I burned them . . . the day we burned the barn."

She studied him, trying to understand the significance of his actions. "Why? You didn't have to punish yourself—"

"I wasn't punishing myself. Burning the barn was a way for you to put the past behind you. Thought it was time for me to put the past to rest, too."

"But you still love her."

His thumb stroked her cheek. "I love the memory of her."

The difference sounded slight to her, if it existed at all. She was no longer competing against a woman—only a memory. Perhaps if she'd loved someone before Austin came into her life, she could better understand how difficult it was to let go. As it was, all she knew was that she wished there'd been no one before her.

"Last night, I was afraid you weren't going to come back," she confessed quietly.

His lips spread into a smile that had warmth swirling through her, from her head to her toes.

"Missed me, did you?" he asked, and she heard the slight teasing in his voice.

"Where did you go?" she asked, not ready to admit how very much she'd missed him.

"Riding." He sighed deeply. "I just needed to ride."

"All night?"

"All night."

She realized then how tired he looked. Shadows rested beneath his eyes. His face remained unshaven. "I'll finish packing if you want to get a little sleep before we leave," she offered.

"What I want is a little kiss." He brought her face closer to his. "I know it's hard, but trust me, Loree."

She nodded hesitantly. "I'm trying."

He joined his lips to hers and rolled back onto the bed, holding her close, bringing her down with him, his mouth never leaving hers. He cradled her head, holding her in place as he plunged his tongue into her mouth.

Awkwardly, she straddled his thighs as his lips worked their magic. The warmth grew through her, and she hoped he'd kiss her forever.

He moaned low in his throat and shifted his mouth from hers. "So sweet," he murmured.

He pressed her face into the crook of his shoulder. She heard his soft even breathing. She lifted her head slightly to gaze at him. He'd fallen asleep.

She eased off him. He tightened his hold, turning onto his side and bringing his legs onto the bed, forming a cocoon around her. "Don't leave yet," he mumbled.

"I won't," she whispered, snuggling against him. She was determined to stop feeling jealousy over the beautiful woman who worked in the general store. She was part of Austin's past. Loree was his future.

Trepidation sliced through Loree as they neared Dallas's house. She saw Austin's brother standing by the corral, a young boy standing by his side. As Austin brought the wagon to a halt in front of the house, they both turned and headed toward them. Loree knew beyond a doubt that the boy was Dallas's son. He had his father's walk.

"Expected you to show up sooner," Dallas said, an authoritative ring to his voice that made Loree think the man always got what he expected.

"I fell asleep," Austin said as he helped Loree climb down from the wagon.

"During the day?" Dallas asked.

"Yep, not everyone works from dawn till midnight building empires," Austin said, giving her a wink.

"Nothing wrong with building empires," Dallas informed him.

"Didn't say there was," Austin said. "Only pointing out that not everybody does it."

Once she was firmly on the ground, Loree glanced around, feeling like a bush surrounded by mighty oak trees. Even Dallas's son stood inches above her.

Dallas swept his hat from his head. "Think I forgot to welcome you to the family yesterday."

Before she knew what he was about, he'd taken her hand, leaned forward, and kissed her cheek.

"It's a pleasure to have you here," he said as he released her hand. "This is my son, Rawley."

The boy swept off his hat in much the same manner as his father had. "We're right pleased to have you here, Aunt Loree."

He cast a furtive glance at his father who gave him a nod of approval, and she wondered how many times they'd practiced his greeting. Two-bits chose that moment to make his presence known. He leapt up, placed his paws on the side of the wagon, and began barking.

A broad smile split Rawley's face as he rushed to the wagon. "You got a dog?"

"Yep. Why don't you take him out?" Austin suggested. "He's probably ready to do some running around."

Rawley lifted Two-bits into his arms. The dog squirmed, snaking out his tongue to get a taste of Rawley's nose. Rawley set Two-bits on the ground and dropped to his knees to rub the dog's stomach as he rolled onto his back.

"What's his name?" Rawley asked.

"Two-bits," Loree told him, an ache in her heart. The boy very much reminded her of her brother. She judged him to be near her brother's age before he died.

Rawley glanced over his shoulder, his face skewed up. "Who named him that?"

"I did," Austin said. "Why don't you take him around to the back? We'll probably need to tie him up for the night so he won't run off," Austin said.

"He can stay in my room," Rawley suggested.

"I don't think so," Dallas said.

Rawley's face fell even as he gave his father a brusque nod. "Come on, Two-bits," he called out as he began running. The dog chased after him like he'd found a new friend.

"Rawley!" Dallas yelled.

The boy stumbled to a stop and spun around. "Yes, sir?"

"It's warm enough, you can bed down on the back porch tonight if you've a mind to."

Rawley smiled brightly. "Thanks, Mr. D!"

Loree turned her attention back to Dallas in time to catch a glimpse of a grimace before he wiped it from his face.

"Still can't get him to call you 'Pa'?" Austin asked.

Dallas shook his head. "Nope, but it doesn't matter. He's my son. I'll find Dee. She's bound to have an empty room or two that you can put your belongings in," Dallas said.

Loree waited until Dallas disappeared into the house before asking, "Why doesn't Rawley call him 'Pa'?"

"Dallas and Dee adopted him. He wasn't treated too kindly before they took him under their wing. Think he still finds it difficult to trust men."

"Did someone beat him?"

"Among other things." As though signaling an end to the conversation, Austin took her hand. "Come on. I'll show you around the house."

Had he not told her, Loree still would have known which bedroom had belonged to Austin. Smiling, she picked his rumpled shirt and britches off the floor.

"Guess Dee hasn't been in here since I left," he said as he set her suitcase on the bed.

She didn't think anyone had been in the room. It carried his lingering scent, faint because of his absences, but ingrained because of the years he had slept here.

He jerked the blankets on the bed up to cover his pillows and grinned sheepishly. "Never saw much point in making a bed in the morning just to unmake it at night."

He wiped his hands on his backside. "Let me talk to Dee about some clean sheets."

He headed out the door, and Loree wandered around the room. She imagined it to be a reflection of the man he'd been before prison. It was sparsely furnished as though he'd never planned to stay: a bed, a bureau, a dresser.

No portraits adorned the walls. Nothing hinted at permanence, but it was his room and on the dresser rested a violin. Reverently, Loree trailed her finger over the dull varnish. A chip here, a scratch there did not diminish the beauty of the instrument. Still, it looked forlorn and lonely.

"Dee thought the maid had cleaned in here," Austin said as he came back into the room. "She said she'll send Maria in to take care of it for us."

"I can change the bed—"

"Enjoy the luxury of being waited on because you'll only get it while you're here."

"Your brother is very wealthy, isn't he?"

"Yep, but I don't envy him that. He worked hard for every penny."

She turned her attention back to his dresser. "Is this the violin your mother played for you?"

Stuffing his hands in his pockets, he slowly approached her. "Yeah, it is."

"My father played the violin. He thought music was important. He'd take me into Austin once a week so I could have a piano lesson. I had no natural talent, but I tried to learn. I could teach you what I know. You could play your mother's violin."

"No."

"But it would be a tribute to your mother, a way—"

"No. I can't play and you can't teach me."

"But how do you know if you don't try?"

"Trust me. I know."

Baffled, she watched him turn for the door. She didn't want the moment to end with disappointment. "Austin?"

He glanced over his shoulder. "I'm just going to get the rest of our things."

She gave him a hesitant smile. "Do you think you could draw me a map of the house so I don't get lost when I wander through it?"

He grinned. "It's god-awful big, isn't it? Dallas doesn't do anything in small measures."

"I guess they're planning to have a large family," she offered.

His grin eased away. "They were planning on it, but Dee had an accident a few years ago. She won't be giving Dallas any more children."

She wrapped her arms around herself. "I'm so sorry. Will my being here and having a baby upset her?"

Austin shook his head. "One thing about the Leigh men, they tend to marry generous women."

He disappeared through the door. Loree crossed the room, opened a double set of doors, and stepped onto the balcony. She was glad they'd left the town. It had stirred up memories that had kept her from sleeping the night before.

She hoped that tonight Austin's presence would hold the nightmares at bay.

Chapter 10

✢

_B_LOOD. IT WAS _everywhere. Rich, red, warm, glistening in the night. Coating her hands, soaking through her clothes._

She couldn't stop it from flowing like a raging river. She was drowning, drowning in the blood.

The scream ripped through the tranquil night. Dallas jerked upright as Dee rolled away from his side and turned up the flame in the lamp.

"What in the hell was that?" Dallas asked.

The terrorized shriek came again.

"It came from Austin's room," Dee said as she headed for the door.

Dallas bolted from bed, rushed after her into the hallway, and grabbed her arm. "Where do you think you're going?"

"To help."

"Let me go first," he ordered, taking the lamp from her. No telling what was waiting on the other side. The woman was always rushing into places where she shouldn't.

Quietly he opened the door to Austin's room and peered inside. The light from the lamp cast a pale glow around the room. He heard a woman's harsh sobs.

Dee edged past him and walked into the room, giving him no choice but to follow.

Sitting in bed, the blankets draped around his waist, Austin held Loree. "It's all right, Loree. It was just a bad dream," he said, his voice low as he rocked back and forth, stroking her back.

"I didn't know where you lived. I didn't know. I shouldn't have come here," she wailed.

"It's all right, Sugar. No one's gonna hurt you here."

She tilted her head away from his shoulder and the light from the lamp glistened over her tears. "I'm so scared, Austin."

He pressed her face back into the nook of his shoulder. "I know you are, but I'm gonna make things good for you, Loree. You'll see."

Dee eased toward the bed. "Why don't I warm up some milk for Loree?" she whispered. "It always helps the children get back to sleep when they wake up with a bad dream."

Austin glanced over his shoulder at her, gratitude etched over his features. "And put a lot of sugar in it."

Dee strolled to Dallas and placed her hand on his arm. "Light their lamp for them, then give them a little privacy while I warm some milk."

When she left his side, Dallas walked to the bedside table and lit the lamp. "Need anything else?"

Shaking his head, Austin settled down on the bed, carrying his wife with him. Dallas heard her stifling sobs and Austin's repeated words of comfort. He strode back to his own room, jerked open the door to the balcony, and stepped into the night. He was trembling almost as much as he imagined Loree was. Taking several deep breaths, he stared at the canopy of stars overhead.

Long moments passed before he heard Dee's soft footsteps. She joined him on the balcony and rubbed her hand up and down his bare arm. "Loree's sleeping. Come back to bed."

"Did you see his back? They beat him in prison."

It wasn't a question, but she answered anyway. "It looks like it."

"When we find the man who killed your brother, I'm gonna string him up from the nearest tree."

"You need to let the law handle—"

He spun around. "The law sent my brother to prison."

"The law isn't perfect, but you have to trust it to serve justice. You have to let the law send the real murderer to prison."

"They had better damn well hang the man, and I want a front row seat."

*   *   *

Austin held Loree as she sipped on the warm milk Dee had prepared for her. She was trembling so hard that the bed shook.

After all she'd lived through, he wasn't surprised she still had nightmares. On the journey, he'd heard her whimper a few times in her sleep. It seemed the farther they traveled from Austin, the more restless she was when she slept. He hoped bringing her here wasn't a mistake, but he'd feared she'd continue living as a hermit if they'd stayed at her home.

She gave him a shaky smile and handed the empty cup to him. "Thank you," she whispered.

He set the cup aside, and with his thumb, he wiped the milky mustache away from her lip. "You're welcome."

She released an awkward chuckle. "I am so embarrassed. Your brother must think—"

"He doesn't think anything," he assured her, lying her down and tucking her against his body. Lord, she fit so nicely, even though she was beginning to swell with his child. As it rested against his chest, her hand curled like the petals of a flower closing for the night. He wrapped one hand around it, while the other lazily stroked her back. He kissed her forehead. "Were you dreaming about your family?"

She moved her head up and down against his chest.

"And the man who killed them. There was so much blood," she whispered hoarsely.

"What did he look like?"

He felt the shiver course through her body.

"I don't want to talk about him."

"While I was in Austin, I talked with a detective about hunting the man down—"

She jerked away and stared at him, fear reflected in her eyes. "What?"

"I thought it would put your mind at peace if the man was found and hanged for what he did to your family. But I couldn't give the detective enough information. If you tell me what you know about him—"

She shook her head violently. "No, no, I don't want him looking."

"Sugar, I'm not gonna let the man hurt you—"

"No!" She buried her face against his chest. "It's been over five years. Please just let it be."

"It's not right that he murdered three people and got away with it."

He felt her tense within his arms as she shook her head. He drew her closer. "I won't press you on this, Loree, but think about it. What if he's out killing others?"

Loree squeezed her eyes shut. She should have told Austin everything before they were married even though she might have sacrificed any affection he held for her. But she'd wanted what he was offering for her baby.

Strange how a little one, not yet born, could bring so many responsibilities with him. She had to do what was best for the baby. She had to put him first. So she held her silence.

A detective searching for the man who had killed her family was a worse nightmare than the one that had woken her up screaming. If anyone tracked down the man who had killed her family, he'd no doubt discover things about her father that Loree wanted to remain a secret.

The only peace of mind she found resided in the fact that she knew the murderer wasn't going to kill anyone else.

"Loree? Is that short for Lorena?" Dallas asked.

Austin watched his wife jerk to attention and glance down the breakfast table at his brother. Shadows rested beneath her eyes. He wished he had the power to rid her of the nightmares.

"Yes, it is," she said. "My father told me it was a favorite song around the campfire during the war."

"Not in my unit," Dallas said. "I forbid my men to play it, sing it, or think about it."

"How come?" Rawley asked.

"Because it made the men miss home so much that they'd end up deserting. Can't tolerate a man shirking his responsibilities."

Loree flicked her gaze to Austin, and he noticed the crimson fanning her cheeks. He gave her wink. Dallas tolerated less than most men, and Austin was glad Loree hadn't shared her father's military history with his brother.

"Can I add taking care of Aunt Loree's dog to my list of chores?" Rawley asked.

Austin sipped on his coffee, watching Rawley wait expectantly for his father's permission.

"Don't you think you got enough chores?" Dallas asked as he scooped up his eggs.

"But I like taking care of dogs, and I don't have one to watch over since Ma's went to live with her friends."

Out of the corner of his eye, Austin saw his wife lean forward and glance down the table at Dee.

"While she carried her litter, she got a bit testy, so I thought it was best to set her free. She still comes up to the house, but not as often," Dee said.

Loree shook her head. "I don't understand why you set if free—"

"It was a prairie dog," Dallas said with disgust.

Loree blinked, confusion mirrored in her eyes. "You had a prairie dog as a pet?"

"Yep," Austin said, grinning broadly. "Dallas even made it a leash. Carved the dog's name right into it."

"Me 'n' Wrawley wanna dog," Faith piped in from her high chair beside Dee.

"Maybe you can borrow your Aunt Loree's for a spell," Dallas suggested.

"Can we, Aunt Loree?" Rawley asked. "I'll take real good care of him."

Loree smiled softly. "I'd appreciate the help."

"Now that that's settled," Dallas began.

Austin listened with half an ear as Dallas rattled off all the things that Austin needed to tend to that day. He remembered a time when he'd handled his chores and still had time to go into town and visit with Becky.

Right now, it seemed his list of responsibilities would leave him with little time to visit his wife. He watched as she sprinkled two spoons of sugar into her coffee and began to stir. Austin reached across the table and took her cup from her. When she started to protest, he silenced her with a lifted brow. Then he scooped four more spoons of sugar into the brew before handing it back to her. "There's no shortage of sugar around here."

Her cheeks took on the hue of a sunrise. "Most people don't use as much sugar as I do."

"Maybe if they did, they'd be as sweet as you are."

Her blush deepened and she lowered her gaze to her plate.

"Have you heard a damn word I've said?" Dallas asked.

Austin shifted his gaze to the end of table. "Heard every word. I want to take Loree over to Houston's this morning so she can pick out a horse."

Narrowing his eyes, Dallas rubbed his thumb and forefinger over his mustache. "Reckon Amelia will have your hide if you don't take Loree out and introduce her."

Austin gave his brother a nod. "I figured the same thing. I'd rather face your wrath than Amelia's."

Dallas leaned back in his chair and laughed.

Austin drew Dallas's buggy to a halt, unable to do little more than stare at the huge unfamiliar house. A balcony jutted out from a room on the second floor. Some sort of fancy railing circled the porch that circled the house. One side of the house eased out into a half circle. Bright yellow curtains billowed out from large windows.

"What's wrong?" Loree asked.

"Houston has always preferred solitude. I just never expected to see him with neighbors."

"It certainly is a fancy house," Loree said.

"Yep," Austin responded, apprehension taking hold of his gut. He slapped the reins, sending the two black mares into a trot. Beyond the corral where Houston worked with a palomino mustang, Austin saw the house he had helped to build. It appeared abandoned. Austin shifted his gaze back to the larger house.

A woman stepped onto the porch and waved, a tiny girl planted on her hip, another girl clinging to her skirt.

"Good Lord," Austin muttered.

Loree leaned toward him. "What?"

He shook his head. "I never would have believed it." He brought the horses and buggy to a halt near the corral just as Houston slipped through the slats. Austin set the brake and climbed out of the buggy. "Tell me that isn't your house?" he ordered.

Houston grimaced. "Disgusting, ain't it? I wasn't looking for it, but success found me. Figured the least I could do was give the woman a fancy house." He rubbed the scarred side of his face. "I hear tell Cupid's cramp got a hold of you."

Inwardly, Austin cringed at his brother's phrasing. Cowboys used it whenever they got an urge to marry. "Yeah, you might say that." Turning to Loree, Austin helped her out of the buggy and slipped his arm protectively around her. "My wife needs a horse."

"Not gonna bother with introductions?" Houston asked.

"I figured it was obvious you're my brother and this is my wife."

Houston swept his hat from his head. Austin heard Loree's tiny gasp. He'd grown up with Houston's scars. He hadn't thought to warn Loree about them.

"Welcome to the family," Houston said quietly.

Loree's lips spread into the most understanding smile Austin had ever seen. "I'm very happy to be here," she said.

Houston gave her a distorted grin. "You have to be the most forgiving soul on earth to say that after meeting Dallas."

"I think our announcement took him by surprise," she said.

"Yeah, you might say it took us all unawares, but then Austin always did have a hard time figuring out when to open his mouth and when to keep it shut."

"How long were you planning to stay out here with the horses instead of bringing your wife to the house so I can meet her?"

Austin spun around at Amelia's welcoming voice. She waddled toward him, a girl in each arm. Houston strode toward her and took both girls from her.

"I told you not to carry them," he said.

"You tell me a lot of things," she said, her voice laced with teasing.

Austin grinned at her swollen stomach. "I'll be. When I was home before, Dallas said you had to be carrying another one 'cuz you weren't eating."

Amelia laughed. "I can't eat anything for the first three months. You'd think I'd get skinny, but I just keep getting more plump with each girl we have." She turned slightly and smiled. "You must be Loree. I'm so grateful Austin has someone to love."

Austin watched his wife's face blush becomingly. "Well, I'm not certain—" she began.

"I am," Amelia said, interrupting her. She threw her arms around Loree and hugged her closely. "Welcome to the family."

Then she stepped back, grinning. "And look at this. Someone I can actually reach. Dee's as tall as a tree, and these men here are no different." She slipped her arm through Loree's. "Why don't you come into the house for a spell? Our other two girls are baking cookies. They won't be edible, but we can pretend to nibble on them."

Austin listened to his wife's laughter as she walked toward the house with Amelia. Amelia had always had a way of putting people at ease. He'd never been more grateful for it than he was now. He glanced at Houston. "Want me to take one of those girls?"

"Sure." Houston handed the smallest one over.

"Which one is this?" he asked.

"A. J."

Austin shifted her in his arms. "Hello, A. J. I bet you don't remember your Uncle Austin, do you?"

She covered her eyes and buried her tiny nose against his shoulder. Lord, she was incredibly small and warm. A knot rose in his throat with the thought that he'd soon have one of these of his own.

"Since you came in Dallas's buggy, I reckon the two of you mended your fence," Houston said.

"He told you about that, did he?" Austin asked.

Houston gave him a lopsided grin. "Yep."

"What's so funny?"

"The whole world is afraid of Dallas. He's only been hit twice in his life—and both times the fist was attached to one of his brothers."

Austin chuckled. "I'd forgotten that you'd hit him. I never knew why."

Houston shrugged and started walking toward the house. Austin took off after him. "Why *did* you hit him?"

"He questioned Amelia's virtue. I took exception to his doubts."

Austin was relieved to know Loree wasn't the only one whose virtue Dallas had doubted, but he also knew that Amelia had been long married before she began to swell with a child. Austin swallowed hard. "Loree's pregnant."

Houston glanced over at him. "I know."

"She's a decent woman—"

"Never doubted that for a minute. Hell, Austin, I took you to your first whorehouse, and you walked out as pure as you were before you went in. Decent women are the only kind that ever appealed to you."

"Don't suppose you happened to mention that to Dallas when he came by."

"Figured he knew since he told me if anyone dared to look at your wife with anything but admiration, they'd answer to him."

The knot in Austin's throat tightened a little. "I wasn't sure how he felt—"

"You're his baby brother. He would have sheltered you from the world if he could have, and that's probably where he went wrong. Some lessons have simply got to be learned the hard way."

Loree folded the blanket, placed it in the box, and lifted her gaze to the woman standing on the other side of the bed who was doing the same thing. "I hope we haven't hurt your feelings."

Dee glanced up. "Of course not. Why ever would you think that?"

Loree shrugged. "You made me feel so welcome, and here we are, after only one night, moving out."

Dee smiled with understanding. "I'm glad that Amelia and Houston offered to let you live in their vacant house. I know it's difficult to marry someone you've only known a short time. I didn't know Dallas at all when I married him. If my family had been underfoot, I don't think I ever would have gotten to know him."

"I feel badly taking the furniture from this room."

"It's always been Austin's. I often thought of replacing it, but I wanted him to come home to something familiar. I was afraid all the other changes would overwhelm him."

Loree picked at a loose thread on the blanket. "You must love him very much to accept what he did."

"I understand why he did it. I hated to see him go to prison, but the decision was his to make, and I respect that."

Understanding, respect, acceptance. She wondered if Austin would give those as easily to her if he knew the entire truth about her past. She supposed one had to build a foundation of love before one's faults could be laid bare and accepted.

"Dallas and Austin should have the table moved out of the shed by now. Do you want to run outside and let them know that we're almost finished here?" Dee asked.

Loree nodded, walked to the doorway, and halted. "Dee?"

Dee glanced over at her, and Loree nibbled on her lower lip. "I appreciate that you don't seem to be sitting in judgment of me."

Dee's brown eyes widened. "Because of the baby?"

Loree jerked her head quickly.

A wealth of understanding and sympathy filled Dee's brown eyes. "A child is a gift, Loree, regardless of the circumstances. And Austin's child at that. We will spoil the baby rotten, I promise you."

Loree didn't doubt it. She'd already seen evidence that every child in this family was considered precious.

She walked into the hallway and down the wide sweeping staircase. The discordant notes of a piano traveled from the front parlor. She ambled toward the room, the off-key chords grating on her nerves before they fell into silence. She peered into the room.

"Did you practice one hour every day like I told you?" a rotund woman asked Rawley.

He shrugged.

"Stand up, young man," she ordered.

Slower than ice melting in winter he slid off the bench and stood.

"Hold out your hand."

She saw Rawley tense as he extended his hand, palm up. The woman picked up a thin wooden stick and raised it.

"Don't you even think about striking him," Loree snarled as she stormed into the room.

Rawley spun around so fast that he lost his balance and dropped onto the bench. The woman's eyes protruded farther than her nose.

"How dare you interfere with this lesson—"

"I'm interfering with your cruelty, not the lesson."

"Mr. Leigh is paying me good money—"

"To teach his son, not to beat him."

"He is lazy and irresponsible—"

"Irresponsible? What time did you get out of bed this morning?"

"I don't see that that's any of your business."

"This child was up before the sun tending to his chores, and he'll sneak in a few more after everyone thinks he's in bed, so don't tell me he's irresponsible. You are irresponsible." Loree snatched the stick out of the woman's hand and snapped it in two.

The woman's jowls shook. "How dare you! Wait until Mr. Leigh hears about this." She stormed from the room.

Loree slid onto the bench beside Rawley, gave him a warm smile, and began to play "Greensleeves."

"Mr. Leigh! Mr. Leigh!"

Standing in the wagon, holding one end of the heavy table, Austin glanced over his shoulder to see something that looked like the beginnings of a dust storm hurling toward them.

"Drop it!" Dallas ordered, and Austin gladly obliged, hearing the wagon groan beneath the weight.

The banker's wife staggered to a stop. "She broke my stick!"

"Who did?" Dallas asked.

She pointed her finger at Austin. "I believe she's his wife."

Austin settled his butt on the side of the wagon. "If Loree broke your stick"—he swallowed his laughter—"I'm sure she had good reason."

"I will not tolerate interference from that hoyden when I'm teaching," the woman said.

"I'll talk to her," Dallas said.

"The hell you will," Austin said. He glared at the woman. "And she's not a hoyden."

"She's married to a murderer—"

"My brother's not a murderer."

"I was at the trial—"

"That'll be enough, Mrs. Henderson. Why don't you head on home, and we'll take this up tomorrow?" Dallas suggested.

She stuck her nose in the air. "I don't think I can teach Rawley. That boy is as lazy as his father—"

"I'm his father."

"Not by blood—"

"By all that matters." Dallas shoved on the table and sent it crashing against the back of the wagon. "Jackson!"

A tall lanky man hurried out of the barn. "Yes, sir?"

"Escort Mrs. Henderson home."

Leaving the woman to huff and puff, Dallas strode toward the house. Austin leapt off the wagon and caught up to him. "You gotta pity poor Lester being married to that."

Dallas just snorted.

"What are you aiming to do?" Austin asked as Dallas stalked through the front door.

"Find out what really happened."

Austin heard the music filtering out of the parlor. Dallas ground to a stop in the parlor doorway. Wanting to ensure that he could get between Dallas and Loree if the need arose, Austin slipped past his brother and froze.

Loree was playing the piano with Rawley sitting beside her, watching as her hands moved over the keys. She struck the final chord and folded her hands in her lap.

"I could never play like that," Rawley said, his voice filled with awe.

"You could if you wanted," Loree said. "But the secret is—do you want to?"

Rawley shook his head. "I'd rather be out tending cattle."

"Then that's what you should do."

"But I don't want to disappoint Mr. D. He ain't gonna like what happened with Miz Henderson at all," Rawley said quietly.

"Of course, he won't like it," Loree said. "She's lucky I walked into this room and not your father. He would have snatched her baldheaded if he'd seen that she was going to strike you."

"You really think so?"

"I know so." She shifted on the bench. "Rawley, he loves you very much."

"I know he does, but I ain't really his son. His son is buried out by the windmill. He died on account of me." Ducking his head, Rawley rubbed his finger along the edge of the piano. "I ain't never said that out loud, but I know it to be true."

"Rawley!"

Rawley came off the bench at his father's booming voice, and Loree looked as though she'd jumped out of her skin.

"Yes, sir?"

"I need to talk to you, son," Dallas said more quietly. "Outside."

Dallas turned abruptly and headed down the hallway. Rawley hurried after him. Austin ambled into the room and sprawled in a chair near the piano.

"What do you think he's going to say to Rawley?" Loree asked, worry etched deeply between her brows.

"Imagine he'd going to explain to the boy that he is indeed Dallas's son."

"How long were you there?"

"Long enough to know Rawley will be herding cattle instead of banging on a piano."

Loree breathed a sigh of relief. "I'm beginning to think your brother is more bark than bite."

"Only where family is concerned. Make no mistake about that."

Austin heard Loree's laughter as he prodded his horse into the corral. Moving into their own place had seemed to put Loree more at ease with her new surroundings. He sauntered to the house, rounded the corner, and leaned against the beam supporting the eve. Contentment stole over him as his gaze fell on Loree, sitting on the ground, her bare toes peeking out from beneath her skirt. Rawley was hunkered beside her while Two-bits yelped and wagged his tail like there was no tomorrow.

"Sit!" Rawley ordered, deepening his voice.

The dog got his shaking butt halfway to the ground before he lifted it back up and began wagging his tail again.

"Sit!" Rawley repeated. Austin thought he sounded a great deal like Dallas.

This time, the dog plopped his butt onto the ground. Loree smiled brightly and clapped while Rawley tossed the dog a scrap of food. Loree glanced Austin's way, and her smile grew warm. "You're home."

He ambled to her, extended his hand, and helped her to her feet. "Yep. What are you two doing?"

"Teaching Two-bits how to sit," Rawley explained as he tossed the dog another morsel. The dog devoured it like he hadn't eaten in weeks when Austin knew that wasn't the case.

"Rawley made him a collar," Loree said as she reached down and petted the dog.

"Used an old belt. Mr. D taught me how to carve into the leather," Rawley pointed. "See, I did the dog's name."

"You did a good job," Austin said, glad to see how his words pleased Rawley. The boy had received too little praise before he'd come to live with Dallas.

"Mr. D said when Two-bits fathers some pups, I can have one."

"That might be a while," Austin said.

"Mr. D said the same thing. Said he'd git me a dog now if I wanted, but I decided to wait on account I want a dog like Two-bits." Rawley backed up a step. "Well, I'd best git home."

"Tell your pa that I'll be checking on the north range tomorrow."

Rawley gave him a quick nod. "Yes, sir. Bye, Aunt Loree."

"Thank you for the collar," she said warmly.

"You're welcome." He hurried to his horse, mounted up, and kicked his horse into a gallop.

Austin watched the dust settle back into place.

"You did that on purpose didn't you?" Loree asked.

He shifted his gaze to her. "Did what?"

"Gave him a message to take to 'his pa.' My guess is Dallas already knows you'll be checking the north range tomorrow."

Austin rubbed the side of his nose. "Was it that obvious I want the boy to realize Dallas is his father?"

"Probably not to him, but I'm beginning to know you a little more. Dallas tells people what he wants. You have a tendency to try and guide them without letting them know that you're guiding them."

Reaching out, he took her hand and tugged her to him until her toes crept over his boots. "So if I wanted to guide you toward an 'I'm glad that you're home' kiss, what would I do?"

"What you do every evening. Put my hands on your shoulders and your hands on my waist. Then lean down—"

He didn't let her finish, just planted his lips over hers, allowing the seed for love to begin taking root. He wished like hell that she hadn't been forced to marry him, but if she hadn't—she'd be in Austin and he'd be here, wishing he were with her.

He kept the kiss sweet and short because his resolve was weakening. What he really wanted was to lift her into his arms, guide her into the bedroom, and make love to her until dawn—but that damn promise stopped him because he hadn't figured out how to convince her that he was only thinking of her.

Loree bit back the whimper when his mouth left hers. She did so look forward to his coming home in the evening. She smiled warmly. "Are you ready for supper?"

"Starving."

Loree strolled into the house. A main living area on the first floor opened into a kitchen area. The bedroom she and Austin shared was off to the side. Stairs within that bedroom led to the second floor where two other rooms waited for them to decide how best to use them.

She had brought a few things from her home near Austin: a rocking chair, her vanity, her music boxes. They had Austin's bedroom furniture, Dee and Dallas's table, and a sofa from Amelia and Houston.

Nothing to hint at permanence . . . and yet, she felt contentment. She was learning a good deal about her husband. He was a man of simple habits. He awoke each morning before dawn and sat on the front porch, waiting for the sunrise, his hands wrapped around a tin cup that held his black coffee. He never started the day with a meal, always ate lunch with the cowhands, and returned in the evening with a voracious appetite.

Night had fallen by the time they finished their meal, and she joined Austin on the porch. She enjoyed these moments when he seemed most relaxed and content. She sat on the top step. "How was your day?" she asked quietly.

A corner of Austin's mouth quirked up. "Tiring. I sure don't remember feeling this tired in the evenings before. Must be age catching up with me."

She laughed lightly. "You are so incredibly old."

Turning, he pressed his back against the beam, straightened his legs, and brought her feet to his lap. He rubbed his thumbs over her sole. "How was your day?"

"Amelia visited."

"Not being a pesky neighbor, is she?"

"No, I think she's purposefully trying to leave us alone. She told me you had helped build the house."

"Helped to add the bedroom and the rooms upstairs."

"I like the thought of our children playing on a floor you may have hammered into place." She gnawed on her lower lip, raised a hand, and squinted into the setting sun. "You see that tree over there?"

Austin glanced over his shoulder. "Yeah?"

The tree was not what she would call beautiful. Bent, gnarled, and crooked, it looked as though it had spent much of its time fighting the lonesome winds and seldom winning.

"Can we hang a swing from it?"

"We can hang anything from it that you want, Sugar."

Two-bits leapt on the porch, wagged his tail, and yipped before settling down beside her hip.

Austin chuckled. "He's such a ferocious guardian."

"He's good company, and he gives Rawley an excuse to visit. He reminds me so much of my brother."

Austin's fingers stilled their soothing journey over the soles of her feet. "You really miss your brother, don't you?"

"Some days are harder than others, but I guess it's always like that when you lose someone you love."

He started rubbing her feet again. "Speaking of someone you love, they're putting the ones they love to bed."

Night had swept over the land. Loree gazed at the house in the distance. Lights spilled out from the windows on the second floor. A window fell into darkness.

"That'll be A. J.," Austin said.

"What does the A. J. stand for?" Loree asked.

"Anita June. Amanda's middle name is April. When it suits their fancy, they have a tendency to name their daughters after the month in which they were born. Hope you're not planning to do that."

"What if I was?" she challenged.

"Then that's what we'd do." Austin pointed toward the house. "They're coming to my favorite window."

Loree glanced back over her shoulder. Two other windows were now ensconced in darkness. She watched as the light from the last window disappeared.

"That was Maggie's room. Give her a minute . . ." The light again burned within the window. Austin chuckled.

"What's she doing?" Loree asked.

"No idea, but she turns that lamp back up every night."

"You love her so much."

"I love 'em all, but I know Maggie . . . and Rawley. But I'm slowly getting to know the others." He yawned and patted her feet. "Guess I'd best get to bed."

He unfolded his body, took her hand, and brought her to her feet. "Don't know if you noticed the theater Dee built in town. It's gonna have its first performance next week. She's invited the whole family to go."

"That should be fun."

"Yeah," he replied, but she thought she heard doubt in his voice. "You go on in. I'll be there directly."

Following their nightly ritual, she went to their bedroom, slipped into her nightgown, crawled into bed, turned down the lamp, and waited. She heard her husband walking the perimeter of the house as though he loathed giving up another day. He joined her a little sooner than he had the night before. Pressing a kiss to her temple, he drew her into the circle of his arms.

As she lay there, listening to his breathing, knowing he was giving as much as he could without dishonoring his vow, she cursed the night she'd extracted a promise from him.

Chapter 11

༚

LOREE GLANCED AT her reflection in the mirror. The yellow ribbon at the end of her braid looked incredibly childish, even if it had been a gift from Austin. She yanked it from her hair and dropped onto the bed, pulling the ribbon through her fingers, over and over.

Austin had gone to Houston's as soon as he'd seen Dallas and his family arrive in their buggy, leaving Loree to finish getting dressed on her own. She didn't want to embarrass him by looking like a little girl when they attended the play at the theater. Only she had no idea how to make herself look grown up. She heard the soft knock on her door. "Come in."

Dee poked her head around the door. "How's it coming?"

Loree held up the ribbon. "I just need to figure out what to do with this ribbon. I don't want to hurt Austin's feelings by not wearing it."

Dee stepped into the room, and Loree wished she could come up with a plausible excuse to get out of going to this affair. Dee's red gown complimented her pale complexion, black hair, and brown eyes, leaving her devastatingly beautiful. "Oh, I'm sure we can think of something to do with it. Don't you think, Amelia?"

Smiling warmly and holding a large box, Amelia waltzed in behind Dee. Amelia's golden hair was swept up into a graceful bouquet of curls. The green of her dress emphasized the green of her eyes. She looked radiant.

Dee pulled out the chair in front of the mirrored vanity. "Loree, why don't you sit here?"

"Why don't we put on the gown first?" Amelia suggested.

Incredibly embarrassed, Loree glanced at her best dress. "I am wearing my dress."

Amelia walked to the bed, set the box down, and ripped off the lid. "I thought you'd want to wear the gown Austin ordered for you."

Loree took a hesitant step forward. "What gown?"

With a flourish, Amelia pulled a rustle of lace and silk out of the box and held it up for Loree to see. "This one."

Tears stung Loree's eyes. The pale yellow bodice dipped down to form a V. Lace decorated the area between the V and ran up along the shoulders. A top skirt was split down the middle and pulled back, held in place with yellow ribbons, to reveal a pleated lace skirt beneath.

"Austin ordered this gown?" Loree asked, touching the soft material with awe.

"In a way," Amelia admitted. "He told me you needed something to wear. He insisted it be yellow because you look beautiful in yellow—"

"He said that?" Loree asked. "That I looked beautiful?"

Amelia smiled warmly. "He said that. But not knowing how his taste in women's clothing runs . . . and having had an unfortunate experience with Dallas's tastes in women's attire, I oversaw the dress maker's efforts."

"I had no idea—" Loree began.

"I think he wanted it to be a surprise."

"Oh, it is."

"Why don't you slip it on," Dee suggested, "and then we'll see about arranging your hair."

Loree grabbed her braid. "I don't suppose we could pile it on top of my head."

"We can do anything you want."

Austin sat in Houston's parlor, sprawled in the chair, gazing out the window, wishing he could think of a way to get out of his family obligation.

The way Rawley was crunching his face, Austin figured he was searching for an excuse, too. Rawley dug his finger behind the collar of his starched white shirt, looking like he might choke at any minute. Then his face brightened. "I should probably check on the herd."

Dallas shifted his gaze from the window and nodded slowly. "You probably should."

Relief washed over Rawley's face as he strode for the door.

"If the herd means more to you than your mother does," Dallas added.

Rawley stumbled to a stop and glanced over his shoulder.

"The theater is one of your mother's dreams. She's a little nervous about tonight," Dallas said.

Rawley took a deep breath. "Then I reckon I oughta be there."

"Reckon so."

Rawley reached into his shirt pocket and pulled out a sarsaparilla stick. Daintily, Faith walked up to him. "Gimme."

"It's my last one," Rawley said, even as he broke it in half and handed a piece to her. Then he glared at Maggie as she sat in the corner, watching over her three sisters. "Reckon you want some, too."

She held up a bag. "We still have the lemon drops Uncle Dallas brought."

"If those women don't hurry, the girls are all gonna have belly aches before we get out of here," Houston said.

"As long as they're riding in your wagon, that's not a problem for me," Dallas said.

"What's keeping them?" Austin asked.

"Hell, you never know with women," Dallas said.

Austin heard the patter of footsteps on the front porch. The door swung open. Amelia and Dee rushed in, looking like little girls trying to hold in an enormous secret. Then Loree stepped through the doorway and Austin felt as though a wild mustang had just kicked him in the chest. Sweet Lord, the little darling he'd married was going to catch the eye of every man in town.

Slowly he came to his feet. Loree's smile faltered and she touched her gloved hand to the nape of her neck.

"You don't like it?" she asked.

"I like it just fine," he said, wondering where that raspy voice had come from.

"Amelia said you purchased the gown."

"I did. I just didn't know it was gonna look like that."

"I could change—"

"No!" three male voices sounded at once.

Loree had seen the outside of the theater from the hotel, but she had never imagined the opulence that had been hidden inside. Candles flickered within crystal chandeliers. A thick red carpet with designs running through it covered every inch of the floor. Gilded mirrors adorned the walls. Wide sweeping stairs on either side of the foyer led to the balconies.

At one end of the foyer was a room where parents could leave their children in the capable hands of women paid to care for them. As far as Loree could determine, Dee had thought of everything and designed the theater to give the people of Leighton a night they'd never forget.

It seemed everyone within a thousand miles had come for the opening performance. Loree had never been in one room with so many people.

Austin took her elbow and leaned low. "They're serving champagne over there. Do you want some?"

"Do you think they have some water?"

Smiling, he tucked a stray strand of hair behind her ear. "If they don't, I'll find some. Why don't you wait here with Rawley until Dee and Dallas get back from taking Faith to that baby room?"

She nodded slightly.

"Rawley, I'm leaving your aunt in your care. You watch after her, now."

Rawley straightened his shoulders. "Yes, sir."

Loree's heart swelled as she watched her husband make his way through the crowd. Tall, lean, he looked incredibly handsome in his black jacket and white starched shirt.

"How long is a play anyway?" Rawley asked, drawing her attention away from Austin.

"A couple of hours I imagine."

"Think there's any chance *Romeo and Juliet* is a story about a boy and his dog?" Rawley asked.

Loree fought back her smile. "No, it's a love story."

"A boy could love his dog," he said hopefully.

Loree's smile broke free. "In this story, he loves a woman."

Rawley grimaced. "They ain't gonna do any kissing, are they?"

"Don't you like kissing?"

"Ain't never tried it, but can't see where it'd be much fun. From what I can tell, looks to me like the two people are just swapping spit. I'd rather swap marbles."

"Rawley!"

Loree turned just as Maggie plowed into Rawley. Breathless, she squeezed his arm. "Rawley, one of the actors is over there showing people his sword. His honest to gosh sword! Come on!"

She tugged on his arm, but Rawley pulled back. He cast a quick glance at Loree, and she saw the longing in his eyes. "I can't. Told Uncle Austin I'd stay here with Aunt Loree."

Maggie wasn't as discreet in her disappointment. "Heck fire, Rawley, we won't be that far away."

Rawley hesitated, then shook his head. "Can't do it. Gave my word."

Loree placed her hand on his shoulder. "Go on. I'll be all right."

"Uncle Austin might not like it."

"I'll explain it to him so he does."

"Suppose I could just run over and take a quick look-see."

Maggie grabbed his hand. "Come on, Rawley. You won't believe how shiny his sword is. Looks like it's sharp enough to cut the head off a Longhorn."

Loree watched them work their way through the crowd. Her brother had been around Rawley's age when he'd died. She couldn't remember if he'd ever looked at a sword.

She felt a light tap on her arm and turned. Her stomach dropped to her knees at the sight of the man and woman standing before her.

"Hello," Becky said smiling warmly. "I didn't know you were still in town."

Loree gave her a jerky nod. "Yes. Yes, I live here now."

"How wonderful! You'll have to come visit some Sunday when the store is closed. Did you find the gun you were looking for?"

"Why would she need a gun?" Austin asked from behind her.

Loree's heart pounded so heavily she was certain he felt it as he clamped his hand possessively onto her waist. "Here's your water," he said quietly.

With a trembling hand, Loree took the glass from him. "Thank you. I was already beginning to miss you."

Austin smiled warmly, dipped his head, and brushed a quick kiss across her lips. "I was missing you, too."

Loree shifted her gaze and watched as understanding dawned in Becky's eyes and the blood drained from her face.

"Austin, it's so good to see you again," Becky said, her voice faltering. "How are you?"

"Wiser."

"Cameron told me you'd gotten married . . . I just . . . I just didn't realize . . . I'd met your wife," Becky stammered.

"She mentioned meeting you. Loree, Sugar, did you meet Cameron?"

"I saw him, but I don't think we actually met."

"He's Dee's brother. I'm not sure I ever mentioned that," Austin said.

"No, you didn't. You only mentioned that he'd been your best friend."

Cameron looked as though he might fall ill at any moment. "Austin—"

"If you'll excuse us," Austin said, "we need to find our seats. Dee would never forgive us for missing the opening scene."

Austin held out his arm. Loree grabbed onto it, afraid she'd sink to the floor if she didn't have his support. The crowd parted as they walked to the sweeping staircase. She heard a mumbled "murderer," and her heart tripped over itself. She glanced at her husband, saw his clenched jaw, and realized people were murmuring about him. She angled her chin proudly.

"I've never watched a play before. I've always wanted to attend one."

Austin glanced down at her.

She smiled with her heart in her eyes. "I'm very glad that you're the one who's taking me."

"Sugar, I don't think I would have made it up these stairs without you by my side."

He took her hand at the top of the stairs. They walked along the landing, passing several curtained entrances before Austin swept back the drapery and led Loree into the darkness of a balcony.

"Thank you, Loree, for looking like you were proud to have me by your side," he whispered.

"I was proud."

She sensed a moment's hesitation before he took her into his arms and lowered his mouth to hers. She twined her arms around his neck, returning his kiss with a fervor that surprised her. She had wanted to scratch out eyes and yank out hair. She'd wanted to ask those two people how they could have betrayed her husband, the father of her child, the man she was coming to love.

Austin grunted and stumbled to the side, taking her with him. The curtain was drawn aside, and Dallas was silhouetted in the doorway.

"What are you doing?" Dallas demanded.

"Looking for our seats," Austin said, his hand skimming over hers before latching securely onto it.

Then mayhem erupted as the family crowded inside the small balcony.

"Everyone take your seats," Dee said excitedly. "They'll be opening the curtains any minute."

"Which chair is mine?" Maggie asked. "I wanna sit in the front."

"Ladies in the front," Dallas said, "Men in the back."

"Loree sits by me," Austin said.

"Yeah, and I want to sit by Amelia," Houston added.

"Fine," Dallas ground out.

"We'll put the children, Austin, and Loree in the back—" Dallas began.

"Then the children won't be able to see," Amelia pointed out.

"I don't care if I can't see," Rawley said.

"But then you won't see the sword fight," Maggie told him. "You gotta see the sword fight."

"I don't mind sitting in the back—"

"Houston and I will sit in the back," Amelia said.

"No, Dallas and I are taller. We'll sit in the back," Dee offered.

"No, Dee, this is your dream—"

"But I want you to see—"

Austin tugged on Loree's hand. "Come on," he whispered. "We'll just sit in the back."

He guided her toward the far side. As they sat, he kept his hand wrapped around hers. She heard his low chuckle. "Guess I started this by wanting to sit by you."

"I'm grateful you did because I really didn't want to sit by anyone else."

He trailed his finger along her jaw. "I'm glad. Loree, I'm sorry it was so awkward down there, with people staring and whispering. They're just not used to me being home yet."

"My home could give us the things we need."

"I want you to have things that you *want* not just things that you need."

"That's it!" Dallas roared. "Everyone has five seconds to plant their butts in a seat. Anyone left standing at the end of that time goes over the balcony."

A mad scramble ensued.

"Come on, Rawley," Maggie cried as she pulled him to a seat in front.

She plopped down in front of Austin. He tapped her shoulder. "Trade places with Rawley so your Aunt Loree can see."

She and Rawley switched chairs. While the remaining adults discussed the seating arrangements, Maggie turned and looked at Austin. "Can me and Rawley spit over the side of the balcony?"

"Sure, especially if your Uncle Cameron is sitting down there."

"He ain't. They got balcony seats, too." She pointed to the side. "They're right there."

Loree watched as Austin's gaze followed the direction of Maggie's finger. He stiffened. Cameron and Becky were sitting alone in the balcony next to theirs.

"You don't like Uncle Cameron anymore, do you?" Maggie asked.

Austin jerked his head around and stared at her. Amelia put her hand on her daughter's shoulder. "Turn around, young lady." She gave Austin an apologetic smile before taking her seat beside Maggie. Houston settled in beside her.

Dee sat beside Loree and laughed lightly. "I didn't realize that was going to be such an ordeal." She patted Dallas's knee. "You handled the situation very well."

"Next time, everybody gets their own balcony."

A man walked onto the stage, and a hush fell over the audience.

"Ladies and gentlemen! The Royal Shakespearean Theater is honored to be in your lovely town. Tonight's performance is *Romeo and Juliet*."

He walked off the stage. The curtains slowly began to open, but Loree found she had no interest in the play. She wondered what thoughts preyed on her husband's mind. His hand had tightened around hers when Maggie had asked her question. His grip had yet to loosen. He stared straight ahead, but she didn't think he was paying any more attention to the play than she was. She leaned toward him. "I want to go outside."

He jerked his head around, and even in the shadows, she saw the concern etched in his face. His hand closed more tightly around hers. "You all right?"

She nodded slightly. "I just need a breath of fresh air."

He leaned low around her and whispered to Dallas, "We're gonna step outside for a few minutes."

Rawley twisted around in his chair. "Can I go?"

Dallas gave a quick nod and stood. Austin helped Loree to her feet and they worked their way between the chairs.

"I'm sorry," she whispered as she stepped on Dee's foot. But Dee didn't seem to notice as she waved them past, her gaze riveted on the stage. They stepped between the curtains, and Loree took a deep breath.

"You sure you're all right?" Austin asked.

"I just felt a little faint."

"You wanna go sit in the buggy?"

"Could we take a walk?"

"Sure." He wrapped his hand around hers, and they descended the stairs.

"Could you understand anything them actors was saying?" Rawley asked as he tromped along behind them.

"Not a word," Austin said.

They walked through the foyer, and Austin swung open the front door. Loree walked through. Austin glanced over his shoulder. "You coming?"

Loree noticed Rawley's hesitation. She peered back inside. At the far end, in the baby room, Faith had her nose pressed to the pane of glass.

"Reckon I'll go be with Faith," Rawley muttered.

"There's women inside watching them," Austin assured him. "She's fine."

"She don't look fine. She looks downright miserable," Rawley said. "I don't like for my sister to be unhappy."

He stalked toward the room. Austin chuckled. "I reckon Faith couldn't have asked for a better brother." He glanced at Loree. "I couldn't have asked for a finer wife."

Loree felt herself blush as she stepped onto the boardwalk. Austin followed her outside and took her hand. "Where do you want to walk?"

"Doesn't matter."

"We'll head for the far end of town, then."

He'd taken four long strides before he adjusted the length of his walk to accommodate her.

"So why did you need a gun?" he asked quietly.

Her step faltered, and she glanced up at him. "I was hoping you'd forgotten about that."

"There's not a lot I forget."

She sighed heavily. "I was in a strange town, I didn't know if you'd come back—"

He came to an abrupt halt and spun her around to face him, hurt evident in his eyes. "You thought I'd abandoned you?"

"No, not really. I was just . . . I was just scared."

She felt him searching her face, searching for something she could never let him see.

"What is it exactly that you fear?"

"The past. I'm afraid it has a stronger hold on us than either of us realizes."

"Because of Becky?"

"Because of a lot of things."

"I can't change my past."

Unfortunately, she couldn't change hers either. She could only hope that it would never lift its ugly head to touch Austin or their children. "Share something good with me."

His blue eyes darkened, and his lips spread into a warm smile filled with impassioned promises. He placed his hands on either side of her waist and drew her against him. "What exactly did you have in mind?"

"A story. Tell me a good story from your past."

Laughing, he released her waist, took her hand, and began walking. "I'm no good at telling stories."

The night closed in around them. The lamps along the street threw ashen light over the abandoned boardwalk. The town seemed almost deserted with most of the residents attending the play. She saw pale lamplight spilling out from the saloon at the far end of town, along with boisterous laughter, and the echo of a tinny piano.

She stumbled when the heel of her shoe hit a loose plank in the boardwalk. Austin steadied her, then knelt and slapped his thigh. "Give me your foot."

"What are you going to do?"

He glanced up at her and she saw the answer in his gaze.

"I'm dressed all fancy. I can't go barefooted."

He angled his head and lifted a brow. "Are we going back into the theater to watch the play?"

She remembered how tense he'd been inside the building, how his body and his hold on her had relaxed once they'd stepped outside. "No."

"Then get your foot up here."

Placing her hands on his shoulders, she planted her foot on his thigh and watched as he nimbly worked her buttons free and removed the shoe from her foot. "You have such nice fingers," she said as he rolled her stocking off.

"You think so?"

"Mmm-uh." She relished the feel of the boardwalk beneath her bare sole and placed her other foot on his thigh. "I wish you'd let me teach you to play your mother's violin."

His hands stilled.

"It takes time and patience, but I have both," she assured him.

He worked her shoe free, grabbed the other shoe, and unfolded his body. "I can't play the violin, Loree."

"If you tried—"

"I can't."

His words were spoken with absolute finality.

"Can't never could," she muttered.

"What?"

She shook her head. "Just something my ma used to tell me."

He shifted her shoes to one hand, wrapped his free hand around hers, and began walking.

"Dallas has his cattle, Houston has his horses. What do you have?"

"You."

His smile was warm, and her heart fluttered.

"Before me, what did you have? What were your dreams?"

His steps slowed as though they followed his thinking, back to a time when he had dreams. "Dallas is a man of powerful influence." He pierced her with his gaze. "I love and admire him, Loree. Don't ever think that I don't."

"I wouldn't."

He gave a curt nod. "I wanted to go someplace where people had never heard of him. I wanted to make a name for myself, knowing I had earned the recognition because of me, not him. Does that make any sense?"

She nodded with complete understanding. "Where would you have gone?"

He shook his head slowly. "Never got that far in my thinking. Once I . . . Once I met Becky, the thought of leaving went straight out of my head."

"She became your dream then."

He stopped walking, leaned one shoulder against the side of the building, and brought her close. "No. No, she didn't. She just made me stop thinking about it." He trailed his long fingers along her jaw. "You made me start thinking about dreams again."

He dipped his head and brushed his lips over hers. "You make me think about a lot of things. You have from the first moment I realized you weren't a boy."

He settled his mouth over hers, drawing her up onto her toes. Her feet crept over his boots, taking her higher. His arm came around her, holding her close while he cradled her cheek with his other hand and tilted her head back. He trailed his hot mouth along her throat.

"Sweet, sweet Loree. God, I need you," he rasped.

Heat swirled through her, around her, over her. Her head dropped back. "Tell me . . . tell me what you would have done to make a name for yourself."

"I woulda—"

He made a guttural sound and stumbled back. Loree went flying off him and landed hard on her backside.

"You goddamn murdering son of a bitch!" a man yelled as he slammed Austin into the brick building.

Austin grunted and slid in a heap to the ground.

"They shoulda hanged you!" The man kicked him in the side. Groaning, Austin curled into a ball.

"No!" Loree screamed as she crawled toward one of the shoes Austin had dropped. She threw it at the man, hitting him squarely on the side of the head.

The man jerked back. She heaved the other shoe at him, grateful to see him run into the shadows.

Loree scrambled across the boardwalk. "Austin?"

He moaned as she rolled him over and gently placed his head in her lap. She felt the warm, sticky wetness coating her hands and released a bloodcurdling scream.

Chapter 12

ॐ

"I CAN'T GET the blood off," Loree ground out through clenched teeth as she washed her hands in the bowl of warm water that the doctor had brought her.

Austin heard the tremor of panic in her voice, watched the way she scrubbed viciously at her hands, and was afraid she was going to peel off her skin. He moved away from the doctor who was examining his head.

"Hey, young fella—" Dr. Freeman began.

Austin held up a hand. "Just a minute."

He crossed the room and took Loree's hands. She snapped her gaze up to his, and he could almost see the horrific memories mirrored in her golden eyes.

"I can't get the blood off," she rasped.

He remembered how she'd continued to scrub herself the night Digger had died, even though she'd washed away all the blood. "I can get it off," he said quietly. He dipped his hand into the water, then slowly, gently trailed his fingers over her clean hands. Tenderly, he wiped them dry. "There, see? The blood's all gone."

Her brow furrowed, Loree glanced at her hands, then lifted one to touch the back of his head. He grabbed her hand before she could get blood on it again. Tears welled in her eyes. "Someone hurt you."

He kissed the tips of her fingers. "I'm gonna be all right. You go sit in the front room with Dee."

She nodded before leaving the room, closing the door in her wake.

He wished he'd been able to spare her the sight of his blood. Austin crossed back to the chair and sat. He grimaced as the doctor dabbed something against his head. "Damn! That burns."

"I just want to make certain the gash is clean before I stitch it up. We don't need any infection," Dr. Freeman said, his tall skeletal frame thinner than Austin remembered.

"Are you sure Loree is all right?" he asked. Afraid she might have been hurt earlier, he had insisted Dr. Freeman examine her first.

"She's fine," Dr. Freeman said. "She just doesn't have much stomach for blood is all."

Austin figured he wouldn't either if he'd watched someone murder his family.

"Who attacked you?" Dallas asked from the doorway.

"I don't know."

"Duncan?"

Austin glared at his brother. "I said, I don't know. He came at me from behind and slammed my head against the wall. Everything went from black to blacker."

"I'll ride out and talk to Duncan tomorrow—"

"And what? Tell him to stay away from me when you don't even know it was him? He's not the only one in town who thinks I should have hanged."

Dallas's eyes narrowed. "Who else?"

"Most of the town."

"Then I'll set them all straight."

"It's your word against a verdict of guilty. Just stay clear of this. You're only asking for trouble if you get involved."

"Goddamn it! This started with me!"

"And it'll finish with me." He heaved a weary sigh. "I appreciate your willingness to take a stand, but the truth of the matter is that I did some stupid things without thinking them through. They were my mistakes, and I'm the one that has to pay for them. Without those mistakes, no jury would have ever found me guilty."

He expected a further argument. Instead, he saw abiding respect delve into his oldest brother's eyes. "Christ, you did grow up, didn't you?"

Austin gave him a halfhearted smile. "Yeah."

The door opened and Dee poked her head through the opening. "Dr. Freeman, Loree said something is happening with the baby."

Austin shot off the table. "Dammit! I thought you looked her over."

"I did," Dr. Freeman said as he shuffled from the room, following in Austin's wake.

Loree was sitting in a stuffed chair in Dr. Freeman's front parlor. Austin knelt beside her and wrapped his hand around her tightened fist. "Loree?"

Tears shimmered in her eyes. "Oh, Austin, I think I'm losing the baby."

Austin heard bones creak as Dr. Freeman made his way to his knees. "How badly did it hurt?" he asked.

A look of surprise swept over Loree's face. "Well, it didn't hurt exactly."

"What exactly did it do?" Dr. Freeman asked.

Loree cast a sidelong glance at Austin before turning her attention back to Dr. Freeman. "Well, it sorta felt like"—she gnawed on her lower lip and furrowed her brow—"you know when you jump into a creek and air gets trapped in your pantaloons and sorta sits there for a minute after you hit the water and then it bubbles out and tickles? That's what it felt like."

Austin thought Dr. Freeman looked as though he were on the verge of busting a gut, his face turned crimson and Austin could tell he was fighting to hold back his laughter. "Can't say I've ever had air get trapped in my pantaloons." He glanced over his shoulder at Dee. "Think she just felt the baby roll over?"

Dee smiled warmly. "I think so."

With wonder reflected in her golden eyes, Loree pressed her hand against her stomach. "I felt the baby roll over? She's all right?"

"I'm certain she's just fine," Dr. Freeman said.

The stymied late August air hung outside the open window, doing little to cool Austin's sweating body. The moon spilled into the bedroom, waltzing with the darkness.

He saw the shadow of his violin as it rested on the top of his bureau. Once he'd been able to hear the music long before he ever touched the strings.

Once, he had dreamed of a special violin—created with his own hands—that made the sweetest music ever heard.

Now, he would be content to play his mother's scarred and scratched violin—if only he once again had the ability to bring the music to life within his heart.

"Austin, what are you doing?" Loree whispered sleepily.

He walked to the bed, stretched out beside her, and spread his fingers over her stomach. "Just couldn't sleep."

"Does your head hurt?"

"Nah, it's fine."

"The man you went to prison for killing—"

"Was a sorry son of a bitch not worth worrying over."

"He must have meant something to someone for a man to attack you. I heard him say you should have hanged."

He cradled her cheek. "I'll tell you how worthless he was. One night behind the hotel, he shoved some wooden crates over on top of Dee and lit out without a backward glance. Dee lost the baby she was carrying and dang near lost her life. Then he paid Rawley's father to kill Dallas. I don't regret his dying. I only regret that I went to prison because of it." Tenderly, he brushed his lips over hers. "I'm gonna be the one waking up with nightmares if we keep following this trail. Let's talk about something else. Tell me again what it felt like when the baby moved inside you."

"It scared me at first because I thought something was wrong. My ma never told me things about having a baby. I didn't know I'd feel her roll over . . . or that it would feel so wonderful." She turned to her side, burying her face in the crook of his shoulder. "I'm glad we're gonna have her. I was embarrassed at first . . . even ashamed—"

He tilted her face back. He couldn't see the gold in her eyes, but it didn't stop him from searching for it. "Loree, the shame is mine, not yours, never yours."

"Austin, I wanted you close to me that night. I'd never felt so alone in my whole life."

He reached through the darkness, found her hand, and brought it to his lips. "In prison . . ."

"What?"

He swallowed hard. If only removing the shackles had removed the memories. "There was this box. The inside was black as tar. If the guard had a toothache or was in the mood to be mean, he'd shove someone into that box." He felt the sweat break out on his skin and he shivered, even though the night was warm. Her fingers tightened around his. "I couldn't breathe in that box. I thought I'd go crazy. The night I got home and Dallas told me Becky had gotten married, I felt like he'd shoved me inside that box."

She pressed a kiss against his chest. "I'm sorry."

"That first night I held you, I felt a flicker of hope that I might be able to escape."

He felt her warm tears slide down his chest. "One of these nights, Loree, I'm gonna leave every memory I have outside that door. When that happens I'm gonna make love to you until dawn." Her arms slid around him and she scooted her body close enough to his that he felt every curve. "Lord, I love it when you do that," he whispered, drawing her closer.

"They're nice people, aren't they?"

His chest muffled her words, but he knew without asking to whom she referred. Becky and Cameron. "Yeah, they are. That's what makes this so much harder. I can't find it in me to hate them."

Her hold on him tightened, and he felt slight tremors racing through her. "I'm glad," she whispered hoarsely. "Hate can eat at you . . . make you do things . . ."

He pressed a kiss to her temple and tasted the salt of a tear. "What do you know of hate, Loree?"

"The man who murdered my family. I wanted him dead. I wanted him dead so bad that it was like he'd crawled inside me."

She started gasping for breath, and he heard a broken sob escape. "Shh. Shh. Loree, don't upset yourself. It's been a bad night. Don't think about the past. Think about the future." He continued to coo to her, feeling her body relaxing within his arms. Her gasping gave way to slow even breathing. "That's it, Sugar. Think about that little girl—"

She sniffed. "Boy."

He chuckled low. "Oh, it's a boy now, is it?"

"I think so."

He drew her closer. The night was warm, unbearably hot, but he kept her within the circle of his arms. He hadn't been lying when he'd told her he'd be the one to wake up with nightmares, but he'd discovered that as long as she was nestled against him, he could hold the hated memories at bay.

"Tell me about your wedding."

Loree stopped kneading the bread dough and glanced up at Maggie's expectant face. The child sat at the end of the table, her legs tucked up beneath her bottom on the chair, the hand holding the stub of her pencil poised above the journal.

"My wedding?"

Maggie nodded briskly. "I want to write a story about it."

Loree glanced at the window. She saw the gray skies. She could not believe how quickly autumn had given way to winter. She turned her attention back to Maggie. "Do you write lots of stories?"

Maggie bobbed her head.

"When do you write all these stories?"

"Nighttime is the best. It's usually the quietest 'cept when Pa gets a hankering for a bunch of kisses. He'll say he wants to see Ma's toes curl, and she'll start giggling. Then suddenly, it gets really quiet. Do your toes curl when Uncle Austin kisses you?"

Loree felt her face warm. She had to admit Maggie wasn't a shy child, but she couldn't wait to tell Austin that she knew what Maggie was doing at night when her light again became visible in her room. She started pounding the bread dough. "Sometimes."

"I bet Aunt Becky's toes curl. When Uncle Cameron married her, he kissed her a really long time. Until Uncle Dallas cleared his throat real loud. Made me jump outta my skin."

Loree imagined any noise Dallas made on purpose would startle her. "Was their wedding nice?"

Maggie shrugged. "It was tiny. There was just us. And Aunt Becky was so silly. She started crying. She said she didn't think we'd come on account of her lovin' Uncle Austin first and then lovin' Uncle Cameron." Maggie rolled her eyes. "But once you love someone, you don't stop lovin' 'em."

"No, I guess you don't." Loree wondered where the child had gained her wisdom, and if she'd lose it once she grew older.

A brief knock sounded on the door before Houston opened it, a panicked expression on his face. His other three daughters were with him, their eyes wide. "Amelia's having the baby. Can I leave the young 'uns with you?"

"Certainly." Wiping her hands on her apron, Loree crossed the room and ushered the children inside.

The cold November winds whipped around Austin as he guided Black Thunder home. He drew up the collar on his sheep skin jacket and pulled his hat lower over his brow. Night was closing in, and he relished its arrival.

Evenings had become his favorite time of day. Loree welcomed him with arms open wide, a warm meal, and a warmer kiss. They sat in front of the fire, curled around each other, waiting for their child to move.

Austin had grown up around a brother who bred cattle, a brother who bred horses . . . and yet the wonder of a child that he'd helped to create growing within a woman he cherished . . . humbled him.

He brought Black Thunder to a halt, dismounted, and impatiently set about the task of tending to his horse before seeing to his own needs. He saw the lamplight spilling out from the window, and the chill of the night gave way to an unexpected warmth.

He finished his task and strode to the house, anticipation hurrying his step. He threw open the door and froze.

"Uncle Austin," three little magpies chirped and raced across the room to wrap themselves around his legs.

"We're makin' baby cookies," Laurel said. "Want one?"

The one she extended toward him had a bite taken from it. Loree strolled across the room and began to tug the girls back. "Come on, girls. At least let Uncle Austin get his jacket off."

He met Loree's eyes as he shrugged out of his jacket. She looked at him imploringly. "Amelia went into labor this morning. Houston brought the girls over so I could watch them."

Austin looked past her to the table laden with cookies. "I said we'd bake cookies until the baby was born. I didn't know it would take all day."

The door swung open catching Austin in the middle of his back. Maggie pushed her way through. "Not yet. Pa says anytime. So can we bake some more cookies?"

"Don't you think you have enough cookies?" Austin asked.

"But Aunt Loree said—"

"She didn't know your ma would take so long," Austin explained. "And Aunt Loree looks mighty tired to me."

"We could play Go Fish," Maggie suggested.

"It's a little late to go fishing," Austin said.

Maggie laughed. "You're so silly, Uncle Austin. It's a game."

Loree sat in the rocking chair, watching her husband play a card game with his nieces. They sat in a circle, drawing cards, laying down cards. She suspected he was cheating because tiny A. J. who sat in his lap while he held her cards, as well as his own, was winning several hands while Austin was repeatedly ending up with no cards to his credit. It was a strange moment to come to the realization that she had fallen in love with him.

Her father had cheated as well—but it was always to his benefit . . . and she had yet to see Austin do anything that put him ahead at anyone else's expense.

As night wore on, he carried each sleeping girl to the bed. Near midnight, a knock finally sounded on the door. Looking exhausted Houston stepped into the house.

"It's a girl. Gracie."

"How's Amelia?" Austin asked.

"She had a hard time of it. Dr. Freeman says this will probably be the last one. Let me gather up the girls—"

"Why don't you let them stay?" Loree said quietly. "They're already asleep. I'll bring them over in the morning."

"If you're sure?"

"We're sure."

"If Maggie turns up the lamp after you've gone to sleep, will you ignore it? I know she slipped into the house and got her journal earlier. She likes to write in it after everyone else is asleep. We're not supposed to know."

Austin patted his brother's shoulder. "Go on. You look like you're ready to collapse."

Houston walked out the door. Austin turned to Loree. "Lie with me by the fire for a little while."

He stretched out on the sofa, and she curled against his side, watching the flames dance within the hearth.

"I'm almost out of sugar," Loree said quietly.

"I'll pick up another ten pounds tomorrow."

"I'm not that bad," she said, knowing he was teasing her.

"You're not bad at all."

Silence wove around them. Reaching down, Austin splayed his fingers over her swollen stomach. "You're tinier than Amelia."

"My mother was tiny. She didn't have any problems."

"Dallas wanted to be a father. Houston wanted to be a father. It's not that I don't want to be a father, but the thought of this little fella coming into the world scares the hell out of me."

"Scares me, too," she admitted.

He wrapped his hand around hers. "I've made a lot of mistakes in my life, Loree. I want you to know that I don't consider this child to be one of them."

She met his gaze, the love she held for him deepening. "I never thought that you did."

Chapter 13

❧

AUSTIN STOOD AGAINST the wall in Dallas's dining area and watched the bustling activity with interest. Christmas had always been his favorite time of year.

Beside him, Loree jostled Gracie. Six weeks had passed since her birth, and it was evident that Houston had finally fathered a daughter who resembled him, with black hair and dark eyes. Austin enjoyed watching Loree care for the children.

He couldn't remember what she thought their baby was going to be this week, but whether it was a boy or a girl, he wanted it to have the one thing he'd grown up without: the comfort of a mother. And he knew beyond a doubt that with Loree, his children would have the best.

"When is Uncle Cameron going to get here?" Maggie asked as she plucked a pecan out of a bright red bowl and popped it into her mouth.

Dee stilled, the dish of applesauce halfway to the table. She cast a furtive glance at Austin before answering. "He's not going to celebrate Christmas with us this year."

A look of horror swept over Maggie's face. "But what about the special reindeer hay?"

Clearing her throat, Dee set the dish on the table between pumpkin pies and candles that smelled of cinnamon. "I'm sure Santa Claus will come even if we don't have the hay."

"No, he won't," Maggie said as she crossed her arms over her chest and pushed out her lower lip.

"Somebody ought to tell her the truth: There ain't no Santa Claus," Rawley whispered beside Austin.

Austin watched Rawley saunter to Maggie and put his hand on her shoulder. He didn't know if he could stand to watch the disappointment reshape Maggie's face when she heard the truth.

"Hey, Brat, we could probably use some of the hay from the barn," Rawley told her in a comforting voice.

Maggie wrinkled her nose. "It's not reindeer hay. What if it gives them a belly ache?"

"Then we'd know for sure there's a Santa Claus."

Maggie laughed, her green eyes sparkling like the candles lit upon the evergreen tree that stood in the corner of the front parlor. Rawley shoved on her shoulder. "Come on. Maybe we can find some that'll work."

"Get your jackets," Dee ordered as she headed back to the kitchen.

As they walked toward the door, Faith scrambled to her feet and raced after them. "Wawley, I wanna go, too."

"Come on then, Shorty."

She squealed as he swung her up into his arms.

"It's a wonder that girl ever learned to walk," Amelia said as she came to stand beside Austin. "The way her brother carts her around."

He shifted his gaze and found Amelia studying him. "Don't look at me like that," he ordered.

"Like what?" she asked, her green eyes containing an innocence he didn't believe.

"Like you know what I'm thinking. It's damn aggravating when you do that, and you've done it for as long as I've known you. Hell, you probably figured out that I lied about Houston's horse breaking its leg all those years ago."

She smiled at him the way he supposed mothers smiled at their errant children. "I suspected it at the time."

"Then why didn't you say something back then?"

"Because I figured it was a dilemma you needed to work out for yourself—just like now." She patted his shoulder before taking her daughter from Loree.

Austin spun on his heel and caught up with the children as they were shoving their arms into the sleeves of their coats. He opened the door and followed them outside, leaned against the veranda beam, and watched them trudge into the barn. The cold wind whipping around him felt warmer than his heart.

He heard the door open quietly and glanced over his shoulder. The woman had a way of walking into his life when he needed her the most. Reaching out, he grabbed Loree's hand and pulled her against his side, her arms forming a cocoon around his chest.

"Special hay for reindeer." He snorted. "Where did Cameron come up with that?" Although she held her silence while he stared at the barn, he felt her scrutinizing gaze delving clear into his soul.

"I love those children," he finally managed to force past the knot that had risen in his throat. "I'd do anything for them." He shifted his gaze to her, taking his time, needing to gauge her reaction in order to find the truth. "I won't go into town and get Cameron and his family if it'll hurt you to have them here."

Warmth and reassurance caused the gold of her eyes to glisten like a miner's treasure as she rose up on her toes. He dipped his head, welcoming the light brush of her lips over his.

"I'll get your jacket," she said, stepping away from him.

He drew her back into his arms, lowered his mouth to hers, and kissed her like a man who had lived too long in the bowels of hell and was only just beginning to see a glimpse of heaven.

Standing on the second floor landing, Austin turned up the collar on his sheepskin jacket. Through the paned glass window, he saw the scraggly boughs of a tree that looked as though it might have been left over from a past Christmas—or brought in quickly to accommodate last minute plans.

Cameron had never celebrated Christmas at Dallas's house before Austin had gone to prison, but he supposed since he was Dee's brother, his family had welcomed him into their home after Austin left. He shoved his trembling, damp hands into his jacket pockets. He should have brought Loree with him. Sometimes he thought he could face anything if Loree stood beside him. What was it Houston had said to Amelia the day he married her? "With you by my side, I'm a better man than I've ever been alone." Austin hadn't understood the significance of the words at the time—but they were certainly beginning to make sense now.

Taking a deep breath, he pounded on the door. The heavy footsteps echoed on the other side. Cameron opened the door, and Austin watched as shock quickly gave way to concern.

"Has something happened to Dee?" Cameron asked.

"Nope. To Maggie."

"Ah, Jesus. What do you need us to do?"

Austin turned away as memories swamped him, and the stinging in his eyes had little to do with the bitter wind. Cameron had been his first—his best—friend, the kind of man who had always put others before himself.

"Let me get the keys to the store and I'll open it up. You can just take what you need—"

"I need reindeer hay."

Cameron's mouth fell open. "What? You said something had happened to Maggie."

"Yep. She got her heart broke when she found out you weren't coming with your special reindeer hay so pack up your family. I want to get back before dark."

"You don't need me. Just put some hay in burlap sacks and tell them it's reindeer hay. I've got some sacks in the store that I can get for you." Cameron turned to go back into the house.

"Not good enough," Austin said. Cameron halted and glanced over his shoulder. "They think you're the only one who can deliver special hay."

"Look, Austin—"

"I figure you've got two choices. You can either come with me now or go with Dallas later because as soon as he sees the sad faces on those children—"

"Becky, pack up!" Cameron called out. "We're going to spend Christmas with my sister."

Austin chuckled low as Cameron disappeared into the house. It felt good after all this time to find something that had remained exactly the same over the years: Cameron was still scared to death of Dallas.

"Uncle Cameron, you came!" Maggie cried as she hopped up from the floor, spilling the bowl of popcorn she'd been threading. "Did you bring the reindeer hay?"

Standing in the doorway of the front parlor, Austin watched with interest as his family welcomed the visitors into their midst. Smiles grew bigger. Laughter erupted along with hugs and backslapping.

Wearing a wide grin, Dee strolled over and kissed his cheek. "Thank you. I know it was hard for you."

He glanced at Loree as she greeted Becky with a warm smile and held a cookie out to Drew.

"You've got no idea," Austin said roughly. "I need to unhitch the horses."

He went outside, taking his time drawing the buggy into the barn and unhitching the horses. The wind howling through the cracks wasn't strong enough to drown the sound of laughter he'd heard inside the house. He slapped each horse on the rump, sending it into the corral through the side door of the barn.

Twilight was closing in. Dallas would have a house full of people tonight. He wondered if he and Loree should head back to their own place rather than sleep in his old room with the new furniture as they'd planned.

"Are you all right?" a quiet voice asked from behind him.

Turning he smiled, took Loree's hand, and drew her near. "I am now."

Her cheeks took on a rosy hue as though she'd spent the afternoon sitting before a cozy fire. Suddenly he wished that they were home, sitting before the crackling hearth, wrapped around each other.

"Was the journey back awkward?" she asked.

He shrugged. "We didn't talk. You would have thought we were heading for a funeral if Drew hadn't been bouncing on the seat, singing 'Jingle Bells' the whole way."

Her eyes widened. "Becky said he's only eighteen months old. I think it's impressive that he can sing a song—"

Austin shook his head. "Not a song. Only two words. Jingle bells, jingle bells, jingle bells. Over and over. All the way here."

"The children are so excited—" she began.

"Yeah. They sounded like a heard of stampeding wild horses when Cameron walked in."

She placed her hand over his heart. "Even if they hadn't come, this Christmas seems difficult for you."

"The last Christmas I had here . . ." His voice trailed off as he shook his head. "It was so different. Dee had just lost the baby. Rawley had been living here for a couple of weeks, but he was still afraid." He grazed his knuckles over her cheek and smiled. "The only niece I had was Maggie. It truly was a silent night. I have a feeling tonight will be anything but quiet."

"My family died shortly after Christmas. I haven't celebrated Christmas in the years since."

He wrapped his arms around her and pressed his cheek to the top of her head. "Ah, Loree, I'm so sorry. I haven't given any thought to what this time of year must mean to you."

She tilted her head back and met his gaze. "It's wonderful to have children around, snitching the candies and shaking presents." Taking his hand, she placed it on her swollen stomach. "I'm glad to be here."

"Ah, Sugar, I'm—" The movement beneath his hand halted his words. He gave his wife a warm slow smile. "Lord, I love it when he does that."

His knees creaked as he hunkered down and placed his cheek against Loree's stomach. She intertwined her fingers through his hair, and he realized that contentment existed in the smallest of moments. Suddenly it didn't matter that he had never before celebrated Christmas with over half the people in his brother's house.

What mattered was that he would be sharing the day with Loree and with a child that was not yet born.

"Uncle Austin!" Maggie staggered to a stop right after she rounded the corner of the stall. Her eyes turned into two big circles of green. "Can I listen?" She didn't wait for an answer but hurried over, two burlap sacks clutched in one hand, and pressed her ear against Loree's stomach. Austin glanced up to see Loree's startled expression.

Maggie drew her brows together. "It don't sound like a girl," she announced.

"I reckon you'd be the one to know," Austin said.

Maggie nodded her head enthusiastically, her blond curls bouncing. "Ma always lets me and Pa listen. Pa even talks to the baby before it's born!"

"I don't believe that," Austin told her.

She jerked her head up and down. "He does so. I 'member when he talked to me before I was born. He told me he loved me better than anything." She thrust a burlap sack into his hand. "We need to get the reindeer hay put out. Come on!"

She raced out of the barn. Austin slowly unfolded his body and took his wife's hand, escorting her outside.

"I cannot picture Houston making a fool of himself and talking to his wife's belly," Austin said.

"He was talking to the baby."

Austin snapped his head around. "You say that like you think the baby could hear him."

Loree shrugged. "Maybe. I don't know."

He glanced down at his wife's rounded stomach. He'd feel silly talking to it. He met her gaze. "I'll just wait until he's born."

He closed his fingers more firmly around hers as they approached the house. Giggling children were digging into burlap sacks and tossing hay over the yard, the veranda, and each other.

"Is there a trick to this?" he asked as he neared Dallas.

"Don't put it in the hands of a three-year-old," Dallas warned as he waited patiently while Faith carefully picked a single piece of straw from the pile he held in his hand. She bent down and placed it on the ground. Then she meticulously sifted through the straw in his hand, searching for another piece to her liking.

Austin cleared his throat. "You'll be here all night."

"Yep, and this ain't the worst part. We gotta remember where they put all the damn hay so we can pick it up in the morning before they wake up." He lifted a brow. "So they'll think the dadgum reindeer ate it."

Austin knelt beside his niece. She stilled, the straw pressed between her tiny forefinger and thumb, her brown eyes huge. He smiled broadly. "You want to put out my hay for the reindeer, too?"

She bobbed her head, took his sack, and held it up to her father. Dallas scowled and ground out his warning through his clenched teeth, "You just wait until next year."

Austin threw back his head and laughed. God, it was good to be home . . . to know there would be a Christmas next year . . . and he would be here.

Breathless, Maggie rushed over, Rawley in her wake. "Uncle Dallas, can me and Rawley go put some on the balcony outside his room?"

"Sure."

"Me, too," Faith said as she held her arms out to Rawley.

He lifted her into his arms. "Get her bags, Brat."

Maggie relieved Dallas of his burden and rushed after Rawley, her short legs unable to keep up with his long strides.

"She never seems to mind that he calls her a brat," Loree said quietly. "Why does he call her that?"

"I think because she's like her mother and speaks what's on her mind—even when he wishes she wouldn't. When Rawley first started going to school, he somehow got on the teacher's bad side. Teacher was punishing him for not learning quickly enough. Rawley was too ashamed to tell me about it. Reckon he thought he deserved it. Maggie thought differently and told me about it."

"So you talked with the teacher and worked things out?" Loree asked.

"Hell, no. Gave him his wages and sent him on his way. Hired another teacher. Nobody, but nobody punishes my children but me. And you were right. I would have snatched that piano teacher baldheaded if I'd seen her lifting a hand to my boy. Never did thank you for interfering there." He walked off, with Loree staring after him.

"I wouldn't want to get on his bad side," she said quietly.

"I don't think you have to worry. That's the closest thing to an 'I owe you' that I've ever heard from Dallas," Austin said.

Austin studied the abundance of food that stretched the length of the heavy oak table. Every time he turned around, Dee or Amelia came through the door that led to the kitchen, carrying more food. He picked up something that looked like a tiny pie, held it beneath his nose, and sniffed. It smelled like raisins. "What's this?"

Amelia stopped slicing off pieces of pound cake and looked up. "Mincemeat pie."

Austin gave her a slow nod and popped it into his mouth. A combination of tangy and sweet hit his tongue. "Pretty good," he said as he swallowed and reached for another one.

"Would you do me a favor and tell Maggie she can come decorate the cookies now?"

"Sure," he said as he snitched another pie and headed toward the parlor. He never would have believed that Dallas's big old adobe house would seem so warm and cozy. Dee had added so many small touches. Wreathes on the doors, greenery here and there, red ribbons, and satiny bows.

He rounded the corner to go into the parlor and staggered to a stop in the doorway, his path blocked by Becky, who had obviously been planning to leave the parlor. Her face burned crimson, reminding him of the stockings Dee had hung over the fireplace. Then her pale blue gaze shot upward. He slowly shifted his gaze to the arch above his head and his stomach tightened like a ribbon wound too tight around a package.

Damn mistletoe!

If it had been anyone else standing there—Dee or Amelia—he would have laughed heartily and given her a sound kiss on the lips. But not Becky. Five long years had passed since he'd held her, kissed her, been close enough to smell her vanilla scent, and count the freckles on her nose.

He didn't have to look into the parlor to know that they'd managed to gain everyone's attention. His mouth went as dry as a dust storm. Becky gave him a shaky smile, and he recognized the silent plea in her pretty blue eyes, but damn if he could figure out what she was asking for.

He swallowed hard, lowered his head, bussed a quick kiss across her cheek, and turned to the side, giving her the freedom to slip past him. He'd never been so glad to hear anything as he was to hear the rapid click of her shoes as she left the room.

Reaching up, he snatched the mistletoe from its mooring and glared briefly at his oldest brother, daring him to say anything about what he'd just done.

"Maggie—" his voice sounded like that of a drowning man coming up for the last time. He cleared his throat. "Maggie, your ma says the cookies are ready for decorating."

Maggie shoved the present she'd been shaking back under the tree and raced out of the parlor.

Austin crossed the room and hunkered down beside the rocking chair. Loree stilled her gentle swaying and met his gaze. He brushed a stray curl away from her cheek. "Think you can give Houston back his daughter and come with me for a minute?"

She nodded slightly and eased up on the seat. Austin slipped his hand beneath her elbow and helped her stand. Houston stopped helping his other three daughters paste bits of colored paper into a chain and stood.

"'Preciate your getting her to sleep. Sometimes there's nothing like a woman's touch."

"Kin Aunt Loree rock me?" Amanda asked.

"Maybe after a while," Houston said patiently. "I think your uncle Austin needs her right now."

His brother couldn't have spoken truer words. Austin wrapped his hand around Loree's and guided her from the room. The women's laughter spilled out of the dining room. He cast a hesitant glance at Loree. "Did you want to join them?"

"Maybe later. I thought you needed something."

"I do," he admitted as he opened the door to Dallas's study.

A low fire burning within the hearth served as the only light in the room. The drapes were drawn back to reveal the cloudless night sky, a thousand stars, and a bright golden moon. "I just needed a little solitude. I'd take you outside if it weren't so cold," he said as he led her to the window that covered most of the wall.

"I like being in here where it's warm, knowing that it's cold out there," she said quietly.

He trailed his fingers along her cheek and cupped her chin. "I wanted to apologize for earlier, kissing Becky in the doorway . . . I didn't know what to do . . . if I hurt you—"

"You didn't. She and Cameron were friends, now they're family. Our paths are going to cross constantly, and not always in ways we'd prefer, but I can accept that." She lowered her lashes. "Besides, she looked as uncomfortable as you did."

"Guess you could kiss Cameron to get even with me."

"Now, why would I want to kiss Cameron when I love you?"

She ducked her head as though embarrassed while his heart pounded like an untamed stallion thundering over the plains. He'd heard those three little words before, in his youth, but they hadn't managed then to bring him to his knees. Right now, he wasn't certain how long he could remain standing. She loved him. This sweet little woman loved him.

"Loree?"

Loree glanced up and watched Austin dangle the mistletoe in front of her nose. She smiled warmly. "You don't need that."

She raised up on her toes, entwined her arms around his neck, and pressed her lips against his. He welcomed her as he had that first night when they had each needed comfort. His mouth was hot and devouring as though he couldn't get enough of tasting her.

She hadn't planned to tell him that she'd come to love him, but she had thought he needed to hear the words as badly as she did. She knew she couldn't compete with his memories, but she'd grown weary of worrying how the past—his and hers—might affect their future.

She had this moment, when he held her as though he would never release her, this moment, when the world contained all that mattered: warmth, security, and the possibility of love. She had no doubts that he cared for her and treasured her. Maybe not in the same manner that he had Becky, but he had been younger then. Now and then, she would catch glimpses of the young man he might have been. She could not return to him his youth, but she could give him her love—unconditionally.

And if he continued to love another, she would not allow her love for him to diminish.

He trailed his mouth along the sensitive area below her ear. She felt as though the fire had jumped from the hearth and was surrounding her, flames licking at her flesh. He nimbly unbuttoned the top buttons on her bodice and dipped his tongue into the hollow at the base of her throat. She dug her fingers into his shoulders, needing his strength to prevent her from melting into the floor.

"Ah, Sugar," he rasped, his breath skimming along the curve of her bosom, "why don't we ever do this at home?"

She dropped her head back, giving him easier access. "Your promise, I guess."

"My promise?" His lips moved lower. "My promise? Dammit to hell!" He pressed his mouth to the valley between her breasts. "I was only thinking of you, Loree. I swear to God, I was only thinking of you."

He pulled away from her, braced his forearm on the window, and pressed his forehead against the glass, his breathing harsh and labored. Studying his tortured profile, she watched his Adam's apple rise and fall as he swallowed. Tears stung her eyes. Without thought she had answered his question with the excuse that she gave herself each night when he simply held her and didn't ask for more.

"Austin—"

Reaching out, he took her hand, brought it to his lips, and pressed a kiss to her fingertips. "We probably ought to get back to the others. I'll need to pass out the presents soon."

Turning he gave her a wayward smile and began to button her bodice. "You make me forget all about propriety, Loree . . . and promises." He slipped the last button through its loop and straightened her collar. "One of these days, Sugar, I'm gonna kiss you until *you* forget about promises."

"Promise?" she asked, a hint of teasing in her voice.

His eyes grew warm. "Promise."

He slipped his fingers between hers, pressing his rough palm against hers. "Come on. My favorite part of Christmas is nearly here."

His excitement was infectious as he led her from Dallas's office. They'd create new memories to replace the old, and she imagined each Christmas would simply be more wonderful than the one that had come before.

They walked into the parlor. Someone had lit the candles on the branches of the evergreen tree. The flames flickered, making the shadows dance around the room.

The drapes were drawn open. The night eased inside. The fire in the hearth burned brightly. Everyone had gathered inside the room, some sitting, some standing, many of the children sprawled over the floor.

"Oh, there you are," Dee said smiling. She took Loree's free hand. "We have a tradition of singing a song before we open presents. We were wondering if you'd play the piano while we sang."

Loree felt the comfort of belonging slip around her like a warm blanket as Austin squeezed her hand. "I'd love to. What should I play?"

" 'Silent Night'?"

"One of my favorites," Loree said as she released Austin's hand and walked to the piano. She sat on the bench and swiped her damp palms along her skirt. Austin came to stand beside her.

"You'll do fine," he mouthed.

She smiled and nodded. "Hope so."

"All right, everyone, Loree is going to play 'Silent Night.' Everyone stand so we can sing together as a family," Dee commanded.

Loree glanced over her shoulder. The husbands and wives had gathered their children around them, distinct families that came together to form one. Where was a photographer when they needed one?

She wiped her hands again on her skirt before placing her fingers on the ivory keys. The notes sounded and the room filled with off-key voices—and for the first time ever, she heard her husband's voice lifted in song. He carried the tune like no one else in the room, as though the melody were part of him.

His gaze captured hers, holding her entranced, and she wished the song would never end, but eventually it drifted away, leaving a moment of respectful silence in its wake.

Austin smiled at her, rubbed his hands together as though in anticipation, and took a step away from the piano. Loree twisted around on the piano bench to watch the exchange of gifts.

"You can help me pass out presents, Brat," Rawley said as he knelt in front of the tree.

"You don't have to tell me," Maggie countered as she dropped beside him. "I've been helping you forever."

Austin still smiling, stepped back, and sank onto the bench beside Loree, his gaze focused on the tree. He took her hand. "Thought you played really nice," he said, his voice low.

She thought her heart might break as she remembered him saying earlier that he needed to pass out the presents. In the years while he was away, the responsibility had obviously fallen to Rawley until everyone had forgotten a time when anyone else had passed them out.

She squeezed Austin's arm. "It surprised me, hearing how well you sang."

He shrugged. "Use to enjoy music."

"I wish you'd let me teach you to play—"

"Here, Uncle Austin, this one's for you," Maggie said, holding out a large package.

"Well, I'll be," Austin said with a smile as he shook the box. "This is almost as big as the box Rawley got the first year that you helped me pass out the presents. You remember that?"

Maggie furrowed her brow and shook her head. "What'd he get?"

"A saddle."

"I don't 'member."

Austin touched her nose. "Doesn't matter. You'd better get back to helping him."

She scurried away. Loree leaned close and whispered, "She couldn't have been very old when you left—"

"Three."

He looked at her and smiled sadly. "Guess we can't always choose which memories we keep when we start growing up."

But she knew she would forever hold the memory of her husband's first Christmas after his release from prison. Even with her by his side, she thought he'd never looked more lonely.

Chapter 14

༂

AUSTIN AWOKE AS he had for several months, long before the sun came up, with his wife curled against his side, her furled hand resting on the center of his bare chest. He loved these first moments of awareness, hearing Loree's breathing, feeling her warmth, knowing they would be his for the remainder of his life.

He pressed a kiss to her forehead and gingerly moved away from her. She sighed softly and shifted over until she was nestled in the spot where he had been. He brought the blankets over her shoulders.

He carried the lamp to the dresser and increased the flame by a hair's breadth. He glanced toward the bed. Loree hadn't stirred. He turned back to his task and ran his hand over the wooden violin case she'd given him for Christmas. On the top, someone had carved his name in fancy script. His gift to her—a small music box—had paled in comparison.

"If you're not going to play your mother's violin, you need to keep it protected," Loree had told him. "Someday, maybe your son will play it."

His son. He thought of Drew's tiny fingers and wondered when a child's fingers would be long enough to play a violin. Houston's daughter Laurel could probably play. She was five now, but still she'd need a smaller violin.

He imagined the joys of teaching a child the wonders of music. He could teach his own children . . . He unfolded one of the sheets of music Loree had given him. All the black dots looked like bugs crawling over the page. Reading them was nothing like reading a book. Loree could teach his children to play.

Quietly he donned his clothes and slipped into the hallway. The house seemed incredibly quiet after all the festivity the night before. The children had finally fallen asleep around midnight, giving up their quest to actually see Santa Claus. Their stockings were now filled with goodies and additional presents were waiting under the tree in the parlor.

He crept down the wide winding staircase and grabbed his sheepskin jacket from the coat rack by the front door. Then he walked into the kitchen, prepared his morning coffee, and stepped onto the back porch.

He settled onto the top step, wrapped his hands around the warm tin cup, and waited . . . waited for the first ray of sun to touch the sky and reveal its beauty . . . waited to hear the music in his soul that had always accompanied the sunrise before he'd gone to prison.

He heard the door open and glanced over his shoulder, anticipating the sight of his wife, rumpled from sleep.

"What are you doing?" Cameron asked.

He averted his gaze and tightened his hold on the cup. "I *was* enjoying the sunrise."

"Mind if I join you?"

Austin shrugged. "It ain't my porch."

Cameron dropped beside him and wrapped his arms around his middle. "Cold out this morning."

Austin watched the steam rise from his coffee.

"Loree seems nice," Cameron said.

Austin sliced his gaze over to Cameron. "She is nice."

Cameron nodded. "She doesn't look like she's got much longer to go."

Austin narrowed his eyes. "You counting the months? 'Cuz if you are, I'll have to take you out behind the barn and teach you a lesson in minding your own business."

"Nah, I wasn't counting. I was just saying. That's all."

"Good, 'cuz I wouldn't like it at all if you were counting months." Austin extended the cup toward Cameron. "Take a sip on that before your clattering teeth wake everyone up. It'll help warm you."

Cameron took the cup without hesitating and downed a long swallow before handing it back. "Thanks."

"Becky would probably never forgive me if I let you freeze to death out here," Austin said, squinting into the distance, searching for that first hint of sunlight.

"She missed you like hell while you were in prison." Cameron clasped his hands between his knees. "So did I."

Austin laughed mirthlessly. "You two had a hell of a way of showing me that."

A suffocating silence wove itself between them, around them. Austin saw dawn's feathery fingers pushing back the night.

"After Boyd died, my pa didn't want anything to do with me since I didn't approve of what Boyd had done—paying someone to kill Dallas. Dallas offered me a job—"

Austin turned his attention toward Cameron. "You would have wet your britches every time he gave you an order."

A smile tugged on the corner of Cameron's mouth. "Yeah, that's what I figured so I went to work for Becky's pa. She and I put a box in the storage room. Every time we got in some new contraption, we'd put it in the box because she knew how much you loved new contraptions."

Austin took a sip on his coffee before handing the cup back to Cameron. "Didn't really care about them one way or the other. They were just an excuse to go into town and see Becky."

Cameron gulped on the black brew and passed it back. "She wrote you some letters. Couldn't bring herself to address them to you in prison, though. She couldn't stand to think of you being there so she just put them in the box so they'd be waiting for you when you got home."

Austin cut his blue-eyed glare over to Cameron. "One of those letters tell me how she fell in love with you?"

"I doubt it . . . since she never fell in love with me." He watched Cameron swallow. "We'd been married a little over eight months when Drew was born."

"Babies come early."

"He didn't. My pa was dying. He asked to see me. I always had the feeling he didn't like me much. Never knew why, but he didn't want to die without telling me that I didn't come from his loins. It took him six years to realize my mother had fallen in love with the foreman. His name was Joe Armstrong. My pa—I can't stop thinking of him as my pa—said he shot Joe Armstrong through the heart and buried him where no one would ever find him."

"You believe him?"

Cameron nodded. "Yeah. Dee remembered the foreman. Said I'd always reminded her of him, but she was so innocent she never put things together."

"And when you found out the truth, you turned to Becky."

Cameron gave him a jerky nod. "Her pa had died a few months before so I guess she knew how I was grieving. I'd loved her forever, but I didn't mean for things to turn out the way they did." He planted his elbows on his thighs and buried his face in his hands. "Christ, I never wanted her to *have* to marry me."

Austin looked toward the golden light sweeping across the horizon—as brilliant a hue as Loree's eyes. He wondered if she was awake yet. It was past time for her to join him on the porch. Lord, he missed her.

"Drew seems like a good kid," he said quietly.

Cameron's head came up. "Oh, he's great. And Becky adores him. I was afraid she might resent him—like my pa resented me—but she doesn't. She loves him with all her heart."

"She loves you, too, Cameron." The words cut deeply, lancing the wound that had been left to fester too long.

Doubt plunged into Cameron's eyes. "You're just saying that."

"Why in the hell would I tell you that if it weren't true? Don't you think it would ease my pride to think she still loved me?"

"I haven't touched her since you got out of prison. I was afraid . . . afraid she'd wish it was you. I couldn't stand the thought that maybe she was thinking of you while I was loving her."

Austin tossed the remaining coffee over the cold ground. He'd made Loree a promise and suddenly, it didn't seem as though it would be difficult to keep. Whatever he and Becky had once had . . . was nothing more than a distant memory.

"A blind fool could see that she loves you more than she ever loved me. Why in the hell do you think I've been so angry all these months? Not because she married you. But because she didn't love me as much as she loves you."

"Yeah?"

Austin gave a brisk nod. "Yeah." He studied Cameron a minute. "You said your pa killed your real father?"

Cameron gave a slow hesitant nod. "Hard to believe I lived with a murderer all those years and never knew it."

"You think there's a chance he might have killed Boyd?"

"It occurred to me, more than once, but why would he have killed Boyd? Boyd could do no wrong as far as he was concerned."

Austin heaved a deep sigh. "Damn. Wish I knew who killed him. I don't like having this guilty verdict hanging over my head."

"Doesn't seem to bother Loree."

"Loree looks at the world differently than most people. Someone murdered her family, but she somehow managed to hold onto a portion of her innocence. I'm afraid if we stay here . . . if she hears too many people whispering about me, speculating on who I might murder next . . . that she'll lose that little bit of innocence."

"You thinking of leaving?"

Austin shrugged. "I don't know where we'd go or what I'd do so probably not, but I think about it sometimes. Houston told me once that when a man loves a woman, he does what's best for her, no matter what the cost to himself. I'd pay any price to see Loree happy."

"She seems happy enough."

"I think I can make her happier. I know I can. Houston told me that he thought he might have fallen in love with Amelia the minute he saw her. I didn't feel that way with Loree, but when she stepped out of that house, I felt as though . . . I'd come home."

"Do you think Dallas fell in love with Dee when he first laid eyes on her?"

Austin shook his head, joyful memories surging through his mind like a kaleidoscope of forgotten images. "Nope. He probably fell in love with her when he discovered she had a nose. Do you remember the look on his face when he lifted her veil and saw her face for the first time?" Austin chuckled.

Cameron started laughing. "His face? You should have seen *your* face!"

"Mine? What about yours?"

Their laughter grew louder, mingling with the dawn.

Loree slipped her fingers between the kitchen curtains and peered through the tiny opening. Austin laughed so hard that he very nearly doubled over, his chin almost hitting his drawn up knees.

"Oh my God!" Becky whispered behind her. "Tell me that's Austin and Cameron laughing."

Loree stepped back, surprised to see tears brimming in Becky's eyes as she peeked through the curtain.

"I could not have asked for a better Christmas present." Becky squeezed her eyes shut and released a quick breath. "It almost killed Cameron to lose Austin's friendship." She opened her eyes and grabbed Loree's hand. "Come on. Let's go sit with them."

"I'm not sure we should—"

"Oh, I am. I know it'll never be like it was . . . but this is sure close." Becky opened the door. "What are you two laughing about?" she demanded of the men sitting on the porch.

Holding her breath, Loree peered around Becky who stood with her hands planted on her hips, her legs akimbo. She saw Austin's smile increase, his eyes grow warm as he held out his hand. She wanted to crawl back into the house and die until she realized that his gaze was latched onto her.

"Come here, Sugar," he said in a slow drawl that sent her heart to racing.

She skirted around Becky and slipped her hand into his, thinking his had never felt so warm or comforting, so right as his fingers wrapped around her hand and he pulled her down to his lap. He opened his jacket and tucked her inside like she was a piece of fine jewelry to be protected between velvet. He held her close with one arm and enveloped her bare feet with his other hand. She was eye-level with him and from the intensity of his blue gaze, she would have thought he were only aware of the two of them sitting on this porch in the cold dawn.

"What were you laughing about?" Becky repeated as she plopped onto Cameron's lap and nearly sent him sprawling backward over the porch.

"We were remembering the day that Dallas married Dee," Cameron said, straightening himself and putting his arms around Becky.

"What was so funny about that?" Becky asked.

"Cameron had told me that Indians cut off Dee's nose," Austin said, his gaze never leaving Loree. She grew warmer, but she thought it had little to do with the heat of his body burning through her clothing. "I told Dallas. It came as a surprise to him to discover his wife had a nose."

"I remember now. Everyone's mouth dropped open when he lifted her veil, but I never knew why," Becky said. She wrinkled her brow. "He married her, thinking she didn't have a nose?"

"He was a desperate man," Austin said quietly. "Desperate men don't always think things through."

Loree wanted to tell him that desperate women didn't think things through either. She had been desperate once, so incredibly desperate that she had done something she never would have believed herself capable of doing. At unexpected times the memory would strike like a rattlesnake . . . only a rattlesnake gave warning. Her memory from hell wasn't as kind.

She heard the tread of heavy feet and twisted slightly. Dallas rounded the corner, burlap sacks bunched in his hand.

"What in the hell are you doing lollygagging back here?" he demanded without breaking his stride. He tossed the burlap sacks onto the porch. "Get this hay picked up."

Reaching behind him, Austin grabbed the sacks and handed a couple to Cameron. "Guess we'd better get to it."

Loree slid off his lap and tightened her wrap around herself. "I need to get dressed."

Austin's hand clamped onto her waist, preventing her from slipping back into the house.

"Me, too," Becky said. "I'll see you in a little bit, Cameron."

"Be sure and get the hay off the balcony in Rawley's room."

She smiled. "Guess he forgot we were going to sleep in his room last night." She disappeared into the house.

Austin shifted his gaze from Loree to Cameron. "Why don't you go on? I'll catch up."

"Sure thing." Cameron hopped off the porch and headed toward a distant scattering of hay.

Austin returned his gaze to her, his fingers tightening their hold.

"Is everything all right?" she asked.

She watched his Adam's apple slowly slide up and down. His blue eyes smoldered like flames on the verge of coming back to life. "Everything is just fine. As a matter of fact, I think it's been fine for a while and I just didn't notice." He cradled her cheek. "I love you, Loree."

Her heart slammed against her ribs. "You don't have to say that just because I did—"

"That's not why I'm saying it." He dipped his head slightly. "I'm saying it because it's true."

He closed the distance between their mouths, their hearts, with a kiss that made her body feel like a melted pool of wax, warm and molten, easily shaped to fit his desires. And more to fit her desires, desires that spiraled through her. She slipped her hands beneath the shoulders of his sheepskin jacket and felt the comforting heat of his body. He brought his coat around her. Her toes crept over his boots. And the baby rolled between them.

Austin drew away and glanced down at the small mound. Then he lifted his gaze. "Figure we'll spend the day here, pack up our stuff, go to that Christmas ball that Dee is giving in town . . . then head home."

She gave him a quick nod.

"Don't remind me of any promises I've made in the past when we get home."

Her voice caught in her throat, forcing her to push out the words. "I won't."

A slow lazy smile spread across his face and in it, she read a new promise, a promise she dearly wanted him to keep.

With long strides, Austin carried the box of presents to the wagon. He and Loree had been blessed last night with an assortment of gifts that ranged from useable items for the baby to a picture from Faith that he suspected was a horse only because it had been scribbled in brown.

After setting the box in the back of the wagon, he dug through the contents until he found one of the music sheets Loree had given him. He opened it and again studied the black ovals with the strange sticks and flags. He supposed it wouldn't hurt to let Loree explain them to him. If they made sense to her, maybe they could make sense to him.

"Austin?"

Becky's serene voice came from behind him. He stuffed the sheet into the box, spun around, and realized that he'd lied to Loree.

He'd told her once that a man couldn't tell if a woman had been made love to, but standing here, staring at the warm glow on Becky's cheeks, he had no doubt that she had just been well and thoroughly loved.

"I just wanted to thank you," she said softly.

"For what?"

"For whatever it was that you said to Cameron that made him stop doubting my love."

"I just told him the truth." He turned and shoved the box farther back into the wagon.

Becky came up alongside him. "I did love you, you know," she said quietly.

He met her gaze. "I know."

"What we had was so incredibly sweet . . . and young." She furrowed her brow. "I don't know if that makes sense."

"It does."

"If we had gotten married five years ago—even without you going to prison—I don't know if our love would have survived the passing years. I think we would have been content, but never truly happy."

Words backed up in his throat and he could do little more than give her an understanding nod.

"I know it's been hard on you since you got back. Cameron and I just finished talking about some things that we hadn't really discussed before. I'm willing to make a public announcement saying I was with you the night Boyd was killed."

Austin felt as though the air had been pulled from his lungs. Emotions clogged his throat. He knew that announcement would cost Becky more than her reputation. It would cost Cameron his pride.

"I appreciate that, Becky. More than you'll ever know, but I think it would cause more harm than good. That's the reason I told you not to say anything five years ago. Most people would think you were lying to protect me, but your words would still plant the seeds of doubt about your reputation in everyone's mind. It's not worth taking the chance of hurting not only you and Cameron, but Drew as well."

He watched as relief washed over her face. "Just so you know we're willing."

He gave her a brisk nod. "Better get back to your husband. Wouldn't want to make him jealous."

"A part of me will always love you, Austin." She leaned over and brushed a kiss over his cheek. His heart tightened.

"Same here," he said hoarsely.

He watched her stroll back toward the house, her hips swaying gently from side to side. Within his heart, he bid the love of his youth a silent farewell.

Chapter 15

✦

THE GRAND BALLROOM of the Grand Hotel had changed over the years—like everything else in Austin's life. If windows didn't grace the wall, then floor-to-ceiling gilded mirrors did. The room seemed larger than it was as Austin stood beside his brothers, Loree at his side.

While Amelia and Dee rushed around the room making certain everything was in order, the children sat in chairs along the wall, like stair steps, from oldest to youngest, with the very youngest nestled in Houston's arms. The girls swung their feet, their heels hitting the underside of their chair. Rawley slumped forward, looking bored as hell. Austin understood that feeling.

Dallas's cook strode in, his legs bowed out like a man who still had a horse sitting beneath him, his fiddle tucked beneath his arm. He wore a fancy black suit that Austin had never expected the man to own.

"The fiddle player's here," Maggie announced. "You're gonna have to dance with me, Rawley."

Horror swept over Rawley's face. "Don't neither."

"Do to." Maggie tipped up her nose. "Uncle Dallas, doesn't Rawley have to dance with me?"

Absently, Dallas waved his hand in the air, his attention focused on his wife. "Can't see that it'd do any harm, Rawley. Probably be good practice."

Groaning, Rawley glowered at Maggie, who wore a smile of triumph. Faith slid out of her chair, tiptoed across the floor, and climbed onto Rawley's lap.

"Dance wiv me, too, Wawley."

He held up a finger. "One dance." He glared at Maggie. "One dance." Holding Faith in place with one arm, he leaned forward and glared at each of his cousins in turn, his finger pointing to the ceiling. "One dance each and that's it."

He slumped back against the wall, reached into his shirt pocket, and removed a sarsaparilla stick.

"Gimme some," Faith ordered.

"It's my last piece," Rawley said, even as he proceeded to break it into six pieces and distribute it to the girls, popping the last and smallest piece into his mouth.

He met Austin's gaze over the top of Faith's head. "I sure hope your baby is a boy."

"Reckon we need to even things out a little, don't we?"

Rawley gave him a brusque nod. "We men folk are sorely outnumbered."

Austin laughed, remembering a time when that was exactly what Dallas had wanted: more women out in West Texas.

Breathless, Amelia rushed over and took Gracie from Houston. "I think we just about have everything ready to go."

"Who's gonna watch the young 'uns while you and me dance?" Houston asked.

"I'll be happy to watch the girls," Loree said, her fingers tightening around Austin's. "I can't imagine I'll be doing any dancing tonight. In this red dress, I look like an apple that's been turned upside down."

Austin gave her a long slow perusal, then leaned over, and whispered in her ear, "I've always liked nibbling on apples."

Her face burned a deep crimson, and he wished he could find some dark secluded corner where he could taste her fully. His only fear was that once he got started, he'd be unable to stop. He couldn't remember ever wanting anything as much as he wanted Loree at this moment.

People began to arrive. The night they'd gone to the theater, Austin had only seen Leighton's successful citizens. They were here tonight, but so were the cowboys, the wranglers, the stonemasons, and the carpenters. The ladies who worked in Dee's hotel and restaurant glided into the room in their fancy gowns and were swept onto the floor to dance before the music began to play.

When the first strains from Cookie's fiddle filled the air, a roar went up and people began to dance in earnest.

"We're gonna take you up on that offer to watch the girls if you're sure you don't mind," Houston said.

"I don't mind," Loree assured him as she released Austin's hand and took Gracie into her arms.

"We'll just dance one dance," Amelia said.

"Dance as many as you like."

"I'm going to make my wife stop working and do some dancing," Dallas said before walking off.

With a huff, Rawley shifted Faith off his lap, stood, and held his hand out to Maggie. "Come on, Brat. You asked first."

Maggie hopped out of her chair and followed him onto the dance floor.

Austin helped Loree sit in the chair Maggie had vacated, then he sat beside her, easing Faith onto his lap. She reached up and planted a sticky sarsaparilla scented kiss on his cheek. "Love ya."

"I love you, too," Austin said quietly.

He glanced over at Loree. "And you."

She pressed her cheek against his shoulder.

"We won't stay long," he promised. He looked toward the waltzing couples.

"They all look so happy," Loree said quietly.

Cameron and Becky passed quickly in front of them before disappearing in the crowd. "Yeah, they do," Austin said.

When the music stilled momentarily, Amelia came over and took Gracie from Loree. "Come on, girls. Let's go get some punch." Houston scooped A. J. into his arms before holding a hand toward Faith. "You thirsty?"

She nodded and slid off Austin's lap. Austin watched his nieces, all in identical red dresses, traipse toward the table like performers in a circus parade. He glanced at Loree, her hands folded over her apple red stomach. He leaned toward her. "Do you dance?"

She wrinkled her nose. "I went to a couple of balls in Austin, but that was a long time back."

He pulled gently on a curl dangling near her temple. "Is that where you met Jake?"

"I told you there was no Jake."

"Who did you dance with?"

Sighing, she narrowed her eyes. "I danced with somebody named John and . . . Michael."

"That's it?"

"I wasn't exactly the belle of the ball."

"What do city boys know?" he asked.

"A good-looking woman when they see one."

"Not on your life." He stood, held out his hand, and helped her to her feet.

"Thought I spotted you over here," Cameron said, diverting Austin's attention away from Loree. "Would you mind if I danced with your wife?"

Austin caught the look of surprise in Loree's eyes, and suddenly, he wanted every man in this room to dance with her. "No, I don't mind."

"You don't mind do you?" Cameron asked Becky. "I'll be leaving you in good company."

Becky smiled. "Go on."

Cameron held his hand toward Loree. She hesitated before slipping her hand into his. "I'm not very balanced these days."

Cameron grinned. "That's all right. Neither am I."

Austin watched Cameron lead Loree onto the dance floor. Their steps were awkward, mismatched. Cameron chuckled, and even with the din of the other dancers, Austin heard Loree's gentle laughter.

"You and I never got to dance," Becky said quietly.

Austin slid his gaze to her. The royal blue of her dress enhanced the shade of her eyes. "No, we didn't."

She licked her lips. "We're not going to dance tonight, are we?"

"No, we're not."

She shifted her gaze to the dancers. "Cameron wouldn't mind."

"But it might hurt Loree."

She peered at him. "Do you love her?"

"Yeah, I do."

"Then she's a very lucky woman."

"She hasn't been up until now, but I aim to change that." He tilted his head as the music drifted into silence. "If you'll excuse me, I think I'll dance with my wife now."

He glanced toward the dance floor, reining in his impatience as Cameron escorted Loree back to him. Her cheeks were flushed, her eyes sparkling. He would have grabbed her and hauled her back onto the dance floor right then and there, but he had something special in mind.

"Didn't topple over, huh?" he asked as they neared. He laughed when Loree stuck her tongue out at him.

"Come on, Sugar, sit down," he ordered.

Loree plopped into the chair, grateful to be off her feet. "Thank you, Cameron," she called out.

Cameron glanced over his shoulder and winked at her before he led Becky back toward the dance area. Loree released a deep sigh. "I didn't want to but I think I like Cameron. He's nice."

"Of course, he's nice. You think I'd have mean friends," Austin said as he knelt in front of her and lifted her foot.

She leaned forward. "What are you doing?"

"Taking off your shoes."

She jerked her foot back. "Austin, not here," she whispered hoarsely.

He looked at her with blue eyes that reflected the innocence of a child. "Why?"

She stared at him, trying to think of an acceptable reason. "It's not proper. A woman doesn't show her ankles in public."

"Your skirt is long enough that your ankles won't show. Besides, your toes have gotta be hurtin'. I've seen Cameron dance before. He may be nice but he doesn't know his right foot from his left."

She slapped a hand over her mouth to stop herself from laughing out loud. Her toes were hurting. He patted his thigh. "Come on, Sugar."

She gnawed on her lower lip. She supposed if she just sat here . . .

"Oh, all right, but don't let anyone see what you're doing," she whispered as she placed her foot on his thigh.

She loved to watch his long fingers nimbly work to unbutton her shoes. She wanted to see his fingers gliding along the strings on his mother's violin. She knew he had been touched by the case she had given him for Christmas, but she'd been disappointed that he hadn't shown more of an interest in the music sheets she'd given him.

He slipped her shoe under the chair, and when she would have brought her foot to the floor, he held it in place on his thigh, rubbing his thumbs in a circle over the balls of her foot. "Oh, Lord, that feels good," she said. "You have such nice hands."

"Wait until you see how nice they're gonna be later on."

She didn't know if the gleam in his eyes spoke of teasing or seriousness, and she wasn't certain she wanted to know. He placed her foot on the floor, brought her other foot up, and removed her shoe. He rubbed her foot until every little pain vanished.

"How does that feel?" he asked.

"Wonderful."

"Good." He stood and held out his hand. "Will you honor me with this dance?"

Loree widened her eyes. "I don't have shoes on."

He smiled warmly. "I know that, Sugar. I just took 'em off."

"I can't dance without shoes."

"Sure you can."

She thought of being held within his arms, her stockinged feet gliding over the smooth hardwood floor. . . .

"Cameron said that you never learned how to dance."

"He doesn't know everything."

The music stilled. "So you have danced before."

"Once . . . with Amelia."

She scooted up in the chair, hope flaring within her. "Only with Amelia?"

"Only with Amelia. I was sharing her with a dozen cowboys at the time, and all we knew how to do was swing her around, stomp our feet, and clap our hands."

"Have you ever waltzed with anyone?"

"Never."

Slowly, she rose to her feet. "What else have you never done?"

She knew from the darkening of his eyes that he understood what he was asking.

"Never danced with a woman I love."

Jealousy was a petty thing, but she'd never known such gladness. She smiled warmly. "I wouldn't want to miss this opportunity to be your first."

"Sugar, it's more important that I intend for you to be my last."

Before she had the chance to respond, he'd placed his hand on her waist and swept her onto the dance floor. The room contained two hearths, but neither fire burned as brightly as his eyes. Her stockinged feet glided over the floor and she wondered why women bothered to wear shoes at all.

When the music drifted into silence, she slipped her arm through his and allowed him to lead her from the dance floor.

Cameron and Becky caught up with them. "I've never seen you dance before," Cameron said. "Didn't know you could."

Austin shrugged. "Now, you know."

"I guess it's because you were always playing the music."

Austin started to walk away, but Loree stood fast, staring at Cameron, her heart thundering in her ears. "What . . . what do you mean he played the music?"

"Austin plays the violin and whenever we had occasion to dance, he provided the music." He glanced at Austin. "I figured you'd be playing tonight."

"I don't play anymore."

"I'm sorry to hear that," Cameron said. "No one played music the way you did. You should have heard it, Loree. It was beautiful."

She felt Austin's gaze boring into her. She slipped her arm from beneath his. "Yes, I should have heard it."

The strains of the waltz floated around the room. She began to tremble from her head to her toes. "I'm not feeling well. Will you excuse me?"

She didn't wait for his answer. She didn't bother to gather up her shoes or her coat. She simply ran. Shouldering her way through the crowd like a mad woman, her heart breaking.

She finally managed to burst through to the lobby. She hurried to the front, shoved open the door, and stumbled into the cold night. Tears stung her eyes. She had told him that she loved him.

And she realized now that she didn't know anything about him.

The ride home was quiet. Too quiet.

Austin had given their excuses and apologies for having to leave early. Naturally, everyone had wanted to check on Loree and make certain the baby wasn't planning to come early.

The one time she had met his gaze, he'd seen nothing but hurt in her eyes. He drew the wagon to a halt. Loree shifted on the seat.

"Loree, wait for me to get over there."

He leapt off the wagon and raced around to the other side. She'd already reached the ground.

"You're gonna hurt yourself with your stubbornness," he chastised.

"And you hurt me with your lies."

"I never lied."

"You never told me the truth, either."

She spun on her heel and headed into the house. Austin grabbed their box of presents from the back of the wagon and traipsed in after her. Shafts of moonlight pierced the darkness.

"Will you start a fire in the hearth?" she asked. "I'm cold."

He set the box on the table, walked to the hearth, and hunkered down. He struck a match to the kindling and watched the flames flare to life. He heard a scrape and bang. He twisted around and watched Loree remove something from the box.

"Your music box is on the bottom," he told her.

"I'm not looking for the music box."

Slowly, he unfolded his body. "Loree—"

She spun around, marched to the hearth, and threw something at it. The sheets of music.

He dropped to his knees, grabbed them from the fire, and beat out the flames that were already greedily devouring the pages. He glared up at Loree. "What did you do that for?"

"You already know how to play the violin. All these months, you let me make a fool out of myself—"

"No, I never meant that."

"Why didn't you tell me? When I asked you—begged you—to let me teach you, why didn't you say, 'I already know how to play, Loree.' "

He saw the tears glistening within her eyes. "Loree—"

"You told me that you love me. Do you think love is supposed to hurt? It's not. Whatever Becky taught you about love is wrong. It's supposed to heal. It's supposed to make you feel glad that you're alive. It's supposed to help you live with the past.

"You can't love me if you won't let me inside your heart. Either open your heart and invite me in or take me back home. But don't tell me you love me when you don't know what it is to love."

She spun on her heel, walked into their bedroom, and slammed the door.

Austin bit back the agonizing wail that would have been her name. What did she know about the things in his heart? What did she know about love? Love looked deeply within a person. Hadn't Amelia looked beyond Houston's scars to his soul? Love understood what others couldn't begin to fathom. Hadn't Dee understood Dallas's hard nature when no one else had?

Loree was the one who knew nothing about love. He stalked to the bedroom door, put his hand on the knob, and heard her wrenching sobs. He pressed his forehead to the door.

Christ, how many times had he made her cry? How often had he hurt her?

She was right. He should take her back home. She had his name. That was all she needed.

He stormed across the room, opened the front door, rushed through it, and slammed it in his wake. The last thing he needed her to hear was his heart breaking.

Loree awoke to the sound of a child crying. She rubbed the salt of her dried tears from the corners of her eyes and squinted through the darkness. Shafts of moonlight sliced through the window, forming the silhouette of a man, standing, his head bowed, his arm pushing and pulling, pushing and pulling the bow slowly across the taut strings of a violin.

The resonant chords deepened and an immense lonesomeness filled the room. Loree sat up in bed, sniffing through her stuffed nose. She clutched her handkerchief as the wailing continued. She wanted to slip out of bed and wrap her arms around someone, ease the pain she heard in the echoing strains of the violin. The poignant melody released fresh tears and caused her heart to tighten. In all her life, she'd never had a song reach out to capture her soul.

The melody drifted into an aching silence. Austin lifted his head, and she saw his tears, trailing along his cheeks, glistening in the moonlight.

She slipped from beneath the blankets, her bare feet hitting the cold floor. "What were you playing?" she asked reverently, not wanting to disturb the ambiance that remained in the room.

"That was my heart breaking," he said, his voice ragged.

She felt as though her own heart might shatter as she took a step toward him. "Austin—"

"Don't stop loving me, Loree. You want me to learn what those little black bugs on those pieces of paper mean, I'll learn. You want me to play the violin from dawn until dusk, hell, I'll play till midnight, just don't stop loving me."

She flung her arms around his neck and felt his arms come around her back, the violin tapping against her backside. "Oh, Austin, I couldn't stop loving you if I wanted."

"I do know how to love, Loree. I just don't know how to keep a woman loving me."

"I'll always love you, Austin," she said trailing kisses over his face. "Always."

She felt a slight movement away from her as he set the violin aside, and then his arms came around her, tighter than before. "Let me love you, Loree. I need to love you."

His mouth swooped down, capturing hers, desperation evident as his tongue delved swiftly, deeply. And then, as though, sensing her surrender, his exploration gentled. His hands came around, bracing either side of her hips, hips that had widened as she carried his child.

His hands traveled upward, until her breasts filled his palms. His long fingers shaped and molded what nature had already altered, preparing for the day when she would nourish their child.

He cradled her cheek, deepening the kiss, as his other hand worked the buttons of her nightgown free. He slipped his hand through the parted material, his roughened palm cupping her smooth breast. She felt his fingers tremble as his thumb circled her nipple, causing it to harden and strain for his touch.

His breathing harsh, he trailed his mouth along the column of her throat. He dipped his tongue into the hollow at the base of her throat.

"I'm only thinking of you, Loree," he rasped.

She dropped her head back. "I know." And she did know, deep within her soul, where his music had dared to travel only moments before, she did know that he was thinking of her. The tears he had shed had been for her. The music he had played had been for her.

His kiss, his gentle touch—they belonged to her now, just as he did. His mouth skimmed along her flesh, between the valley of her breasts, his breath warm like a summer breeze. He trailed his mouth over the curve of her breast. His tongue circled her nipple before he closed his mouth around the taut tip and suckled.

Like a match struck to kindling, her body responded, heat flaming to life. Her knees buckled and he caught her against him, steadying her. Slowly, he unfolded his body and within the faint moonbeams, she saw the deep blue of his smoldering gaze.

He slipped his hands between the parted material of her gown, spreading it over her shoulders until it was free to slide down her body and pool at her feet. She heard him swallow.

"God, you're beautiful."

His voice sounded as thick as molasses, and his gaze spoke more eloquently than his words. Her fingers trembled as she ran her hands over his wide shoulders and along his broad chest, knowing that she was on the verge of sealing forever the vault that held old promises. One movement, one touch, one word . . . and they could never return to what had been.

"Tell me again," she whispered.

"I'm only thinking of you, Loree," he said, his voice ragged, his breathing uneven.

She smiled warmly into the face of the man she loved. "No, tell me you love me."

"I love you."

She wrapped her hand around his, took a step back toward the bed, and watched his lips spread into a slow, seductive smile. Another step back and she sank onto the bed.

Austin tore his shirt over his head and dropped his britches to the floor. She watched the moonlight play over the hard muscles of his body before he stretched out beside her on the bed.

"Now, you gotta tell me," he said as he nipped on her earlobe and swirled his tongue around the shell of her ear.

"I love you," she whispered as her body curled.

"Ah, Sugar, I'm gonna make you damn glad that you do."

His promise carried assurances that she didn't doubt. "I'm already glad."

He rose up on his elbow. "Everything is gonna be better, Loree. Everything."

He lowered his mouth to hers with a renewed urgency. She touched her hand to his chest and felt the hard steady pounding of his heart. Where once he might have lain over her, now he only pressed his body against her side, his warm hand gliding over her stomach to the juncture between her thighs.

She moaned as his fingers imitated the action of his tongue, sweeping, plunging, warming, heating. She ran her hand down his side, dug her fingers into his lean hip, and rolled to her side, needing him close, knowing a moment of regret with the realization that her swollen stomach would never allow him to be as close as she needed.

Need spiraled through her, desire flamed. She trailed kisses over his face, his dew-covered throat and chest, wanting him as she'd never wanted anything. He fell onto his back and tugged on her hand. "Come here, Loree."

His shoulders rolled off the bed as he leaned up slightly and put his large hands on either side of her hips, guiding her until she straddled him. She watched the shadows and moonlight caress his magnificent body as she wanted to and knew a moment of doubt. Keeping one hand planted on her hip, he cradled her cheek with the other and held her gaze. "Stop me if I hurt you."

She trailed her gaze along the length of his body to the place where her body met his. She wrapped her fingers around him. He groaned and she felt a tremor wrack his body. Cradling her hips, he lifted her and eased her down as easily as the dawn met the day until they were one.

He released a long deep sigh. "Oh, Sugar, you feel so good."

She rolled her shoulders forward. "So do you."

Chuckling low, he threaded his fingers through her hair, bracketing her face between his palms. "I don't want to hurt you, so I need you . . . to do the ridin'."

She wished she could double over and kiss the furrows between his brow. He looked as though he were afraid he might have disappointed her. But how could he disappoint her when he loved her?

She ran her hands over his chest, along his side, leaned forward slightly, circled her hips, and relished the sound of his sharp intake of breath. He had given her so much: the power to love him, the power to satisfy him.

Keeping her eyes trained on his, she began to rock her hips. His hands glided to her breasts, the long fingers that she loved taunting and teasing, and she realized he had not relinquished all power.

Unbridled sensations ripped through her, and she felt as though he played her as easily as he played his violin. The sensations rose until her body went taut, and she uttered a cry of ecstasy.

She heard Austin's guttural groan as he shuddered beneath her, and into the stillness that followed, she heard their harsh breathing. Supporting her shoulders, he gently rolled them to their sides, his body never leaving hers. He threaded his fingers through her hair, his palm resting heavily upon her cheek as though all strength had been drained from him. Beneath her hand, his heart thudded.

Her lips spread into a contented smile and she sighed. Then her smile disappeared and her brow furrowed. "Austin?"

"Mmm?"

"What little black bugs?"

"What?" he asked sleepily.

She lifted her head, trying to make out his features in the shadows. "Earlier you said something about bugs on paper—"

"Oh, that. I was talking about those sheets of music you gave me for Christmas. I'll let you teach me how to read them."

She came up on her elbow. "Don't you know how to read music?"

"Nope."

"But that song you played—"

"Told you . . . it was my heart breaking. And I hope I never hear it again."

She sat up completely, drawing the blankets around her bare shoulders to ward off the chill of the room. "Austin, I don't understand."

"I don't know if I can explain it."

"Try."

He placed his hand on the back of her head. "Cuddle up against me first."

She nestled her cheek against the crook of his shoulder as his arm came around her, his hand trailing from her shoulder to her elbow. She spread her hand over his chest, her fingers toying with the light dusting of hair that sometimes tickled her nose.

"Don't know where to start," he finally said into the silence.

"At the beginning would be nice."

"Explaining things with words has never come easy for me. I don't know if what I say will make sense."

"I'm a patient listener."

"You are that, Sugar. All right. I'll try." He cleared his throat. "I reckon I was about seven the first time. We were herding cattle north along the Shawnee Trail."

"You were herding cattle when you were only seven?"

"Mostly I followed Dallas and picked up cow chips for the camp-fires at night. Anyway one night I'd been sleeping under the chuck-wagon. I heard this noise. It sounded like the wind, but there was no breeze that night. It was still as death, like something was waiting. So I got up. Cookie—that's the man that played the fiddle tonight—was fixin' food for the men about to come off the two o'clock watch. I asked him if he'd heard anything. He wanted to know what it sounded like. I couldn't describe it. He always kept his fiddle nearby so I picked it up . . . and played what I heard."

"Just like that?" she asked in awe.

"Just like that."

She lifted her head. "How could you do that?"

"All I can figure is that all those nights I watched my ma when I was a boy stuck with me."

She'd never heard of anything like it, but she couldn't discount the fact that the song he had played earlier had been flawless.

"Cookie taught me a few notes, a couple of songs, but he doesn't have your patience. Then one Christmas, Dallas and Houston gave me a violin, but I was sixteen before I found out it had been my ma's."

"But you told me you couldn't play. Why did you lie—"

He rolled her over, rising above her, cupping her cheek. "I wasn't ly-ing, Loree. I've always heard the music in my heart . . . but I lost the abil-ity to do that when I went to prison. It was like the music just shriveled up and died. I thought I'd never hear it again. How could I play the vio-lin if I couldn't hear the music? Then lately, I started going crazy because I'd hear snatches of music—when you'd look at me or smile at me. But I couldn't grab onto it, I couldn't hold it. Then last night, you told me that you loved me and I heard the music, so sweet, so soft. It scared me to hear it so clearly after I hadn't for so long.

"Tonight, I hurt you—again. I was going to let you go, Loree. I was gonna take you back to Austin. But I heard my heart break . . . and I knew that's all I'd hear for the rest of my life. Don't leave me, Sugar."

Joy filled her and she brushed the locks of hair back off his brow. "I won't."

She saw his broad smile in the moonlight.

"You should hear the music filling my heart right now," he said quietly.

"Will you play it for me?" she asked.

"Sure will, Sugar, but not with my violin."

His mouth descended to cover hers, and his hands began to play a song of love over her body.

Chapter 16

✤

THE JANUARY WINDS blew cold and bitter as Loree scooted across the bench seat of the wagon and snuggled against Austin.

"Stubborn woman," he mumbled as he slipped his arm around her. "You could be at home sitting in front of a nice warm fire."

"I'd rather be sitting beside you."

He leaned toward her and brushed a quick kiss over her lips. "I'm glad."

She tucked her shawl beneath her chin, bringing it in closer around her ears. The winds howled across the plains like a woman mourning a lost love. She imagined Austin would play the tune for her when they got home.

The town came into view. Her stomach always knotted at the memory it brought to mind. She brought the chilled air deep into her lungs, blowing it out in a smoky breath.

"Looks like Santa brought Cameron a new sign," Austin said.

Loree looked toward the general store, her breath hitching.

MCQUEEN'S GENERAL STORE.

Her fingers tightened on Austin's arm. "I thought their name was Oliver."

"No, that was Becky's pa." He glanced sideways at her, an incredulous expression on his face. "All this time you thought their name was Oliver?"

She nodded, fear clogging her throat. "So Dee is a McQueen, too?"

"No, she's a Leigh. Used to be a McQueen."

"Do they have other family?"

"They have a brother, Duncan."

"And that's all?"

"As far as I know."

He drew the wagon to a halt in front of the store, clambered down, and held his arms up to her. She scooted across the bench and he helped her down to the ground, his arms coming around her.

"Good God, Loree, you're shaking like a leaf in the wind."

"I'm just cold," she lied.

"Let's get you inside."

He headed for the store—the last place she wanted to go. He shoved open the door and hustled her inside. The bells above the door clanged and nearly made her jump out of her skin.

Cameron walked out from the back, drying his hands on a towel. "You picked a bad day to come into town."

"Wasn't this cold when we left," Austin said as he led Loree to the black potbellied stove. "Sit here, Loree."

She did as he instructed and gave him the freedom to remove her gloves.

"There, just rub your hands in front of the stove."

"I'll be all right," she assured him.

He smiled and leaned low. "I'll warm you up all over when we get home. How's that for a promise?"

She returned his smile. "I'll make you keep it."

He touched his finger to her nose before turning to Cameron. "You still carry violin strings?"

Cameron's face split into a wide grin. "You playing again?"

Austin shrugged. "A little. Now and then. When the music comes over me."

Loree listened with half an ear as their conversation continued. She had once known a man named McQueen, but Cameron didn't favor him in the least, not in looks or temperament. Maybe they were cousins or distant relatives or had nothing more in common than the same name.

She rubbed her hands together and almost imagined she saw the blood—bright red, glistening in the moonlight. "Austin, could I please have my gloves back?"

"Sure."

He handed the thick gloves back to her, and she slipped her hands inside. She always felt safer when her hands were covered.

"Did you want to get that rattle you were telling me about?" he asked.

She nodded and forced herself to stand on trembling legs. She glanced at Cameron. He gave her a warm smile that calmed her fears.

No one as nice as he was could be related to the devil who had murdered her family.

"Oh, come on, Loree. Please!"

Loree pursed her lips, crossed her arms over her stomach, and fought hard to resist the plea in those mesmerizing blue eyes. He'd replaced the string he'd broken two days before, and no longer had an excuse not to practice. "No. Not until you've mastered this."

Austin slumped back in the chair like a petulant child and started to randomly pluck the strings on his violin. "It's such a boring song. Just the same sounds over and over and over. No wonder Rawley hated his piano lessons."

"You can't play the complicated songs until you've learned the easy ones."

He sprung forward. "Take pity on me, and just let me try. If you're right . . . I'll go back to 'Mary Had a Little Lamb' . . . unless I kill the lamb first."

Loree couldn't stop her laughter from bubbling up. How could she expect a man who played from his heart to be content with other people's music? For the first time, she was catching true glimpses of the young man he had been before he went to prison.

When he awoke at dawn, he still carried his coffee out to the porch and sat on the top step, but instead of staring into the distance, he'd tuck his violin beneath his chin, and Loree would hear the sunrise as well as see it.

She knew the sound of twilight and midnight . . . and her husband's easy laughter. The ranch chores that had once exhausted him no longer phased him. He came home, anxious for her kiss and her arms around his neck. Through his gift, he would give her an accounting of his day until she could hear the bawling of the cattle he'd branded or the snap of the barbed wire he'd mended. He might not be a man who could explain things with words, but with his music, he had the ability to create worlds.

Against her better judgment, she unfolded a more complicated piece of music and slapped it down in front of him. "There. Play that."

Eagerly, he scooted up and studied the sheet of music. Then he took a deep breath, lifted his violin, and without shifting his gaze from the notes, he began to play—the most beautiful melody she'd ever heard.

She sat in awe, watching his fingers coax the notes from the strings, following the path of the bow as he stroked it—slow and long—over and over. It was little wonder that the man was skilled at stroking her.

She lifted her gaze to his only to find his eyes closed, his expression serene. He stilled the bow, opened his eyes, and met her gaze.

"You were right," he said quietly. With a sigh, he tossed the sheet of music aside and turned his attention back to the tune he'd been playing earlier.

"I was wrong," she said as she pulled the sheet away from him. "What were you playing?"

"Did you like it?"

"I thought it was beautiful."

"How beautiful?"

"How much praise do you want?"

"A lot. How beautiful was it?"

She sat back in the chair, narrowing her eyes, wondering if the truth would go to his head, but how could she lie? "I thought it was the most beautiful song I've ever heard."

A slow warm smile spread over his face. "I call it 'Loree.' It's what I hear in my heart whenever I look at you."

"Either you or your heart needs spectacles."

He set the violin aside, came out of his chair, and knelt beside her, wrapping his hands around her arms. "Why can't you believe that you're beautiful?"

She had become angry at him for not telling her that he played the violin. How would he feel if she revealed the truth about herself now? She had just gained his love. With a few well-chosen words, she knew she could lose it . . . and never regain it.

He leaned forward, latching his mouth onto hers, sweeping the past and the doubts away. Her bones turned to mush, her thoughts scattered like autumn leaves before the winter winds. She dug her fingers into his shoulders.

"You are beautiful, Loree," he rasped as he trailed his mouth along her throat. "God, I want you."

She loved those words, whispered from his lips. "I know, but the doctor says we have to practice abstinence now."

With a heavy sigh, he rocked back on his heels. "That's worse than practicing 'Mary had a Little Lamb.'"

"It won't be for much longer."

Reaching behind him, he grabbed the violin and tapped the bow against her protruding stomach. "Listen up, young fella."

Open-mouthed, Loree stared at him as he slipped the violin between his chin and shoulder. "You said it was foolish to talk to a child before it was born."

"It is foolish to talk to it," he said, grinning. "But I'm going to play for him. That ain't foolish at all."

"What are you going to play?"

"Something fast and spirited to take my mind off the long slow kiss that I want to play against his mother's lips."

Sipping on his coffee, Austin sat on the porch in the predawn darkness. His coat warded off the chill in the late winter air. Spring would arrive soon. Last year it had heralded his release from prison. This year he would celebrate the coming of spring with a wife and a child.

And an uncertain future.

Fewer people stared at him than before. He no longer heard whispers behind his back. But the fact remained that in the eyes of the law he was a murderer.

That fact had reached out to touch Loree.

He feared it would touch their child.

He understood ranching, but Dallas was the only rancher he knew who would hire on a family man. He hated ranching, but it was the only skill he possessed. He wanted to give Loree the world, but he couldn't see that ever happening.

He heard his wife's gentle footsteps. Smiling, he twisted around. The fear on her face sent panic surging through him. He came to his feet. "Loree, what's wrong?"

"I felt a pull in my stomach and heard a loud pop. When I slipped out of bed, water ran down the inside of my legs. There was a little blood."

"You think maybe the baby's coming?"

Her eyes grew wide and she gripped the doorjamb. Austin rushed to her side, holding her while she breathed heavily. Finally her breathing eased and she looked up at him. "I think the baby's coming."

"All right. Don't panic."

"I'm not," she assured him.

He scooped her into his arms and started down the steps.

"Where are we going?" she asked.

"I'm gonna take you to the doctor."

"What if there's not time? I don't want to be out on the prairie—"

"You're right. You're right. We'll just—" He turned and headed into the house. "We'll just put you back into bed . . ." Gingerly he laid her on the mattress. He wrapped his hand around hers and pressed his forehead against her temple. "Sugar, I don't know what to do."

"Go get Amelia and send Houston for the doctor."

Relief coursed through him, and he wondered where the hell his common sense had gone. He lifted his head and brushed the hair from her brow. "I can do that."

Her hand tightened around his, and she began to breathe harshly again, her face a grimace of pain. What in the hell had possessed Houston to put his wife through this five times? Austin planned to practice abstinence for the remainder of his life.

Her hold on him loosened, and the fear reflected in her eyes was deeper than before. "I don't think the pains are supposed to come this fast, this soon."

"Sure they are," he lied. "I remember when Amelia had Maggie, it all happened so fast that we barely had time to catch our breaths."

"I want a girl," she said breathlessly.

"Then that's what we'll have."

"Or a boy."

He chuckled low. "It'll be one of the two, Sugar. That I can promise you."

"I don't understand why we have to be out here while she's in there," Austin said as he wore down the weeds in front of his porch with his constant pacing. Two-bits shadowed his every step as though he, too, realized there was cause for concern. Twilight was settling in. What was taking so damn long?

"That's just the way it's done," Houston said.

"I think it's a dumb way to do it," Austin said.

"I agree," Dallas said. "I think if you want to be in there watching her suffer, you ought to be in there."

Austin staggered to a stop. "How much do you think she's suffering?"

Dallas shrugged. "Well, she's not screaming . . ."

"That don't mean anything. Amelia never screams and she suffers plenty," Houston said.

"Then why do we do this to them?" Austin asked.

His brothers stared at him as though he'd just eaten loco weed.

"Why does it take so long?" he asked.

"That's just the way it is," Houston said.

He glared at his brother. "Think you could come up with some better answers?"

"Nope. I ask these same questions every time."

"I'm never touching her again," Austin swore.

"You'll touch her," his brothers said in unison. And damn it, he knew he would, first chance he got. He leapt onto the porch, stormed into the house, and threw open the door to his bedroom—and wished to God he hadn't.

Loree's face was contorted with pain as she strained and pushed, grunted and groaned. Then she dropped back on the bed, breathing heavily. Austin heard a tiny indignant wail, and Loree's lovely face filled with wonder and love.

"It's a boy," Dr. Freeman announced.

Austin watched the physician place the child in the crook of Loree's arm. Loree smiled softly, then she looked at Austin, her eyes brimming with tears through which the gold glistened like treasure.

But the treasure was nestled within her arms.

"It's a boy," she said breathlessly. "I knew it would be."

Smiling, Austin walked toward the bed like a man ensconced in a dream. He had a wife. He had a son. The responsibility should have weighed heavy on him, but he thought he might actually float to the clouds.

He knelt beside the bed. She touched the child's head. "Look, he has black hair just like you." Her smile was radiant as she proceeded to stroke the baby's hand. "And your long fingers."

She snapped her gaze to Austin. "I'm so glad he has your hands and not mine."

He cradled her cheek. "He's beautiful, Loree. Just like his mother." He brushed his lips over hers. "God, I love you."

"Do you want to hold him?"

He jerked his gaze to his son. "Hold him?"

"Uh-huh." She moved the child closer to him. "Surely you want to hold him."

"What if I drop him?"

"Did you ever drop your nieces?"

"I never held them while they were this tiny. I waited until they were big enough to latch onto me."

"He doesn't have teeth yet, so he won't bite," she assured him.

He swallowed hard and gave her a nod, not wanting to disappoint her after she'd worked so hard. He slid his hands beneath hers.

"His head is kinda wobbly so be sure you hold it."

"Won't fall off or nothing, will it?" he asked.

She laughed with joy. "No."

He brought the boy into the crook of his arm. "Hello there, young fella."

The babe blinked his blue eyes.

"He's looking at me, Loree. Look at that." He tilted the baby toward her. "He's looking at me. You think he knows who I am?"

"I'm sure he does."

"Can I show him to Houston and Dallas?" he asked, feeling like a child with a new toy.

"I don't see why not."

With the greatest of care, he stood and turned toward the door. His brothers were already standing there, grinning almost as much as he was. "I've got a son. Can you believe that? A son."

He looked over his shoulder at Loree. "What are we gonna name him?"

She licked her lips. "I'd like to name him after my family—Grant."

"Grant," Austin repeated. "I like it."

That night after everyone left, while Loree listened with tears in her eyes, Austin played his violin, lulling his son to sleep with a song that bore his name.

Chapter 17

ᔓ

THE COOL BREEZE blew over the front porch as Loree rocked, her son cradled within her arms. Three weeks had passed since his birth, and she didn't think she'd ever anticipated the coming of spring more.

She heard the rumble of carriage wheels and glanced up from her sleeping son's face. She smiled and waved as Becky brought the horses to a halt.

Loree sent the spark of jealousy she usually felt when she first saw Becky to oblivion. She had given Austin the one thing Becky never had: a son.

Becky bounced up the steps and leaned over, slipping the baby shawl away from Grant's cheek. "Isn't he precious?" Becky whispered. Smiling broadly she met Loree's gaze. "I think he looks like Austin."

"He has his eyes," Loree admitted. "When they're open."

Becky straightened and leaned against the porch railing. "I always thought Austin had the prettiest eyes—too pretty for a man really." She sighed as though blowing away a memory.

"Would you like something to drink?" Loree offered as she started to rise.

Becky placed her hand on her shoulder and guided her back down. "Don't get up. I just brought you a few things. I wanted to come sooner but Drew got the chicken pox. Then Cameron got them. I've never seen anyone as sick as he was. I wanted to wait until I was certain I wouldn't bring them out here, but it was hard not to come."

"I appreciate your coming out."

Becky smiled. "I can't tell you how happy I am for Austin." Her smile grew. "You should have seen him, strutting through the town, passing out cigars. I've never seen him so proud and it's been a long time since I've seen him so happy. It did my heart good to see that."

She gazed off into the distance. "I always felt so guilty."

"For marrying Cameron?"

Becky shifted her gaze back to Loree. "No. For not telling people that Austin was with me the night Boyd McQueen was murdered."

Loree felt her heart slam against her ribs, and the blood drain from her face. Becky's eyes widened.

"Oh my goodness. Didn't he tell you? I was certain he would have, you being his wife and all. I'm so sorry. I should have kept my mouth shut. Let me get the items I brought out of the buggy."

Loree surged to her feet and dug her fingers into Becky's arm to halt her leaving. "Why . . . why would people care that he was with you the night Boyd McQueen died?"

"If they knew he was with me, then they might have believed that he hadn't killed Boyd."

Loree released her hold on Becky and sank into the rocker. "Boyd McQueen? He went to prison for killing Boyd McQueen?"

"Surely you knew that," Becky said.

Loree shook her head. "I knew he'd gone to prison for murder. He never told me the name of the man he was supposed to have murdered. I never thought to ask."

"Well, let me tell you right here and now that he did not murder Boyd McQueen."

Loree lifted her gaze to Becky. "I know that. With all my heart I know that."

Austin sauntered into the house, the first flowers of spring clutched in his hand. He spotted Loree sitting in a rocker before the empty hearth, rocking back and fourth.

He knelt beside her, the sadness in her eyes causing a knot to form in his chest. "Where's Grant?"

"Sleeping in his cradle."

He extended his gift toward her. "I brought you some flowers."

She shifted her vacant gaze to his hand. "You were innocent."

Reaching across, he grabbed the arm of the rocker and turned the chair so he could see her more clearly. "Pardon me?"

She lifted dull eyes to his. "Becky came by today."

"Did she say something to upset you?"

She shook her head slightly, tears brimming within her eyes, and she touched her trembling fingers to his shadowed cheek. "You went to prison for killing Boyd McQueen. I didn't know. All these years, I didn't know."

"All these years? Sugar, you've known me less than a year. If I never mentioned his name, it was because I didn't figure it would mean anything to you."

"I didn't know you were innocent."

"I told you I wasn't a murderer."

"I thought you meant you hadn't killed anyone in cold blood. I thought it had been self-defense."

"And you married me anyway, thinking I'd killed someone?"

"It was your eyes, your dang blue eyes. They weren't the eyes of a killer."

He smiled warmly. "There, see. You did know. You just didn't listen to your heart. I was doing the same thing with my music. Not listening."

"They beat you in prison, didn't they?"

"Loree, that's all in the past. It doesn't matter anymore. I've got you and Grant—"

"Who gave you that cut on your back? The one I tended."

He gave a deep sigh wondering why she was hanging onto this discovery like a starving dog with a bone. "Duncan McQueen. Boyd's brother. We got into a fight right after I got out of prison. Seems he thinks I should have hanged."

"Is he the one who attacked you the night of the play?"

"I don't know who attacked me that night. It was dark."

"But it could have been him—"

"What does it matter—"

She shot out of the rocker like a bullet fired from a gun and turned on him. "It matters. God, you don't know how much it matters and you'd hate me if you did."

She ran into the bedroom and slammed the door. He heard his son give a pitiful wail. Silence quickly followed, and he knew instinctively that Loree had carried his son to her breast.

Right now he wouldn't mind being held to Loree's breast, comforted, and loved.

He looked at the sagging flowers in his hand and somehow felt as though they reflected his life.

Austin knocked on the door and waited an eternity for Becky to open it. "What exactly did you tell Loree?"

Becky grimaced and groaned. "I told her we were together the night Boyd was killed."

Austin cursed harshly and jerked his hat from his hat.

"I thought she knew!"

"Thought who knew what?" Cameron said as he came to stand in the doorway.

Austin watched the blood drain from Becky's face.

"I thought Loree knew that Austin was with me the night Boyd died." Cameron's cheeks flamed red and he averted his gaze. "Oh."

"I don't want to cause you any embarrassment, Becky, but is that all you said?"

"That's all I said."

"You didn't say anything specific, anything that might have . . . hurt her?"

"Nothing. I am so sorry."

Austin settled his hat onto his head. "It's not your fault. For some reason, this damn thing won't go away."

"You and Loree break a fence?" Houston asked.

Austin glanced toward the front porch of Houston's house where his wife sat in the rocker. He couldn't tell if she was talking to Amelia. Damn he wished she'd talk to someone.

He hefted the board for Houston's new corral and held it in place while Houston hammered one end to the post and Dallas hammered into the other end. "I don't know what happened. It makes no sense to me. She married me, thinking I'd killed someone. She found out I didn't and now she won't talk to me. I can't figure it out."

"That's 'cuz she's a woman," Dallas said around the nail protruding from his mouth. He removed it from between his teeth and pointed it at Austin's nose. "You can't figure women out so don't even try. I was married to Dee for weeks before I realized when she said something was fine—it wasn't fine at all."

"But wouldn't you be happy if you discovered that you weren't married to a murderer?" Austin insisted.

"It's the baby," Houston said.

Austin jerked his head around and glared at Houston. "What's Grant got to do with it?"

Houston gave the nail a final whack and stepped back to inspect his work before waving the hammer at Austin. "Whenever Amelia has a baby, she gets . . ." He scraped his thumb over the scars on the left side of his face, just below the leather eye patch. "She gets . . . difficult. Yep, that's the best way to describe it."

"Can't imagine Amelia being difficult," Dallas said. "She wasn't when I was married to her."

"She didn't give you any young 'uns either. Trust me. She gets difficult."

"In what way?" Austin asked, thinking maybe Houston had hit upon his problem.

"Well, as you know Gracie was born in November. About a week after she was born, Amelia hollers for me. Almost broke my neck gettin' to her, and you know what she wanted?"

Austin glanced at Dallas who was shaking his head.

"She wanted me to sit down right then and there and order Christmas presents from the Montgomery Ward catalog. Got it into her head that we had to order them that day or they wouldn't get here in time. Had to take the blasted order into the post office in Leighton—that day mind you. It didn't matter that I had horses to work—"

"You coulda just told her no," Dallas said.

Houston looked at Dallas as though the man had gone loco. "I suppose you tell Dee no all the time."

"Never tell her no, but we're not talking about me. We're talking about you—"

"Actually, we're talking about me," Austin reminded his brothers with disgust.

They both snapped their attention to him. Houston rubbed the side of his nose. "That's right." He squinted. "How'd she find out she was wrong about you after all this time?"

Austin dropped his gaze and kicked the toe of his boot into the dirt. "Becky. She visited Loree and somehow it came up in conversation that she and I were together that night."

"She's probably just feeling slighted then," Dallas said.

"Why would she feel slighted? That was six years ago—"

"Like I said earlier, you can't figure women out. They make no sense."

"Then what do I do about it?"

"Talk to Dee."

"Talk to Amelia."

His brothers offered their advice at the same time, and he wondered why they hadn't just told him that to begin with.

"You're both useless, you know that?" he said.

"Well, this might cheer you up," Dallas said. "I got a telegram from Wylan. He was playing in a private poker game and Boyd's name came up. Something about cheating someone out of some land. So he's gonna see what else he can find."

Austin shook his head. "I'm sure he's a good man, but after this long, he's not gonna find anything. Whatever trails were left behind are nothing more than dust in the wind now."

"I don't want to go," Loree insisted.

Austin sighed heavily. "Dee says you need to get out of the house—"

"I got out of the house last Sunday when you went to help Houston with his corral," she pointed out.

She watched him work his jaw back and forth. She knew what she needed to do. She needed to tell him the truth and ask him for forgiveness. But what if he were unable to forgive her?

He held the tickets toward her. "This is a special performance. They're only going to be in the theater tonight. Amelia offered to watch Grant—"

"And what if someone attacks you—"

Sympathy filled his eyes and he cradled her face. "Is that what's worrying you? Now that you understand why I was attacked, you're afraid I'll get hurt?"

She nodded briskly. "Let's just stay here, Austin."

"Sugar, don't you see? If we hide out here, then whoever attacked me has won. Whoever killed Boyd has won. And I'm not gonna let either of those bastards run my life."

She turned away, wrapping her arms around herself. "I can't go."

She expected further protests, but instead she only heard the echo of his boot heels as he left the room. She could stop people from staring at him. She could stop people from whispering about him. She could stop people from attacking him. But she couldn't give him back the five years she had unknowingly stolen from him. And without that, what good were the others?

She heard the sharp brief whine of the violin and spun around. Austin stood in the doorway, instrument in hand.

"Please?" He gave three quick strokes to the strings. "Please? Please? Please?"

She bit back her smile. "No."

Three more quick strokes as he stepped into the room. "I'll have to play something sad." A forlorn sound filled the room. "And I'd rather play something happy." He played a quick fast tune. "Give me a reason to play something happy."

For him, she forced herself to set her fears aside. "All right."

He whooped, tossed the violin onto the bed, clamped his hands on her waist, and lifted her toward the ceiling. "You'll be glad, Sugar."

She looked into his beloved face, his shining blue eyes, and wished to God that she'd never fallen in love with him.

The lobby was nearly empty when they arrived, and Loree couldn't have been more grateful as Austin took her hand and rushed up the sweeping staircase to the balcony level.

He drew back the drapes and she stepped into the dark alcove. She barely made out Dee's silhouette as the woman turned, smiled, and motioned them over. Loree eased down to the chair beside Dee.

Dee squeezed her hand. "I'm so glad you could come. This is a special performance."

Austin leaned forward. "What play is it anyway?"

Dee's smile grew. "It's not a play."

The stage curtains parted to reveal a group of people sitting in a half circle, instruments poised. Loree's breath caught as Austin wrapped his hand around hers and shifted up in his chair.

A man walked onto the stage, bowed sharply from the waist, then stepped onto a box. He lifted a long thin stick, swept it through the air, and music reached up to the rafters.

Austin's hand closed more tightly around hers, and she knew he had spoken the truth. She was glad that she came, glad that she'd given him the opportunity to hear a symphony. She eased up in the chair, tears stinging her eyes at the sight of awe and wonder revealed on his face.

"Look at all those violins," he whispered. "They're all moving the same, like a herd of cattle heading to pasture."

"They're following the same music."

"Reading those little black bugs. How long do you think it took them to learn to play together like that?"

"Years."

"It's mighty fine sounding, ain't it?" he asked.

She brushed her fingers through his hair and pressed her cheek to his shoulder. "Mighty fine."

They arrived home with no mishaps. Loree wished she could believe that Austin was safe. It had been a year since his release, six months since someone had slammed him into a building. If only she knew for certain that no harm would come to him, she could keep her secret buried deep within her soul.

Grant released a tiny mewling sound. She sat on the bed, unbuttoned her bodice, and smiled as he rooted at her nipple, his mouth working feverishly. "Got hungry, did you?" she asked as she brushed her fingers over his black hair.

"When you get bigger, you can help your pa put the horses away after we go to town." Leaning down, she pressed a kiss to his forehead. "I'm gonna get better, Grant. I'm gonna stop worrying. I can't change the past, but I can be a good wife and make everything up to your pa that way. I realized that watching him tonight. Oh, you should have seen his face—"

She heard the front door close and shifted Grant within her arms. Austin walked into the room, dropped onto the bed, and tossed the sheets of music toward her hips.

"Teach me, Loree."

She blinked her eyes. "What?"

"Teach me. I won't complain. I'll play the same song over and over and over—just like you wanted me to. I'll do whatever it takes."

"It takes time—"

"Which is the one thing I haven't got so just for tonight, teach me one song, one fancy song."

She shifted Grant to her shoulder and began to rub his back. "You want me to teach you tonight?"

He rolled off the bed and began to pace. "All my life, Loree, I've been searching for something, wondering where I belonged. Dallas always knew that he belonged with cattle and Houston . . . hell, he practically becomes a horse when he's working with them. But I never knew what I should do. Not until tonight.

"There was a time when I thought if I could make a violin I could find a way to live on forever. It never occurred to me that I could stand on a stage and fill people's hearts with music."

He dropped to his knees by the bed and wrapped his arm around her waist. "I want to go see Mr. Cowan—the conductor—tomorrow. I wanna play for him. I wanna ask him to take me with him, to let me be part of his orchestra."

"What about us?"

"You and Grant will come with me. We might have to leave Two-bits with Rawley, but the boy loves him. He'll give him a good home. And I'll show *you* the world."

The world. She would miss Two-bits, but she saw Austin's dream reflected so clearly in his eyes of blue—burning brighter and hotter than any flame in the center of a fire, and she knew deep within her heart that every dream he had ever lost had been because of her.

This one last dream he had found was hers to give.

She laid Grant, asleep, on the bed beside her and combed her fingers through Austin's dark, curling locks. "No," she said quietly.

"No?" Confusion mired his eyes.

"No, I won't teach you to play a song. If you're going to impress Mr. Cowan, you're going to have to play from your heart, and you'll only be able to do that if you play the songs that are within you."

She watched him swallow. "What if he doesn't like what I play?"

"How can he not like it? You have a rare gift. Your heart isn't in any of the songs I gave you for Christmas. You need to play one of your songs."

"Which one?"

"The one that means the most to you."

He gave a slow hesitant nod. "How can I convince him that I'll be able to play with the others?"

"You just play for him, and he'll find a way to make it work."

"Will you iron my Sunday-go-to-meetin' shirt?"

She smiled. "And I'll cut your hair and trim your nails."

He chuckled. "You probably ought to shave me, too." He lifted his hands. "Look at how much I'm shaking."

She wrapped her hands around his. "Just play from your heart."

"I want this, Loree, like I've never wanted anything."

She saw him off at dawn, his violin safely housed in the wooden case she'd given him for Christmas, tucked beneath his arm. Then she sat on the top step, Grant in her arms, and waited.

She gauged the distance into town, the time it would take him to play, and figured he'd ride home at a gallop. It was late morning before he returned, and she'd never been so glad to see anyone.

He dismounted, set the violin case on the porch, and sat beside her.

"Brought these for you," he said, holding out a handful of red and yellow flowers.

"They're beautiful," she said as she took them.

"I couldn't find you any that were blue."

"That's all right. I like these."

He touched Grant's tiny fist. The boy's fingers unfurled and wrapped around the larger finger that was waiting for him.

"He's got a strong grip," Austin said quietly. "It won't be much longer, and he'll be able to hold a bow."

"I didn't think it'd take you this long," Loree said, anxious to know all that had transpired. "I guess you had a lot of details to work out, traveling to arrange—"

"He can't use me, Loree."

She couldn't have been more shocked if he'd told her the sun was going to start setting in the east. "Is he deaf?"

He gave her a sad smile. "No."

"Why didn't he want you?"

She watched his Adam's apple bob. "He didn't think the people in his company would be comfortable traveling with a murderer."

"But you're not a murderer!"

"The law says I am and that's all that matters." He unfolded his body. "I need to change clothes and repair some fence for Dallas on the east side."

She watched him disappear into the house, and even without the aid of his violin, she heard his heart breaking.

Loree drew the wagon to a halt and studied her husband, standing with one leg straight, one leg bent, his elbow resting on the gnarled and crooked fence post, the barbed wire curling on the ground like a ribbon recently removed from a girl's hair.

His hat shadowed his face, but she knew he was staring in the distance, toward the railroad tracks that he couldn't see, but knew existed. She heard the lonesome train whistle rent the afternoon air.

Austin stepped back, turned, slid his hat up off his brow with his thumb, and gave her a warm lazy smile. "Hey, Sugar, wasn't expecting to see you out here."

He ambled to the wagon and Loree's throat grew tight. "I brought you some lunch."

"I sure could use some."

He put his hands on her waist and lifted her off the bench seat. "Could use a little sugar, too," he said, his gaze holding hers.

She raised up on her toes and wrapped her arms around his neck, kissing him as she hadn't in weeks.

"Mmm, I've missed that." Reaching around her, he grabbed the picnic basket while she picked up Grant.

She sat on the quilt Austin had spread over the ground and laid Grant near her hip. Austin stretched out beside her.

"You caught me daydreaming," he said, his voice low.

"What were you dreaming?"

"Different things. I ran into Houston on my way back from town this morning, and we got to talking."

"About what?" she asked, handing him a hunk of cheese. She'd thrown the picnic together as hastily as they'd thrown their marriage together.

He set the cheese aside as though it really held no interest for him. "He's gaining a wide-spread reputation for having the best horse flesh this side of the Rio Grande. He's needing some help so I offered to start working for him on my off-day. I thought we could set the money aside until we have enough to go somewhere on a little trip."

"Where would we go?"

"Wherever you want." He leaned toward her and cupped her chin. "I'm gonna give you a good life, Loree. You'll see. It might never be filled with any of the things you dreamed of, but it'll be good."

"If they found the person who killed Boyd McQueen—everything would change for you, wouldn't it?"

"Damn sure would. But that's not gonna happen, Loree. It's been six years. The fact of the matter is that man got lucky, and I didn't."

Chapter 18

꙲

*A*USTIN SAT ON the porch, staring at the moonless sky, knowing sleep would be as elusive as his dreams.

He heard the door open, but he didn't bother to turn around. Dallas had once told him that a man had to learn from the mistakes he made. Austin had never expected the lessons to be so damn hard.

He caught a glimpse of bare toes as Loree sat beside him. He felt a ghost of a smile touch his lips. He turned slightly and brought her feet to his lap, rubbing his thumb over her sole.

"Daydreaming again?" she asked.

"You can't daydream at night," he said quietly. "But I was thinking—there's no reason I couldn't play in Dee's theater." He leaned toward her and smiled. "A special performance."

"Would that make you happy?"

He moved his thumb in an ever widening circle. "You make me happy."

She jerked her feet off his lap. Even in the shadows, he could make out tears glistening within her eyes. "I told you that I'll make everything all right."

"It'll never be all right. Oh, God, Austin. I didn't know, and now I'm so afraid, more afraid than I was then because I have so much more to lose."

"Loree, you're not making any sense."

She scooted across the porch until their thighs touched and took his hand in hers, holding his open, rubbing her fingers over it again and again, as though she wanted to memorize every line and callus.

"My mother hated West Texas."

His gut clenched, and he wished he'd kept his dream of playing for the orchestra to himself. He'd given her hope of leaving only to disappoint her with mistakes from his past. "We'll travel, Loree."

She shook her head. "Let me say everything before you say anything."

"All right."

She cleared her throat. "My father bought some land after the war. He got it cheap, and it wasn't a lot of land. So he extended his boundaries and posted a notice in a newspaper."

"Your father was a land grabber?"

She nodded. The practice had been widely used following the war, saving men considerable time and effort in filing deeds. Dallas had always cautioned his brothers that the practice would bring trouble. He'd filed legal claims for every inch of land he owned.

"My father used to say that land grabbing was like gambling—sometimes you won, sometimes you didn't. He was a good man, but gambling was his weakness.

"When my mother refused to move out here, he put his deed and his dream of ranching away. He used to take them out on my birthday, show me the land on the map, and tell me that I could be a rancher.

"One night he got involved in a private high stakes poker game in Austin. He ended up owing one of the players a great deal of money . . . money he didn't have. So he handed over the deed to the land, claiming the boundaries went farther than his original entitlement.

"The land was so vast. Many successful ranchers had extended their boundaries through land grabbing so my father felt confident that Boyd McQueen would be satisfied with the bargain they'd struck."

Austin's stomach clenched. "Boyd McQueen got his land from your father?"

"A little west of here. My father didn't know that someone had a legal claim to a good portion of the land, the best part where the river flowed. I don't know why it took McQueen so long to exact his revenge once he realized my father had deceived him. He didn't strike me as a man of patience—"

"He's the one who killed your family?"

"And I killed him."

She spoke the words with no emotion: no hatred, no anger, no fear.

Austin stared at her, and then he burst out laughing. "God, Loree, you scared me to death there for a minute. You were so serious." He took a deep breath. "I appreciate that you're willing to lie and take the blame for Boyd's murder so I can—"

"I'm not lying. It took me three months to get strong enough to travel after he shot me, another month to track him down."

He jerked his hand from hers and surged to his feet. "You're telling me that you honest to God shot Boyd?"

"Shot and killed. Dewayne was with me."

He trembled so hard that he thought the ground might shake. His wife was a murderer. His *wife* was a murderer!

No matter how he repeated it in his mind, no matter how he thought of it, he couldn't see Loree murdering anyone. He began pacing. The music thundering through his soul was hideous. He wanted to cover his ears to block it out. He had wanted to find the person who had killed Boyd so he could clear his name.

Not only had he found the person, he'd married her and fallen in love with her. He brought his pacing to an abrupt halt and glared at his wife. "Forgive me for doubting your word, Loree, but you are the sweetest—"

She surged to her feet. "I was seventeen, trussed up like a pig for slaughter, along with my ma and pa. He took my brother outside and God only knows what he did to him. All we heard were his screams. Then he brought him back in and hanged him. He was fourteen, Austin. Look at Rawley and imagine what McQueen might have done to him."

Austin didn't have to imagine. He knew exactly what Boyd had done to him, something no man should ever do to a boy.

"Do you know how long it takes for a person to die when they're hanged?" she asked. "My brother didn't deserve to die that way. My pa didn't deserve to watch his son suffer like that."

She dropped onto the porch, wrapped her arms around herself, and began to rock back and forth. "I know I should have gone to the authorities, but . . . I didn't want my father's name dragged through the mud. And I didn't want people to know what McQueen had done to my brother. There were no witnesses. It was just my word against his. I didn't come here with the intent to murder him. I wanted a fair fight. But then he started to laugh . . ."

Crouched in the dimming twilight, she and Dewayne waited. When Boyd McQueen slipped from the house, mounted his horse, and road north, they followed until the ranch was no longer in sight and Loree had gathered her courage. Then she spurred her horse into a gallop, Dewayne following in her wake.

She yelled his name. McQueen circled about and brought his horse to a halt. Loree drew her gun. "Get off your horse."

He did as she instructed, and Loree dismounted as well.

"You're Grant's daughter. I thought I'd killed you."

"You thought wrong," she replied with false bravado.

Her heart was pounding, and her hands shaking. She'd practiced drawing her gun from the holster, but she feared when it came right down to it, she wouldn't be able to do it. "I'm gonna give you what you didn't give my family. A chance."

He flashed a sardonic smile that didn't reach up to touch his eyes. "Oh? Like a duel? I draw, you draw, and the one left standing is the winner? And what about your friend here, do I get to kill him, too?" He snorted derisively. "You haven't got the guts to kill. Want to know what I did to your brother when I took him outside? I enjoyed hearing him scream." He started to laugh. "Your brother wanted me to stop"—his laughter grew harsher—"begged me to stop—"

Loree didn't realize she'd pulled the trigger until she heard the explosion and watched McQueen's arms flail out as he staggered backward to the ground.

"Oh, God," she cried as she dropped beside him, jerked free the linen sticking out of his pocket, and pressed it to the dark stain spreading over his white shirt. He groaned.

Dewayne knelt beside her. "You gut shot him, Loree. He's as good as dead. We gotta get out of here."

"Help me stop—"

Then McQueen released a deep roar and grabbed her wrist. The blood coating her hands made it easy to slip free. She stumbled back.

"You bitch! I'll drag you into hell with me." He started to laugh. "Mark my words! I'll drag you into hell with me!"

"And he did. He did drag me into hell. I lived alone, afraid that if I had a family, what I'd done would reach out to hurt them. I didn't know I'd already hurt you." Tears streaming along her cheeks, Loree doubled over and pressed her face to her knees.

"You thought you could outdraw him?" Austin asked stunned.

"Blame it on my youth, my grief, or my shame. I just didn't want anyone to know everything that led to that night, all that happened that night. And I couldn't *not* do anything."

"So once you shot him, you left?"

Wiping at her tears, she nodded. "He was fumbling to get his gun out of his holster so we mounted up and rode out. We came to a river. I couldn't get his blood off my hands. I tried and tried, but I couldn't." She started wiping her hands on her gown. "Sometimes, I feel like his blood is still there."

Austin had listened with increasing horror and dread . . . and more, with the realization that she spoke the truth. She was tied to the land . . . the missing link the detective had uncovered. He dropped beside her and took her ice cold, trembling hands into his. "Loree, listen to me." He shook her until her head snapped back and the vacant gaze left her eyes to be replaced by tears.

"I'm so sorry, Austin. I never knew anyone went to prison for killing McQueen. I thought we were safe. I would have come back and confessed if I'd known—"

"It doesn't matter, but I gotta talk to Dallas right now. I want you to go into the house and take care of Grant. Can you do that for me? Trust me to take care of everything. All right?"

"You'll tell the sheriff, won't you? We'll clear your name—"

He pressed his finger to her lips. "I need to talk to Dallas tonight. Then we'll decide tomorrow what we're gonna do." He put his arm around her and helped her stand. She was trembling as badly as he was. He escorted her into the house, eased her into bed, and brought the blankets around her, tucking them below her chin.

"Don't hate me, Austin," she said quietly.

"I don't hate you, Loree. You take care of Grant if he wakes up. Remember months back, before he was born, when we said he has to come first? That still holds true. Nothing's changed that."

She gave him a weak nod. Lord, he didn't want to leave her, but he knew it was imperative that he talk to Dallas as soon as he could. "I won't be long," he promised.

He hurried from the house, saddled Black Thunder, mounted up, and rode through the night like a man hounded by demons.

*   *   *

Dallas loved those first few moments when he crawled into bed and his wife cuddled up against him. She purred like a contented kitten, and he hadn't even gotten around to ensuring her contentment yet.

He covered her mouth with his, drinking deeply of the glory she offered.

The bedroom door banged against the wall, and he shot out of bed, naked as the day he was born. He jerked a blanket off the bed to cover himself and glared at his baby brother. "What in the hell do you think you're doing?"

"I need to talk to you," Austin said, his breathing labored. His worried gaze shifted to Dee. "You, too."

"Do you mind if we get dressed?" Dallas barked.

Austin looked him over as though just noticing his lack of apparel. He gave a brusque nod. "That'd be fine." He disappeared down the hallway.

Dallas looked at Dee. "The last time one of my brothers burst into my bedroom like that, I lost a wife."

Smiling, she slipped out of bed and reached for her wrapper. "Well, you don't have to worry about that happening this time."

He pulled on his trousers before following her to his study. Like a caged animal, Austin paced back and forth in front of the window that ran the length of the wall. He pointed to the desk without breaking his stride. "Why don't you sit down?"

Dallas dropped into the leather chair behind his desk, propped his elbow on the armrest, and rubbed his thumb and forefinger over his mustache while Dee sat in her chair beside the desk and drew her legs up beneath her. Austin continued his pacing.

"You had something you had to tell us at this ungodly hour?"

"I don't rightly know how to say it."

"Straight out is usually best."

Austin nodded and came to an abrupt halt. "I killed Boyd."

Dallas grew as still as death and stared at his brother. "I beg your pardon?"

"I killed Boyd."

Dallas planted his hands on his desk and slowly brought himself to his feet. "Let me make sure I understand everything you just said. For six years, you claimed to be innocent, you allowed your family to stand by you and proclaim your innocence, and I have been paying a man to find proof of your innocence. And now you're telling me that you're guilty of murder?"

He watched the blood drain from Austin's face before he gave a brusque nod. "That's right."

"But you were with Becky that night," Dee reminded him.

"Afterward. I killed him and then I fetched Becky, planning to use her as my alibi, but I couldn't bring myself to do it. I know I've destroyed your trust in me, and I can never regain that. Tomorrow, I'll pack up my family and we'll leave—"

"Let's not do anything rash," Dallas ordered. "We'll just sleep on it. Things will look clearer in the morning."

"In the morning, I want you to telegraph Wylan and tell him to stop his search for the murderer."

Dallas narrowed his eyes and gave his brother a long slow measuring nod. Austin took a step toward the desk. "Give me your word that you'll send that telegram first thing in the morning."

"Give you my word."

He watched relief course down his brother's face like water rushing over rocky falls. Austin turned to Dee. "I know I owe you the most, Dee, Boyd being your brother and all. I don't know how, but I'll find a way to pay back all I owe."

"You don't owe me anything, Austin," she assured him.

"I need to tell Houston and Amelia. I'll do that tomorrow. And Cameron." He jerked his gaze to Dallas. "I could take out an announcement in the newspaper, couldn't I?"

"Like I said, let's not do anything without thinking it through."

Austin slipped a hand into his hind pocket and took a step backward. "I need to get home to Loree."

"I'll come by in the morning and we'll work this out."

Austin nodded. "I'm really sorry."

"So am I," Dallas said quietly. He watched his brother high-tail it from the room. He walked to the window and caught sight of Austin galloping into the night. "So who the hell do you think he's protecting now?"

"If he's following in the footsteps of his older brothers, it would have to be the woman he loves," Dee said softly as she came up behind him and wrapped her arms around his chest.

"Christ, I hope you're wrong."

Loree heard the footsteps on the porch and slowly brought herself out of the rocking chair. The door opened quietly, and Austin slipped inside. He hung his hat on the peg by the door and stood staring at his boots. He looked like a man who had just taken the weight of the world on his shoulders.

"Austin?"

He snapped his head around and gave her a weak smile. "Thought you'd be asleep. Must be near midnight."

"Almost. What did Dallas say?"

"That we'll take care of it."

She furrowed her brow. "What does that mean?"

He crossed the short expanse separating them. "It means we'll take care of it. I don't want you to ever tell anyone what you told me tonight."

"How will that clear your name?"

"Don't you be worrying about my name. You worry about that little boy that's sleeping in the cradle in our room."

"You didn't tell Dallas, did you?"

He dropped his head back and plowed his hands through his hair. "He'd hired the detective I told you about. Recently he notified Dallas that he thought he'd discovered a link to the land. I don't know why it took him so long—"

"Because my father bought the land under a false name. So many men used different names after the war, especially if they had something to hide. He'd deserted. He was afraid they wouldn't sell him the land if they knew the truth . . ." She looked at him imploringly. "Honestly my father wasn't a bad man—"

"He just lied and cheated."

Tears burned her eyes. "I never wanted anyone to know—"

"No one will know. I told Dallas to send a telegram to the detective and tell him his services were no longer needed."

"And he agreed to do that . . . on your say-so?"

"He's my brother. He trusts me." He hunkered down before the hearth. "I'll bank the fire. You go on to bed. I'll be there directly."

She padded into their bedroom and clambered onto the bed, drawing the blankets over her. Relief swamped her when she heard his footsteps and saw his silhouette in the doorway. As though she'd never see it again, she watched the way he held onto the doorjamb while slipping the heel of his boot into the bootjack and jerking his boot off. She listened to the thud of one, then the other, and the soft tread of his stockinged feet as he walked to the bed, yanking his shirt over his head as he went. She watched his shadow as he dropped his britches onto the floor. In the morning, she'd gladly pick up all his clothes and check them for tears and missing buttons before she laundered them.

The bed sank beneath his weight as he stretched out beside her, folded his arms beneath his head, and stared at the ceiling.

"Why did they think you killed McQueen?" she finally dredged up the courage to ask.

She heard him swallow in the silence that followed her question.

"Lots of reasons."

"You said you'd made some mistakes—"

"Yep."

"What did you do?"

He sighed deeply. "The land your father claimed was his belonged to Dallas. Boyd and Dallas fought over it. Dallas made a pact with the devil. He'd marry his sister and when she gave him a son, he'd deed the land over to Boyd. I told you what happened behind the hotel.

"We didn't know it was Boyd at the time. Dee had heard a child cry out—Rawley. Boyd had hurt him in ways a boy should never be hurt. When Rawley confided in me, I went into the saloon—like a big man—fired my gun right over Boyd's head and told him that I'd like nothing better than to rid the ground of his shadow.

"There were plenty of witnesses. So when he showed up dead, they figured I'd carried out my threat."

"But Becky knew differently," she said softly, understanding the full extent of his love for Becky. He had to have known what their silence might cost him.

"I didn't think they'd find me guilty so I told her not to say anything."

"But after they found you guilty—"

"Didn't see that it would have made any difference. Boyd wrote 'Austin' in the dirt before he died."

"I wonder why he didn't write my name."

"My guess is that he planned to but he died before he got around to it. Writing your name wouldn't have helped if no one knew where to find you so he wrote that first." .

Her heart slammed against her ribs with the realization of what had brought him to Austin. "The man you were looking for in Austin—"

He rolled over and cradled her cheek. "Seems he wasn't a man at all."

She squeezed her eyes shut. "How you must hate me."

His thumb circled her cheek in a gentle caress. "Loree, make no mistake. I would have killed him that night but Becky sidetracked me. Boyd had paid some men to kill Dallas, and they'd lashed him to within an inch of his life. We couldn't prove anything because he'd murdered them in their sleep. He was spawned by the devil, and I'm damned tired of him reaching out from hell and touching our lives. We're gonna put this behind us. I'm not saying it'll be easy, but by God, I'm not going to let him steal something else away from me." He dropped his hand down to her shoulder and squeezed gently. "Come here."

She scooted over until she was nestled in his embrace.

"Tomorrow, we'll decide what we're gonna do," he told her. "But right now I gotta get some sleep." She heard his deep yawn. "Last night, I didn't sleep at all, worrying about this morning."

This morning. How long ago it seemed since he had set out in search of his dream. Every dream he had ever dreamed, she had stolen from him.

His hold on her loosened, his fingers unfurling from around her shoulder. She heard his breathing deepen and slow. She was amazed he slept after all that she'd told him, and thought how much easier it would have been if he'd ranted and raved and told her that he hated her.

She could only surmise that the full implications of her confession hadn't hit him yet. Sooner or later, he would look across the room and realize all that she had cost him.

She heard the small cry, tempered by the night. She slipped from beneath the weight of Austin's arm and walked the familiar path in the darkness, lifting her son into her arms and settling into the rocker near the window. She held him to her breast. His tiny fist pressed against her flesh as he suckled greedily.

She loved the child as much as she loved the father. Her gaze traveled across the room until she saw the dark shadow of her husband, asleep. She wondered what he would dream tonight.

She wondered how long before his love turned to hate. How long before he ticked off and counted all the things she'd stolen from him.

Five years of his life spent in prison, and she could only imagine what horrors he'd experienced there—a man with a heart that heard music as beautiful as his did. Little wonder the music had died within him.

She couldn't give him back those years. She couldn't remove the scars from his back . . . or return to him the woman he had once loved—a woman he would be married to today if only Loree had known they had arrested someone for killing Boyd McQueen. She would have turned herself in six years ago, confessed then had she known.

She couldn't give Austin back anything she'd unknowingly taken from him, but she could return what she'd recently taken. With his innocence proven, he would be truly free of the walls that still held him. He could pursue his dream and there would be nothing to stop him from reaching it.

She glanced down at the bundle of joy in her arms. How could she leave him? If she turned herself in, she had little doubt she would leave her son. She would go to prison just as Austin had. To give Austin his dream, she had to give up hers. Her heart shattered with the thought of never holding this child again, of not watching him grow, of not watching him take his first step. But each day she waited, the debt she owed for killing McQueen increased.

And she could no longer tolerate the thought of Austin continually paying for her actions. Tears streamed along her cheeks. How was she to have known that Fate was more cruel than Boyd McQueen?

Austin awoke to a strangeness that he couldn't identify. He heard birds chirping outside the window. He heard his son gurgling in the cradle nearby. But he couldn't hear Loree.

He threw back the blankets and swung his legs off the bed. His gaze landed on his son, his blue eyes wide, his fists and feet swinging at the air. "Hey there, young fella. Where's your ma?"

Grant cooed and his feet kicked excitedly. Austin yanked on his trousers before lifting his son into his arms. "Well, you're dry and you ain't hollering so she must have fed you." With his thumb, he wiped the drool from his son's mouth.

"We got a lot of things to work out—your ma and me—but I don't want you to worry none. I'm doing enough worrying for all of us."

He padded into the front room. Morning light slanted through the windows. A chill swept through him that was as cold as the stove. He headed for the door. Something on the table caught his eye. He ambled back and picked up the paper. With uneven lines as though she'd been trembling at the time, she'd scribbled, "Forgive me."

Dread shot through his vitals like the well aimed bullet of a Winchester rifle. He tore through the front door and stumbled onto the porch. "Loree!"

Holding his son close, trying not to jar the boy, Austin rushed to the corral as though going nearer would change what he was already seeing. Her horse was gone. He slammed his palm against the post and screamed her name, knowing even as he did so that it was pointless. She couldn't hear him.

Grant started to fuss. Austin jostled him slightly. "It's all right. I'm sure your ma just went for an early morning ride." Dear God, he hoped that was all she'd done.

He walked back into the house and stared at every inch of it as though just seeing it for the first time. "Reckon we missed the sunrise. I don't hardly know how to start the day without seeing the sunrise, but I still need my morning coffee."

He set Grant down on a pile of quilts, but the boy started hollering like his heart would break. Big fat tears rolled down his cheeks.

"All right, all right," Austin said as he tucked his son into the crook of his arm. The tears and hollering stopped as quickly as they'd begun. "I'll wait until your ma gets home to have my coffee." He plowed a hand through his hair. "She can't be much longer."

He heard a horse whinny and relief surged through him. He rushed outside and stumbled to a stop at the sight of Dallas sitting astride his horse.

"Did you send that telegram to Wylan?"

Dallas swept his hat from his head and draped his forearm over the saddle arm. "Sure did. First thing this morning, just like I promised."

"Good."

"Ran into Sheriff Larkin while I was in town. Seems your wife paid him a visit bright and early this morning."

Austin felt all the blood drain from his face, his knees went weak, and his heart was pounding like stampeding cattle.

"She told Sheriff Larkin that *she* killed Boyd McQueen."

Taking a deep breath, Austin swung open the door to the jail and stepped into the front office. The cells were kept in the back behind another door, which Austin knew from experience Larkin kept ajar. Sweat popped out on Austin's brow and he trembled as though he were the one to be locked up.

He had no fond memories of jail. His trial had been held in the saloon. The judge presided from a stool behind the bar. Austin sat at a table, humiliation wrapping itself around him because Larkin wouldn't unshackle his hands. He rubbed his wrists now as though the cold metal still bit into his skin.

Larkin was sprawled in his chair, his feet on his desk, his belly lapping over his belt. Austin knew that somewhere behind that insolent gaze the man had some redeeming qualities or his brother never would have hired him.

Austin swallowed hard. "Heard my wife came in this morning with some tale about killing Boyd McQueen."

Larkin removed the match from between his teeth. "Yep."

"She lied."

Larkin raised a graying brow. "Do tell."

Austin felt a spark of hope ignite within him and he stepped nearer. "I wanted to leave town with that orchestra that was here a few days back, but they didn't want a man who'd been convicted of murder traveling with them. Loree, bless her sweet heart, thought if she said she'd killed Boyd, they'd let me go with them." He scoffed and shook his head. "Women. They don't understand the intricacies of the law."

Larkin pointed the match at him. "So you're telling me you killed Boyd?"

"That's right. When you arrested me six years ago, you sure knew what you were doing. I resented like the devil that you figured out it was me—but I had to admire you as well."

Larkin dropped his feet to the floor. "Well, I'll be damned. Your wife sure did tell a convincing story."

"I'll bet she did."

Larkin stood and picked his ring of keys off his desk. He ambled toward the back door like a man in no hurry. Then he stopped, turned, and rubbed his ear. "Suppose you told her where you hid the gun."

Austin felt as though Larkin had just gut-punched him. "What?"

"The gun you used to kill Boyd. Your wife knew exactly where it had been all these years. Reckon you must have told her."

"Yeah, I did."

"And where was it?"

Austin slammed his eyes closed. Hell, he didn't even know where Boyd had died. "I buried it under some sagebrush—" He opened his eyes and breathed a sigh of relief as Larkin slowly nodded.

"And you'd wrapped something around the gun before you buried it. Want to tell me what that was?"

"A strip of blanket."

He knew from the hard look in the sheriff's eyes that he'd given the wrong answer. "A linen handkerchief that had Boyd's initials sewn into it and his blood soaked through it," Larkin said.

"Larkin, let her go."

"Can't do that. My job is to see that justice is served, and six years ago an injustice was done that I can't overlook." He jerked his head to the side. "You want to talk to her?"

"No, I don't by God want to talk to her." He spun on his heel, stalked through the office, and slammed the door in his wake.

If he saw her, he was afraid he would tell her that by turning herself in, she had taken from him the most precious dream he'd ever held.

And what good would that knowledge do either of them?

Austin laid his sleeping son in the cradle. Three days had passed—three days without Loree—and every minute had been hell. He wanted to see her like he'd never wanted anything in his life, but he was afraid looking at her behind bars, caged like an animal, would bring him to his knees.

As quiet as a mouse, he tiptoed from the room.

"You look like hell."

His head came up, and he glared at Houston, standing in the front doorway. "I feel like hell. You want some coffee."

"Nope." Houston stepped inside, his hat in his hand. "Just thought you'd want to know that the circuit judge arrived. Loree's trial will be tomorrow."

Austin's stomach clenched. "Considering the fact that McQueen killed her family, maybe they'll let her go," he said hopefully.

"If you'd been meeting with her lawyer like the rest of the family, you'd know Boyd ain't the one on trial here."

He didn't like the censure he heard in his brother's voice. "What do you want me to do, Houston? My responsibilities didn't go away just because my wife decided to clear her conscience. I've got chores to take care of along with a baby. Takes me hours to get any milk into him. Every time I go to change him, he pisses on me—"

"I knew he was smart."

"What does that mean?"

"You told me once that if a woman loved you as much as Amelia loved me, you'd crawl through hell for her."

"I've crawled through hell. I don't recommend the journey." The fury that had been building inside him burst through unexpectedly like a raging river. He planted his hands beneath the table and sent it crashing to its side. "And now Loree's gonna crawl through hell. I told her I'd take care of everything." He spun around, the anguish nearly doubling him over. "Why did she have to confess?"

He heard Grant's startled cry and felt as though the roof would cave in on him at any moment.

"Let me get him," Houston offered, crossing into the bedroom without waiting for an answer. Austin heard the blissful silence and wondered how long it would last. Houston came out of the bedroom, holding Grant in his arms. "Why don't I take him home? Amelia can feed him—"

"I don't know what I'm gonna do, Houston. I can't stand the thought of her going to prison."

"See if you like this thought better. Duncan has petitioned for her to hang."

Chapter 19

❧

AUSTIN STOOD INSIDE the doorway, staring along the length of iron bars that made up the jail cells. He saw Loree in the cell at the far end, the cell in which he'd once slept, ate, and worried while awaiting his trial. He hadn't meant to abandon her, but he realized now with startling clarity that he had.

She stood on her cot beside the brick wall, stretched up on her bare toes, hanging on to the bars of the window, and looking into the night.

"What are you doing?" he asked as he ambled toward the last cell.

She spun around and nearly toppled off the cot before catching her balance. Her eyes wide, her hand pressed just below her throat, she grabbed onto one of the iron bars and stepped off the cot onto what he knew was a cold stone floor. "I was looking for a falling star so I could make a wish."

"What'd you wish?"

She angled her head slightly and gave him a quivering smile. "If I tell you, it won't come true. But then it probably won't come true anyway. I was wishing you'd forgive me."

She looked so damn tiny standing in that cell in her yellow dress and bare feet. He furrowed his brow. "That a new dress?"

She nodded quickly. "Dee brought it over. She made Larkin take me over to the hotel so I could have a bath. He didn't want to, but when she started shouting, he jumped. I wish I had her courage."

He smiled slightly at a distant memory. "You should have seen her when she first married Dallas. She hid under his desk on their wedding night."

Her eyes widened. "I can't imagine that."

"That's the way it was."

She gnawed on her lower lip. "How's Grant?"

"Missing his ma."

Tears brimmed in her eyes.

"He wouldn't eat much so Houston took him to Amelia so she could nurse him."

"I wouldn't be able to do him any good anymore. My milk dried up . . . on account of the worry I guess."

Against his will, his gaze dropped to her breasts . . . and her tiny waist . . . and her rounded hips. How would she survive the harshness of prison?

"Why did you have to come here and confess? I told you I'd take care of it."

"By admitting that you'd killed McQueen. Isn't that how you took care of it? Isn't that what you told Dallas to make him send the telegram to the detective?" Wrapping her arms around herself as though she were in pain, she spun around. He saw her narrow shoulders shaking. Even if he reached through the bars, he'd be unable to touch her.

"Loree?" he rasped.

She turned slowly, tears spilling onto her cheeks. She walked toward him, and her hands clasped the bars until her knuckles turned white. "Austin, don't you see? You lost five years of your life because of me. If it weren't for me, you never would have lost the music to begin with, you could have your dream of playing your violin with an orchestra. If it weren't for me, you would be married to the woman you love."

Tears clogged his throat and burned his eyes. Reaching through the bars, he cupped her cheek. "Loree, I *am* married to the woman I love. Have I been so poor at showing you?"

A ragged sob broke through from her chest. Austin pulled her close and felt her arms go around his back.

"Larkin!"

The sheriff ambled over and leaned against the doorway.

"Unlock the cell so I can go in."

Larkin removed the match from between his teeth and shook his head. "Can't do it."

"She's not going to escape. Just let me go inside."

"Every time some member of your family walks in here, I'm having to bend the rules. Not this time." He walked away.

Loree sniffed. "It's all right, Austin."

"No, it ain't."

He released his hold on her, walked to the wall, and slid down it until his backside hit the floor. Loree strolled over and did the same. He slipped his hand through the bars and wrapped it around hers.

"You scared?" he asked quietly.

"Terrified."

A suffocating silence began to spread between them.

"Will you do me a favor?" Loree asked.

"Anything."

"Will you think of something nice to tell Grant about me when he's growing up? I think that's gonna be the hardest part, having to miss watching him grow up . . . and watching you grow old."

He couldn't argue with that. He thought of all he'd missed out on—how quickly his nieces and nephew had grown and changed and become people he'd barely recognized. "I'll tell him how much you like sugar and how sweet it made you."

A corner of her mouth lifted momentarily, then dipped lower than before. "I want you to divorce me."

"What?"

Her fingers tightened around his. "My lawyer thinks I'll get at least five years, maybe more. I've already told him to draw up the papers so we can sign them before I go. I want you to marry someone who'll be a good mother for Grant."

He shifted onto one hip so he faced her squarely. "No. I'm gonna wait for you, Loree. The day you get out of prison, I'll be standing at the gate with Grant beside me."

She shook her head vigorously. "We both know how easy that promise is to make and how hard to keep."

"Ten years, twenty, twenty-five. It won't matter, Loree. I'll wait."

He reached through the bars, drawing her as closely as he could with the damn iron separating them, wishing he had the power to hold back the dawn.

Dawn arrived, shafts of sunlight piercing the gloom of the jail. Austin had brought Loree a meal from the hotel and watched as she nibbled on the toast he'd coated with butter, sugar, and cinnamon. He'd poured so much sugar into her coffee that the bottom of the cup felt like the silt of a river when he'd tried to stir it.

Now they stood, toe to toe, fingers intertwined, words insignificant as they waited for Sheriff Larkin. The only thing Austin found to be grateful for was the fact that Leighton now had a town hall and her trial wouldn't be held in the saloon.

"Aunt Loree?"

Austin jerked his head around at Rawley's hesitant voice. He felt Loree's fingers tighten around his, and he knew she wished the boy hadn't seen her here. "Hey, Rawley, shouldn't you be in school?" Austin asked kindly.

Rawley took a step toward him. "Ain't no school today on account of the trial."

Loree looked at him as though she wished she were anywhere but where she was.

"Aunt Loree, they're saying you killed Boyd McQueen. Did you?"

"Rawley—" Austin began, but Loree pressed her finger to his lips.

She angled her head, tears glistening within the golden depths of her eyes. "Yes, Rawley, I did."

He removed his dusty black Stetson as though he'd just walked into church. "Then I'm obliged to you."

Loree jerked her baffled gaze to Austin, then looked back at Rawley. "Rawley, I'm not proud of what I did."

"Didn't figure you were. Once Mr. D told me that there's a difference between being good and doing bad things. Sometimes, a person does something because he don't have a choice. He might not like what he did . . . but it don't make him bad. I reckon that's the situation you're in, and I've been there myself." He settled his hat into place. "I aim to take good care of Two-bits for you till you get home so you don't have to fret over that."

"I appreciate it," Loree said softly, giving him a warm smile.

He gave her a brusque nod before walking out.

She squeezed her eyes shut. "At least McQueen will never touch our son."

Heavy footsteps echoed outside the hallway. Larkin strolled in, twirling the key ring around his finger. "Well, it's time."

Austin stepped aside and Larkin jammed the key into the lock. He grated and ground it until an audible click echoed between the cells. He swung the squeaking door open. "Step out."

Loree walked hesitantly out of the cell. Austin drew her into his arms, ignoring the scowl Larkin threw his way.

"It's gonna be all right, Sugar."

She nodded against his chest.

"Remember that I'll wait, no matter how long."

She lifted her face away from him, tears brimming in her eye. "I wish you wouldn't."

He gave her a warm smile and wiped a tear from the corner of her eye. "You were right, Sugar. If you tell me what your wish is, it won't come true."

He heard the clanging of chains and looked over Loree's shoulder to see Larkin unlocking the shackles.

"Jesus, Larkin, don't put those on her."

"I've got no choice. It's the rule."

"Whose goddamn rule?" Austin demanded. "She turned herself in, for Christ's sake. Show her some respect for doing that."

Larkin rolled the match from one side of his mouth to the other. "All right," he said reluctantly. He jerked his head to the side. "Let's go."

Loree took a step forward, halted, and glanced over her shoulder. Austin shook his head. "I can't go, Loree."

She gave him a smile filled with sympathy and understanding. "I know."

She angled her chin proudly, squared her shoulders, and followed Larkin down the hallway and into the front office. He waited until he heard the front door close before he gave into the pain. His agonizing wail echoed between the empty cells. He pounded on the brick wall until his knuckles were scraped raw and bleeding.

Somehow, in spite of all she had endured, Loree had managed to maintain an aura of innocence and sweetness. Prison would do what Boyd McQueen had been unable to do: It would kill her spirit and rip every shred of kindness from her.

He slammed his palm flat against the wall and pain ricocheted up his arm. Even knowing the hell that waited, he'd gladly go to prison in her place.

Loree decided it wasn't a trial, but more of a hearing. People got to hear her say how she'd killed Boyd McQueen. They got to hear Duncan demand that she hang for killing his brother. And they got to hear her lawyer ask for leniency because she'd confessed.

And now Judge Wisser was pondering her fate, although it looked to her like he'd fallen asleep, his hands crossed over his stomach, his lips pursed, his eyes closed. Only the flies in the crowded room dared to make a sound.

She was glad that Austin hadn't come with her. She thought she could accept hearing her sentence with dignity as long as she didn't have to see how much her going to prison would hurt him.

Judge Wisser popped his eyes open and leaned forward. "Loree Leigh, it is the decision of this court that you are indeed guilty. Do you have anything to say on your behalf before I pronounce your sentence?"

Loree's mouth went as dry as the parched earth, and her heart was pounding so hard against her ribs that she was certain they would crack. She could do little more than shake her head.

"Very well, then. In light of the circumstances—"

"I've got something to say."

Loree twisted around. Austin walked down the aisle between the bench seats, a purpose to his stride, while people craned their necks to see around each other, whispering and muttering.

"Six years ago you sent me to prison for a murder I didn't commit."

"An injustice I intend to set right today . . ."

"You can't set it right," Austin told him. "No matter what you do, you can't undo what you've already done. I lived in hell for five years, not because of Loree, but because of Boyd McQueen. He was a mean-spirited man who hurt children for the pleasure of it. She listened to the screams of her fourteen-year-old brother while McQueen tortured him. Then she had to watch while he hanged him. McQueen shot her, her mother, and her father. He paid a man to kill my brother, slit the throats of three men on the prairie—"

"You can't prove that!" Duncan roared.

Austin spun around. "Then who did it, Duncan? You? Cooper told Dee that her brother paid him to kill Dallas. If it wasn't Boyd, then it had to be you because I damn sure know it wasn't Cameron."

Duncan paled and dropped back into his chair. "It wasn't me."

Austin turned back to the judge. "I know we can't take the law into our own hands. I'm not saying Loree should have gone after Boyd, but I know the man isn't worth all our worry. An injustice was carried out here six years ago. Don't worsen it today by seeking justice for a man who didn't know the meaning of the word.

"I gave up five years of my life for his murder. Let those years serve as Loree's and if that's not enough then send me back to prison—"

Loree jumped to her feet. "No!"

"Duncan wants somebody to hang, then hang me—"

"No!" Loree cried.

"Because by God if you take her from me now I'm gonna die anyway—and where's the justice in that?"

Loree had never been so terrified in her whole life because it looked to her as though the judge was seriously contemplating what Austin had just said.

Judge Wisser sliced his gaze over to her. "Loree Leigh, I sentence you to life . . ."

Austin slammed his eyes closed, bowed his head, and clenched his fists.

"With this man."

Austin jerked his head up.

"May God have mercy on your soul." Judge Wisser slammed his gavel down. "This court is adjourned."

The courtroom erupted with shouts and cheers. Loree looked at her lawyer. He smiled and nudged her arm. "Go on. You're free."

She turned and found Austin waiting for her. He spread his arms wide and she fell against him, entwining her arms around his neck. He enfolded her in his embrace.

"Ah, Loree," he whispered near her ear. "You should hear the music."

*   *   *

Exhausted, Loree sank into the steaming hot water. The day had been spent enjoying her freedom: feeling the breeze blow over her face, listening to each of the children tell her how much they'd missed her, holding Grant close, enjoying the warmth of Austin's hand wrapped around hers.

And now they were home, and he was rubbing the soap filled cloth over her limp arm.

"You don't have to wash me," she said softly although she wasn't certain she had the strength to do it herself. She hadn't slept at all after she'd turned herself into Sheriff Larkin.

"I want to."

He stroked the cloth slowly over the curve of her breasts.

"Dr. Freeman said if I let Grant suckle, my milk might come back." Her eyes drifted closed. "I'd like that."

"Then I hope it happens."

"You . . . don't . . . have to wash me."

"So you said," he reminded her and she heard the smile in his voice. "I don't *have* to love you either, but I do."

She forced her eyes open. "How can you love me when I took so much from you?"

"How can I not love you when you gave me so much back?"

Tears welled in her eyes. "It would have killed me if they'd hanged you."

"Well they didn't. Cameron and Dee had a long talk with Duncan after the trial. Think he just couldn't accept the kind of man his brother was."

"So he'll leave you alone?"

He combed her hair back from her face. "He'll leave us alone."

"What about your dream?"

"I'm gonna finish washing her up and put her to bed."

She smiled tiredly. "I meant your music."

"I'll play for you. I'll play for Grant. I'll play for my family."

She wondered if he would be forever content with that, knew that if she asked him, he would tell her yes whether it was the truth or not. She held her doubts and worries to herself, and relished the attention he paid her as he washed her, dried her, and carried her to bed.

He tucked the blankets around her, and as she drifted off to sleep, she heard him stroking the bow over the violin creating music that sounded very much like contentment.

"It was the most beautiful song I'd ever heard," Mr. Cowan said as he reached for another cookie. "Couldn't get it out of my mind."

Bouncing Grant on her lap, Loree smiled. "Austin has a way of playing music that comes from his heart. I think it makes it unforgettable."

"And if the music is unforgettable, so shall he be, my dear." He leaned forward and winked. "And me, right along with him."

Loree heard the footsteps on the porch and rose from the chair as Austin stepped through the doorway. She smiled brightly. "Austin, look who's here."

Austin removed his hat and studied Mr. Cowan skeptically. "What brings you out here?"

"You do, my dear boy. As I was telling your lovely wife here, your song has been haunting me ever since I heard it. I want you to come play for me."

Austin hung his hat on the peg. "Appreciate it, Mr. Cowan, but I'm not interested."

Mr. Cowan looked taken aback. Loree simply stared at her husband. "What do you mean you're not interested?"

"I wasn't good enough before. Nothing's changed that."

"Everything—"

"No, Loree. This isn't what I want."

With pleading eyes, Loree looked at Mr. Cowan. "Let me speak to him privately about this opportunity—"

"I'm not going to change my mind," Austin insisted.

At that moment she wished she had a skillet in her hand so she could bang it against his hard head. She knew pride was making him cast his dream before the wind.

Mr. Cowan brought himself to his feet. "I know this isn't a decision to be made lightly. It'll affect your family for many years. I'm staying at The Grand Hotel in Leighton—finest hotel this side of the Mississippi— and I have to confess it was part of the reason I didn't mind traveling back to this area. But I must catch the train in the morning so I'll leave a list of my destinations with Mrs. Curtiss at the front desk. If at anytime you change your mind, you just send me a telegram." He held up a finger. "But you'll need to decide before next spring because we'll be leaving for Europe then and it'll be harder for me to make the arrangements."

He lifted his bowler hat from the table. "Mrs. Leigh, it was a pleasure to spend the afternoon in your company."

He strode out of the house like a man without a care in the world.

"You shouldn't have sent him a telegram without discussing it with me first," Austin said.

"I didn't send him telegram."

"You didn't tell him that I was innocent?"

"No."

Austin rushed outside, Loree in his wake. Mr. Cowan was climbing into the buggy.

"Mr. Cowan, how did you hear about my innocence?"

Mr. Cowan pulled his foot out of the buggy and straightened. "Didn't hear about it until this very second. But that's excellent news."

"You came here still thinking I was guilty of murder?"

"That's right."

"I don't understand. A week ago—"

"A week ago your song hadn't kept me awake with regret every night."

Austin glanced over at Loree and slipped his hand around hers before looking back at Mr. Cowan. "I don't know how to read music. Loree's been teaching me, but I'm not a very dedicated student."

Mr. Cowan shrugged. "Doesn't matter, dear boy. You won't be playing with the orchestra."

Austin furrowed his brow. "You've lost me again. Why are you here—"

"Because I want you to be my soloist. It's your songs I want. Your gift."

"What about my family?"

"They'll come with you, of course."

Austin gave him a nod. "Let me talk it over with my wife this evening, and I'll let you know in the morning."

"Good enough."

The night was pleasant as Austin drew their horses to a halt. They had left Grant with Amelia so Loree and Austin could have some time to sort things out. She had allowed him to lead the way in silence because she sensed that something was bothering him.

After all that had transpired in the past few days, she would not blame him for seeking a divorce.

She heard water rushing over rocks. Through the darkness, she saw a series of waterfalls in the moonlight. Austin helped her dismount, then he guided her onto the quilt he'd spread near the falls. He dropped down beside her.

"This is beautiful," she whispered in awe.

"Houston married Amelia here. I didn't even know the place existed until that day."

A moment of silence echoed between them before he said quietly, "This is where I was the night Boyd died."

Her heart slammed against her ribs. "Austin—"

"I want to tell you about that night—"

"You don't have to. Becky did—"

He cradled her cheek. "Loree, I *need* to tell you about that night."

She dropped her gaze to her lap and nodded. "All right."

"Dallas had always been there for me—so strong. I began to think of him as invincible. Rawley's father had taken a whip to Dallas's back until it looked like raw meat. Dee managed to get Dallas home, but he was fighting a fever. He'd lost a lot of blood. I was terrified that he'd die . . . and then who would we turn to? We knew Boyd was behind it and I planned to confront him. But I stopped to see Becky first and we came out here."

He tilted her face until their gazes met. Holding his gaze was the hardest thing she'd ever done.

"I want you to understand that I was twenty-one and scared. I loved Becky as much as a twenty-one-year-old man who knows little of life can love. When she offered comfort, I gladly took it."

She heard him swallow.

"Whores had never appealed to me . . . until that night, I'd never . . ." His voice trailed off.

"You don't have to tell me."

"I'd never been with a woman until that night—not in that way. And I never touched another woman until you."

He released his hold on her and reached for his violin. "Listen to this," he ordered. He began to play a soothing melody, over and over. "That's Becky's song."

She licked her lips. "It was lovely."

"But it never changes. It stays the same. It doesn't grow. It doesn't deepen. It doesn't challenge. It never did." He placed his violin on his shoulder. "I want you to hear the song I played for Mr. Cowan, the song he couldn't forget."

She drew her legs up to her chest and wrapped her arms around her knees. The music began softly, gently, and she imagined a child discovering the wonders of a dandelion, blowing the petals, and watching them float upon the breeze. As smoothly as the dawn pushed back the night, the song grew deeper, stronger. The chords echoed around them, thundering against the falls, filling the night until chills swept through her and her heart felt immense gladness. The song rang of destiny and glory and splendor.

She marveled that the melody came from within the man she loved, and she knew that she would forever remember it even as the final chords vibrated into silence.

She knew no words worthy of his efforts, no praise adequate enough for what he had just shared with her, so she said inanely, "That was beautiful."

"I call it 'My Loree.' That's what I hear in my heart when I look at you, when I hold you, when I love you." He set the violin aside and scooted up until they were connected hip to hip. He framed her face with his hands. "Becky was a part of my youth and I'll always love her—just as I'll always love my mother. That doesn't mean that I love you any less. She was the first woman I ever made love to, and that memory will never leave me. But everything about her pales in comparison to all that I hold dear regarding you. I loved her as much as a boy can love." He trailed his thumb along her cheek. "I love you as much as a man can love."

He settled his mouth over hers with a tenderness that mirrored his words. He removed her clothes in the same manner that dawn removed the darkness, calmly, quietly, with reverence and tranquillity. Then he tore off his own clothes and gently eased her down to the quilt.

The night air carried a hint of spring, and she knew she should feel cold, but all she felt was the glorious warmth of his body covering hers.

She touched her fingers to the old scar on his shoulder. "You never told me who shot you."

He pressed a kiss to the puckered flesh on her shoulder. "The same man who shot you."

"He was so intricately woven through our lives—"

"Through our pasts, Loree. He'll never touch us again."

She was weary of the past having a tight hold on her present. She wanted a future rich with the love this man could give her. "Love me, Austin."

He gave her a warm lazy smile. "Oh, I do, Sugar. With all my heart."

He lowered his mouth to hers, and their tongues waltzed to the music created by their hearts. She threaded her fingers through his thick hair, holding him near. He nipped at her chin, before trailing his mouth along the column of her throat.

"So sweet," he rasped.

And she felt sweet. For the first time in over five years, she truly felt sweet and untainted by the past. He knew her ugly secrets, her foolish mistakes, accepted them and loved her in spite of them. For both of them, she knew the innocence was forever lost, but together they could regain the laughter, the joy, and the promise of tomorrow.

And the music. Although he wasn't playing his violin, she almost imagined that she heard the chords thrumming through her heart as he brushed his lips over the curve of her breast. His tongue swirled around her nipple, taunting, teasing. She rubbed her hands along the corded muscles of his shoulders, shoulders that had tried to carry her burden.

"Hear the music, Loree," he whispered before returning his mouth to hers, hot and devouring, his fingers stroking, bringing to the surface the symphony housed within her soul.

Then he eased his body into hers and the crescendo reached new heights, thundering around her, with the force of his love. Each thrust carried her higher, farther, until she reached the tallest pinnacle. As he rose above her, she held his startling blue gaze and felt the heat of the hottest flames as he carried her over the edge into fulfillment.

Her body arched as his did, both quivering like the taut strings of a violin, masterfully played. With his final thrust, he cried out her name.

It echoed over the falls and through her heart in such a way that even when it fell into silence . . . it remained.

Epilogue

～

April 1898

"BLIMEY? WHAT'S THAT!"

Austin's fingers tightened around Loree's hand, and she knew he was cringing at his eight-year-old son's choice of words. He leaned forward slightly to look out the window of the passenger car as the train rumbled over the tracks.

"A cow," he told Zane.

"But it's got such long 'orns."

"That's why we call it a Longhorn. If we could see its backside, we'd know from its brand who it belongs to."

"I'll wager it belongs to Uncle Dallas," Grant said. At ten, he was the authority on all things.

"Father, can I ride one of Uncle 'Ouston's 'orses?" six-year-old Matt asked.

"Sure can. I wouldn't be surprised if he gives you one."

"To keep?" Matt asked, his eyes wide with disbelief.

"To keep."

"I'm going to name 'im 'Is 'Ighness," Matt said, his blue eyes gleaming.

Austin leaned toward Loree. "Please tell me that somewhere in all our luggage you packed their *H*'s."

Laughing, she squeezed his hand to offer reassurance. "I'm sure they'll show up once our sons have spent some time with their cousins."

"We shouldn't have stayed in London as long as we did."

"Does that mean we'll never go back?"

"Sugar, if you want to back, we'll go back. I'll give you whatever you want. You know that."

Yes, she knew that. In the passing years, he had given her the world—Rome, Paris, London, among others—his hand within hers more often than not, and five sons.

Joseph slipped out of his seat, crossed the short expanse, and placed his small hands on Austin's knee. Unlike his brothers who had inherited Austin's long slender fingers, Joseph had Loree's short stubby fingers. "Can I be a cowboy?" he whispered.

Austin lifted him onto his lap. "You can be anything you want to be."

"I don't play music so good," he said as though sharing a secret.

"You play better than I did when I was four."

Joseph's golden eyes widened as the sun glinted off his blond hair. "Truly?"

"Give you my word."

Loree flashed her husband an appreciative smile. At four, Austin had never played the violin, but she knew he would never mention that fact to Joseph. He loved Joseph because the boy favored Loree. He loved all his other sons because they resembled him in looks, temperament, and talent.

The train whistle pierced the air.

"I see the town!" Zane cried, and the boys scrambled to the window and pressed their noses against the glass.

Austin took Mark from Loree's lap and held him up so he could see over his brothers' heads.

"Is that big building Aunt Dee's theater?" Zane asked.

"Yep."

"Are we going to perform there?" Grant asked.

"We might. We'll have to discuss it with your Aunt Dee."

"I'll wager that she'll let us," Grant assured him.

The train lurched to a stop. Giving the other passengers time to disembark, Loree gathered up the boys while Austin reached for his violin case. Along with the instrument nestled within it, it had gained a few scars to remind them of its journeys over the years.

With two-year-old Mark firmly placed on her hip, she allowed Austin to herd the boys onto the wooden platform. He reached for her hand.

"Not nervous, are you?" she asked.

"It's been a long time."

"Uncle Austin?"

Austin turned at the deep slow drawl. Loree watched recognition and surprise dawn in his eyes as he stared at the tall, lanky man dressed as though he'd just come in off the range.

"Good God! Rawley?"

The man smiled and extended a hand. "Yes, sir."

Austin jerked him into his embrace. "Good Lord, boy. You grew up."

Rawley stepped back. "Yes, sir, I reckon I did." He removed his hat and gave Loree a warm smile. "Aunt Loree."

Austin took Mark from her. She stood on the tips of her toes and wrapped her arms around Rawley. "It's so good to see you."

He hugged her close. "You're a sight for sore eyes, that's for sure."

He released his hold on her. "Ma said the platform would break beneath the weight of the whole family so everyone else is waiting in the ballroom at the hotel."

"Blimey! Are you a cowboy?" Zane asked.

A slow smile tugged at the corner of Rawley's mouth. "I reckon I am."

"Have you got a gun?"

"Yep, but I can't wear it into town on account of the city ordinance that prohibits guns."

"And a 'orse?"

"Yep." Rawley reached for the violin case. "I'll carry that for you."

"Thanks," Austin said as he handed it over.

Rawley jerked his thumb back. "We'd best head to the hotel before Ma sends the posse out lookin' for us."

"You ever seen a posse?" Zane asked as he hurried to keep pace with Rawley's long strides.

"Once I rode with one. Some men held up the bank here in town, and that didn't sit well with us."

"Did you catch them?" Zane asked.

"Nope. Last I heard they were hiding out in some hole in the wall." Rawley stepped off the platform and hit his thigh. "Two-bits!"

The dog eased out from beneath the shade and trotted to his side. Loree knelt in the dirt, laughing with the delight as the dog licked her face.

"You 'ave a dog?" Zane asked as the boys began petting Two-bits.

"Nah, he's your ma's dog. I've just been taking care of him."

"Does that mean 'e gets to live with us?" Matt asked.

"Reckon it does," Rawley said.

Loree rose to her feet. "Won't you miss him?"

Rawley glanced over his shoulder. "We really need to get to the hotel."

"Is Two-bits going to live with us, Mother?" Zane asked.

"I don't think so. I think he'd miss Rawley too much." Rawley turned his head, and she saw the relief in his eyes. "But I'm sure we can find another dog somewhere."

"That's if we decide to stay," Austin reminded her and the boys.

"I want to stay," Zane said, "if it means we can have a dog."

"And a 'orse," Matt chimed in.

Austin slipped his hand around Loree's. "Come on."

The town had grown, and Austin couldn't help but feel that his brother had done himself proud. And any man would have busted his buttons to have fathered the young man who patiently answered the boys' questions as they entered the hotel.

Rawley threw open the door to the ballroom. Tightening his hand around Loree's, Austin took a deep breath and stepped beneath the archway. Screams and cheers resounded around him. Tiny bits of paper and ribbon flew in front of his face.

More than his family welcomed him home. It looked as though most of the damn town had crowded into the room.

"Uncle Austin!"

Turning, Austin felt as though he'd been thrown back in time— over twenty years—looking at Amelia again, smiling and radiant . . . only he had never been Amelia's uncle. "Maggie May?"

She nodded briskly and threw her arms around his neck. "I missed you so much," she cried.

"I missed you, too," Austin said hoarsely.

Rawley leaned close. "Watch what you say to her. She thinks she's smarter than all of us now that she's going to that university in Austin."

"You could go, too, Rawley," Maggie said, a daring glint in her green eyes.

"Not on your life, Brat. I got cows to watch."

"You and your cows." She looked at Austin's sons. "Are you boys gonna help Rawley take care of his cattle?"

All his sons bobbed their heads excitedly.

"Good God, don't you know how to make girls?" Houston asked.

Austin smiled at his brother. "You don't look like you've changed at all."

"It's just not as noticeable when a face is as unattractive as mine."

Austin saw tears spill from the eyes of the woman standing beside Houston. Her hair wasn't as blond as it had once been, but he thought it still looked as though it had been woven from moonbeams. He held out his arms. "Amelia."

She hugged him closely.

"You started all this you know," he whispered. "You were the first, the one who taught us that we didn't have to be so strong."

She patted his back. "I wouldn't have missed it for the world."

"I need a hug."

Austin looked over Amelia's head and smiled at Dee. "Who would have thought you'd turn out to be so bossy?"

Her arms came around him in a fierce hug. "You haven't seen me be bossy yet. I have you scheduled for three performances at my theater."

"Dee—"

She wagged her finger at him. "I am not going to have a world-famous violinist in our town and not have him play in my theater."

"I don't know how world famous I am—"

"Loree sent us all your newspaper clippings—"

He glanced at his wife, who simply smiled at him.

"Of course, we can't read most of them what with their being written in a foreign language and all—"

"I can read the ones from France now," Maggie said.

Rawley rolled his eyes. "See, I told you she thinks she's smarter than us—"

"Not smarter, just more educated," she said.

"Experience is the best educator," Rawley said. "Dallas taught me that."

"And here I didn't think you were paying attention."

Austin turned at his oldest brother's booming voice. The years had turned Dallas's hair silver and shadowed his mustache with varying shades of gray. The creases had deepened around his eyes and mouth. Dallas's gaze slowly roamed over Austin, and he hoped with all his heart that his brother didn't find him wanting.

A slow smile eased onto Dallas's face. "I always knew your dreams would take you away from us. Just didn't expect them to keep you away so long."

"Well, we're home now." He hadn't known the words were true until he embraced his brother. He had given Loree the world . . . and now he wanted to give her and their boys a home.

Rawley stepped out of the ballroom onto the veranda. "Faith, Uncle Austin and Aunt Loree are here. Aren't you gonna come in and welcome them home?"

She spun around, tears brimming in her eyes. "Oh, Rawley, I don't want him to see me like this, not after all these years."

He looked her up and down. He didn't understand ladies' fashions, but he thought she looked beautiful in the red gown. "Nothing wrong with the way you look."

"I've got no bosom."

His gaze fell to her chest, flat as a well-sanded plank of wood. Irritation surged through him because he'd looked. "Jesus, Faith, you're only thirteen. You're not supposed to have a bosom."

"I'm almost fourteen. A. J.'s only eleven and she has a bosom."

"I wouldn't call those two little bumps on her chest—"

"You noticed!"

He slammed his eyes closed. "You're gonna get me skinned alive." He opened his eyes. "It's not like I was lusting after her or anything. She's my cousin, for God's sake."

"But you noticed."

And who wouldn't? All of Uncle Houston's daughters had nice curves, but it didn't mean he had lascivious thoughts just because he'd noticed. He leaned against the wall, dug the heel of his boot between the bricks, and decided to hold his tongue because there was no way in hell he could win an argument with her. He pulled a sarsaparilla stick from his pocket.

"Gimme," she ordered holding out her hand.

"It's my last one," he said as he broke it in half and handed her a piece. "Want to tell me what's really bothering you?"

"I love John Byerly and he loves Samantha Curtiss. I know it's because she already has a bosom and I don't."

"What do you want with John anyway? He's a runt."

"All the boys are runts next to me."

He couldn't argue with that. She already came up to his shoulder, and he had a feeling she wasn't finished growing.

"No one is ever gonna love me, Rawley."

He shoved himself away from the wall and put his arm around her. "I love you, Faith."

"But you're my brother so that doesn't count."

He cupped her chin. "You don't want somebody that's just looking at the outside of you. You want somebody who cares enough to look inside because what's inside never grows old or wrinkled or gray."

She sniffed. "If no one asks me to dance, will you dance with me?"

"Why, Miss Leigh, I'd be honored."

He slipped her arm through his and led her into the Grand Ballroom. He had a feeling in future years, Faith was destined to break an abundance of hearts. His greatest fear was that one of them would be his.

With his brothers flanking him on either side, Austin allowed his gaze to wander the room. Cookie played his fiddle and couples waltzed. Men still outnumbered women, but not by much. His nieces were growing into young ladies, his nephew a fine young man.

"Is this what you envisioned when you answered Amelia's ad all those years back?" he asked Dallas.

"Nope. I had no idea it would turn out this good," Dallas said.

"Even if you didn't end up with her?" Houston asked.

"Even though you stole her from me," Dallas emphasized.

"I always thought that worked out for the best," Austin said.

"It did," his brothers concurred at once.

Austin watched as Rawley sauntered over. "Dallas, I need to get back to the ranch and check on the herd."

Dallas gave him a long slow nod. "Whatever you think best."

Rawley held his hand out to Austin. "Uncle Austin, it's good to have you home. Reckon we'll see you up at the house later."

"Reckon so."

"Uncle Houston, I'd keep an eye on that fella dancing with Maggie."

"Him and the other three that followed her home from school. I told her she could miss school because this was a special occasion, but those fellas . . . not dedicated to their studies from what I can tell."

"They're dedicated to her." Laughing, Rawley patted Houston's shoulder before wandering out of the room.

"Still can't get him to call you 'Pa'?" Austin asked.

Dallas shook his head. "Nope, but it doesn't matter. He's my son and he damn well knows it."

Austin caught sight of his own son ambling toward him, a young girl in tow.

"Father, this is Mary McQueen," Grant said.

The girl had eyes the blue of a summer sky and hair that glinted red. Austin hunkered down. "Hello, Mary McQueen."

"Your boy talks funny."

"That's because he hasn't been in Texas very long."

"You aim to remedy that?"

At the sound of an old friend's voice, Austin slowly unfolded his body and held out his hand. "Cameron."

Cameron's handshake was firm. "Austin, you look like a man who has met with a great deal of success."

"I could say the same for you. How's the general store business?"

"Booming, although he's too modest to admit it," Becky said as she stood beside him. "He expanded the store to include the second floor and has all the merchandise divided into departments. We actually live in a house now." Her smile softened. "We've been so proud following you around the world. Dee has all your news written up in the newspaper."

"You look happy, Becky."

"I am." She turned slightly to the young boy standing beside her. "Do you remember Drew?"

"I sure do."

"And you've just met our Mary."

"I told Mary that you would play for her," Grant informed him.

Austin raised his brow at his first born. "Oh, you did, did you?"

His son nodded. "If you'll play for her, then I'll play for you because I know Mother wants to dance, and the gentleman who's playing hasn't quite got the knack of it."

"Don't tell him that."

"No, sir, I wouldn't want to hurt his feelings. So will you play for Mary?"

"I think that's a wonderful idea," Dee said as she slipped her arm through Dallas's. "You could play for all of us. I realize we're not royalty—"

"How can you say that, Dee, when you're married to the king of West Texas?"

Dallas snorted. "If you're gonna play, get to it. I've got a hankering to dance with my wife."

Loree knew the moment when the crowd hushed that Austin intended to play for them. The reverence he held for his gift was apparent as soon as he stepped on stage and lifted his violin to his shoulder.

The first strains of the sweet music filled the air, and Loree smiled. She knew the song. It always began the same, but the ending had changed over the years, growing deeper and stronger, a reflection of their love. She never tired of hearing it. Never tired of watching her husband coax the melody from the strings in the same way that he elicited passion: with care and devotion and attention paid to the tiniest of details.

His three oldest sons already exhibited a preference for music. Grant had, on occasion, joined Austin on the stage and wooed audiences with his talent.

"He'll go farther than I ever dreamed," Austin had told her once. And she wondered if it was that revelation that had brought him back home, so he could give his sons roots as well as wings.

The music drifted away like dandelion petals on the wind. An awed silence permeated the air before someone dared disturb it by clapping. Austin smiled and bowed. The cry rose up for another song, and her husband simply shook his head.

"If you'll excuse me, I'd like to dance with my wife now." He handed his violin to Grant and whispered something into his ear before stepping down from the makeshift stage.

Loree's heart warmed as he approached, knelt in front of her, and slapped his thigh. "Come on, Sugar."

He removed one shoe, then the other before standing and signaling their son. The music floated toward them, and Austin swept her onto the dance floor. His blue gaze never strayed from hers, but grew warmer and held promises she knew he would keep.

She had toured the world. She had waltzed with royalty.

But she was happiest when Austin held her within the circle of his arms, and she was surrounded by the splendor of his love.